Also by Colin Bateman

Cycle of Violence
Empire State
Maid of the Mist
Wild About Harry
Mohammed Maguire
Chapter and Verse

Martin Murphy novels
Murphy's Law
Murphy's Revenge

Dan Starkey novels
Belfast Confidential
Divorcing Jack
Of Wee Sweetie Mice and Men
Turbulent Priests
Shooting Sean
The Horse with My Name
Driving Big Davie

For Children
Reservoir Pups
Bring Me the Head of Oliver Plunkett
The Seagulls Have Landed

I PREDICT A RIOT

BATEMAN

with illustrations by John McCloskey

headline

First published in 2007 by
HEADLINE PUBLISHING GROUP

1

Cataloguing in Publication Data is available from the British Library

978 0 7553 3465 0 (hardback)
978 0 7553 3466 7 (trade paperback)

Typeset in Meridien by Palimpsest Book Production Limited,
Grangemouth, Stirlingshire

Printed and bound in Great Britain by
Mackays of Chatham plc, Chatham, Kent

Headline's policy is to use papers that are natural, renewable and recyclable
products and made from wood grown in sustainable forests.
The logging and manufacturing processes are expected to conform to
the environmental regulations of the country of origin.

HEADLINE PUBLISHING GROUP
A division of Hachette Livre UK Ltd
338 Euston Road
London NW1 3BH

www.headline.co.uk
www.hodderheadline.com

For Andrea and Matthew.

For Austin Hunter and everyone at the
Ulster News Letter without whom
this would not exist.

For my Christian name, gone but not forgotten.

Prologue

The Mariner of the Seas, huge and white and beautiful, is the largest cruise ship to sail into the port of Belfast since the *Titanic* sailed out. While its 1200 crew is drawn from 65 different countries, its 3000 passengers are almost entirely American. Their plan – at least for those who intend to get off – is to see the city, and the rest of the country, in a few hours and still be back in time to eat. Eating is important. In the past week on board they have consumed 69,000 steaks.

The main problem for those planning the on-shore itineraries is a chronic lack of capacity. Belfast has an efficient tourist infrastructure, but it mostly caters for small parties interested in the thrill of poking around a former war zone; it is not set up for thousands of American tourists descending all at once. For example, the open-top tours run by Belfast Big Red Bus (or BBRB – it's a city famous for its acronymns, and it's useful to recognise as many as possible to avoid confusion, and death) – normally runs only one bus, on a four-times-a-day basis in the summer season. But here it was being asked to provide fifteen buses. It normally employs one, sometimes two, out-of-work actors to act as guides. Now it has been forced to employ the entire cast of Frank McGuinness's *Observe the Sons of Ulster Marching Towards the Somme* from the Lyric Theatre to perform an only marginally less gloomy travelogue to the largely bored tourists. Bored because they've spent the past week *doing* Europe and can really do without much more local history. What they're really here for is the Terror Tour.

Take bus number 5, driven by a moonlighting Ulster Bus driver and with a guide in the slightly rotund shape of Martin McBurney, who plays a bitter old man called Kenneth Pyper in *Observe the Sons of Ulster Marching Towards the Somme*, which to some of his colleagues almost constitutes typecasting. Martin gruffly begins to work his way

1

through the script as the BBRB swings away from the harbour; he has a microphone, but can still barely be heard above the busily chatting tourists. They're not paying a blind bit of notice, at least until they get to the good stuff. He tells them that the name Belfast derives from *beal feirste*, which more or less means 'mouth of the sandpit'. He informs them that the settlement originated from a castle built in the twelfth century by John de Courcy, but didn't start to develop until the early years of the seventeenth century, when Sir Arthur Chichester began to plant the land with settlers from Devon and Scotland, thus sowing the seeds of all the trouble that was to follow.

Digital video cameras are duly brought out to record the massive cranes at the Harland & Wolff shipyard and there are many *oohs* and *aahhhs* when it's pointed out that this is where the *Titanic* was built, although it's hardly much of an advert for quality shipbuilding. Beyond the shipyard, there is precious little with which to impress the Americans; it is, like any other previously industrial city, in terminal decline. No ships are built now. The great linen mills and ropeworks are long closed. It would be the most boring of all their tours if it wasn't for The Troubles, and this is where their interest really picks up. The BBRB turns onto the Falls Road, and Martin gets to act a bit, detailing the terror and killing and insanity that enveloped these dark streets for thirty years. Now of course it's all over, he tells them, though he knows this is not exactly true.

'We're going to stop here,' he says, 'and you can have your photos taken beside the war murals. Look – there's one commemorating the death of Bobby Sands. He starved himself to death, you know, on hunger strike,' and the tourists trundle out and shake their heads at the tragedy and smile for their photos, and Martin helps them out by taking their pictures for them. The very mention of hunger strike has reminded them that they're missing their daily buffet on the ship, and they become restless. Luckily, a stop at a traditional Belfast bakery is built into the tour, and they rush off the bus and are talked through soda farls, potato farls, wheaten bread and Veda by an old lady with flour on her face. But the terror is not yet over, because Belfast is a city where everything has to be balanced – if you see the Republican murals on the Falls, you must see the Loyalist murals on the Shankill.

Except today, with a driver unused to the regular stopping points, they turn onto the Shankill and miss the local guide waiting to explain the history of Loyalism, and stop instead half a mile further up beside some of the more garish and offensive murals. (None of them, strictly speaking, are politically correct, but some are more so than others.)

I Predict A Riot

'This is the Shankill Road,' Martin begins, 'and the murals here depict the local working-class population's appreciation of their ties with the British Empire. They commemorate soldiers who died in the First and Second World Wars, soccer heroes and soldiers who have fought to retain the local culture and protect religious—'

Martin stops suddenly, as a stone strikes the window behind him. Then there's a second stone. The tourists peer out of their windows, and see that a crowd has gathered.

One kid, who can hardly be more than twelve, screams: 'Why don't youse all just f**k off!'

A hail of stones strikes the bus. Luckily, it is a new bus, and the windows are built to withstand attack. Martin, although shaken, comes from a school of acting where improvisation is encouraged, so he manfully tries to cover up. 'No need to be alarmed,' he says. 'This is just the interactive part of our tour, as local boys strive to recreate some of the rioting which took place here in the seventies and eighties.' Lowering the microphone for a moment, he hisses at the driver, 'Get us the f**k out of here!'

'The driver, who, being experienced in these kinds of things, has kept the engine running, doesn't need a second invitation. Unfortunately he immediately finds his way blocked by a twisting snake of purloined Tesco's shopping trolleys. Kids begin to hammer on the bus doors. The tourists press their video cameras to the glass, then duck down as another fusillade of stone and brick rocks their vehicle. They let out little whoops of excitement and clap their hands. The crowd outside has grown in strength to around fifty. Many are wearing football scarves tied up around their faces, and some appear to be carrying bottles half-filled with transparent liquid. The doors of the bus are now forced open, and two of the bigger kids, one brandishing a hatchet, and the other a baseball bat, climb up the steps and shout, 'Everyone off the f**king bus!'

The tourists dutifully stand and begin to make their way down the aisle. One of them says to Martin, 'Should we leave our coats and bags?'

Martin says, 'No, I'd bring them with you, it might rain.'

The boy with the baseball bat ushers the last of the tourists off, then hauls the driver out from behind his wheel and pushes him down the steps. Then he strikes him hard with the baseball bat. The driver sinks to his knees, bleeding from the forehead. The boy with the hatchet takes a bottle and sets fire to the tea towel tied around the top of it; then he hurls it halfway down the bus. It explodes, the force of it blowing out half the windows and spraying liquid flames around the interior. In moments, the bus is a blazing

3

inferno. A cheer goes up from the crowd, and after a few moments the tourists, lined up on the pavement, break into a spontaneous round of applause.

'Now that's what I *call* interactive,' says one.

Meanwhile, in another part of the city, Superintendent James 'Marsh' Mallow, drives hopelessly around, his wife in the glove compartment. More of this later.

1
Let's Be Mates

Walter was nervous.

It wasn't a blind date, exactly, because they'd examined each other's pictures and profiles on the website for *Let's Be Mates*, a Belfast dating agency. He knew her height and weight, what she did for a living, what her interests and hobbies were, her personality, the kind of man she was hoping to meet.

Walter presumed that she'd made most of it up. He certainly had. It was, after all, only a bit of fun. Exaggeration. Distortion. Half-truths. He was sure everyone else did it as well.

They'd even exchanged a few emails. She seemed bright and interesting. And keen. If she really was nice, and they hit it off, he would confess all. He had described himself as a property developer. In fact, he was a Civil Servant in the Department of Education in Bangor. But he had ambitions.

Margaret Gilmore had described herself as a fashion designer. Walter wondered what she really was. Perhaps the closest she got to fashion designing was sitting at home, lonely, with a ball of wool, knitting. He couldn't imagine that a successful fashion designer would have to resort to an internet dating agency to meet men.

In fact, Margaret Gilmore worked as a security guard in Primark on Royal Avenue. But she too had ambitions.

Margaret had endured another miserable morning in work. She caught a Millie with two shoes stuffed inside her fake Burberry raincoat. Two left shoes, as it turned out. The girl wasn't ever going to be recruited to *Ocean's 11*. She couldn't have been more than fourteen. She'd screamed about being 'connected', lamped Margaret, then charged out of the store cursing her head off and leaving Margaret with a rapidly swelling left eye. It was all she needed, going on her big date later. She'd booked an appointment at Toni & Guy for the afternoon – she normally wouldn't dream of spending that much on her hair, but it was a special occasion. She quite liked the look of this Walter McCoy. Perhaps he was the *real* McCoy. She promised herself not to crack that one. He'd probably heard it a million times.

In fact, he hadn't, as McCoy wasn't his real name.

It was a typical May evening in Belfast: raining heavily, and cold with it. Walter got out of work early, and caught the train back to Botanic. He'd worn his best – and only – suit to work so that he wouldn't have to go home before the big date, but now he had a couple of hours to kill. He ducked into Lavery's bar. He was feeling nervous, a pint would calm him down. He could buy some Polos later. He hoped she'd be nice. He prayed that he wouldn't say something stupid. He usually did. Nerves.

It was still bucketing when Margaret eventually emerged from the hairdressers looking as well as she possibly could, under the circumstances. The cut was such that it swept down over her by-now half-closed left eye, so with luck, Walter mightn't even notice. She'd also camouflaged the bruising with heavy make-up. She checked her watch: it was only half an hour until she was due to meet him outside the Grand Opera House. She tried calling a cab, but with the bad weather and the rush hour there was nothing available for at least twenty minutes. She didn't want to take the chance of being late for her big date, so she decided to walk.

It wasn't her brightest idea.

Before she'd gone 100 yards, a sudden gust blew her umbrella inside out, then she got drenched as she fought a losing battle to get it back into shape. By the time she threw its remains angrily into a bin, her elaborate new hairstyle had collapsed around her face, in the process smearing her carefully applied eye make-up across her cheek.

Margaret hurried on, but by the time she was halfway down Great Victoria Street, she was soaked right through, and the colour from her turquoise blouse had begun to seep into her beige jacket.

She glanced at her watch. She still had time. She could nip into the Europa toilets and attempt emergency repairs. Everything could still turn out all right. But then she stepped off the pavement and her right shoe immediately lodged itself in a grating. In freeing it, she bent the heel to one side. When she tried walking on it, it made her look slightly disabled.

So it was with some trepidation that Margaret Gilmore limped towards Walter McCoy on a rain-swept Belfast night outside the Grand Opera House. She wasn't hoping for true love. At the beginning of the day she would have settled for a free show, a nice meal and perhaps a bit of a snog afterwards. But with her hair hanging round her, her eye almost completely closed, her jacket dyed a weird two-tone colour and limping like an idiot, she realised she didn't look so much like a woman going on a special date, but one who'd recently escaped from a high security hospital.

'It's Walter, is it?'

Walter turned. It seemed to Margaret that his face fell. That he was truly horrified. In fact, he was just stifling a yawn.

It seemed to Margaret that, as well as being horrified, he looked desperately disappointed. But the fact was, he was half-cut. And he wasn't wearing his glasses. She might have looked like the Elephant Woman and he wouldn't have noticed.

'I'm . . . Margaret.'

Walter put out his hand. 'Yes indeedy,' he said, grinning widely.

Margaret limped forward and clasped it. 'I got caught in the rain,' she said.

'Have a Polo,' said Walter.

2
Kangaroo

Walter began to snore midway through the first act, his mouth hanging open, his head occasionally lolling from side to side. Once in a while he mumbled something that sounded like, 'Maradonna,' but Margaret couldn't be sure.

As a first date, it left something to be desired.

But then she thought, as a first date, *I* leave something to be desired. Sitting here soaked from the rain, hair plastered to my face, my eye closed over after getting thumped by that Millie, my shoe pointing north, its heel pointing west. He's probably not asleep at all. He's just pretending; he's so horrified at being here with me he's trying to scare me off.

She was tempted to go. To just quietly shuffle out and disappear back into the stormy night. She lifted her handbag. But then set it down again.

I may look like I've been dragged through a hedge backwards, she thought fiercely, but if I go now he'll always have that image of me. I know I'm better than this. You have to hang in there, girl, let him find the real you.

Except she'd no idea who the real Margaret Gilmore was. Was she a security guard at Primark? Yes, she was. Was she a fashion designer? Yes, she was. Had she ever actually had any of her designs professionally produced? No, she hadn't. But one day, she would. She was sure of that. Or, she was *quite* sure of that . . . No, she wasn't sure at all. Sometimes she was sure, sometimes she wasn't. She just needed a break.

She glanced across at Walter. Now he was mumbling. 'Best . . . Best to Law . . .'

Football.

Luckily the show, which was a musical based on the life of a 1980s pop group called Kajagoogoo, was fairly loud and raucous, and nobody seemed to mind that Walter was snoring his head off.

I Predict A Riot

It was the kind of behaviour she might have expected on a last date. A splitting-up date. Or after twenty years of marriage when you just didn't care what your other half thought.

That's why he's single, she decided. That's why he uses a dating agency – because he can't meet women any other way. Oh, God, how desperate am I?

She lifted her handbag again. She was in an end-of-aisle seat. She could be away and out the door in a few seconds.

Margaret started to rise. Then sat down again. How could she just give up so easily?

Walter might be drunk and asleep, but he'd been quite charming on the way in. He'd made her laugh when he said he'd been to see The Isley Brothers at some bar in town last year and wasn't convinced that they were even distant cousins. And Walter was handsome enough, even if he looked nothing like his photo on the *Let's Be Mates* website. She didn't either, did she? Maybe he was a bit heavier than she usually liked. But the love of a good woman would soon sort that out.

No!

She picked her bag up again. Who did he think he was, showing her such a lack of respect? Turning up drunk – falling asleep! She thought: *I can do better than this!* Then: *Run away!*

She glanced at Walter again, and saw that he was now awake, and looking at her. He sat up straighter in his seat. He brushed out a crease in his trousers. He nodded his head in time to the music. Then he leaned closer.

'I'm sorry,' he whispered. 'I dozed off.'

Margaret nodded.

'I had a couple of beers before we met. I was nervous.'

Margaret nodded again.

'I'm sorry. It wasn't the right thing to do. And also, this show is rubbish.'

She smiled at that. It was.

'Why don't we slip out and go for something to eat?' Before she could respond, he leaned even closer, and kissed her lightly on the cheek.

Margaret blushed to her kidneys, then nodded.

It had stopped raining. The wind had died down. They strolled along, close, but not too close.

Walter pointed up at one of the dozens of slightly battered election posters, still attached to lampposts the length of Great Victoria Street. 'You think they'd have taken those down by now.'

'I think they get fined if they don't,' said Margaret. Actually, she had no idea.

'Gerry Adams,' said Walter, pointing up again, this time at the Sinn Fein President. 'Don't you think he looks like Rolf Harris?'

She stopped and looked. 'I suppose he does.'

'And the interesting thing is, you never see them in the same place at the same time.'

'I'd never thought about that before,' Margaret admitted.

'Maybe that's the problem with the whole Army Council business. Perhaps he'd *like* to be on the Army Council . . .'

'But he's too busy saving animals and can't spare the time.'

They were both laughing now. It was nice. Walter began to hum 'Tie Me Kangaroo Down, Sport' and she was just about to join in when he stopped abruptly.

'I'm sorry.' He touched her arm, and looked sympathetically at her. 'I can't go on like this.'

'You . . . what?'

'It's just not working, is it?'

Her mouth fell open slightly. The blush, which hadn't quite faded from earlier, was back and beaming.

He moved closer. 'But it doesn't mean it can't be fixed, right?'

'I . . . I . . .'

Walter dropped to one knee and grabbed Margaret's ankle.

She was about to whack him with her handbag. But even as she swung back, he lifted her foot gently and slipped off the shoe with the bent heel.

'I'm sorry,' he said, 'but it's like going out with Hopalong Cassidy.' And with that he bent the heel back into place.

'Oh,' said Margaret.

'Try that,' said Walter, kneeling again, and slipping it back onto her foot.

Margaret tried it out. 'That's perfect,' she said.

'We aim to please,' said Walter. 'Now then – what do you fancy? Chinese, or a cowboy supper?'

3
Bread Rolls

Walter McCoy joked about taking Margaret to a Chinese or a chip shop, but he actually steered her into one of Belfast's more expensive restaurants in Shaftesbury Square. They'd no reservation, of course, and the restaurant appeared full, but Walter charmed the maître d' into bringing out an extra table, and Margaret found that very impressive. He ordered wine with casual self-assurance, tasted and approved it, then they perused their menus. Walter had his glasses on now, and he suited them.

They sipped their wine. Their eyes met over the top of their menus. They studied their menus some more.

A waiter appeared and asked if they were ready to order.

'I think we need another few minutes,' said Walter.

Margaret nodded in agreement, then accepted a bread roll. She was starving. Hadn't eaten all day. She liked her food plain and simple, and wasn't ashamed of it. She would play safe, and order steak. She glanced at Walter again. His lips were forming up the words as he read the menu. His brow was slightly creased. He liked his food plain and simple as well, but was slightly ashamed of it. But this woman, whom he was liking more and more as the evening wore on, she was probably used to dining in expensive restaurants like this. He felt desperately out of his depth. Even when he'd slipped the maître d' a £20 bribe to ensure they got a table, it seemed to Walter that the man had responded more out of pity than genuine appreciation.

Walter had tried to take command of the situation by ordering an expensive bottle of wine. He'd pointed at it on the wine list so that he wouldn't have to pronounce it, then when he tried a sample he almost gagged. He had no idea if this was how it was supposed to taste or if it was corked. But he smiled anyway and allowed the waiter to pour. How much simpler it would be, he thought, if beer could be ordered in the same way. *I'll have a pint of your Harp '87.* Then he'd be on safer ground.

'Think I'll go for the steak,' said Walter.

'Me too.'

He smiled. She smiled. She took a sip of her wine. It tasted *rotten*, but she persevered.

They ordered. Margaret accepted another bread roll.

'So,' she said, 'you're a property developer.'

'Oh, in a small way,' said Walter.

Modesty is very attractive, thought Margaret.

Please don't ask me for details, thought Walter.

'Do you employ many people?' asked Margaret.

'No, it's a very tightly run operation.'

'That's probably a good thing.'

'Yes, it is. And you – fashion designing. That must be exciting. Paris, Milan . . .'

'Cullybackey,' said Margaret.

They laughed.

She was, actually, telling the truth. She had knitted some jumpers a couple of years back and they'd been shown at a Women's Institute Fashion Night in Cullybackey. Then they'd been auctioned for charity. For her trouble she'd been given a bottle of home-made ginger wine and a £20 voucher for The Body Shop. The wool alone had cost her more. She still had the wine, and the voucher was out of date.

The waiter brought their starters, and some more bread.

Walter shifted the conversation to movies. He liked Spielberg and *The Godfather* and Al Pacino. She liked *Casablanca* and Tom Hanks, although 'not for sex'. She said it without really thinking, and immediately blushed again. She urgently buttered another roll.

Walter was very kind. 'I know exactly what you mean,' he said. 'I feel the same way about Maureen Lipman.'

'Who?'

'You know, Maureen Lipman – off the TV. She used to do those adverts. And she always pops up on panel shows and prize-givings. She's very funny. But not in a sexy way. And Kathy Bates.'

'Kathy Bates – from . . . I know, *Misery*, wasn't it?'

'Yes, that's her!' exclaimed Walter, a trifle too enthusiastically. 'I think she's fantastic. Remember how she broke James Caan's ankles?'

Margaret shuddered. 'She'd get a job over here no problem,' she said. 'You know, one of those punishment squads.'

Walter nodded thoughtfully. 'Yes, she would. I can just see the trailer now.' And he slipped into the big American voice you hear on the movie trailers. 'Coming soon – *Misery Two*. She's back, and this time she's in Dundonald.'

Margaret laughed. The waiter appeared at her side, and she accepted another bread roll.

'God,' said Walter. 'It's like feeding-time at the zoo.'

Margaret paused just as she began to tear the roll apart. 'Sorry?'

Walter was immediately flustered. 'I didn't mean . . . I meant, they don't half keep the bread coming.'

Margaret put the roll down.

'I mean . . . good service. Please, eat the roll.'

'I've had enough.'

'No, really – I didn't mean . . .'

'It's fine.'

Walter took a sip of his wine. It tasted like vinegar.

Margaret wanted the floor to open up so that she could be consumed by the fires of hell. She'd eaten four bread rolls. And was tearing into a fifth when he'd made his comment.

He thinks I'm fat.

I'm fat and my hair's a mess and my eye's closed over.

He's not interested at all. If he was *interested he would have asked about my eye by now.*

They ate the rest of the meal in relative silence.

Walter tried his best, but he barely got more than a few sentences out of her. It was a familiar situation. He was always putting his foot in it. Most of the time he didn't really care, but this was different. He liked Margaret. He wanted to talk to her some more. They laughed together. That didn't happen often. Usually he made a joke and they just looked at him like he was mental.

When they'd finished the main course, Margaret declined a dessert.

When the bill came Walter handed over his credit card. He included an impressive gratuity, but didn't mention it to Margaret. He was classy, that way.

The waiter returned with the credit card. As he went to hand it over he glanced at it and said, 'Thank you very much, Mr North.'

Walter blinked at him.

Margaret's eyes narrowed. 'I thought your name was McCoy?'

Walter gulped for air.

4

A Moment for Mr Trimble

Walter North had already had his feet up on his desk for twenty minutes when his colleague came bustling into the office. Even before he had his coat off, Mark was eagerly enquiring how the big date had gone.

'Well, I wouldn't—' Walter began.

'Hold it right there.' Mark opened his desk drawer and took out a framed photograph. He studied it for a moment, before setting it down where they both could see it.

It was a picture of David Trimble.

Mark had been doing this every day since the Unionist leader's downfall. Walter had joined in willingly at first. It was just a bit of fun. But now he was rather tired of it.

'A moment's silence, please,' said Mark, 'for the Trimble.'

Walter nodded.

Mark, as usual, ignored his own request. 'The Trimble – survivor of more coups d'états than many a small African country.'

'Praise the Lord,' said Walter.

'Won as many Nobel Peace Prizes as Nelson Mandela.'

'Praise the Lord,' said Walter.

'Held hands with Bono, and it was a good thing.'

'Praise the Lord.'

'Held hands with Paisley, which wasn't so smart.'

'Praise the Lord.'

'Embraced an original hairstyle which was briefly more popular than the Rachel cut from *Friends*. Although only in Banbridge.'

'Amen to that.'

Mark replaced the photo in his desk and stood by the window. They were on the ninth floor of the Department of Education's HQ in Bangor.

'What has the world come to, ruled by Paisley and Adams?'

'Well, it's early days yet.'

I Predict A Riot

'Before you know it, McGuinness'll be back in town, and how long before we're all talking camogie then?'

Walter wasn't entirely sure what camogie was, but he was fairly certain it wasn't a language. More like something you'd order in an Italian restaurant. And thinking of restaurants reminded him of Margaret, and their disastrous date. She had stormed off into the night after discovering that he was using an assumed name. He had tried to explain, but she was having none of it.

So that was that.

Except.

She was nice. She was funny. She looked a bit strange, with her straggly hair and her half-closed eye. Strange, but attractive. He'd wanted to ask her about the eye, but he'd read once that lawyers were taught never to ask a question in court unless they already knew the answer to it, and as their date had in many respects been something of a trial, he had decided to allow her to explain the state of her eye in her own time. What if she was suffering from some mortifyingly embarrassing disease? Where could the conversation possibly have gone after that revelation? Or worse – what if she wasn't even aware of her eye?

Hump? What hump?

No, he'd done the right thing, not asking about it. And the wrong thing, handing over the credit card like that. The waiter was only being polite, calling him by his real name.

'So – how *did* the big date go?' Mark was now sitting on the edge of his desk.

'Fine.'

'You seeing her again?'

Walter shrugged nonchalantly. 'I might.'

Mark winked. 'That's what I like. Playing hard to get.'

'Very hard,' agreed Walter.

'Well,' said Mark, getting up and sauntering back to his desk, 'we've a country to run, might as well get started.'

Walter switched his computer on, then logged onto *Let's Be Mates*. They had emailed each other several times before the big date and the exchanges were always conducted through this dating website. Now that a weekend had passed, and she'd had time to cool down, he could apologise properly. Put it into words. He was good with words.

Walter nervously typed in Margaret's name and the password to her page. He had an odd feeling in the pit of his stomach. It was a strange mix of love, lust and a crushing desire for a gravy ring.

INCORRECT PASSWORD.

Walter stared at it. *She's changed her password! She wants nothing more to do with me!* He sighed.

Mark looked up. 'Ah,' he said. 'Young love.'

Walter managed a smile, but inside he was in turmoil. He had been reasonably keen to make amends with this Margaret, but now, suddenly denied the opportunity, he was absolutely *determined*. But how to contact her? He tried to recall the information that had been on her page, but quickly realised that it had all been quite vague. And on the date itself she'd played her cards close to her quite nice-looking chest.

He stared at the screen. INCORRECT PASSWORD. He had to find her.

'Mark?'

'Mmm?'

'You wouldn't know how to hack into a computer database, would you?'

'Are you joking? I can hardly switch the bloody thing on. Why, what's the prob?'

Walter shrugged.

'Anyway,' said Mark, 'even if I could, wouldn't do it in here. They caught you, you'd be out on your ear.'

Walter nodded.

'Unless, of course, you're in Office Twelve.'

Walter's eyes flitted up, towards Mark, and then across to the open door and down the corridor towards Office 12. He swallowed.

'If it's *that* important,' teased Mark.

Walter had never been in Office 12. Nobody he knew had ever been in Office 12. It was a Department within a Department. Nobody knew what went on in there. All they knew was that any information that had to reach the outside world had to be channelled through Office 12. And that whatever perfectly good, clear and precise information was delivered to Office 12 somehow emerged for public consumption as confusing, contradictory and invariably misspelled. Rumour had it that Office 12 had been set up to undermine the performance of Martin McGuinness when he was briefly Education Minister, but that after he was chased out, someone had forgotten to shut it down. On the bright side, however, it was still meeting all its targets.

Walter sat where he was for a further ten minutes. Then finally it got the better of him. He *had* to see her again. And if it meant approaching Office 12, then so be it.

Walter jumped up and marched straight out of his office and down the corridor. He could feel the eyes of his colleagues following him all the way. He stopped outside Office 12, took a deep breath, and knocked on the door.

5

Compensation

By Monday morning the swelling to Margaret's eye had largely receded, leaving behind it a yellowy-black bruise which sat like an aging banana just above her cheekbone. Margaret sighed, then tutted as she examined her reflection in the staff toilet mirror. It wasn't just her eye that was annoying her. It was her lips. And her eyelids. And the way her hair, which had looked so well in the hairdressers, now looked like a cracked bowl.

What I need is a full time hairdresser at my beck and call, she thought. Donatella Versace probably has one. Anne Robinson too.

A new hairstyle, she decided, was rather like buying a new car. The moment you stepped out of the salon, it lost a third of its value.

The door opened behind her and Maeve came in. Margaret and Maeve had been security guards in Primark for the past two years together. Maeve had hair like an explosion in a mattress factory.

'So, how did the big date go?' Maeve began, coming up to the mirror, lipstick in hand.

'Well, I wouldn't . . .' But Margaret trailed off. The tears were already rolling down her colleague's crumpled cheek.

'I'm sorry,' wept Maeve.

'It's all right.'

'I keep trying to put a brave face on it.'

'I know you do. Still no word?'

Maeve shook her head dolefully. Margaret felt genuinely sorry for her. Although they came from very different parts of the city – Margaret off the Holywood Road, Maeve from the Falls – they got on like a house on fire, at least in work. Maeve's husband Redmond was a builder, but his real passion was ornithology. He made regular trips abroad to study the birds. Except he had failed to return from his last expedition, six weeks ago.

'And nothing from the Colombian authorities?'

'They weren't even aware he was in the country. Some of these countries are *so* disorganised.'

'Well, in a way that's good, isn't it? He may be perfectly fine. Perhaps he's just somewhere that doesn't have good communications.'

'I know. But it's been so long. And those places can be so dangerous. All for some little yellow bird. Anyway . . .' She wiped at her eyes, then held the lipstick up again. 'Tell me about your date.'

'Oh, what's to tell? The usual disaster.' Margaret told her about the downpour and the hairstyle and the bent heel and her date falling asleep and using a false name.

'Oh, what a prick,' said Maeve. 'And it could only happen to you.'

'Don't I know it.'

They examined their reflections.

'Do you know what we need?' Maeve said.

'Counselling?' suggested Margaret.

'A make-over.'

Margaret shook her head. 'Tried that. It's a temporary fix.'

'No – I mean one of those *extreme* make-overs. You know, where they suck your guts out into a jar and pull your face so far back that every time you smile your thong vibrates.'

Margaret giggled.

'At the very least,' Maeve continued, 'we should go for the Botox. And maybe the breast implants.' She turned a little, taking a side-on look at herself. 'I could maybe just get one boob done – be nice to give Redmond a bit of variety. What do you think?'

'I think it might look a little strange.'

Maeve touched her expansive mane. 'Hair like this, love, I'm way past worrying about looking strange.' She winked, then turned for the door.

Margaret spent a few more minutes plastering make-up over her bruise, then headed back out onto the shopfloor.

Margaret chased a pervy man out of ladies' underwear. She placed an epileptic who was causing havoc in the changing rooms into the recovery position. A child got her anorak stuck in the escalator. She directed. And sometimes she misdirected.

She window-shopped at lunchtime, while eating a sausage roll and half of a Twix. She would have eaten the other half, but a homeless man asked her if she would give him something for a cup of tea, and she had felt compelled to oblige. The man called her a patronising fat cow.

She deliberately tried not to think of Walter. She'd stormed home, drunk herself to sleep, and spent most of Saturday in bed with a hangover. When she had recovered sufficiently, she logged onto the *Let's Be Mates* website to see if Walter had by any stretch of the imagination been in touch to apologise or explain. But nothing. Another timewaster. Cute, but still a timewaster. It was the final straw. She was never going to find a soulmate that way. So she thanked *Let's Be Mates* for their efforts and cancelled the direct debit.

In late afternoon, Maeve joined her for a patrol through the Men's Briefs, Boxers, Jockeys and Gunks Department – which, one might argue, served as a bit of a metaphor for the post-Ceasefire city itself. That is, generally quiet, but prone to sudden explosions of violence. The problem was that the Men's Briefs, Boxers, Jockeys and Gunks Department had been erroneously listed in one of the world's most popular gay guidebooks as the perfect place to meet a potential partner; this had led to quite a few misunderstandings, and not a few headbutts. Now the security staff, especially the men, had to travel in pairs. And avoid eye-contact.

'I was thinking some more about the make-over,' said Maeve.

'Yeah, I wish,' said Margaret.

'But what if you could afford it?'

'On these wages?'

'Wouldn't cost you a penny.'

'How's that?'

'Just one word. Compensation.'

'Compensation?'

'Oh, Margaret – that's just you all over. You nearly lost an eye on Friday, and you haven't even thought about compensation? Annie McDuff stubbed her toe last year, got a whole new kitchen from MFI out of it. The very least you'd get is your wart sorted out.'

'What wart?' Margaret gasped.

Maeve cackled, and led her into Fluffy Slippers and safety.

6
Office 12

There was no response from within Office 12, the mysterious Department within the Department of Education. Walter knocked on the door again, this time a little louder.

Still nothing.

He glanced nervously back. His friend and colleague Mark was now standing in the doorway of their office, watching curiously.

Take the bull by the horns, he urged himself. *It's only an office. How bad can it be?*

Walter knocked again, but this time he simultaneously twisted the door knob. He had half-expected it to be locked, but the door opened straight away. Almost before he saw anything, he became aware of an odd smell – like . . . burning candles? Incense? But with a hint of something savoury? It smelled a bit like The Body Shop, where the shop assistant had gorged herself on Tayto Cheese and Onion crisps.

There were five desks within, but only one, closest to the window, was occupied. The man behind the desk was wearing headphones and nodding his head gently; Walter could just about hear the tsk-tsk of music.

Walter cleared his throat. The man looked up, suddenly panicked, pulled the headphones off and made a dive for his desk drawer. He pulled it open and rested his hand on something inside.

'Who are you?' he snapped. 'What do you want?'

'No, no . . . I'm from down the corridor.' Walter thumbed behind him.

'You're not Special Branch?' Walter shook his head. The man visibly relaxed. He moved his hand from the open drawer.

'I just wanted a hand with my computer.'

'Wrong floor. IT's downstairs.'

'I know. It's not that sort of help I wanted.'

The man's head turned a little, more interested now. 'I see.'

'It's kind of – you know, personal.'

'You have pornography on your computer and you're scared of it being discovered.'

'No, it's not that.'

'You've been sending filthy emails to a colleague and now—'

'No, it's not that either. You see, I think I'm falling in love.'

It sat in the air for a moment. He couldn't believe he'd said it. Or even thought it. The man clasped his hands, and raised an eyebrow.

Walter quickly explained about his disastrous night out, the dating website and his urgent need to hack into it. The man, who appeared to be in his early thirties, nodded throughout. When Walter had finished, he said, 'So you come to me in your time of need.'

'Well, I was told . . .'

'What exactly were you told?'

'Nothing – just that you might know something about . . .'

'We know something about a lot of things, Walter.'

'Yes. I'm sure you do.'

'And this woman . . . she's spurned you and now you want me to destroy her life?'

'No, I—'

'Cancel her credit cards?'

'No, I—'

'Have her house repossessed?'

'No, really I—'

'If she has a relative on life-support I can—'

'*No.* I just want her phone number. Maybe her address.'

'Oh. Right. You're sure?'

'Yes. Absolutely.'

'Because we can do many things.'

'I'm sure you can.'

'A cup of coffee might have been nice.'

'I'm sorry?'

'Even though I have been just down the corridor from you all this time, you have never put your head around the door and said good morning, or asked me if I wanted a cup of coffee or enquired after my wife.'

Walter cleared his throat. 'How is your wife?'

'My wife is dead.'

'Oh. I'm very sorry. Would you, ahm, like a cup of coffee?'

'I have one already. Thank you.'

Walter looked at him. He looked back.

'Is – is there any chance you *could* help with my computer? If it's a question of, you know, a couple of quid . . .' Walter knew instinctively that it was the wrong thing to say, but it was out before he could help himself. The man's face seemed to freeze. He had been listening attentively, but now his eyes returned to his computer screen.

'I'm sorry,' Walter began. 'I didn't mean—'

'I am not the sort of person who thrusts his friendship on those who do not value it. But what have I ever done to make you treat me so disrespectfully?'

Walter swallowed. The man behind the desk was not large. He was wearing glasses and there was a half-eaten packet of Starburst and a coffee mug beside his computer. He appeared normal, in other words. But there was something deeply unsettling about him.

'We, uh, maybe we could go for a pint one time?' Walter suggested. 'Watch a match or something.'

The man nodded slowly. His eyes flitted up again. 'When?'

'Uh, well. Let's see. Ahm . . . Thursday?'

'I'm busy Thursday.'

'Ahm . . . what about, say, Saturday?'

'Busy.'

'Well . . . when suits you?'

'I'll have to check with my wife.'

'I thought your w—'

The man cut in. 'Who do you support?'

Walter hesitated. It suddenly struck him that it might be a loaded question. If he gave the wrong answer, he might never see Margaret again. He made a quick calculation. The man had to be talking Premiership, not the dodgy local teams. And there was probably a 75 per cent chance that he was a Man United supporter. But what if he wasn't? What if he followed Liverpool, their mortal enemies? Or, God forbid, Leeds? Walter's eyes fell on the coffee mug. He could just make out the very edge of a club crest.

'Oh, I'm a Chelsea man,' said Walter.

The vaguest hint of a smile appeared on the man's lips. An almost imperceptible nod.

'Give me the website address, I'll see what I can do.'

'Brilliant. Thanks a bunch.' Walter gave him the address.

'Okay, give me ten minutes.'

'Cheers, mate.'

Walter turned for the door. But the man wasn't finished. 'Walter?'

Walter turned, and realised in almost the same moment that he hadn't exchanged names with the strange man in Office 12. Yet he'd called him Walter. Twice.

'Mmm?'

'Some day, and that day may never come, I will call upon you to

22

do me a service in return. Until that day, consider this a gift from me, and my dear departed wife.'

Walter nodded, then hurried out.

That evening, on the way home on the train, Walter studied Margaret's file and tried to devise a strategy. He not only had the information she'd contributed to her webpage on *Let's Be Mates* but also her home address, phone numbers and bank details. If she didn't forgive him, he would order himself a toolkit from Argos using her credit-card information.

7
Every Cloud

Margaret was summoned to the Security Manager's office. His name was Peter Kawolski. His family had come to Belfast from Poland during the Second World War. (This has no bearing on anything.) He sat behind an untidy desk, facing a bank of CCTV monitors which covered each Primark floor. He offered Margaret a coffee. She accepted. As he poured he said, 'Margaret, I like to think of the security staff here as being like a family.'

'You mean we argue all the time, then someone runs off and gets pregnant?'

'No, I mean we're close. There are no secrets.' He looked her straight in the eye.

'Secrets?' asked Margaret. 'Why, have you heard something? You can tell me, I'm the soul of discretion. Redundancies, is it?'

Kawolski set the coffee-pot down. 'Not my secret, Margaret, *yours.*'

'I'm not sure I follow.'

Kawolski winked at her. She winked back. Kawolski winked again.

'Is this, like, *Candid Camera* or something?'

Kawolski sighed, and sat down heavily. 'Margaret – your eye.'

'Ah – gotcha. What about it? If it's putting people off I can wear an eye-patch. Or a paper bag with holes cut in it.'

'It's all over the shopfloor you're suing us for compensation.'

'Well, I—'

'You know, in my day a security guard could expect to get both arms broken in the morning and carry a ticking bomb out of the shop in the afternoon.'

Margaret blinked. 'How exactly would—'

'But these days all you have to do is sneeze and next thing you're suing Mother Nature for malpractice.'

'I really haven't decided to—'

'Look, there's no point in messing around, Margaret – this is how it works. You can sue us and it'll take eighteen months and all right, so maybe you'll get a couple of grand out of it, but half of that will go on legal fees, and you might be dead or a living vegetable by then anyway, or I can write you a cheque now for £250 and that's the end of it.'

'I'll take the cheque,' said Margaret.

'All right. Very businesslike. Do you want a Jammy Dodger?' He pushed the packet towards her, then took a chequebook out of a drawer and began to fill it in.

Margaret and Maeve went for a drink after work in Morrison's. Maeve had half a dozen leaflets for beauty salons and cosmetic surgeries. They spent twenty minutes going through them with mounting incredulity.

'The world is your oyster, kid,' said Maeve. 'So what's it to be?' She began to read down another one of the leaflets. 'Are you going for breast enhancement? Reduction? Uplift? Fat removal, liposuction? Tummy tuck? Face, neck or brow lift? Upper or lower eye bags? Calf implants?'

'Calf implants? What on earth . . . ?'

'God, I don't know.' She returned her attention to the list. 'Laser skin resurfacing, nose reshaping, ear correction, lip implants, cheek and chin implants, cyst and mole removal, thread vein removal, semi-permanent make-up, colonic hydrotherapy, lip dissolve, skin peeling . . .'

'Okay – enough! My head's spinning. Maeve, I only have £250. Tell me what I can afford.'

Maeve scanned the leaflet. 'Two-fifty . . . two-fifty . . . right here we are – two hundred and fifty pounds will get you . . . a good scrub with an old flannel. Margaret, they never put their prices on the leaflets, it's just to lure you in.'

'But £250 isn't going to get me very far, is it?'

'Well, if you were prepared to go off-menu it would go a lot further.'

'Off-menu?'

'Well, these places are all well and good, very flash, lovely carpets – and that's what you're paying for – but if you were to go off-menu, you could get a lot more for your money.'

'You mean, like paying wholesale?'

'Exactly. You go to someone's house instead of some glitzy clinic, your money goes twice as far.'

'Someone's house? I'm not sure . . .'

'It's fine, it's perfectly safe. Everyone round our way does it. You pop out for a cup of coffee, a bit of gossip and a spot of Botox or some collagen in your lips.'

'And it's safe enough? You hear these stories . . .'

'Of course it's safe. I mean, there are always a certain number of rogue beauty therapists. You only have to look at Gerry Adams.'

'*Gerry Adams*?'

'Oh God, yes. You ever wonder how he keeps that poker face when he gets accused of this or accused of that? Fact of the matter is, he *can't move* his face because he got a dodgy consignment of Botox. But apparently that's all been sorted out now. Everyone's at it. Licence to print money.'

Margaret took a sip of her drink. 'If it's all the same to you, I think I'd prefer to go somewhere, you know, *official*. At least if something does go wrong, I'll know who to sue.'

Maeve nodded. 'Aye, suppose you're right.'

Margaret didn't like to say, and she'd nothing against Maeve or the Falls Road where she lived, but she really didn't want to go to some back street Botoxist. Even if it was a good job, you heard things about that part of the world. She could never be certain that at least some of the proceeds wouldn't find their way back into the coffers of the IRA. And how could she possibly kiss anyone with her beautiful new lips if she knew that they were partially funding terrorism?

8

The Master Plan

Walter had worked out a long and quite complicated strategy for winning Margaret back. It involved a lot of surveillance. It meant following her to and from her job. Working out who her friends were. Where she socialised. Seeing by how much the information she'd volunteered to the *Let's Be Mates* website differed from the reality. He would become an expert on every single part of her life, and in knowing her so thoroughly he would be perfectly equipped to slot himself into her life. If she was interested in movies, he would invite her to the QFT or the Warner Village at the Odyssey. If she was an expert in wine, he would attend classes and try not to get drunk. If she liked mountain climbing he would wait at the bottom until she came down. It would be like Romeo and Juliet.

Except, these days, you'd call it stalking. He was aware of this, but it did not deter him.

Nevertheless, he did not undertake any of it. Because, he reasoned, at the end of the day, if she was really not interested, what was the point? And also, he had no patience at all. He never had had. It was a fact of his life that he always went for the quick solution, the easy option; if it didn't happen there and then – *now* – then he lost interest. It was the same at school. He had the intelligence, his reports said, he just lacked application. And the same with his hobbies. He had over-whelming, passionate interests right up to the point where any genuine work was involved, and then he lost interest. Once he was going to be a rock star. He thought about it eighteen hours a day for months, what he would wear, the songs he would write, how to get over that difficult second album syndrome. Eventually he put his money where his dreams were and went out and bought a synthesiser. It cost him £800 and the instructions all but boasted that even a moron could learn to play it. Walter wasn't even up to that level. He messed around with it for three days, but could only ever manage to make a sound like a car alarm. He tried to follow the first tutorial that came with it on a CD-Rom, but quickly lost his way, and then he was distracted by the football on TV.

Shortly after Wayne Rooney scored another wonder goal for Manchester United, Walter decided that being a rock god wasn't for him. It was a little late to become a professional footballer, but there was nothing to stop him getting fit. So he sold the keyboard to a gay Christian, losing £300 in the process, and reinvested most of what was left in a year's membership of an upmarket gym in the Culloden Hotel. Despite all advice to the contrary, Walter went hell-for-leather on every piece of equipment the gym had to offer, squeezing into one weekend what wiser bodies might have slowly built up over months.

Walter strained every muscle in his body, and could hardly walk for weeks. He never went back to the gym.

He was aware of all of these things, but seemed helpless to do anything about them. Because there was always the next time: he had learned his lesson, he would take things more easily, he would be patient, he would chill.

But here he was, marching up to Margaret's front door carrying flowers, chocolates and a bag of Ormo hamburger baps. This last was a bit of a joke. His crack to Margaret about 'feeding time at the zoo' on their first – and only – date had revolved around her prodigious appetite for bread rolls, and had caused considerable embarrassment. This was meant to show that they could laugh about past faux pas.

He was an eternal optimist, that way.

The house was semi-detached, with a well-kept garden in front. There was no gate. The drive undulated softly. Gypsy tarmac, thought Walter. They'd probably drunk the spirit level.

He was wearing a black sports jacket, white shirt, and black jeans. The chocolates were Milk Tray and the flowers were orange lilies.

Only as he reached the front door did Walter suffer a crisis of confidence. Why had he picked Milk Tray? Margaret was roughly his age, so she would have the same childhood memories of the Cadbury's TV advert, the mysterious man in black slipping into the beautiful model's luxury apartment and leaving the chocolates on her pillow, with the catch line, *All Because the Lady Loves Milk Tray*. The Milk Tray Man was tall, dark and handsome and Walter felt himself to be none of these things. He was wearing his glasses and they were speckled with rain; he felt heavy and vaguely ridiculous.

Walter stared at the front door. What if he left it until midnight, broke into the house, sneaked into her bedroom and left the chocolates on her pillow? *No*, Walter. Or he could race back to the shop and exchange them for . . . what? A Toblerone, so she could break her teeth?

Relax, relax, it'll be fine.

He looked at the flowers. God Almighty! Orange lilies! What was he thinking of!? They were undoubtedly the most beautiful flowers available on the garage forecourt. But what did they say? *Hello, beautiful lady, and No Surrender!* They were only flowers, but they symbolised so much! He might as well be wearing a sash! And . . . and . . . what had he read in the paper, just the other day? That cats who rubbed against lilies, and then licked themselves clean, were dropping dead all over the country, poisoned. What if she accepted the flowers, and they killed her cat?

My God, if I ditch the Milk Tray and the orange lilies, he thought, I'll only be left with the hamburger baps. She'll take one look at me and phone for the men in white coats.

Settle, Walter, settle! She is a nice woman, she will take it all in the spirit in which it is intended. She will accept your apologies and your gifts, and everything will work out just fine.

Walter raised his hand to ring the bell. Then he hesitated. He took the bag of hamburger rolls and tossed them over the hedge into the next-door neighbour's garden.

Then he rang the bell. He had the Milk Tray in one hand, the flowers in the other. He really needed to clean the spits of rain off his glasses. If only they had miniature windscreen wipers . . . Walter shook his head, amused, then straightened up, pulled himself together as he heard footsteps on a wooden floor.

Walter smiled – but not too widely. Didn't want to look like a grinning idiot.

The door opened.

'Hi – hope you don't mind—' But then he stopped. The man standing opposite him did not look happy.

'I . . . I . . .' Walter gasped. 'I was . . . is Margaret in?'

'No, she's not. I'm her husband. Who the hell are you?'

From next door, a woman shouted, 'Did you throw these bloody baps in my garden?'

9

By My Own Fair Hand

At nine o'clock on Monday evening, Margaret and Maeve were still sitting in Morrison's. What was supposed to be a quick drink after work had turned into a session, for the third Monday in a row. Margaret had tried telling herself that she was only there to show a bit of support for Maeve, whose husband was missing on that bird-watching trip to Colombia, but deep down she knew it wasn't true. She was there because she was lonely. She liked to think of herself as basically an optimistic person, but lately things just hadn't been going well. And that farrago with Walter McCoy or North or whatever the hell his name was, hadn't helped. Now here she was, the week hardly started, and she was already drunk.

Margaret glanced up from their corner table, and along the bar. It was lined with hopeful men in nice suits. None of them were paying even the occasional compliment of looking in her direction.

Am I really that bad? she thought, and she looked at Maeve. Maybe it's not me. She does look kind of scary, like she's escaped from the Hair Bear Bunch.

She'd been a security guard for too long. It was supposed to have just got her through the first few months after the break-up with her husband, but somehow it had stretched to two years. She quite enjoyed the work, but it was going nowhere.

Was this going to be the pattern? Hanging out in bars, looking for true love? She hadn't exactly exhausted the local dating agencies, but her experience with Walter had put her off trying again, at least for a while. What did that leave? Cruising around Tesco's, trying to pick up any one of the dozens of single men pushing their trolleys forlornly along the aisles? Or eating burgers in McDonald's in the hope of bagging a recently divorced father trying to bribe his offspring with a Happy Meal?

I'm getting old and bitter, she decided. I'll probably end up drinking

Meths in Botanic Gardens. She looked across at Maeve. She'd gone quiet as well. Soon she'd be blubbering about her missing husband. Normally Margaret was sympathetic, but she couldn't handle it now. She signalled to the quite cute waiter she'd put on a promise of a good tip earlier that they needed another round, then hurried off to the Ladies.

'Excuse me?'

Margaret had just emerged from the cubicle, and was washing her hands. Her first instinct, which she followed, was to check the back of her dress in case she was trailing a long stretch of toilet roll. She'd managed to do that once before, on another disastrous blind date. The fella hadn't pointed it out for thirty-seven minutes because he thought it was 'a good laugh'. No second date there.

Now there was the tall, blonde, slightly snooty-looking woman she'd seen in the bar earlier, sitting with another stick-thin woman, ordering cocktails, staring at her.

'Uhuh?' said Margaret, quickly drying her hands and making fists of them. That's what two years in Primark did for you.

'I hope you don't mind,' said the woman, moving closer – within inches of death, since Margaret had had three lessons in unarmed combat – 'but I couldn't help but notice your dress.'

'Uhuh?' said Margaret.

Oh great, some drunk, stuck-up cow's going to have a go at my dress.

At work they were occasionally allowed to rifle through the returns bin and buy whatever they fancied at a staff discount; they also had to discount the smells of BO and the unmistakable evidence of bodily secretions while making their selection. This dress, luckily, hadn't been too bad. There was just a small rip in the material you would hardly notice.

'Could I be really cheeky and ask where you got it?'

'Primark,' Margaret replied bluntly.

The woman laughed suddenly. 'No – really.'

Margaret was about to punch her in the throat.

'I just think it's absolutely beautiful.' The blonde moved closer still, and this time she reached out to touch the material. 'The cut of it, the design – it's gorgeous. I'm Emma Cochrane.'

Margaret looked blankly at her.

'Emma Cochrane – I own a boutique on the Lisburn Road.'

'Ah. Right.' She had heard of it. Out of her league. Margaret relaxed, slightly. She wasn't being assaulted, or insulted.

Emma Cochrane was all big eyes. 'I do all the shows,' she gushed, 'but I haven't seen anything as nice as this in a long time. It must have cost you a fortune.'

£8.99, with the staff discount. 'Well, you know . . .'

'Indeed I do. Please. You simply *have* to tell me the designer.'

She almost – *almost* – blabbed it out. But then, from nowhere, she had a sudden moment of clarity, a Road-to-Damascus moment, although if she'd been driving she would have been hauled over.

'Actually, to tell you the truth,' she began, a sure indication that there was a colossal whopper on the way, 'I made it myself.'

'You *did not.*'

Margaret nodded. 'I did. I design all my own stuff.'

'You mean there's others? As good as this?'

Margaret shrugged. 'I couldn't really say.'

'Well, who do you normally sell through?'

'I don't . . . I'm just waiting to meet the right people.'

'Oh, my goodness – I'm getting goose bumps. This is so lucky, meeting you like this. I'd kill for this dress, and there are others! Darling, we simply have to talk! Come and join us for a drink. I'm in with my fashion buyer – we're just over in the corner. Please, promise me you'll come.'

'I, ah – well, I suppose it couldn't do any harm.'

Emma Cochrane clapped her hands together, then surprised Margaret by kissing her on both cheeks. 'This is going to be so fantastic! Come on.'

Margaret hesitated. 'I just need a minute to . . .' She nodded at the mirror.

'Of course. I'm sorry. Please – as soon as you can.'

Margaret nodded, and Emma Cochrane hurried out of the Ladies. Margaret hurried back into her cubicle and ripped the Primark label out of her dress.

10
The Tears of a Clown

Walter did what all normal men do when confronted with the truth. He ran away.

One moment he was done up like a dog's dinner, bearing gifts of chocolate, flowers and hamburger baps, hopeful of a reconciliation with a lovely woman; the next he was confronted by her angry husband and flying up the road like Billy Whizz.

And what hurt more than anything?

Not the fact that his relationship with Margaret was on the darkest side of doomed.

Not the fact that she had clearly misled him about her marital state.

But the fact that her husband screamed up the road after him: 'That's right, run, you speccy fat git! I can walk quicker than that, Fat Chops! You come round here again, you four-eyed clown, I'll break your friggin' neck.'

Two references to being fat. Two references to his glasses.

I walk up to a door like Casanova. I run away like Krusty the Clown.

Walter adjourned to a pub. He sat in the corner, drinking pint after pint, orange lilies on the chair beside him, the Milk Tray open on his lap.

I need to turn my life around. I need to get fit. The diet will start. Tomorrow. He slipped an orange creme into his mouth. It tasted good.

A barman came over and said, 'You can't eat chocolates in here.'

Walter said, with something of a slur, 'But I'm the Milk Tray Man.'

The barman rolled his eyes and walked away, muttering under his breath. Walter couldn't be sure, but it sounded like he said, 'More like the Michelin Man.'

Walter glared after him. He moved the chocolate box under the table. His fingers snaked into the second layer.

*　　*　　*

Walter was late for work the next day, his head busting with a hang-over. Mark got him coffee, then went and stood looking out over the dual carriageway to Newtownards as Walter recounted the harrowing events of the previous evening. He let it all hang out. The rush of adrenaline on approaching Margaret's house. The last-minute nerves. The sheer horror of confronting her husband. The total embarrassment of charging up the street. The cutting remarks. His glasses. His weight. His storytelling was so compelling that by the time he was finished he had managed to bring himself to the verge of tears.

Silence hung like a wet blanket over the office. Thirty seconds. A minute. Eventually Walter spoke, his voice small, chastened.

'So – what do you think?'

Mark turned from the window. 'I'm thinking of standing as an MP.'

'What?'

'I know – but the Trimble's gone and the Party's in disarray; now's the time to get in.'

'I meant about last night.'

'Oh, for godsake, Walter, you're so self-centred.'

'What?'

'The country's going to wrack and ruin and all you're worried about is your love handles! Go on a diet! Go and get your eyes fixed!'

Walter glared at him. They had been friends for fifteen years, but they occasionally had bust-ups like this.

'Well, I'm not flippin' voting for you.'

'You never vote anyway.'

'Well, next time I will. And I'll vote for someone else. The DUP.'

They lapsed into a moody silence. Mark went back to his desk and struck his keyboard with even greater fervour than usual. Walter went onto the internet and looked up 'laser eye-surgery'.

Eventually Walter said, 'It says here that ninety-five per cent of laser eye-surgery operations are successful.'

'Does that mean that the other five per cent are catastrophes?' Mark didn't look up, but he sounded more like his old self.

'Please don't. I'm serious about this.'

Now Mark peered over the top of his monitor. 'Oh yes, I've heard that if the surgeon sneezes or someone nudges his arm, the laser can shoot right through the eye and blow the back of your head off.'

This didn't much help Walter's hangover. He sought refuge in a can of fat Coke and a gravy ring. The diet was now scheduled to start the day after tomorrow. You couldn't start a diet with a hangover. You needed grease and sugar. Everyone knew that. It probably said it in a book somewhere.

'Perhaps,' Mark suggested, 'you could just get one eye done. Then if something goes wrong you'll only be hideously disfigured on one side of your face.'

It was time to change the subject.

'Are you really serious about becoming an MP?' Walter asked. 'Wouldn't you have to be selected?'

'Oh, God aye, but the way things stand, Hermann Goering could get signed up. What's wrong with your glasses anyway?'

Walter shrugged.

'It's this bloody Margaret woman, isn't it?'

'No – she's dead and gone now.'

'Then what's the point?'

'I need to change, Mark. Something dramatic.'

'And getting your eyes done counts as dramatic?'

'Well, it's a start. And you can just go in and have it done, it's not like piano lessons.'

Mark blinked at him. 'You what?'

'I mean, it's not going to take years to achieve. You just go in and they laser your eyes and you're done in five minutes, and then the world's your lobster.'

'Providing nothing goes tragically wrong.'

'I'm going to have it done. I've decided.'

'Well, more power to your elbow. Which, by the way, you'll need to help control the guide dog.'

'They'll never select you,' said Walter. 'They're desperate, but they're not *that* desperate.'

'You just wait and see. Or in your case . . .'

Walter was about to snap something back when a sudden movement along the corridor grabbed his attention. The door to the very mysterious Office 12 was opening and the creepy little man who'd helped him hack into Margaret's website appeared. He was looking directly up the corridor towards Walter. Walter concentrated his attention on his computer screen, but then he couldn't help but glance up again, and the man was still there, and now his hand was raised, and his index finger was pointing directly at Walter. The finger slowly curled back towards Office 12, then pointed at Walter again.

'Oh *hell*,' said Walter.

11

The Eagle Has Been Arrested

Margaret bounced into Primark the next morning, despite the fact that she had an enormous hangover. She was humming 'The Only Way Is Up'. Before she clocked on, she yanked three dresses similar to the one she'd rescued from the returns bin off the rails and paid for them, not forgetting to use her staff discount. She immediately took them into the toilets and removed the Primark labels.

She knew, of course, that this wasn't quite right, passing off these cheap, mass-market dresses as her own designs, but as far as she was concerned it was only a mild deception. It was her *in* to the fashion business. She'd been waiting all her life for a break like this, and she wasn't going to waste it. She would turn up at *Emma Cochrane* to meet Emma Cochrane and her fashion buyer Louise, sell them the dress she'd worn last night plus the three she'd now bought, for some exorbitant price, and then show them her own designs she'd been working on at home for years. Hopefully Emma and Louise would be just as excited about them. Who knew where it would all lead? Walter had joked about Paris and Milan – and she had put herself down by mentioning Cullybackey. Well, she would soon show him.

Margaret's walkie-talkie crackled and she was summoned urgently to the Security Manager's office. At first she was panicked that her subterfuge with the Primark dresses had somehow already been rumbled, but as she approached the office she saw that Mr Kawolski was standing in the doorway waiting for her, but also that he was keeping an eye on Maeve, who was sitting slumped in a chair opposite his desk. All Margaret could see from the back was Maeve's expansive, voluminous hair bobbing up and down, like a bush blowing in the wind.

'What's . . . ?' Margaret began.

Mr Kawolski put a finger to his lips, and gently closed the door. 'It's her husband.'

'Oh my God. Is he dead?'

'Worse. He's been arrested in Colombia.'

'What? What on earth for?'

'Training guerrillas.'

'Gorillas? But it's birds he's interested in.' Mr Kawolski gave her a look. And the penny dropped. '*Guerrillas*? You mean—'

'Terrorists. She woke up this morning and there were reporters camped outside her house. Seems he got picked up in a restricted area.'

'Oh my God. And she had no idea?'

They both looked through the glass panel in the door at her.

'What do you think?' asked Mr Kawolski.

'I don't know. No, I *do* know. She was always talking about Redmond and his birds. She *couldn't* have known. But all this time he's been . . .'

'Well, there's a lot of unemployed terrorists out there. They can't all become politicians.'

'But that's presuming . . . I mean, it could be some kind of mistake.'

'Well, according to what I heard on the news he had half a kilo of Semtex in his backpack. And that's not something you would normally associate with ornithology.'

Margaret took a deep breath. 'The poor woman,' she said.

'Aye,' said Mr Kawolski. 'That's why I called you up. There's only so many *there, there*'s I can say. I'll send some coffee up. Take as long as you want. Although I should warn you, if the press arrive you'll have to take her out the back way. Can't have Primark being associated with . . . well, you know.'

Margaret stood straight and tall. 'Mr Kawolski, whatever happened to "innocent until proven guilty"?'

Mr Kawolski raised his eyebrows. 'Just do what you can, Margaret.'

He beetled away along the corridor.

'Do you know what my first thought was when I heard he'd been arrested?' Maeve wiped at her eyes with one hand, and raised her coffee with the other. 'Eggs. Birds' eggs. Rare birds' eggs. Not bloody Semtex. Oh, how could I have been so bloody stupid?'

Margaret tried her best to be reassuring. 'He's only been arrested. It doesn't prove—'

'But it all makes sense now!' Maeve exploded. 'All those trips abroad. I mean to say, who could be that interested in bloody birds?'

'Well, people travel to football matches.'

'Not for months at a time! Not using a false passport!'

'He had a—'

'Well, not false. His twin brother's. Redmond had a couple of convictions, and it sometimes made travelling awkward. So he would put the priest's outfit on and fly through passport control.'

'A priest's outfit?'

'His brother's a priest – Father Damian. Margaret, please, it made perfect sense at the time.'

'And you had no idea he was . . .'

'Training guerrillas? Of course not! My God, he couldn't train a Jack Russell.' She let out a loud, long sigh. Then shook her head. 'He'd bring all these hundreds of photographs of rare birds home. I wasn't really that interested. I used to say, "They all look the same to me". And now that I think of it, they probably were all the same. One man, a camera and a stuffed parrot. But I still love him.'

'I know you do.'

'But what am I going to do?'

Margaret drummed her fingers on Mr Kawolski's desk. She really liked Maeve, but she didn't know her husband from Adam. And if he was training guerrillas then he deserved all he got.

'Well, as I see it,' she began, 'you can either do a Tammy Wynette and stand by yer man, or you can sell your story to the Sunday papers and reinvest the money in a fashion design business I'm starting.'

Maeve blinked at her, not quite believing what she was hearing.

'I'm sorry,' Margaret said quickly. 'I shouldn't have said that.'

Maeve wiped at her eyes again. She put her coffee cup down and stood up. She too had endured three lessons' worth of unarmed combat training, Margaret reminded herself, and prepared to receive another bruise.

'How much do you think they would pay?' Maeve asked.

12
Doing Bird

Sunday is visitors' day at La Picota prison outside Bogotá, Colombia, but Redmond O'Boyle was not hopeful. His nearest and dearest were thousands of miles away in Belfast, and probably hated his guts. He spent the morning sitting in his single cell, which he shared with fifteen others, nearly all of them narco-traffickers. They believed he was also in the drugs business. If they knew that he was suspected of training FARC guerrillas, they would probably have stabbed him. News had not yet leaked out. But it soon would.

The heat was stifling, and so was the conversation. Redmond knew very little Spanish. He had picked up enough to say, 'There goes another lovely bird,' and 'This is a mercury tilt, very old-fashioned,' but neither phrase was going to get him very far in La Picota.

Redmond had been in prisons at home, but this place was something else. There'd already been a number of raids by the prison guards which had recovered computers, mobile phones, an AK-47 (minus ammunition), dynamite, shovels, a billiard table, alcohol and three women. Many of the prisoners seemed free to conduct their nefarious business from within their cells, and the more they could afford to pay in bribes, the better their conditions.

Redmond had bugger-all money with which to pay bribes. When he had sought payment from FARC for his explosives expertise, they had paid him with cocaine.

In the early afternoon, when they were finally allowed out into the crowded exercise yard, Redmond was able to cook a little of his own rice, and barter some of the cocaine he kept in the false heel of his shoe for some chicken. But before he could actually eat any of it a squad of guards came and kicked it over, then told him he had a visitor.

He was escorted into an administration block away from where the normal visits took place, so he knew something was up. The man waiting in the small interview room introduced himself as Martin

Brown, the British Ambassador. He was a large, florid man, in a white suit. He was sweating heavily. He shook Redmond's hand and said, 'This is a bit of an awkward one, eh?' and indicated that he should sit down. There was a desk between them. There were bloodstains on it. 'Sorry it's taken me so long to see you,' Brown said wearily, 'but it's chaos out there, bombs going off here, there and everywhere. Still, I expect you know more about that than I do.'

'I'm an ornithologist.'

'Yes. Quite. So, how are they treating you?'

'I haven't had a proper meal in a week, I share a cell with fifteen drug dealers, I'm covered in flea bites, the place is crawling with roaches, if I don't succumb to the disease and squalor I will undoubtedly be murdered.'

'Well. Yes. The ahm good news is that your people back home – Sinn Fein – have already started a Bring Him Home campaign. The not quite so good news is that the DUP have launched a Leave Him There campaign. They're rather crossing each other out.'

'Has my wife been in touch?'

'No, I'm afraid not.'

'I have to speak to her. Explain. She had no idea. If I had a phone card, I could call and explain. But I don't have a phone card.'

It was a hint. It was ignored.

'I understand that your people will be organising your legal representation. In the meantime I've brought you some bits and pieces to see you through.' He lifted a cardboard box from the floor beside him. It was sealed with Scotch tape. The Ambassador patted the top of it. 'There's quite a good Agatha Christie in here. Fiendishly clever. That headmaster had me fooled.'

Then he stood and held out his hand. 'Well, duty done,' he said.

'What about my wife?' Redmond asked, clasping it.

'Pen and paper in there, old chap,' said the Ambassador, nodding down at the box. 'That's your best bet.'

He smiled, then strode to the door. He knocked twice, and a guard opened it. He stepped forward, then hesitated for a moment. He looked back at Redmond. 'We will do everything in our power to help you, Redmond, but the fact is that your kind make me sick. And you give ornithologists a very bad name.'

He nodded again, then hurried out.

The box contained a Fray Bentos Steak & Kidney Pie, a small tin of shoe polish, the aforementioned Agatha Christie, a notebook, two pens, a lengthy London *Times* report of a cricket match between Sri Lanka and Bangladesh, eight tiny containers of raspberry jam most probably

purloined from a hotel breakfast buffet, a Lynx deodorant, a Head &
Shoulders shampoo, for frequent use, and a Gideon Bible.

Redmond looked forlornly at the contents of the box and wondered
if by any stretch of the imagination he could construct a bomb out of
them. He could possibly make some kind of deadly weapon with the
Fray Bentos lid, since they were notoriously difficult to get off and
sharp as hell, and the deodorant probably had some explosive qualities. However, before he got much further than thinking about it, his
cellmates came back in from the exercise yard and stole it all.

Except for the notebook and pens.

It was pointless protesting. They would chop his head off, and not
even bother to make it look like a suicide.

Redmond settled himself on the floor of his cell, with the notebook
in his lap. He was concerned for the state of his marriage. He'd had
no choice but to keep Maeve in the dark. *What you don't know can't
hurt you.* Also, she was a bit of a blabbermouth. But he loved her, and
wanted to explain. He would write her a very long and impassioned
justification of his actions. He would also apologise profusely and beg
her to forgive him, and swear his undying love. He was going to fill
every single page; he would overpower her with the strength of his
argument, the depth of his love.

Except then someone slapped his head, stole the notebook and
charged out of the open door of the cell. By the time Redmond tracked
him down to a dark corner of the exercise yard he'd sold off all but
one of the pages for use as cigarette papers. Even then he had to pay
him with lashings of cocaine to get the single remaining page back.

Redmond returned to his cell floor, placed the single page on the
cracked tile, and lifted his pen.

Dear Maeve, he wrote. *Am up s**t creek without a paddle. Please send
paddle. All my love, Redmond.*

13

The Odd Number

The man in Office 12 was still the only man in Office 12. The four desks which had been empty before were still empty. Walter stepped through the opening and the man in Office 12 closed the door behind him. This was quite unsettling.

'Take a seat,' said the man.

Walter sat at one of the empty desks. The man crossed to his own desk, lifted a notebook, then ripped a sheet out. He placed the sheet face up in front of Walter. Walter looked down. There were two lines of writing in red felt tip. The top line said *Psyclops* and the second *Malone Road*.

'This is . . . what?' Walter asked.

'Plastic surgery, beauty treatments, and the best laser eye business in the city. If I was getting my eyes done, that's where I'd go.'

'But how did you even know I was contemplating . . . ?'

The man, by now back behind his desk, patted his computer monitor. 'There's very little goes on in this building I don't know about.'

'Oh.'

Walter folded the sheet of paper. 'Well,' he said, beginning to rise from his chair, 'I'll certainly bear it in—'

'Where are you going?'

Walter hesitated. 'I thought . . .'

'No.'

Walter sat again. Apart from the folded sheet, the desk was empty. Pristine, in fact. He scanned the room, and saw that all of the walls were bare. He was aware that the man was looking at him rather intensely. Walter's shirt was sticking to his back.

'So,' said Walter.

'So?'

'I, ah, don't even know your name.'

The man nodded. 'You can call me Steve.'

'Steve. All right, Steve. How's it going, Steve?'

'It's going all right, Walter. We should get out for that drink one night.'

Walter cleared his throat. 'Yes, that would be nice. I, ah, only ever see you in here. So, ah, why are there five desks?'

'Why are your eyes blue?'

'Excuse me?'

Steve smiled. It wasn't a very pleasant smile. His mouth went down at the corners.

'So, how did the big reconciliation go?' he asked.

'It didn't, really.'

Steve frowned. 'Was there a problem with the information I retrieved for you?'

'No, the information was fine.'

'Well, that's good.'

Walter nodded. Steve nodded. There was a lengthy silence. Walter desperately wanted to get back to his own desk, but couldn't.

'So, uh, what exactly is it that you do in here?' he asked eventually.

Steve smiled again. 'I could tell you, but . . .'

'Then I'd have to kill you,' Walter finished, and smiled.

Steve did not. He suddenly looked quite angry. And a little bit hurt.

'Sorry,' Walter said quickly. 'Didn't mean to cut you off.'

Steve shrugged. 'That's all right. Maybe I need some new lines. Are you good at new lines, Walter?'

'I'm not sure what you—'

'Are you good at making things up?'

'Well, I . . .'

'I looked at your website on that dating agency. You're quite the little fabricator, aren't you? An elastic approach to the truth. We could do with a man like you.'

'You could?'

'Don't you get tired, just ticking boxes all day?'

'I don't tick them all day. Just part of the day. And, and, like, don't you . . . just tick boxes as well?'

'No, Walter. That's not what we do. You tick the boxes. We untick the boxes.'

'I'm sorry, I don't quite . . .'

'If you say up, we say down. If you say left, we say right. If you say live, we say die.'

It sat in the air for perhaps ten seconds. Then Walter gave a little shrug. 'I thought we all just collated exam results and worked out school budgets.'

'Yes, well, there's many a slip between an exam result and a school budget.'

'There is?'

'Walter, can I be frank with you?'

'Yes, of course.'

'And it won't leave this room?'

Walter shook his head.

'Think about it. Last year, the Department spent eighteen million pounds on building new school playgrounds. Did you ever stop to think how anyone could *possibly* spend that much on a few sets of swings and a slide? It's used for *other things*.'

'What sort of . . . ?'

'That's not for you to know, Walter. Not yet. But in time, perhaps. You see, this building is the HQ of the Department of Education. But the moment you stepped through that door there, you entered the Department of Re-education.'

'Re . . .'

'Black propaganda, Walter. We're a specialist unit. The élite. We can use a man like you, with a cavalier approach to the truth. We have a desk available – right where you are. At least until Number Three comes back.'

Walter shifted uncomfortably. 'Number Three. That's like, his codename or something?'

'No, Walter, that's his job.'

'I don't . . .'

'His job is to remove the number three from all official documents.'

'Remove it? I don't quite . . .'

'He removes the three from all phone numbers issued to the public. He removes it from press releases. When the Department announces its works budget for the coming year, all financial projections are devoid of the number three. Do you get the picture, Walter?'

'I . . . I think I do, but why would you do that?'

'Because it is our job. Our role. Our contribution.'

'To what?'

'To the Department of Re-education.'

'But you can't just . . . I mean, people must notice. Don't they phone up and complain?'

'Of course they do, Walter. But they phone the wrong number.'

Walter nodded, as if everything suddenly made sense. It didn't, of course. He wanted out of there more than ever. But still he couldn't move. Instead, trying to change the subject, he nodded at the next desk along.

'So who, uh, sits there?'

'Number Four,' said Steve.

14
A Design for Life

Margaret walked along the Lisburn Road with a spring in her step. This could be her big break. Her defining moment. She was nervous, excited and confident. She *deserved* this. *Emma Cochrane*, the upscale boutique where she hoped to make a killing, was only a further 100 yards along. Margaret glanced at her watch. She was forty-seven minutes early for her appointment.

She had told herself in the staff changing room in Primark that it wasn't smart to appear too keen, yet here she was already outside the shop with the best part of an hour to kill. She spotted a café on the opposite side of the street, and nipped across.

The café was called *Irma La Deuce* and it served sixteen different kinds of carrot cake. Margaret tried two – one with coconut, and one with something vaguely orangey. She had an espresso as well. She liked the new Belfast, with its hundreds of cafés. They'd all sprung up since peace had broken out. In the old days you'd be lucky to get a cup of instant, a sausage roll and a thorough body search. Now there were a thousand new smells to appreciate, exotic imported coffees and chocolates, all produced by natives who weren't quite as exploited as they previously had been.

And thinking of distant, exploited people reminded Margaret of her friend and colleague Maeve, trying to sell her story to the press. She wondered if she'd had any joy. Certainly the local papers might be interested, but the big money would come from the nationals. How keen would they be on the story of a wife whose husband had fooled her into thinking he was going away on bird-watching trips, when he was actually training FARC guerrillas? Not very, Margaret reflected. If he'd been having an affair with some dusky Latin babe, then perhaps they might shell out. But it seemed Redmond O'Boyle was just another ex-terrorist showing entrepreneurial spirit, and they were a dime a dozen.

46

She stared across the road at *Emma Cochrane*. It looked so *chic*. Three-quarters of the women she knew pronounced it *chick*.

Be confident.

Act like you're in control.

Take no bulls**t.

Margaret had the four label-less Primark dresses in a plastic bag, and an A4 envelope containing twelve of her own designs.

What if they love the Primark dresses, and hate my own designs?

My career will be over before it's even started.

Sure I'll make a little bit on the dresses, but that's not what it's about.

Margaret launched into her second slice of carrot cake. It was a little sour, and she thought that what had appeared to be orange, wasn't. But it was still quite pleasant. And she didn't want her tummy rumbling during her big interview.

Carrot cake.

Why take a chance with the designs?

Sell the dresses, and offer them the carrot of further designs?

Yes! But make them pay upfront. Or offer some kind of a deal. A licensing agreement. A development deal.

That's the way to play it!

Margaret checked her watch again. Ten minutes to go, but that wasn't so bad. Nothing wrong with being a little keen. She took the envelope containing her own designs and folded it into the inside pocket of her knee-length leather coat. She was also wearing a black T-shirt and jeans. Smart but casual. Her stomach rumbled. Nerves.

Don't be over-awed.

You are every bit their equal.

Margaret felt her throat go dry as she approached *Emma Cochrane*. A trickle of sweat ran down her brow. She opened the door and stepped inside. Emma and Louise, her fashion buyer, were standing behind the counter. There were two customers. Emma's face immediately broke into a wide smile and she hurried across. She planted a kiss on either cheek.

'Oh, you are *such* a joker!' she exclaimed, nodding down at Margaret's bag of dresses. 'A Primark bag!'

Margaret laughed, but inside, her stomach turned over. *What a fool I am!*

Louise came over and repeated the kiss-kiss routine, while Emma took the bag out of Margaret's hand.

'Oh, I can't resist another moment!' She opened the bag, peered in, then lifted the dresses out with the delicacy a priest might reserve for the Turin Shroud. 'Look at them, Louise!' she cried. 'Just look at them!'

The two customers in the shop turned to watch.

'Truly a star is born!'

Margaret smiled. Or she tried to. Her throat was not only dry now, but tight. And her tongue felt *thick*. She could only manage a mild grimace. She felt cold. Yet she was sweating. *God, I don't handle pressure well at all.*

Louise was looking at her now quite oddly. 'Are you all right?'

Margaret nodded.

'Your eyes – they look a little puffy.'

Who're you to talk? You've crow's feet, and legs.

'Just a late night last night.' She heard her own voice. It was a dry rasp. She looked at Emma. There were little pings of light flashing about her head.

That's not right. That's ... really ... not ... right ...

Suddenly she felt very, very dizzy. She staggered. Then she threw up.

Not just threw up. Projectile vomited. It was completely beyond her control.

She was sick on Emma's legs and shoes. She sprayed poison over the last of the Winter Collection. She stumbled towards the counter, grabbed onto it for support, then boked up over the cash register.

Everything was revolving.

Margaret forced herself to turn round; she tried to utter an apology, but the only thing she could emit was another long stream of stinking fluid, this time over the summer dresses and a fake fox fur.

Her legs gave out then, and she slithered to the ground. In the background, someone was crying. She couldn't make out who. Her eyes were by now completely swollen shut.

Margaret lay flat out on *Emma Cochrane's* soiled floor, too ill to even begin contemplating the scale of the disaster.

Emma Cochrane herself, flecks of sick across her blouse and dripping from the Primark bag in her hand, stood over her. 'Would you like a tissue, darling?' she asked.

15

The Eye of the Beholder

All in all, after a shaky start, it wasn't turning out to be such a bad week for Walter North. He had a job offer. The fact that it was quite a dodgy job offer was neither here nor there. It was an offer; somebody valued him. It was a light at the end of the tunnel, even if it was a tunnel he chose not to venture down. After all, who in their right minds would want to work in Office 12, the Department of Disinformation within the Department of Education? Of course he'd made all the right noises. *Oh yes, I'll think about it.* But no, it wasn't for him.

It was still a good sign.

Now he was taking another step in the right direction. He was never going to look like Brad Pitt, but every little helped. Get the eyes sorted out, then the rest could follow. Psyclops Surgeries was housed in a plush private hospital on the Malone Road. A plaque outside was like a *Who's Who* of top Indian surgeons. Psyclops not only specialised in laser eye-surgery, but also plastic surgery. It had Ear, Nose & Throat Specialists, a children's ward with a McDonald's franchise and also claimed to house Ireland's top private Allergy Research and Confinement Suite. The carpets inside were so thick you could have used a Strimmer on them. And the women behind the counter were *gorgeous*. Walter told them he was here for a consultation about his eyes, and they gave him a form to fill in.

This time he told the truth. He was through with lying. He'd learned his lesson with Margaret. He'd lost her because he'd been cavalier with the truth on his form for the *Let's Be Mates* website. Besides, there was nothing to be gained by lying about his health. That said, he shaved a couple of pounds off his weight, and rather exaggerated the amount of exercise he took. There wasn't a specific question about gravy-ring consumption.

While he waited to be called, Walter picked through the magazines on a table in the waiting area and settled on a copy of *Big Houses*. It had a strapline which said, *Properties You Probably Can't Afford*. Walter wasn't sure if it was meant to be ironic. He flicked through, growing more and more depressed. His big idea, to get out of the Civil Service, was to become a property developer. To buy houses, do them up, sell them on. Or rent them out. But he had managed to squirrel away precisely nothing during his long years ticking boxes in the Department of Education. Walter sighed. These houses were huge. Five bedrooms minimum. Swimming pools. Snooker rooms. Tennis courts. When was he ever going to have enough money to get his foot on the property ladder? Unless . . . Office 12?

'Mr North? Mr Benson will see you now.'

Walter stood and followed the pretty nurse down a short corridor and into a small room packed with hi-tech equipment. A teenager in a white smock smiled hello and told him to sit on a leather couch. While Walter made himself comfortable the boy examined Walter's form. Then he looked up and said, 'Relax, Mr North. This is just a preliminary consultation. And I'm sure we can get that nose sorted out for you.'

Walter's mouth dropped open. 'It's not my—'

The boy smiled. 'Only rakin'.'

'That's not funny,' said Walter. 'I'm nervous enough as it is.'

'Sorry. No offence. Let's take a look, eh?' As the boy moved closer, he reached up and began to move a piece of equipment on a mechanical arm towards Walter's eyes.

'Shouldn't . . . shouldn't we wait for the optician?'

'I am the optician.'

'Seriously?'

Benson cleared his throat. 'Yes, Mr North.'

'Are you some sort of child prodigy?'

'No, Mr North.'

'But you only look about twelve.'

'I can assure you, I'm fully qualified.'

'Okay. All right. I'm sorry. I'm just nervous.'

'There's nothing to be nervous about. It's only an examination.'

'I know that. I'm sorry. You just look so young.'

'Healthy living. Now, if you'll just move your head forward a little . . . and yes, rest your chin there . . .'

'And I'm sure you have all the certificates and all. You know. In case anyone wanted to see them.'

'Yes, I do, Mr North. They're on the wall of my study at home. Perhaps you would care to come round?'

'That, ahm, won't be necessary.'

'Because I could ask Mummy to show you them.'

Walter concentrated on a series of red dots now appearing on a small screen before him. 'Point taken,' he said.

'Now then, you'll see a series of red dots . . . Every time a green dot appears anywhere on the screen, I want you to click that little button beside you – see it?' Walter nodded. 'Good. It'll help us check your field of vision. At least, I think that's what it does.'

Walter moved his head back a little and looked at the young optician. 'We got off on the wrong foot. That's my fault. I apologise.'

'All right. Let's just get started.' Benson indicated for Walter to move and retake the position.

Walter moved forward. Then back. 'It's just my friend says these operations are only ninety-five per cent successful and—'

'You're worried about the five per cent.'

'Yes.'

'Mr North, the five per cent refers to the very small number of people who experience no significant improvement in their eyesight as a result of their treatment here. If your eyesight doesn't improve significantly, you get a full refund.'

'Ah. Right.'

'Has that put your mind at ease?'

'Yes, it has. Absolutely.'

'Good. Now if you'll just . . .'

'So I don't have to worry about the five per cent.'

'No.'

'And nobody's head just explodes if you miss the target.'

'No.'

'And there's no disfigurement or horrific scarring.'

'No!' The optician took a deep breath, and appeared to be counting to ten under his breath. Or at least seven. Then: 'Mr North, if five per cent of our patients suffered damage to their eyesight as a result of our procedures, don't you think there'd be huge gangs of blind people roaming the streets of Belfast bumping into things and demanding justice?'

'I suppose.'

'Very well, then, might we continue?'

Walter nodded. He set his chin on the little cushion and tried to concentrate on the red dots. Then he moved back again and said, 'Just one more thing.'

'*Yes*?'

'You're wearing glasses.'

'Yes, I am.'

'And yet . . .'

'Mr North, it's a free world.'

'But it's not a very good advertisement.'

'Mr North, one of my colleagues does fourteen breast enlargement procedures every day. He does not feel the need to enlarge his own breasts.'

'Well, that's hardly a comparison.'

'Another colleague does penis extensions. He has so far resisted the temp—'

'Well, he mightn't need it.'

Benson folded his arms. 'Do you really want this done, Mr North?'

'Yes, I do.'

'Then either shut your cake-hole and let me get on with the examination, or get the hell out of my chair!'

Walter cleared his throat again and moved forward.

Walter returned to the front desk to arrange a date for his laser treatment. There was a cancellation the following week, but Walter lied and said he was off on holiday. They gave him one in a month's time. There was no need to rush.

As he made his way out of the reception area an ambulance roared up to the entrance, siren blaring. Paramedics leaped from the back, slid a stretcher out and hurried it through the sliding doors. Walter stepped back to let them pass, glancing curiously down at the poor woman lying on it. Her eyes were bulging, her lips were blue and her skin was deathly white.

But he knew who it was.

'Margaret?' Walter whispered, even as she was carried away out of sight.

16
A Matter of Life and Death

In retrospect, one could argue that Emma Cochrane, of extremely expensive clothes and shoes fame, insisted on the violently ill Margaret Gilmore being taken to Belfast's most exclusive private hospital not out of concern, but to protect her prospective investment. She had discerned a remarkable talent in the designer, and how would it have looked if she'd merely bundled Margaret into an NHS ambulance and left her to the mercies of the Ulster Hospital? Margaret could end up like a James Dean of the fashion business – three remarkable dresses, huge potential and then a tragic accident (plus, in all possibility, MRSA). The Superbug simply wasn't allowed in the private hospital on the Malone Road, at least not without an appointment.

In fact, Emma Cochrane insisted on first-class treatment for Margaret Gilmore because she was a decent woman. Only a very small percentage of herself considered it as a smart business move. Certainly not more than 17 per cent. Also, it would hardly have helped her business to have someone dying on the premises. She knew from past experience – a stick-thin model had given birth to a stick-thin child, a Twiglet, in one of her changing rooms – that the Psyclops Surgeries paramedics were first class.

Emma and her fashion buyer Louise followed the ambulance directly to the hospital, pausing only to close up the store, phone their cleaner, supervise the cleaning, return to their prospective homes to shower and change into clothes more fitting to a hospital environment – comfortable but stylish, colourful enough to suggest hope, but with a black top underneath in case mourning was required.

And it looked like it might be.

The doctors did a lot of headshaking. It was clear that there had been some sort of massive allergic reaction – but to what? There were standard procedures, which were followed meticulously, but Margaret showed little sign of improvement.

'It is vital,' said Professor Thompson, the head of the Allergy Research and Confinement Suite, 'that we establish what has caused this dreadful reaction. Do you know what she might have eaten, immediately prior to this happening?'

Emma shook her head. 'We've only just met her. We were having a business meeting and then she suddenly started throwing up. It was horrific.'

'The Winter Collection's ruined,' said Louise.

'This kind of reaction,' Professor Thompson continued, 'would have happened within just a few minutes of consuming whatever she consumed. So if she wasn't actually eating anything when she came to your meeting, she must have done so only moments before. We've been through her effects, and there's no sign of any car keys – just this.'

He handed Emma an A4 envelope. She quickly peered inside, and her heart skipped a beat. Designs.

'I'll look after these.' She folded the envelope and carefully placed it inside her handbag.

'So if she was walking,' said the Professor, 'she might conceivably have stopped for something to eat somewhere nearby. Can you think of anywhere, close to your business?'

Emma looked at Louise. '*Irma La Deuce*?'

Louise nodded. '*Irma La Deuce*.'

'That's nearby?'

'It's just over the road,' said Emma.

'Their menu is limited,' said Louise, 'although the interior design is quite interesting.'

'They specialise in carrot cake,' said Emma.

'Carrot cake?' said the Professor.

'Yes. Apparently it's a niche market but growing. They advertise sixteen varieties.'

'Of carrot cake?' Emma nodded. '*Are* there sixteen varieties?'

'Oh, yes. We have a model we use who's thrown up every single one of them.'

'You mean this has happened before?'

'Oh, no. She's bulimic. Loves her food, but only for about five minutes.'

Professor Thompson scribbled a note on a file. 'We'll have to contact them urgently – get a sample of each and every variety of carrot cake – then we might be able to work out which one has done this to her.' He began to turn away.

'Professor?'

'Mmm-hmm?'

'She is going to be all right, isn't she?'

'Well, fingers crossed.' He hurried away.

Emma and Louise took a seat along the corridor.

Louise said, 'Not exactly inspiring that, is it? "Fingers crossed".'

Emma smiled. 'Just an expression, I suppose. That poor girl – I don't think I've ever seen anyone so ill.'

Louise nodded. 'And the carpet's ruined.'

Emma lifted her handbag and took out Margaret's designs. She flicked through them, with Louise looking on.

'What do you think?' Louise asked.

Before Emma could respond, swing doors opened beside them and a slightly rotund man in glasses appeared. He stopped a nurse coming down the corridor and said, 'There was a woman just brought in – Margaret Gilmore.'

'Margaret – oh yes.'

'Is she okay?'

'Are you her husband?'

'No. No. Just, you know, a friend.'

'I'm sorry, I can't really discuss it unless you're next-of-kin.'

'Oh. All right. But she will be . . . you know, all right?'

'Well,' said the nurse, raising her eyebrows, 'fingers crossed'.

Emma and Louise exchanged glances. As the nurse walked off, leaving Walter standing there rather forlornly, Emma said, 'That's what they said to us as well – "fingers crossed". Hardly inspires confidence.'

Walter nodded. 'You're with Margaret?' he asked. Then: 'Do you know what happened?'

'Allergic reaction to carrot cake, apparently.'

Walter sat down beside them. 'Carrot cake?' he repeated.

Louise nodded. 'You can be allergic to anything. I have a friend who's allergic to zips.'

Walter shook his head. Then he glanced down at the designs in Emma's lap. 'You're in the fashion business as well?'

'Oh, yes.' Emma introduced herself. Walter pretended to have heard of the shop. Then she patted the designs. 'She's a fantastic designer; it'll be a terrible loss.'

Walter turned a little paler. 'Is it really that serious?'

'She could die,' said Louise, 'or suffer some kind of irreparable brain damage, or be paralysed down one side, or lose the motor function in her arms and legs, or be blind or deaf.'

'Crikey,' said Walter. 'Carrot cake has a lot to answer for.'

All three of them stared at the floor for a while.

Eventually Walter said, 'Has anyone told her husband?'

'Didn't know she was married,' said Emma.

'Don't know where she lives,' said Louise.

Walter looked at the floor for another thirty seconds, debating with himself. Then he stood up. 'I – well, I know where he lives. I can, ah, go and get him if you think it would be a good idea.'

They both nodded. Walter thrust his hands into his pockets. On their last meeting, Margaret's husband had called him a speccy fat clown. Now he would have to inform him that his wife was at death's door because of a rogue carrot cake.

17

Yourself Alone

Redmond O'Boyle was summoned from the exercise yard of La Picota prison, outside Bogotá. Once again the guards waited until he was in the middle of preparing his food. They knocked over the chicken and stamped on it. They kicked gravel into the rice. Then they marched him across to the Administration Block. The other prisoners watched him with ill-disguised contempt. Word had leaked out that he was being held for training FARC guerrillas. Overnight, his single cell's population had gone from fifteen to two. He was now sharing it with a Frenchman called Marcel, who spoke even less Spanish than Redmond, and so wasn't aware that the other prisoners had decamped because they feared that extreme violence was about to be visited on their Irish cellmate. Marcel's English was passable, but Redmond decided to maintain the pretence that he had been arrested for illegal bird-watching activities. He detested the overcrowding in La Picota, but also didn't want to be left alone.

Redmond was shown into the same small, bare interview room. A young, freckled woman with a bad case of sunburn stood and held out her hand as he entered. She was wearing a white linen dress which was sweat-stained at the armpits. A fan revolved lugubriously overhead, shaking and rattling. Its only function seemed to be to provide annoyance.

'Siobhan O'Rourke,' said Siobhan, reaching out a hand. 'Sinn Fein Flying Squad.'

Redmond shook it. 'It's good to hear a friendly voice.'

'Caught the first flight I could. Horrible journey. Had to overnight in Rio. Have you ever been to Rio?'

'No, I can't say I—'

'Put you to shame, those girls. Those guys. On the beach. The thongs!'

'Well, I—'

'But it was so crowded, honestly! And you have to keep your eye on your purse the whole time and you never really relax. Tell you the truth, I think the beach at Portstewart is better, but we don't get the weather, do we? Maybe a couple of days a year. God, it's hot in here, isn't it, I'm sweating like a hoor. So how are you?'

'I think they're going to try and kill me.'

'I mean, food and fresh water – getting enough?'

'Yes, but they know what I'm here for. It can't be long before they try and—'

'But you've enough water. That's good. And access to a church or Bible?'

'Yes, of course.'

'Well, there's no of course about it. Those are your fundamental basic human rights. Although if you saw the state of the swimming pool at my hotel – I'd almost swap places with you. It's a disgrace, I tell you. Supposed to be five star. It can't be more than four, I swear to God. There's *things* floating in the water. And room service, don't get me started. But you're surviving all right, aren't you?'

'I'm okay for the moment, but you have to get me out of here.'

'Well, it's not quite as simple as that, Redmond. As you may know, we are supporting a Bring Him Home campaign, but metaphorically rather than physically.'

'I'm not sure if I—'

'Times have changed, Redmond. We've embraced democracy. If you can put your hand on your heart and tell me that you are an innocent man, then I – *we* – as a Party, will be in a much stronger position to offer you help.'

Redmond looked at her, not entirely sure if she was serious. She didn't crack a smile. She had a yellow legal pad in front of her, and had been making odd notes, but now she turned it round so that he could read it. It said *I think they're listening to us.*

Redmond nodded. He slowly raised his hand to his heart and said, 'I am an innocent man.'

'And the Semtex they found in your rucksack? Did you pick somebody else's up by mistake?'

'That's all I can think of.'

'And you're an innocent victim in all of this?'

'Yes, I am.'

'You were merely on an ornithological visit?'

'Yes, I was.'

Siobhan turned a page in her notebook. There was a list of names. She quickly wrote above them *Birds. Try and sound like you know what you're talking about.*

'And did you find any interesting species?' Siobhan asked.

'Oh yes. The Rufus-naped Grand Torrent.'

'The Rufus-naped *Ground Tyrant*?'

'That's what I said. And also the . . . the Coppery-headed . . . Emerald.'

'The Coppery-headed Emerald. That sounds interesting. What do you know about that one? What does it eat, for example?' Siobhan's hand made a suddenly crawling motion across the top of the desk.

'Creeply crawlies,' said Redmond.

Siobhan did it again, but this time using both hands.

'Loads of them,' said Redmond. 'There are so many insects, I don't want to blind you with science.'

'Did you manage to see a Golden-browed Chlorophonia?' Siobhan underlined the name of the bird twice with her pen, then wrote: *Very rare!*

'I believe it's extinct,' said Redmond.

Siobhan stabbed her pen at her instruction again.

'Or at least that's what some people think because it's so rarely spotted. Nothing would make me happier than to be released from this prison – where incidentally the guards and prison staff have treated me with nothing but respect – to return to the jungle and find the Golden-browed . . .' he twisted his head to read the name again '. . . Chlorophonia.'

Siobhan nodded enthusiastically. 'Redmond, I believe you are innocent, the people back home believe you are innocent, and I can assure that I – we – the Party and the people will do everything in our power to see that justice is done. In the meantime you have to remain resolute. Have faith in the great Colombian justice system.' She wrote quickly in her book again. *I just have to find the right person to bribe.*

Redmond nodded. Then he remembered the letter in his pocket. He had been endeavouring to post it to his wife, to explain his current situation, but his dire circumstances had prevented him from scrawling anything other than a basic appeal for help. He fished it out. The envelope was sweat-stained and badly creased.

'Please, can you give this to my wife?'

Siobhan took it.

'Have you heard from her?' he asked.

Siobhan looked rather pained. 'We spoke to her, Redmond. She's very angry. But she also is putting her faith in the fabulous Colombian judiciary.'

'No visit then,' said Redmond. He couldn't even begin to hide the disappointment in his voice. 'I suppose it's better that she doesn't see me like this.'

'Nor the children.'

'The children?' Siobhan quickly wrote a number in her notebook, but before she could turn it round Redmond leaped in. 'All nine of them.'

Siobhan turned the notebook round. She had written the number six. Redmond rolled his eyes. 'They send their love, and hope that you will remain resolute, though God knows what they'll do without their father to provide for them.' With that Siobhan closed the notebook. She stood. She extended her hand. He clasped it.

'Thank you for coming,' said Redmond.

'No problem,' said Siobhan. 'And don't worry, we'll get you out, Redmond.'

'I'm sure you'll do your best. In the meantime, you wouldn't happen to have any cash on you? I need to buy food.'

'They make you pay for your own food? Although of course that's quite understandable.'

Redmond nodded forlornly. 'I'm stony broke.'

'Well, how have you survived up till now?'

'Oh, I've some coke in my shoes.' It was out before he even realised. Siobhan shook her head. Redmond shrugged helplessly.

'I would lend you some,' said Siobhan, 'but I used all my spare cash to buy souvenirs. Next time, I promise.'

When they were walking him back to his cell, the guards stole his shoes.

18
Journey into Fear

Walter had never been the bearer of bad tidings before. Throughout his life he had scrupulously avoided taking that kind of responsibility. You could argue that he was a coward. But although accurate, that is much too simple. The fear he had was not a fear of death or illness, it was not a fear of standing up and being counted, it was an abject terror of saying the wrong thing. Of laughing at the wrong moment. Of getting his words back to front. He lacked confidence, and that manifested itself in frequent and embarrassing communication breakdowns in relatively trivial situations. This one was about life and death, and he was terrified. He had volunteered to tell Margaret Gilmore's husband that she was lying unconscious thanks to an allergic reaction to a slice of carrot cake.

So he approached the front door with some considerable trepidation. He bit down hard on his lip to remind himself how grave the situation was. He kept saying to himself, over and over, 'Don't mention carrot cake, don't mention carrot cake.' He knew if he did, he would only start laughing. Even in the hospital he had struggled to contain himself. It was a nervous thing.

He hesitated before ringing the bell.

What am I even doing here? I've met Margaret once. It has nothing to do with me. Run away! Run away now! Or leave a note. Why give him any respect at all when only the other day he was screaming up the road after you that you were a speccy fat clown?

Because it's the right thing to do.

Walter rang the bell. He stepped back. He bit on his lip again. *Calm, calm, calm, calm, calm, calm . . .*

The door opened. The husband was standing there, a newpaper in his hand and a snarl already on his face.

'What the hell do you want?' he growled.

'Carrot cake,' said Walter.

'What the . . . ?'

'Your wife – carrot cake – the hospital – you have to . . .'

'Hospital? What about a hospital? Is Margaret . . . ?'

'Life support. Excuse me one moment.' He was beginning to hyperventilate. Walter closed his eyes and took several deep breaths. *Control yourself. Calm. Calm. Calm. Look at him. Look him in the eye. He's just another human being.*

'Are you pissed or something?'

Walter's eyes flashed open. 'No, I am not.'

'Then what the bloody hell are you talking about? What's this about my wife?'

Calm, control, calm, control.

Walter stared wide-eyed while he grasped for the right words, in the right order. Now that he looked at him, the husband didn't seem that threatening. In fact, he was quite a lot smaller than he remembered. His hair was receding and his eyes were hooded. His nose was a little too long and his wrists thin. Suddenly Walter felt an awful lot calmer. From his slightly hunched position, Walter's back began to straighten. His posture improved. He spoke clearly and precisely. 'Sorry, it's been such a panic. Margaret's in hospital; she's had an allergic reaction to something she ate and she's in a bad way.'

'Oh.' The colour had now drained from the husband's face. 'I'll get my coat.' He disappeared for a moment, then came back, putting on a black sports jacket. He pulled the door closed after him. 'Where's your car?' he asked.

'*My* car?'

The husband stopped. He poked a finger towards Walter. 'Listen, mate, I don't like this any more than you do, but if she's sick I have to get there, and my car's being serviced. If you're the one she left me for, if you're the one destroyed our marriage, then the least you can do is drive me there. Now where's the bloody car?'

Walter blinked at him for several moments, then nodded a little way along the street. 'Just over there.'

Walter's mind was in turmoil as he drove. Margaret had left her husband. The man was plainly upset about it, but Walter didn't care. She had left him. She was *available*. Virtually in a coma, but available.

Walter became aware of the husband watching him as he drove. He glanced across. 'What?'

'You're not what I imagined.'

'I'm not what *I* imagined.'

The man's brow furrowed. 'What the hell does that mean?'

'It means, when you start out in life, do you ever become what you imagine?'

'What a lot of crap,' said the husband.

Walter shrugged, and concentrated on the traffic. He wanted to sing 'If You're Happy and You Know It Clap Your Hands' and it was all he could do to stop himself from humming it. When he next chanced a look across, there were tears rolling down the husband's cheeks. Walter felt suddenly very sorry for him.

'Look,' he said, as sympathetically as he could, 'not only am I not what you or I imagined, I'm not who you think I am.'

'What the hell are you talking about?' The man wiped at his cheeks.

'Margaret didn't leave you for me. I only met her a few days ago. Through a dating agency.'

'Only sad bas**rds use dating agencies.'

'That may be. My point is, I had nothing to do with her leaving you. It's none of my business.'

'Well, you made it your business, didn't you? Embarrassing me in front of the entire street. Rubbing my nose in it. See all the neighbours out having a great laugh, did you?'

'No, . . .'

'Yeah, right.'

They drove on in silence.

When they reached the car park behind Psyclops Surgeries, Walter took some time to find a parking space, then, aware of being watched by Margaret's husband and feeling under pressure, took half a dozen goes to manoeuvre into it. Successful at last, Walter began to open his door. But the husband wasn't moving. Walter settled back in his seat.

'You all right?' he asked.

'I still love her.'

'I'm sorry,' said Walter.

'When she left, she said she'd never loved me.'

'Oh.'

'Ten years we were together, and she never loved me.'

'That's hard.'

'I keep hoping she'll come back to me.' He glanced up at Walter. 'And it will happen, I swear to God.'

'Well, I hope . . . Well, I mean, in my position, I can hardly say I hope it all works out, but if I wasn't in . . . my position, I would hope that it all works out for you, if I wasn't, you know . . .'

'Sleeping with her.'

'God no, not yet. One date we've had.' Christ, thought Walter, I'm starting to talk like Yoda.

The husband began to tap his fingers on the dash. 'Did you kiss her?'

'No. It didn't come to that.'

'So if nothing happened, and you've had one date, how come you know about her being in the hospital before I do? I'm her friggin' husband.'

'I know that. It's purely coincidental. I was getting my eyes checked, and I saw them bring her in. Swear to God.'

The husband nodded slowly.

Walter moved his fingers to the door handle again. 'Should we . . .'

'I'm an accountant,' said the husband.

'That's good,' said Walter.

'I still do her accounts. It's one way of keeping in touch.' Walter nodded. 'Not very exciting, is it, accountancy?'

Walter shrugged. 'I'm in property.'

The husband nodded. 'At least, you wouldn't think it was exciting. All those figures. Tax. I do big companies. Little ones too. Tinker, tailor, soldier, sailor. But there's others too. You know, the dark side. Gangsters. Paramilitary. Think nothing of having you knocked off if you cross them.' He looked directly at Walter. 'Wouldn't think twice.'

Then the husband climbed out of the car.

Walter took a deep breath and followed.

19

The Sentinel

'I'm going to be late,' said Walter, down the phone to his colleague Mark in the Department of Education in Bangor.

'How late?' Mark asked.

'Tomorrow,' said Walter.

'That's late. And it'll also be two days in a row.'

'I know. I'm sorry. It's just—'

'No need to explain. Sixty-three per cent of people in Northern Ireland are employed by the Civil Service; they're not going to miss Walter North for a couple of days. Besides, that's what flexitime's for.'

'What about my work?'

'Done.'

'You did it for me?'

'No, Walter, I moved it from the in-tray to the out-tray. Haven't heard a complaint yet.'

'Well, whatever you're doing, thank you.'

'No problem. How's Carrot Cake Kate?'

'It's Margaret. And she's still, you know . . .' Walter trailed off. He was standing at a payphone in a hospital corridor. He hadn't washed or shaved for three days. Margaret was in a private room – they were all private, of course, this being the Psyclops Surgeries, the most exclusive private hospital in Belfast – and hadn't batted an eyelid yet.

'I thought they found the culprit. I thought a carrot cake was arrested at the scene of the crime.'

'They did. And they didn't. Turns out she's allergic to coconut carrot cake, which was responsible for half of the symptoms. The other half, and by far the most serious, were caused by a poison, a toxin with some very complicated name which somehow found itself embedded in the coconut carrot cake. A combination of things, really. Plus they say her cholesterol is quite high.'

'You're *joking*.'

'Yes, I am.'

Mark sighed. 'Mate – what are you doing there? You hardly know her.'

'I know. It's just . . . hard to explain.'

'What about her husband?'

'They're separated.'

'Well, what does he say?'

'Billy blows hot and cold. He loves her. And he hates her. He's not too fond of me either.'

'Why, has he said anything?'

'No. But he scratched *Fruit* on my car.'

'You're sure it was him?'

'Yeah. I think.'

'Because pretty much anyone could have done that. It's the popular opinion.'

'You're funny.'

'Walter – he's still her husband. Is it really helping to have you hanging around as well?'

'I'm not hanging around. Not exactly. And even if I was, there's hardly anyone else coming to see her. Billy comes twice a day, at visiting time, just after lunch and just after dinner. He's an accountant, Mark, he sticks to the rules. Rest of the time I have her to myself.'

'You have her to yourself? Have you heard yourself lately?'

'I don't mean it like that. I'm just trying to help. The nurses don't mind. When Billy's here I make myself scarce. I just sit with her. Read her the paper. *Vogue*. Did I tell you she's a fashion designer?'

'Yes, you did.'

'And the swelling is starting to go down. And her colour's a lot better.'

'But she hasn't woken up.'

'No. But the body's a wonderful thing, apparently. It's healing itself.'

'Anything to stop it waking up and healing itself?'

'I don't know, Mark.' Walter sighed. 'I know this is crazy.'

'I didn't say you were crazy.'

'It's just like – you know sometimes late at night, and you start watching a movie, and you're knackered, and you just want to go to bed, but you have to know what happens in the end, so you have to stay up, and even though the movie's really, really bad, and you can guess what's going to happen, you still have to stay up? Do you know that feeling?'

'Yes, Walter. You know what I would do in that situation?'

'No.'

'I'd set the video. You know, find out in the morning.'

'I wouldn't be able to sleep for thinking about her. And at least part of me would think that they'd somehow change the ending of the movie if they knew I wasn't watching. To something sad.'

'Let me take that back. You *are* crazy. But I think that if I was in a coma, I would be pleased to learn later that you'd kept watch over me.'

They were both silent for half a minute.

Then Walter said, 'If you were in a coma, I wouldn't bother.'

Walter was dozing next to Margaret's bed when there was a gentle knock on the door and a man in an impressive-looking uniform appeared. He looked like he belonged to a branch of the armed services that hadn't been invented yet. Walter thought he might have come to throw him out, that they had twigged to the fact that he had only ever stood next to someone who was the next-of-kin.

'Sorry to disturb,' said the man. 'Are you Billy?'

Walter shook his head.

The man extended his hand. 'Name's Kawolski. I work with Margaret.'

'Walter. Come on in.'

Kawolski edged into the room. He had a big bunch of flowers and a card with him. 'I'll just set these . . .' And then he looked at Margaret for the first time. 'Oh dear God,' he said.

'She's actually looking a lot better,' said Walter.

Kawolski shook his head. 'No one at work knew what happened. We were very worried.'

'She's getting better now.'

'That's good. Place isn't the same without her. She's a bit of a live wire. First thought I had when I heard she was in hospital, was that it was that Millie who done it.'

'Millie?'

'Aye, she got thumped by some Millie, caught her shoplifting. Her eye all swole up. Thought maybe it was concussion or something, delayed reaction.'

Walter shook his head. 'It was a carrot cake.'

'Aye. So I heard.'

They sat quietly for a few minutes.

'Happen often, does it?' Walter asked after a while. 'Getting thumped?'

'You'd be surprised.'

'Not something you associate with – you know, fashion.'

'Everywhere, these days.'

'Suppose.'

They lapsed into silence again. After five minutes Kawolski glanced at his watch, then stood up. 'I should be off.'

Walter nodded.

Kawolski looked at the flowers, sitting on the end of the bed. 'Should I . . . ?'

'Don't worry, I'll sort them out.'

'Cheers, Walter. You'll let her know, if she . . . when she . . . ?'

'No problem.'

Kawolski smiled, then slipped out of the room, gently closing the door after him. Walter got up and lifted the flowers. He'd ask the nurse for a vase. He took the *Get Well Soon* card out of the envelope and went to set it on the locker beside Margaret. He opened it up so it could stand, and read the inscription: *Margaret, thinking of you, get well soon, from all your colleagues at Primark Security.*

Walter's brow furrowed.

20

Nuns with Fashion Sense

The café in Psyclops Surgeries served fresh Italian breads and cream-filled scones and steaks with delicious pepper sauces. There were linen table-cloths that were changed after every meal. The maitre d' was French with a slight Irish accent, or Irish with a slight French accent, depending on his energy levels and his commitment to the fraud. Walter spent most of his time by Margaret's bed, but even though he was dog tired and had little appetite, he knew he had to eat something. He was a connoisseur of plain food, and this place was a little too rich for him, but he had no choice but to dine at the *Ristorante Piccoli*. It was either that or the McDonald's franchise in the Children's Wing, but the security there was overbearing, and it was a little too far away from Margaret's room.

He was halfway through his first course when Billy arrived, scanned the restaurant and spotted him. For one terrifying moment, Walter feared that Billy had come to tell him that something awful had happened to Margaret, but then, after the briefest moment when their eyes met, Billy continued to scan the rest of the room. But the café was packed and there were no other seats. He came up and stood by the chair opposite Walter.

'Is this free?' he asked.

Walter nodded. As Billy sat, Walter said, 'Better the devil you know, eh?'

Billy stared blankly at him and lifted a menu.

'How is she?' Walter asked.

'Don't know, haven't been down yet.'

Walter checked his watch. Normally Billy arrived dead on the start of visiting time, and left on the first ring to signal it was over. 'You're early.'

'Traffic was unusually light.'

A waiter approached, and Billy ordered a small bowl of pasta and an exotic-sounding dessert.

'Ah yes,' said the waiter. 'The carrot cake.'

As he hurried away, Walter said, 'I hope they make it *here*.'

'Why?' asked Billy.

'Well – you know what happened to Margaret.'

'Don't be ridiculous.'

Walter continued eating. Billy looked everywhere but across the table. His pasta and then his carrot cake arrived quickly, and the dessert then became the focus of his attention. Walter would have been quite happy to leave the unsmiling accountant to his own devices, but there were things he needed to know about Margaret. He set his knife and fork down. He dabbed his lips on a linen napkin, which had an embroidered eye in the corner. 'So,' he began quite nonchalantly, 'Margaret works in Primark.'

'Uhuh.'

'In security.'

'Yeah.'

'She enjoy that?'

Billy shrugged. He cut another forkful of carrot cake, but then paused. He looked up at Walter. 'She didn't tell me she was working there. One Saturday afternoon I was in buying some new gunks, and she suddenly shouts behind me, "Freeze! Put down the pants and raise your hands!" and I nearly had a heart-attack. Why would you embarrass anyone like that? And then when I was leaving the shop she gave out over the tannoy, "Missing you already". Everyone was looking at me.'

Walter studied Billy's face. He was still angry about it.

'Perhaps she was just having a laugh,' said Walter.

'More like making a show of me.'

Walter wondered how they had ever got together in the first place, and for a brief moment he considered asking. But when he thought about it, he realised that although he did want to know, he didn't want Billy's take on it, for it would surely be suffused with anger and bitterness. He would much prefer to hear it from Margaret herself.

'I had thought she was a fashion designer,' said Walter.

'Aye – in her dreams.' It was heavy with sarcasm. 'I've seen nuns with better fashion sense.'

'I happened to see some of her designs.'

'Yeah? So what?'

'They looked quite good.'

'Yeah. Right. Listen – when I'm drunk, I get up and do a bit of karaoke Rod. I don't think I *am* Rod. I know who I am. Get the difference?'

'Well, you know – a bit of encouragement mightn't have gone amiss.'

Billy jabbed his fork at Walter. 'She's not your friggin' wife, right?'

'And she's not yours either.' He snapped it back almost without thinking.

Billy glared across at him. The pulse in the side of his head was visibly throbbing. His elbow was on the table, the fork still clutched in his left hand, but he raised one of his fingers and said, 'See that? See that wedding ring? Long as that's on there, she's still my wife.'

'I'm not sure if it works like that.'

'You bet your sweet life it does. Put it this way: if she dies, it'll be me carrying the coffin, not you, right?'

'That's nice.'

Billy shook his head. 'You know something? First time I clocked you, I thought you were a big fat speccy clown. Now I *know* you are. And I don't like you sucking round her. She probably hasn't a clue who you are.'

Walter, mindful of the fact that Billy occasionally worked for gangsters and paramilitaries and was thus in Belfast street parlance 'connected', tried to calm the situation. Also, most of the other diners were watching them.

'Look, we're both tired . . .' he began.

'*I'm* not tired!'

'Well, we're stressed, concerned and worried, then.'

Billy finally put down the fork. He wiped the back of his hand across his mouth and stood up. 'Don't you friggin' tell me what I am, you speccy git. She's my wife, you leave her alone.' Then he threw his napkin down and strode away across the café.

As he reached the entrance, Walter shouted suddenly, 'Billy!'

Billy stopped in the doorway and looked back. 'What?!'

'Missing you already.'

The man looked stunned. But just for a moment. Then his eyes blazed and he silently mouthed a series of expletives at Walter and gave him the fingers. Walter waved.

When Billy stormed out, Walter decided that he wasn't really frightened of him. He wasn't even convinced that he *was* 'connected'. Billy was hurt and angry and bitter about his break-up with Margaret, but even though he tried to act tough, Walter believed that, like himself, inside every tough guy there was an accountant fighting to get out. It must have made it doubly hard if you actually were an accountant already. You'd have to act *really* tough . . .

21

The Quick and the Dead

Given the furious manner in which Billy had stormed out of the hospital café, Walter thought it was better to linger at his table for a while. He had only picked at his food. He put his elbow on the table and rested his head on his palm. He had barely slept for two nights, and it was dark again outside already. He closed his eyes. He imagined Margaret in her sickbed, surrounded by monitors, and her husband glaring down at her.

'Put it this way: if she dies, it'll be me carrying the coffin, not you, right?'

How could anyone say that? And especially about someone you professed to love.

'Excuse me, do you mind if I sit down?'

Walter jerked upright. 'Mmmm – what?'

A young nurse smiled down at him. 'Is there anyone sitting here?'

'No.' Walter glanced quickly around the restaurant. It was considerably less busy than when he'd arrived, and there were a number of empty tables. The nurse looked vaguely familiar.

'Food in here's great, isn't it?'

Walter nodded, aware of the half-eaten meal before him.

'I just wanted a wee word.' She gave a little laugh then. 'It's nothing to be worried about. You're very devoted to her.'

Walter shrugged.

'Not like that obnoxious bag of weeds down there now.'

Walter managed a smile. 'He's an accountant.'

The waiter smiled familiarly as he put a cappuccino down before her. 'Cheers, Pepe,' she said. He blushed, then lifted Walter's plate and turned away. 'You don't remember me, do you?'

'Sort of.'

'We met the first day she was brought in. You said you weren't next-of-kin, so I couldn't let you in to see her. Then, when I came back on duty there you were, in with her, so I presumed the Sister had okayed it. But then just this afternoon she asked me who you were and if I'd checked you out.'

'So here you are.' Walter glanced around him. It was never going to be a case of making a dash for the exits. He hadn't actually done anything wrong. It wasn't his fault if their vetting procedures were lax. And he wasn't entirely sure if the stalking laws applied if the subject of the stalking was in a coma. But still.

'I'm not here to chase you away,' she added gently.

'You're not?'

'Nope. Wish I had a boyfriend like that. I just thought – you've been here three days straight, you can't have slept much, you must be knackered. You know, it's okay for you to go home. Get cleaned up.'

'I'm starting to smell, you mean.'

'No! I mean, you could just do with a . . . you know. Shower, and stuff.'

'I *am* starting to smell.'

'You just look a bit crumpled and homeless and they don't really like to encourage that here. If you wanted to pop home, that would be all right – with her, I mean. She won't mind. She won't *know*.'

'*I'll* know.'

'Well – give me your number, and I'll phone if there's any change.'

'Look, I know I probably am a bit whiffy. But I just . . . can't.'

The nurse smiled sympathetically. She reached out and patted his hand. 'You must love her very much.'

Walter didn't quite know how to react to that one. So he looked down at the table. The nurse got up – then sat down again. 'Tell you what – if you're absolutely determined to stay, you could have a shave and a shower here. I can slip your clothes into the laundry, it would only take an hour. Do you the world of good.'

This didn't seem a bad idea at all. Except. 'I don't have a spare . . .'

'You don't need a change of clothes, we're coming down with pyjamas and dressing-gowns. Pop them on till yours are done. You'll look just like one of our own. How about it? Might even get a free dinner out of it. What about that, eh?'

'Well, if it's not too much trouble.'

'It's no trouble at all, love.'

Walter's clothes were taken to the laundry while he had a shave and shower. He returned to the corridor outside Margaret's room, wearing his hospital-issue pyjamas, with an embroidered eye on the jacket pocket, a dressing-gown, with a large eye on the back, and the slippers, with an eye on either foot, and sneaked a peek through the glass panel in the door. Billy was standing at the foot of her bed, and even though Walter couldn't see his face, he was sure he was glaring down at her, just as he had imagined earlier.

Walter thought that Billy probably just needed somebody to give him a bit of affection. A hug and an ice cream. But walking around with a face-ache like that was hardly going to attract anyone. Neither was accountancy, no matter how intriguing he managed to make it sound.

Walter sat on a chair in the corridor for a while, then decided it might be better if he wasn't there when Billy came out. He didn't need another confrontation. There was a waiting room just around the corner, where he'd be out of sight, so he padded along there and sat on a chair in the corner. He tried reading a magazine – *Big Houses* again, but a more recent issue. The strapline said *Properties you still can't afford*. But he couldn't concentrate. His head began to loll forward. He would doze for a few moments, then give a sudden start when someone coughed or a trolley was pushed past outside, and find that he had drooled down one side of his face. This happened again and again, until a distressed elderly couple came in followed by a nurse with a tray and biscuits and sympathy. Walter padded back down the corridor.

He looked back into Margaret's room, but Billy was still there, staring at her, as if he was daring her to open her eyes and confess that she'd been faking all along, that it was one of her jokes.

Missing you already.

Walter smiled to himself, then stood rather forlornly in the corridor. The seat he'd occupied before was now taken. He yawned. Perhaps that pretty young nurse had a point. What was he achieving here? What harm would a night in his own bed do? He could come back tomorrow. The shower and shave had freshened him up, but done little to resolve his underlying fatigue. Now the cumulative effect of the smell of antiseptic and the glare of the strip lighting was beginning to hurt his head. He badly needed to lie down. Yet he couldn't go anywhere without his clothes.

Walter moved slowly along the corridor, peering into the private rooms. Six doors along he found a recently vacated and newly remade bed. He looked both ways, then slipped into the room.

Ten minutes, he promised himself. Just ten minutes.

The top cover was dominated by a large eye. He pulled it back and crawled under.

Fifteen, tops.

Walter pulled the cover back up and over his head. Hopefully nobody would notice. Not for twenty minutes at least.

Two hours later, with the visitors long gone and normality restored, a

I Predict A Riot

Sister on patrol happened to look into Walter's room and saw the outline of his body beneath the sheet. She immediately turned back to the corridor and hollered: 'Nurse! I thought I told you to get that stiff down to the morgue!'

Six doors further along, Margaret Gilmore opened her eyes.

22
The Sleeper Awakes

Margaret Gilmore had been unconscious for three days, thanks to a slice of rogue carrot cake. She didn't know this, of course. As far as she was concerned, she was waking from a heavy sleep filled with disturbing dreams, but, nevertheless, in her own bed, snug and secure. So, naturally, when her eyes flickered open and she found herself in a strange room, hooked up to all kinds of machines, and with a tube stuck up her nose and an IV in her arm, she screamed.

The nurses came running. They clucked around, trying to calm her down. One, trying to stop her climbing out of bed and ripping out the tubes, cried, 'Please! We'll call your husband!'

'No! Get this out of my nose! Get it out of my nose!'

'Just take it easy . . .'

'Get it *out*!'

The house doctor arrived, quickly surveyed the situation, then stepped forward and removed the tube. It wasn't pleasant; tears rolled down Margaret's cheeks. Nevertheless, she rattled her wrist at him.

'And this, and this!'

The young Indian doctor shook his head. 'That requires to stay.'

'It's hurting!'

'It still requires to stay. We will give you a painkiller. You have been very sick.'

This stopped her in her tracks. 'Me?'

'Yes, Margaret. You. Why do you think you are here?'

Margaret blinked at him. 'I thought I was kidnapped by aliens and you were doing experiments with my ovaries.'

The doctor blinked back. Then quietly and efficiently he explained what had actually happened. Margaret nodded along in semi-disbelief – she remembered the projectile vomiting in *Emma Cochrane*'s boutique, but nothing else. The doctor said she would have to continue with the intravenous supply of fluids for another twenty-four hours at least, and that she would have a more thorough examination in the morning, together with some scans.

'For brain damage?' Margaret asked.

'No,' said the doctor.

A nurse asked if there was anyone she wanted contacted. Margaret was lucid enough now to experience the acute embarrassment that comes with realising that you don't actually have any really close family or friends. In the end she dredged up her work colleague Maeve O'Boyle's number, and a different nurse scurried off to contact her.

Margaret had slept for three days, but she could hardly keep her eyes open. This wasn't a bad thing, the doctor explained; her body was just exhausted. As she drifted off to sleep again, she was almost sure that she heard one of the nurses say, 'What about Walter?' but then she heard another say, 'What is the capital of Patagonia?' and knew that she must be dreaming.

In the corridor outside, another nurse responded, 'I've told you a million times, I'm crap at crosswords,' but Margaret was already asleep.

She woke again shortly before midnight.

'Aha – the sleeper awakes!'

She turned groggily, her eyes opening just a slither. A bush on a chair. She fought to open her eyes fully; she concentrated on focusing in.

'What a fright you gave us,' said Maeve, shaking her big hair.

'I'm sorry,' Margaret said weakly.

'Don't be daft! I'm just so pleased you're back!'

Maeve poured her a glass of Lucozade, then helped her to sit up. 'Remember how they used to do Lucozade with all that cellophane stuff round the top? *Lucozade aids recovery.* Remember that? Anyway, how do you feel?' she asked.

'Like I've the mother of all hangovers, without having enjoyed the night before.' Margaret drank greedily. 'I hope you didn't waste a lot of time coming to see me while I was asleep.'

'Margaret, darlin', it was no bother.'

It was no bother because she hadn't. Maeve came from West Belfast, where pragmatism was a requirement rather than a choice. What was the point in babysitting a vegetable? However, she was genuinely happy that Margaret was awake. She opened her handbag and fished out a somewhat crumpled quarter of Jelly Babies. As she passed them across she said, 'You don't see them like this any more, you know, in a paper bag, poured in and weighed by the shopkeeper himself. They're all in presealed plastic bags these days. You miss the personal touch.'

Margaret looked at the bag, then into it. 'Well, it might have been the personal touch that got me here in the first place. You know – the carrot cake.'

Maeve smiled. 'Funny you should mention it. I was going to keep this for a couple of days, till you felt a bit better. But you might as well have it now.' She delved into her bag again and produced a sheaf of stapled A4 pages. 'Got them off the internet.'

Margaret tried to focus on the information they contained. Her eyes were still not quite right. The pages appeared to contain lists of names, dates and amounts of money, all neatly set out in columns, but she couldn't quite make out the details.

'I don't follow,' she said.

Maeve moved to sit on the edge of the bed, then pointed down. 'It's a list of people who've sued restaurants and cafés for food poisoning. These are the dates, and this is the amount of compensation they were paid. The last few pages have accounts of some of the court cases, and believe you me, yours is one of the worst examples. You'll make a *fortune* out of this.'

'Maeve, I'm not even thinking of . . .'

'Well, you should. I thought you let Primark off with murder, but these guys really did nearly kill you. You have to hit them, Margaret, and you have to hit them *hard*.'

Sometime after midnight, a nurse brought her tea and toast.

'Where am I?' Margaret asked. For a moment the nurse feared that she was slipping away again, but Margaret quickly explained. 'I mean – what hospital? I thought there was a bed shortage in all these places, yet here I am, private room and all.'

'Psyclops Surgeries.'

'*Psyclops*? I can't afford Psyclops.'

'Well, someone can. We don't do charity cases. Let me check.' She came back five minutes later carrying a file and said, 'Your employers are paying for it.'

'*Primark?*'

The nurse's brow furrowed. 'No. Says here, . . . Emma Cochrane Ltd.'

'Oh. *Right.*' Margaret had presumed that her display of projectile vomiting and subsequent collapse in the trendy boutique on the Lisburn Road would automatically have spelled the end of her briefly promising career in fashion design. But if Emma Cochrane was paying for her treatment . . . *My God, they must have been really impressed.* After a moment of elation she remembered that she hadn't even shown Emma or her fashion buyer Louise the designs, only the dresses she'd bought in Primark and passed off as her own. It was a fraud. It was all based on a fraud. Margaret slumped down in her bed. But where were her own designs? She'd intended to show them to Emma, but then had a last-minute change of heart and put them in her jacket pocket.

When a different nurse came in to remove her tray she asked where her personal effects were.

'Not sure there were any love.'

'I had a leather jacket.'

'Oh, your clothes – they stank of boke. They're in the laundry. I can have them picked up in the morning.'

'Was there an envelope in the inside pocket?'

'Anything like that, be in your locker there.'

Margaret checked her locker. It was bare.

'So,' said the nurse, plumping her pillows as Margaret leaned forward. 'Where's he got to then?'

'Where's who got to?'

The nurse smiled. 'Here all day every day, all night – like a devoted puppy, he was.'

Margaret rolled her eyes. 'My husband doesn't normally like hospitals.'

'Not him, silly. Walter.'

'*Walter?*'

23

The King of the Underworld

Even in private hospitals, patients occasionally die. They just do it more discreetly. In normal hospitals – that is, those establishments that still hang on by their cracked fingernails to the crumbling cliff-face of the National Health Service – the recently departed are normally heaved down a maintenance chute then transported by shopping trolley to await pick-up by a prune-faced man in a black suit. At Psyclops Surgeries the dead are treated with a little more respect. After all, they are still paying for it.

The climate-controlled basement mortuary was known throughout the hospital as the Upstairs Room. It was known as this because bereavement counsellors, of whom there were half a dozen on the payroll, preferred not to refer to recently departed loved ones as having died, but as having just 'popped upstairs'.

It was not a huge room, because there was not much daily traffic. Barney was the Chief Mortuary Technician. It was a grand title for someone who did little more than wash the bodies down and prepare them for collection by an undertaker. But it sounded a lot better than saying, 'I wash dead bodies.' He had difficulty enough keeping girls when he said he was Chief Mortuary Technician.

Barney mostly worked nights, starting at 9 p.m. and continuing until dawn. It was a simple fact that most people died in the early hours of the morning, and it was best, like wills and pizza, not to leave them lying around. The secret was to whip them out of their beds and get them down to the Upstairs Room as quickly as possible. Once they were on the slab he could work at his own pace, although of course rigor mortis did not recognise flexitime.

Tonight, however, was a bit of a shocker. It was rare for him to have more than two bodies to work on in the course of his shift. This night there were four. And then a nurse came hurrying down pushing another on a bed, complaining that she'd been chewed out by the

I Predict A Riot

Sister for forgetting about him when really, it wasn't her responsibility.

She shared a cigarette with Barney. He made her coffee. She quite liked him, but had twice refused to go out with him. Like all of the others, she had difficulty getting past what he did for a living. She never put it into so many words, but Barney knew. He could have responded with, 'You clean up old people's poo all day and it's not a problem for me.' But the comment was never made, the response was not required, and a romance that might have been incredible withered and died before it even began.

Nurse Rachel, lighting another fag, and nodding around the room, said, 'Busy tonight.'

'Yeah, there's a lot of it going around.'

There was a body on a slab before her. It was an elderly woman. She was completely naked. Her eyes were open. She had an ash tray on her chest. Nurse Rachel wasn't altogether comfortable about using it, but this was the only room in the entire hospital where you could enjoy a fag without setting off the smoke alarms – it was something to do with the climate control – so she had to bide by Barney's rules if she was to enjoy her fix of nicotine.

Behind her, a low rumble issued from one of the bodies, and Rachel jumped. Barney laughed.

'God,' said Rachel, pressing her hand to her chest. 'I never get used to that.'

'Ach, you do, you do. There's that much gas in some of them, they're fartin' all night.'

Rachel smiled. 'Maybe we shouldn't be smoking then. One spark, an' this whole place could go up. Explain that to your boss!'

She was funny, Barney thought, and pretty, but he wasn't going to risk a third round of humiliation. If she was interested – and flirting away like this he was quite sure she was – *she* could do the asking.

The ominous rumble sounded again.

Rachel, glancing across, was astonished to see the body move slightly under its cover.

'Jesus! . . . Did you see that?! It moved!' She stepped closer to Barney, put a hand on his arm. 'Is that normal?'

Barney didn't even look round. 'Relax,' he said.

'I don't like it,' shuddered Rachel. 'Gives me the creeps.'

'Ah, you get used to it.' He put his fag out in the ash tray on the old woman's chest. 'Secret is, you give them a good telling-off, they don't do it again.' He winked at her, then moved towards the third of the waiting trolleys.

Rachel, aware that he was going to do *something*, instinctively said, 'Don't!'

'Shhh,' said Barney. He took hold of the top end of the sheet covering the body, then suddenly whipped it back and wagged an admonishing finger down at the corpse. 'Would you ever quit it with all the bloody farting!'

The corpse opened its eyes.

Barney's mouth dropped open.

The corpse sat up.

Rachel screamed, then hurtled across the room and out of the door.

'Please, . . . don't,' Barney whispered, terrified but frozen to the spot.

Walter North, the corpse in question, still half-asleep, rubbed at his eyes. 'It's bloody *freezing* in here,' he mumbled.

As he began to climb out of bed, Barney fortuitously discovered the power of his legs and staggered backwards.

'Any chance of a cup of—' Walter began.

Barney gave him one more terrified look, then charged out of the room. Walter yawned, stretched, blinked against the strip lighting, then took his first proper look at his surroundings. The three other beds, with dead feet sticking out of the bottom. And the naked woman on the bed with a half-full ash tray on her chest.

'Oh, holy crap,' said Walter, then shuffled his slippers quickly towards the door.

Walter knew one thing: he had to get out of the hospital. It was one thing hanging around Margaret. Or sneaking into an empty room for a sleep. It was something entirely different to wake up in a morgue with only corpses for company. To wake up dead. What if they'd tried to drain him of bodily fluids? Or harvest his organs? Or have him stuffed and mounted on casters? Or what if he'd slept through it all and somehow woken up in a coffin? He could have been buried alive! Or cremated!

Walter hurried along a labyrinth of basement corridors, trying door after door until he found a back way into the car park. His car was still there, but it had been clamped and plastered with prosecution warnings. Someone – Billy, in all probability – had added *Speccy* to the *Fruit* that had previously been scratched into the paintwork. Even if it hadn't been clamped, he didn't have the keys anyway; they were with his wallet and jacket in a locker that nice nurse had organised for him while the rest of his clothes were put through the laundry. But there was no way he was going back in for them. The morgue attendant had probably recovered his senses by now and would have alerted hospital security. How could he explain it away? *I was visiting a friend, but I decided to stay for three days, and then I pretended to be a patient, and then I decided to go sleep with the corpses.* They would cart him off to the mental wing. And how would it go down at work? And what would Margaret make of it?

Margaret.

What was it about her?

He was normally so *boring.* He was, after all, a Civil Servant.

And now here he was, standing on the Malone Road, in his Psyclops Surgeries pyjamas, dressing-gown and fluffy slippers, vainly trying to wave down a taxi.

Margaret definitely had a lot to answer for.

24

Big Foot

Margaret was making remarkable progress. She had, according to the young Indian house doctor, been at death's door. Or if not exactly at its door, then just along the hall from it. Waiting on the landing. It was one of the most serious cases of food poisoning he had ever seen, and that was saying something, coming from the land of the Delhi belly. Now, apart from extreme fatigue, it was almost as if the past three days hadn't happened.

'You look as good as new,' one of the nurses told her.

'I've never looked as good as new,' Margaret replied. She still wanted to do something about her drooping eyebrows and the bags under her eyes, and her lips and cheeks and forehead and maybe her bum and her boobs. But she had seen enough of hospitals for a while. She was even going to put the Botox needle on the long finger. Or with her luck, through it.

What was concerning her more than anything was the man in her room.

Nurse after nurse was telling her about the pleasant young fella who'd shown her such devotion while she was unconscious. Sitting by her bed, reading to her, arranging her flowers, talking away. They seemed to think he was called Walter. And they were certain that they weren't getting him mixed up with her soon-to-be ex-husband Billy. But the only Walter she knew . . . well, she hardly knew him at all. They'd endured one date together and parted acrimoniously. Why on earth would he choose to spend days watching over her? How did he even know she was in hospital?

Unless he poisoned me in the first place. But no, she'd chosen the café and the carrot cake at random. There was something more to it. She thought back to their abortive date – she had caught him out in a lie and stormed off even though he had been apologising profusely. Perhaps this was another way of saying sorry, mounting a vigil.

84

I Predict A Riot

Is that something I should feel good about? Or is it a bit weird?

Every nurse she spoke to confirmed Walter's devotion, but they all seemed to have slightly different impressions of him. He was fat. He was well-built. He wore glasses. He didn't. He was cleanshaven. No, a moustache. He chatted amiably. He was quiet and morose. One claimed to have seen him wearing a hospital dressing-gown. Another said he hadn't washed or slept or eaten the whole time. It was like sightings of Big Foot. Too many to dismiss his existence out of hand, but no hard physical evidence either.

If it was *the* Walter, and he was supposed to be so devoted, where was he now that she was awake? More to the point, what sort of a hospital would allow a complete stranger to hang about in a patient's room anyway? Anything could have happened! She'd seen a Pedro Almodóvar movie once where an obsessed man had done the business with a woman in a coma, and she'd become pregnant.

What if I'm pregnant?

Margaret knew she was getting a bit ahead of herself, but she had a point. She raised it with the Sister next time she called in.

'But he was so lovely,' the Sister said.

'Well, that's all right then,' said Margaret.

The Sister turned to leave.

'I was being sarcastic,' said Margaret.

'Well, it doesn't become you.'

'I was just making the point that—'

'If you're not happy, tell whoever's paying for your room. I'm sure they can negotiate a discount.' The Sister flounced out.

Who the *hell* did she think she was? Margaret swung two feet out of bed. *Nobody* talked to her like that. Except for her husband. Sometimes Mr Kawolski at work. And the robbing Millies who plagued her every day in Primark. But apart from them – oh, and Mrs Morrison, who owned the apartment she rented – *nobody* talked to her like that.

As soon as she tried to stand, Margaret immediately felt a little woozy. She grabbed the end of the bed for support, but was determined to stand upright. She took a deep breath and staggered forward. Then the door opened again. Margaret expected it to be the Sister again, thinking better of her attitude, but instead an extravagant bunch of flowers entered, followed a moment later by the tall, blonde, lithe Emma Cochrane.

The boutique owner smiled widely. 'Look at you!'

'Look at me,' Margaret said weakly, then staggered backwards.

'Just like Bambi!' Emma gushed.

Margaret collapsed back on her bed. 'Sorry, I . . .'

'It's all right! It's all right!' Emma rushed forward. 'You lie back, darling! You're so weak! What a dreadful experience! But you're alive! My little genius is alive!'

'Well, I don't know about that.'

'Yes, you are! Oh darling – I have a confession to make!' She dropped her Prada handbag from her shoulder, unclipped the logo lock, and produced a creased brown A4 envelope.

Margaret was feeling a little better now. 'You took my designs.'

'Only for safekeeping – and I couldn't help myself. It was the dresses – they were so fantastic, the thought that there might be more . . . Please forgive me!'

Margaret nodded, then ventured a hesitant: 'What did you think?' Her heart was beating twenty to the dozen, and it was nothing to do with her weakened state. This was her big moment. Did she have what it took to be a fashion designer?

Emma set the flowers on a chair and came and sat beside her on the edge of the bed. She put her arm around her and gave her a little squeeze. She smelled of expensive perfume or fabric softener. Margaret sometimes found it difficult to tell the difference.

'Margaret, darling, the designs . . . I'm just lost for words.'

What? Words like crap or rubbish or amateurish or rip-off or pathetic?

'Well, they're fairly basic, I'm sure.'

'They are *magnifique*!'

'What?'

'Magnificent! Fantastic! Superbly original! Dynamic!' Emma Cochrane didn't appear to be lost for words after all.

'*Really?*'

'Darling, I've been looking for designs like these for twenty years!' She gave Margaret another squeeze. 'Do you know what I'm going to do?'

'No.'

'I'm going to make us both rich and famous.'

Margaret blinked at her in disbelief. 'Can I have that in writing?'

25

Dr Chicago

Dr Manuel Speranza had been Chief Medical Officer of La Picota prison, outside Bogotá, for three years. He was a handsome man with short grey hair and a pristine white coat. Although he had a team of four nurses and a junior doctor to assist him, he was primarily responsible for the health of the three thousand inmates with just nineteen beds at his disposal. He had an ulcer. (There is probably a Colombian equivalent of 'physician heal thyself', but that should not detain us.) His medical wing had state-of-the-art equipment, thanks to a United Nations grant, but it continually broke down, and even when it was working, the power surges and blackouts meant it was either unreliable or downright dangerous.

La Picota was cramped, dirty, sweaty and provided perfect incubation for 127 different diseases. Competition was intense amongst the prisoners to catch the most virulent and deadly of these, as suffering in the medical wing, with its air conditioning and pretty nurses and decent food was infinitely preferable to suffering in the prison itself, which lacked air conditioning and decent food, and where the pretty nurses were invariably transvestites or transsexuals who, although attractive in a certain light, usually fading, weren't the same, no matter how willing they were.

Redmond O'Boyle was in the medical wing, recovering from a stab wound to his left buttock. Three men who either disagreed with his training of FARC guerrillas, or just wanted to steal his chicken, had attacked him and he had suffered his wound while running away. If he had stayed to argue either politics or fowl, he would undoubtedly have died. Now he lay face down on a soft bed and sipped warm Coke through a straw. The wound was not particularly serious or painful, but it had to be watched carefully to make sure that infection did not set in. A nurse called Maria was assigned to watch his buttock. She was very pretty, but did not say much. Redmond talked away to her, although she didn't appear to understand even the most basic English. He told her about his life at home, about the Mourne Mountains in the spring and Van Morrison, and because Maria had brown eyes, he sang her 'Brown-Eyed Girl'. He also gave her his version of 'Star of County Down'.

On his third day in the prison hospital wing Dr Speranza arrived at Redmond's bed shortly after lunch. He examined the wound.

'How's it looking?' Redmond asked.

Dr Speranza's English was reasonably good, if quite slow. He stood back, scratched at his brow for a moment, then said, 'Do you have . . . English word . . . for *gangrene*?'

Redmond swallowed. 'Ahm, "gangrene" works in English.'

'Really? It is the same word?'

'Yes.'

'I wonder what the origin of it is? Do you think, French?'

'I don't know. Doctor, do I—'

'I do not think Spanish, and it is not harsh enough for German.'

'Doctor . . .'

Dr Speranza bent to the buttock again. 'I am pleased to tell you that there is no sign of *gangrene*. However, the wound has not yet healed.' He turned to Nurse Maria and said in Spanish, 'Maria, you must keep a very close eye on our esteemed guest's buttock.'

Maria nodded.

'She is very pretty nurse, no?'

Redmond glanced at Maria, who continued to watch his buttock. 'Yes,' he said.

'Very pretty indeed,' said Dr Speranza, 'but I do not make love to her.'

'Oh,' said Redmond.

'Though I very much want to.' Redmond nodded. Dr Speranza smiled. 'Do not worry, Redmond, she does not speak English. You may speak freely on the subject of her loveliness.'

'Well, yes. She certainly is lovely.'

'I think this also. I am married, alas. You are married, Redmond?'

'No. Yes. I mean – I'm not sure.'

'Ah – yes, I know. Do you think I look like George Clooney? Many people remark that I look like George Clooney.'

'Well . . .'

'I big fan of George Clooney. I learn my English from DVD of *ER*. First season.'

'Ah. Right.'

'George Clooney – I think he has his pick of nurses. You think?'

'I would imagine so.'

'I think he will be a big star.'

'Well, I think he actually . . .'

'But he will have to leave *ER*. Perhaps I could be his replacement?'

'Well . . .'

'I have good bedside manner, no?' Redmond nodded. 'And I very popular with the pretty nurses, no?' Redmond nodded again. 'And I act as well. Just a little. Very small. Colombian TV – not pay well. You think *ER* is . . . ambitious?'

'Well . . .'

'Perhaps *Chicago Hope*. I also have this on DVD. Not as good but perhaps a better place to start?'

'Could be,' said Redmond.

Dr Speranza's brow furrowed suddenly, and he bent back down to examine Redmond's wound. 'Oh, my goodness,' he said. 'How did I miss *that*?'

Redmond glanced at Maria. She too was looking concerned. His stomach turned over.

Dr Speranza grabbed the young nurse's elbow, 'Maria – I have not seen anything like this in thirty years,' he said in English. 'We must operate immediately—!'

Maria jumped to her feet. She was just hurrying away when Dr Speranza caught her arm again and almost twirled her back towards him. 'Hush, child, hush,' he said dramatically, then spoke rapidly to her in Spanish.

Anger flashed across her face. Dr Speranza patted her shoulder.

Redmond was beside himself. 'What's wrong?'

The doctor looked sympathetically down at his Irish patient. 'You see, Redmond? I think I make good actor. You both believe. It's all in the eyes – and intonation.' He laughed, then moved on to the next bed.

Redmond's own eyes blazed. He was on the verge of snapping something not very pleasant after the doctor, something which would undoubtedly have resulted in a speedy return to his prison cell, when Maria stopped him, by simply by putting her finger to his lips.

'Shhh.'

'But—'

'Do not lose your temper,' Maria whispered. The finger lingered where it was for a moment, then slowly dropped away. She had spoken English. Perfectly. Redmond could only wrinkle his brow in a mix of surprise and confusion.

Maria smiled. She moved closer, and began to smooth down his blankets. Then she knelt down by his pillow and lifted his hand, as if she was checking his pulse. 'Yes, I do speak English, Redmond O'Boyle. And Doctor Speranza is an idiot.'

'I had no idea.'

'I wanted to see what kind of a man you are.'

Redmond looked at her oddly. 'And what kind of a man *am* I?'

'You are romantic. Doctor Chicago – that is what we all call him – he thinks he is romantic . . . but no, you sing to me and you talk even though you do not think I understand. But he is right about one thing – it is in the eyes. That is how you tell if a person has a good soul. You have a good soul, Redmond O'Boyle.'

Well, thought Redmond, who could occasionally be as shallow as a dried-up riverbed, I may be stuck in a Colombian prison with a stabbed buttock, but things are starting to look up.

'I think you have beautiful eyes,' he said.

'Save your bulls**t. I am FARC, and I am here to get you out.'

'Oh,' said Redmond.

26

Tomorrow Is Another Day

Later, Walter decided that he'd been drunk with fatigue. How else to explain running away from the hospital like that? Leaving his clothes and wallet and car keys behind like that? And his car clamped and Security probably charging about looking for him, thinking he was a weirdo who sneaked around morgues poking at the dead bodies. In fact, he should have stood his ground and reported *them* for shipping him to the morgue in the first place, when all he'd done was lie down for a bit of a kip on a spare bed.

Now he was back home, having climbed through the window he'd left ajar for three days and nights. Luckily no one else had climbed in during his absence, although there were paw-prints on the kitchen counter. Probably the neighbour's cat. He moved along the hall into the lounge. He looked at the newspapers spread across the sofa, the foil dish stained with curry lying on its side on the carpet, the curtains hanging loosely off the rail, the TV with the thin coating of dust, the clock on the wall still not adjusted for summertime. He felt deeply, deeply depressed. He trod up the stairs to his bedroom. The sheets which hadn't been changed in months, the Venetian blinds bent from poking out to see what the kids in the street were up to, and to watch that twenty-one year old in the mini-skirt from three doors up walking for the bus in the morning.

Is this what my life is?

Yes, it is! The answer seemed to scream from every cobwebbed corner of his house and heart.

I must change this, he decided. Starting tomorrow. Tomorrow will be the first day of the rest of my life.

And if not tomorrow, because I'm going to be absolutely knackered and I need to get to work, then certainly the next day. Or definitely Monday. Get the weekend out of the way first – never a good idea to start—

No!

NO! NO! NO! NO!

It *has* to be tomorrow. *For once in my life, I have to follow through on something.*

Walter crawled into bed and immediately fell into a deep sleep. He dreamed of gerbils eating their young and naked old women with ash trays on their chests. He was drenched in sweat when he woke shortly after 10 a.m. He made himself do fifteen sit-ups, then showered. He had Rice Krispies for breakfast. He sprinkled on Canderel. It was a year and a half out of date, but he doubted somehow that fake sugar really could go off. Unlike the milk, which was slightly turned.

Then he phoned work.

'Let me guess,' said Mark. 'You're going to be late.'

'Yes, I am.'

'In fact, you may not make it in at all today.'

'That's a distinct possibility.'

'Oh, Walter. What are we going to do with you?'

'Shoot me,' said Walter.

'That's a bit harsh. Although your flexitime is so far into the red you'll be paying it back till Christmas. That is, if you ever turn up. The good news is, nobody's missed you yet.'

'That is good.'

'The bad news is, that's not quite true. That funny guy in Office Twelve was asking for you.'

'Steven?'

'Is that what you call him? Anyway, he knows you've not been in. Don't know if that's good or bad, but forewarned is forearmed, or something like that. Meanwhile, back at the ranch, how's "Girlfriend in a Coma"?' He sang the last bit. It was an old Smiths' song.

'Just the same.'

'Did you ever see that De Niro film where he was in a coma for like thirty years and then he suddenly woke up and fell in love and then fell asleep again?'

'No.'

'Yeah, wasn't much cop, but just warning you, you might be in it for the long haul.'

'I know that.'

There was silence for a few moments. Walter didn't quite know what to say – or how to explain how he was feeling. He felt like he was standing at the edge of a precipice, and the wind was at his back. It would be so easy to fall over. The only thing was, he didn't know if he was in for a soft landing, in warm water, with bubbles, far below, and that it was therefore something to be embraced, or if he would be dashed to pieces on the rocks.

Mark said, 'Just to let you know, I passed the first hurdle.'

'The what?'

'You know, with the Unionist Party. I went down for a chat and they're all for building me up as a potential candidate. They think the local council first – they say any idiot can get elected there.'

'Well, that's good.'

'Yeah, I suppose.'

'You don't sound over-enthusiastic.'

'Well, you know – councillors. What do they do? They deal with drains and speed humps. I'd prefer to be where the action is. But they say I have to learn to walk before I run. But what if you're a natural athlete?'

'Well, I'm sure there's things you still have to learn.'

'Yeah, I know. Although going by the ones I've met so far, I have to ask exactly what that might be. Half of them are farmers and the other half are doting.'

There was a pip-pip sound on the line to indicate there was someone else trying to call, so Walter made his usual promise – he'd be into work tomorrow – and rang off. Immediately the phone rang again and a woman said: 'Is that Walter North?'

'Possibly,' said Walter, who was naturally suspicious.

'Walter from the hospital?'

Walter cleared his throat. 'I didn't do anything. I just went to sleep and woke up there. I never interfered with anyone.'

'What are you talking about?'

'What are *you* talking about?'

'Walter – this is Jenny. Nurse Jenny? I spoke to you in the café, got your clothes washed?'

'Oh yes. Sorry. Of course.'

'You just disappeared on us.'

'Yes, I know – sorry. Bit of a mix-up.'

'Didn't know where you'd got to. Had to get the maintenance guy to break into that locker, get your wallet. Luckily found your Xtravision card.'

'My . . . ?'

'Phoned them, they gave us your home phone number – although they say you're overdue with that dirty movie . . .'

'What dirty movie?'

'Only joking. But your clothes and all your stuff's here – are you not going to come and get it?'

'I . . . Yes, of course. Sorry – I'm just very tired.'

'That's all right. I understand that. But still, you must be delighted.'

'Delighted?'

'About Margaret being awake and all.'

Walter was silent for a moment, wondering if she was winding him up again. 'She's *awake*?'

'Yes. Didn't you know?'

'No, I . . .'

'Oh yes, she's awake all right.'

'And no . . . ?'

'Brain damage? Paralysis? Not a sausage. She's full of the joys of spring, so she is.'

'Well, that's good,' said Walter.

'So you'll be coming to see her? Will I tell her?'

'No,' said Walter. 'Don't tell her.'

'But why not? She's been asking for you.'

Walter's heart skipped a beat. 'She has?'

27

Prelude To A Kiss, Or Something

At first Walter was going to bring Margaret a Get Well Soon gift of hardboiled eggs and nuts, just like in the Laurel & Hardy film. But then he was worried that she wouldn't get the joke and would think he was an eejit. He'd already made a fool of himself by trying to bring her a bag of hamburger baps – thank God only her estranged husband and his neighbour had been a witness to that one. Perhaps Billy had told her about it – chasing him up the street like the coward he was and yelling dog's abuse after him. Maybe they'd laughed about it. Maybe they'd looked into each other's eyes and decided that yes, despite everything, they really did love each other and had now promised eternal devotion. What if Billy had also promised to permanently get rid of that creep who was hanging around the hospital?

But no. Nurse Jenny had said it: *She's been asking for you.*

Which meant: She *wants* to see you. That was a good thing. *Unless it was some kind of a trap.* An ambush. Perhaps it wasn't Nurse Jenny at all, but an undercover cop setting a honey trap. *Sex-Stalker Trapped by Heroic Coma Girl.* Or if Billy had anything to do with it: *Fat Speccy Sex-Stalker Trapped by Heroic Coma Girl.*

No.

I have to go and see her.

It was just a feeling. In the pit of his stomach, in the cavities of his brain. An instinct. A desire. Their entire history comprised of one miserable date. He had no way of knowing if she was feeling any of the same things he was feeling, but there was only one way to find out.

Or I could phone her, he thought. Send her a letter. A bunch of flowers, and include my phone number. Put the ball in her court.

No.

Today is the first day of the rest of your life, he told himself. You have done your sit-ups. You have sprinkled Canderel on your Rice

95

Krispies. You are sorting your life out and this is one step you have to take yourself. You have to walk in there and use everything in your power to convince her that you are genuine and sincere.

Walter put on his suit. Then he took it off. He put on an open-neck black shirt with short sleeves and a pair of black jeans. He pulled on a Pringle jumper over the shirt, then took it off again. *Not playing golf.* He tried on a navy zip-up jacket with yellow piping around the collar. There. What they call 'smart but casual'.

Walter took a taxi into town, then bought an understated bunch of flowers from a proper florists. He went into Waterstones and picked out a biography of Tom Hanks. He stood outside Bar Bacca for ten minutes, debating whether to go in for a steadying drink. Then proudly decided against it. He caught another taxi up to Psyclops Surgeries on the Malone Road. He went straight in. He still had his clothes and watch and wallet to pick up, and the clamped car to sort out, but he could do that later. It was important not to be deflected now. It was a little after 2.05 p.m. Visiting had been underway for five minutes. Walter approached Margaret's door and peered nervously in.

Billy was standing at the end of the bed.

Walter cursed silently, then hurried on down the corridor and took up a position where he could see if her room door opened, but in the opposite direction to the one Billy would take when leaving. The last thing he needed was another confrontation, or a hiding.

Walter knew from past experience that Billy never spent the full hour visiting. He always left ten minutes early to beat the rush in the car park. He was an accountant.

'Nice flowers.'

Walter jumped. He turned. The girl from the café. Nurse Jenny.

'Oh – thank you.'

'You're not going in?'

'Her husband.'

'Oh right.' Then Nurse Jenny said: 'Do you want me to throw him out? I could go in and say she needs her rest or an enema or something. I can do that. I have the power.' Walter smiled, but shook his head. 'Well, seeing as you're here, do you want to come and get your stuff?'

'No, I'll wait.'

She nodded, understanding. 'All right. Well, I'll be around. Just ask for me. And, well – good luck.' She gave him a wink, then walked on.

No honey trap there then. Walter felt more confident now. He took a deep breath. He needed to use the bathroom, but knew if he did, he was taking the risk of something going wrong. He was that kind of a guy. The guy things happened to. He would be locked in. His trousers would be ripped off in a bizarre hand-dryer malfunction. But he had to. Wouldn't be able to settle otherwise. Nothing worse than trying to have a life-changing encounter while busting for a pee.

He went. He washed his hands. He dried them carefully. He checked his hair, his face for dry skin, his jacket for dandruff. There, perfect. He took his glasses off and polished them. Then decided to keep them off. Then decided to put them back on again.

Okay.

Walter took up his position again. The only way of being sure that Billy hadn't slipped out while he was in the Gents was to go right up to the window and check, but that would run the risk of bumping into him. He'd only been gone for a minute. Chances were, Billy was still in there.

Be patient. For the patient.

A few minutes later, the door opened. Walter stepped back, out of view. He counted to ten. When he chanced another look, Billy was just passing through the swing doors and taking the stairs down to the Exit.

This is it then.

Margaret hated him.

He was a sanctimonious, pompous, nit-picking, whiny knob. He had snapped something snidey at her on the way out, and now here was the door opening again and it would be him back to take a final parting shot.

Except it wasn't her husband Billy, it was Walter. He stood in the open doorway, his hair combed impeccably, his face flushed, a small bunch of flowers in one hand, a Waterstones bag in the other.

'Hello,' said Walter.

'Hello,' said Margaret.

''Scuse me.'

Walter turned. A nursing assistant was trying to push a trolley into Margaret's room.

'We're ju . . . we're just . . .' Walter stuttered.

'Tea's up, love.'

He stepped into the room and looked helplessly at Margaret. She was blushing. The nursing assistant pushed the trolley ahead of her.

'Cuppa tea, love?'

'Please,' said Margaret. She couldn't take her eyes off Walter.

'What about you, love?'

It took a long moment for Walter to realise she was talking to him.

'No – yes – thank you.'

The woman set Margaret's tea down on her locker. Then she poured one for Walter and turned to hand it to him. But then she stopped, smiled, and said, 'Spurs are at the bottom of the league.'

Walter blinked at her. 'I'm sorry? What?'

'*Zip*-adee-do-dah, love.'

Walter looked at Margaret in confusion. She had lifted her tea, and now seemed to be giggling into it.

'I'm sorry – you've lost me completely.'

The woman rolled her eyes. 'For godsake, man, pull your zip up before your willy falls out.'

Behind her, Margaret erupted.

Walter looked down at his flies in horror, at the square inch of tartan boxer short poking out, then backed out of the room.

28

Talks About Talks

'Well,' said Walter, 'that didn't quite go according to plan.' He had prepared scrupulously for his big moment with Margaret Gilmore, and then forgotten to make sure his flies were done up.

'I think that's what Janet Jackson called a wardrobe malfunction,' said Margaret.

Walter stepped fully into her private room in Psyclops Surgeries. He was, of course, very familiar with it, having recently performed a seventy-two-hour vigil by her bed while she hovered on death's landing. But now that she was awake again, it felt very different. While she'd been unconscious, he had been in control. He decided what they did. When she needed to be read to. If a window needed opening. When she needed to hear another tale of woe from his sad life. But now *she* was back in charge. He stood awkwardly at the foot of her bed, just as he had seen her husband Billy do. As if he was waiting for punishment.

'Well,' said Margaret.

'Well,' said Walter. He had written down a list of thirty-seven interesting conversation-openers, but now couldn't think of one. Apart from: 'Well, uhm, how are you feeling?'

Margaret just looked at him.

'Not so good, eh?' Walter volunteered.

'No. Not so good.'

'I understand it was carrot cake.'

'Yes, it was. What are you doing here?'

'Visiting.'

'Someone else?'

'No. You. Oh.' He came forward and thrust the flowers and the Waterstones bag at her rather too enthusiastically. She took them, but looked at the flowers without reacting, and set the bag down by her side. She returned her attention to Walter.

'Aren't you . . . going to look inside it?' he asked.

'No.'

'Oh.'

'So what are you doing here, Walter – if that indeed is your real name?'

'Yes of course it's my real name.' He stopped and shrugged. 'Well, I was passing, and . . .'

'You've been here three days and three nights.'

'Well yes – like I say, I was passing.'

'*Why* are you here?'

'I, ah, – well, I thought we might have gotten off on the wrong foot. Our big date wasn't exactly . . . We argued.'

'And do you do this with everyone you have a cross word with? Camp out on their doorstep until they forgive you?'

Walter cleared his throat. 'I don't want you to forgive me.'

'What?'

'Well – yes, I do, but also, ahm, I don't think you were, ahm, exactly honest either.'

Margaret sat up further in the bed, her brow furrowed, her nostrils flared. 'What exactly are you implying?'

'I'm not implying anything.'

'Insinuating then, is that a better word?'

'No – yes – it's just . . . well, you never said you were, you know, married, or working as a security guard in Primark.'

'So you've not only been plaguing me day and night, you've also been sticking your nose into my affairs?'

'I never mentioned your affairs.'

It sat in the air for a moment, then Margaret shook her head and a smile almost appeared. She took a deep breath. 'Well,' she said.

'Well,' said Walter.

'You spent three days and nights here, you hardly ate, you hardly slept, you read to me and you talked to me.'

Walter shrugged. 'Yeah,' he said, avoiding eye-contact.

'I wasn't aware of any of it. None at all.'

'That's all right. They say it helps. And you never know. Subconsciously.'

She looked at him doubtfully. 'I don't know whether you're sicker than I am, or if it's quite the nicest thing anyone's ever done for me.'

'I would, you know, incline to the latter.'

'I'm sure you would.' Margaret shook her head again, then lifted the Waterstones bag. 'This had better not be something weird.' She removed the biography of Tom Hanks. 'You remembered.'

Walter nodded. 'And I thought this whole thing was a little bit like *Sleepless in Seattle*.'

'It's nothing like *Sleepless in Seattle.*'

'Okay.'

'Although there was one with Sandra Bullock. And that actor who's in everything but nobody knows his name. Do you know who I mean?'

Walter shook his head.

'*While You Were Sleeping,* that's what it's called. But it was really nothing like this.'

'I'll . . . ah, look out for it.'

She opened the book and began to leaf through the pages.

'I thought that we could start again,' he said suddenly.

Her eyes flicked up to him. 'You thought that?'

'Yes, I did. Only this time with absolute honesty. And I am sorry for telling fibs.'

'Fibs, were they? Not lies?'

'The point is, I was kind of embarrassed and we all buff up our CVs, don't we?'

She nodded a little reluctantly.

'But if we could start again, well – it was good fun before you . . .'

'Caught you out?'

'Yes, but—'

'You made fun of me eating so much bread.'

'I didn't mean to.'

Margaret sighed. 'I looked such a mess.'

'Yes, you did.'

'Don't beat around the bush there.'

He smiled. She smiled.

'Ahm – what do you think?' Walter asked.

'Absolute honesty?'

'Absolute.'

Margaret looked back down to the book. Then, after several long moments, and still not looking up, said, 'I suppose.'

Walter smiled again. There was hope. There was a God. He went to sit on the end of the bed but she suddenly stretched her legs out in front of her to stop him. He moved to a chair opposite.

'I'm not a property developer,' said Walter.

'Mmm-hmm?'

'I'm a Civil Servant.'

'Uh-huh?'

'But there's a possibility of me becoming a spy.'

Margaret's eyes flicked towards him.

'Only kidding,' said Walter.

And he was. Sort of.

29

Tripping the Light

He could have danced all night.

Or something like that.

Walter skipped ecstatically down the hospital corridor. He wanted to hug nurses, but didn't. He really wasn't touchy-feely. He wanted to embrace old folk and reassure them that everything would be all right, but couldn't, because he felt a bit weird about old people. Inside, though, *inside*, he was on fire. Walter was tripping the light fantastic. He was walking on air. It was like that scene in *It's a Wonderful Life* where James Stewart realises that it is indeed a wonderful life and he charges down the main street in celebration. Just like it. Except for the snow.

Walter retrieved the clothes, wallet and car keys he had left in a locker the night before, then waited patiently in the car park while the clamp guy freed his vehicle. He even tipped him. The poor guy didn't know where to look. When Walter had reached for the fiver the clamper had instinctively stepped back, half-expecting a knife to be pulled. And even when Walter had handed the tip over, the clamper had examined it doubtfully, nipping it between the very tips of his fingers, convinced that it was either a joke note that would explode in his face, or that handling it would somehow automatically tie him into the latest IRA bank heist.

'It's fine,' Walter tried to reassure him. 'Just printed it this morning.'

The clamper didn't smile. Of course, it wasn't in his nature. Or if it had once been, it had long since been driven out. Or not driven out, as the case may be.

And the reason for Walter's happiness? He wasn't a proud new father. He hadn't had a marriage proposal accepted. There wasn't even the promise of a date. He had asked Margaret if he could visit her again that night. Her first reaction was to shake her head. But it wasn't a no. It was half-surprise, half-exasperation. But then she'd shrugged and said okay, and it might as well have been a resounding yes to a proposal, the effect it had on Walter.

It meant they were back on an even keel. That he was forgiven.

They had laughed together. They had sworn to be honest with each other. It was a new dawn. A new beginning. He had come so close to ruining things, but now he was back, better than ever. He was on top of his game. He was cool again. He was Steve McQueen in *The Great Escape*. And now, as he gunned his vehicle out of the car park, he was *Bullitt*.

He saw her – but too late – a little old lady crossing the exit lane from the car park. There was just a fraction of a second where she looked up, and saw death approach.

Walter slammed on the brakes, there was a screech of rubber on tarmac, and the car came to a violent stop.

Walter hardly dared open his eyes. He hadn't been aware of a thump. Or a scream. But there must have been both.

He had screamed, anyway. Perhaps death had come too suddenly for her to make any noise.

He knew, he *knew* if he opened his eyes, she would be plastered across his windscreen. Or parts of her would be. Or perhaps he had struck her so hard that she still hadn't landed. That even now, as he was thinking *this*, she was descending from space, just about to crack through the roof of his car and kill him as well.

Walter's heart was beating ninety to the dozen.

I should have known, I should have known, things were going so well. Thank You God! Thank You! Show me heaven, then condemn me to hell.

Walter opened his eyes. The windscreen was clear. The traffic ahead of him was flowing normally. Surely if he'd struck her, people would have stopped, if not to help, at least to gawk.

Unless she was *under* the car, and nobody saw. Squashed to a pulp.

Walter looked left and right. There were no pedestrians. People didn't walk on the Malone Road. His luck was in. If he just eased the car forward, slipped into the traffic, he could get to the car wash and—

No! How callous and evil was that? Much better to drive home, clean it up there. Too many people at the car wash.

No – *no*! He'd have to drive *over* the body, and he couldn't do that. No – he'd have to get out, drag the body free and stuff it in the boot. Work out some way to dispose of it later. There was a lake near—

No!

What if she's not dead? What if even as I sit here tuning in my radio, she's struggling for her last breath?

He'd only had the most fleeting glimpse of her, but she was definitely old. Old women have brittle bones. Even if he'd only touched her, the force would probably have been enough to shatter every bone in her body.

If I try and pick her up, she'll shatter in my hands. What if she needs the kiss of life?

Walter didn't think he was up to kissing her. She probably smelled of old woman. Either pee or *Youth Dew* like his own granny used to wear. She would slobber all over him when he was a kid, and it terrified him. And every time he'd smelled *Youth Dew* since, it reminded him of moist old women. And in the Belfast way it had always been pronounced *Youth Jew* and for many years it had made him vaguely anti-Semitic until he'd finally seen the label and realised his mistake.

There was a sudden tap on the driver's window. Walter's heart, which had been racing out of control, threatened to explode. Not more than thirty seconds had passed since he had struck, squashed or shattered the old woman, yet it felt like a lifetime.

Slowly he turned his head.

She was there. Her face was white. Deathly white.

My God. My God.

Walter touched a button, and the window eased down.

'Are you all right?' It was the old woman asking. Not him.

'I . . . I . . .' Walter stammered.

'I'm so sorry. I stepped out without thinking. I'm such an idiot!'

'No, no,' said Walter. 'I should have . . .'

'Nonsense. I need to take more care. Are you okay? You look very pale.'

'I'm fine.' He put his hand to his chest. 'Just . . . shock.'

She touched her own chest. 'Well, thank God. I thought my number was up.' She blew air out of her cheeks. 'Well, sorry again.'

She nodded, and began to turn away. She stopped again and took a deeper breath.

'Miss . . . Missus?'

She turned.

'Can I . . . can I give you a lift home?'

She studied him.

'I'm not a pervert or anything,' said Walter.

30

Just Friends

It was a curious thing, Margaret thought. Prior to her extreme allergic reaction to a slice of carrot cake she had only met Walter once, and they hadn't exactly hit it off. Yet she was quite calm and relaxed about the fact that he had mounted a vigil in her hospital room for three days and nights. Of course, if he had turned out to be a murderer or pervert there was nothing she could have done about it, being in a coma and all, but when she did wake up, and discovered what he'd done, it had made her feel good instead of worried, reassured instead of concerned. Her soon-to-be ex-husband Billy had also visited conscientiously, yet the realisation that he had been there while she was unconscious still filled her with a kind of dread, mostly because she did not doubt that he had the capacity to do some kind of harm to her. Not murder her – but if he had been given the choice of switching off her life-support or waiting to see if she ever came out of her coma, she did not doubt for one moment that he would have chosen to switch it off. Walter, she thought, would probably have sat with her until he was an old man.

She didn't hate Billy. She just didn't like him, and that was a terrible thing in a marriage.

Had she changed? Or had he?

They had married young. Probably they had both changed. They wanted different things. They'd just got caught up in the excitement of a first proper relationship. Sex, really. Nobody called it courting any more. Then he'd asked her to marry him, and she'd said yes straight away. She thought now that it had been about getting an engagement ring. About being able to show it off to her friends. And she'd loved planning the wedding and choosing the dress and walking down the aisle. But the reality had set in not long after they'd come back from honeymoon.

No – in fact, it had set in on their honeymoon. They were in Spain, and it was about the outdoor restaurant and the breakfast buffet.

It was, basically, your Ulster fry – save for there being no soda or potato bread, and the addition of beans. It was now 'the full English'. Billy had once taken her on a weekend to Jury's in Dublin and made her laugh by asking for 'an unoccupied twenty-six counties fry'. And then when they'd gone back to the hotel after a night on the tear the doorman had asked if they were residents and Billy had shot back, quick as you like, 'No, mate, we're Protestants.'

Margaret smiled at the memory of it. There had been good times. But how long had it been since Billy had made her laugh? More than a decade, she thought.

On the honeymoon she'd watched him eat his breakfast, his plate piled high, shovelling it in as fast as he could, and it made her feel sick. She'd wanted it to be romantic, sitting on the veranda, facing the sea, the gentle breeze, holding hands. Not sitting opposite Igor, with bean juice rolling down his chin.

'Couldn't you slow down?'

'It'll get cold.'

'Couldn't you just . . . talk to me?'

'It'll get cold. It wasn't hot to start with. It'll be bloody freezing. They should heat those things a bit better. What do you want to talk about?'

'Doesn't matter.'

'Yes, it does. Just let me finish this. I hate cold food.'

'Okay.'

'Don't look like that.'

'Like what?'

'Sulky. I'm just trying to eat my breakfast. What's so important it can't wait until I finish my breakfast?'

'Nothing.'

'Well then. Their bacon is really crap.'

'So why are you eating it?'

'It's free, isn't it?'

'No, Billy, it's not free. We're paying for it.'

'Yeah – all right, smarty pants, I know the breakfast's included. But the amount I'm eating, there's actually about four breakfasts here. So, as far as I'm concerned, three of them are free. And I won't need any lunch, 'cause I'll still be stuffed, so I'll be saving money there as well. You've only had cereal. You should go and get a fry. Fill your plate. That'll mean we've had eight breakfasts between us, six of them free, and we'll save on two lunches. First day of our honeymoon, and we're already into profit. This is the life, eh?'

Margaret sat back in her hospital bed and picked up the book

Walter had brought her. Tom Hanks would have held her hand and talked to her. He wouldn't have shovelled in his food like that. Neither would Walter. They'd only had one meal together, and he'd eaten it like a perfect gentleman, never putting so much into his mouth that he couldn't swallow it quickly and respond to whatever she said.

He was coming back that night. *And so was Billy.* Damn.

Her ex-husband had been bad enough earlier. *'Who is he? Why's he hanging around? He arrived at my front door with a bag of baps!'* She'd laughed out loud at that. She'd been so nervous on their one and only date that she'd eaten every bread roll she'd been offered in the restaurant. This was Walter's little joke. She liked his sense of humour.

'Are you having sex?'

'No, of course not.'

Why had she said *of course not*? It was nothing to do with Billy who she had sex with, or how often. Not any longer. It was entirely her decision. If she chose to have sex, then she bloody well would have sex. With Walter. Or with a passing traffic warden. Anyone. The fact was, she hadn't had sex with anyone since she'd left Billy. She just hadn't met the right person yet. Or maybe she had.

'He's just a friend.'

'Oh yeah?'

'I swear to God.'

'You've been seeing him since before we split up. You left me for him.'

'No, I didn't. I only just met him.'

'You're a liar.'

She took a deep breath. 'Billy, you'll meet someone else.'

'No, I won't. I love you.'

'No, you don't. You're just lonely.'

'Yes, of course I'm f**kin' lonely – you left me.'

'I had to.'

'Yeah, right. A big boy made you do it.'

'Billy, please. Not here. Not now. We've been through this a thousand times.'

Billy stared at the ground. 'Sorry,' he said.

'It's okay.'

'I miss you.'

She nodded. She did feel desperately sorry for him. And there were occasional moments when she did miss him. But the problem was, she really didn't miss him enough. In fact, she wasn't sure if it was even Billy that she missed. It was *someone*. Someone to laugh with. To share things with. To eat toast and jam with in bed and not worry about the crumbs. To go onto the second layer of Milk Tray without finishing the first, and without worrying about your husband slapping your fingers for doing it.

He had done that, her Billy. Slapped her hand like she was a baby. She couldn't imagine the real Milk Tray Man doing that.

Or Walter.

31

DIY

The old woman was called Bertha James, and she lived in an impressive three-storey terraced house in South Belfast. She was from Omagh originally, and although she'd been in the city for sixty years, she still retained a country twang. Walter parked outside. They had chatted amiably enough on the short drive home.

When she'd told him her name, he'd smiled and said, 'Good job you're quite small.'

'Why?'

'Well – you know – *Bertha*.' And he'd winked. She'd stared at him blankly, and he'd flushed, because he was coming across like Eric Idle. *Nudge, nudge, wink, wink, say no more.* But he had persevered. 'You know – Big Bertha.'

Then she'd nodded.

'Heard it once too often,' said Walter.

She nodded again.

'Name you don't hear that often, these days,' said Walter. 'Bertha. And Hilda. And Sadie. And Wilhelmina.'

'And Walter,' said Bertha.

'Aye,' said Walter. 'I suppose.'

She said, 'Do you want to come in for a cup of tea?'

Walter had an immediate image of turned milk and rock-hard scones.

'No, thanks, I should—'

'Just to check for burglars.'

'You've had . . . ?'

'Lock on the back door's broken. Would you mind?'

'No. Of course not.'

He followed her up the drive. She fumbled with a key for several moments, then handed it to him.

Walter unlocked the door and pushed it open. He stepped into the hallway and shouted, 'Give yourself up, the house is surrounded!'

109

His voice echoed along the wooden floors, and up the stairs, and rattled off the hundreds of shelves lined with vases and china and ornaments. From where he stood, and then as she led him through the house to the kitchen, there was hardly an inch of wall or floor which was left bare. The house was crammed with every single commemorative plate ever advertised in a Sunday supplement. Every leather-bound volume ever offered as a extra special free gift by a dodgy book club. Every priceless antique ever sold at a once-in-a-life-time price by a market-stall huckster. It was a museum of tack.

'I collect things,' said Bertha. She set about making a cup of tea.

'So I see.'

'It passes the time, since Frank . . .'

'Your husband?'

'He passed away. 1973. Just up those stairs. He was bringing me up a cup of tea. My legs were bad, even then. He was singing. "I'll Be Your Long-Haired Lover from Liverpool" then there was this tremendous crash and when I hobbled out to see, there he was, bottom of the stairs, scalded with tea and his head squashing the Swiss roll. He'd had a massive heart-attack. Just like someone switched the light off. Sad.'

'Sad,' agreed Walter.

'Never been able to hear that song again, without feeling sad.'

'Me neither,' said Walter. 'You never remarried?'

'Nah. There was only one Frank. They broke the mould when they made him. Plenty of proposals, mind.'

'But no one measured up.'

Bertha gave a little shrug. As she poured a cup for Walter she said, 'Are you married, Walter?'

'No. Not yet.'

'No children?'

'No. Not yet.'

'You wouldn't want to be leaving it long.'

'No, I suppose.'

'Who were you visiting at the hospital?'

'How do you know I'm not a brain surgeon?'

'Are you a brain surgeon?'

'No. Not yet.'

Bertha smiled. Walter added milk from a semi-skimmed plastic bottle. He surreptitiously checked the date before he poured and was pleased to see that he had at least twenty-four hours before it became poisonous. Just as he lifted the cup to his lips, Bertha said, 'Would you take a look at the lock?'

Walter set the cup down. He nodded at the back door. 'This one?'

'If it's not too much trouble.'

'No. No trouble at all.'

There wasn't much the matter with it. Two of the four screws holding it in place had slipped, shifting the locking mechanism slightly. Once he tightened it up, and added a little oil to smooth the action, it worked just fine.

She poured him a fresh cup of tea, and offered him some short-bread. He declined the biscuit, because he could see that the seal on the tin was broken, and shortbread is notoriously difficult to keep fresh. He was looking forward to the tea, but even as he raised the cup she caught his eye, and he hesitated. 'Is there something else?' he asked.

'I hate to ask.'

'No – not at all.'

'There's a window upstairs. It bangs. Slightest breeze sets it off. Keeps me awake all night.'

'Would you like me to take a look?'

'Only if you have time.'

Walter set his cup down. He had time. There were still four hours to go before evening visiting time at the hospital.

Three and a half hours later, Walter was just finishing off the grouting around Bertha's ancient bath. He had sweated through his shirt and grazed three of his knuckles badly enough to bleed. He had fixed curtain rails, chipped ice out of a freezer, re-hung thirteen paint-ings and removed the skeletal remains of a mouse from under a Super Ser gas-heater. Bertha had hovered over him throughout, lavishing him with praise and thanks, yet he had still not managed a sip of tea.

'It's just so long since I had a man about the house,' she said, several times.

'Don't worry about it. I nearly killed you this afternoon. Look on this as my penance.'

'Well, if you really don't mind.'

And then she remembered something else that needed fixing. It went on and on, but finally, when she remembered another last thing, Walter called a halt. 'Sorry, I'm going to have to get going.'

She looked rather crestfallen. 'Oh, of course. I understand.' She looked at the floor.

Part of him wanted to say, 'I don't know you from Adam, you old bat, and you have me working like a slave all because you walked out in front of *my* car. I've done my bit.' He didn't, of course. 'I'm sorry,' he said again, 'but I have to meet someone.'

'Of course, of course. I'll be fine. You've done a grand job. Do you think I might have your telephone number?'

'My . . . ?'

'It would just be reassuring to know there was someone I could call. You see, The Samaritans, they only listen, they're not allowed to have a proper conversation. Might as well not be there. When you get to my age – I'm eighty-five, you know – talking is about all you have. And the Samaritans, they're all very well if you want to jump off a cliff, but you can't invite them round for a cup of tea and some shortbread.'

No – and they won't fix your windows either.

'It's no problem,' said Walter. 'Call any time.'

He wrote down his number, and she thanked him profusely. She waved from the door. Walter waved back as he drove away. It was nice seeing her smile. He wondered if she'd be smiling so much when she phoned the number and discovered it was for a kebab shop.

32
The Impending Death of Redmond O'Boyle

Maria, the incredibly attractive nurse who was also working for the FARC guerrillas, crouched by Redmond O'Boyle's bed in the hospital wing of La Picota prison and whispered, 'Tonight you die.'

Redmond, face down on the bed because of his stabbed buttock, looked shocked. 'Oh,' was all he could manage.

Maria's eyes flicked towards Dr Speranza, chatting animatedly to another prisoner who had been hovering between flu and cholera for several weeks, at the far end of the ward, then back to Redmond. Her face was grave, but her eyes were smiling. He liked that. It warmed his cockles the way his wife Maeve's eyes never had. Redmond was falling in love, which made it all the more depressing that Maria was planning to murder him.

'It is essential,' said Maria.

'Okay,' said Redmond.

'I will administer the drugs at ten o'clock.'

'All right.'

'You will fall asleep. There will be no pain.'

'Okay.'

'Dr Speranza will be off duty. Dr Mendoza will issue the death certificate. He has been bribed, and also his qualifications are fake. You will be removed from the prison. Then you will be revived.'

'Oh right,' Redmond whispered. 'You're not actually killing me then.'

This time she really did smile. 'Of course not.'

'I thought maybe it would be easier – just to knock me off.'

'Yes, it would. But you are FARC. You will be taken to a safe place.'

'Are you coming with me – to the safe place?'

'Yes. I cannot return here. Also, I must supervise your medication. Reviving you will not be as easy as putting you to sleep.'

'You've done this kind of thing before?'

'Yes, of course.'

'Successfully?'

'That depends on your definition of success.' He thought that her English was getting better and better. If Dr Speranza had learned his from pirate copies of *ER*, he guessed that Maria might have learned hers from Alistair Cooke's *Letter from America* on the BBC World Service. Clear and crisp and precise. 'If we get you out, the cause of FARC will be advanced. It will show our ability to infiltrate Government installations at the highest level. If you can walk and talk, that will also be good.'

'Is there a possibility that I won't be able to walk and talk?'

'If you had to choose, which one would you prefer?'

'Are you serious?'

'No, of course not. You will not have the choice. These drugs are inexact, but it is better to take the risk than rot in here, no?'

Redmond nodded, although he wasn't entirely convinced. Earlier in the day he had received another visit from Siobhan, Sinn Fein's representative in Latin America. Her sunburn had given way to a vague kind of tan. She was much happier with her hotel. She'd told him about the football results from back home, the weather, the price of petrol, her auntie's heart condition, how much extra tax had been put on cigarettes in the budget. Eventually Redmond was forced to ask, 'But what about me?'

'What about you?'

'Are they any closer to bringing me home?'

'Home?'

'The campaign – they're working hard? They're lobbying heads of state and staging fundraising concerts?'

'Well – no, frankly.'

'But *why*? I'm here because of you.'

'*Me*?'

'Not you personally – the cause.'

'What cause?'

'Irish liberation.'

'You what?'

'Ireland United. Free. The British jackboot et cetera . . .'

Siobhan laughed. 'Well, wouldn't that be better achieved in Ireland?'

Redmond gritted his teeth. 'Yes, I know that. But you have to keep your hand in, don't you? What if the call to arms suddenly went out again and no one had any idea how to handle explosives? Then you'd feel pretty bloody silly if your leading expert was rotting away in this dump, wouldn't you?'

'Well, now, Redmond, as you know, we don't have anything to do with that kind of thing any more. We're a political party now.'

Redmond shook his head. 'It's okay – I'm virtually certain there's no bugs in here. You can lay off on the psychobabble.'

'I'm serious, Redmond. We're bigger than the SDLP and we're giving the Unionists a run for their money. We really are a proper political party now.'

'Get away.'

'Really.'

'I've only been gone a few months, what's changed?'

'Well, you get older, you want to settle down.'

'Seriously? What about Gerry – and Martin? They're still on the Army Council.'

'Well, obviously. But just until their pensions kick in. Once the bank thing settles down and they have their lump sum, they'll retire.'

'Okay, well, fair enough, they've put their time in. But still . . . I mean, I'm here and they're there – they must be able to do something.'

Siobhan raised her hands in a helpless gesture. 'That's the problem, Redmond. You see, now that we've embraced democracy and the judicial process, it's important that we be seen to support Colombian democracy and judicial process.'

'But there is no Colombian democracy or judicial process!'

'That's not our fault.'

'Then how can you support it!'

'We support the *idea* of Colombian democracy and judicial process – much as we support the *idea* of democracy and judicial process back home. By supporting the *idea*, we can hold our heads up in any company. But we still need funds, so we sanction a certain number of bank raids, extortion, kidnappings, blackmail, drug dealing and protection rackets, but on the strict understanding that they are to raise funds to help promote the idea of democracy and judicial process.'

'So where does that leave me?'

'Well, you can hardly claim that bomb-making classes promote democracy, can you?!'

'If they bring down the Colombian government and it's replaced by something truly democratic, then yes I can!'

Siobhan shook her head. 'Oh Redmond, don't be so naïve. This is South America. Terrorism cannot lead to democracy here, they're not civilised enough. You can't have a bunch of murdering psychos running a country. It just won't work! That's why we cannot be seen to be supporting you.'

'But last time you promised you'd get me out.'

'Well, see, there you are. It shows you how much we've changed.

We're politicians now, we make promises like that all the time. It's in our nature.'

'But you won't do anything to get me out.'

'Our hands our tied. But on the bright side, I brought you some Tayto Cheese and Onion crisps from home. Had them flown out special.' She reached into her handbag and produced three yellow bags of crisps. 'There would have been more, but I couldn't resist!'

Redmond took the bags wordlessly.

'Go on,' said Siobhan, 'open one now. Diet starts on Monday!'

She'd laughed long and hard, and if Redmond hadn't had a very sore arse he would have got up and slapped her.

'You are joking, aren't you?' Redmond asked.

Her smile faded. 'Joking.'

'Very funny, Siobhan, but it's gone on a bit long. I'm knackered; I'm in pain. Please be serious for a moment. How are you going to get me out, and how long do you think it will take?'

She cleared her throat. 'Redmond – we're not. It's just too risky.'

'You're washing your hands of me?'

'Until the climate is right.'

'The climate is *f***ing* killing me.'

Siobhan sighed. 'And some people are banking on that. But not me, I assure you. I like it here, Redmond.'

'I'm sure you f**king do.'

Redmond boiled at the memory of it. He turned his head slightly so that he could see Maria again. She was now standing at the other end of the ward beside Dr Speranza as he continued his rounds.

Redmond's mind was truly made up. He had been abandoned by Ireland. Now he must place all of his faith in the ability of this beautiful young nurse to kill him, and then bring him back from the dead.

33
Burger Or Steak?

That night, Walter and Margaret got on like a house on fire. She said this to Maeve, who arrived after visiting time was over. As she was more or less fully recovered, they were a bit more lax with her visiting hours.

'You mean like when a house gets burned down and people get horribly maimed and the insurance company won't pay up and you end up on the streets? And the only way to make ends meet is to sell your body and this pimp with a big Afro beats you up every night but actually deep down really loves you?'

'No,' said Margaret.

Maeve looked a little disappointed. 'Oh,' she said. 'It's a good thing, then.'

'Yes, of course it is.'

'What's he look like then? Is he a bit of a ride?'

Margaret spluttered into her tea. 'Maeve, please.'

'Well – is he?'

Margaret, a little flushed, shrugged and said: 'Beauty is in the eye of the beholder.'

'What's that supposed to mean?'

'Well, it means some people prefer Tom Hanks to Tom Cruise. Some people prefer the Isle of Man to the Caribbean. Some people prefer hamburger to steak.'

Maeve nodded vaguely. 'So is he a bit of a ride?'

'Maeve, for godsake. I like him.'

'Okay. All right. I suppose there's all different sorts.'

'Yes, there are.'

'There's those hamburgers that are a hundred per cent beef but have no flavour, and then there's those you buy out of the chip van that probably don't have any meat in them at all but taste lush.

And then there's those Birds Eye ones which taste all oniony then you grill them and they disappear to nothing.'

Margaret sighed.

'Then there's sirloin steak and rump steak and T-bone and—'

'Maeve.'

'Whatever. But youse are getting on?'

'Yes, we are.'

'You and this lying weirdo pervert.'

'He's not.'

'He lied. And he came to see you with his todger hanging out.'

'He did not! His zip was down! It was an accident!'

'That's what they all say.'

'Maeve. For goodness sake.'

'Whatever. Mr Kawolski was asking for you. He came to see you, you know, when you were dead to the world.'

'Did he?'

'Oh yeah. He met your Walter as well.'

'Did he now? What did he think?'

'Thought he was a bit odd.'

Margaret sighed again. 'He's really nice. Honestly. We just got off on the wrong foot.'

'Mmm,' said Maeve.

'He may not be perfect, but then he's not bunged up in a Colombian prison either.'

Maeve's mouth dropped open a fraction.

'See?' said Margaret, examining her nails. 'You've got to be able to take it as well as dish it out.'

Maeve had indeed sold her story to the newspapers. She had initially been quite attracted to the idea of opening her *News of the World* on Sunday and seeing herself spread across the centre pages in a skimpy bikini and all her make-up done and her stomach flattened by computer technology, proclaiming that five-times-a-night Redmond had left her for some dusky Latin babe, but the attraction soon wore off when the best offer anyone would come up with was a £25 book token for Easons. The fact was that the initial flurry of interest had quickly receded. Redmond was like one of those Japanese soldiers who went on fighting years after the war was over. He had curiosity value, but no one was going to get into a lather over whether he lived or died or received a fair trial. He was yesterday's news before today had even finished.

Now, sitting in this private room in this plush hospital, Maeve had to admit to herself that she felt quite jealous of Margaret. Not the vomiting-carrot-cake-and-coma side of her colleague, but her new and recent flirtation with romance and ambition. Even if this Walter sounded a bit suspicious, at least it had added some excitement to Margaret's life. Maeve had excitement, but it was the wrong kind. And as for this dress designing . . . Margaret sure was a bit of a dark horse. But talented, it seemed.

Redmond was in prison, and the chances were he wasn't coming home any time soon. The sad thing was that she was hardly depressed about it at all. While he'd been missing, she had of course been distraught. It was the not knowing. Now that she did know, she was actually quite calm about it all. He had lied to her. She had been foolish to believe him. Her position now was: *You've made your bed, and now you can lie in it.* (He had literally made Maeve's bed as well. *Their* bed. He was handy with his hands, Redmond. He liked to build things. Shelves. Sheds. Dolls houses. And, as it turned out, bombs. But never a bird table, curiously enough.) She'd grown quite used to living by herself. When he was here they argued all the time. When he was away on his bird-watching trips he sent quite affectionate letters home. While he was gone she had enjoyed three affairs.

Well, affair was probably a bit strong.

Three one-night stands.

And 'enjoyed' was slightly wide of the mark as well. None of them had been particularly satisfactory in the bed department – but they'd been *different*. One had been a colleague from work. Another, a taxi driver taking her home after a works outing. And the third was Mr Kawolski, her boss. He was married with five children, and she had told him it wasn't going to happen again, but he still gave her one leg of his KitKat every day. 'Where there's chocolate there's hope,' he would say with a twinkle in his eye.

'Do you find chocolate a bit of a turn-on?' Maeve asked Margaret now.

Margaret could feel her eyes going together; she still wasn't back to full strength, and talking to Walter had used up a lot of nervous energy, but she was too polite to let it show. 'Mmm . . . what? Chocolate?'

'You know, if a man feeds you chocolate, does it help get you in the mood? Or do you start mentally calculating calories and fat content?'

'Depends on the man. Or the chocolate, for that matter.'

'So, say for the sake of argument if Richard Gere came up to you, you know, in his white uniform, would it make any difference whether he offered you a Terry's Chocolate Orange or the leg of a KitKat?'

'If it was Richard Gere, I'd be prepared to forget about the chocolate entirely.'

'If it was someone you quite liked, but weren't sure about, would the quality of the chocolate have any bearing on the outcome?'

Margaret had to think about that. 'Well,' she said eventually, 'if he was offering me a Revel he found in his pocket, that wouldn't be much of a turn-on. Or a Cadbury's Creme Egg which was slightly dented, then I'd probably turn him down. But if he bought me a huge Easter Egg, he'd be in with a better chance.'

'So size matters.'

'Yeah. I suppose. And shape. You wouldn't get much snogging done if you'd just broken your jaw on a giant Toblerone.' Margaret smiled sympathetically at her friend. 'It's Redmond, isn't it?'

'What's Redmond?'

'This talk about chocolate.'

Maeve snorted. 'It's nothing to do with him. Although that said, he used to save the two end bits of a Fry's Chocolate Cream and tease me with them. Never once let me have them. He was very cruel that way. But I wasn't even thinking about him.'

'Deep down, I think you were.'

'Deep down, I think I wasn't.'

'Don't you see the connection?'

'*What* connection?'

'Between Redmond and chocolate. Colombia – that's where chocolate comes from. Your mind made the connection, even if you didn't.'

'What a lot of crap,' said Maeve.

'I'm serious.'

'Anyway – chocolate comes from Switzerland.'

'South America – the cocoa bean.'

'Yeah, the bean. But then they send it to Switzerland. Their chocolate scientists pound up the beans – I mean, the scientists aren't made of chocolate – but they add milk and stuff and then they design the packaging and put it all together into something attractive people want to buy. Not attractive people, ordinary people. But attractive people as well. Anyway – it's the whole kit and caboodle. Not just a pile of beans. So you have to agree, chocolate comes from Switzerland more than it comes from Colombia.'

Margaret thought about that for a little while, then nodded. 'You're right. It's not just about the bean. It's what you do with it. And the packaging. Don't underestimate the packaging.'

'It's half the battle. I like a good wrapper.'

'Like Eminem,' said Margaret.

I Predict A Riot

'He's from Detroit,' said Maeve.

'Maybe you need a new car,' said Margaret.

'Maybe I need a new life,' said Maeve.

'Maybe you do,' agreed Margaret. 'Maybe we both do.'

34

You Can Run But You Can't Hide

Mark was standing by the office window, staring out, when Walter finally returned to work at the Department of Education in Bangor. Walter sat behind his desk and began to look through the papers in his in-tray. He had expected the work to be piled up, but there were only half a dozen files. Mark had evidently done what he'd said he'd do: simply transferred everything to his out-tray. Walter cleared his throat. Mark didn't seem to hear, so he did it again, and finally his colleague turned. He looked at Walter for several moments, as if he was a complete stranger, then slowly a smile spread across his face.

'You're back,' said Mark.

'Yes, I am.'

'And how is *Girlfriend in a Coma*?'

'She's fine and dandy.'

'And are you very much in love?'

'Well, I wouldn't go that far.'

'But everything is going well?'

'Yes, it is.'

Mark came and sat on the edge of Walter's desk. He did not appear to be his usual ebullient self. They did not often speak on a very personal level, and on the few occasions when they did, it was always in a bantering, jokey way.

'So,' said Walter, 'how's it been going?'

'Oh, fine. Yeah.'

'I haven't been near a doctor, but I can still self-certify, can't I?'

'Yeah, but only for the first six months.'

'And how's the political career?'

'Well, it's early days yet.'

'They say a day is a long time in politics.'

'Not with local councils it's not.'

They lapsed into silence. Walter lifted some papers from his in-tray.

He looked at the first page, without really comprehending any of it, then transferred it to his out-tray. When he glanced up at Mark, his colleague was staring down the corridor towards Office 12.

'What do you make of that guy?' Mark asked.

'Steven?' Mark nodded; Walter shrugged. 'Dunno. What do *you* make of him?'

'He offered me a job.'

Walter immediately felt quite proprietorial. 'As Number Three?'

'Number Four. He offered you Number Three?'

'Only temporarily.'

'Number Four's on paternity leave.'

Walter nodded. 'Did he tell you what they do in there? With the numbers?'

Mark nodded. 'It's a bit odd, isn't it?'

'You're telling me.'

'But at the same time, it explains a lot.'

'You can say that again. What did you tell him?'

'That I'd think about it.'

'Yeah. Same here.'

They both stared at Office 12.

'You tempted?' Walter asked.

This time Mark shrugged. 'I don't know. He strikes me as someone who knows how to pull a few strings. I was thinking of the politics. Be nice to leapfrog a few levels. I sympathise entirely with the plight of the working man, but I don't want to tramp round some dodgy housing estate in the middle of the night like I'm selling pegs.'

'Maybe he could leapfrog you straight into the Cabinet.'

Mark gave him a sarcastic smile. 'What about you? He sorted out your lovelife, didn't he? He's like your pimp.'

Walter snorted. 'Yeah, right. I don't think so. But – it's kind of tempting, isn't it? Do you think he's like MI5 or something?'

Mark shook his head vaguely. 'He's something all right.'

They both jumped as Walter's phone rang. They looked at each other, then back towards Office 12.

'Do you think . . . ?' Walter hissed.

'I don't know,' Mark whispered back. 'Answer it.'

Walter just stared at it.

'Go on!'

But he couldn't bring himself to lift the receiver. Mark sighed, then lifted it himself.

'Yo,' he said. He listened for a moment. 'Yes, he's here. Hold on a mo.' He held the receiver against his chest. Walter was just raising his hands to say he didn't want it when Mark said, 'Someone called Bertha?'

'Bertha?'
Mark nodded and handed him the phone.

Walter caught the train home as usual after work, took a quick shower, then drove out to Bertha's house. If he was lucky he could fix her shower in twenty minutes then go on to the hospital to see Margaret. In fact, it would be better if he was late. He was desperate to see her, but not quite so keen to bump into her husband. He wasn't afraid of Billy, exactly, but it was early days with Margaret, and until he was sure where they were going there was no point in getting involved in a slanging match, as they surely would.

Walter parked and nipped up the steps to Bertha's front door. He rang the bell, and it opened almost immediately. She was a slow mover, so it appeared she'd been waiting for him in the hall.

'Oh Walter,' said Bertha, smiling extravagantly, 'it's so good of you.'

'No problem,' said Walter. He was thinking about that old Country and Western song where a child rhymes off all the things it – she or he, he couldn't remember – has done for its mother and how much it's owed, and the mother comes back with all the things *she's* done, but for her there's 'no charge'. Walter had nearly knocked Bertha down, but far from there being 'no charge', he suspected he would be paying off the debt for the rest of his natural life.

Or hers.

'Just up here . . . but can I get you a wee cup of tea first?'

'No, thanks, I'm in a bit of a rush. I'll go on up.'

Walter took the stairs two at a time. He already knew his way around the house. He went straight to her bathroom and began to examine the seal around the shower which was apparently leaking and causing water to drip down the living-room wall directly below. In the background Walter could hear Bertha's electric lift humming as it slowly brought her upstairs. She didn't need it. The social services had insisted because they had money left in their budget which they'd lose if they didn't spend it before the end of the financial year. She could run up the stairs quicker. But she could be lazy like the rest of us.

Walter saw that the seal had indeed come loose, but all he had to do was ease it back into place. By the time Bertha stepped into the bathroom, he was already finished.

'All done,' he said, standing up.

'Already?'

'Yeah – should be fine now.'

'Oh dear. I feel so silly, bringing you round just for that.'

'Nah, don't worry. You weren't to know.'

'Well – you'll take that cup of tea now.'

He had no choice really. And he wasn't in *that* much of a rush. He helped her back onto her lift, then patiently moved one step at a time beside her as she descended. As he did, she smiled patiently across at him. 'I must admit, I felt a bit like Sherlock Holmes,' she said, 'tracking you down like that.'

'Right enough. Or *Columbo*, remember him?' Bertha nodded. He had already apologised to her half a dozen times on the phone, but he did it again. He did feel kind of bad, but probably only because he'd been caught out. 'I'm just sorry about the mix-up with the number. Don't know what I was thinking.'

'It was quite a surprise,' said Bertha. '*Abrakebabra* – is that what they said? I've never had a kebab. Too old now, I expect. But they were very helpful. I only knew your Christian name, but as soon as I mentioned it, they knew exactly who I was talking about. You must go there all the time. The food must be delicious.'

'Not that often,' said Walter.

Walter found it an incredibly sad statement on his life so far, to be recognised so easily by the staff of a fast-food joint. If it had been somewhere else, say – the library, then that would have been different. 'Oh yes, Walter. He's in here all the time, such a bright fella, six books a week he gets through.' Or if he'd left her the number of the Ulster Orchestra and the chief conductor had said, 'Walter! Ja! He iz such an expert in German music of ze seventeenth century!' Or even Donald Trump's number. 'Walter? He's the only other property tycoon I have any respect for!' But no. A kebab shop.

Bertha climbed off the chairlift, with a little assistance from Walter, then slowly led him down the hall towards the kitchen. It was an old house, and appeared to be solidly built. Walter thought that if there was a sudden earthquake, they wouldn't be killed by the building coming down around them, but by the thousands of commemorative plates and dodgy antiques that filled the shelves.

As if she could tell what he was thinking, Bertha paused in the kitchen doorway and looked back up the stairs. She tutted. 'It's such a pity,' she said. 'Since Frank passed on I've devoted my life to this little house of mine. And now I've no one to leave it all to.' She shook her head, then managed a little smile. 'Listen to me wittering on, and you dying for a cuppa.'

Walter placed his arm gently around her shoulders and gave her a little squeeze. 'You sit yourself down,' he said. 'Let me get it.'

35
Please Release Me, Let Me Go

'I don't want you to come to the hospital tonight,' said Margaret.

Walter, sitting in his office, felt his stomach lurch. His shirt stuck to his back almost instantaneously. The receiver felt slippery in his hand. What had he done?! What had he said?! What had she found out?! His face burned with assumed guilt.

'But . . . but . . . but . . .'

'They're sending me home!'

Relief surged through him. *Thank God!* He could hear the pure joy in her voice. He pictured her lovely, smiling face. 'That's fantastic. Are you sure you're okay? You were quite weak.'

'Walter, just because you beat me at arm-wrestling, doesn't mean I'm still ill. You're a lot more muscular than I am.'

Walter blushed. Was that a compliment? *No, no, she doesn't mean it like that.*

'Well, yes, I take your point. You, ah, gave it your best shot, but I think you'll find that there aren't many women I can't beat at arm-wrestling.'

Margaret giggled. Across the office, Mark raised a concerned eyebrow. Walter winked at him, then swivelled his chair in the opposite direction.

'Do you want me to pick you up?' he offered. 'You can't always depend on the taxis up there and I could be with you in half an hour.'

'No, Walter. I'm fine. Billy's taking me home.'

'Oh. Right.'

She could hear the disappointment in his voice. Maeve had said to her, treat 'em mean, keep 'em keen. She didn't really agree with that. In her experience it was more like treat 'em mean, lose 'em. But she really didn't want Walter taking her home, because then she would feel obliged to invite him in, and the house was in a complete mess. At least, it had been in a complete mess when she'd left for her appointment at Emma Cochrane's boutique. So unless a burglar had broken in and tidied up, it most certainly still was. Billy, on the other hand, could give her a lift home no problem, and although he might make hopeful eyes at her about coming in for coffee or sex, she would feel no qualms at all about turning him away. That's what ex-husbands were for. Treat 'em mean and . . . well, just treat 'em mean.

'But you could call by later on, if you liked.'

'Really?'

'If you felt like it.'

'Well, obviously I'd need to check my diary. Let me see . . . ah yes, I have a window between seven-fifteen and . . . Well, actually it seems to be clear for the next fifteen years.'

'You can't stay for the next fifteen years.' She said it quite abruptly. Her voice was a little cooler.

'I was only joking.'

Margaret giggled exquisitely. 'So was I! See you later!' She laughed again, then the line went dead.

Walter replaced the phone and turned his chair around to face Mark again.

'Chuck E's in love,' sang Mark.

Billy arrived at visiting time as usual, and was a little surprised to find her packed up and waiting expectantly on her bed.

'I thought you could give me a lift home,' she said.

'Did you.'

'It's on your way back to work.'

Billy shrugged. 'You're better then.'

'So they tell me.'

'And where's Lover Boy?'

'Which one?'

He glared at her. But then he took hold of her bag and turned for the door. She followed him out and down the corridor to the reception desk where she'd been told to sign out. Billy stood by the doors while the receptionist got her to sign her medical release forms and then called up her file on the computer.

'All right then,' said the receptionist, 'a clean bill of health. And talking of bills, if I could just have your credit card, we'll have you on the road in a jiffy.'

'My credit card?'

'We accept Visa, American Express, Mastercard. But not Kidney Donor Cards.' She smiled up at Margaret.

Margaret frowned. 'It's being paid for by someone else. Emma Cochrane?' She nodded down at the screen.

The receptionist scrolled further down her file. 'Oh – right. I see. Ahm. Well. I see what's happened. This Miss Cochrane, she has our Family and Friends emergency cover, but unfortunately that only extends to emergency treatment and one night's stay in a private room. After that, it automatically reverts to the patient. Sorry. There's also the supplemental charges – lab tests and X-rays, consultant's report, second opinion, plus food and cleaning and laundry.'

Margaret gave a little cough. She glanced around at Billy, tapping his foot impatiently, and lowered her voice a little. 'How much are we talking about here?'

'£3223.56.'

'Holy shit!'

'Plus an optional fifteen per cent service charge.'

'Service charge? It's not a bloody restaurant!'

'Well, actually, it is. We have the finest chefs and—'

'Okay, okay, all right.' Margaret rubbed at her brow. She had a Visa card in her purse, but she most certainly couldn't afford three grand. She could hardly afford the service charge. If she handed over her card it would either be rejected or Mr Visa would send the hard men round in the morning to confiscate her house. 'I . . . I . . . just don't understand how this could happen. I mean, shouldn't someone have told me that I was being charged for all this?'

'We tried, but you were in a coma.'

Margaret snorted. 'So if I'd stayed in a coma for another year, you'd have charged me the full whack?'

'Oh no.' The receptionist shook her head vigorously. 'Anything over three weeks and we offer a discount. It can be as much as twenty-five per cent.'

Margaret just stared at her. The receptionist looked back to her screen. 'As the booking was made by Miss Cochrane, I could try reverting the charges to her account. I'd probably have to phone her though, just to confirm?' She smiled hopefully.

Margaret shook her head. She wasn't going to put Emma Cochrane in that position. Emma had already done so much for her, she couldn't possibly sting her for another three grand. She'd got her into this wonderful place when she could just as easily have left her in a skip outside some other of Belfast's collapsing hospitals. She'd saved her life. Perhaps she'd also had one eye on their future business relationship, but it was still a more than generous gesture. At the end of the day, Emma's boutique was just that – a boutique. It wasn't some massive chainstore that could just write her a big cheque and think nothing of it. Three thousand pounds probably represented a fair whack of her monthly profit. She had done her bit for Margaret, and now Margaret would have to sort this out herself.

'Is there a problem?' It was Billy, at her shoulder.

'No, nothing. I just . . .' Margaret trailed off. She was on the verge of tears. Everything had been going so well.

'It's just a matter of settling the bill,' said the receptionist.

'How much?' Billy asked.

The receptionist turned her screen around so he could read it.

'Christ,' said Billy. 'You could bury someone for that.' He gave Margaret a hard look, then reached for his wallet.

'Billy – don't, please.'

'It's no problem.' He handed over his credit card.

'Thank you,' Margaret said weakly.

'You can thank me later,' said Billy.

He didn't even look at her. But she knew exactly what he meant.

36
The House of Love

This is my defining moment. I have at last met a woman who can change my life. And now fate, fatigued by repeatedly slapping me in the face, has been sent to motivational classes. It is now a power for good. How else to explain Bertha being thrown into my life like this?

Walter was driving over to Margaret's, Milk Tray and flowers on the passenger seat. In some ways it was a good thing that he wasn't actually thinking about her – because then he'd get nervous and panic about what he was going to say or how he was going to put his foot in it. By concentrating on Bertha he could just turn up at Margaret's and be himself, not some babbling fool.

Bertha. Eighty-five years old. Nobody to leave her house to. The moment she'd said it, it was as if a huge great light bulb was switched on in his head. Not even a light bulb – a nuclear-powered chandelier. *Nobody to leave it to.*

He had been fantasising for years about getting into the property game, and now an opportunity had presented itself out of nowhere. *She has no one.*

If I keep calling round and fixing things, she'll grow to depend on me. She'll change her will. She'll do it of her own accord, No pressure. I'll drop a few tiny little hints. Subtle.

And then she'll go to her solicitor's. I'll give her a lift.

The solicitor will say, 'Are you sure, Bertha?'

She'll say. 'It's my house! It's my money! Walter means everything to me!'

Walter forced himself to concentrate on his driving. He tried to not let himself get carried away. That had been a major failing in the past. Getting over-excited about things, getting obsessive, then spoiling them.

First of all, she said she had no one to leave it to, but that didn't mean there weren't people who wouldn't make a claim on it. There were bound to be grandchildren or nieces or nephews. They might not have spoken to her for years, but they would still come out of the woodwork once she popped her clogs. Perhaps she didn't even have a will. How to find out?

Walter tried to picture the scene. He's just finished fixing something else, he's sitting having tea with Bertha. 'So, Bertha, you're eighty-five, you're bound to die soon, have you made a will yet? And could you put me in it? Just the house. You can keep the commemorative plates.'

Walter smiled. *I don't think so.*

He would probably have to introduce the subject of the will himself. He would drop it nonchalantly into the conversation. 'Sorry I was late, had to call in to see my solicitor. He's been on my back about making a will. I said to him, "What's the hurry?" and he said, "Well, Walter, you never know." I suppose he has a point.' Then he would look across at Bertha and say, 'I presume you're sorted?' And she'd say, 'Actually, yes I am, but I think I'm going to change it. I'm going to leave this beautiful, expensive house to charity, but that vase has your name on it, Walter.'

Yeah, with my luck.

No!

My luck has changed.

And because at heart I am a good person, God, after years of taking the p**s, has decided that I am worthy of favour.

I didn't give her a lift home and fix her shower because I knew about her big house, I helped her out because that's the kind of guy I am. If she chooses to reward me, then that is her affair.

Walter nodded self-righteously. He drove a little further, he changed the radio station, he tapped along in time to Abba. And then the dark side began to creep in again. What if he did manage to insert himself into Bertha's will? Her obscure relatives would certainly contest it. And they'd go to the press. He'd be portrayed as the scheming handyman who forced a senile old woman to change her will.

What would Margaret think of that?

And what if Bertha changed her will, and then didn't oblige him by dying quickly? What if she lived to be 125? That wouldn't be fair, would it? After all, she'd had a good innings.

No! Don't even think it! But Walter couldn't get the thought out of his head. What if she changed her will and then *accidentally* fell down the stairs? Or what if she was bending to get chips out of the chest freezer and she *inadvertently* lost her balance and fell in, and somehow the lid came down on top of her? Or what if that nice handyman insisted she hadn't taken her medicine that morning and somehow persuaded her to take 200 times her normal dose?

Walter sighed as he stopped at a traffic-lights. Who was he kidding? He wasn't a murderer, and he wasn't a property developer, and you needed the killer instinct for both. It was a nice house. It was a *lovely* house. But Bertha wasn't just going to give him it, no matter how many curtain rails he straightened out.

As he waited for the lights to change, he glanced to his left. There was a tiny terraced house, close to the road, with a For Sale sign screwed to the side of it. Beneath it there hung a small appendage: *Under Offer*. He wondered how much it was worth. And then how much had been actually offered.

What if he made Bertha an offer for her house? It was a huge old place, and clearly too big for her to cope with. What if he found out the true value of the house, and then made her a somewhat lower offer? He wouldn't be cheating her. He would be doing exactly what a property developer would do. It was just business. He wouldn't pressure her into selling. He would say, 'If you ever felt like selling, then I'd love to buy it.'

And she would say, 'Well, I really don't know what it's worth.'

Walter would say, 'I've been checking around, and I reckon it's worth such and such.'

Bertha, having lived through wars and rationing and being able to get into the movies in exchange for a jam jar, would say, 'That sounds like an awful lot of money,' and sell it to him there and then. She would add, 'You will look after the old place, won't you?'

'Of course I will,' he'd reassure her, while picturing the bulldozers moving in to flatten it, and the luxury apartments he would build.

There was a blast from behind; the lights had changed. Walter waved an apology in the mirror, and drove on.

Who am I kidding? he thought wearily. It's not going to happen. She's an old woman. Old women spend their lives complaining. She has no intention of selling. She was just moaning for the sake of it.

In fact, she's the smart one. Pretending to nearly get knocked down, then using me to fix every damn thing in her house. She's saving herself a fortune. She probably has half a dozen guys coming round doing things for her, all in the hope of some day getting their hands on her property.

Five minutes later, still alternating between wild ambition and doomed reality, Walter parked outside Margaret's house. Perhaps he should talk to her about it. She seemed to have her head screwed on. Yeah. Maybe she'd like to get involved – they could pool their resources, make a combined offer for the house. They could live there together while they fixed it up. And then they'd fall in love with it themselves and instead of selling it on, it would become their home.

132

Walter sighed. One step at a time.

He checked himself in the mirror. Glasses on, glasses off? He left them on. That reminded him, he had to decide whether to go back for his laser eye-surgery. So much had happened since, with Margaret falling into a coma and then his hanging around the hospital, that he'd quite forgotten about it.

Walter climbed out of the car.

Here I go – the Milk Tray Man.

It was different this time. Before, he'd been chancing his arm. This time he was invited.

She liked him. She fancied him. They were a couple, almost.

Walter rang the bell. He heard footsteps on the stairs. He had a Polo in his mouth. He crunched as much as he could of it, then swallowed the rest. *She might kiss me.*

Walter smiled widely as the lock was turned and the door opened. 'Hope I'm not—'

But it wasn't Margaret. It was Billy. He had no shirt on. There was sweat on his brow.

'Oh,' said Walter.

Billy smiled. 'What do you want, you speccy fat clown?'

Walter shook his head. 'Nothing,' he said.

'Then f**k away off.' Billy closed the door.

Walter stood there, completely frozen, his head pounding. He heard Margaret's voice, calling from inside, upstairs. 'Who is it?'

'No one,' Billy shouted back.

37

Reap What You Sow

Billy came back into the bedroom. She recognised his supercilious
I've got one over on you grin immediately, but couldn't think what it
might be in aid of. He went to pull the quilt back, but she held onto
it.

'Who was it?' she asked.

'Ah, some clown.'

'What did you say?'

'I told him I was upstairs shagging.'

'You did *not*.' He pulled at the quilt again. She held fast.

'Give me some credit. Said I was in the shower.'

'So who was it really?'

'Take a wild guess.' He pulled, she held on. He let go and folded
his arms.

'The Jehovah's Witnesses?'

'Nope.'

'The Osmonds?'

'Nope.'

'Gypsy pegs?'

'Getting colder.'

'It wasn't *actually* a clown? Are Fossett's back in town?'

'Let me into the bloody bed and I'll tell you.'

'Tell me now.'

'No.'

She pulled the quilt firmly down and tucked it beneath her bum
on either side. 'It's time you were going anyway,' she said.

Billy looked surprised. 'Aye, right.'

'Please, Billy.'

'Wise up,' he said.

'We've done what you wanted. So please.'

'You don't want to go again?'

134

She started to laugh, then stopped herself. But not soon enough to prevent him from looking hurt. 'It's not a good idea,' she said quickly. 'You know that.'

'Please yourself,' Billy snapped. He turned to look for his trousers. They were in a crumpled heap on the floor at the bottom of the bed. Margaret looked across at her own clothes, folded onto a chair. Their neatness reminded her of the way a suicide might fold their clothes on the beach before walking into the sea.

Billy giggled suddenly.

'What's so funny?' Margaret wanted to know.

'Nothing.' As he pulled on his shirt, he laughed again, but it wasn't a nice laugh. Kind of mean. She recognised it. 'You should have seen his face.'

Margaret's brow furrowed. 'What?'

Billy just kept smiling. He pulled a shoe on, then put his foot down on top of Margaret's clothes as he bent to tie it.

Behind him Margaret suddenly shrieked. 'Oh my God!'

Billy snorted.

'It was Walter – I completely forgot!'

'Sure you wouldn't have been up for another shag so soon anyway, would you?'

'You b***ard!'

'Whatever.' Billy pulled on his jacket.

'What did you say to him?'

'Didn't have to say anything. He's a man, after a fashion, so he could tell.'

'You complete and utter b***ard!'

Billy shook his head. 'I'm not a b***ard, Margaret. I'm a bloody fool. I've just paid three grand for a crap shag with my ex-wife. I feel pretty bad about it, but I'm sure you feel a hundred times worse. Even at three grand, you must feel pretty cheap.'

With that, he walked out of the room and down the stairs. When he reached the bottom he shouted back up, 'Call me when you want to do it again!'

She heard the door slam. She buried her head in the pillows and cried, and cried, and cried, and cried.

Oh, what a fool I am, she thought. Oh, what a bloody fool.

Walter was in a bar off Great Victoria Street. He'd downed three pints and three shorts and was now sitting with a pint of Guinness. He was shell-shocked. He was still trying to compute what had happened, desperately trying to concoct an alternative explanation for Billy's half-naked presence at Margaret's house:

He was having dinner with his ex-wife, and spilled gravy on his shirt. It was being cleaned when Walter called.

Billy's shower is broken, so Margaret allows him to call round and use hers.

Billy had stripped off in an attempt to seduce his ex-wife, but she had rejected him.

Margaret was giving him a massage.

She had a sudden urge to count the freckles on Billy's back.

She hurled *The Da Vinci Code* across the room, yelling, 'I'd rather have sex with my ex-husband than read any more of this crap!' and he was round like a shot.

Or, Margaret was making love with her husband because she felt like it. It was her perfect right to do so. She hardly knew Walter. Okay, so it was a bit sordid, having sex with anyone immediately before your 'date' was due to arrive, but it wasn't illegal.

Walter sighed. He couldn't get Billy's smug grin out of his head. He ordered another drink.

This was his life. He built himself up. He built other people up. And always, always, there was disappointment. It was like football. It was ultimately disappointing, because in the end, your team always got beaten. Of course, some teams were better than others. (And Chelsea won nearly all the time, which probably made the occasional loss easier to bear.) But if Walter had to be a football team, it would be one that had just been relegated from the Irish League, and its top player had had his legs broken by a gang with baseball bats.

Walter hated himself, and his life.

Then his mobile phone rang. He didn't recognise the number – although, that said, being three sheets to the wind, he could barely make it out.

'Yes?' he said.

'Walter? It's Margaret.'

Silence.

'Walter – I'm so, *so* sorry.'

Silence.

'Please, Walter – I can explain. I . . . he . . . shouldn't have . . . He wasn't meant to . . . I mean, I didn't mean to . . . Oh Christ, will you say something?'

Silence.

'Walter, please. I'm really sorry and I can explain. I was stuck, I didn't have enough money and . . . No, look, it just doesn't come out right. I mean, it can never come out right because I've done a terrible thing – but if I could just talk to you face to face . . . Oh God, Walter, I'm sorry, please talk to me.'

I Predict A Riot

Walter cut the line.

He stared at his phone. Then he stood and hurled it at the bar. The barman ducked down just in time and it smashed into one of the optics behind him. The barman raised himself slowly, then threw himself to the ground again as Walter's empty pint glass crashed into the optics as well. Another empty glass followed, then another; then he lifted a full pint from the next table and threw it. Walter picked up a table. It sailed through the air and shattered the huge mirror. Half a dozen chairs followed. Everything he could find, he launched at the bar. All around him, other drinkers dived for safety as Walter screamed in agony and torment, the heartbreaking screech of a damaged soul.

Then the bouncers came in and punched his lights out.

38
Fly Away Home

They opened the cell door at six the next morning. The Legal Aid solicitor had been and gone, having witnessed Walter make his tearful statement of admission, during which he had apologised profusely and wailed about the treachery of women and the inevitability of losing his job if this got out. He had destroyed property worth thousands of pounds and was resigned to a life sentence without the possibility of parole, but the cops kind of peed on his dizzying spiral of paranoia by merely cautioning him and telling him that he'd been a *very* naughty boy.

'What about all the damage?!' Walter protested.

'It's only some glass, a table and some spilled drinks. Relax. It's not the end of the world.'

But it was the end of the world. *His* world. He actually *wanted* to be punished, he felt so miserable. He deserved it for being such a meaningless, hopeless, spineless specimen. He was a pathetic human being. Everyone thought so. Especially Margaret, who had all but laughed in his face. *Screwed* in his face. But the bar-owners weren't interested in pursuing him because their licence was up for review soon and they didn't want anything to leak out which might place their upmarket drinking establishment in a poor light, like their bouncers pounding on a poor heartbroken man's face. If a passing police patrol hadn't intervened, Walter would have looked even more horrendous than he currently did. As it was, his nose was crushed and his eyes were swollen, and he'd a long scrab wound along his cheek. One of the bouncers was a woman. She was built like a brick sh*t-house, but still fought like a girl.

'So you're free to go.'

'Free to go?'

'Yes, your lift is here.'

'I didn't—'

'Yes, you did.'

Walter had been very drunk when they brought him in, and had only the vaguest of memories as to who he had given as his next-of-kin. Mark, he supposed. Great. That was all he needed now. He liked Mark a lot, but didn't want sarcastic comments with his life in such a dire state.

Walter signed some papers, and was given his meagre belongings back. They had even retrieved his mobile phone. Then he limped through the front doors of the Donegal Pass police station and saw Bertha standing there, smiling at him.

'Oh God,' he groaned.

'Walter,' said Bertha.

'I'm sorry – I was drunk. I didn't even know I called you. You really don't have . . . I mean, I can get a taxi.'

'Nonsense. Is there anyone at home to make you a cup of tea?'

Walter shook his head.

They drove towards Bertha's house. It was early yet and there was little traffic. Walter sat slumped in the passenger seat, his head down, morosely staring at the floor.

'You must be exhausted,' said Bertha.

'I'm not exhausted,' replied Walter. 'I'm mortified.'

'I'll make you a nice cup of tea, and you can tell me all about it.'

'What sad state is my friggin' life in that you're the only person I can think to call to get me out of jail?'

Bertha smiled. 'Well – what sad state is *my* friggin' life in that I'm so happy to do it?'

Walter looked up at her and smiled at last. 'Seriously?'

'Seriously.'

He shook his head. 'What are we like,' he said.

They sat at the kitchen table, which itself sat slightly unevenly on the linoleum floor. Walter said he would fix it later. His nose throbbed and he had difficulty breathing through it because it was clogged with dried blood. His head was sore. And he was exhausted, but he couldn't face sleeping because he knew he would have nightmares.

'You think you've got problems?' said Bertha. 'I'm eighty-five years old. I'm in perfect health, but it's like someone's set the oven. It's only a matter of time.'

'Not if I'd set it. It would never go off.'

'So a long time ago I decided to live every day as if it was my last.'

'You mean lie in bed and moan a lot.'

'No, I mean, enjoy myself.'

'You mean buying plates and vases and shi— stuff like that.'

'Yes. And paragliding.'

'Paragliding?'

'It's fantastic. Have you ever tried it?'

'No, nor will I. Far as I'm concerned, there's but a short step from paragliding to paraplegic. Anyway, where'd you paraglide round here? Didn't think we had the weather for it.'

'Not here. Florida. I spend six months of the year on the Gulf Coast.'

'Oh. Right. Fantastic.'

'Yes, it is.' She smiled at the memory of it. Then, when they'd been silent for a couple of minutes, she reached across and gently put her hand on top of Walter's. 'What's the matter with you, son?'

He looked at her and suddenly felt like crying. 'Nothing. Everything. What can I say? My life's all fu**ed up, and has been for as long as I can remember. This, with her, was just the final straw.'

He had told her briefly about Margaret on the way home. She had merely nodded, without commenting.

'You seem such a nice man.'

'Well, you don't really know me.' He sighed. 'It's just . . . I've always had all these dreams and plans, you know, about meeting the right woman, settling down and having children, and getting out of the bloody Civil Service and getting into property and becoming really rich and successful. Becoming *someone* – but that's all they ever bloody are, dreams. You wake up in the morning and they're gone.'

Bertha nodded slowly to herself. Then she gave his hand a gentle squeeze and said, 'Do you have any idea how many cars I had to throw myself in front of before I found you?'

Walter smiled. 'Yeah, right.'

'I'm serious.'

'No, really.'

'Really, really.'

'You've done this before?'

'I have. Half a dozen times.'

'Seriously?'

'Seriously.'

'But why? Why would you do that?'

Bertha shrugged. 'I don't really know. I suppose it's like when rich people get caught shoplifting. It's not what they're stealing, it's why. I just – I don't know. I like to see how people react.'

'But you could *die*.'

'Well, I suppose that's part of the attraction. It would be a better way to go, wouldn't it, instead of going mad or wasting away? Short, sudden shock. But I haven't been hit yet.'

'God. And how *do* people react?'

'Most of them just scream about me being a stupid old bat. One got out of his car and I thought he was going to help me up, but he stole my handbag and drove off. You're the first one to offer me a lift home. And certainly the first to come in and fix my shower.'

Walter shrugged. He stared at his tea. Bertha stared at him.

After a while she said, 'Can I tell you something?'

Walter nodded without looking up.

'You remind me of my husband.'

'Sorry.'

'Oh no – it's a good thing. In fact, to tell you the truth, I've been finding reasons to call you.'

Now he *did* look up. 'You . . . ?'

'There wasn't anything wrong with the shower till I pulled up the seal.'

'Seriously?' Walter's brow furrowed. 'What about the tumble-dryer?'

'I stuck a spoon into its inner workings.'

'And the back-door lock?'

'I hit it with a mallet.'

Walter took a deep breath. 'Why would you do that?'

'Lonely, I suppose.' She took a sip of her tea. Walter found it quite hard to look at her. 'Walter, I like you, and you do remind me of my husband. But I don't want to scare you. I'm not going to suddenly demand sex or anything. I'm eighty-five. Sex for me ended in 1974.'

'I thought he died in seventy-three.'

'He did. And I went a bit mad in seventy-four.'

'So, what are you saying exactly?'

'I'd like to help you.'

'Help me?'

'Invest in you.'

'I don't follow.'

'Walter, I've a bit of money put away. It'll be eaten up in death duties when I die, and this place'll be fought over by my two thousand nieces and nephews till it's not worth having. And there aren't many commemorative plates left in the world for me to buy; besides, I absolutely draw the line at that damned *Star Trek* series. What I'm saying is that I've a certain amount of money to play with. If you really want to get into the property game, then I'll put some money up. If you'd be interested.'

Walter stared at her, beaming. 'Is the Pope a Catholic?' he asked.

39

Regrets, I've Had A Few

Margaret tossed and turned all night, then gave up her efforts to sleep and lay in the grey stillness of the dawn, her face crushed into her tear-stained pillow. She was an idiot of epic proportions. If there was an Olympic event for idiots, she would be disqualified for being professional. In future dictionaries she would be the very definition of idiot. It would also say, *see: slapper*.

What had she done? What had she been reduced to? Was there any justification for having sex with your ex-husband as a thank you for paying off your hospital bill? No, of course there wasn't. Even if the sex was *fantastic* there could be no justification. The fact that it had been utterly cr*p made it even worse. But what made it so soul-destroying was the fact that the one man with whom she did want to have sex had caught them at it.

So, farewell then, Walter North.

Of *course* he had put the phone down on her. They had not known each other for very long, and she wasn't overly familiar with his personal life, but he struck her as someone who had been badly hurt in a previous relationship, and now she had done it again. Little wonder he had curled himself up into a spiky hedgehog ball and was refusing to talk to her.

I just need the chance to explain.

Margaret allowed herself a few blissful seconds to imagine that this might just be possible, then groaned. Of course it would never happen! What she had done was unforgivable. In fact, she wouldn't respect the man who could even contemplate forgiving a woman who had treated him the way she had. He was quite right not to want to speak to her, not last night, not today, tomorrow or ever again. She had slammed the door on their relationship with a violence that even a grinning Mormon would interpret as final.

Margaret rolled out of bed and into the shower. She'd forgotten to set the timer, and the water was cold.

I Predict A Riot

It was her first day back at work, and she received a right royal welcome from Mr Kawolski and the rest of her colleagues. That saw her through the first thirty seconds of her day, and then it was back out onto the shopfloor and dealing with everything that one of the biggest and busiest department stores in Belfast could throw at her. Often, quite literally.

Maeve, her usual partner on these patrols through bandit country, could see that she wasn't happy, and probed mercilessly.

'Walter mess you around again?'

Margaret shook her head.

'So when are you seeing him again?'

'I'm not.'

'So what happened?'

'Nothing.'

'Nothing happened, or something happened and you don't want to talk about it?'

'Nothing happened.'

'So why the long face?'

'It's just my face.'

'He dumped you.'

'No, he didn't.'

'You dumped him.'

'Not really, no.'

'Not really? What's that mean?'

'It doesn't matter.'

'Well, it obviously does.'

'No, it doesn't.'

'Look, if you don't want to talk about it, that's all right. Just tell me to mind my own business.'

'Mind your own business, Maeve.'

They walked on. Maeve spotted a Millie pocketing a pair of socks. She pretended she hadn't. Margaret was much more interesting.

'So you're together, or not together?' Maeve asked.

'Not together,' said Margaret.

'Friends or enemies?'

'Neither.'

'Crap in bed, was he?'

'Do you mind?'

'Not at all. So, marks out of ten?'

Margaret sighed. 'Have you heard from Redmond?'

Maeve shrugged.

'You don't want to talk about him?'

'We're finished. I'm focusing on the future. Moving on.'

'Good. So am I.'

'It's really over?'

'Yes, it is.'

'That's a pity. You had high hopes.'

'Well, that's life, Maeve. But tomorrow is another day.'

'That's the spirit,' said Maeve, and gave her a mock punch on the arm. 'We'll move on together. Our little business enterprise.'

'Our what?'

'You know – the designing.'

Margaret stopped by a display of lacy bras. 'Oh yeah. Well, it's like, early days yet. I mean, I know what I'm doing, but where do you see *yourself* in our little business enterprise?'

Maeve shrugged. 'Where do *you* see me?'

'Well, you could do security.'

Maeve gave her a sharp look. 'You better be f**king joking.'

Margaret smiled quickly. 'Relax, would you?' She hadn't actually been joking. She had no idea what Maeve could do. Or any particular desire for her to do anything. 'What would you like to do?'

'I'm like, your enforcer.'

'Enforcer? I'm not sure if a fashion . . .'

'Course they do! Margaret, open your eyes – the fashion world's as cut-throat as any, even if the half of them are fruits and lezzies. You need someone who can call a spade a spade. Like this afternoon.'

'Eh?'

'This afternoon. I've an appointment with Jack Finucane.'

'Who's he?'

'Owner of *Irma La Deuce*, purveyors of poisonous carrot cakes.'

'*Maeve*, what are you up to?'

'I'm going to thrash out a deal.'

'What on earth are you talking about?!'

'Compensation! Margaret, for Christ's sake, he nearly killed you. And if we sue him and it gets to court, the publicity will destroy his business. So he'll pay us off.'

'Us?'

'Yes. You're on seventy-five per cent and I take the rest. It's my fee for representing you.'

'But I never asked you to.'

'And that's why you need an enforcer, darlin'. If I left it to you, you'd never get round to it. You concentrate on the designing, love, leave the business side of things to me.'

'Well, I—'

'Come on, would you? We're talking thousands here, and what we do is re-invest it all in the business. Today the Malone Road, tomorrow the world.' Maeve winked, and turned out of Lingerie.

Margaret hurried after her. 'But Maeve, wait, I'm not even sure I want to do that.'

'Well, I am. And that's the end of it. Besides, what if he does it again, and somebody dies next time? He needs a shock – and short of whacking his goolies off, you have to hit him where it hurts most, and that's in his bank account.'

Margaret sighed, but she didn't say no. She wasn't even sure if she was going to proceed with this designing thing and maybe some carrot-cake money might come in handy. The carrot-cake thing, and then the Billy thing, and then the Walter thing, had really knocked her for six.

When they reached Children's Wear Margaret's mobile rang, and for a moment she hoped that it might be Walter, calling to forgive her, but it was a text message from her husband.

Hi sxy, njoyed lst nite, r u up 4 more? Lve Billy xxxx.

Margaret texted back: *F**k off and die!*

40

Nerves

Billy was on top of the world, sauntering down the Lisburn Road towards his office, a definite spring in his step. He'd won Margaret back, hadn't he? His wife had dumped him, she'd gone out into the world all by her lonesome and discovered what a hard, cruel place it could be. Then, when she could hardly sink any lower, she had succumbed to a poisoned carrot cake and ended up at death's door. *Who you gonna call?* Your husband. Your true love. When it came down to it, she'd needed him. He was her rock. Billy whistled. *I'm singin' in the rain.* Of course it was one of Belfast's rare sunny mornings, but nevertheless, that was how he felt. A night of hot sex! He'd sent her a loving text first thing and she'd responded by telling him what he could do with himself, but that was just her raking around. He'd never quite 'got' her sense of humour. Billy himself had never knowingly cracked a funny in his life.

What he really wanted to know was when she was moving back in. As he walked, he thought about sending her another text. *If you're worried about eight months worth of dishes, relax. I didn't marry a dishwasher, I bought one!* That would impress her. In fact, there were two or three other things around the house that were bound to lure her back – the widescreen plasma TV, the DVD recorder, the big . . .

'Hey – Billy.'

Billy turned to his right. There was a blue Jaguar idling by the kerb, against the traffic, so that the fella in the passenger seat was facing him. The fella was in his fifties, probably, wearing a shirt and a tie and a smile.

Billy put his official face on, friendly, approachable. 'All right? How's it going?' He didn't know the man from Adam. It was probably a client. How was he supposed to keep track? He smiled and moved closer to the car.

'Do you want a lift?' the man said.

'Nah – sure, I'm only round the corner.'

'Let me put it another way – jump in.'

The man wasn't smiling now. He had his wallet out and he was showing Billy his ID. Billy stepped closer to examine it, a cold sheen of sweat already beginning to form up on his back. Friends didn't flap their IDs at you. Potential clients didn't introduce themselves like this. And the murky paramilitaries Billy occasionally worked for didn't carry ID, unless it was tattooed on their arms. Billy squinted. There was a slight glare from the morning sun off the embossed plastic, which was also quite badly creased. The photo, probably quite deliberately, had red eye. The name said Superintendent James Mallow, PSNI. Beside Billy a passenger door swung open; there was a fella back there as well, stretching across.

'B . . . but I . . .'

'I'll count to three.'

Billy got in before he said one. There was something about James Mallow. What annoyed Billy was that he hadn't recognised him straight off. He'd seen him a hundred times on the news. Jimmy Mallow. 'Marsh' Mallow, he was known as. It was a sarcastic nickname. Belfast had the most sarcastic police force in the world.

The car pulled out. It was this year's model. Everyone in Belfast seemed to be doing well these days. The driver and the guy beside Billy were both about his age. He only gave them a cursory glance. He was drawn to the back of Jimmy Mallow's crumpled neck. Muscle or flab? Muscle, he thought. His hair was cropped short. A number two. Mallow didn't look back. His voice was calm, confident. 'So how's life treating you, Billy?'

'It's all right.' He could hear a slight quaver in his own voice. 'What's this about?' He already knew the answer. How could he not?

'It's about you and Pink Harrison.'

'What about me and Pink Harrison?'

'About how you cook his books.'

'I've never cooked a book in my life.'

The driver snorted. Mallow gave the driver a look, then turned slightly in his seat. 'Let me put it this way, Billy-boy. *I* know what you've been doing, and *you* know what you've been doing, and we'll save ourselves a lot of trouble beating around the frigging gorse-bushes if we acknowledge that and get on with it.'

Billy cleared his throat. 'I don't know what you're talking about.' His shirt was now completely stuck to his back. The knowledge that this day might come had always been there at the back of his mind. The moment he'd broken the Arithmetic Oath by taking Pink Harrison's shilling was the moment he knew that one day, one day . . . Jimmy Mallow would come calling.

Mallow sighed. 'Where do you want us to start, Billy? Do you want us to take your car? The plasma? Do you want us to walk into your office and take your friggin' Oxford brogues? Because I'm telling you, we can trace every single thing you own back to Pink Harrison if we choose to. You do know that, don't you?'

Billy tried holding Mallow's glare. He managed about four seconds, then nodded.

'How's your wife?'

'My wife?'

'Aye, heard she was in hospital.'

'She's fine.'

'You still together?'

'Yes, of course.'

'You just maintain separate homes.'

'I . . .'

'What's that – another tax dodge? We can take her place as well.'

'It's rented.'

'Well. You would say that. Maybe it is. We can take her shoes. They rented? We can take her handbag and her groceries. We can take everything. You know that, don't you, Billy?'

Billy nodded again. 'What do you want?'

'What do you think we want, Billy?'

'I don't know.'

'Billy.'

'You want Pink.'

'Of course we want Pink.'

'That's not possible.'

'Excuse me?'

'He'd kill me.'

'It's a distinct possibility.'

Billy was wide-eyed. He wanted to *bolt*. Only he could hardly move a muscle.

'Ah, Billy son, I know how it is. Godsake, you're an accountant. Not the most exciting, is it? Then Pink Harrison walks into the office and asks you to cook the books and you can hardly say no to that, can you? You're scared, but you're a bit excited too, aren't you? He takes you out, wines you and dines you, maybe he fixes you up with a couple of Millies and some speed and—'

'There was nothing like that.'

There had been, of course. He'd strutted around for a couple of days afterwards like *he* was the drug-dealing UDA Chief, not Pink Harrison. Billy Gilmore, Mob Accountant. It sounded considerably more exciting than Billy Gilmore, Financial Advisor to the Ulster Farmers Union.

'You don't think we know? You don't think we watch? Get a grip, Billy.'

Billy shook his head.

Mallow smiled back. 'Relax, son,' he said. 'We're only asking a little favour.'

Billy swallowed. 'Like what?'

'We need you to get a little closer to Pinky. We need eyes and ears.'

'Closer?'

'Hang out with him a bit more. Socialise. He has a lot of fingers in a lot of big fat pies. You're not the only crooked accountant he uses, you know.'

The proper answer should have been, *'Crooked?'* But Billy said, *'I'm not?'*

'Oh no. Lessens the risk. That's why we need you to find out more.'

Billy sighed. 'I'm screwed if I do, and I'm screwed if I don't.'

'That's about the sum of it.' Mallow glanced across at his driver. 'Stop the car,' he said. They were more or less back to where they had started, 100 yards down from his office, as if they'd known exactly how long the conversation would take.

'And what would you say if I said no?' Billy asked, somewhat tremulously.

'I'd say, "Billy, don't be a hero. Don't be a fool with your life".' Marsh winked, and nodded his head to the side, indicating for him to get out.

Billy stepped out. He closed the door.

'We'll be in touch,' said Mallow.

As they drove away, Billy let out a long and loud fart of relief.

41
Carrot Confidential

Maeve stood on one side of the counter, sixteen different varieties of carrot cake between her and Jack Finucane.

'I'm here about the poisonous carrot cake,' she trumpeted.

Finucane, a big man in his thirties with a shock of black hair, visibly flinched. Half a dozen of his customers in *Irma La Deuce* looked at Maeve, then Jack, then the carrot cake.

Maeve addressed them directly. 'It's all right,' she said, 'it wasn't all the flavours – only the one.'

A girl in a Boots uniform said, 'But which one?'

'Ah now,' said Maeve. 'That would be telling.' She raised a see-what-I-can-do eyebrow at Jack.

Jack recovered his composure quicker than she'd hoped. He smiled at the customer. 'When she says poisonous, she means in the French sense, from *poisson*, the fish. You've tried our salmon carrot cake? It's very popular.'

The Boots girl looked at Maeve, who smiled. No point in going too far. She'd shown him that she meant business. She had on a grey trouser suit and she'd moussed her expansive hair down so that it looked less like an Afro and more like a Bonsai tree in bloom.

Jack Finucane left his counter staff to deal with the perplexed customers, then led Maeve through the small but busy kitchen at the back, along a short corridor, then left into a cramped office. There was a paper-strewn desk and two chairs. They sat.

Maeve said, 'You've spelled it wrong.'

'I've what?'

'*Irma La Deuce*. It should be d-o-u-c-e. Like the movie.'

The carrot-cake chef shook his head. 'You think I don't know that?'

'Then why don't you fix it?'

'Because it's intentional. It's a play on words.'

'How exactly is it a play on words?'

'Is that relevant? Or any of your business?'

Maeve snorted. 'Boy, you're touchy. But then I suppose nearly killing someone can do that to a bloke.'

'I didn't nearly kill someone.'

'Oh yeah, right, I forgot. It was the carrot cake. "Your Worship, I only made the bomb, I didn't actually blow anyone up".'

Jack Finucane clasped his hands. 'Well, you would know more about bombs than I do.'

That caused a sharp intake of breath. *Damn it – how did he know?* And then: *Of course he knows.* Her mug had been all over the papers. Because like a fool she'd blabbed her mouth off to reporters when she'd been emotionally fragile, and they hadn't offered her a red cent. Redmond was stuck in a Colombian prison with no hope of release. She would never see him again. He was being tortured and starved and robbed of the freedoms he had spent many years trying to destroy. But he was still Redmond. He used to bring her cups of tea in the morning and he knew how burned to make her toast and when there was an occasionally sunny day in July he used to put her sunbed out in the back garden and place the towels on it with the fleecy side up and bring her a cold drink in a foam rubber cooler with ice cubes and a striped straw.

Maeve looked at the untidy desk. She saw receipts and a flattened crisp packet and a *Daily Mirror* and a John Grisham novel with a Twix wrapper in it as a bookmark, and she burst into tears. She couldn't help herself. Her shoulders juddered and she gulped for air. She could hardly see Jack Finucane. Her eyes had instantly clogged up, thanks to the cheap mascara wand she'd purchased in a Poundstretcher. It had been like pasting damp coal-dust on a gobstopper.

'Are you okay?'

'. . .'

'I didn't mean to—'

'I'm sorry.'

'Here.' He was holding a tissue out to her.

'It's just . . .' She took it. She dabbed.

'Don't worry about it.'

She blew into the tissue. Wasn't the smartest move. Jack Finucane smiled.

'What's so funny?' Maeve moaned.

'Nothing. Sorry.'

'I'm falling to bits and you're laughing your head off.' She sniffed up.

'I've just never sat doing business with a panda before.'

Maeve opened her bag and took out her compact and urgently studied her face. 'Christ,' she said.

Jack Finucane handed her another tissue. 'Relax,' he said. 'I'll get you

151

a coffee. There's a bathroom just down the hall if you want to clean up.'

Maeve pushed her chair back. She paused by the door. 'You're being very nice. It doesn't mean I'm not going to screw you into the ground.'

He burst into laughter.

'I mean financially,' said Maeve, and hurried away.

She studied her face in the mirror, which appeared to be slightly magnified. She could see every crevice and cranny. Every blotch and bag. She had bottled Redmond up inside her and now the pressure was beginning to crack the glass. It wouldn't shatter yet, perhaps it never would, but little bubbles of hate and bile and disappointment and frustration were beginning to leak out. Redmond had had the best years of her life, and even the best years weren't that good.

Look at you, Just bloody look at you. Come in, all guns blazing, you end up firing blanks. Bloody, bloody, bloody Redmond. She gripped both sides of the sink. *Sort yourself out.*

She had to think positive. Redmond getting arrested could never be a good thing, but she realised now that it was vital to look upon it as God's way of presenting her with an opportunity. To change her life. To get her act together. But that in itself wasn't enough. She couldn't just start a new life like *that*. Her mate Margaret had presented her with another opportunity, but for either of them to realise it, they needed money. And Jack Finucane was such an obvious first step. Yet she'd already messed it up.

And also, he was quite cute.

She returned to his office. There was a cappuccino and a slice of carrot cake waiting for her. He was back behind his desk.

'Sorry about that,' she said.

'Don't worry about it.'

She examined the carrot cake with a mock pathology.

He smiled – good teeth, she noted – and said, 'Don't worry, I had some this morning, and I'm not dead yet.'

'It might be slow-acting,' said Maeve.

'Well, only one way to find out.'

She took a bite. It was very nice. She tried her best not to show it. She said, 'So have you been doing this long?'

'Making carrot cake?'

Maeve nodded. 'And this place.'

'Oh, a few years. I saw a gap in the market.'

'And is there?'

'And is there what?'

'A gap in the market.'

'Well, "gap" might be a bit strong. There's like a crevice – you have to get in and push both sides, make a little space. But we're getting there.'

'We?' Maeve had a sudden image of a glamorous showbiz chef couple. It made her feel curiously sad.

'That's the Royal we. Just me and my lonesome.'

'Aw,' said Maeve, with slightly sincere sympathy and some little relief. 'Does that mean you're not going to try and screw me into the ground? Financially speaking, of course.'

'Of course not. You nearly killed a good woman.'

'It was food poisoning. It happens.'

'I'm sure it does, but the fact is, she almost died. Unless you're going to put a disclaimer up, then you leave yourself open to this kind of thing.'

'What would you suggest? A big sign with *There's an outside chance of dying if you eat in this restaurant*?'

Maeve smiled indulgently. 'Nevertheless,' she said.

'Nevertheless, you want me to write you a big f**k-off cheque.'

'That would be nice.'

'Well, I'm not going to do it.'

'Oh.'

'Because what you're doing is blackmail. If I gave the police a tape of this conversation, they'd have you behind bars before you could scramble eggs.'

'You're taping this?'

'You'll find out.'

'It's not blackmail anyhow. You nearly killed my friend. If it goes to court, and it gets in the papers, that crevice is going to slam shut, on your head.'

'That's a chance I'll have to take.'

'Is that your final word?'

'No.'

'What is?'

'Let me take your friend out to dinner, by way of apology.'

'Absolutely not.'

He clasped his hands again. 'Well, let me take you out then.'

'Okay,' said Maeve.

42
Marsh Mallow at Rest

Jimmy 'Marsh' Mallow – although you wouldn't call him that to his face, unless you were very big, with a Black Belt, or a nut in search of a hiding – kept his wife in a wardrobe. Caroline, currently, was about twelve inches tall and weighed ounces rather than pounds. He didn't quite know what to do with her. She'd been dead for eight months now, cremated at Roselawn. They'd given him the option of scattering her in the Garden of Remembrance up there, or, 'If you wish, you could scatter her somewhere she loved.' Jimmy wasn't sure how they'd take to that in Marks & Spencer. So she remained in the wardrobe with her dresses and shoes and handbags and little trinkets and shells and Quality Street jars full of coppers (that's small coins, not tiny policemen smelling of chocolate). She was a continued presence in his life, and although it gave him more pain than comfort, he found it difficult to part with her.

A well-meaning colleague, aware of his predicament, had, over whiskey, tried to tell him that it probably wasn't her ashes anyway, that all the corpses got burned together because it didn't make financial sense to fire up the incinerator for each individual body, and that all the ashes therefore got mixed up, so that what you got at the end of the day was a crematorium version of a 10p mix. Jimmy had decked his colleague. It might have been over the ashes, it might have been over a dozen things. He tended to get violent with drink on-board, which was one reason that nowadays he drank alone.

Like this evening, sitting in his front lounge. He loved The Beatles. He had all of their albums, on CD as well as vinyl, and since he had discovered eBay he had dozens of bootlegs as well. Not only The Beatles. The Stones, The Kinks, The Move, The Faces. He liked his rock'n'roll. He even had an album by Oasis. He was fifty-eight years old and could have retired at any stage over the past twelve years. But he held on and on. He was the oldest in the Department by far;

all of his superiors were younger. He loved his job. Always had. Even in the dreadful, harrowing times when he couldn't have felt any lower, deep down, he still loved it. He was a good man. He had loved his wife, even though she drove him to distraction. He had been injured three times in his career: Grazed by a sniper's bullet in the Short Strand. Hit with a brick during a peace march through Wellington Place. Blown across the road when a bomb went off in the city centre in 1978, his back peppered with shards of glass, any one of which might have killed him. He was the last of the die-hards. Most everyone of his vintage hadn't wanted anything to do with the Police Service of Northern Ireland when it was set up. They thought the lunatics were taking over the asylum. But Jimmy hadn't minded. The law was the law. Bad guys didn't go away. They just changed their clothes. That's what drove him. He was determined to get Pink Harrison. Pink with his myriad little businesses, his fat fingers in greasy pies, his sordid veneer of respectability.

The phone rang. Jimmy set his whiskey down on the arm of the chair, used the remote to turn down the TV – a DVD of *Paul McCartney Live in Red Square* (it was good to hear some of the old Beatles songs played live, with decent sound; he liked to close his eyes and pretend it was the four of them, not just Paul and some talented pick-up band) – and went into the hall. He looked at the caller ID. Someone – Pink Harrison, he suspected – had posted his home phone number on a UDA website, and he got abusive calls from time to time, so he had taken to screening them before he answered, but when he saw who it was, he smiled and sighed at the same time.

'Hiya, Dad.'

'Daughter of mine,' he said.

'I haven't heard from you, I was worried.'

'I spoke to you on Tuesday.'

'I know.'

'I'm a big boy – I can look after myself.'

'I *know*. I just . . . are you eating?'

'Yes, I am.'

'And sleeping?'

'Yes. Often at the same time.'

'Dad. When are you coming to see us?'

'When hell freezes over.'

Lauren had gone to university in Sunderland, and hadn't come back. She'd met a doctor over there and married. She was a midwife. She had a three-year-old son called Michael. She had held onto her accent, but there was no trace of Belfast in Michael. She'd brought him over for the funeral. It was surprising, the difference the accent made. Jimmy could hardly relate to him at all. Jimmy had been to Sunderland once, and didn't like it. There wasn't anything particularly wrong with it, he just didn't like it. It wasn't home. People laughed sometimes when he said he loved Belfast.

'How are you doing, really?'

'I'm fine.'

'Truth?'

'Yes.'

They were on familiar ground. Lauren would find a dozen more ways to ask the same question, and he would respond minimally.

'And are you getting out?'

'Of course.'

'I don't mean to work.'

'I get out.'

They fell silent. It felt slightly uncomfortable. The distance between them was more than just geographic. He knew he'd been quite stern as a father. Caroline had been softer and was always telling him off for being hard on Lauren. He knew she was right, but couldn't help himself. He'd blamed it on the stresses of the job – murder, mayhem, bodies, grief, shock – but she'd said it was more than that. It was his nature. Lauren loved him, without a doubt, but sometimes there was an awkwardness.

She said, 'Dad, don't be angry.'

'I'm not angry. What have you done?'

'It's your birthday next week.'

'Uhuh.'

'And it's always a struggle to get you something.'

'Record tokens are good.'

'Oh, you and your bloody music.'

'Lauren, you're sounding more like your mother every day.'

'Anyway – I worry about you. Being alone. You need someone to look after you.'

'I'm fifty-eight, love, not a hundred and three.'

'You know what I mean.'

He sighed. 'What have you done?'

'You promise you won't shout?'

'No.'

'Well, I was surfing. I mean, the internet . . .'

'I know what it is.'

'And I came across this website.' Lauren took a deep breath, and then spoke twice as quickly. 'There's a Belfast-based dating website. I signed you up for it as your birthday present.'

'What?!!'

'I signed you up. I sent in your photo and filled in the form and you went live last night.'

'Jesus Christ, Lauren! Are you bloody mental or what?'

'Dad, you need to meet someone.'

'It's not about that! Jesus Christ – you stop it, you stop it now!'

'I can't, Daddy, it's on there now.'

'Lauren! Good God!'

'You're lonely.'

'It's not about that! I'm the Head of CID! If the press get hold of this they'll tear me to pieces.'

'They *won't.*'

'You don't know them!'

'It's okay, Daddy, I didn't use your real name.'

'Jesus H! That's even worse! Have you any idea how bad this will look? Not to mention how dangerous it is. Jesus, love, have you learned nothing, all those years checking under the bloody car for bombs, never going the same way to school in the morning? Didn't you learn—'

'Daddy, The Troubles are over and you need to meet someone!'

'They're not bloody over! They're still out there!'

'Yes, they *are* over, Daddy! You're the only one still fighting them!'

Jimmy slammed the phone down. He slapped his hand hard against the wall. *Jesus Christ.* She had no idea, no bloody idea of the damage she'd done. Physical violence was one thing – he'd lived with the threat of that for years. But he couldn't live with ridicule. Who would take him seriously now? How could he scare the *bejesus* out of people if they read about him trawling for girlfriends on some dodgy website like a lonely, desperate, sad old man?

He had to get it off. He had to get it off *now*. Except he didn't know the name of the website. He called Lauren back. He would apologise, try to explain, attempt to keep his temper. But it rang and rang and rang.

Huffing. He was quick to explode, but she was a huffer, like her mother.

Bloody hell. Bloody, bloody hell.

He would just have to track it down himself on the web. Belfast was a small city – there couldn't be that many dating agencies.

He logged on. When he went to check his email there was a welcome message from *Let's Be Mates*. It cheerily informed him that he already had three responses to his posting.

Bloody, bloody, bloody hell.

43
The Player

Walter didn't even bother with the pretence of doing any work. His in-tray was piled up to overflowing. Once in a while his EO1 would come past and glare at him, but there was nothing to be done. The Civil Service was a job for life. Only murderers and Catholics had previously been sacked. Instead Walter studied the *Big Houses* website. This week's catchline was *Don't Even Think About It*. This week's difference was that, for the first time in his life, Walter *could* think about it. He had backings. A little old lady was putting up the dough. He was a player now, a man of substance. He felt six inches taller, as opposed to the six inches wider he usually felt on a Monday morning after a weekend on the beer and curries. When a girl came round taking orders for pastries, Walter declined. This was enough to make her back out of the room in genuine shock. Somewhere, shares in gravy rings began to tumble.

Mark wasn't doing any work either. He paced by the window.

Walter said, 'Ants in your pants?'

'Big killer scorpions,' said Mark.

'It'll be fine.'

'That's easy for you to say.'

Walter smiled. Mark was due to appear before a Unionist committee after work, and if he passed muster he would be appointed as an assistant to a working councillor, to get him trained up before the next election, when they would hopefully run him as a candidate.

'I know bugger-all about anything,' said Mark.

'I know that.'

'I mean, I know it in my head, but it never comes out right. I've always been crap at job interviews – why do you think I've been here so long?'

'You'll sail through. You said yourself, they're desperate.'

'What are you saying? I'm that bad?'

'No.'

'You're meant to build me up, not knock me down.'

'You'll be great. I have every confidence. But just remember – power corrupts, and absolute power corrupts absolutely.'

'You're very funny.' Mark had now wandered in behind Walter. He glanced down at his computer. 'This mad old biddy is serious, is she?'

'Seems to be.'

'She's just going to give you the money?'

'Well, I expect there'll be some papers to sign.'

'You know it'll end in tears.'

'How do you work that out?'

'Because doesn't it *always*?'

'Christ, and you want me to build *you* up.'

'I just want you to keep your feet on the ground. Chances are she's got Alzheimer's. You'll go round there tomorrow and she'll think you're her dad. Or if she hasn't gone loopy she's one of those professional conmen, you know, comes on like your granny but actually she's playing you like an oboe. She'll get you to sign those papers and then you'll go home and find your house has been sold out from under you.'

'Yeah. Right.'

'I'm serious, Walter. I'm only trying to protect you.'

'Right. I'll bear that in mind. Good luck with your interview, you dough-bag.'

Walter gave him a look. Mark shrugged and went back to the window to contemplate his political future. Walter clicked onto the next page on the *Big Houses* website. He wasn't quite sure where to start. Buy an old house, fix it up, make a profit? Buy a couple of apartments, rent them out? What about commercial property? Or property abroad?

Walter had never bought a house in his life. He'd inherited his own house from his late parents. Most of the drawers were still crammed with their knick-knacks. He had never paid a mortgage. The ground rent was £25 a year, and he was usually three months late paying it. Investing in property might have been completely new to him, yet if filled him with a tremendous excitement. This wasn't like dreaming of being a rock star, or transforming his body in the gym. This was do-able, this was real life. He was within spitting distance of turning his life around. He just had to take the first step. But he would be cautious. No point in rushing in like a head-the-ball. Study the market. Establish where property prices were rising. Consult experts. Weigh up the pros and cons. The different sorts of mortgages. How to manage a bidding war.

There was a sudden *ping* and a small box appeared on his screen, showing that he had an internal email, and asking if he wanted to accept it. Walter glanced up at Mark, but he was still by the window. He clicked yes.

A message appeared. *Looking at houses, are we?*

Walter looked down the corridor. The door to Office 12 was closed, but he couldn't imagine that it could be anyone but Steven, its mysterious occupant. With everything that had happened in the last few days he hadn't got back to him about his generous but somewhat creepy job offer. And now, with the backing of a rich old woman, and the confidence and opportunity that gave him, he no longer felt quite so intimidated, or awkward about rejecting it. He would make his fortune on his own terms now.

He wrote back: *Yes, I am.*

A minute later the message box appeared again, and again he accepted.

Kill someone, did you? Come into some unexpected cash?

Yes, wrote Walter. But before he sent it he thought, No, that's not very clever. Who knows what someone like Steven might use such an admission for? There was, he thought, no real sense of humour in an email, because they could always be interpreted in so many ways. So he deleted his answer, and instead typed: *Just looking for a new house.*

Steven typed back, *It's a jungle out there.*

Walter typed: *I know that.*

You should be careful.

I will be.

You never came back on my job offer.

I've been tied up.

It was impolite.

Walter stared at that one for a while. He felt a little queasy. He typed: *Sorry. I appreciate the offer, but I've decided against it.*

Almost as soon as he sent it, the response came: *You owe me.*

Walter looked up at the door again. He half-expected it to open, but there was no sign of movement. He stared at Steven's message. He desperately wanted to ignore it, but he couldn't. It demanded a response.

So he typed: *What about that drink?* Again, he hesitated before sending it. The last thing in the world he wanted to do was go out with Steven for a drink, but he felt he had to do something. He had, after all, gone out of his way to help Walter track down Margaret, even if it had ended in tears. So he *did* owe him. But still . . .

Mark said, 'Why the long face?'

Walter shrugged. He stared at the message. His finger hovered over the *send*. Then he quickly deleted it and wrote: *We should go out for a drink*. Then after a further bout of contemplation, he added, *sometime*.

Walter took a deep breath, then pressed *send*.

He stared at the screen for the next two minutes, his fingers crossed that Steven would respond with equal vagueness. But no response came. Not in the next five minutes. Or ten.

Or in the two hours that were left before lunch, nor when he hurried back to his screen after devouring a salad in the canteen, nor before he left for home. As he walked down the corridor he couldn't take his eyes off the door to Office 12. He gave a sigh of relief when he was finally out of the building and waiting at the bus stop opposite. But when the bus came, and he took his usual seat near the front, he kept glancing over his shoulder, and it was the same on the train on the way home.

44

In the Pink

Billy Gilmore always felt naked when he wasn't wearing a tie. Sometimes even in bed, when he literally *was* naked, he would wake up in the middle of the night and feel for the knot at his throat. There was something reassuring about it. Something civilised. It wasn't like he was a tie *nut*. He didn't have a huge collection of ties; he didn't have brightly coloured or polka-dotted or hugely wide or shoestring-narrow ties, or ties for every occasion; nor did he have seasonal ones – in particular he didn't have any ties with Santa Claus – just a handful of your normal, common or garden ties. Without a tie he felt robbed of his identity. And also, people could mistake him for what he wasn't. Like today, nervously approaching the Shankhill Road Rangers Supporters Club, wearing jeans and a Rangers top. No tie. With his short hair and his prominent brow, which seemed to freckle up on the least possible exposure to sunlight or even sometimes to a strong light bulb, he could just as easily be taken for one of *them*, with their skinheads and tattoos, crowding around the entrance, an hour before kick-off, wanting to get their cheap pints in and start singing their harsh sectarian songs. He hated having to sit amongst them, hated pretending to love the football, hated the fact that he had forced himself to learn the words to all the songs, hated the fact that he screamed *you Fenian bastard* at the Ref in order to blend in, hated their hard faces, their violence, hated the flags and the emblems and the UDA regalia, and he hated not having his suit and his tie. But he quite liked being in Pink Harrison's company.

This was Pink's place. You wouldn't find his name anywhere, of course, but it was his – like a dozen other places were his. He was always here on a Saturday for the football, drifting in and out, shouting at the TV with the rest of them but really not having much of a care one way or another. It was his *presence* that was important. They were his people. They loved him. They loved him for his blond hair and his pink shirts, for his soft South Belfast accent and manicured nails; they loved him because he bought rounds and provided Es and protected them from the Republicans and kept a squad of men to break the kneecaps of joyriders and petty thieves and men or women who disagreed with him. They loved him so much that they'd even voted him onto Belfast City Council. The Official Unionists loved him because he got votes, and ignored the fact that everyone who wasn't in love with him was too scared to vote against him. Vote once! Vote often! Oh yes, they loved Pink Harrison. Yet he was so utterly unlike them. They said on the Shankhill that they broke the mould when they made Pink Harrison, and Billy quite agreed. One of a kind.

Billy was without his tie, and half-heartedly drinking pint after pint of Harp, and shouting at the TV, because that's the way Pink wanted it. It was his *arrangement*. At some point during the match Pink would catch his eye, give him the nod, then Billy would make his way towards the toilets. But instead of going in, he'd slip inside the storeroom next door. A few minutes later Pink would join him, and together they would go through the accounts of whichever of his many and varied businesses Pink needed attending to. Perhaps today he was trying to avoid paying tax or VAT, or laundering money or illegally purchasing shares or setting up a company as a front for purchasing property. Pink, Billy thought, was quite an astute businessman, and had the knack of making whoever he worked with feel like his partner when really he was the only one in charge. He would clap his arm around Billy and shout: 'Pink and Billy – ruling Belfast through fear and accountancy!' Billy would laugh along with him. It felt great, but he would also flush with sweat. It was intoxicating, but scary. They met in the storeroom because Pink was convinced the cops were bugging his office. He also thought there were undercover cops in the bar. And in cars outside. And in the office across the road. He knew his people loved him, but he expected to be killed by them. He said it was the nature of his business. He was worried about going bald, and about skin cancer, and the price of his pink jumpers. He was worried that people would think he was gay.

Billy wanted to say, 'People *do* think you're gay. It's the pink jumpers.' But he didn't dare.

'I'm not gay, you know,' Pink would say, unprompted. 'I'm just a character.'

Billy knew they would kill him if he was gay. It was the nature of the beast. But as long as he remained just vaguely effeminate, like a pier-end comedian, and protected them from Republicanism and bought them cheap alcohol and drugs, and broke enough knees from time to time, Pink would probably be all right.

Pink gave him the nod halfway through the second half, Rangers two up against Hibs and the crowd in good form. Billy squeezed his way through to the toilets, then slipped into the storeroom. Pink arrived a few minutes later, all smiles.

'How're you doin', fella?' he said.

'Okay. All right.'

Pink reached behind a stack of toilet rolls and produced a familiar thick file. He handed it to Billy.

'Get your head stuck into that,' he said.

Billy hadn't slept for the previous two nights, ever since Jimmy Marsh Mallow had tried to turn him into a police informer. A tout. Before his Marsh encounter he had taken some comfort from the theory that, as Pink's accountant, he knew all the secrets, and therefore was indispensable. But Marsh's revelation that Pink ran more than one crooked accountant meant that his position wasn't quite so secure. For all he knew, the baying crowd in the room next door was *entirely* made up of accountants, all acting the part of rabid Rangers supporters. If he told Pink about Marsh, then what was to stop Pink merely moving his files to one of his other accountants, and quietly disposing of him, under concrete? Conversely, if he didn't tell Pink, and Pink somehow found out, then he'd *certainly* form part of the new motorway to Dublin. He was damned if he did and damned if he didn't. At his worst Marsh could only put him in prison, or take away his earthly goods. But still, Marsh was a legend, a timeless threat; he would be there or abouts, able to haunt Billy long after Pink had gone the way of all gangsters.

A rock and a hard place, thought Billy. A rock and a hard place.

Thing was, he had nowhere to turn for advice. Margaret was his closest friend, and despite his high hopes of the past few days, it was becoming clear that she wasn't that close at all. One night of hot sex. Then the cold shoulder. After her 'funny' reponse to his first text, she had ignored seventeen others.

As Billy scanned down the first page of figures, there came a violent uproar from the other side of the wall. Clearly Hibs had scored and the accountants were trying to outdo each other in the vehemence of their reaction. Billy took a deep breath. He had to do something.

'Pink,' he said.

'Mmm?'

'Got picked up by Marsh Mallow yesterday.'

Pink's eyes held steady on the list of figures he was studying. 'Mmm-hmm?'

'Wants me to become an infomer.'

'Hmmfh. Only a matter of time.'

'You knew he would . . . ?'

Pink glanced up, smiled. 'Well, he watches me like a hawk. Bastard.'

'So, what should I do?'

'Well, you must become one.'

'You what?'

'If you don't, Marsh will twist all my secrets out of you. But if you do, and give him all the wrong information, then he'll leave you alone until he thinks he has enough to get me – which, of course, he never will have, as you'll be feeding him three kinds of crap.'

'But . . . won't he realise that?'

'Of course he will. Eventually.'

'What happens then?'

'Well, who knows. That's the beauty of it. Nobody wins, but nobody loses, and the game goes on forever. It's like The Sims. Now relax. I'm not going to carve you up into little pieces, burn them to a crisp and bury what's left in a landfill site. We're partners. Now, take a look at these.'

Pink passed him a handful of crumpled receipts from the boss of one of his taxi companies. 'He's trying to diddle me,' said Pink. 'I'm convinced of it.'

Billy began to flatten them out with one hand. The other went to his throat, instinctively feeling for the comfort of the noose that wasn't there.

45

The Magician's Apprentice

Mark arrived at Unionist Headquarters at exactly three minutes to 8 p.m. He strolled through the front door with a casual confidence which belied the fact that he had spent the past three-quarters of an hour sitting in his car doubled up with cramps. Nerves. It was natural. He was setting out to change the world.

Entering Unionist HQ was a bit like entering your mad old auntie's house. You could see that it had once been young and thrusting and powerful and possessed of an impressive pair of breasts, but it had now gone to seed, and clipped money-off coupons from knitting magazines and smelled vaguely of cat urine, and its breasts had dropped so far that they were in danger of causing the entire edifice to topple over. At least, this was how Mark saw it. And he was the man who would apply the Wonderbra to the sagging breasts of Unionist power in Ulster.

Mark was wearing a light blue suit and polished brogues. His teeth were clean, his breath fresh. He looked around the reception area for some sign of life, then called, 'Hello.' There was an almost palpable heaviness in the air, a pungent mixture of political decline and dry rot. He shook his head slightly at the dusty portraits, then called again. His voice echoed softly. Or at least he thought it did, but then there came the soft clump of leisure shoes on deep shag and another, 'Hello,' came back at him from the top of a curving set of polished wooden stairs.

'Hello?' Mark ventured again.

'Hello!' A small man, or of medium height but rather stooped, in a dark jacket, finally appeared and smiled crookedly down at him. 'That will be young Mark, will it?'

He almost responded, 'That it will,' but managed to restrain himself. God, he thought, what am I getting myself into? He was led up the stairs and down a long corridor lined with more portraits of powerful-looking dead men. The man didn't bother to introduce himself; he appeared to think that Mark should recognise him, and certainly there was a vague resemblance to someone who had once featured on *Inside Ulster*, but politicians are a bit like film stars: you tend to remember them in their prime, not with the inevitable physical decline which comes with age and the lack of public office.

'Now, if you'll just take a seat there, we'll be with you in a little mo.' The old man indicated a chair opposite the open door to what appeared to be a well-stocked library. Besides the books, Mark could see a desk with three chairs behind it, and one in front. Two other elderly men were sipping tea. The man who had led him up the stairs stepped into the room and half-closed the door behind him. Mark sighed.

'Nervous?'

Mark looked sharply to his right. Another man he vaguely recognised, but couldn't quite place, was smiling at him. He was a good six feet tall with sandy, well-cut hair. Probably about forty. He was wearing track shoes, a pair of black jeans, and a pink short-sleeved shirt. He had a mug of coffee in his hand. At last, Mark thought, someone who hadn't fought the Hun.

'No, not really,' said Mark. 'A little.'

'Nothing to worry about, really,' said the man. 'But let me guess – you're brimful of ideas about how to reinvigorate the Party, how to win the next election, how to pull this country together. You've been working on your spiel for months, you're going to dazzle them with your grand vision.'

Mark cleared his throat. 'Well, something like that. Not quite as—'

'Let me give you a word of advice.'

Mark nodded.

'I have found that if you give answers which are what they want to hear, rather than what you genuinely believe, then you'll do a lot better. Quite often, that will mean saying precisely the opposite of what you feel.'

'But why would I do that?'

'Because they are old men and are scared of change. And as a rule, people don't like to hear that they've been doing a bad job. Especially from someone who has never held public office or run a campaign or gone knocking from door to door. Do you get what I'm saying?'

'Yes – yes, of course. It's just not a very good way to start out – I mean, telling lies, and shouldn't I be, you know, true to my beliefs?'

'Of course you should – but later. You have to get past this hurdle first. It's just the way the Party's set up; the old fogies do all the administrative stuff. They do it out of love of Ulster; there's plenty of young pups would do it quicker and better, but they'd want to be paid. These guys do it for nothing. So if I were you I'd just grin and nod and tell them what they want to hear.'

The guy took a sip of his coffee, winked and backed into the other room, just as the first man reappeared at the door of the library.

'Now, son, come on in.'

Mark stood up and followed him. He had been preparing his grand political vision for weeks and months, and now one fella with a cup of coffee had shattered it. But what did he know? Maybe that was all he did, make the coffee. Maybe he was some kind of half-wit who hung around Unionist HQ cleaning the sinks. Yet, just like the old guy who'd welcomed him, there was also something quite familiar about him. And also appealing. They had only exchanged a few words, but he already seemed like he would be a good man to go on a long drive with. Entertaining, funny, charismatic, with good stories, who could hold his drink and keep your secrets.

Mark took his seat. The old men shuffled papers. They pointed at things and whispered. Then one said, 'Mark – you work in the Department of Education in Bangor.'

'Yes, I do.'

'Martin McGuinness was in charge there for a while. Tell me, how did you find him?'

Mark blinked at him. What he wanted to say was, 'Contrary to expectations, he was a breath of fresh air.'

But he couldn't. And then it came to him suddenly who it was he'd been talking to outside. Jesus Christ. The pink shirt! Pink Harrison. Pink bloody Harrison. He was a Unionist councillor! Of course he was! One of the things Mark had intended to say, if pressed upon the future of the Party, was that they shouldn't recruit just anyone in order to get elected, and he would have used Pink Harrison as an example. Once a gangster, always a gangster, was his view on it.

'Well,' said Mark, 'obviously his IRA background was very difficult to ignore. We all like to move on, but even so.' He cleared his throat. The three men looked at him expectantly. 'He had some interesting ideas, but really, he wasn't going to last. I mean – signs in Irish, what next?'

The men smiled and nodded. And that was the pattern for the next forty-five minutes. He became quite comfortable with all the lying. When they finally ran out of questions, the man in the middle stood and without consulting with his colleagues extended his hand and said, 'Welcome to the Party, Mark.'

Mark gave it a firm shake, then repeated it with the others.

'You seem like a fine young man,' said the one on the left.

'Exactly what this Party needs,' said the one on the right.

'Good chap,' said the one in the middle.

'Now then,' said the one who had brought him in. 'You should meet the man you'll be working with. It'll be no picnic, mind – you're prepared for hard work?'

'Yes, I am.'

'For God and Ulster?'

'Absolutely.'

They all smiled and nodded.

'Good man. Now you wait here, I'll go and get Pink.'

46
The Name of the Game

Margaret checked her appearance three times in shop windows on her way to *Emma Cochrane*. She was wearing a white T-shirt, black jeans, Jimmy Choo heels (or at least a knock-off version she'd bought at Knutts Corner) and a determined smile. This was make or break. Like many people with big dreams she lacked confidence, and was willing to accept defeat at the first possible opportunity. For every positive that found her, there was a larger negative she could provide all by herself. Yes, she had been given an astonishing opportunity to kick off her career as a fashion designer, yet it was based on a lie. She had got rid of her very annoying husband and strode out bravely into the world – then had sex with him as soon as she faced her first real crisis. She was talented and ambitious, but also quite pathetic.

Her stomach rumbled. She'd been too nervous to eat breakfast, and had slipped out of Primark on her lunch break. She was now just a couple of doors down from *Emma Cochrane*. She could really do with something to eat to settle herself. She peered across the road at *Irma La Deuce*. Perhaps she could pop over for a slice of carrot cake and a coma. She wondered how things had really gone with her colleague Maeve and her attempts to screw some compensation out of the café's owner, Jack Finucane. Maeve had been curiously reticent, merely saying that 'negotiations were continuing'. Somehow, she doubted that. More that Maeve wasn't quite as smart or ruthless as she thought she was.

Margaret took a deep breath.

Okay, be strong. Be confident. You're a winner. Think of Oprah! Maggie Thatcher! Martha Stewart!

And then she remembered that Martha Stewart had ended up in prison for something fairly trivial. What would happen to her if they found out she'd ripped off her dress designs from—

'Margaret!'

I Predict A Riot

The shop door was already open and Emma Cochrane came charging out, or at least moving as fast as she could on towering heels. She enveloped Margaret in her sinewy arms. Margaret wasn't overweight by any stretch of the imagination, but compared to Emma Cochrane she felt like a rhino. As Margaret hugged her back, it felt like she was embracing a birdcage.

'Oh, it's so good to have you back! Come in! Come in!'

Emma took Margaret by the hand and led her into the shop. Louise, her fashion buyer, was behind the counter. 'Welcome home!' she cried. 'It only took us three days to get rid of the smell of boke!'

'Oh shush, Louise. It's been like forever, Margaret darling. And you're well? You're looking well. That's a lovely top – is it one of yours?'

'No, no . . . I . . .'

'This is so exciting!'

Emma asked for all the details about her health and recuperation, but before Margaret could properly respond she rushed onto the designs and whether she'd had any further inspiration. Margaret said no, she'd been in a coma, and since then, a bit fatigued, a bit down. Emma made big sympathetic eyes, then produced the original designs Margaret had given her. They discussed some minor changes, then moved onto materials and production costs and who was best to do the actual physical dressmaking. It went extremely well, and after an hour or so of discussion, everything seemed to be agreed. Margaret had relaxed considerably, and they laughed and joked and joshed like old pals. Margaret glanced surreptitiously at her watch – she was well past her lunch hour by now – but Emma noticed and said, 'We must let you go.'

Margaret shook her head. 'No panic.'

'Well, I know what it's like – rushed off my feet, I am. Let me just get you this . . .' She reached behind the counter and pulled out a Manila envelope. From within she produced quite a thick document and handed it to Margaret. 'I had my solicitor draw this up. He's a whiz at business things, and he's worked with all the big fashion houses in Belfast. It's just to clarify what we've discussed really, how much you'll get. I think you'll find it's a rather satisfactory amount. Obviously there's not that much upfront, but it's a royalty thing really. If you just look – there . . .'

Margaret studied the figures. Emma was right. There wasn't much upfront. Five hundred quid. But she thought the royalty rate was quite generous.

'That looks fine, fine,' said Margaret. 'Do you have a pen?'

Louise laughed.

Emma said, 'Oh no – no rush, darling. You take it away and study it, get your people to check it out, but I'm sure they'll say it's more than fair.'

'Yes, I mean, I just need your email address so I can . . . You know, if I have any new ideas I can send them over.'

Louise quickly handed her a pen and she wrote it down on the back of the envelope.

'So all that leaves really is the name,' said Emma.

Margaret looked up. 'The name?'

'Do you know, I'm completely torn. Do you think it should be just *Emma*, or *Emma Cochrane*?'

Margaret found herself momentarily speechless.

'Louise thinks *Emma Cochrane* is fine for Belfast, but to go international, *Emma* might be better. Or perhaps *emma*, you know, with a small *e*. Or even *M*, capital letter, and the word *Ah*.'

'Or *Cochrane* on its own,' said Louise. 'Although women might be put off by anything with a cock in the name.'

Margaret stared at Louise for a moment, then returned her attention to Emma, who could clearly see that she wasn't happy. 'What's wrong, darling?' she asked.

'Well, sorry, but I sort of presumed . . . well, they're my designs.'

'Yes, of course they are.'

'Well, I thought they would carry my name.'

'*Your* name?'

'Yes. Of course.'

Emma looked genuinely surprised.

'Call them *Margaret*?' asked Louise.

'Well, not necessarily *Margaret*, but . . .'

'*Gilmore*?' asked Louise. She was starting to annoy Margaret.

'And why not?' said Margaret, with slightly more resolve. 'They're my designs.' She was aware that it sounded petulant. She was aware that she was looking a gift horse in the mouth, and sticking spurs into its flanks.

Emma said, 'But, darling . . .'

'You're separated from your husband, aren't you?' Louise asked suddenly.

'Yes, but . . .' Margaret said in surprise.

'Just thinking. If you had a sexier maiden name, we might be able to work with that.'

Emma gave her a frosty look.

Margaret said, 'Margaret Wilson.'

Louise snorted. Emma laughed. Even Margaret couldn't resist a smile. An international fashion line called *Wilson*.

I Predict A Riot

Emma sighed. She took Margaret's hand. 'Look, darling, I understand how you feel, I really do, but to be perfectly frank, this isn't open to negotiation. I've been building awareness of the *Emma Cochrane* brand in Belfast for nine years. If I'm going to invest in this line, then it absolutely has to carry my name.'

There was an undoubted coolness in the air now. Margaret took her hand back.

'Believe me, darling,' said Emma, 'it'll be for the best. And I have to tell you, the top fashion houses employ designers all the time, and they're delighted just to be there. They don't even consider the possibility of using their own name, not when they're just starting out.'

Margaret looked at her. She wanted to say, 'But you're not one of the top fashion houses. You're a little boutique on the Lisburn Road in Belfast that nobody's ever heard of, and these are my designs and they should carry my name.'

Instead she said, 'I understand completely. But I'll have to think about it.'

Emma nodded. 'We'd really like to get started as soon as we can.'

'Absolutely,' said Margaret.

Five minutes later, they'd hugged and said their goodbyes. But outside the shop, Margaret found that she was shaking. Her legs felt suddenly weak. She hated the fact that she was still called Margaret Gilmore, because it reminded her of that creep she'd married. But it was still her name, and she would be damned if she was going to give it up for Emma bloody Cochrane, *darling*.

47

Rest in Peace

The call came shortly after midnight on a Friday, long after Martin Brown, the British Ambassador to Colombia, had let the staff go home. He was already dozing off in the master bedroom of his official residence in Bogotá. A fan spun relentlessly above him, like a crashed helicopter, but never seemed to make the room any cooler. He found the heat oppressive but the women beautiful. There was one beside him in the bed right now. She had lovely olive skin, and in his half-asleep state he began to wonder how the name Olive had ever come to represent plainness in British women. He tried hard to think of anyone even remotely pretty who had ever been called Olive. It wasn't a name you heard any more. Like Bertha and Cecil . . .

He was still thinking about names, and only vaguely aware of a ringing sensation, when the olive-skinned girl growled angrily and snatched the receiver off the bedside table and spat something guttural into it. Then she listened for a moment and wordlessly began to tap the receiver on the Ambassador's brow, each tap a little harder. Eventually his eyes opened.

'What?' he mumbled, batting at his head as if a big fly in steel boots was dancing on his forehead. Then he focused enough to become aware of the girl glowering down at him. She wasn't much more than seventeen. She had cost him the equivalent of £5.50; she was cheaper than cocaine. Brown groggily took the receiver.

'Ambassador Brown?'

'Yes? What time is it?'

'Ambassador Brown, this is Doctor Mendoza at La Picota prison. I regret to inform you that the British citizen Redmond O'Boyle died this evening.'

'Oh Christ,' said Brown.

The Ambassador got off the phone as quickly as he could, then hustled the olive girl out of bed. She wasn't happy at all, but was placated by another £5.50. He let her out of the back door himself, then called his driver. By the time he'd showered and changed into a dark suit his car was waiting out front. The journey to La Picota could take up to two hours during the day, depending on the traffic, but he was whisked there in thirty minutes on largely empty roads. On arrival he was hurried into the administrative block, then ushered into a small office. Dr Mendoza introduced himself, then nodded at the tanned young woman sitting opposite him.

'And you've met Miss O'Rourke. Sin Fine.'

'*Sinn Fein*,' Siobhan corrected.

'Yes, of course,' said the Ambassador.

Siobhan wiped at a tear. 'Poor, poor Redmond.'

'It is unfortunate.'

'It's a bloody tragedy!'

He blinked at her for several moments, then returned his attention to the doctor. 'You say it was an infection?'

'Yes, Ambassador – regrettable but unfortunately very common. It is the climate. And the prison, it is not perfect, no? I signed the death certificate at ten-thirty p.m. Now if you will accompany me, you may examine the body.'

Dr Mendoza led them down a short corridor. Flies buzzed. Brown's suit was already stuck to him. As they walked he noted Siobhan's flowing earth-mother skirt and cheesecloth shirt. No bra.

Dr Mendoza nodded at the guard standing outside the makeshift morgue and opened the door. Brown wondered why they needed a guard outside a morgue, but didn't ask. It was Colombia. Inside, it was scarcely any cooler. A young nurse sat by a trolley on which there was a body covered by a green sheet.

Dr Mendoza said, 'Maria?'

The nurse nodded, stood, took a deep breath then pulled back the sheet far enough to reveal Redmond O'Boyle's face.

The Ambassador had been in this job for many years, in many countries, and had had to bear witness to many sudden and tragic deaths of British citizens. Experience had taught him never to actually look at the corpse. He always suffered nightmares afterwards, sometimes for weeks and months. It simply wasn't worth it. And what did he know about these poor dead people? What difference would his staring into their still faces make to their loved ones? None at all. So he merely tutted sympathetically and focused on the young nurse holding the sheet up. She really was very pretty. Olive, he thought.

There was a sudden flash of light. Brown's head shot to his left.

'Please – no!' Dr Mendoza shouted, waving angrily at Siobhan.

She had a disposable camera in her hand. 'Just one more,' she said quite calmly.

'Really, I must insist,' said Dr Mendoza.

'What on earth?' said the Ambassador.

Siobhan changed her angle. 'We must have a record of this. It's like Che Guevara.'

She flashed once more before Dr Mendoza stepped in front of her. 'No camera,' he said. Then he nodded at Maria, and she quickly dropped the sheet back down over the corpse.

'Really,' said the Ambassador, 'this is most inappropriate.' He didn't like her at all. They had had several brief telephone conversations about Redmond O'Boyle since she'd arrived in the country, and she had always come across as rather haughty and insincere; in reality, that was *his* job. Also, there always seemed to be water lapping in the background, as if she was talking to him from a lilo. 'The poor man should be allowed his dignity,' said the Ambassador.

Siobhan exploded: 'A dignity you robbed him of by allowing him to die in this rat-hole!'

The Ambassador shook his head sadly.

'Just you wait!' Siobhan shouted. 'Don't you realise how bad this is going to look in the newspapers back home?'

'Not in the papers I read.'

Siobhan glared at him, then slipped the camera back into her handbag.

Dr Mendoza raised his hands apologetically to the Ambassador, then said, 'Now if we can go back to my office, there are some papers to sign, then I can release the body to the mortuary.'

'If you don't mind,' said the Ambassador, 'I'd much rather you released the body into my custody.'

Dr Mendoza glanced automatically at Nurse Maria, his boss in the FARC guerrillas, then shook his head. 'That is impossible, Ambassador. There are certain . . .'

'Nonsense, Doctor. Whether I like it or not, Mr O'Boyle was a British citizen and I have a duty of care to the family. I must take responsibility for the body.'

'Ambassador, you misunderstand. There are procedures which must be carried out if the body is not to—'

'Doctor Mendoza, they can just as easily be carried out on sovereign British territory. Mr O'Boyle passed away in your care, and although we do not doubt for one moment your own thoughts on the cause of his demise, we must satisfy ourselves – on behalf of his family, of course – that this was indeed the cause. We will fly in our own pathologist. It is standard practice, I assure you. I'm sure you'll concur with me on this, Siobhan?'

'Concur that you should seize our martyr's corpse?'

Ambassador Brown shook his head. 'Really, Siobhan. You're staying at the Hilton, aren't you? Do *you* want to take him?'

She blanched at this. 'Well, of course not, but that doesn't mean I should trust him to you.'

The Ambassador turned back to the doctor. 'Obviously I understand your concerns, Doctor. If it's a problem, then let me speak to your superior. I'm sure we can get this cleared up quickly.'

Mendoza's mouth opened slightly, but he was lost for words. The fact was that Redmond O'Boyle was as alive as any of them, merely drugged to give the effect of death. If the Ambassador had felt for a pulse, he would have found it. Dr Mendoza glanced again at Maria, who gave a short nod.

The doctor sighed. 'Very well, Ambassador, if you will accept full responsibility, I will sign the body over to you.'

The Ambassador nodded curtly. Dr Mendoza hurried out of the room, followed by Nurse Maria. Siobhan gave him a hard look, then patted the camera in her pocket and followed. As the door swung closed Brown caught the briefest glimpse of Mendoza and his nurse gesticulating angrily at each other.

Alone, the Ambassador stood looking down at the outline on the trolley. It appeared that for the next several days he would be sharing his official residence with the mouldering corpse of Redmond O'Boyle. There would be no more sleep for the Ambassador now. How ironic that a man who had claimed to be on a bird-watching tour was about to be picked apart by the vultures of the press.

48
The Marsh of Time

They say that time is a great healer, but they never specify exactly how much time – days or weeks, months or years. Jimmy 'Marsh' Mallow was a methodical man whose career lived or died by evidence and certainty, but there was no certainty to his current situation, a widower with his wife in an urn in the wardrobe, no evidence that he was ever going to feel better about losing the woman he had loved, and treated so miserably. There was a massive hole in his life which he filled with work. He worked more overtime than anyone in the Department, and he pursued Pink Harrison relentlessly.

The gangster had run out of fingers to have in pies. Toes, even. As if being a paramilitary kingpin, drug dealer and dispenser of arbitrary street justice was not enough, he had connections to literally dozens of businesses which were either legal but used for money laundering, or semi-legal and keeping just one step in front of the law. Marsh was sure he was only aware of about a quarter of them. To make matters worse, Pink had for the past eighteen months been an Official Unionist councillor. There was something very 'Pink' about the fact that he had chosen the Official Unionists – and it was very much *his* choice – and not one of the really hardline Parties which were little more than fronts for the paramilitaries. No, Pink had chosen to throw his lot in where the money still lay, where influence wasn't about shouting through a megaphone, it was much more subtle. The Unionist Party was looking for a saviour, and it was misguided enough, and just desperate enough, to believe that Pink might have changed his spots. A physical impossibility, of course. Leopards creep up on you. Then they eat you.

Jimmy Mallow sat in his car opposite *Lemon Grass*, a smart restaurant close enough to Queen's University to be trendy, but too expensive to attract students as customers. He was thinking about his wife and how they'd never really gone out for meals. It was always home cooking. He liked it that way, and he had presumed she had as well.

But now that he thought about it, he wondered why he had never taken her out to restaurants like *Lemon Grass*. He had always used the excuse that it wasn't safe for him to go out somewhere conspicuous: between the first course and dessert, word could have gone out and by the time they returned to their car there could easily have been a gunman lying in wait to blow their heads off. That excuse had carried him through the 1970s, maybe the 1980s. He had seen too many colleagues die. Friends who'd let their guards down; who didn't always check under the car. He had been careful. But maybe too careful – certainly in the years since the Ceasefire. He tried to think of treats they had shared as a family, but could hardly think of a single one that didn't involve being in the house, in front of the telly. No drives in the country, no picnics. *Too dangerous*. No late-night shopping for Christmas presents. *Too dangerous*. No trips to the cinema. *Never know who's waiting in the dark.* They had lived like prisoners. He was a cop, fighting for something that he had never experienced – a quiet, normal family life. No wonder his daughter had upped sticks at the first possible opportunity.

Oh, daughter of mine.

But *this* is *your* fault.

Marsh unfolded the sheet he'd printed out, a head and shoulders shot of a woman called Linda Wray. Over the years he must have looked at ten thousand perp sheets just like this. Put so many men and women away. She had that rabbit-in-the-headlights look. Short hair, a sharp nose. Early forties. He was good at faces: pick them out in a crowd, no trouble. How many stakeouts had he gone on where he had a sheet just like this, and the photo was invariably years out of date, the hair different, or gone, yet he could still pick them out, still zoom in like a seagull at a dump. He was the best. He hadn't lost it. He scanned down the information, looking for her previous convictions, then he laughed out loud and slapped the wheel. There were no convictions. There were *hobbies*. There was no list of time served, there was *star sign*, and *favourite movies*. Christ, his daughter was right, he had to get out more.

His Jag was six months old now, blue. The tax was up to date. The inside was immaculate. There was a CD player which held five discs in the glove compartment. He was currently listening to a CD of the Rolling Stones live. It had been recorded recently and the sound was perfect. He liked 'Angie' and 'Brown Sugar' and 'Satisfaction'. Some of the young pups he worked with now wouldn't have believed he liked his rock'n'roll. Jimmy Marsh Mallow was feared throughout the Department; he didn't wear a uniform, but he might as well have done. He looked starched. He looked like someone who went to church every Sunday and liked easy listening music, or Country, or both. He looked straight. He *had* in fact gone to church every week with Lauren, but hadn't bothered since. When he had gone, he'd prayed with his eyes open. Jimmy Marsh Mallow had seen too many horrors to believe that there was a God.

Jimmy folded the sheet and slipped it inside his jacket. He checked the dashboard clock. Eight thirty-one. She was a minute late.

Linda Wray had sent him a chatty email and suggested this restaurant. He had responded with equal enthusiasm. He had raged at his daughter about hooking him up with *Let's Be Mates* but hadn't been able to resist looking at the three responses he had already received. Of the three of them, this one looked the least desperate. She worked for an estate agent. She liked long walks. Jimmy tried to think of the last time he'd had a long walk. He wasn't unfit. He worked out in the gym at the office. He was *tough*, tough as f***ing nails. He just didn't like to go out. He didn't like to be seen. He wasn't paranoid; it was just a hangover from the old days. He knew things weren't quite so bad now, but he still had enemies – new ones, and old ones with good memories. Why give them the opportunity? Why expose himself? Linda Wray said she liked The Beatles. There, there was something to talk about. And she loved *Casablanca* and *The Cincinnati Kid*. Something else. His full name was James Michael Mallow, but Lauren, to protect his identity, had filled in the on-line form as James Michael. Like George Michael, she'd quipped. It wasn't a lie – it was just an edited version of his life, like the rest of the info she'd provided. *A widower.* Truth. *A Civil Servant.* True, kind of. *Interested in – photography.* Yes, but mostly surveillance. *In property.* Yes, but mostly to do with confiscating it. *Outgoing personality?* Yes, particularly in an interview room, when he could go through you like a ton of bricks.

Eight thirty-five. Five minutes late.

Then he saw her, hurrying along the footpath. Her hair was longer. She was thinner of face. Even from this distance, she looked prettier in real life. She stopped short of the restaurant door, opened her handbag, took out a compact, examined her reflection, fixed her lipstick, patted her hair down. She put a hand on the door, took a deep breath, then pulled it open. Nerves.

Jimmy Marsh Mallow took his own deep breath. He reached for the door handle, hesitated. He could see her through the restaurant's front window, handing her coat to the maitre d', then being led to a table. She was smiling, making small talk.

Jimmy started the engine. He looked at her once more, her fingers smoothing down the tablecloth, then drove home.

49

M & Emma

The only thing Margaret could thank God for, in retrospect, was the fact that she wasn't still wearing her Primark security guard uniform when Emma Cochrane, of *Emma Cochrane* and greedy bitch fame, came marching up to her front door. The rest she could quite comfortably curse Him out for – the fact that she was wearing a horrendous *101 Dalmations*-style dressing-gown, the fact that she was living in near squalor in a rundown part of town, the fact that she hardly earned a living wage, the fact that she'd spent several days in a carrot-cake coma, the fact that she'd been forced into sleeping with her ex-husband in order to settle her hospital bill, the fact that her dreams of being a world-class fashion designer to rival Donatella Versace or Giorgio Armani or Stella McCartney – or even whoever the hell designed the dresses she'd tried to rip off from Primark – were on the verge of extinction. All of these things and many more. But the most pressing was the fact that the boutique owner with her finger on the doorbell was clearly here to force a showdown, or read the riot act, or demand to know why Margaret was throwing the opportunity of a lifetime back in her face.

Fear. That was why. Margaret knew that.

She might have kicked up a fuss about the name Emma wanted to use – anything but Margaret's, basically – but it was really all about fear. She was scared to grasp this opportunity. She was not worthy. She felt like one of those sad women who spend their days reading sexed-up versions of Mills & Boon novels, dreaming of being swept up by their prince but who would, in reality, run a mile if he came knocking.

Now Emma Cochrane was banging on the front window. Margaret could just see the stick-thin boutique owner through the crack in the kitchen door.

Oh God. What am I going to do?

181

She turned and despairingly surveyed the tragedy around her. The Pisa Tower of dishes in the sink. The Rice Krispies scattered across the table, the most recent blowing gently back and forth in the ever-changing draught from the cracked back window; others stuck fast for weeks. The bottom layer of a Black Magic box lying on the floor by the pedal bin, with two uneaten black cherry sweets sitting abandoned in their plastic nest.

Emma knocked again on the window. Margaret wondered if it would be easier just to let her in, then kill her. Bludgeon her with something. But she'd been in such a rush to depart the marital home that she'd left all of her knives and most of her cooking utensils behind. If she was going to commit murder, it would be death by potato peeler. Or cheese grater. Far from providing an instant solution, it would require a considerable investment of both brute strength and time. She'd probably have to stop for snacks.

Then her eyes fell on the fridge. It was the one major item she'd insisted on bringing from the old house, but she hadn't yet got around to removing the family snaps stuck to the front – including the one of her and Billy, capturing what she now thought must have been the only occasion on which she had smiled during the last five years of her marriage. He was throwing up, moments after coming off the roller-coaster at Barry's Amusements in Portrush. She'd actually given the camera to someone to take the photo, so keen was she to feature in Billy's moment of supreme embarrassment. Even now, with the enemy at the gates, she smiled at the image of Billy being sick on his favourite suede shoes while still managing to hold his precious tie up and out of the line of fire, and at herself grinning widely and giving a thumbs up.

The doorbell again.

Christ – what was she thinking of? She was being given the chance to become a fashion designer. It was her dream! Did she want to end up with someone like Billy again?

No! This was her chance!

Get your friggin' act together, girl!

Margaret charged across the lounge and yanked open the front door. Emma Cochrane was just climbing into her car. A silver Porsche.

'Emma!'

The boutique owner turned, surprised, then smiled as Margaret hurried towards her.

'Margaret, I thought—'

'I was on the bog!' It was out before she could stop it.

Emma burst out laughing. 'Too much information, darling!' She came forward and gave Margaret a hug, which felt odd, then held her at arm's length. She looked the dalmation dressing-gown up and down. 'Please tell me it's not one of yours.'

Margaret smiled as she shook her head. 'Of course not.'

'Margaret, sweetie – I must have phoned a hundred times.'

'I know. Well, actually – twenty-three times. Or twenty-four if it was you doing the heavy breathing.'

'So you were in, but avoiding me. Huffing.'

'I wasn't huffing.'

Emma folded her arms. 'No?'

Margaret looked at the pavement. She was also wearing bunny slippers.

Emma said, 'Do you want to do this out here, with half the street watching you?'

'Well, it's probably tidier out here.'

'Oh, stuff and nonsense. Let's have a nice cup of tea.' Emma brushed past her and headed for the front door.

'Emma! Please.' She turned and hurried after her. 'Emma – I've made my mind up.'

'No, you haven't.'

'Yes, I have!'

Emma was through the front door now, and into the living room. There was no hall, as such. After the briefest look around, she began to make her way towards the kitchen, but this time Margaret caught her arm.

'No!' she said firmly. Emma stopped; she raised an eyebrow. 'You sit down,' said Margaret. '*I'll* put the kettle on.'

Margaret pushed her gently down into a chair, then scooted off into the kitchen, quickly closing the door behind her. The living room was a mess, but *nothing* compared to the kitchen. She shouted back in, 'How do you like your tea?'

'Weak,' said Emma, 'like my men.'

Margaret squeezed through the narrowest possible opening with the tray, and set it on the coffee-table. She was using her finest china, which in this case was two mugs; one had *Rangers For Ever* on the side, the other had once been white but was now permanently stained. Three chocolate chip cookies sat on a side plate. Emma picked one up.

'In case you're wondering,' Margaret said, before her guest could take a bite, 'they're supposed to be soft. They're not stale. You get different types of chocolate chip cookies. Some are soft and chewy and some are quite crisp. Those are the soft ones. They're not off.'

Emma took a bite. She sipped her tea. She smiled and said, 'Margaret, what are you so worried about?'

Margaret shrugged. 'What have you got?'

'Margaret, I love your designs. I think we could do something really special.'

'I know that.'

'So what's the problem? Is it just the name?'

'I suppose.'

'I explained to you how important it was to me to hold onto the name.'

'Yes, you did.'

'And you would still walk away?'

Margaret studied the carpet.

'I don't wish to pry, darling, but it seems to me that you don't have much money coming in. And this area – it can't be easy.'

'I'm fine.'

'Well, you don't look fine. This is a marvellous opportunity for you, could lift you out of all this – and I hate to see you throw it away over something so silly.'

'It's not silly to me.'

'I understand that. And that's why I think you should give some ground. If I give some, you give some.'

Margaret's eyes flicked up. 'What will you give?'

'A lot more money upfront. And I'll compromise on the name.'

'Compromise?'

'Yes, compromise. Not capitulate. Louise came up with it. We call the line *M & Emma*. M for Margaret, Emma for me. *M & Emma*. It's catchy, and it's a true partnership. You'll have a one-third ownership.'

'One half would be a partnership.'

'But you like the name?'

'I can put up with it.'

'So we have a deal?'

'You're giving in on the fifty-fifty?'

'Yes, I am.'

'Why would you do that so easily?'

'The truth?'

Margaret nodded.

'Because at the moment I don't own *any* of it. You could just walk away with those designs and take them somewhere else and still own one hundred per cent of them. I'm not giving you fifty per cent, Margaret, you're giving it to me. I'm the winner here.'

'That, or you're just a fantastic bullshit artist.'

'Well, that's for you to decide, but I think we'd make a fantastic team.' She held out her hand. '*M & Emma*, darling, what do you say?'

Margaret stared down at Emma's fine, shapely hand and manicured fingers, then at her own, bitten to the quick.

'Bloody hell,' she said.

50

A Past Master

Mark could scarcely believe it. Here he was with the legendary Pink Harrison at a secluded table in *Past Masters*, the exclusive private members' club, smoking a cigar and drinking Irish whiskey, swapping political theories and insider gossip as if they were firm friends. Sitting at tables all around, or staring down from portraits on the wall, were the movers and shakers of the Northern Irish business world. Every few minutes some familiar face or other would come up and say hello to Pink, shake his hand warmly – and then Pink would introduce Mark, *little me*, as a future star of the Party.

Mark had to admit he had harboured certain reservations – or indeed experienced sheer horror – when Pink had first been revealed as his political mentor. After all, it was Pink Harrison, *Headline* Harrison, paramilitary leader, gangster and deliverer of summary justice standing beaming before him. But now that he thought about it, who better to guide him? Better Pink Harrison than some faceless nonentity who was never going to rise above debating dog-fouling at the local council. And if Pink did have a shady past, so what? Hadn't McGuinness come from an equally dubious background, and he'd ended up Education Minister. The times certainly were a-changin', and if you had a short memory and no personal grievance, why not give them a second chance? And at least Pink Harrison had been consistent in his beliefs, not blowing this way and that like their previous leaders. Little wonder the Party had got itself into such a state. It was crying out for someone like Pink Harrison. And now, Mark Beck.

Pink offered him another cigar; Mark declined. Pink stuffed it into Mark's breast pocket.

It was like déjà vu. Like a scene from some movie. A Western. He smiled to himself. That's what he was in, a Western. No – a Northern. The Wild North. It was finally being tamed and civilised. He was a homesteader. No, a railroad man. Which made Pink – Custer or Buffalo Bill or Sitting Bull – someone brave and fearless.

Crazy Horse. Drinking firewater.

He knew he was drunk. He wasn't used to whiskey. He leaned forward, gave a little hand signal for Pink to move closer. 'I gotta ask . . .'

Pink raised his hand. 'Have I really changed? Said goodbye to the bomb and the bullet? Can a man really change? Pull on a new persona the way I pulled on this nice pink jumper in the morning? Well, let me ask you this, Mark. Do I really want to change? Do I want to change the fact that I've fought to protect our way of life? That I've fought to protect our community? People deserted this Party because it didn't represent them any more, Mark. It got fat and lazy and out of touch, but deep down, at the grassroots – that's where I come from, that's where my people come from – we still believe in the Party and what it stands for. That's why I'm here, not just to reclaim past glories, but to lead it forward, do you understand what I'm saying?'

'Sure,' said Mark, 'but I was only asking where the toilets were.' He laughed out loud, and immediately regretted it. Anger shot across Pink's face.

Oh Christ, what have I said?

Pink pointed. 'Over there,' he said.

Mark tried to mumble an apology, but the words wouldn't form up right. He stumbled slightly over his chair, then hurried away. When he reached the toilets he went straight into a cubicle, locked the door, and sat down heavily.

Not smart, not smart at all. Get your act together, he told himself. Go back out there, say you're sorry. God, it had all been going so well.

When he eventually opened the cubicle door, Pink was standing there, arms folded, leaning against the sinks, clearly waiting for him.

'Oh,' said Mark.

'Aren't you going to flush?'

For a moment Mark didn't fully comprehend, then he nodded and turned back into the cubicle. But before he could reach the handle he was yanked suddenly backwards, then hurled forwards again; in the same movement his feet were whipped from under him and he was plunged headfirst into the toilet bowl. As he opened his mouth to scream, it filled with his own urine.

Mark heaved and fought at the same time, but he was helpless. Pink plunged him in once, twice, three times, then held him up by his hair. 'You want to play the funny bugger with me?!' he screamed.

'N . . . n . . .'

Mark coughed up, then as he gasped for another breath, Pink forced his head back into the toilet bowl.

This time he flushed it.

Mark felt his whole life pass before him. It was comprised mostly of paper clips and Toffee Crisps. His hands fought for a grip on the smooth circumference of the toilet bowl, but Pink was overpowering. Again he was plunged into the maelstrom. Then out again. As the water poured out of his ears, Pink yelled: 'You think I lived through thirty years of shit to have the piss taken out of me by a little prick like you?'

'No . . . Pink . . . honest,' Mark gasped.

This time Pink pulled him backwards, then hurled him against the thin metal wall of the toilet cubicle. Water sprayed around them.

'You gonna sell me down the river to the cops?!'

'No!'

'You breathe a word about this, you'll end up under the Lisburn flyover!'

'I wouldn't! I swear to—'

'What year was Partition?!'

'What?'

'Partition between the North and South! What year?'

'1920! But what's—'

'Name the last three leaders of the party!'

'Last . . .'

Pink battered him against the cubicle wall again, then slapped him hard. 'Last three leaders – tell me now!'

'Empey! Trimble! Molyneaux!'

Pink grabbed him by the lapels and thrust him out of the cubicle with considerable force. Mark stumbled across to the sinks; he caught a momentary glimpse of his dank-haired self before he was spun around again. Pink stuck his face into his and spat: 'I'm going to take my gun out now and blow your f***in' head off if you don't tell me about Office Twelve!'

'Office Twelve?!'

'Tell me about it. Tell me now, you little piece of s**t!'

Mark did not doubt for one moment that Pink had a gun, nor that he had the capacity to use it. But he had a sudden, miraculous moment of clarity.

It's a test. It's a god-damned test!

Pink's reaction to his cheeky riposte had been so monstrously over the top that there had to be more to it. *He can't be that much of a psycho!* This wasn't life and death, he was merely sorting the wheat from the chaff. Seeing if he had a backbone!

But what was the correct answer? Give up the information Pink obviously knew he had, or hold back?

'So help me!' Pink exploded. He held Mark with one hand and began to pat his pockets with the other. 'I will blow your eyeballs out of your bloody sockets! Now tell me, you buckin' little midget creep!'

'I've never heard of Office Twelve!' Mark suddenly bellowed. 'I don't know what the hell you're talking about!' He slapped Pink's hand away then shoved him in the chest. As Pink took a surprised step backwards, Mark made a charge for the door. With every step he expected to be felled – chopped or stabbed or shot. But he made it to the door and pulled it open.

Then he was out, hurrying down the short corridor and turning into the main bar, already scanning for the quickest route to the exit.

But they were waiting for him. It seemed like every single member of *Past Masters* was standing there.

Mark stopped, dripped, and stared around at their grim faces. There were footsteps behind him. Mark glanced round as Pink approached. There wasn't any point in running. There were too many of them.

He jumped as Pink brought his arm down forcefully on his shoulder. He tried to move, but an iron grip kept him rooted firmly to the spot.

'Don't you know, Mark, that in politics, no one can hear you scream?'

Mark stared into his murderous eyes. Pink glared back for an ominous few seconds, then broke off to address his audience.

'Gentlemen,' said Pink, 'he has passed with flying colours!'

They burst into applause. Suddenly he was confronted with a sea of smiling faces.

Pink hugged him close. 'I knew you had it in you,' he beamed. 'Didn't doubt you for a moment.'

Mark nodded thankfully and forced himself to smile, but his legs felt weak; his heart was thumping out of control.

Another, vaguely familiar, voice came from behind. He turned and saw Steven, from Office 12, the Department of Re-Education, with his hand extended. 'Welcome to the Party, Mark,' he said.

51
Knowing Me, Knowing You, Ahaaa

Jack Finucane and Maeve O'Boyle actually lived quite close to each other in West Belfast, but Maeve was astute enough to know it wouldn't look good to be spotted being picked up for a date, even by one of their own. Only a few days ago the IRA had finally announced, after more than a decade of the Ceasefire, that it was going to dump its arms. Theoretically it was all *completely* over, but everyone knew that wasn't the case. There were dozens of splinter groups who would continue to rattle their collection tins. And to them Redmond O'Boyle was a star, and she was his wife and she should remain good and true. So she had to be careful. She didn't want her windows put in or her knees cracked with hurley sticks; she didn't want *Irma La Deuce* burned down. Instead, the couple arranged to meet at a restaur-ant Jack recommended.

Lemon Grass gave Maeve a little frisson of excitement. She hadn't eaten in a proper restaurant in years. Jack, also, gave her a little frisson, or 'the horn' as she might have described it to Margaret. He sounded like he came from Belfast, but there was something in his colouring, his tousled hair, his dark eyes, that spoke of hot sun and mad passion. As if his father had been a merchant seaman, his mother a Brazilian beauty. Or, she supposed, the other way round.

As far as possible they kept off the elephant in the bedroom that was Redmond O'Boyle. Jack talked about carrot cake the way other men obsessed about Manchester United. But not just carrot cake. He had a consuming passion for all types of food, and dreamed of one day opening a restaurant of his own in the centre of Belfast. Not just a carrot-cake café. He wanted to create his own lines and market them internationally. He wanted to be a brand. He wanted some old woman to be pushing her trolley through Tesco one day and have her stop one of the staff to ask, 'Where's the Jack Finucane?'

'I want it to become a generic term for quality food.'

Maeve smiled. 'That would be fantastic. Although the name . . . I don't know.'

'What's wrong with it?'

'It's just not very . . . ' She was going to say sexy, but decided against it. 'Catchy.'

'Is *Bernard Matthews*? Or *Linda McCartney*?'

'But that's all crap. This should suggest quality.'

'What about *Paul Newman* – good quality and it goes to charity. And Lloyd Someone.

'Grossman,' said Maeve.

'Grossman. That's upmarket.'

'And George Formby.'

'George Formby? With the ukulele?'

'No, with the lean mean, grill machine,' Maeve said.

'George Foreman. The boxer.'

'Big fat coloured fella who never grilled a thing in his life?'

'That's him.'

'And Duncan, of course,' she added.

'Duncan?'

'Duncan Doughnut.'

He laughed out loud. Some of the other diners looked round. Maeve smiled at one of them, a woman sitting by herself six tables away who smiled quickly back then returned her attention to slowly revolving the stem of her wine glass. Maeve leaned forward and whispered: 'What do you think her story is?'

He studied Linda Wray. 'Waiting for her boyfriend?'

'It has to be more exciting than that. I think this is where she used to come with her lover, and one night he didn't turn up and she never heard from him again, but still she turns up here every night at the same time, hoping he'll appear. Perhaps he was killed in a tragic accident.'

'A tragic *skiing* accident,' Jack suggested. 'Although if it was round here it would have to be that fake bloody ski-jump in – where is it?'

Maeve shook her head. 'Never done it.'

'Oh, it's *fantastic*. I go to Switzerland twice a year.'

'Well for some.' She looked away. The woman was rolling up the corners of her napkin, then smoothing them out.

'You should come.'

'To Switzerland? We always go to Portstewart. Used to.'

Jack smiled. 'There's a whole big world out there, Maeve.'

Maeve nodded. He was lovely. And yet if there was a whole big world out there, and he went skiing twice a year, and had a fashionable carrot-cake café, what was he doing here, sitting with her? What did *she* have to offer? She'd told him she was really a security guard in Primark and that she'd been chancing her arm over the compensation, given up all that information without her arm being twisted at all, because she really was attracted to him. But the question was, what on earth did he see in *her*?

Her mobile rang. She ignored it. Their meals came. Maeve had steak. He had pasta.

'So,' Maeve said, 'you're divorced. What happened? Couldn't she keep up on the slopes?'

'She had an affair.'

'Oh.'

'On the slopes.'

'Seriously?'

'Well, not literally on the slopes, you'd freeze your bollocks off. But yeah, more or less.'

'And how did you find out? I'm sorry. It's none of my business.'

'Yes, it is. You should know. I visit a lot of restaurants when I'm away. Research – the grand scheme. I left my wife in the ski-resort and was travelling to see a chef in Berne when I got a call from him to say he was unwell. So I turned round and went back to the cabin – and there they were. Their skis were outside, side by side.'

'Was it the ski instructor?'

'"Fraid so.'

'My God, it's like something you make up.' There was a glint in his eye and she said, 'You *are* making this up.'

He laughed. 'Okay. So it was her driving instructor.'

'Naw.'

'Seriously. A Volkswagen with a giant L on top of it parked outside the house. So we got divorced. On the bright side, when she got the car, at least she knew how to drive it.' He gave a little shrug. 'Nah. You know. We grew apart. Didn't get on. Acrimonious. My solicitor described her as "a pain in the hole". And that pretty much sums her up.'

'You must have loved her once.'

'Well, you would think that. But I don't think I did. We were very young. It was about sex, and I think she wanted to be the first one in her class to have a baby.'

'You have a baby?'

Jack shook his head. 'Didn't work out.'

'Didn't work out for me either. Ironic that, isn't it? A terrorist like Redmond? First time he's ever shot blanks.'

Jack roared at that. He had a great laugh. And strong-looking arms. She wanted to be enveloped in them. She wanted him to lick Pooh

Bear ice cream off her breasts and do kinky things with a Cadbury's Flake. She wanted to spend Sunday mornings making Rice Krispie buns with their children. She wanted them to go skiing, her and Jack and all four of their cute kids.

Her mobile rang again. This time she switched it off. They ate dessert. Jack ordered a slice of carrot cake.

'Are you never off duty?' Maeve joked.

He smiled, and gave it eight out of ten. She had Sticky Toffee Pudding.

When he excused himself to go to the Gents, she wanted to follow him and leap on him, but she restrained herself. They would probably break the toilet. Or be captured on CCTV and their antics displayed on an obscure digital channel. She wondered what it would be like to kiss him, and if he would try. Perhaps he would be too much of a gentleman. How would he react if she clamped him in a headlock and planted one on him? She wanted to invite him back to her place for coffee and sex, but there was too much danger of them being lynched. He was single, he had his own apartment. She imagined it was spotless, with a glass coffee-table and glossy magazines sitting in neat piles. There would be no football posters or Virgin Mary icon staring down from the wall. No great heap of video tapes by the telly. A white leather suite. There would be no KitKat wrappers stuffed down the back.

She glanced back down the restaurant, and saw that the single woman was gone now. Poor cow, thought Maeve. She took another sip of her wine, then lifted her handbag. She checked her lipstick and make-up and patted down her mane. When he returned, Jack had already settled the bill. 'I hate all that standing around,' he said, 'trying to catch the waiter's attention, sorting out the tip. When I open my restaurant . . .'

'The international one.'

'. . . You'll pay before you eat, then you can relax and enjoy it.'

'What if you don't like the food? Or you poison someone?'

'It took us all night to get back to the poison.' But he was smiling. 'Like you said, I'll have a disclaimer. *You take your life in your hands, but the chances are you'll enjoy it.*'

'And you tip before the meal as well?'

'Yes, you do. And if they don't measure up you get to slap their faces on the way out. They'll have to line up.'

'And what if you're just some sort of pervert, and like slapping people.'

'Then you'll have a grand time, won't you?'

He held her coat for her. When they were outside, she slipped her arm through his. They walked down past Morrison's, where she usually drank with Margaret. They reached Shaftesbury Square, with Kentucky Fried Chicken on one corner. Behind and above them, a huge video screen silently played out the day's news over the quiet hum of the late traffic. It was a warm, pleasant night for walking. They were both slightly drunk. She was just in the middle of saying something as they reached the far side of the square when he gently caught hold of her and kissed her lightly on the lips. They separated briefly, then she moved forwards, already bending her back slightly, happy to melt into him. Her eyes flicked up, anxious to record the scene in her own mind, because it was fantastic and dreamy and she wanted to remember it forever, but in drinking in his marvellous, slightly flushed face her eyes couldn't help but also be drawn to the kaleidoscope of colours dancing on the giant video screen behind; the talking head, the scrolling text and then, suddenly, a thirty-foot image of her husband lying dead on a slab in darkest Colombia.

Maeve screamed.

52

The Body

Cars were burned overnight in West Belfast, and wisps of smoke still hung over the area as Jimmy Marsh Mallow drove along the motorway to work the next morning. It was a reflexive thing, this rioting when one of their own died. Barely half an hour after the photo of Redmond O'Boyle flat out on a slab appeared on TV, dozens of teenagers erupted onto the streets, burning, smashing, throwing, yelling. Jimmy didn't mind that much. It was a working-class letting off of steam. In South Belfast they might have gone out for a jog, or had a massage. The rioting was easily contained, and both sides were happy with that. For the kids it was an excuse to respond to petty grievances – smashing a neighbour's window, setting fire to a shop where they'd been caught stealing, throwing a petrol bomb at the Sinn Fein rep who acted up worse than the cops. Half of them didn't know who Redmond O'Boyle was. It was an excuse.

Halfway there, Marsh got a call redirecting him to the Ormeau Embankment. In the old days it had been pretty much of a wasteland, running along the edge of the River Lagan as it wound its way calmly down to the sea, a place where things happened in the dead of night and the cry of seagulls and wild dogs brought anxious relatives looking for missing loved ones in the early light, but in the past ten years dozens of apartment blocks had sprung up, the whole area gentrified beyond recognition. It was a good thing, of course. He knew that. In fact, he and the wife had looked over one of the apartments, with one eye on their retirement, but he talked her out of it. Too expensive.

There were half a dozen other police cars there, plus an ambulance and some TV people. Scenes-of-Crime tape had been set up at either end of a 100-metre stretch of riverside walkway.

Gary McBride, the DI he worked most closely with, stiffened visibly as he approached. Everyone did. It was a good thing, Marsh thought, to inspire this kind of reaction. They weren't his friends. He didn't have to impress them with the warmth of his personality; all he had to do was make sure they did their jobs properly. And sometimes he had to show them. He'd been doing it so long it was second nature to jump into the heart of an investigation. Only now he had to keep reminding himself to give others their head.

'Where is he?' Marsh asked.

No greeting. No handshake, familiar wink, no coffee thrust into his hand, no joshing over last night's football or cracks about another terrorist stiff on a slab.

'Along here,' said Gary. 'Guy out walking his dog found him, tangled up in weeds.'

Marsh followed him along the embankment. He nodded to a Forensics guy who then stood back to show them the body.

'Christ,' said Marsh.

'Aye.'

No head. No feet. No hands. Naked. Bloated from the river.

'Anything?'

'Fifteen, sixteen maybe. Been in the water a few days. Divers on their way. Going through Missing Persons, but it'll take a while. Most of them run away, that age.'

Caroline had run away, he remembered that. Fifteen. Sixteen. A fight over what? Spending too much money on make-up? Not phoning home three times a night when she was out? You could argue she'd never stopped running.

Gary said the press wanted a word.

'You do it,' said Marsh.

Gary looked surprised, then hurried away. He faced the cameras and said what a shocking crime it was, and appealed for witnesses, and said there was no place in society for anyone who could do something like this, though he didn't specify what the *this* was or say that divers were about to start searching for hands and feet and a head. This was somebody's son, somebody's brother, he said.

Marsh stared down at the water. He felt bad about last night. He wondered how the woman had felt, sitting in the restaurant all by herself. She'd looked nice enough. But what was he supposed to talk to her about? Movies? How far would that get them? How long before he got onto the subject of his wife? Why did she need to hear all that? And worse, what if she'd had a similar, sad story? You didn't get to their age without baggage, without divorce and death and disease. What could be worse than sitting in a restaurant with a complete stranger, taking it in turns to unburden yourself, neither of them particularly interested in the other's story, but nodding and making sympathetic noises, waiting for the next opportunity to dive in and steer the woe back to their own personal experience.

No. Better off by himself. Listening to the music.

Still, he'd left her sitting there. Hadn't even sent an email. Should have come up with some excuse.

Lauren would be on the phone soon, all full of the joys of spring. 'What was she like? What did you talk about? Did you snog her, Daddy, did you?'

Snog. What a word. When was the last time he'd snogged anyone? Did kissing your wife on the brow, on her cold brow, for the last time, did that count? No, of course not.

He missed kissing his wife. He missed listening to music with her. He missed saying who'd written the song and where it was recorded and who did or didn't play on the track. She wasn't interested, he knew that, but she pretended. In the early days she'd sit for hours while he played her this or that. Not so much in the later years. But still.

Jimmy Marsh Mallow caught his breath. *Christ.* He had a lump in his throat. He gripped the handrail, stared down into the murky water. It had been his personal mantra during the bad years, to treat every death as if it was one of his own – that's what had driven him to such success. That poor sod with his head blown off, that was his son, his brother; you have to find out who did it, you will not rest until an arrest is made. And even the ones who got away, it remained personal for years afterwards. But the years had passed now, and death had finally visited his own home, and now this poor kid, this headless, handless, footless kid lying under a sheet, hardly raised a flurry of interest. Was it indifference? Or was he just numb?

'Divers are here, boss,' said Gary.

Marsh could hardly take his eyes off the water.

'Boss.'

'I hear you.' He turned. He had never been able to tell his wife about *this*, and now he never could.

53

A Shoulder To Cry On

Margaret was never much of a news junkie, so it was only the next morning, sitting in her dalmation dressing-gown in front of *Breakfast*, with a bowl of Special K in her lap, that she discovered that Redmond O'Boyle was dead and that West Belfast had endured a night of rioting. She had in fact been perilously close to it, though blissfully unaware. She'd gone out with Emma to celebrate their new partnership and sworn undying allegiance over several bottles of wine. Emma had chosen a chic new place on the very edge of West Belfast – 'It's wonderful, darling, although another hundred yards down the road and it'd be a chip shop' – and when they'd emerged, the air had been decidedly smoky but Emma had passed it off with a mild admonishment, 'Barbecues, and it's not even summer!' and Margaret had laughed hysterically because she was pissed.

Now, however, with her head rattling, and spooning in the Special K as if it was some kind of cure rather than treated cardboard, she stared in disbelief at the oft-repeated photograph of Redmond O'Boyle dead on a slab in some remote corner of the world, and immediately thought of her colleague Maeve and what she should do. The most practical, and easiest option was to phone, but Maeve's mobile was switched off and her home number wasn't responding. *Damn!*

So she showered and fixed her hair and drove straight into West Belfast, stopping only to peruse the houses on offer in an estate agents in South Belfast. Emma had repeatedly driven home the fact that Margaret lived in a shit-hole and needed to get out *right now*. And with a big fat cheque in her bag, why not? A nice swish apartment somewhere, that's what she needed, somewhere down by the river, quite high up, with views over the city. A penthouse. She liked the sound of that. But then the very next item on the news was about some poor soul being found in the river right where those new apartments were and she laughed immediately at the thought of some grinning estate agent leading viewers out onto the veranda and saying, 'Here's your stunning view out over Belfast, the shipyard where the *Titanic* was built, the beautiful Cave Hill watching over our city, the Lagan winding lazily to the ocean, and just over there the Crime Scene Investigation team trying to solve the mystery of the headless, handless, footless corpse.'

Margaret had no idea where she was driving. All she knew was that there were lots of police on the streets keeping their eyes on teenagers with smoke-blackened faces and tired eyes, and the further in she got, the more lost she became and the fewer police she saw, so that she had to stop every few hundred yards and ask those hard-looking boys if they knew where Maeve's house was. She always added in, 'I'm a friend of the family,' and despite her best efforts, always found herself giving a little wink as if she was in with them on some grand conspiracy.

Eventually, she found her way to Maeve's front door, which was open, and into the house, which was packed with wellwishers and friends and old war buddies. The air was ripe with booze and fags. Gerry Adams was just going out as she was going in. He was looking grave but she still winked at him. If he noticed he didn't respond (probably the botched Botox job). Women were probably winking at him all the time. Then finally she spied Maeve across the small, crowded lounge, and Maeve saw her about the same time and pushed her way over, and they hugged and Margaret tried to make all the usual noises but Maeve shushed her and led her out of the room and up the stairs, past the queue waiting to use the tiny bathroom, and into their bedroom. Maeve closed and locked the door, then sighed and said, 'Thank God.'

'I'm really sorry—' Margaret began, but Maeve cut her off again, with, 'He's such a big ride.'

Clearly it hadn't sunk in, or she was drunk.

'Maeve . . .'

'We went to *Lemon Grass*. I could have jumped him there and then.'

'Maeve?'

'Jack. Jack Finucane – we went on our date last night.'

'But . . . Redmond . . .'

'Like he was watching! Just as we move in for the big snog, Redmond appears right above me. I screamed and screamed!'

'Like a ghost?'

'No – on that giant TV thing in Shaftesbury Square. It was just the shock of it, but that wore off in about twenty minutes.' She made a thumbing gesture downstairs. 'But then all this circus started . . .'

'Well, it's nice that people—'

'Margaret, dear, it's a bloody nightmare. I gave up on Redmond ages ago, and so did most of them down there, but now they're fighting over his corpse like it's the Christmas turkey in the poorhouse.'

Margaret took hold of her hands. 'It's a delayed reaction, love. You're in shock.'

'I'm really not.'

'Yes, you are. Have you heard what happened?'

'Well, I know his arse went septic after he got stabbed, and in the climate out there they couldn't control the infection and it was too much for his heart. He's in the British Embassy. They won't pay to ship him home though, they made that clear. Those lot down there, they'll pay, but I don't want that either. The old fighters want a big military ceremony. I think they just want one last excuse to pull on the black berets and shoot their guns over the coffin. The Shinners just want to wave their fingers and say, "Look, he used to be one of ours but this is what happens to *very naughty boys*".'

'Well, I'm sure you can't afford it.'

Macve looked at the ground.

Margaret couldn't help but blush. She had a cheque for a large amount of money, at least by her standards, burning a hole in her handbag. There were at least a dozen things she'd thought about spending it on, but it's safe to say paying for a dead terrorist to be shipped home from Colombia wasn't one of them. But she was nice, and she felt slightly guilty that she wasn't at least making the offer. Maeve would surely say, 'No, but I appreciate the thought.' But what if she said yes? Margaret really liked Maeve, but she knew for a fact that the people of West Belfast weren't the type to look a gift-horse in the mouth. They would have it straight down to the knacker's yard and sell it for glue. So Margaret sucked on her bottom lip and said nothing.

Maeve looked up from the carpet. 'I haven't told them what I'm going to do yet.'

'What are you going to do?'

'Margaret – they're all waiting for Red to come home so they can start the wake.'

'I thought *that* was the wake.'

'Oh no, that's just the *pre*-wake. The wake'll only start when the body arrives. Then there'll be the *après*-wake – like skiing, I imagine, but colder – after the funeral; that'll be another couple of days. I don't want it, Margaret, none of it. I want my home back.'

'So what are you going to do?'

'I'm going to tell the British Ambassador to have Redmond cremated out there.'

'Oh,' said Margaret.

'You think that's terrible, don't you?'

'No. I don't really know. It just seems . . .'

'Callous.'

'No.'

'I didn't love him, and he betrayed me, and I don't want all the crap that goes with having a martyr in the house.'

'I understand that, love, but still . . .'

'If it was your Billy . . .'

'If it was my Billy I'd have him cremated whether he was dead or not.'

'Well then.'

'I know – but my Billy's not all over the news like your Redmond. What if it turns ugly?'

'Well,' Maeve began, and then hesitated. 'You'll think I'm awful.'

'Tell me.'

'I have a plan. I think it'll keep everyone happy.'

Margaret shook her head. 'It would have to be some plan.'

'I'll let the British Embassy go ahead and cremate him. *Then* I'll announce that they did it without my permission.'

'You can't just—'

'Yes, I can! It'll keep everyone happy! Sinn Fein will have something to moan about and everyone else can go out and have another riot. It's perfect!'

Margaret had never really appreciated how difficult life must have been living in an area like this, and how it couldn't help but corrupt your sense of right and wrong, but looking at Maeve now with her hopeful eyes and absolute incomprehension that there might be anything immoral or soulless about what she was planning to do, she began to understand.

54
A Room With A View

The estate agent Linda Wray had endured a miserable day. Partly it was her own fault, for getting drunk by herself in that restaurant – but who could blame her – but mostly it was because of the police and what they were doing to her. She'd been showing clients around the Towerview Apartments for several weeks now and she had her script off pat. The flats were quite expensive, but they were undoubtedly luxurious – the kitchens especially. None of your MFI tat. She wouldn't go so far as to say that they sold themselves, but the kitchens certainly contributed. What mostly did it was her smooth delivery, her winning smile, her enthusiasm and then finally, when she opened the doors onto the veranda and they got their first look at the view. It was stunning. She always said, 'And at no extra cost . . .' before opening the doors, though of course that was a lie. There was a huge extra cost, it just didn't show up on the paperwork. But today, with her raging hangover, the 'dry bokes' as her mum used to call it, what she especially did not need was a body in the river and the PSNI swamping the whole area, making it look as though the apartments had been thoughtlessly flung up in the middle of a war zone.

Every single one of her clients today had stared down at the crime scene, transfixed, neglecting the beautiful Cave Hill and the harbour and the Waterfront Hall just across the way. People's memories were so short; used to be you'd see that kind of a thing every day, but since The Troubles had ended, any sort of police presence – apart, obviously from in the Wild West – had seemed to evaporate. But now they were very definitely back, buzzing around the corpse like flies and scaring off her clients.

Now, thankfully, with the end of the day in sight, her head finally lifting and only one more client to see, the police were packing up and moving on. With any luck there'd be no trace of them by the time she brought this Walter North out onto the veranda.

She went into the bathroom to freshen up before he arrived, and wondered what he'd be like. Because you never knew when the right one would come along. Maybe one day she'd score the double whammy – sell the property *and* marry the client. It was as good a way as any to meet eligible men – certainly better than that bloody *Let's Be Mates*, sitting in there like a prune all night. Maybe Walter North would be a rich businessman looking to add another property to his portfolio, and in the market for a trophy wife as well. Linda smiled. Trophy wife! She wasn't bad-looking – *age shall not wither her!* – but if she was a trophy, she was the sort that got given out at school sports days, not the European Cup; small and valuable only to the person it was awarded to. She shook her head. She just hoped he wasn't a time-waster. Half her day was taken up with clients who clearly couldn't afford such a property, but just fancied a mosey.

The doorbell went, and there was Walter North, smiling broadly. She smiled back. He was quite nice, albeit a trifle overweight. He seemed momentarily reluctant to enter the apartment, but then she realised he wasn't alone. An elderly woman was just appearing at the top of the stairs.

Walter shook his head. 'She's a marvel – insists on taking the stairs at her age.'

Linda showed them into the apartment, fussing over the old woman, then led them from room to room. Everyone said the same things, whether they meant them or not: *It's lovely! So spacious! I love the design! Look at the size of the bath!* And this pair, the mummy's boy and the sprightly old woman, weren't any different. Linda hadn't worked out who the apartment might be for yet – a retirement place for her, a bachelor pad for him (she'd checked for a wedding ring) – and they'd been too busy clucking about the delights of the property to divulge much about themselves. However, now was as good a time as ever, because the old woman had moved into one of the bedrooms and Walter North was examining the electronic display on the front of the cooker. It was always better to divide and conquer.

Linda came up behind him. 'If you don't mind me asking, is it for yourself or your mother?'

'She's not my mother.'

'Oh, sorry, I thought . . .'

'She's my lover.' Linda blanched. Walter winked. 'Only rakin'', he said.

Linda forced a smile. She didn't think it was funny *at all*.

'We're partners. *Business* partners,' he went on.

'Oh, I see.'

He was looking at her a little more closely now. 'Do I know you?'

'Excuse me?'

'I'm sorry – you just look like someone.'

'People say that to me all the time. But I'm just little ol' me.'

He was sure he did. Then he thought that he knew so few women that she had to be one of the women he'd thumbed through on *Let's Be Mates*, and she was quite pretty, so if he'd emailed her his details, the chances were that she'd rejected him. Of course she hadn't recognised him, because his photo had been ancient and his name had been different, and anyway, good-looking women tended not to remember bad-looking men. But he'd be damned if he was going to give her a percentage on this one. Nice place but, he thought, not quite what he was looking for. More expensive places, like this, took longer to sell, and apartments weren't showing the same increase in prices the way traditional houses were. Bertha had wanted to take a look.

He turned his attention to the microwave. It was state of the art.

Linda moved into the bedroom. Bertha was checking under the beds. (It was furnished to a 'showroom standard'. They all were. People no longer seemed to keep their old furniture. They threw it out.) She straightened with some difficulty.

'Lovely,' she said. 'I think my son could be very happy here.'

Linda glanced back to the kitchen. Walter was pressing buttons. 'Your son?'

'Mmm. Shall we?' Bertha indicated the sliding door which opened out from the bedroom onto the veranda.

'Of course.' Linda unlocked it. She was trying to decide whether it was kind of cute, a grown man being embarrassed to be seen house-hunting with his mum, or deeply, deeply sad.

'Oh, would you look at that,' said Bertha, her hands excitedly clutching the rail. 'That's exactly where they found that headless corpse.'

Linda fought valiantly to retain her smile.

55
Muttering

Billy said, 'Well, can we meet somewhere where at least I won't be recognised?'

Marsh said, 'What about down at the Accountancy Club? They won't recognise you in there once they hear what you've been up to.'

'That's not funny. And there is no Accountancy Club.'

'Tell me where you'll be comfortable, Billy. We aim to please.'

'I don't know. Maybe if we just go for a drive.'

'That's okay by me. Do you want me to pick you up?'

Billy hesitated. 'What sort of a car do you have?'

Marsh laughed. 'So you can pass it on to Pink and he'll have me topped the minute I pull up?'

'No! *God*. I'm into my wheels.'

Marsh sighed. 'That figures. It's a Jag.'

'Nice one. What's it got under the bonnet?'

'A f***ing engine, what do you expect?'

'I mean—'

'I know what you mean. Be outside your office in fifteen minutes.'

'I can't just—'

'Trust me, you can.'

Marsh was about to go when Billy rasped an urgent, 'Don't pump the horn!'

He told the others he was taking an early lunch, and such was his devotion to the job that it didn't surprise them that he took some of his files with him, to work on as he ate. Pink's files.

Jimmy Mallow was double-parked thirty yards down. He flashed his lights. Billy climbed in, surprised that this time the cop was by himself.

'Nice wheels,' said Billy.

Marsh grunted. He drove down through the city centre. Billy sat with his elbow on the window, his head resting on his hand and turned sideways, so that no one could see his face properly. Marsh drove along the Sydenham by-pass, through Holywood, then turned up into the Craigantlet Hills. It was a bright, sunny June morning and the view from the lay-by across Down was breathtaking.

'One day, son, all this will be yours.'

Billy looked at him, like he was mental. 'What?'

'Must have been like that, don't you think, when the old knights came over and saw this view. Didn't have to bother with a bloody estate agent then, did you?'

'I suppose not.'

'I hear Pink's got his fingers in an estate agent's.'

'Not exactly.'

'Not what I heard.'

Billy sighed. 'His sister is married to an estate agent.'

'Yeah. He's opened a couple of new offices recently.'

'Belfast's booming.'

'He's laundering money.'

'Well, you're clearly better informed than me, which makes this a waste of time.'

'Don't get snotty with me, Billy.'

Billy nodded. There was a huge vista before him, yet he felt desperately claustrophobic. He wanted to open the door and run, tumble down the fields, scramble over hedges, disperse grazing cattle. But he sat, closer to the Pine Fresh tree hanging from the mirror than he was to nature.

'So what do you have for me, Billy?'

Billy patted the files. 'I have his accounts. The ones I work on.'

'And is there anything in there I don't already know about?'

Billy stared at them for several seconds, then slowly shook his head.

'So what's the point?'

'Just so as you can – you know, build a picture of—'

Marsh suddenly slapped the wheel, setting off the horn, and Billy jumped. 'I don't want a f***ing picture. I've hundreds of pictures! I want something I can use!'

'But you said—'

'I told you to bring me stuff or I'd take your telly, that's what I f***ing said!'

'Okay! All right!' Billy fingered his tie. 'He – look, he was drunk. I don't know if it means anything, but he said something about an Office Twelve?'

'Office Twelve?'

'That's what he said.'

'What's Office Twelve?'

'I've no idea. But he said it in a way that, I don't know, sounded important.'

'In what way?'

'I don't know. He just sort of said it. I'd given him some bad news about his tax return, something he couldn't avoid paying, and I was a bit wary because I've seen him explode over less, but he just took it on the chin and muttered something about "Office Twelve can sort it".'

'He muttered it?'

'Yes, he muttered it.'

'You said before, he *said* it. But now he muttered it.'

'Well, he muttered it. I don't see what the difference is.'

'There's a difference. Saying it is definite, muttering it is a throwaway. See, Billy, if you have ten thousand hours of wiretaps, you have to be able to tell the difference between the definites and the throwaways, because you can't pursue everything. You have to pick and choose.'

'So muttering's no good?'

'If it really *is* a mutter. If you can make it out on the tape, then it's not a mutter, it's a said thing that sounds like a mutter. Do you follow?' Billy just stared at him. 'If it's a said thing, you can pursue it, it's evidence, but if it's a mutter and you think he said it, but he could well have said something that just sounds like it, well that's no use at all. So, your Office Twelve – was that a mutter, or did he say it?'

'I'm pretty sure he said Office Twelve.'

'Pretty sure, or certain?'

'Certain. I suppose.'

'Don't suppose, Billy. You're talking man hours here.'

'I'm certain then. Office Twelve.'

'Good. See – that wasn't hard, was it?'

'No.'

'So how come we didn't hear it?'

'Hear what?'

'Office Twelve. We have the whole Supporters Club wired, yet we didn't hear it.'

'The storeroom. He says there's no bug in there.'

Marsh nodded. 'Okay, Billy. Well done.'

Billy smiled; he even flushed a little. It was like being in school, and the bully wants to be your friend.

Marsh's phone rang. He listened then said, 'No, I should do it. Give me the address.'

He patted his jacket, searching for a pen. He looked about for something to write on, then clicked his fingers and pointed at Pink's files, sitting on Billy's lap. Billy slid one across. Jimmy Mallow quickly scrawled down an address in Bangor, five miles down the road. He cut the line, then repeated the address several times before passing the file back to Billy.

'You can walk back from here,' he said.

'What?'

'Walk. Jesus, man, don't look at me like that. Are you made of cheese or something? Ulster Hospital's about a mile along the road, and it's all downhill. There's a million taxis, and it's not exactly Bandit Country.'

'But why?' Billy ventured. A few moments ago he'd have given anything to be let off the hook, but now that he was off it, he didn't really fancy a walk in the country.

'Because I'm going to tell a woman her son's dead, and I'm not sure what support a crooked accountant can exactly offer her right now, okay?'

Billy gathered up his files. He opened the door. 'I'm not crooked,' he said flatly, then climbed out.

'That's right, Billy,' Marsh said after him. 'You're more like Pink. Just slightly bent.'

He laughed, then performed a three-point turn on the narrow road, and roared off towards Bangor. Billy, clutching Pink's files to his chest, started walking in the opposite direction.

56

On the Move

Walter stayed up late into the night, studying lists of property, and even when he went to bed he couldn't sleep. His head was buzzing. This was going to be *brilliant* – Walter North, *property magnate*. And Bertha had been great – good advice, but never interfering, never insisting on her own way, constantly saying that the final decision was his.

When he arrived, yawning, at work the next morning, Walter was surprised to find Steve, from Office 12, standing by Mark's desk, sharing a joke with him. But their laughter faded quickly as Walter approached.

'All right,' he said, 'how's it going?'

'Great,' said Mark.

'Fine,' said Steve.

Walter nodded from one to the other. They nodded too. Mark's eyes flitted up to Steve, and then they both smirked.

Steve said, 'Well, see you later,' and turned away.

Mark wagged a finger after him. 'Not if I see you first!' and they cracked up again.

Walter concentrated on his in-tray until he heard the door to Office 12 close, then he glanced up. Mark stood by the window, staring out. *'Not if I see you first,'* he mimicked.

Mark ignored him.

'So what's that all about?

Mark shrugged. 'Nothing.'

'Didn't think you were pals.'

'Well, there you go.' Mark turned from the window. He sat behind his desk, but made no effort to turn his computer on. 'How did the house hunting go?' he asked.

'Getting there. What about your interview? Was it the blue-rinse squad?'

'Yes and no. Anyway, I'm in. They've asked me to work with one of their councillors.'

'Excellent.'

Mark reached forward and switched on his computer. Without looking up he said, 'Pink Harrison.'

If he'd been eating his usual gravy ring, Walter would have choked on it. Fact was, his diet had started on Monday and he was three days into it without a wobble.

'I hope you told them where they could stick Pink Harrison.'

'Actually, he's a nice bloke, and he has lots of good, forward-thinking ideas about how to save the Party.'

'What, like shooting the leadership?'

'You're not funny. He's changed.'

'Ah, Mark, catch a grip.'

Mark shrugged.

'Mark. Seriously. You're winding me up.'

No reponse.

'Pink Harrison. He's a born-again Democrat?'

'Yes, he is.'

'And you buy that?'

'Everyone can change. Look at you, Donald Trump.'

'That's different.'

'How is it different?'

'Well, I never killed anyone.'

'And neither did Pink.'

Walter raised his eyebrows.

'Anyway,' said Mark, 'that's in the past. D'you think if everyone who was ever involved was excluded from politics, that we'd be where we are now?'

'And where exactly are we now, Mark?'

'Ask me next year, when we come to power.'

'We? You and Pink?'

'The Party. He's only a small cog in a big machine.'

'Pink Harrison was never a small cog in anything.'

'Why do you have to be down on everything? I'm trying to make a difference. So is Pink. So is the Party. A bit of support wouldn't go amiss.'

Walter shrugged. Mark stared at his screen.

Walter offered him a Polo. Mark nodded. Walter got up and crossed to his colleague's desk. As Mark took one, Walter said, 'It's good you got in. I'm just not sure about Pink.'

'Thanks. And that's fair enough. Time will tell.'

Walter sat on the edge of the desk. 'So what's up with your man, Steven?'

'Steven? Oh yeah – Steve. Well, I told you he offered me a job.'

'I think he's offered everyone that job – just hasn't found the right sucker.'

'I'm thinking about accepting it.'

Walter laughed. 'No, seriously.'

'I am serious.'

'Well, why the hell would you want to do that? You know he's going to be arrested one of these days. You can't mess with things the way he does and not get into trouble. Anyway, I thought you were into helping the country, not causing chaos.'

'Yes, but it's organised chaos.'

'Organised chaos? What the hell are you talking about?'

'Chaos from which our side benefits.'

'Our side? Which side is that?'

'The Party. You cause enough havoc, people are going to vote for change.'

'People voted for change and got Hitler.'

'Well, at least the trains ran on time.' He held his stern look for a moment, then suddenly smiled. 'Chill, would you? It's a hike in wages, and I can do with it. He just bullshits a lot. You didn't fall for all that crap, did you? He was just winding you up.'

'Oh, so it's not like Black Ops or something.'

'Of course not. This day and age, out in the open like that? Christ, man, it's not the eighties any more. He does the same shit we do, just gets paid more, so I'll be having some of that. You should have taken your chance while you had it. Do you want me to put in a word?'

Walter shook his head. 'Nah.'

'Oh aye – forgot. You're the property tycoon now. Well, at least when I get into power, and you want to build some huge housing estate, you'll know who to bribe, eh? And I'm not talking a couple of gravy rings, either.'

'I'm off gravy rings,' said Walter.

'Right. Like that'll last.' Mark laughed.

Walter laughed. But not inside. He didn't like the fact that Mark was moving. And he didn't trust Steve, believed he was up to no good in Office 12. But most of all he resented the fact that Mark didn't believe he was serious about his diet. Because this time he was determined. He was turning his life around.

As he crossed back to his desk, Walter suddenly realised that he hadn't thought about Margaret all day. Good. He was getting over her. Although he had to admit that thinking about the fact that he *hadn't* thought about her, did technically constitute thinking about her – so perhaps he wasn't out of the woods yet. And from further down the office came the smell of a gravy ring, and his stomach rumbled. Walter pulled himself in tight against his desk, put three Polos in his mouth and steeled himself for a day of fighting incredible temptation. Jesus Himself had survived forty days and forty nights of temptation, although probably there weren't any gravy rings in those days.

57
Redmond and the Elephant

YOUNG REDMOND LEARNED FAST....

*BUT YOU CAN'T DESTROY THINGS
24 HOURS A DAY. THERE WAS ALWAYS
ROOM FOR ROMANCE....*

THE WAR WAS WINDING DOWN ...

...AND REDMOND, UNQUALIFIED FOR ANYTHING BUT DESTRUCTION.....

...HAD TO CONSIDER HIS OPTIONS...

SO IT WAS THAT REDMOND SET OFF FOR SOUTH AMERICA....

IT WAS A WILD EXOTIC COUNTRY .....

IT WAS EXACTLY THE SAME, AND YET IT WAS DIFFERENT ....

HE BEGAN TO
APPRECIATE THE
WONDER OF NATURE....

....AND UNDERSTAND
THE SANCTITY OF LIFE ....

THERE ARE NO ELEPHANTS
IN SOUTH AMERICA.....
WHICH MEANS.....

I'M ALIVE! I'VE DONE IT!
I'VE ESCAPED!

58
Bad news

Marsh had been delivering bad news all his life. He had heard other cops say, 'You never get used to it,' but he had. It was all about putting on an act. It was his duty to be professional about it. You might have wanted to say, 'Actually I don't give a damn about your husband. He was a head-case and you're better off without him,' but you couldn't, so you just played it straight. Official. Maybe it came across as cold, but that's the way it had to be. Because every head-case had a mother or brother. And for every head-case there was one innocent kid, one paragon, one saint or scholar in the wrong place, wrong time, and breaking that kind of news could absolutely break your heart, if you let it. Marsh didn't. He put up a shield. The thing was, sometimes he forgot to lower it again.

When his wife went to hospital that last time, they kept him in a waiting room while they fought to save her. It was a useless, pointless battle. She'd been trying to surrender for months. But at the end, when the doctor came out, and he gave his spiel, all platitudes and stutters, Marsh had nearly slammed him against the wall, nearly yelled, 'You f***ing amateur, that's not how it's done.'

Now here he was again, outside the smart bungalow in Bangor West. As soon as he stopped the car a policewoman came hurrying up; she'd been there for a while, trying to keep out of sight so that the family inside wouldn't guess and come wailing out. Marsh would have preferred to do it by himself, but there were regulations. Something about a woman being there was supposed to make it easier.

The boy's name was Michael Caldwell. Fifteen years old. Still at the local grammar school.

A nice home. Photos of the kids – there were two brothers, one sister – all over the walls. The mother, Irene, was in bits; the dad was holding it together better, but his eyes were red.

They'd known that this day would come. He was a good boy, and he wouldn't go anywhere without calling, would never stay out all night, certainly not four nights.

Then the body on the news.

It's a boy. A teenager.

The sheer horror.

They sat Jimmy Mallow down in the lounge and he explained methodically where the investigation was at, that it was possible the boy had drowned before he was dismembered, that it could conceivably have been an accident, perhaps even an industrial accident of some kind, but that in the meantime they were treating it as a murder investigation.

That seemed to give them a little hope – that somehow their son had died first, and that it might not have been a bloody, gruesome end.

They talked about him as if he was still alive. What he wanted to be. How school was. His favourite movies. How addicted he'd been to his X-Box.

It wasn't just to break the bad news, this visit was to collect photographs, and to clear the way for Marsh to send his detectives in and then they could ask the really hard questions. Because even as he looked at them, for all the world a family in the midst of grief, he had to consider the possibility that *they* might have killed him. They might have all got together to kill their son. Or the dad might have had a row with him and drowned him in the bath. Or the mum might have had a stand-up fight and clubbed him with a vase. Stranger things had happened. You never ruled out anything. Ever.

The doorbell went, and a Minister came in. Marsh took this opportunity to make his excuses and leave. He nodded at his colleague; she would wait behind, smooth the way for the detectives when they arrived. He shook hands gravely with the Minister in the hallway. Marsh went outside with the photos. He flicked through them on his way down to the car. Michael Caldwell had been a good-looking boy, blond hair cut short, a cheeky grin.

If this was a movie, Marsh thought, it would be my last case, the one I had to solve before retiring. But it wasn't a movie, and it wouldn't be his last case. However, he'd crack it. His strike rate was good, and he had a good team.

As he approached the gates he saw that someone had placed a bunch of flowers there since his arrival. He stopped for a moment, then bent and examined the card. It said, *Good lad, Michael, we'll miss you. Carl, Alan, Bix.* Marsh repeated the names to himself. They would be checked out. The florist would be tracked down. Sometimes the devil was in the detail.

Then his name was called from behind, and he straightened as the mother hurried down the drive.

'Superintendent. Thank you for coming to see us. Yourself. Personally.'

'It's no problem, Mrs Caldwell. Just sorry to be the bearer of such terrible news.'

She nodded, folded her arms, took a deep breath, tried to hold back the tears. 'We're a Christian family, Superintendent. I will forgive whoever has done this.'

Marsh nodded.

'But I have to know who it is and why they did it.'

'We'll find out.'

'He was only a baby.'

'I know.'

'Why would somebody do that?'

'There's a million reasons, Mrs Caldwell.'

She stared at the ground. No make-up, her hair all over the place. 'I want him back,' she said quietly.

'It'll be a few days before—'

'I mean all of him. Every bit.'

'We'll find him.'

'Do I have your word?'

He wanted to tell her that his word was valueless. That it meant nothing.

'We'll do our best.'

'He was our youngest. Didn't expect to have him. We spoiled him.'

Marsh sighed. 'We always do.' He nodded, then turned back to the car. She stood and watched him drive away. In the mirror he saw her husband come out and begin to guide her back towards the house.

Marsh had set the photos on the passenger's seat. Face-up. When he stopped at the first set of traffic-lights, he turned them over.

59

Smoke on the Water

'So what line are you in anyway?'

Linda Wray was standing with Walter on the veranda of the penthouse apartment at Towerview. He'd decided to take a second look, this time without Bertha.

'Is she not well?' Linda had asked.

'Tae kwon do class,' said Walter.

She looked at him as he gazed out over Belfast. She wasn't sure if he was winding her up.

'Tae kwon do?'

'Aye.'

So she didn't pursue it. There was something attractive about this Walter North. He was reasonably quiet, but quite sharp when he did open his mouth. His clothes were understated. He wasn't unkempt, neither was he overly groomed, like so many of the moneyed men she encountered these days. He was just . . . normal. And he had money to spend.

'Line?' asked Walter. 'Oh – bit of this, bit of that.' He held her gaze for a moment, then abruptly broke it. He flushed a little and in keeping with his new policy of not lying through his teeth said, 'Actually, I work in the Department of Education in Bangor.'

'Oh right.'

'But the big plan is to move into property. Always been fascinated by it.'

'Well, it's a good investment. The prices are shooting up.'

Walter nodded down at the Lagan. 'I see they've moved the body. Can't have been good for sales.'

She smiled. 'A nightmare.'

'Do you see they've started putting flowers down there?' He pointed, and she saw that about a dozen bunches were spread out along a 100-yard stretch of the riverbank. 'That all started with the Princess Diana thing, didn't it? I mean, in a big way, putting flowers down at the death scene. Now anyone who pops their clogs, and it's like the Chelsea Flower Show. Wouldn't surprise me if the flower companies got together and knocked her off themselves. Here we are, all looking at vast conspiracy theories, and it's some tulip-grower from Amsterdam responsible.'

Put a sock in it.

Walter gripped the handrail. He just had to learn when to be quiet. Inscrutable. Not blabber away like an eejit. He was sure Donald Trump didn't run off at the mouth like that. Or if he did, he did it because he could afford to do it. If he'd run off at the mouth like that when he'd started out, he wouldn't have got anywhere. So zip it. Be businesslike. He glanced across at Linda Wray. She was biting down on her lower lip, as if she was trying to stop herself from saying *'Shut the f**k up.'*

'Sorry,' Walter began. 'Hope I didn't—'

She waved a hand at him. 'No, it's just that you mentioned Princess Diana – and that always brings a lump to my throat. You see, I got married the day of her funeral. It cast a gloom over the entire day, which never really lifted. We barely lasted a year and a half.'

Walter nodded.

'Oh Christ,' said Linda, 'I'm really sorry. You're trying to buy an apartment and I'm rabbiting on about my crap marriage and non-existent lovelife. Come on, I'll show you the bedroom.'

She stopped suddenly, they looked at each other, then burst into laughter.

'What am I like!'

'It's fine – honestly.'

'I'm *really* sorry. It's been a long day. Just one more appointment. But I could murder a fag.'

'Feel free.'

'You're sure?'

'Of course.'

She took the pack from her handbag and offered him one. He shook his head.

'Then I won't,' she said.

'No, seriously, it's fine.'

She lit up, inhaled deeply, held onto it, then slowly exhaled. 'It's a disgusting habit,' she said.

Walter shrugged. 'We've all got disgusting habits,' he said. Then he thought he'd better qualify that. 'I've been on a diet since Monday. You should see the crap I used to get through.'

'You're on a diet? Why?'

He patted his tummy. 'This is why.'

'That's not so bad.'

'It's hardly Brad Pitt.'

'Nobody is Brad Pitt. Brad Pitt probably isn't Brad Pitt. His six-pack is probably a special effect.'

The doorbell rang. Linda looked at her watch, then, panic-stricken, threw her cigarette over the side. 'Christ,' she said, 'I'm running late. That's my next appointment.'

'But I haven't finished.'

'I know. I know – of course you haven't. I just hate showing two parties round together. It's always awkward.'

'I could hang around until they're gone.'

She looked at him. Was he interested in the apartment, or her, or both? Did she want him hanging around waiting? What if he was a serial killer?

He looked at her. Why had he said that? The apartment was nice, but it wasn't *that* nice. It was Linda. But what if she was as mad as a bag of spiders?

The doorbell rang again.

'If you really don't mind waiting,' said Linda.

'It's no problem. But maybe I should pretend that I'm leaving, and then I'll hang about downstairs till they go. On the way out now, will I sound like I'm dead interested? Maybe that'll make them keener to buy.'

Linda, laughing, shook her head as she ushered him towards the door. He was funny. He gave her a conspiratorial wink as she opened the door. 'Well, thank you very much, it's a wonderful apartment, let me talk to my people.' He pumped her hand enthusiastically then turned to say hello to her incoming clients.

Walter stopped dead.

'Hello Walter,' said Margaret.

60
Walter & Margaret & Linda

Linda looked from Margaret Gilmore to Walter North. Walter looked from Margaret to Linda and back. Margaret glared at Walter, smiled apologetically at Linda and then looked back to Walter.

'You know each other?' Linda asked.

'I thought we did,' said Walter.

Margaret tutted. 'Never mind him. We went on a date once, it didn't work out.'

'Because you had sex with your husband!'

'Because you spent three nights in my bedroom while I was in a coma!'

Linda swallowed. This was a bit weird. The pair of them were staring angrily at each other. 'Do you want me to give you some time alone?'

'No!' they both said at once.

'Well, Mrs Gilmore, would you like me to show you the—'

'I want it,' said Walter.

'I'm sorry?' Linda asked.

'I want to buy the apartment. I'm putting an offer in. Take it off the market, please.'

'Well, that's very . . . but ahm, you would need to, you know, make a formal offer and—'

'I want it now. I'll pay the asking price.'

Margaret shook her head. 'That's pathetic,' she said.

'What's pathetic?' Walter snapped.

'Pretending to buy this apartment just to piss me off.'

'Don't overrate yourself, missus, I'm buying it because I like it.'

Margaret smiled sarcastically. 'Yeah. Sure.'

'Yeah, sure yourself.'

'Well,' said Linda. 'If you're serious—'

'Of course I'm serious,' snapped Walter.

'Then I'll communicate that to my boss.'

'Good. Then take it off the market, please.'

'I can't do that, not until—'

'That's the condition of my offer. It's the full asking price. A definite sale. Now, *please*, take it off the market.'

'Pathetic,' repeated Margaret.

'I can't – until I confirm it with my boss.' This was too weird, Linda thought.

'Well, do that.'

'I'd like to see the apartment,' said Margaret.

'No *way*,' hissed Walter.

'I might make a higher offer,' said Margaret.

She was half-smiling. There was smoke coming out of Walter's ears. He knew he was being ridiculous, but he was mad. Mad because he'd forgotten about her and now here she was, like a sign from God, and his tummy was churning, and she had led him on, made him think there was a chance and then laughed in his face by screwing her half-wit husband right in front of him.

'Look at the f***ing thing then!' Walter shouted. He stormed out into the hall; Margaret had to move sharply to one side to avoid him.

Linda called after him, 'Walter – Mr North! Are you serious about this offer?'

'Yes!' he called back as he angrily jabbed the lift button. His face was burning.

Margaret emerged thirty minutes later. She had barely been able to concentrate on the apartment. Especially when they went out onto the veranda and saw Walter leaning on the fence by the river. Margaret had apologised already to the estate agent, but now that they could see Walter, she felt the need to do it again. But she added, 'We hardly know each other.'

'It happens,' said Linda. 'And also, men are such bloody eejits.'

Margaret nodded.

'He seemed so nice, though,' said Linda. 'Then just to explode like that.'

'Well, I don't really blame him.'

'Do you think he really wants this place? You don't seem that keen.'

'It's nice, but it's not for me. I don't know about Walter.' Margaret sighed. 'I'll go and talk to him.'

Margaret had heels on, so Walter was bound to be able to hear her approaching, but he didn't turn. She stood beside him at the railings.

'You shouldn't have bothered,' she said.

'I shouldn't have bothered *what*?'

'Getting me all these flowers.'

He continued to stare at the water. 'They're not for you. This is where that boy was washed up with his head and hands and legs cut off.'

'Oh,' said Margaret. 'I thought it was some sort of council initiative.' She watched him. Then she put a hand on his arm. 'Look, this is silly. I'm sorry for what happened.'

Walter shrugged.

'And if I try to explain, it'll just make matters worse. I made a mistake. I am not back with my husband. I will never be with him again.'

'It's got nothing to do with me.'

'Walter. Come on. You sat by my bed all that time.'

'That was then, this is now.'

'Walter.'

'Margaret.'

'What can I do to change things?'

Walter shrugged.

'Come on.'

'Jump in the river.'

'What?'

'If you're serious, jump in the river.'

'*This* river?'

'This river. Right now. Just jump in.'

'Walter, we've only ever been on one date, and that was a disaster. I'm not jumping in a river for you.'

'Okay. Please yourself.' Walter turned and began to walk away. He felt good and strong and superior.

'Hey!' He stopped, looked back. Margaret was perched precariously on top of the fence, like a woman who had never seen a horse before trying to ride side-saddle.

'I'll do it!' she shouted.

'Okay.'

'Come back here and talk to me sensibly. For Christ's sake, we're both adults.'

He started to walk again.

'Walter!'

When he looked back she was gingerly lowering herself over the side of the fence. She set one sharp heel down on the shiny cobble of the man-made riverbank, but it immediately slid out from under her. She gave a little shriek, then skidded down the bank on her arse and went feet-first into the river.

Walter stood stunned for a moment, then charged across. He vaulted over the fence, but kept one hand on top so that when he landed he was able to stay upright. He carefully stepped down the bank and held his hand out to Margaret, who was sitting in the water, which was only a foot deep so close to the bank, beating it and screaming, 'I hate you! I hate you! I hate you!'

When she paused for breath, he said quietly: 'Do you want a hand?'

She turned, sodden, towards him. Her face was wet and her hair straggled and her clothes clung to her. 'No, I don't want a f***ing hand!' she yelled, and tried to get to her feet. She put one hand down to steady herself as she pushed up, but the rock she was trying to get a grip on rolled to one side; everything else was silt and sludge, so she felt for the rock again, her fingers coiling around it looking for a proper grip. Except as she turned it in her hand, she realised it wasn't a rock, but a child's head with staring eyes, and she screamed and screamed and screamed.

Up on the veranda, Linda Wray said, 'Oh Christ.'

61

A Last-Minute Reprieve

Ambassador Martin Brown almost had a heart-attack when his visitors were shown in. Siobhan he knew, of course, but the priest . . . the priest was the spitting image of the corpse he had only an hour previously sent off to be cremated. And only marginally a better colour.

Siobhan was ranting and raving before she sat down. 'You can't . . . how dare . . . we have rights . . . you will burn in hell for this!' but the Ambassador only had eyes for this Father Damian.

'I'm his brother,' Father Damian said finally.

'It's *uncanny*. Are you identical twins?'

'Yes.'

'It's funny how two brothers can take very different paths.'

'Who says we took different paths?'

'Well,' the Ambassador began, and then stopped. 'Fair point,' he said.

'But as a matter of fact, we did,' Father Damian said. 'We were not close, Mr Ambassador, but nevertheless, I flew here immediately I heard about his deteriorating condition.'

'Yes, of course you did. We're all dreadfully—'

'Don't give me that s**t!' Siobhan exploded. 'If you cared a fraction, you would not have treated Redmond like some kind of a bad smell and shipped him off to be burned.'

'The fact is, Miss O'Rourke, and with all due respect to you, Father, he *was* becoming a bad smell. *Nothing* keeps in this climate. But besides that, we have clear and direct instructions from Mrs O'Boyle to cremate her late husband, so we had no option but to obey them.'

'It's not too late,' said Siobhan. 'We can still stop this. We need the address of the crematorium.'

'I'm afraid I can't give you that.'

I Predict A Riot

'This is his *brother*!'

'I'm aware of that. And I'm sorry, Father, but in cases like this a wife takes precedence and therefore I must see that through. We really don't need any kind of disruption.'

Father Damian clasped his hands gravely. 'Mr Ambassador, Redmond is – was – my brother. And a human being. I should at the very least have the opportunity to say goodbye to him, and to conduct a short service.'

'I understand completely, Father, but his wife was quite clear on this subject. Redmond is to be cremated. She did not wish his body to become – well, a political football. Certain people have what I would call an agenda . . .'

'That's outrageous!' cried Siobhan.

He ignored her, while nodding sympathetically at the priest. 'If it's of any value to you, I myself said a few words over the body before sending it on its way.' The words he had said were: *'Burn in hell, motherf***er!'* But they didn't need to know that.

In fact, he had said the words, especially the last one, very quietly. It was an act of bravado, but one without a living audience. Ambassador Brown now patted his brow with a crisply folded handkerchief. Siobhan was also sweating profusely. When he had first met her, her skin had been red and blotchy, then it had been sunburned, but now it was finely tanned. Father Damian looked uncomfortable in his collar and black shirt; the sleeves rolled up to the elbow. There was an air conditioner, but like democracy, it only worked occasionally, and even then it was never quite satisfactory.

'It really is most unfortunate,' Ambassador Brown continued, 'but on the bright side, I have had no instructions as to how to dispose of the ashes. Father, it might be possible to release them into your safe-keeping. Granted it's not the same as getting . . .' Ambassador Brown trailed off.

Siobhan stamped her foot. Literally. 'You can still do this, Ambassador. Phone them now and stop the cremation – at least until we can reason with Mrs O'Boyle.'

The Ambassador glanced at his watch. 'I'm afraid it's too late for that.'

'Rubbish! Nothing works on time in this country! I demand—' At that moment, her mobile phone rang. She removed it from her bag, answered it, looked at the Ambassador, then said, 'Excuse me,' and hurried out of the office.

She was strident, very annoying but utterly predictable, as if she was playing a role, espousing a script. But in leaving the office, she'd left the Ambassador alone with a real, grief-stricken human being.

'I'm very sorry about this,' the Ambassador said weakly. 'You say you weren't close?'

'Not at all.' The priest leaned forward. 'Mr Ambassador, can I ask you something?'

'Yes, of course.' Martin Brown lifted a cup of tea and sipped. It was the only cool thing in the office, and quite dreadful, but he felt the need to hold onto something.

'If your brother died, and you were denied the opportunity to say goodbye, how would you feel?'

The room, which was quite spacious, suddenly felt claustrophobic. He had dealt with many bereaved relatives in his time as Ambassador both here and in other countries, but had always been able to retreat into meaningless platitudes when faced with a difficult situation. But now, one on one with this austere-looking priest with a genuine tear in his eye, Ambassador Brown realised that his only refuge was the truth.

'I don't have a brother,' he said.

The door opened, and Siobhan strode in, holding the phone out before her as if it was Chamberlain's scrap of paper or a telegram from the top of Everest.

'It's the Minister of the Interior, Señor Valdez. He's ordering you to stop the cremation!'

It was. The reasons were 'political and regrettable'.

The Ambassador first tried to usher Siobhan and Father Damian out of his office, so that he could phone the crematorium in private, but they refused to move. Siobhan beamed triumphantly as he lifted the phone and then spoke in fluent Spanish to the head of the crematorium. When he replaced the receiver, she said: 'Never underestimate the influence of my Party.'

The Ambassador nodded gravely. 'That may be, but you also should never underestimate the determination of a crematorium superintendent who wishes to knock off early for the weekend. I'm afraid Mr O'Boyle was cremated a quarter of an hour ago.'

The young woman's hand went to her mouth in disbelief. Father Damian sighed.

'My condolences to you, Father. This has been most regrettable. May your brother rest in peace.'

Siobhan rattled on for a while, but her heart wasn't in it. She was beaten. When they'd gone, the Ambassador settled back behind his desk and called for fresh tea. He shook his head. *Rest in peace.* Redmond O'Boyle had spent his life in pursuit of precisely the opposite. The Ambassador opened a drawer and took out a fresh box of Jaffa Cakes. He put his feet up on his desk. Redmond O'Boyle's arrest, incarceration and death had upset his rather sedentary life. At least now things could get back to normal.

His phone rang.

'Yes, Catherine?' he said to his young receptionist.

'Ambassador, I have a Redmond O'Boyle on the line.'

62
Tales of the Riverbank

Margaret had to give a statement to the police, explaining how she came to be sitting in the River Lagan at all, and confirming that no, she had no idea there was a child's dead head there, and no, she had never met the deceased or been involved in any way in the circumstances of his suspicious death or indeed had any idea where the rest of him was. 'We have to ask,' the nice policewoman said, the same one who'd got her the blanket to keep her warm – though it wasn't doing much good; what she really needed was to get out of her sodden clothes. When she'd said, 'Occupation?' Margaret had said, 'Fashion designer,' and then looked away, embarrassed, half-expecting the cop to laugh or suddenly demand evidence or treat it in some way as proof that she was involved in the murder of the boy because she'd clearly lied about how she earned her living. But the policewoman had merely written it down and moved quickly to the next question.

There were police swarming all around. The head remained in the water where she'd found it. The whole area was being minutely examined by the very same forensics experts and divers who'd failed to find it earlier. Walter, who had called the police on his mobile, had also given his statement, but he and Margaret were kept apart. His tan trousers were damp up to the knees where he'd leaped into the water to haul her out. It had taken the police ten minutes to arrive. For nine of those minutes she had wept silently against him. He had patted her back.

Later, as Margaret sat in the back of a police car, awaiting permission to go home, she watched as the mother and father of the dead boy were escorted down to the riverbank by the police officer in charge. It was grim. When they'd gone, broken and hysterical, the same police officer came over to her car and climbed into the back seat beside her. His eyes looked dead.

'That must have been dreadful,' Margaret said.

I Predict A Riot

He nodded. He said who he was – Inspector Gary McBride.

'That must have been very frightening, finding . . . that,' he said.

'It's the single worst thing I've ever seen in my life. That poor child. The worst thing—' She stopped suddenly at the memory of it.

'It's all right,' said Gary.

She nodded gratefully, but couldn't find her voice for a moment.

'I'd get you a coffee, but they're not here yet.'

'It's okay,' she said. 'The worst thing – his eyes were open.'

'I know.'

'I only looked for a moment – but it was like he wasn't dead at all, and wanted to tell me what happened, but couldn't. I'll have nightmares tonight.' She shivered.

'It's not easy,' said Gary. He nodded vaguely towards another of the police cars. 'This Walter North – your boyfriend?'

'Did he say he was?'

'No. Said you were friends.'

'Huh.'

'I asked him why you jumped in the river and he said because your lift doesn't go all the way to the top.'

'The bugger.'

'I think he was only joking. Why *did* you jump in the river?'

'I didn't jump. I fell. Off the top of the rail.'

'And what were you doing on top of the rail?'

'I honestly don't know.'

Gary smiled. 'None of it's easy, is it?' Then he climbed out of the car.

She wanted to call after him, 'None of what's easy? What are you talking about? I've just seen a dead head, I don't need someone to be cryptic, and you're ten years too old for me, but you're quite nice.' But she just sat there until the policewoman came back and told her she could go.

She was offered a lift but said, 'Sure, my car's over there.' Then she was asked if she was okay to drive, or if there was anyone they should call, but she couldn't think of anyone. Billy? Of course not. Maeve – I don't think so! No, it was just her by her lonesome, trudging damp and deflated towards the newly laid car park at the Towerview Apartments. Hers and Walter's were the only two vehicles left now, and he was already standing by his, clearly waiting for her.

'All done then?' he said, as she stopped beside him.

She nodded. 'You?'

'For now, yeah. Bit of a turn-up for the books, eh?'

'Well,' she said, 'that'll teach me to make a show of myself.'

'You couldn't have known.'

233

'I know, but still. Who feels foolish now?'

'You shouldn't.'

'It was your fault, losing your temper, then playing hard to get.'

'I think if you ask around, you'll find I'm extremely easy to get. As you are, apparently.' It was out before he could stop himself. He hadn't really meant it that way, but it was out there and she visibly stiffened. She shook her head.

'I'm sorry,' Walter said quickly.

Margaret took a deep breath. 'Once bitten, twice shy is the expression. Not once bitten, shy for the rest of your life. I'm traumatised enough, I don't need you sticking the knife in.'

'I know that. I'm sorry, really I am. You're soaking wet.'

'Yes, I am.'

'Do you want to get into my car and I'll turn the heater on?'

'I don't think that's going to fix it, Walter. I need to get home.'

'Okay.' He nodded. He jangled his keys nervously. She turned to go, then stopped.

'Well?' she asked.

'Well?'

'Aren't you going to say anything?'

Walter looked lost for a moment. 'Have a safe journey home.'

She raised her eyebrows. She started walking. The penny dropped.

'Do you want . . .' he called after her.

Margaret stopped. 'Do I want what?'

'Ahm. Do you want – you know, a drink. Something to eat. A pizza.'

'I'm all wet, Walter.'

'I know. Later. When you get dry. I could . . . follow you home.'

Margaret folded her arms. 'If I say no, are you going to stand outside my house for three days and nights?'

'Probably,' said Walter.

63
Second Chance

Jimmy Marsh Mallow had a thousand things running through his mind to do with the head and the body and the missing bits and possible suspects and the way his team of detectives didn't seem as energetic or keen as he had once been, so the last thing he needed was a blind date with another woman. She was the second of the three who had contacted him as soon as his file appeared on the *Let's Be Mates* website. Having stood up the first one, and despite being widely regarded, not least of all by himself, as a standard-bearer for strong morals and honesty in Northern Ireland, he had not yet found the guts or gumption to email her explaining his reasons for no-showing. Nor would he. Perhaps because he didn't want to admit any kind of a weakness. Jimmy Marsh Mallow didn't apologise.

Number two was called Tracey Hill. She described herself as a widow, forty-one years old, worked two jobs – on the till in a Mace shop during the day and then as a barmaid in Robinson's in the city centre, usually at weekends. She liked long walks in the country and reading history books. She was carrying a little excess weight, and her red hair was flecked with grey. She looked exactly like her photograph, sitting opposite him now in Deane's on the Square.

He was mildly surprised to be there. He'd said on the phone to his daughter Lauren that he was tired, didn't fancy it, he would call and cancel, but she shouted at him, said she hadn't spent all that money for him not to at least try it, and he yelled back that he'd never asked her to do it in the first place and what he did with his life was *his* business. But he didn't hang up, and eventually they calmed down. Lauren said she was only thinking of him, that he sounded tired and tense, and getting out and meeting someone new – other than someone he would arrest – would do him the world of good.

He felt at least a little like that now, cutting into his first-course salmon fishcake. Tracey'd ordered the same. She was funny – talking

235

about the drunks in Robinson's and the old women smelling of pee who came into the Mace for their cat food. Both of them steered clear of the fact that their other halves were dead. At least for the moment. The wine flowed. Marsh had parked the car outside, but he would leave it there, pick it up in the morning. He wasn't stupid. More than one of his colleagues had lost their jobs over one extra drink, trusting on their colleagues looking the other way if they did get stopped. Misplaced trust, usually.

'So walks in the country and history books,' Jimmy said.

'Not at the same time,' Tracey laughed.

'Where do you walk?'

'Oh, up over the Cave Hill. Down to Newcastle sometimes. The Mournes. Not so much since Danny . . .'

Marsh nodded. 'It's lovely down there,' he said. 'And the Silent Valley.'

'Gorgeous,' said Tracey. Then she put her knife and fork down, took a sip of white wine and said: 'It's odd this, isn't it?'

'How so?'

'You know, two complete strangers sitting down for a meal. I mean, unless you excuse yourself after the first course and climb out of the Gents window, we're going to be stuck with each other for at least a couple of hours.'

'Well actually,' said Jimmy, 'I've been here before, and I can tell you for a fact that the Gents window isn't big enough to climb out of.'

She roared at that. He glowed. He liked to make a woman laugh. It had been a long time.

'But yes, I know what you mean,' he went on. 'You could be smiling at me, but thinking, What a moron, let me out of here.'

'And you could be thinking, Christ, she looks nothing like her photo, who's she kidding?'

'You do look like your photo.'

'It's ages old.'

'Well, you do. Very nice.'

He averted his eyes to his plate. She looked at her own.

'Thank you,' she said.

He smiled. After a few moments he said, 'I was leaving a space there for you to say that I look exactly like mine.'

'Yes, you do. Is your hair always so short?'

'Easily maintained.'

'It suits you.'

'My wife used to say . . .' He stopped. 'Sorry.'

'No, it's okay, we're both kind of beating around the bush, aren't we?' He nodded. 'Neither of us wants to, you know, ruin things by getting all morbid, yet it's natural. We spent so long with our partners, they're a part of us and always will be, and when we talk about things, of course we have to mention them. It's not a problem, really. How long were you married?'

'About three hundred years.'

She smiled. 'Yeah, I know how that feels. Do you mind my asking what happened?'

'Cancer. It was horrible.'

'God, I'm sorry.'

'That's all right. What about you?'

'Danny was murdered.'

'Oh, God. What happened?'

'He was shot by the police. The RUC. One of the last people they murdered before they became the PSNI.'

Jimmy Marsh Mallow set down his own knife and fork and clasped his hands. 'How exactly was he murdered?'

Tracey dabbed carefully at her lips with her napkin. 'He never really supported the Ceasefire. He was all for keeping things going. There was a bank robbery in South Belfast to raise funds – except someone squealed on them and the police were waiting. Danny tried to surrender, but they shot him anyway.'

'Was he carrying a gun?'

'Yes, he was. But Danny wouldn't have hurt anyone. Of course he shouldn't have been there, but there was no need to kill him.'

Their main courses arrived then. They'd both ordered steaks. Jimmy ate because he was hungry, but what he really wanted to do was grab her and shake her and tell her to stop bloody fooling herself, that her husband wasn't murdered, he was shot dead because he walked into a bank with a gun. And he deserved it.

Marsh finished first. He waited for Tracey to finish, then excused himself to go to the bathroom. Except instead he walked to the front desk, paid the bill, retrieved his coat, then slipped out into the darkness. He'd only had two glasses of wine, so he might have been okay to drive. But he wasn't going to take the chance. Jimmy Marsh Mallow started walking.

64

Suicide Is Painless

Pink Harrison was in good humour, showing Billy around his house in Holywood, a small garrison town six miles out of Belfast. Pink didn't need to tell him that this was one of the most expensive parts of the Province in which to buy property. But he did. He showed him the Jacuzzi, the gym, the walk-in dresser, the king-sized bed, his collection of wine, his immaculate lawn, the pond with koi carp, the cobbled driveway, 'none of yer f***in' gypsy s**t', and his Ferrari. Pink smoked a cigar, and offered Billy one. Billy accepted readily.

Billy knew it was worth just over a million, as he'd seen the paperwork. He also knew it was held in Pink's wife's name. A lot of his business assets were. Thing was, nobody had ever seen Pink's wife. He never talked about her and he had no photos of her on public display. Occasionally he alluded to the fact that she was on holiday, or was abroad. Anyone who knew Pink presumed that if she existed at all, it was a marriage of convenience, merely a device to protect what he had earned illegally from the assets recovery people and the taxman and the CID, and that she never would show her face in the home she owned. Twice a year, Pink took long holidays in the Philippines.

'Okay, let's see what we've got,' Pink said, finally settling on a sunlounger in the conservatory at the back of the house, patting the one beside him for Billy to sit on. Pink had on a white T-shirt, shorts and sandals. Billy wore his usual grey suit and tie. He looked and felt uncomfortable in the heat which, although cool outside, had built up steadily behind the glass. He pulled his shirt out at the neck slightly, but didn't otherwise bother with the top button.

'Is it safe to talk?' Billy enquired immediately.

'Safe as houses. I have it swept for bugs once a week.'

'You ever find any?'

'Oh yes, I have a cupboard full. They keep trying; I keep finding.'

238

'How do they get in to do it? I mean, I can understand at the club, it's public, but here?'

'Postman, gardener, milkman – who knows. They just keep turning up. Fresh done this morning, so we're fine for a couple of days.'

Billy knew the stories about Pink being paranoid, or mad, but he thought on the balance of probability, and knowing what he knew about Pink's business activities, and even then only a fraction of it, that the chances were that he *was* regularly bugged by Jimmy Marsh Mallow. Besides, Marsh Mallow had told him so.

'Tell me about your drive with oul' Jimmy.'

'Nothing much to tell. He asked me all about you, I didn't say much.'

'But you let it slip about Office Twelve.'

'Yes, I did.'

'And?'

'You were right. He wanted to know all about it, and he came on quite heavy, but I couldn't tell him what I didn't know.'

'Very good, very good indeed.'

'He's a bully. And self-important.'

'And pride comes before a fall!' Pink clapped his hands together, then rubbed them fast enough to cause a spark, if they'd been made of stone or wood.

'Have you ever actually met him?' Billy asked.

'Well, no. Why do you ask?'

'I just thought – you seem to dislike each other so much.'

'I don't dislike him, Billy. I respect him, as an adversary. It's like we're playing chess, you know? Or Draughts. Or Monopoly! *Go direct to jail*!' He laughed, but just for a moment. 'You know, a few years ago, we were on the same side.'

'He was a criminal?'

'Please don't make jokes, Billy. The road to hell is paved with dead accountants who make jokes, you understand me?'

'Yes, of course. I didn't mean—'

Pink held up a hand to stop him. 'And don't apologise, it's a sign of weakness.'

'Yes, of course. Sorry. I mean . . .'

Pink took another long suck on his cigar. With the heat of the conservatory, and the pungent smoke having nowhere to go but into Billy's lungs, he was beginning to feel ill. But it wasn't just the atmosphere. It was Pink's whole demeanour. In the club he'd been one of the lads, but separate as well. Here he spoke like the Lord of the Manor, yet not quite. He seemed always to fall short of the desired effect, and that led to uncertainty and awkwardness in those he dealt with. Perhaps that was what he was aiming for.

'Oh yes, me and Jimmy Marsh. We were both defending our country against the rebels. And our methods weren't greatly different. He always understood that men could be broken, that they didn't have the same conviction as they do in, you know, Iraq or Palestine or somewhere.'

'I'm not sure I—'

'Suicide bombers, that's what I'm talking about. We never had that here, did we? We all believed so passionately, it was all No Surrender! And Not Another Inch! But we never had suicide bombers, did we? Jimmy knew that; knew there was always a point where we'd back down or cave in.'

'The hunger strikers?'

'Aw, fuck them. Miss a few meals and then you black out so it stops being your choice and becomes someone else's – that's not brave, that's just stupid. Brave's walking into a restaurant with a bomb strapped to your belly and blowing yourself and everyone else to hell. But we never had that. So Jimmy knew all he had to find was the breaking-point, and he did – that's why he scared the shit out of everyone. But now . . .' Pink sighed. 'It's just not the same. The cops, sure the half of them are *Fenians* these days anyway. They think the war's over, and even when they do find someone, their hands are tied. Jimmy Marsh Mallow, in his day, his *pomp*, he knew where the bodies were hid, and if he didn't have enough to arrest you, he wasn't shy about tipping off this side or that and you ended up with a bullet in the neck – you know what I mean?'

Billy nodded.

'Yeah, oul' Jimmy's the last of a dying breed. Surprised they haven't put him out to seed already. Sometimes I think he's hanging on just so as he can put me away, you know what I mean?'

'You'll never let him do that.'

'With your help, Billy, with your help. Now, what have you got for me?'

'Just a few things I need you to initial. Everything's in order – I don't foresee any problems.' Billy extracted a folder from his briefcase, opened it at the correct section and passed it across. 'I've x'd where you need to sign.'

Pink quickly scribbled his name, then flipped the cover back over and smiled benevolently at Billy. 'You're doing a good job, son.'

'Thanks, Mr Harrison.'

'Anything I can do for you? You need another TV?'

'No, thanks. With that cop watching me, it's better not.'

'The money's still going into the account?'

'Yes, Mr Harrison, regular as clockwork.'

'Sometimes if I don't actually hand it over in a paper bag, I don't feel like you're getting it.'

'Don't worry. It's fine.' As Pink went to hand the file back to Billy his eyes fell on the words scrawled upside down close to the bottom corner of the front cover. He turned it round. 'What's this?'

Billy squinted at it. 'Oh, nothing. Your man Mallow had a call, needed to write an address down. I think it's that wee lad's family – you know, the one who had his head cut off?'

Pink nodded. 'Right. Sad.'

He handed the file back, then stubbed his cigar out on the tiled floor of his conservatory. He stood up and yanked the door open. 'All right, mate, keep me posted.' His dismissal was abrupt, but not unusual. Billy pushed the file into his briefcase, and jumped to his feet, already drinking in the cool air as it rushed into the hot-house. As he stepped into the opening, Pink suddenly spoke his name. Billy stopped.

'Yes?'

'Don't call us, we'll call you.'

Billy forced a smile, then hurried up the lawn towards the house, certain that Pink was watching him every step of the way, but too nervous to glance back and check.

65

On the Run!

It wasn't as if you could look up FARC in the telephone directory. If it had been Belfast, then clearly he would have known where to go, who to phone, the safe houses, the right codewords, but this was Bogotá, Colombia, as wild as any city on earth.

Redmond O'Boyle hadn't a clue. He wasn't even sure that he wanted to deliver himself back into FARC's hands, because he knew what he would do in their position. Use him. Parade him like the Elephant Man. And he couldn't face that. Sure, they'd got him out of the prison, but they hadn't foreseen that the British Embassy would claim his body, nor had they been able to do anything about his being shipped to the local crematorium. They probably weren't even aware of it, yet. Redmond was, because of the cremation instructions taped to the side of his coffin, personally signed by Ambassador Brown. He was now alive and free because of his own training, his own finely honed survival instincts – and because the coffin they'd transported him in wasn't much stronger than cardboard. Sensibly, the undertakers had reasoned, if they were going to burn the coffin, what was the point in making it out of valuable wood? That, or the Brits were real cheapskates. Whatever, it had saved Redmond's life.

Borrowing some clothes hadn't been a problem. He was now wearing a very fine suit, although it was slightly large and smelled of death. Purloining a few dollars from the crematorium staff while they ate lunch was easy enough, and sneaking out was straightforward; although security in all buildings in Colombia was pretty tight, it was designed to keep people out, rather than in. Even sauntering down the street towards the city centre wasn't difficult. He had tanned up during his time in South America, and with that and the ill-fitting suit and fading light, passed quite easily for a local businessman, and thus avoided the traditional greeting for footloose foreigners of being kidnapped and held for ransom. But the fact was, he was quite alone. He could turn to

Siobhan, that was true. But what use had she been? With Sinn Fein's shift to 'democracy' she would as likely rat him out as anyone. No, the only person he could turn to, the only person who he might conceivably have any leverage over was that pompous oaf Ambassador Brown.

'Who do you think you are, calling me a pompous oaf?' was the Ambassador's initial reaction.

'I'll tell you who I f***ing am, Ambassador. I'm the man you sent to be cremated without checking whether he was f***ing alive or not! I'm the man you would have burned to a crisp if I hadn't had the f***ing wherewithal to get out of a f***ing coffin. Do you hear me?'

'I hear you,' the Ambassador said down the line, already sweated through his shirt.

'And what's more, you fat p**ck, unless you help me out, it's you who'll be wishing you were in a f***ing coffin, do you hear me?'

'I hear you.'

Redmond told him what to bring, and where to meet him. The Ambassador said it would take him several hours to organise. Redmond told him he had sixty minutes, or he was calling Reuters.

This sent Ambassador Brown into a blind panic. There were contingency plans for these kinds of situations. British citizens abroad were always getting into trouble of some kind which required their being spirited out of the country, so there would not ordinarily have been a problem with issuing a new passport, but this was different. If he was simply to hand over the passport Redmond was demanding, and the fugitive then got caught, it would be immediately traced back to him, and his mishandling of the cremation would be exposed, together with this cover-up. No, a British passport would certainly not do. There was also a fund he could draw upon to deliver the cash Redmond was demanding, but everything had to be signed for in triplicate and justified further down the line. How much worse would it look if Redmond's flight had actually been financed by the British Government?

One and a half hours later, Ambassador Brown hurried into the smoky interior of O'Houlihan's Irish Pub, and found Redmond sitting in a window seat sipping a pint of Guinness.

'You're late,' Redmond snapped.

'Sorry,' Martin Brown gasped, wiping a handkerchief across his brow. 'It just took a little time.' He glanced nervously about him. 'You're sure this is a good idea?'

'You never heard of hiding in plain sight, Ambassador?'

'Well, I—'

'Besides, it might say Irish over the door, and this might well be Guinness, but the barman's French and every other customer's gibbering in Spanish, so relax. Did you bring?'

Ambassador Brown pulled out a chair and sat heavily. 'I brought.' He took a Manila envelope from his jacket pocket and slipped it under the table for Redmond to take.

Redmond shook his head. 'This isn't f***ing Graham Greene, Ambassador. Just f***ing give it to me.'

'Oh. Yes. Of course.' He handed it across the table.

Redmond glanced up at the bar. 'You want a drink?'

'No, really, I'm fine,' the Ambassador responded, although he could barely swallow. 'Must be going. Everything all right?'

Redmond appeared satisfied by the large wedge of dollar bills Ambassador Brown had withdrawn from his own personal bank account twenty minutes previously. Then he removed the passport with its mauve EC cover and flicked it open. The Ambassador held his breath. Redmond's brow furrowed.

'What the f**k's this?'

'It's the best I could do at such short notice.'

'I'm not f***ing Swedish.'

'Yes, you are. You were brought up in Ireland, but you're a Swedish national. We have a reciprocal agreement to get each other out of trouble.'

Redmond examined the photograph, which was his, clearly drawn from his old passport, but then his lip curled as he tried to pronounce his new name. 'V . . . Viggo Mortensen?'

'Viggo Mortensen,' agreed the Ambassador.

'Why does that sound familiar?'

'I'm given to understand it's a very common name in Sweden.'

Redmond looked at it doubtfully. 'This wasn't what I asked for.'

The Ambassador nodded. 'I know that. But you have to realise – I can't just give you a fresh British passport. I'm helping you on the understanding that you disappear without trace. If by chance you are discovered, it can't be traced back to us. To me, in fact.'

Redmond shook his head. 'You didn't even check if I was dead.'

'I had no reason to doubt—'

'I could have been burned alive!'

'I realise that. Most regrettable. But your wife was most insistent.'

'Maeve? You spoke to her?'

'Yes, of course, I was merely following her precise instructions.'

'How was she?'

'Well, upset obviously, I think, but hiding it well, bravely. She said she was under tremendous pressure to have you flown home and there was rioting going on and she didn't want a martyr made of you.'

'Rioting?'

'Oh yes, I believe they're tearing Belfast up.'

'So they're getting behind me at last.'

'Well, I wouldn't go that far. I'm given to understand that last time they had a riot it was because Celtic lost a football match, and that lasted longer. Redmond, please, your wife was right. They wanted to use you, as a symbol, but they were quite happy to leave you here to rot. Which in fact, you did. It's what killed you. But you're free now, you have money, and you're Swedish. You can start again. A completely new life. If only we all had that chance, eh?'

Redmond turned the passport over in his hand. He hated to admit it, but the Ambassador was right. It wasn't just the British who had tried to cremate him, it was his wife as well, and, ultimately, the entire Republican movement. He had no family now, no cause but his own. And if that meant being Swedish, by God, then he would be Swedish. He raised his glass and tilted it across the table. 'All right, Ambassador,' he said. 'We have a deal.' He even gave him a wink.

Ambassador Brown breathed an audible sigh of relief. Excellent! He had at least bought himself some time. The Swedish Embassy had only lent him the passport. It was due to be collected the following day by Viggo Mortensen, the visiting star of *The Lord of the Rings* trilogy, who held dual American and Swedish citizenship, and who had lost his original passport while whitewater rafting. Now the Ambassador had twenty-four hours to find and recruit an assassin who could remove the problem of Redmond O'Boyle for good, rescue the passport and retrieve his retirement fund. How difficult could that be? It was Bogotá, for godsake. Probably the first person he stopped in the street would do it.

66

Carrot Cake and Caresses

Maeve knew it was time to get out when a brick came whizzing through her front window. There was an angry crowd outside. She yelled through the jagged hole, 'Why don't youse all just f**k off!' but they paid no heed. They were upset that she'd had their hero and her husband cremated. Great plans had been laid by certain elements within the Republican movement to stage an elaborate funeral for their new martyr. Sinn Fein and Amnesty International had each issued statements pointing out that Redmond had not been convicted of any crime and had died alone and abandoned by the British Government, who had to take full responsibility, along with naturally, the Colombians who'd thrown him into prison in the first place on the basis of disputed evidence; and while they were at it, Amnesty International had a swipe at Colombia's history of legal corruption and its place at the head of the international league table of states up to their oxters in the drugs trade.

What all of this boiled down to was the fact that there were a lot of angry people outside Maeve's house. They were baying for blood.

Maeve, who was no stranger to rioters baying for blood, hurried upstairs, packed a bag and hightailed it out the back way. She wore a hooded anorak. When she got down onto the Falls Road proper she stopped a black taxi and asked to be taken to the Lisburn Road. The driver eyed her in the mirror, but if he recognised her he didn't say. But just in case, she got him to drop her well short of *Irma La Deuce*. She didn't want him taking his suspicions back to West Belfast, and then have a mob rampage through Jack Fincucane's carrot cakes.

Jack himself was pleased – and surprised – to see her coming through the doors, at least until he saw her suitcase. He thought she was lovely, but wasn't ready to have her move in on the basis of one date and a snog which had ended with her screaming her head off.

He sat her down at a table he had brought out especially for her –

246

the café was crammed – and cut her a slice of coconut carrot cake and brought this over, together with a cappuccino.

She wailed, 'What am I going to do?'

'Things will settle down.'

'No – you don't understand. I can never go back.'

'They'll forget about it.'

'They *never* forget. I had a neighbour who once criticised Gerry Adams, and he hasn't been out of the house since, and that was 1974.'

Jack patted her hand. She looked at him with big, pleading eyes.

'Don't you have friends, relatives?'

'No!'

'What about the girl I poisoned – s**t, I mean she had an allergic reaction – can't you stay with her?'

'Margaret? No. I don't know. She only has a wee place. And I hardly know her.' Maeve dabbed at her eyes. 'Right enough, only the other day she said if there was anything she could do to help, I should call her.'

Jack had his mobile phone out in a flash. 'Here,' he said.

She took it. She turned it over in her hand. 'You don't want me here.'

'Of course I want you here.'

'When I walked through that door with my suitcase, you nearly had a heart-attack.'

'I was just surprised to see you. But it's great that you're here. Honestly.'

'We kissed.'

'Yes, we did.'

'It was really nice.'

'Yes, it was.'

'But at the end of the day, it's a first date, and now I land in on you like I expect you to let me move in.'

'No, not at all.'

'I'm sorry, I'm just upset . . .'

'No, really . . .'

'I just had this kind of a fantasy, with your big safe arms around me and us having sex all night.'

'Well, there's no harm in you staying for one night.'

'No, it wouldn't be right. I'll phone Margaret.'

'No, look, what harm can it do, a couple of nights. Here, give me the phone.'

'No, seriously, we hardly know each other. Why take the chance of ruining something before it's hardly started. I'll phone her.'

'No, come on, give me the phone. I should've been more—'

'It's all right. I *understand*. It's no problem.' She took her own mobile out of her handbag and checked Margaret's number. Then she jabbed it into Jack's phone and replaced her own phone. This didn't strike her as odd. It was training. Waste not, want not. She took another bite of carrot cake while she waited for a response.

'There's no need, Maeve,' said Jack.

Maeve held up a placatory hand, and mouthed, 'Here we go.'

Jack sat back in his chair, frowning and horny.

'Margaret – it's me.'

'Me?' Her voice sounded slightly echoey.

'Maeve. Christ, Margaret, I need your help.'

'Why, love, what's the matter?'

'They went and did it, with Redmond.'

'They . . . ?'

'Cremated him.'

'Oh God.'

'I know, but even worse, everyone round here's gone mental on me.'

'Mental?'

'They've smashed my windows and I had to jump out over the back fence or they would've strung me up.'

'Christ, Maeve, that's terrible.'

'I know, but I'm stuck, Margaret. I've nowhere to go.'

'. . .'

'It would just be for a couple of nights until I sort something out.'

'. . .'

'Even just for tonight.'

'Maeve, I can't.'

'. . .'

'It's not that I . . .'

'. . .'

'Honestly, did you not hear what happened to me?'

'To you?'

'Yes, love. And where do you think I am now?'

'I've no idea.'

'Well, to cut a long story short, I'm in the cop shop. Maeve, I swear to God you wouldn't believe it, but it'll be on the news by now, I'm sure. I was down looking over this apartment, and guess who was there as well? Swear to God, your man Walter looking at it at the same time, and we had this row and I ended up in the river.'

'He *threw* you in the river?!'

'No, no, I slipped – but that's not what it's about. I was sitting on my arse in the water and I put my hand down to help me out except

I thought I was putting it on a rock but it wasn't, it was a head – a dead head. Maeve, do you hear what I'm saying? That wee lad whose body they found, well, I found his head.'

'Christ, Margaret.'

'So now I'm down the police station doing statements and stuff and I've no idea how long I'll be here. I mean, it's not like they think I'm involved or anything, but that's never stopped them before, has it? Think of your poor dead husband. They're just taking forever so I can't let you sleep at my place. Ordinarily it wouldn't be a problem, you know that. Do you understand?'

'Of course I do, love. God, what are we like, the two of us, eh? Front-page news, that's us.'

Down the line Maeve heard what sounded like a door opening and heels on tiles, then Margaret whispered urgently, 'Have to go – I'll give you a buzz tomorrow, all right?' Then the line was cut.

Maeve closed the phone and handed it back to Jack. She said, somewhat sarcastically, 'Well, it looks like it's your lucky night.'

Jack nodded gravely, but leaped about inside.

Less than 200 yards away, Margaret strode out of the Ladies toilets in Pizza Hut, determined that she wasn't going to let anything spoil her second date with Walter North.

67

Democracy at Work

It took Mark some considerable time to decide what to wear for his first night on the campaign trail. In fact, there was no campaign as such, as the elections weren't long over and his man, Pink Harrison, had enjoyed a comfortable majority, but it felt like a campaign, because it was his first night 'on the stump', the beginning of his own political career. He had to talk to the people, thank those who had voted for Pink and re-assure them that good times were ahead, and try to convert those who hadn't. But deciding what to wear was a pain.

Pink's council ward was very definitely working class, which Mark very definitely wasn't. He wore a designer suit to work and had half a dozen pairs of expensive shoes at home. What he needed to do was relate to the voters without condescension while still communicating the fact that because he was clearly much better off and had gone to university and had enjoyed a gap year helping Guatemalan orphans, he was in a much better position than they were to get things done. It was, of course, a predominantly Protestant, Unionist area, so he could have worn a Rangers top and added 'mate', in the local parl-ance, to try and ease things along, but he was not naïve enough to believe they would fall for that any more than the blackest ghetto would fall for a white rapper. (Apart from Eminem.) But an expen-sive suit and tie and sharp shoes – what would that say? That was back to the days of the *old* Unionist Party, when it was little more than a genial social gathering for the horsey set. Better something off the rack, and not just any rack, something out of say, Primark – cheap 'n' cheerless. But even then, how would they know the difference – unless he left the labels on, or allowed his jacket to flap open from time to time so that they could see a 25% *off* sticker. No, that just wouldn't do.

In the end, he settled on transparency: he wasn't ashamed of his expensive suit or his sharp shoes. But no tie. An open-necked shirt.

Informal. He thought about a gold chain for his neck, but rejected it. He thought about a temporary tattoo – *For God and Ulster, No Surrender* or *I Love Me Ma*, but that was too tacky, and would also have meant him having to push up the sleeves of his suit as if he was in *Miami Vice*, which was just not going to happen.

He set out at 7 p.m. in the company of Jinko, Marty and Bull, three chaps who worked exclusively with Pink Harrison. Jinko, tall and thin in black jeans and a hooded sweatshirt, handed out photocopies of the electoral register for the area, then gave each of them three streets 'to work'. Mark studied his list quickly – there were about seventy houses.

'All right,' said Jinko, 'I'll see you back here in an hour.'

'An *hour*?' said Mark, surprised.

'Well, if you're any quicker, get us a Twix from the shop.'

Mark blinked at him. Bull, who naturally looked a bit like a bull, with the bulk and two large freckles on his forehead where horns might once have jutted out, looked Mark up and down and said, 'Where's the party?'

Before Mark could respond, they all chorused, '*We're* the Party!' then split off in their various directions. Marty and Bull were wearing tracksuit bottoms and trainers; Marty had on a Linfield shirt and Bull a grey T-shirt which had once been white.

As he approached Del Rosa Avenue, the first of his three streets, Mark made a mental calculation, entirely based on probability. He reckoned about a third of the houses would be empty – down at the pub, or in the chip shop – another third would just say 'No, thank you for calling, we're fine, Pink's great, good night,' so there'd be no delay there, which left another third who might want to stand and chat or have a problem. A third of seventy was twenty-three and a third-ish, which over an hour meant just under three minutes each. He could do that. Time management was one of his strong points. (He had once marked the A-level English papers for an entire Education Board Area in seventeen minutes.) He had thought about bringing a notebook to write down any grievances, complaints or relevant comments to take back to Pink, but in the interests of speed he decided on an iPOD, with an iTalk Dictaphone attachment. He kept it in his pocket, out of sight, switched on.

The houses here were small, ancient terraces, tightly packed. That would help with his timings. No long walks up driveways, no locked gates to struggle with.

Here I go! This is real politics! Out on the streets, helping the people!

Mark rang his first doorbell. He fixed his hair and smoothed out a crease on his trousers. The door did not open. Instead a voice called out, 'Hello?'

'Hi. I'm working with Councillor Harrison and—'

'Hold on.'

Mark stepped back, expecting the door to open. Instead he heard whispered voices, and then a few moments later the letterbox opened and a crumpled envelope was pushed out. Before Mark could catch it, it fell to the ground, hitting the footpath with a definite clink of coin. Mark picked it up. 'I'm sorry, I—' he began, addressing the closed door, but all he could see through the glass panel was the glimpse of a TV and then an inner door closing. Mark examined the envelope. *Pink* was scrawled on the front.

He didn't quite know what to think. Obiously they didn't want to talk directly with him, choosing to write to their Councillor instead, and making a small financial donation to the Party as well. Well, fair enough.

Mark went to the next house – nobody in.

The next – nobody in, although he had the definite impression of a curtain moving as he passed.

At the fourth house the door opened and a hard-looking woman with a jam-faced child in her arms rolled her eyes when he introduced himself, then turned back into her living room. *Emmerdale* was blasting out of the TV, and was being watched by three other children, a grandparent and a bull terrier. The woman began shifting the children off the sofa, then looking under the cushions, straining as her fingers pressed down the sides. Eventually she came up with half a dozen coins, which she jangled in her hand while she looked around for something. Eventually she came back out into the narrow hall, lifted a red-tinged envelope off the telephone stand, ripped it open, allowed the bill to drop to the floor, then slid the coins into it. She held it out for Mark, snarling, 'Tell him those f***ing bins aren't sorted out yet.'

Mark nodded, took the envelope, then stood speechless as the door was slammed in his face.

In the following fifty minutes, Mark collected fifty-three envelopes. When he walked, he jangled like a porcelain piggy bank. He never once got beyond saying, 'I work for Councillor Harrison,' before money was thrust into his hands. Several people didn't even bother with envelopes so that his pockets bulged with crumpled notes and coins of every denomination. When he returned to the rendezvous point the others were already there and similarly weighed down. Mark was too stunned to even ask. He had kept a check on which houses he had failed to get a response from, and Jinko compared this with a list of his own. Then he jabbed a finger at one name and said, 'Right, that's two months in a row.' He turned to Bull and Marty. 'Okay, lads – the Martins at seventy-two.' Bull went

252

over to the ancient Metro they'd arrived in and popped open the boot. He lifted out a baseball bat and handed it to Marty, then took one for himself.

Mark's mouth worked, fishlike. He finally managed an elongated, 'W.w.w.w.w.w.w.wait a minute.'

Bull and Marty had no intention of waiting anything. Mark urgently studied his list again, then looked sharply up at Jinko. 'Did you say seventy-two?'

'Aye.'

'You know, I think I missed seventy-two.'

'You missed it?'

'Yes. Aye, I think so. The Martins, you say?'

'The Martins. F***ing tightwads.'

'I really think I did miss them. Just give me a moment, and I'll check.'

Jinko shook his head, but then nodded at Marty and Bull. 'Houl' your horses, then.'

'Sorry,' Mark said as he backed away towards the street corner. 'My fault entirely. First night.' He waved apologetically, then hurried back into Del Rosa Avenue. The Martins – one of the curtain-twitching houses. What was he supposed to say? What was he supposed to do? My God, what had he got himself into?

Mark quickly felt his jacket pocket, then pulled out an envelope containing an invitation to a wedding disco which was several months out of date. He took out the invitation and crushed it into his trouser pocket. Then he took a handful of coins from his other trouser pocket and slipped them into the envelope and sealed it as best he could. He loitered there, out of sight of his Party colleagues, for another three minutes, then sauntered back around the corner, holding the envelope aloft as if he'd just discovered peace (and to a certain extent he had). Marty and Bull reluctantly returned their sporting weapons to the Metro and then all four of them drove back to the Rangers Supporters Club on the Shankhill Road to count the money. Pink was nowhere to be seen.

Eventually Jinko lifted a metal cash-box, with some difficulty, and nodded at Mark. 'You did good tonight, son,' he said. 'I'm gonna run this down to Pink. You want a lift?'

'I've a migraine,' said Mark.

68
Clues

Marsh knew that even people from Belfast tended to forget how small the city actually was. Granted, it punched above its weight in many respects, including in music, boxing, snooker, football and extremes of violence, but from whatever perspective you looked at it, it was undeniably compact. This was advantageous to police work. It also helped that it was a divided city, so that, particularly since the end of The Troubles, crimes which were committed in one part tended to be committed by people from that part. There was very little travelling between the two. The dead boy, although his family now lived in nice, prosperous Bangor, had been brought up in the city, in Rathcoole, which had once been described as the largest subsidised housing estate in Western Europe, as if it was a good thing. Rathcoole was 83 per cent Protestant. The other 17 per cent were Chinese, Indian or Pakistani. There are no agnostics or any atheists in Belfast.

Marsh was philosophical about many things, but was not a believer in, say, the theory that if a butterfly beat its wings in London, it might have repercussions in, perhaps, Peking. However, he was willing to concede that it could work on a smaller scale. If something, anything, happened on an estate like Rathcoole, there was always a knock-on effect. Someone would know about it. It was merely a case of pinning down the butterfly, and burning its wings with a match until it talked. Metaphorically speaking.

Michael Caldwell had gone to Rathcoole Primary, and although his parents had done well for themselves and moved down the coast, the fifteen-year-old's heart had remained in the housing estate. He kept in touch with his old muckers. *Good lad, Michael, we'll miss you. Carl, Alan, Bix.* It wasn't difficult to track them down. They said on the night he disappeared he was supposed to meet them in the city centre, but he never showed up. He got the train from Bangor all right, and they'd CCTV footage of him getting off alone at the Botanic halt rather than at Central Station, probably to avoid walking past the Nationalist Markets area. No trace of him after that. They'd intended going to a club, the boys said. They'd fake ID, and when pressed they admitted they'd bought speed and blow. But Michael hadn't shown, so what did it matter?

Well, it mattered because Michael Caldwell's blood tests showed he was drugged up to the point of OD on the night of his death, and he got it from somewhere, and probably took it with someone, on his way to someplace.

Marsh watched their interviews through the glass, and he read their statements. His crack team said, 'We let them go now, boss?' and he just handed back the paperwork and said, 'Try again.'

The kids, they were cocky, but shocked as well. The Ceasefire had been around long enough for them not to have experienced the worst of it, but there was hardly a week went by without someone getting shot or pulverised on the estate. There was always a feud going on between the UVF and the UDA or the LVF or the UFF, usually about drugs. When one group was doing particularly well, the other would launch a campaign to 'free our streets of these anti-social delinquents' and there would be a spate of knee-cappings, beatings and occasionally murders. Power would shift for a while, and then another campaign to free the streets would be launched. Marsh was constantly surprised that with so much dealing/vigilantism going on, the Protestant paramilitaries had any time left at all with which to defend Ulster from Republicans.

Another six hours went past while the butterfly boys were pinned again. Marsh spent time at his computer. He found the *Let's Be Mates* website oddly addictive, which was frustrating, because there was no way he was going to access it at work. Nothing was secret in the PSNI, and if it got out that he was dallying with a dating service he'd be hauled up before the bigwigs and accused of breaching the Official Secrets Act. That's what it was like. Always looking over your shoulder.

He had laughed – to himself, obviously, because looking at his face you'd think he was reading the Death Notices in the local paper – at the filmic notion of either Michael Caldwell or Pink Harrison being his 'last case', the one he had to solve before he hung up his badge. Because the truth was that there never could be a last case. There would always be one more. He couldn't imagine retiring. To do what – the garden? To work as a f***ing security guard? No. He would die in the saddle. He knew that. And although he had done his best to pass some of it on, most of his knowledge would die with him. How he had led the battle against anarchy. How he had defied politicians and paramilitaries and parasites alike. He had helped to keep this country alive. It was all in there, in his head, how it was done, the harsh lessons learned, the sacrifices made, the glorious triumphs. Yet there was a reluctance to come to him, to ask for the benefits of his experience. He was from a different era. *Times have changed, old man.* No one would say that to his face, of course. But he sensed it. They were just waiting for him to go. He was the police equivalent of a salesman laboriously hauling every single f***ing volume of the *Encylopædia Britannica* from door to door, only to find that not only was it out of date, but that every single person he spoke to was already wired for sound, just needed to *Ask Jeeves* or type it into some other f***ing search engine. They didn't want what he was peddling. And were blissfully unaware of how quickly it could all slip back to the way it was. And then where would they be? Lost, that's where.

There was still a third woman to try on the website. The first he had stood up, the second had been a gunman's widow, like vengeance for the first. The third would be fine. She had to be.

The door opened and Gary McBride came in. 'Your fella Bix gave up the name of their dealer – works out of one of the amusement arcades down Castle Street. Benny Caproni.'

'I know Benny, don't I?'

The Capronis had immigrated to Belfast a hundred years before to sell ice cream and had made a fortune. Benny was an adopted son, gone bad and disowned.

Gary nodded. 'Drugs, sure, but he runs hookers and some boys as well.'

'Bix?'

Swears to God he never turned a trick in his life. But then he would.'

In the paramilitary handbook, sodomy was right next to Republicanism. Which made it particularly brave of Pink Harrison to play camp. Pink, up to a point, could protect himself, but there wasn't much a fifteen-year-old could do if word got out.

'What's he say about our boy?'

'Says Michael didn't either, but who knows.'

'Let's talk to Caproni then.'

Gary turned for the door, then hesitated. 'Let them go?'

'You think there's anything else?'

'Hard to tell.'

Marsh thought for a moment, then nodded. 'Let them go. But let it be known we've spoken to them – see what that flushes out.'

Gary nodded.

When he'd gone, Marsh took out the photographs Michael

256

Caldwell's mum had given him, then spread them out face-down on his desk. He turned them over, one by one, saying, 'Talk to me, Michael. Talk to me.'

You wouldn't get that on *Ask Jeeves*.

69

O Brother, Where Art Thou?

Redmond, in keeping with a man who had recently escaped from prison, defied death and finagled many thousands of dollars out of the British Government, probably drank a few more pints of Guinness than was strictly wise. He sat in the corner, talking to no one but watching the endless stream of humanity flowing past outside. It was, literally, the first day of the rest of his life. It was as if he had not previously existed. He was nobody. Or Swedish, which often amounted to one and the same. He was Viggo.

I am Viggo.

I am Viggo Mortensen.

He practised saying it. He tried it with his own accent, then with an American accent, and then with his approximation of a Swedish accent. He ordered another pint in this accent, and although in truth it sounded a little bit like a Muppet ordering Guinness, the message got through to the French barman. He tried it again half an hour later, but this time being more adventurous. He ordered chilli and rice from the menu. When he handed over his crisp new dollars, the barman said, 'Merci, Father.'

Redmond blinked at him uncomprehendingly for a moment, then returned to his seat. As he ate his meal, he became aware that several of the customers were glancing across at him. Then, when he went to the toilet, and another customer was just coming out and he held the door for him, the customer nodded and said, 'Thank you, Father,' in English but with a Spanish twist.

When this customer got up to leave half an hour later, he nodded again at Redmond, then tapped the newspaper sitting at his table and shook his head sympathetically. Redmond nodded back. Then he scurried across to retrieve the paper. It was the main local daily. And there, on the front page, was his photograph. Or what would have looked like his photograph to anyone who wasn't family. It was his brother,

I Predict A Riot

Damian, Father Damian, standing with that useless Sinn Fein bitch Siobhan, outside the British Embassy, obviously giving off s**t about their treatment of Redmond O'Boyle.

Redmond took a long drink. He was nobody, with no history and a potentially wonderful future. But he was also a brother, and that brother was in this very city.

He and Damian had always chosen very different paths. There were many in Belfast who considered the Catholic Church to be little more than the religious wing of the Provisional IRA, but Redmond knew that wasn't strictly true. They were just accommodating. Christian people were supposed to be. Even Hitler had never been excommunicated, though he had received several written warnings. But Damian had always been against violence of any hue. They had fought about it, literally, when they were younger, and then talked about it, as adults, never agreeing, often shouting and pointing, but never, ever falling out to such an extent that they stopped talking or going out for a drink. Now Damian was in this very city. Probably heartbroken, as Redmond himself would be if anything ever happened to Damian. He was a priest, the pride of their family. Every Catholic mother wants a priest for a son, although also one who can provide for them in their retirement, which neither of these brothers was likely to manage. The best Redmond could hope for now was to make his fortune under his new identity and then wire his mother anonymous cash from Stockholm.

Redmond scanned down the article, looking for some clue as to where his brother might be now, whether or not he had already left the country. But finding none, he racked his brain to try and recall where Siobhan had been staying. He remembered her complaining about the hotel, and then saying she'd moved to somewhere much more luxurious, and there couldn't be many of those in Bogotá. The Hilton, the Marriott perhaps?

Redmond drained his pint, left a healthy tip, then reconsidered and reclaimed it. There was no telling how long the dollars were going to have to last him. Outside, in the sticky swirl of downtown Bogotá, he hailed a taxi. A moment after he had climbed in and was driven off, a second taxi was hailed down outside the same bar.

The man climbing in said, 'Follow that cab,' although in Spanish, which didn't sound half as impressive. He had two hundred dollars in his left pocket, and a gun in his right. In his back pocket he had a photograph of Redmond O'Boyle. In his heart he had nothing but the desire for indoor plumbing.

Father Damian was a good man, and had a way with people. But he was neither decisive nor commanding, and was well suited to his small country parish in a remote part of Tyrone which The Troubles had scarcely troubled. He believed in God and the Pope and Ireland, and was occasionally known to drink and wax lyrical about the God-given powers of George Best. Though he had grown up amidst the turmoil of West Belfast in the 1970s, he was not really a city boy. Belfast, even now, made him nervous. How much more nervous then was he in Bogotá, the kidnap capital of the world (still, despite Baghdad), with his brother cremated and his only company the cloying, whining bag of wind that was Sinn Fein Siobhan? The words of anger and frustration he had spoken on the steps of the British Embassy had been delivered in little more than a tremulous whisper; what had made them sound strident was their translation, yelled with furious abandon, like gunshots over a martyr's coffin, by the gregarious Carlos, earning $30 an hour, and who apparently performed in this manner on every occasion, be it a political polemic or reading the latest weather reports on *Voice of America*.

There were not many television channels in Colombia, and the death of Redmond O'Boyle and his rapid cremation had caused a stir. Everywhere he went, police warned Father Damian to stay indoors because people hated FARC; yet each time he ventured outside, people clapped their hands, smiled and crossed themselves. It made him think that perhaps revolution was in the air. Even now, sitting in the bar of the Bogotá Hilton, everyone was all smiles and waves. Siobhan, thanks be to God, was lounging by the pool outside. Father Damian sipped at his Guinness and thought of poor departed Redmond, the black sheep of the family, but still *of* the family. He became aware of the barman waving at him, so he waved back. But no, more than a wave, a phone was being held out to him. Father Damian looked behind him, in case it was for someone else, then pointed at himself; the barman nodded extravagantly. Father Damian wiped his lips on the back of his hand and hurried across. He was sick of talking to the press, but too polite to refuse.

He said a tired, 'Yes, Father Damian O'Boyle,' into the receiver.

'How're you doin', you old bollox?'

Father Damian said, 'Excuse me?'

'Excuse me? Who do you think you're talking to, you old b***ard.'

Father Damian glanced about him; his face had reddened considerably. 'Well, I'm really not sure.'

'Do you not recognise the voice?'

'It's certainly familiar, but . . .' It was a voice from home, that's all he could say with any certainty.

'I know things about you, Father.'

Father Damian cleared his throat. 'I, ah, don't really know what to say to that.'

'You've a scar on the back of your head where Seanie Morrow hit you with a brick when you were seven, and you only ever told one other living soul how you got it.'

'Why, yes I have. And I did. Who *is* this?'

'Have you no idea at all?'

'I'm sorry, it's been a confusing few days.'

'When you were eleven you stole a Slade album out of Woolies and gave it to your ma for her birthday.'

'My goodness – yes, I did. But I never told anyone.'

'Anyone?'

'Well, no one apart from . . .' he began. Then he stopped. 'I'm sorry, I've really no idea.'

'And you've a large brown freckle on your left bollock – now who the hell else is going to know that but your sainted mother who'd never mention it in a million years, and the brother you shared a bath with?'

For several moments there was only the slight hiss of a pre-war Colombian telephone exchange. And then Father Damian whispered with quiet disbelief, 'Is it Father Benedict?'

'No, you friggin' idiot, it's your brother Redmond.'

Father Damian caught his breath. 'That's not possible . . . This isn't funny, this isn't funny at all.' He had gone deathly white.

'Damian, for Jesus sake, it's *me*! Do you not recognise my voice at all?'

'But you're . . . you're . . .'

'I'm upstairs.'

'Holy Mother of God.' There was a bottle of beer sitting on the bar before him, awaiting delivery to another table, but Father Damian grabbed hold of it and took a long swig. Then he spoke slowly and deliberately into the receiver. 'And . . . they . . . have . . . telephones . . . up there . . . do they?'

'What the hell are you talking about? For Jesus sake, Damers, will you put the phone down and get up here now. I can't get your friggin' minibar open without your key.'

The line went dead. Father Damian held onto the bar for support while the world spun out of control around him.

70
Jumping the Gun

Walter was surprised to see Mark sitting at his desk when he arrived in work the next morning. 'I thought you were moving to Office Twelve?'

'I am,' Mark said sullenly.

'Then why the long face, as the barman said to the horse.'

'No reason. Why should there be a reason? I haven't a long face.'

Walter switched on his computer. 'So, how did it go last night, then?'

'Fine.'

'Pounding the streets, were you?'

'Yeah.'

'And?'

'And what?'

'What was it like, meeting the people, hearing their problems, seeing democracy at work? Did Pink show his face?'

'That's Councillor Harrison to you.'

'Well, did he?'

'No.'

'But it went all right?'

'Yeah. I suppose.'

'And when are you doing it again?'

'Tonight.'

Mark looked glumly down at his screen. Walter looked glumly down at his desk, where the gravy rings traditionally sat.

'You know,' Walter said, 'I wouldn't worry about it. Some politicians have the common touch, but then they're crap at everything else, and some just can't handle people at all, and they change the world.'

'You haven't a clue what you're talking about.'

'I know that. I'm only trying to help.'

I Predict A Riot

Mark sat back. Folded his arms.

'So what about Office Twelve? When are you moving?'

Mark shrugged. 'I don't know. Maybe later. There's paperwork to be sorted.'

'You know – you don't have to go.'

Mark nodded slowly. 'I know that.' But he did have to go. He *definitely* knew that. He was in now, he was part of it, and he didn't like it one bit.

The estate agent Linda Wray called Walter on his mobile in the early afternoon. 'Your offer has been accepted,' she said.

'What offer?' asked Walter.

'For the apartment – the penthouse apartment at Towerview. You were most insistent. Well, it's been accepted.'

'Oh,' said Walter. Truth be told, he'd entirely forgotten about the apartment and his grand plan; even Bertha had fallen by the wayside. His pizza with Margaret had been wonderful. Not the pizza, which had been hard as a discus, but sitting with her chatting, as if none of what had happened to them previously had happened at all. He had driven her home afterwards and they had kissed in the front seat of the car, like teenagers. There was even romantic music on the radio. He hadn't tried to go in, and she hadn't encouraged him. It was just nice the way it was. They had arranged a second date. Everything was going to work out fine.

'You've changed your mind?' Linda asked, slightly panicked because she was depending on the commission.

'No, no, not at all. Sorry, my mind was elsewhere. That's great, that's fantastic.'

'Oh, that's good. I was worried you would be put off by that – you know . . .'

'The dead head in the water.'

'The dead head in the water. Wasn't it awful?'

'Bit of a shock to the system.'

'Your girlfriend must have been horrified.'

'She's not my girlfriend.'

They had had one date, snogged, and set up another, so technically she *was* his girlfriend. But they hadn't exactly said it: *You're my girlfriend. Let's be boyfriend and girlfriend.* And also Walter had detected an ever so slight interest from this Linda Wray, and as lightning had never in his life struck twice in the same place, and given the already bumpy history of his short relationship with Margaret and the racing certainty that it would all go pear-shaped again in the near future, he decided that it was better to keep all options open, all bases covered.

'Oh. I thought, from the way you . . . like a lover's tiff . . .'

'We went out twice, that's all.'

'I thought you had a row, and you pushed her in the river. I was watching from the balcony.'

'Good God, no! She jumped in! She's as mad as a bag of spiders.'

'Oh I see. She did seem a bit flighty.'

'So there you go.'

'Oh. Well. Anyway. So your offer's been accepted.'

'Excellent. What happens next?'

'Well, you'd need to get your mortgage confirmed and—'

'It won't be a problem. As you know, Bertha is financing a lot of it.'

'Oh yes, of course. Bertha – I'd forgotten. How is she?'

'She's fine.'

'Great. Excellent. There's a few things I need you to sign . . .'

'I'd really like another look at the penthouse.'

'Well, why don't I meet you there? You can sign—'

'—and have another look round at the same time.'

'Excellent,' said Linda.

They arranged a time after work. Walter felt quite flushed when he came off the phone. He glanced across at Mark, who was smiling.

'What?'

'I have a Margaret Gilmore holding for you.'

'Oh. Right.'

Mark shook his head, then transferred the call.

'Hello you,' said Walter.

'Hello *you*,' said Margaret.

'Sorry, I was tied up.'

'You're a busy man.'

'Well, I wouldn't go that far. How're you doing?'

'Fine. Great, yeah, tired though. Last night was nice.'

'Good pizza,' said Walter.

'I was thinking,' said Margaret.

'That's always dangerous,' said Walter.

She laughed. 'I was thinking – and this is really, really forward, and I won't be offended if you tell me to catch myself on. But I was thinking, this apartment – you're still buying it?'

'Well, there's a few things to sort out, but yeah, I think so.'

'And you're buying it to let it out, aren't you?'

'That's the plan.'

'Well, I'm looking for a place.'

Walter hesitated, just for a moment, but long enough for her to leap in.

'I *am* being forward, I shouldn't have said anything.'

'No, no.'

'I am. You hardly know me and here's me trying to—'

'No, seriously.'

'I just thought, obviously it would all be done properly, with proper contracts and a rent book – the whole thing. I really like it you see, but I'm not in a position to buy at the moment and I just thought, what's the harm in asking. But now I wish I hadn't.'

'It's fine. Honestly.'

'Honestly?'

'Yeah. But I haven't bought the place yet. It could be a couple of months before all the paperwork gets sorted.'

'That's no problem. As long as I know I've somewhere to go.'

They were quiet for a few moments then.

'Are you all right?' Margaret asked.

'Fine. Yes. Just work – difficult to talk.'

'I know. Look, I really enjoyed last night, and I didn't even have a nightmare about the head, so that's how good it was. So let's not . . . let's not ruin things again. Honesty is the best policy.'

'I totally agree.'

'And I'll see you tomorrow night.'

'Tomorrow night.'

She gave a little kissing sound, and he gave one back. She put the phone down. When Walter looked up, Mark made a little kissing sound, but didn't take his eyes off his computer screen.

'Shut your face,' said Walter.

'Shut your own,' said Mark.

71
Extreme Make-over

Mr Kawolski had been pacing back and forth all morning, making them all nervous. It was an open secret that he had a bit of a thing for Maeve, and even though he had been hopelessly inadequate when it came to showing support for her while her husband lay in a Colombian prison, they knew that was only because he had difficulty expressing his feelings, and because he was the boss, and because he was married with five children and a wife with rheumatoid arthritis with whom he hadn't had sex in thirty-six months. But he'd helped in his own way. By not keeping too much of an eye on her when she clocked in and out. Fending off press enquiries. Getting her sandwiches from the canteen. But he had heard on the news that her house had been burned down in rioting in West Belfast, and now she hadn't turned up for work, and he feared the worst.

Margaret kept quiet. She felt dreadful. Maeve had appealed to her for help and she had turned her down. She had been so focused on her date with Walter that she had underestimated the gravity of the situation. It was only when she saw Maeve's house on fire on the breakfast news that she realised how serious it was. And now Maeve hadn't turned up for work.

What if she'd been forced to walk the streets all night?

What if she'd been captured by some mad gang and even now was one of The Disappeared?

Margaret was torn. She should have been feeling lighter than air. Everything was going so well. It was funny, the way things could turn round. One moment in a coma, then having sex with her hated husband, then finding a dead head, the next her fashion line being signed up and even now being secretly designed, Walter snogging like a professional and then offering her somewhere to live. Her! In a penthouse apartment! With a new man! And a bright future!

In some ways it was good that Maeve had disappeared. It kept

I Predict A Riot

Margaret tethered to reality. Life was short and precarious. She still needed to earn a living. It could be months, years before the money started rolling in. So she hadn't resigned her job. It was early days yet, but the force was with her. She was sure of that.

Poor, poor Maeve. How callous was I? In her very hour of need, I preferred pizza and a snog.

Out on the floor, a blonde woman in a white trenchcoat slipped a set of white briefs into a carrier bag, then moved on. She'd done it casually, but professionally, dropping the briefs in while reaching forward to look at something else. Another shopper might not have noticed anything, but Margaret was a professional. It wasn't the three days of training, or the lessons in unarmed combat; it was working on the front line, day in, day out. She was the pile 'em high sell 'em cheap equivalent of a three-tour Gulf War vet. And it was only slightly less dangerous.

Margaret moved towards the thief. She was tall, five ten, her hair cut short and angular. Attractive, confident, even from the back. She wasn't a one-stop shoplifter, that was for sure, and that was all the better from Margaret's point of view. One packet of briefs could be an accident, or forgetfulness, but a jumper, a bikini, a pair of shoes and two pairs of black jeans, there was no mistake there. Nor was there a particular pattern to it. As the thief moved from counter to counter, she appeared to lift items at random, irrespective of size or price. She mixed the cheapest T-shirts with the high end stuff (or as high end as Primark got). By the time she began to move towards the exit, her bag was bulging.

The rule was, you had to wait until they went outside. Only then was it theft, and you could challenge them. But you had no legal powers whatsoever. It was a citizen's arrest. They'd every right to smash you in the face. Margaret had surreptitiously radioed it in, and now as she followed the thief towards the front doors she made furtive hand signals to three of her colleagues, including Mr Kawolski. She would move in, the others were to lend physical support if needed.

Butterflies flapped in her stomach. This was the exciting bit, this was what made it all worthwhile. Actually – nothing made it worthwhile, but it was the only bit of her work that was vaguely interesting. The fact that she got punched or otherwise assaulted in more than half of these cases only increased the adrenaline.

Just as she was about to take the crucial final step out of Primark, the woman suddenly stopped. 'God!' she announced. 'I nearly forgot to pay!'

Margaret let out an audible sigh as the woman turned slowly – and was surprised to find her smiling widely at the small phalanx of security guards.

'If you could see your faces!' she laughed.

Margaret's mouth dropped open. 'Maeve?!'

Maeve cackled.

'Maeve?!' said Mr Kawolski, moving forward. 'But—'

'Your hair!' cried Margaret.

'Your hair!' cried Mr Kawolski.

'What have you done!' cried Margaret.

'Your hair!' cried Mr Kawolski.

Maeve patted her hair, though there wasn't much of it to pat. 'Jack took one look at it this morning and said it would have to go.'

'Your hair,' whispered Margaret.

'*Jack?*' said Mr Kawolski.

'And with half of West Belfast after me, I thought a new look might help.'

'It takes twenty years off you!' cried Margaret.

'Twenty-five!' cried Mr Kawolski.

'And I had all my make-up done.'

'It's fantastic,' said Margaret.

'Jack paid for it all.'

'Jack?' whispered Mr Kawolski.

'The hair, the make-up, the clothes. But he hasn't seen it yet. What do you think – will he like it?'

'He'll love it!' exclaimed Margaret. She gave Maeve a hug, she couldn't help herself. The transformation was incredible. It really did take years off her. She'd been a sad refugee from the Hair Bear Bunch. Her hair had frightened men off. But now she was *gorgeous*. She looked so sophisticated.

'Yes,' said Maeve, patting her hair. 'It's amazing how shagging all night will encourage a man to get his wallet out.'

Mr Kawolski said, 'You're late again, Maeve. This can't go on.'

'Oh dry up,' said Maeve, thrusting the bag of clothes into his chest. 'I was only seeing how alert youse all were. Excellent work, everyone!'

And with that she strode back through the store towards the staff entrance, her head held high and proud.

72

By Hook or By Crook

Marsh's first thought was, My God, she's ravishing.

Photographs did not do her justice *at all*. Julie Mateer was the third of his admirers from the *Let's Be Mates* website, and the moment she stepped through the door into *Lemon Grass*, and began the short walk towards his table, she turned heads. Even the women watched her pass. She was tall, slim, her black hair cut short, a wide smile, short nose, electric eyes. The seventeen-year-old boy couldn't even get the, 'I'll be your waiter tonight,' out; he just flushed and mumbled and took her coat, and he could hardly stop himself from pressing it against his face and breathing in deeply as he carried it to the cloakroom. There was just something about her.

Julie Mateer's website entry said she was thirty-seven and single. She was a sales rep.

Almost before they got started she said, 'You look sad.'

'What, at my age, on an internet dating site?'

'*No*. I mean, just sad.'

'Well,' Marsh laughed, 'that's the Civil Service for you.'

She smiled. Obviously he hadn't mentioned his specific job. And being a police officer was a Civil Service job.

She asked him about his wife, and he began with the usual few, vaguely dismissive details; but she kept asking more questions, and before he was really aware of it he was telling her about how they'd met and his daughter and how they didn't really get on and how just when things were finally starting to work out, when he was more relaxed about his work – he didn't mention the Ceasefire and the subsequent drop in body count – and was getting good promotions and the pay that went with it, that that was when his wife had got sick. He'd tried to make up for lost time, but it was too late.

At one point, a tear ran down his cheek and Julie reached across and wiped it away, her touch, and smile, loaded with sympathy and compassion. He hardly remembered what he ate. Outside, she slipped an arm through his and kissed him lightly on the lips.

He said, 'Do you fancy a drink?'

Julie nodded.

'It's late though,' said Jimmy Marsh Mallow. 'I'm not sure we'll get in anywhere.'

'Let's go to your place.'

'You're sure?'

Julie nodded.

In the car on the way over – he'd had three drinks, but she made him want to chance it – he said, 'I'm sorry, I must have bored the pants off you, talking about – you know . . .'

'No, it was fine.'

'You hardly got a word in.'

'I was interested. It hasn't been easy for you.'

Marsh shrugged. 'At least I'm here.'

She put her hand lightly on his leg. 'I know.'

Marsh could feel sweat dribbling down the back of his neck. He hadn't felt like *this* in so long. It was like being a teenager again. He had talked ceaselessly of his wife through the three courses of their meal and it had been oddly cathartic to get it out, to finally utter all the depressions and deficiencies of his personal life, while still being careful not to reveal the truth of his profession and the horrors that came with it. But now, on this journey home, which was just a couple of miles, it felt like he was drifting across a continent, that every red light was against him, every roadworks was designed to stop him from having fantastic, wonderful sex with this beautiful woman beside him.

As if she could tell, she said, 'Relax.'

He nodded. There was no guilt now, about his wife. Or daughter. He just wanted this to be good.

He parked in the driveway and hurried round to open her door. He took her by the hand and led her inside, then hurried into the kitchen to fix her a drink.

She sat in the lounge and called in, 'I wasn't expecting it to be so tidy, or to smell so nice.'

He appeared in the doorway, with two drinks. 'I'm well trained,' he said.

He gave her her drink, then crossed to the CD-player and put on some early Stones blues covers. They danced. She kissed him long and soft. And then whispered huskily, 'Where's your bedroom?'

He swallowed. 'Top of the stairs, first left.'

She took his hand and led the way. He stumbled once, halfway up, and giggled. She laughed too. He'd made the bed. She smiled and slipped into the en-suite bathroom. He sat on the edge of the bed, not sure what to do. He dived across and splashed on after-shave. He took his tie off. Then his shoes. She emerged from the en-suite and sat beside him. She nuzzled his neck, kissed his cheek and his ear.

She whispered, 'We should get the money out of the way first.'

'What?'

She kissed his cheek again. 'It just saves – you know – any awkwardness later. I'm really up for this.'

Marsh's heart was threatening to burst out of his chest. He was drunk, he knew that. She was beautiful, he knew that. But she was – Christ Almighty!

Marsh shot to his feet.

'What's wrong, love?' She reached out to caress the front of his trousers.

He sprang back. 'Don't!'

'I thought you wanted this.'

'No! Not with . . . Christ!'

'What is it?'

'I didn't know you were . . . I didn't realise you were . . . You'll have to go.'

She looked coyly at him. 'Is this part of your game?'

'No! Now get out!' He grabbed her arm and yanked her to her feet.

Her smile faded immediately, her eyes cooled. 'Get off me!'

'Then get out!' He pushed her in front of him, out of the bedroom door towards the stairs.

'I didn't come all this way for nothing.'

'Yes, you did.'

She tried to stop, grabbing the wall on both sides of the stairs, and this time there was a hint of desperation in her voice. 'Please. Look, you know it'll be good; it's only two hundred.'

What scared him more than anything was the knowledge that the money was in his wallet and he desperately wanted to.

'No!'

He pushed at her, she held on; he peeled the fingers of her left hand off the wall. She let out a little yelp of pain, then let go with her other hand, but she was quite drunk as well and misjudged her step and balance. Before Jimmy could do anything, she was tumbling down the stairs.

He thundered down after her. She was at the bottom, in an untidy heap; deathly still, but only for a moment. She slowly uncurled, sobbing and cursing at the same time. The way she'd fallen, she'd managed to knee herself in the face. There was blood dribbling from her nose and her top lip was split.

'Oh Christ, oh Christ, look what you've done,' she wailed, although she couldn't see the damage, and would probably have wailed louder if she could have.

'I'm sorry, you just slipped,' said Marsh, kneeling briefly beside her, then rushing into the kitchen to get kitchen roll.

She sat where she was at the foot of the stairs.

'I'll drive you home,' said Marsh, pushing the paper towels into her hand.

'Get me a taxi!'

Marsh fumbled for a taxi number.

She had a mirror out now, and there came a renewed series of curses.

'L-look,' Marsh stammered, 'it was an accident. I just didn't know you were . . .' He turned to his jacket on the couch, pulled out his wallet. Then he cursed. The cash he'd thought he'd had was mostly Euros left over from a trip to Dublin, and the few sterling notes had been used up on the meal. He had barely enough for a taxi.

'Listen, let me . . .' He reached out to her, but she pulled away.

He hurried upstairs, then reappeared with his cheque book. He wrote her a cheque for £300. She looked at it for a moment, then crushed it into her handbag.

There was a taxi on the way. She sat at the bottom of the stairs, sniffing and dabbing. He stood in the doorway. It seemed to take about four hours for the car to arrive, but it was only a few minutes. It pumped its horn outside. He opened the front door for her.

'I'm really sorry,' he said again.

She shook her head and went to leave. Then she stopped and said, 'I know it was an accident. That's all right. But a word of advice. Cut the crap about your dead wife, it's not much of a turn-on. And another thing. I've never met a man so desperately in need of a shag. You should get out more.'

With that she hurried out and down the drive.

Marsh closed the front door and leaned against it. When he went into the lounge and picked up his drink, he noticed that his hands were shaking. The Stones were singing 'Under My Thumb'.

73

O Brother, There You Are

Father Damian was on his knees giving thanks, while Redmond busied himself at his mini-bar.

'You sure you won't have one?' Redmond asked.

'Yes, I'm sure,' said Father Damian, then added, 'or just a small one.' He moved from the floor to the bed and looked at his twin brother in disbelief. 'This is just so amazing.'

'Yeah, I know. I'm James Bond in *You Only Live Twice*.'

'It's *fantastic*.'

'These last few days have been like a bad dream.'

'Tell me all about it.'

So, nursing their drinks, Redmond told Damian about his time in Colombia. His training of the FARC guerrillas, his arrest, his incarceration in La Picota, being drugged by FARC agents and smuggled out, only to have his body seized by the British and rushed off to be cremated. 'If I hadn't woken up when I did, I'd be ashes to ashes by now.'

'Thank the Lord,' said Father Damian.

'Thank the Lord indeed. Damian, I've seen the error of my ways.'

'Thank the Lord.'

'People, you just can't trust them. FARC or Sinn Fein or the British or even your wife.'

'Poor Maeve.'

'Poor Maeve nothing, she's the one gave the go-ahead to have me cremated.'

'It was a difficult decision for her, Redmond. I understand fully why she did it. And why Sinn Fein hate her for it. And the people here are repressed, at least some of them are.'

'Your problem, brother, is that you can see every side of the story.'

'Why should that be a problem?'

'Well exactly. But it is. That's the way of the world.'

Father Damian picked up Redmond's new passport and flicked through it. 'This won't do, you know, Redmond, travelling the world as Viggo Mortensen. You're not Swedish.'

'He has dual citizenship. I can do American all right.'

'It's still not right. Look at it, there's no entry stamp. If you're stopped at the airport or—'

'I can't go back to the way it was. I'll be thrown in prison, or shot, or both.'

Father Damian nodded gravely. He closed the passport and flicked it between his fingers, thinking. 'Redmond,' he said eventually, 'the Catholic Church is universal. In any country in the world I can call upon it to help me. The Archbishop of Bogotá himself telephoned to offer support when I arrived here. Let me go to him. Let me sort something out.'

'I'm not going back to prison.'

'I know that. At the very least we can get you out of the country, take you to somewhere remote. You may have to stay there for a very long time.'

'That's okay.'

'Without contacting anyone.'

'I understand that. And it's fine. I'm starting a new life.'

Father Damian nodded. 'I will take this. I can probably secure the necessary visas through the Archbishop.' He slipped it into his inside pocket.

Redmond lay back on the bed and sipped at his whiskey. 'Damian, how are Manchester United doing these days?'

'They're doing fine.'

'And what about Celtic?'

'Good. They have a new manager.'

'It's getting on for summer at home. Remember those day trips to Bangor?'

'Aye, I do.'

'Thieving all round us.'

'You more than me.'

'But they were great days. Carrickfergus Castle with the school.'

'Aye.'

'And that year we went camping in the Mournes.'

The priest nodded sadly. 'Redmond – you can't go home.'

'One day.'

'No, not ever. They'll send you straight back, or disappear you. You stand for too much now. You're a martyr. You have to start a new life, wherever we send you.'

Redmond nodded. 'But you'll keep in touch?'

'If I can.' Damian sighed. 'Redmond – you chose this path.'

'I know that.'

'You have killed people.'

'I know that.'

'Are you sorry now? Will you seek forgiveness?'

'This is me you're talking to, Damian. I'm not sorry. What's done is done. If I had it all to do over again, maybe I'd do something different, but I can't, so it's not worth talking about, and if I seek forgiveness from anyone it'll be me and the Big Fella, not you with your one freckled bollock, all right?'

Damian sipped his drink. He nodded.

Father Damian's appointment with the Archbishop of Bogotá was set for 7 p.m. To avoid attracting press attention – Damian had received eighteen requests for interviews alone since Redmond had appeared in his bedroom – it was agreed that the Archbishop's driver would not pick him up from hotel reception, but from a street at the rear of the building. It was also thought wiser for him not to wear his priest's habit. Damian left Redmond lying on the bed, watching South American football on the TV and eating a hamburger. His brother had ordered it on room service, then hidden in the bathroom while it was delivered.

The priest took the staff lift downstairs, then walked out past the swimming pool to a small gate. A security guard was perched on a stool beside it. He said something in Spanish, then waved the priest away with his gun. Father Damian produced ten US dollars, and he was allowed out with an *it's your funeral* shrug. There was a battered-looking Sedan waiting on the other side of a dusty track, its engine running and a nervous-looking driver peering out of a half-wound-down tinted window.

Damian hurried across.

'Father?' asked the driver.

Damian nodded and climbed into the back. As the car pulled out, Miguel del Sanchez, the man with a picture of Redmond O'Boyle on his lap, a gun in his pocket and indoor plumbing in his heart, leaned forward and said, 'Follow that car,' to his taxi driver.

Redmond was by now drunk as a skunk; he was trying to concentrate on the football, but the phone kept ringing. His brother had been most insistent that he ignore it, and he did for the first hour, but then he got thirsty and wanted a Guinness so he phoned room service and had a broken-English conversation, the upshot of which was they weren't sure if there was Guinness in the bar, but they promised to phone him back or deliver it. So when the phone did ring the next time he supposed it was room service with bad news, but it wasn't, it was Phillip Grey from the *Daily Mirror* in London.

'Honestly, Father O'Boyle, I know you're upset, but if you could just spare me five minutes of your time.'

'I've nothing to say,' said Redmond.

'I understand your reticence, it's just that I try to be fair in everything I write. It's important to have balance, and the things people are saying about your brother, it's only right that you have some comeback.'

'What things?' Redmond snapped.

'That he was a callous murderer and he deserved to die. That he wasn't interested in peace or democracy or even freeing Ireland, he just liked blowing things up because he was a psychopath.'

'I'm not a—' Redmond began, before suddenly catching himself on. 'I'm not *at all* happy with that. It's a disgrace to talk about my brother like that.'

'I quite agree.'

'He had very strong beliefs, and he feels . . . felt betrayed by those who sent him here in the first place. They left him here to die, and they didn't try to get him out because they knew that he knew all their dirty little secrets. He knew where the bodies were – do you know what I'm saying?'

'Absolutely. Father Damian, is there any chance I could come up for a chat?'

'I'm afraid not.'

'Or would you care to join me? They have some excellent Irish whiskey down here.'

'Give me five minutes,' said Redmond.

74
The Anger of the Righteous

Jimmy Marsh Mallow hardly slept a wink, even with the amount of booze he put away after the hooker left. He tossed and turned, all the time the anger steadily growing in him. Of course he had been tempted by her, what man wouldn't be? She was stunningly attractive, but he had stood firm, done nothing wrong and yet, through no fault of his own, it had almost ended in tragedy. What if her fall down the stairs had ended with a broken neck, and not merely a few cuts and bruises? It would have been the end of him, his career down the Swanee because of an innocent desire for female companionship. How many other lonely men had she exploited? And how the hell did *Let's Be Mates* let her get away with it?

He got up at the first hint of dawn, shaved, showered, made breakfast, tried to forget about it, dismiss it as a close call, but he couldn't; it ground away at him. He had been put in a desperate situation through no fault of his own, and something had to be done about it. He had nothing in particular against the girl; she was doing a job, and he supposed it was safer than hanging out behind the BBC with the rest of Belfast's streetwalkers, but she was perpetrating a fraud, with or without the connivance of *Let's Be Mates*. He had been strong and rejected her, but how many other men were going to fall into her penis fly trap?

He wasn't due in work until later, but he phoned anyway. There wasn't any movement on the Caldwell case. Michael's three friends had been released from custody, and his men were looking for Benny Caproni, the Castle Street dealer and occasional rent-boy supplier.

Jimmy Marsh Mallow spent forty minutes on an exercise bike, listening to some early Clapton, then showered again. Downstairs he settled himself at the kitchen table with the phone beside him and a notebook and pen. He checked his watch: five past nine. He called *Let's Be Mates*. A woman answered and he told her his name, at least the one Lauren had used when subscribing to the service, and asked to be put through to the manager or supervisor. A few moments later the same voice returned.

'This is the manager.'

'I just spoke to you.'

'No. This is the manager.'

'Your name is?'

'Patricia. Patricia Craig.'

'You're the manager?'

'Yes, I am. What can I do for you, Mr Michael?'

'This is what you can do for me. You can refund whatever money my daughter paid you to join this agency, and then you can go through your files and chuck out every single whore you've got working for you, 'cause if you don't I'll have the police down on you like a ton of bricks.'

Patricia did not immediately respond.

'Do you hear me?'

'I hear you, Mr Michael. And I must reassure you that every site we run is maintained to the highest standard and all of the entries are vetted for—'

'Then explain to me how come some *hoor* demanded two hundred quid off me for sex last night?'

'I – I'm very sorry if that has happened, Mr Michael. We've had no previous complaints.'

'Well, it didn't strike me like it was the first time she'd done it. If you're running an escort agency down there, then you should be upfront about it.'

'I can assure you, we most certainly are not.'

'Well, what are you going to do about it?'

'Certainly we will have to investigate further. The woman's name?' He told her, and then she asked him to wait for a moment while she looked it up on her screen. 'Right. I see. Well, I can assure you we've had no previous complaints about this lady.'

'If it got out that I was consorting with prostitutes, my career could be ruined. If my daughter found out, how would she feel? If I contracted some kind of disease ... do you understand what I'm saying?'

'Yes, I do.'

'So what are you going to do about it?'

'I'll have to speak to the boss.'

'I thought you were the boss.'

'I'm the manager. I have a boss.'

'Do you want me to speak to him? I want a full refund or I'm reporting this.'

I Predict A Riot

'I understand what you're saying, Mr Michael, and your complaint will be investigated thoroughly. Just leave it with me and I'll get back to you as soon as I possibly can.'

He wasn't about to give his work number over. He gave her his mobile. As he left the house half an hour later, Jimmy Marsh Mallow paused to wipe a set of bloody fingerprints off the doorframe.

Across town, Patricia Craig had spent thirty minutes trying to track her boss down, but he was as elusive as ever. He had half a dozen mobile phone numbers, none of which were accepting even voice-mail. He ran many other businesses in the city but when she tried them he had either just left or was expected at any moment. When she called back he had invariably failed to arrive, or changed his plans. She didn't like speaking to him at the best of times and normally would have handled this herself, but the client was threatening to bring in the police and she had instructions always to refer those ones back.

Eventually, shortly before lunch, he answered one of his mobiles.

'Councillor Harrison,' said Pink.

'Mr Harrison, it's Patricia.'

'Oh hi Pat, what's cookin'?'

She told him.

He said, 'Jesus Christ. Who is it?'

'Julie.'

'Might have guessed. She had a warning already, didn't she?'

'Yes, Mr Harrison.'

'How much did he say she was charging?'

'Two hundred.'

'So she's pocketing a hundred for herself, cheeky bitch.'

'Yes, Mr Harrison.'

'All right. Thanks, Pat, leave it with me. I'll get someone to have a word with her.'

'Will I take her page down?'

'Aye, do that.' He was about to cut the line.

'Mr Harrison?'

'Yep?'

'What will I do about the client?'

Pink Harrison sighed. 'What's he say?'

'He's talking about a refund or the cops.'

'Is he a regular?'

'Not really. We've had one complaint about him failing to show for a date, but that's it.'

'Ah.' Pink hesitated. He didn't usually allow refunds of any descrip-tion, but he was too busy to really think about it, and besides, he had enough cops in his life without inviting some more in. 'Sure, why not,' said Pink. 'Refund it – there's plenty more fish in the sea.' He cut the line.

Patricia gave a little shiver. She didn't like or trust Pink Harrison. He had come to her when *Let's Be Mates* hit a cash crisis, coming on like a blessed angel, but his benevolence came with a price. Before she knew it, he was not only calling the shots, but also running escort girls out of her website.

He was right about one thing, though; there *were* plenty more fish in the sea. It was just a matter of being able to tell the sharks like Pink from the minnows like James Michael.

75
Room at the Top

Linda Wray, wearing a less businesslike outfit than last time, and a little more perfume, gave Walter another tour of the penthouse apartment at Towerview. She looked a little flushed and nervous when he entered the kitchen because she'd slipped a bottle of Asti Spumante into the fridge, but he went past it twice without opening the door. He had his head practically in the oven when she said, 'And the fridge is especially spacious.'

'Mmm-hmm,' said Walter, 'and what about the immersion heater?'

She showed him where the switch was located in the kitchen, and then said, 'You did note that it's an ice-making fridge – it'll always be on tap?'

'Really?' Walter opened the top, freezer door, then nodded. 'Wonderful,' he said. Then, thankfully, he opened the main door and said, 'Oh look – what's this?'

'Well, I thought we should toast the sale,' said Linda, blushing again.

'Excellent,' said Walter, quickly tearing at the foil top. 'Although,' he hesitated, then gave her a hard look. 'I suppose I'm actually paying for this. It'll be included in your fee somewhere.'

'No, really, I—'

'In fact, you'll probably mark it down as a bottle of expensive champagne, or you'll have worked some deal with Winemark to—' He saw that she was looking horrified, and stopped, smiled. 'I'm only raking, Linda.'

'Oh.'

'It's a nice touch.' He twisted the wire around, but didn't pop the cork.

'You're really not paying for it.'

'I know.'

'The company doesn't even pay for it either. I just thought it would be nice.'

'Glasses.'

'Sorry?'

He set the bottle down and began opening cupboards. 'It's a furnished apartment, but not *that* furnished. We've nothing to drink out of.'

Linda moved to her handbag, sitting on the counter. 'I brought these.' She produced a small funnel of slightly squashed paper cups.

'Excellent! Now we're in business!'

He returned to the bottle and popped it open as Linda squeezed the cups back into shape before extracting two and holding their bases as Walter poured.

'I actually prefer Asti to champagne,' said Linda. 'Sweeter taste.'

'Horses for courses,' said Walter. His eyes flicked up to her. 'I mean, it's good to be honest about things, isn't it? If you don't like something you should say so. I can't stand mushrooms.'

The wine fizzed up over the edge of both cups and spread out across the counter. Linda immediately removed a kitchen roll from her handbag.

'Everything but the kitchen sink in there,' said Walter.

'Oh, it's like the Tardis. There *is* actually a kitchen sink in here. Just in case of emergencies.'

They lifted their cups and knocked them gently together.

'Congratulations,' said Linda.

'Fandabidozi,' said Walter.

'To your wonderful penthouse!'

'To you for setting it all up.'

'And your brilliant career as a property tycoon.'

'And to yours. It's like that film . . .'

'*Glengarry Glen Ross*. There's not an estate agent in the world hasn't seen that.'

'That's the one. You get all the leads, and you're a real closer. You're like Al Pacino, but much prettier.'

She smiled. They both drank. An hour later, Walter popped out for another two bottles. An hour after that, they were lying in bed together. Sex had been frenetic and awkward and strange.

Walter was thinking: This never happens to me.

Linda was thinking: I am cheap and horrible and he'll think this is part of the deal.

Walter was thinking: Great breasts.

Linda was thinking: What the hell else did I expect, flirting away with him like that, getting him drunk. He's nice but he's not *that* nice, and he's not exactly in shape, and he's a three-minute wonder – but then who the hell am I to talk. Look at the state of me. Thank God the lights are off. How am I going to get my clothes on without him seeing me?

Walter was thinking: I hardly had to do anything, she really fancies me. Is this what it's like when you have money behind you – women just fall at your feet? She's nice 'n' all, and she's very serious, but the sex was good. Let's face it, it's been years, so any sex is good – but what do I do now? How do I get out of here? And how do I get back into my clothes without her seeing the size of my belly?

They lay in the darkness of the penthouse master bedroom, the curtains open, the lights of Belfast spread out below the shadow of the Cave Hill with its single red light flashing to stop aeroplanes crashing into it. The paper cups, half-empty with flat wine, sat on matching bedside tables. Their heads were beginning to ache.

Linda said, 'It's a fixed mortgage you're going for.'

'I thought it was better. We're putting half the money down, and then we'll hopefully pay off the rest with the rent.'

'It's a good market at the moment.'

They were silent for another little while. There wasn't even the ticking of a clock, or the murmur of life in other apartments. They were all still empty.

'That ice-maker is a cracker,' Walter said eventually. 'The parties I can have here.'

'But aren't you renting it out?'

'Yeah, but in between I can. Every time I buy another property I'll have a party here. And of course I'll use you every time.' It sat in the air for several long moments. Then Walter added: 'I mean I'll use your company. You. And your company. I think this is the beginning of a beautiful friendship.'

Linda thought: You're no Humphrey Bogart.

Walter thought: I'd love to fly one of those old planes.

Linda thought: He's not even Paul Henreid.

Walter thought: Across the desert, with the Nazis in pursuit.

Linda thought: Maybe a younger Claude Rains, not in looks, temperament.

Walter thought: That Ingrid Bergman, I'd have her.

Linda thought: Not completely trustworthy, but his heart in the right place.

Walter thought: Mile High Club.

Linda thought: A bit of a rogue.

Walter thought: With Nazis in pursuit.

'What time do you think it is?' he asked aloud.

'Don't know. Must be late.'

'Still. No one to go home to.'

'No. No one to go home to.'

'We could make love again,' said Walter.

'Yes, we could.'

'And then I could murder a fish supper.'

'So could I. But only if you go and get it.'

'All right then,' said Walter. 'That's a deal.'

'You're a real deal-maker,' said Linda.

Walter nodded in the darkness. *That's what I am. A real deal-maker. And the diet starts again on Monday.*

76
Father Redmond

Father Damian O'Boyle a.k.a. his twin brother Redmond O'Boyle, was three sheets to the wind and slabbering to anyone who would listen to him in the bar of the Hilton Hotel in downtown Bogotá. Phillip Grey of the *Daily Mirror* had long since stopped taking notes. He'd only been looking for a few quotes, not a f***ing lecture on British imperialism in Ireland, not to mention India and South Africa. He could understand the priest being upset over the death of his brother, but he found it rather unsettling to see so much anger, hate and barely restrained violence in a man of God. He'd thought a drunken Irish priest was nothing but a movie cliché, but here was the living, breathing proof of it.

Half a dozen other reporters were subjected to his gale-force opinions before the priest finally passed out on a red leather banquette. When he woke, two hours later, his shirt-front soaked in drool and his head rocking, Redmond at first had no idea where he was or why he was wearing priest's garb or why he had a peanut stuck to his forehead. He wasn't sober, but he was slightly less drunk. He staggered across the bar to the lifts. Everyone he met, he made the sign of the cross: The businessmen, going up to their rooms; The reporters venturing back down to the bar to see if the coast was clear of him; The cleaners in the corridor outside his room; The rotund little security guard who let him in because his hammering on the door was waking the other guests up.

Redmond supposed Damian would have returned from his appointment with the Archbishop of Bogotá by now and had most probably gone straight to sleep – even as a kid, once he laid his head on a pillow, you could never raise him – but was pleasantly relieved to find that the room was empty. Redmond knew he was in a state. He had promised not to leave the room. And his brother was going out of his way to help him. He really didn't want to let him down, albeit in retrospect, but he was pretty sure he had. He had a vague recollection of standing on a chair and lecturing the bar about interrogation methods at Castlereagh Holding Centre, which even drew a round of applause from the bar staff, although probably more for delivery than content, but their support was quickly diluted by his immediately pissing into a plant pot and then demanding a line of coke in a stage whisper which could be heard out on the street. Redmond crawled into one side of the double bed and prayed for a few hours' grace before his brother returned.

In fact, his brother never returned.

While Father Damian conversed with the Archbishop, setting up an escape route into Argentina and securing permanent lodging at a seminary on the Pampas, Miguel del Sanchez, the man with the gun, approached the Archbishop's driver and, after a brief discussion, agreed a fee of $50. When Father Damian emerged, beaming, his faith in human nature restored and the power of the Catholic Church confirmed, he climbed into the luxury Sedan and was immediately clubbed with the butt of Miguel del Sanchez's pistol. As the car set off he was struck again, and again. The Archbishop's driver drove to the edge of a vast and stinking municipal dump and kept the engine running while Miguel del Sanchez hopped out of the car, ran around to the other side, and hauled out the man he presumed to be Redmond O'Boyle.

Father Damian, dwarfed by the vast mountains of waste behind him, stood shaking and wounded. But still he demanded to know what was going on. One might argue that it was bleeding obvious. Miguel del Sanchez, of course, spoke no English, and Father Damian spoke no Spanish. Miguel, who was nervous enough, shook the gun at him and issued precise instructions. Father Damian crossed himself and waved a finger the way he did to miscreant boys back home. Miguel del Sanchez grew angrier and angrier. He was happy enough to shoot this Redmond O'Boyle, and had already retrieved the Swedish passport he'd been told Redmond was carrying, but there was no trace of the money the Ambassador had given him. Miguel knew he couldn't go back without it or he'd be accused of taking it himself. And that would mean another drive out to the dump, only this time it would be *his* body that would be picked over by the seagulls.

So he yelled some more in Spanish, and Father Damian remonstrated.

They only stopped when the Archbishop's driver clambered out of the car, waving the small black Spanish-English phrasebook he kept in the glove compartment at Miguel del Sanchez. This led to a long, loud argument between them, during which they shoved each other several times. Miguel del Sanchez eventually peeled off another $50, and then they both huddled around the book, speed-flicking through the pages and exchanging excited whispers. Eventually the driver straightened and nodded at Father Damian.

'He say – give me money or I kill you.'

'I have no money,' said Father Damian. 'I am a man of God.'

The driver's brow furrowed. He studied the phrasebook again, rapidly flicking through the pages, then turned to Miguel del Sanchez and said something in Spanish. Miguel snapped something back. The driver shrugged. Miguel waved the gun. The driver turned back to Father Damian: 'Man . . . of . . . God?' then held up the phrasebook and shook his head as if it was useless.

'Priest. Father – ahm – *padre*,' said Father Damian.

'Padre?' the driver repeated. He turned to Miguel. 'Padre.'

'Padre?' Miguel shook his head.

'*Padre, padre*,' said Father Damian.

Miguel took out the Swedish passport and opened it to the correct page. He held it up to Father Damian. 'Viggo – Viggo Mortensen.'

'Viggo Mortensen?' asked the driver. He moved across and took a closer look at the passport. His eyes flicked up to Father Damian again. He said, in Spanish, 'Movie star?'

Father Damian said, '*Padre – padre?*'

The driver said, 'Hollywood? *Lord of the Rings*? Frodo Baggins?' He held up a finger. 'Ring? One ring?'

Father Damian shook his head uncomprehendingly. All he knew was that he was being mugged at a most inopportune time. His twin brother's salvation was at hand, but it was imperative that he got him out of the hotel immediately. Redmond wouldn't be truly safe until he was out of the country.

Damian pointed at his neck and repeated, '*Padre*,' and patted his pockets to show that he had no money. He dearly wished that he'd kept his habit on.

The driver turned to Miguel. 'Dunno – maybe big movie star. Maybe padre. Archbishop don't tell me nothing.'

'He don't look like no movie star. Ask him where the money is again.'

'You searched him already, he has no money. I have to get back to the Archbishop. You do what you have to do.'

Miguel shrugged. Then he shot the driver through the temple. He crumpled straight down.

Father Damian staggered backwards. 'Good God.'

287

Miguel stepped after him. Father Damian lost his footing and fell. He looked up, half-blinded by the sun, the caw of surprised gulls all around.

'*Padre . . . padre,*' he whispered.

77

Hurricane

Benny Caproni didn't like being driven around East Belfast with someone as familiar as Jimmy Marsh Mallow up front. So he was squirrelled down in the back, effing and blinding every time the vehicle stopped at lights or got stuck in traffic. Gary McBride, sitting beside him, said, 'A quid in the swearbox every time, Benny,' and Benny would respond with another flurry of curses. He kept insisting he didn't know anything about Michael Caldwell, nor his mates Carl or Alan or Bix, or if he did they were just kids who came into the arcades from time to time; he might know their faces, but nothing else.

'I don't deal to kids, you know that.'

When they'd stopped laughing, Jimmy said: 'We've got you for the hotel job, and we're talking to your friend Bellow.'

'*What?* What the f**k are you talking about?'

''Nother quid in the swearbox,' said Gary.

'You ever heard the song "Hurricane" by Bob Dylan, Benny?'

'I don't know anything about Bob Dylan.'

'Well, you should,' said Jimmy. '"Hurricane" is about Rubin Carter, who was a contender for the world middleweight crown till he got framed by the cops for a murder and robbery in a bar in New Jersey, and he got put away for life. Bob Dylan wrote this very fine protest song – it's one of my favourites.'

'So the f**k what?'

'You think anyone would write a protest song for you, Benny? With your dope and your crack and your rent boys?'

'I don't do none of that stuff, not any more.'

'You think Van Morrison would conjure something up? "The Ballad of Benny Caproni", eh?'

'I think youse are the ones on f***in' drugs.'

'You know, maybe he would. But the thing is, Benny, Bob Dylan wrote about Rubin Carter 'cause there were so many f***in' holes in the case you could drive the Boston Pops Orchestra through it, and it still took twenty-five years to get him out. Do you hear what I'm saying?'

'I've no f***in' notion.'

'I'm saying, we've been doing this so long we can put a case together against you that even Sherlock Holmes couldn't deconstruct, you hear me. I'm saying it doesn't matter if Van Morrison writes a song about you and he gets you out in five, because once you're inside you wouldn't survive more than a few days. Rubin Carter was *tough*. I've seen pints of milk with more colour than you, Benny. I've seen Biafrans with better muscle tone. This wee fella, Michael Caldwell, someone chopped him up and dumped him in the river; you were his dealer, and we think you set him up with someone. We want to know who that was.'

'And I'm telling you I don't f***in' know.'

'You know something, Benny? Far as the press knows, we've recovered this boy's torso and his head, but the other day we found one of his hands as well. And you know something else? Chances are we're going to find the other hand, and it'll probably be in your fridge.'

'My what?'

'Oh yeah, it'll be on the news – police acting on a tip-off searched the apartment of drug-dealing gay pimp Benny Caproni and found evidence linking him to the brutal murder of schoolboy Michael Caldwell.'

'You couldn't do that, I'm not stupid.'

Jimmy turned suddenly in his seat. His right hand shot out and grabbed Benny's shirt. He dragged him forward, then stuck his face right up close. 'Yes, you f***ing are, Benny, that's what's so nice about it. See, I've seen seven kinds of s**t in this job, I've been doing it for near on thirty years, but this one, this one, I don't know, maybe I'm growing old, but this one is really getting to me. He was only a kid, his mum can't even bury him till we get all the bits of him back. So I want it sorted out. I want whoever did it. But I'm a realist, Benny, I have to be. If I can't have whoever did it, I'll need someone else, and a lowlife piece of s**t like you will fit the bill good as anyone, you hear what I'm saying? And maybe twenty years down the line some smart-arse lawyer will find out that we did frame you, but by that time you'll have been dead for nineteen years and eleven months, Benny, nailed to a table because they hate fruits like you.'

Jimmy Marsh Mallow didn't wait for him to respond; he thrust him back into his seat, then turned back to face the traffic.

'I'm not a fruit,' Benny said weakly.

Gary McBride snorted.

'So what's it to be, Benny-boy?' Marsh demanded.

Benny shrugged. He stared out of the window. 'So I deal some stuff, it's not a crime.'

Gary snorted again.

'I mean, sure, but it's not like . . . hell, I only do a few quid, you know that.'

'What about Michael Caldwell?'

Benny sighed. The hot air created a little cloud on the window. He rubbed at it. 'Okay. So. Right. He was just one of the lads. But, you know, good-looking.'

Marsh felt a little twinge at the back of his neck. He always got that at the point of breakthrough.

'He was more into getting high than the others, but couldn't afford it. So, you know, I said to him, maybe there was a trade-off.'

'You pimped him out.'

'He owed me, all right? He said he would only do it this once. And it was, it was his first time. Maybe he couldn't do it, maybe that's why . . .' He shrugged again.

'Who was it, Benny?'

'I don't know.'

'You better know.'

'I swear to God, it was a phone call; a car arrived, he got in. That's all I know, swear to God.'

'And you never saw anyone, or the car before, or again?' Gary asked.

Benny shook his head. 'I never saw, and next thing I know the wee fella's all over the news. It wasn't my fault.'

Marsh gritted his teeth. He'd had thirty years of morons saying it wasn't their fault. He told the driver to pull over. They were just at the bottom of the Newtownards Road, an area rich or poor, depending on your point of view, in paramilitary war murals. Marsh climbed out, went round to Benny's door and opened it.

'What?' said Benny.

'This is you,' said Marsh.

'Not here,' said Benny, panicked.

'Here,' said Marsh.

'For Christ sake.' His eyes darted about to see if anyone was watching. It was a busy road. 'Take me back to Castle Street, or home – don't leave me here.'

'This is it, Benny. You've been very helpful. We'll be in touch.' Marsh put his hand out. Benny just stared at it. Marsh kept it there for a moment. Then he said, 'Who'm I kiddin'?' and moved forward. He yanked Benny out of the vehicle onto the pavement. Then he enveloped him in a bear hug. 'Thanks, Benny,' he said, real loud. 'Thanks for everything.'

Marsh let him go, winked, then jumped back into the car. As he drove off, he reached across and pumped the horn. Benny put his hands in his pockets and started walking, quick as he could, but people noticed. They always did. It was a small city.

78
Bull by the Horns

Julie Mateer had an eight o'clock appointment, and the taxi was due at any moment. But she was still in the bathroom upstairs, fixing her face. And she really was fixing it. Normally she didn't wear a lot of make-up, but ever since that cretin had knocked her downstairs and bust up her face she'd been forced into a big cover-up. Nobody wanted to pay good money, or even average money, to bed a woman with a bruised-up noggin. It *ached*. Her lip was cut inside, and her nose was slightly swollen.

Ordinarily she would have taken a few days off, but she had bills to pay. So she forced herself up out of bed. Two lines of coke helped get her in the mood. She practised her smile. *There, Perfect.* In a dull light, with a few drinks, she'd wing it. Beggars can't be choosers, and it applied to both sides of the equation.

Julie had always been a girl up for anything, and prided herself on knowing the risks and being able to skate clear of trouble. She was independent, vivacious, witty and stunning to look at. She had known she was beautiful from an early age, and also that she was bright, therefore she had presumed her life would be easy. That she could afford to float for several years before choosing a career and marrying a quality guy. She had the chance to go to London to model, but instead fell for a fella called Paddy Long, who had everything she was looking for. He was rich, handsome, a chemist with a string of pharmacies across Belfast, but also the life and soul of the party. She shared a grand house with him, enjoyed a life of leisure, and it was only when the cops bust down their door in the middle of the night that she discovered Paddy was the leading manufacturer of Ecstasy tablets in the Province. The thing was, he wasn't in the least bashful about misleading her. He said he was just 'filling prescriptions' and asked her to wait for him. Eight years, to be precise. In Jimmy Marsh Mallow's *Big Book of Bad People*, Paddy's nickname was 'Boots'.

Without her man, Julie didn't know where to turn. Boots's friends, *their* friends, disappeared the moment he was arrested. The big house was seized by Criminal Assets, and she was lucky to hang onto her Prada handbag. She'd no job, and little cash, but she'd lived life too well to go looking for any normal kind of a job. She was beyond working the sweet counter in Woolies. And yet, standards are a curious thing.

The way it happened was like this. Their favourite bar had always been the first-floor lounge in the Europa Hotel. A better class of clientèle went there – their kind of people. Moneyed, but not awfully-awfully. She and Boots would invariably go there on a Friday and Saturday night and drink into the early hours. Once Boots got put away, Julie still found herself drawn to the place, and, inevitably she attracted her fair share of attention, although mostly from morons. On this particular night she was being bored stupid by this car salesman, and drinking too much of his champagne – his plan was to get her drunk and sleep with her, obviously, although she'd no intention of it – but when he darted off to the toilet his place was immediately taken by a medium-sized, plain-looking man in glasses.

He said, 'Could I talk to you for a moment?'

'Sure. But he'll be back in a minute.'

'A minute's all I need.'

'Quick worker,' Julie laughed.

He didn't smile. He was nervous. 'I've been watching you all night – you're beautiful. But I know, someone like you, you're not going to be interested in someone like me.' She didn't quite know what to say. He was right, after all. 'But I know who you are, and I know what happened to Paddy, and I know things can't be easy for you right now.'

She didn't much like that, him bringing up her personal life. She said, 'What's your point?'

He said, 'I've never done this before. I own a graphic design company, I finished a job today and the guy paid me in cash. Two grand.' He patted his pocket.

Julie's eyes darted towards the toilets to see if the salesman was on his way back yet. 'So?'

'So, it's my birthday, and I'm single, and I'll give you the two grand if you'll come to bed with me for thirty minutes. I have a room upstairs already.'

She stared at him, her mouth dropped open a little. 'You are joking, aren't you?'

'No. Swear to God, I'm absolutely serious. Don't be offended.' She'd been propositioned before, but never so audaciously, never with cash.

'I know you're shocked, and I am as well in a way, but I have the money, and why not spend it on something fantastic that I'll remember for the rest of my life?'

Julie half-snorted into her champagne. 'Fantastic for you or fantastic for me?'

'Well, for me, obviously. But I'll do my best for you, if you like.'

Julie spotted the car salesman, pushing his way through the crowd towards them. She was drunk and miserable, and the salesman was smarmy and full of himself and sure he was on to a winner; while this spunky little guy with his envelope of cash was clearly batting way out of his league. But he was a trier, and God loves a trier. So without thinking about it any more deeply than that, she grabbed his hand and said, 'You're on – let's go.'

There was a momentary look of stunned disbelief and then his face exploded in happiness. He led her away through the crowd towards the lift.

She was back in the bar in forty-five minutes. She'd given him an extra fifteen. It wasn't satisfying in the slightest, but he'd been nice and attentive and keen and said nice things and she didn't feel too bad about it. She kissed him goodbye in the doorway, tongues and all, and with the envelope safe in her Prada bag, returned to the bar downstairs, intending to treat herself to one last drink. She ordered a Pimms and handed over a £20 fresh from the envelope. She was just taking her first sip when the barman came back with the note and said, 'I'm sorry, madam – it's a forgery.'

'Oh, God . . . sorry.' She fished another one out. But it was fake as well. So was a third and a fourth and she was feeling suddenly hollow and then she was physically sick, there at the bar, over the bar stools.

When she'd recovered sufficiently she found enough change in her purse to cover the drink. Then with as much dignity as she could muster she walked out of the lounge, and took the lift back up to the graphic designer's room. He opened the door, smiled at her, then told her to f**k off. Then he slammed the door shut.

She felt about *this* high. There was nothing she could do, no one she could tell. She slunk out and cried herself to sleep.

But it was the beginning of a shift in her approach to life. Even though she'd been stitched up, it made her really aware for the first time that she could actually exploit her good looks rather than just coast along on them. She had something to sell. So she did some research, found an agency specialising in escorts and companions and tried it out. She didn't earn two grand a pop, but still, it was a reasonable living. But that was seven years ago. Boy bands and prostitutes don't have a long shelf-life. She was now down to as little as two hundred a go, and skimming half of that off her bosses.

When the doorbell rang, she shouted, 'Be there in a minute!' then hurried down the stairs. She stopped to check her reflection one last time in the hall mirror, then opened the front door. But instead of seeing the taxi idling outside, she saw Bull. He didn't say anything. Bulls rarely do. He just smacked her once in the mouth and stepped into the hall after her as she fell backwards.

79

The Collector

Mark had read many political biographies, and knew the value of the experience to be gained by going from door to door, meeting the people. Everyone started that way. Churchill. Kennedy. Thatcher. Even Stalin had knocked on a few doors – in fact, he kept it up for decades, although not always personally. If it was a case of merely listening to problems or taking dog's abuse, well, Mark accepted that that was part of the learning process. But the raw fear and desperation he encountered on each of his nightly tours of Pink Harrison's City Council Ward shook him to the core. These were people on the lowest possible rung of society, struggling to make ends meet, yet they felt obliged to hand over money to Harrison's collectors. Bull called them political contributions. Mark called it protection money, although not out loud, or even in a whisper. He was distraught. He didn't know where to turn. Walter was sitting across from him in the office now, looking pretty pleased with himself, but he couldn't ask him. Mark had talked his political career up so much he didn't want to turn to his old friend and admit that he was floundering before he'd hardly begun.

Walter said, 'I'm going down to the canteen for a salad, do you want anything?'

On cue, Mark's stomach rumbled. 'No, I'm fine,' he said weakly.

When Walter left, Mark walked down the corridor to Office 12. He had been elated to join the Party, but surprised to see that Steve, his mysterious colleague, was also a prominent member; however, the more he thought about it, the more it made sense, and the more it creeped him out. As Steve had explained it, the disinformation that issued from Office 12 was calculated to cause disruption and confusion, therefore creating a climate of dissatisfaction that might benefit the Party. At the moment the real political power in the Province was held between the twin extremes of the Sinn Fein Republicans and the Democratic Unionists; the Official Unionists were largely excluded, but reasonably happy to give the others their moment in the spotlight – as long as that spotlight proved to be faulty. When Sinn Fein and the Democrats proved that they couldn't run a country between them, the time would be right for the re-emergence of the Official Unionists.

Mark knocked once and waited to be asked to enter. Steve was behind his desk, but had one hand resting in the open drawer to his left. When he saw who it was he closed the drawer and smiled, waving Mark forward into a chair. Mark closed the door behind him and sloped forward. When he sat down he looked everywhere but at Steve himself, who clasped his hands before him and waited patiently. Finally Mark's eyes met his.

'I have a problem,' said Mark.

'I fix problems,' said Steve. 'Is it work-related? Personal?'

'Political.'

'Are we talking political philosophy, theology or history?'

'We're talking about Pink Harrison.'

'Councillor Harrison.'

Mark nodded. 'Can I talk to you, you know, in confidence?'

'Yes, of course.'

'It's just . . . not what I expected.'

'What did you expect?'

'To work for the Party.'

'And aren't you?'

'No, I seem to spend all my spare time collecting money for Pink Harrison.'

'You mean political contributions?'

'No, I mean protection money.'

Steve unclasped his hands. 'Tell me more,' he said.

So Mark told him about the envelopes, and how on the first night he had to contribute his own money in order to stop one family getting a beating.

'That's not good,' said Steve.

'And then I went back last night, and word must have spread, because there were eight or nine families who wouldn't pay up, and I couldn't let them be attacked, so I paid their contribution as well. It's costing me a fortune.'

'That's terrible,' said Steve.

Mark shook his head. 'It's not what I signed up for. And I think the Party should know what Harrison is doing. Those people are scared stiff of him. He needs to be stopped. I was prepared to give him the benefit of the doubt, but you know what they say about leopards and spots and all that.'

I Predict A Riot

Steve was silent for several long moments. Then he sighed. 'Mark, I know what you're saying, but I wouldn't be too quick to jump to conclusions. I know Pink, I know him well, and the Party took a considerable risk in allowing him to join and stand for us, but he's worked hard, he has some bright ideas, and he is without doubt a star of the future.'

'But not if he's—'

'Let me finish. And yes, he has raised more funds in his ward than probably any other councillor, but you've got to remember, the Party can only function if it has a lot of people working for it at grassroots level, and the problem with that is, particularly in some of the tougher areas, that you have to take what you can get. If you vetted every single person who volunteered, then you'd end up with no one. This Bull guy, and the others, they may have overstepped the mark, but that doesn't mean that Councillor Harrison is even aware of it. Why would he jeopardise his political career like that?'

'But the money goes directly to him. I saw him with it.'

'Yes, and it's all accounted for at Party HQ. It's like Scouts on Bob-a-Job week, Mark, performing a worthwhile public service, but sometimes they get over-enthusiastic.'

'They don't threaten people with baseball bats.'

'In Pink's area, they do. It's part of the culture.'

Mark sighed. 'I hear what you're saying. And if you're sure Pink doesn't know about it, well, that's a bit better. But something has to be done about Bull and his mates, they're terrorising people.'

'And something will be done, believe you me, Mark. You're right to bring this to me. It will be sorted out.'

'But you'll – you know – keep my name out of it?'

'Yes, of course I will. Not only that, I'll make sure you get back whatever money you contributed on behalf of those poor people.'

'Well, that's not necessary. As long as it's going to a good cause. I just couldn't, you know, keep it up.'

Mark felt much better. It all made sense now. Pink *had* turned his back on violence, but some of his followers were finding the transition to democratic means slightly more difficult. But the Party was bigger than any one, two or three individuals, and the problem would be sorted out. Steven was a man who could get things done. Moving into his office would clearly have its benefits.

'I was thinking I could move on Monday,' Mark said.

'Move?'

'In here.'

'Yes, of course. Monday would be ideal.' Then Steve looked down at a sheet of paper on his desk. 'Oh no, wait a minute. Perhaps Monday's not so hot.'

'Tuesday then. I want to be in an office where things happen, you know?'

'Tuesday's much better.' He examined the sheet again. 'Damn – no, Tuesday doesn't suit either. Tell you what, let me check it out and I'll get back to you.'

Mark nodded. He stood up and reached across to shake Steve's hand. 'Thanks,' he said. 'I really appreciate it – it's a load off my mind.'

'No problem,' said Steve. 'Talk to you soon, Mark. And relax, I'm onto it now.'

Mark left the office. In the corridor outside he took out his wallet and checked how much cash he had left. A fiver. Good. He could go to the canteen now and buy himself some lunch, confident in the assumption that he wouldn't be contributing the last of this month's cash to Pink Harrison.

Back in Office 12, Steven clicked a number on speed dial. It was answered straight away.

'Pink,' said Steven, 'we have another whiny whinger.'

80
Pride, in the Name of Love

Walter wasn't aware of the origin of the word 'cocksure', but he presumed it was something sexual. If it was, that was how he had felt, waking up this morning, back in his little house, having made love to a beautiful woman for much of the night in a luxurious penthouse he nearly owned, and with the full knowledge that he had another beautiful woman waiting in the wings. Walter had never had it so good. Now he sat in the Department of Education canteen, grazing on a salad, contemplating his good fortune. It was amazing how quickly your life could turn around. One moment a sexless drone, the next an entrepreneur with women falling at his feet. Power was a superb aphrodisiac. He was human Viagra. Another phrase whose origins he wasn't familiar with was 'pride comes before a fall'.

Walter's mobile rang. 'Walter North,' he purred.

'Hi there.'

'Margaret,' said Walter.

'Linda,' said Linda.

'Linda?' said Walter.

'Linda,' said Linda, already deflated. 'From last night, remember?'

'Yes, of course. I'm sorry – just force of habit. Linda, how the hell are you?'

'I'm fine. Bit of a sore head.'

'Tell me about it.'

She told him about it. At great length. He couldn't remember her talking this much last night. Linda was aware she was overdoing it, but that happened when she was nervous. She told him about her dry throat and her throbbing head and trying to show clients around when she felt like death, and then for some unaccountable reason she told him about her hysterectomy.

Walter pushed his salad to one side. He said, 'That must have been painful.'

'Oh God, yeah; couldn't ride a horse for months.'

'You have a horse?'

'No, I mean, metaphorically speaking. Oh God, I'm babbling. What I'm trying to say in a roundabout way is that you don't have to worry about . . . You know, last night, we didn't use any, you know, *protection*. So I can't get – you know, *pregnant*. I could make love to the entire cast of Tandragee Amateur Operatic Society's production of *Oklahoma* and it wouldn't make a damn's worth of difference. I thought you should know. Put your mind at ease. And also, if you were thinking longterm, and about children and things like that, that I've had it done and there's no going back and it's not perfect, but there you go, that's life, or not, as the case may be.'

'Well,' said Walter, 'that's me in the picture.'

'Yes, it is. I, ah, enjoyed last night.'

'So did I.'

Silence. She was giving him the opportunity to say, 'So what about tonight?' Or, 'So let's do it again.'

'Walter?'

'Yes, uhuh?'

Again she gave him the space. Then she took a deep breath. 'What with all that happened, there's still paperwork to sign.'

'Oh, right. Well, we should do that. Do you want to send it over?'

'No, I would really need to be there.'

'Oh right. Okay. Fine. Do you want me to come to the office?'

'Well, we could meet at the apartment.'

'Okay. Yeah. That would be fine. Only I'm in work now.'

'Well, after work. Say, six?'

'I've some things to do – seven?'

They agreed on seven. There were a few more awkward exchanges, then Walter said he had to go. He cut the line and pulled his salad back into place. What was wrong with him? She was practically offering more sex on a plate, and he was already getting cold feet. This from a man whose entire sexual history could be written on a Christmas postage stamp. But as much as he had enjoyed the previous evening, at least a part of him was going, 'So that's what all the fuss is about?' His desires and lusts were sated, however temporarily, and nice as she was, he did not think she was the *one*. He had forgotten about Margaret in the excitement of the moment, but now that he had had his wicked way with Linda, he was thinking about her again. Only a few days before, they had promised each other a bold new era of openness and honesty, but now he had betrayed her at the first possible opportunity.

I Predict A Riot

Or evened the score. Now he'd had a fling, they were quits.
Self-delusion can be an incredible thing.

When Emma Cochrane phoned to say that her dresses were in the window with an £800 price tag, Margaret nearly had a stroke. £800! Margaret had barely paid £15 each for them, thanks to the staff discount at Primark.

'Eight hundred?' she repeated. 'Are you absolutely sure?'

'Oh I know, but it's like an opening offer, just to test the water. Once they start to sell and word spreads and the publicity kicks in, we'll increase the price substantially.'

Margaret was on a fifty-fifty split, so she should have been dancing in the aisles – literally the aisles, as she was patrolling through the Lingerie Department, keeping an eye out for the pervs – but that wasn't what made her stop in her tracks.

'Publicity?'

'Of course, darling, it's the lifeblood of our industry. We put these dresses in the window now, they're snapped up, word of mouth spreads – and there are simply no others available. And there truly aren't. It'll be a fortnight before your new designs are run up, and by then word will have filtered back to the fashion press. Then when we mount our first show . . .'

'Show?'

'They'll be battering down the doors to get in. Margaret, it's going to work like a dream. Margaret?'

'Sorry. I just kind of thought I'd stay in the background.'

'Margaret, darling, listen to me. I know you're nervous, but the moment I put those dresses in the window, that's the moment your life changed for ever. It'll start small, but it'll grow, I have every confidence. I just can't wait to see you walk down that catwalk, milking the applause. You're a star, darling, get used to it!'

Ever since she'd been a little girl Margaret had lain in bed at night dreaming of catwalk shows and the press and the fame and the glamour of it all, but this was different. This was real. The limit of her true ambitions had not extended much beyond seeing one of her designs made up into something real, but now Emma was talking as if all this other stuff was really possible. Margaret didn't feel remotely qualified for any of it. All she'd really done was make a few drawings and colour them in. A million kids had done that. Perhaps Emma was getting carried away. *Emma Cochrane* was a nice little boutique on one of Belfast's more up-market shopping streets, but it was still in Belfast, hardly the fashion capital of the world. Or even Ireland. All this talk of fame and glory – it was just pie in the sky. The dresses would hang in the window and attract not one iota of attention. Or even worse –

be recognised for what they were – Primark rip-offs bearing *M & Emma* labels. This wasn't the start of some illustrious career, it was the beginning of a short walk down to the Magistrate's Court. The moment some unsuspecting thin woman clapped her hands in excitement, then handed over her credit card – that was when the fraud would really begin.

'Emma, maybe we should wait for the new designs to—'

'Nonsense! The dresses are fantastic! They'll sell like hot cakes.'

Nobody buys hot cakes any more.

'It's just, they're not really representative of my work. They're very, er, derivative. I really think it would be better to—'

'Margaret, those dresses are *stunning*. They are so *you*, they have your personality stamped all over them; no one else in this whole damn world could have made them but you. Be proud of them!'

'Yes, I know, I'm just—'

'It's natural to be nervous, darling, but believe me, this is going to be fantastic. A few days from now, some beautiful young woman is going to be walking down Royal Avenue turning heads and people will say, "Hey, isn't that an *M & Emma?*".'

Margaret felt sick to her stomach. 'I have to go,' she said abruptly and closed her mobile.

Partly it was the fear of arrest and exposure, but mostly it was the sight of an elderly man standing with his hand moving rapidly in his trouser pocket while he fingered a display of women's briefs. Seeing Margaret approach did not deter him. He just got quicker. And then began to sing 'Jesus Loves Me for a Sunbeam' at the top of his voice.

81

Stars in their Eyes

Margaret and Maeve hightailed it to the Lisburn Road on their lunch-break so that they could see the display at first hand. Maeve, who saw identical dresses hanging in Primark every day of her life, failed to recognise them at all. Margaret thought this was because their vantage-point was a window table in *Irma La Deuce* and her companion only had eyes for Jack Finucane, the Carrot Cake King.

Jack, having been reluctant to allow Maeve to stay the night in his swish apartment, was now determined to have her move in. The sex had been that good. And his mouth had dropped open when he'd seen her new look. Before, she'd been reasonably attractive, but her expansive hair had dominated everything. It had been more of a personality thing. Which was good, in a way. But now the big hair was gone, replaced with a short blonde crop, he could really see how beautiful she was. He wanted to pick her up and take her into the kitchen and ravish her. He wanted to cover her in fresh cream and lick it off with tiny little cat darts. But as the hygiene inspectors had visited three times since he'd put Margaret in a coma, he didn't suggest it. She'd be up for it though, he was sure. She was insatiable. She said she hadn't had an orgasm since the first Gulf War, and had then experienced three in twenty minutes.

'Or was it four?' she said to Margaret.

Margaret said, 'Four what?' She only had eyes for *Emma Cochrane*.

'Oh, never mind,' said Maeve, smiling widely as Jack approached. He set another slice of carrot cake before her. 'Bavarian Chocolate,' he said.

'You're a feeder,' said Maeve. 'I'll be the size of a house.'

'Or at least a chalet bungalow,' said Margaret.

'Chocolate is like sex,' said Jack. 'You can never have too much of it.'

Maeve gave him a look. 'Yes, you can, it makes you boke.'

'And gives me a migraine,' said Margaret.

'The sex or the chocolate?' asked Maeve.

'Depends whether it's plain or dark,' said Margaret.

'The sex or the chocolate?' Maeve asked.

Margaret flushed; Maeve giggled; Jack shook his head. 'You two . . .'

'Anyway, is that how you talk to all the girls?' Maeve asked. '"Sex is like chocolate",' she mimicked. 'You'll be wise to stop all that crack if you want to get into my pants again.'

Behind them, an elderly woman half-choked on a mouthful of carrot cake and turned round for a glare. Maeve gave her a hard look, and only broke the connection when Margaret suddenly pointed across the road.

'Look!'

Louise, Emma Cochrane's fashion buyer – at least, that was her title, but as far as Margaret could determine she just worked behind the till – was in the window, removing one of the Primark dresses off a mannequin.

'Do you think . . .' Margaret began.

'I *do* think,' said Maeve.

'It's too soon,' said Margaret.

'Not if they've been on sale all morning.'

'But they're eight hundred quid!'

'Some people have money to burn.'

'We should go over,' said Margaret.

'No – wait here. Whatever will be, will be.'

'We should definitely go over.'

'You don't want to appear too enthusiastic.'

'I'm going,' said Margaret, lifting her bag and sidling out from the table.

'I'm coming with you,' said Maeve. She stopped only to kiss Jack. Her tongue went right in. 'See you later, *lover*,' she purred.

As they hurried out of the door, the old woman at the table behind said, 'That's disgusting.'

'I *know*,' Jack grinned, and floated back to the kitchen.

Margaret and Maeve charged across the road like harpies, but when they actually reached *Emma Cochrane* they entered with the timidity of kittens. Margaret, shaking, went first. There was Louise, standing behind the desk, there was Emma herself, stocktaking. But there was no sign of the prospective purchaser of Margaret's first designer dress (although, obviously she had not actually designed it). For a panicked moment Margaret thought she must have imagined seeing it being removed from the mannequin in the window. Then she thought it had been removed, but only because Emma had reconsidered and now thought it was rubbish, or looked like something out of Primark.

Her heart soared when she saw Louise smile widely, then whisper urgently, 'She's trying it on!' Margaret looked towards the single changing room, which was little more than a curtain stretched around a corner of the stockroom, and saw two bare feet. Across the store Emma held up her hands: all of her fingers were crossed.

The curtain began to move back. Maeve and Margaret busied themselves searching through a rack of summer dresses; Emma studied her stock-list, while Louise came out from behind the counter and stood beside the thin young lady with braided hair as she studied her reflection in a full-length mirror.

'Well, what do you think?' Louise asked.

'I think I need bigger boobs,' said the girl.

'It looks *fantastic*,' said Louise. 'It's so *you*.'

'I bet you say that to everyone.'

'No, really. There's just something about it – maybe it's your eyes, but it's just as if it was made especially for you.'

Margaret had heard a similar spiel a million times before, even in Primark, where the staff were as likely to mug you as talk to you, yet it still sounded fresh and sincere.

'You know something?' the girl said, then paused, deciding. 'I love it, and I'm going to have it, and I don't even want to know the price.'

'Great,' said Louise. 'And it's three million pounds.'

Margaret's heart flipped, but the girl roared. Margaret and Maeve gave each other high fives.

When the girl reached the counter, brandishing her credit card, she suddenly examined the label. '*M & Emma* – never heard of them.'

Louise smiled. 'It's a new partnership,' she said. Then she pointed. 'Her over there – and her over there.'

'Really?'

'And you're our very first sale,' said Emma, darting over excitedly. 'They only went in the window this morning! Congratulations. And if you really like it, please, tell all your friends.'

The girl shook her head. 'No way – this secret I'm keeping to myself.'

Margaret felt ecstatic, and guilty. It wasn't her dress at all, but if this was a taste of things to come, when her own designs really did make it into the shop window, then her life was going to become the stuff of fantasy. When the girl turned for the door, Margaret couldn't help but run up and give her a hug. 'Thank you so much,' she gushed.

When she'd gone, all four of them danced around the shop. Emma turned up the background music, and Louise opened a bottle of champagne from the fridge. They hardly heard the shop door open again.

Another young woman in expensive heels came in, and stood somewhat awkwardly. 'I'm sorry – you are open?'

'Yes, of course,' said Emma. 'Sorry . . . we're having a bit of a celebration. Is there anything I can help you with?'

'That dress in the window – it's gorgeous. I'd love to try it on.'

Emma moved towards the display. 'Which one – the *M & Emma*?'

'That one there – yeah. Isn't it beautiful?'

'Isn't it just, darling,' said Emma.

Maeve turned to Margaret. 'We're going to need more champagne,' she said.

82

Police Cheque

Bull sometimes worked as Pink's unofficial chauffeur – that is, when he wasn't busy collecting money for him or beating people up on his behalf. He liked to think of himself as his right-hand man, although *red*-hand man might have been more appropriate. Tonight he was taking him to City Hall and the monthly meeting of the Planning Committee to which he had recently been elected. Pink took his council obligations seriously, particularly when there was a profit to be made. Of course he didn't discuss bribery and corruption with Bull. Bull was strictly small potatoes, like beating up hookers.

'But you left her face alone?' Pink was saying, although really only half-paying attention, choosing to study instead the minutiae of the planning documents on his lap.

'Course I did,' said Bull. He sat up front. The radio was tuned to *Citybeat* and Rod Stewart came on.

'Turn that *Fenian* off,' Pink commanded.

'You bet.' Bull hit the switch.

Pink smiled to himself. He had no idea if Rod Stewart was a *Fenian* or not, but the singer had antagonised Belfast's Protestant community – or at least that part of it which gave a damn – at his last gig at the Odyssey Arena by shouting out his support for Celtic, which was a sin worse than, or sometimes equal to, death in certain parts of the city. In fact, Pink had quite a few Rod albums and wasn't at all bashful about blasting them out in the privacy of his own swanky home, but out in the heartland, or travelling with his people, he had to play the game.

'He can stick "Maggie May" up his friggin' hole,' Bull sneered.

'He shows his face round here he'll soon know all about "The First Cut is the Deepest",' added Pink.

'It won't be "The Killing of Georgie",' said Bull, 'it'll be the f***ing killing of Rod.'

'He won't be f***ing "Sailing", he'll be sleeping with the fishes,' promised Pink.

'"If you want my body", it won't be that f***ing sexy by the time we're finished with it,' Bull half-sung.

Pink decided to change the subject. 'So what did she have to say for herself?'

'Ah,' Bull sighed. 'The usual crap.'

'She come up with the *spondulicks*?'

'Nah, no cash on her. Ars***le paid her with a friggin' cheque.'

'You're kidding me.'

'Nah, straight up. Apparently they had some bust-up and she went arse over tit down the stairs, and he panicked and wrote her a cheque. To cash, fortunately.' Bull delved into his jacket, and pulled out the cheque. 'You want me to cash it?'

Pink reached forward to take it. 'Nah, I'll sort it.'

Billy was the man to deal with it. He'd be seeing him later. Bull pulled the car into the side of the road without indicating. A horn sounded from behind. Bull gave the driver the finger as he passed by, then nodded ahead: 'There's the yuppy w***er now.'

They were outside Mark's house. He was waiting at the bottom of his drive, wearing a face that suggested all the enthusiasm of a dyslexic going for an eye test.

'Don't talk about him like that,' said Pink. 'He's the Great White Hope of the Unionist Party.'

'Great White W***er,' said Bull, then smiled widely and raised his hand to the sorcerer's apprentice as he approached the car. 'Jump in the back there, mate,' Bull shouted.

Mark climbed in beside Pink.

'Marky-boy,' Pink said warmly, 'how's it going? Coming to see the master at work?'

'Not bad, not bad,' said Mark.

Bull pulled the car back out into traffic. There was another flurry of horns.

'It's just a planning meeting,' said Pink, 'no great shakes, but it's useful to get to know the way of things, get your face known. What's wrong, son? You don't exactly look like the joys of spring, do you?'

'Nothing,' said Mark, then added: 'Nervous.'

'Nothing to be nervous of.' He put his hand on Mark's leg and gave it a squeeze. Mark jumped. No one but his dad had ever squeezed his leg like that. Pink laughed and returned his eyes to the papers on his lap, but his attention remained with Mark. 'So,' he said, 'how has the door-to-door been going?'

*Oh s**t*, thought Mark. 'Fine, yeah,' he said.

'No problems?'

'No, great, just great.'

'No one giving you any hassle?'

'No – no, just the opposite. Hardly anyone answers their door. They just push their envelopes out.'

Pink nodded. 'Well, that's good, isn't it? Must be doing me job right then, eh?'

Mark nodded. He cleared his throat. 'I . . . I . . . it's different from what I expected.'

'Mmm-hmm?'

'I mean, it's fine, but I'm just surprised, in such a deprived area, that they're so keen to – you know, contribute.'

Pink looked at him again. 'Deprived? You think they're deprived? I'll tell you what deprived is, Mark. Deprived is sitting in some s**t-hole in Africa with bugs crawling over you and your children starving to death. We don't know the meaning of it here. Okay, so maybe there's some of them got no jobs, but you take a look down those friggin' *deprived* streets, Mark, and you count the number of houses that haven't got friggin' satellite dishes or cars sitting outside them. They've all got money to burn, son, and it's only right and proper that they burn some of it in my direction. You've heard the expression "democracy has a price"? Well, I've put a friggin' figure on it, and it's not going to break anyone's bank. Seven quid a month. Seven quid a month – what's that? I'll tell you what it is. It's an insurance policy.'

'Like third-party fire and theft,' said Bull from the front.

'Exactly. They put their trust in me and I never, ever let them down. I'm like f***ing Lloyds of London.'

Mark nodded. 'And do the rest of the Party see it like that?'

'Absolutely,' said Pink. He kept eye-contact with Mark, until Mark blushed and looked away.

Bull finally pulled the car up outside City Hall. Mark moved to open his door, but before he could grasp the handle Pink brought his hand back down on his leg. This time he didn't let go; this time the pressure was much greater. He brought his face close. His brow was furrowed, his nostrils flared, his breath smelled of mint.

'People need to be led, Mark; they need reassurance and discipline. If they think they can get away with something, they will; if they think you're weak, they will break you down, and that undermines democracy, do you know what I'm saying?'

Mark didn't really have a clue. He neither shook his head nor nodded. Just emitted a strange kind of grunt.

'Point is, I understand what you did, Mark, filling their envelopes for them, but what if everyone did that? What if everyone thought they could just rip me off like that? There'd be anarchy. How long do you think you could keep it up anyway? What were you going to do, sell your friggin' house?'

Mark shrugged.

Pink squeezed his leg one last time. 'Your heart's in the right place, Mark, but your brain's up your a***hole. Try not to think too much. It never did Bull any harm – right, Bull?'

'Right, boss,' said Bull, laughing.

'Okay, let's go then.'

Pink released Mark's leg, then climbed out of the car. Mark wanted to get out of the other door and *run away*. Instead, he followed Pink meekly into City Hall.

An hour later and Pink was in full flow. Mark thought he was quite an impressive speaker, a decent enough debater, but he got hot under the collar (and arms, clearly) quite easily, and now there were patches of deeper pink on his shirt, and his perfectly coiffured hair sat slightly dank on his head. But still, there was a certain amount of charisma, a good sense of humour; his origins were still clear but his demeanour and delivery were cultured enough and he showed both a definite grasp of detail and a true sense of the bigger picture. Mark thought Pink could make a very good politician indeed, that he was capable even of high office, so it confused him utterly as to why Pink was still clearly up to his oxters in protection money. It didn't strike Mark that Pink was unduly careless – cavalier perhaps. Mark had been determined that this would be his last night with Pink. Steven in Office 12 had more or less promised to sort things out, and perhaps he would, but now, seeing politics actually in action, Mark felt slightly better. It was the streets where he felt uncomfortable. Perhaps what Pink was up to was no different to what any other politician did, that it was an open secret to which the law turned a blind eye.

A vote was called, and Pink's motion was passed to an accompanying round of applause. Pink sat back, basking in it, then glanced round at Mark and winked. Mark smiled back.

Another councillor came over and patted Pink's back, then bent to ask quietly if he could help out a pensioner who lived in his ward but ran a business in Pink's. Pink nodded, then checked his pockets for something to write a telephone number on. The only thing he had was the cheque Bull had given him. He turned it over, then quickly jotted down the number and promised to get right onto it. The councillor pumped Pink's hand and turned away. Pink examined the number for a moment, then absentmindedly turned the cheque over again. His eyes flitted across it, confirming that it was crossed for cash, that the date was on it and finally that it was properly signed. Bull was good at getting money out of people, but sometimes the little details passed him by.

The signature was a careless scrawl, but the printed name below said: *James Mallow*.

No, Pink thought, no *bloody way*.

83

I'm in Heaven

Maeve returned to work, quite plastered, but Margaret couldn't drag herself away. Maeve promised to smooth it with Mr Kawolski, and Margaret had no doubt that she would. New Maeve was different to old Maeve. She'd always been brash and loud, but now she oozed confidence, and even if Margaret felt funny about admitting it, sexuality. She had been transformed by a haircut, a little care and attention, the demise of her husband and her encounter with the King of Carrot Cake.

Margaret was still bouncing with excitement by 4 p.m. One more dress was sold and another woman had promised to come back the next day with a final decision. Emma thought their first day's business was *remarkable*.

'And all without press or publicity – oh darling Margaret, the sky's the limit.' Then she glanced at her watch. 'I nearly forgot – May Li is due.'

'May Li?'

'She's making your designs up. She's *fantastic*, darling. She really *can* make a silk purse out of a sow's ear.'

'You mean my—'

'Oh darling! Don't be so defensive! If she can make a silk purse out of a sow's ear, think what she can do with your designs!' Emma sashayed away across the shop singing, 'Heaven, I'm in heaven . . .'

Margaret stepped outside and phoned Walter. She felt slightly odd doing it. Maeve had experienced the thrill of the first sale with her, but it wasn't enough. She wanted to share it with someone who wasn't there. Like exam results or passing your driving test. She wanted to call and say, 'I did it!' How sad was her life that the only person she could think of was Walter, with whom she had only had two dates?

No, that's the wrong attitude, she decided. How splendid is my life that I have this great news and someone to share it with. Walter is special. I know he is. I jumped in a river for him.

'Walter North,' said Walter.

'Hello stranger,' said Margaret.

'Linda,' said Walter.

'Margaret,' said Margaret.

'Oh – oh hi! How are you? Sorry, I thought it was . . . you know – the estate agent.'

'No,' said Margaret. He'd called the estate agent *Linda*. She didn't like that *at all*. There was no need for him to be on first-name terms with her. That suggested intimacy. She had a radar for that. After all, she never went in to see her bank manager and called him Jimmy or Ricky or whatever the hell his name was. She felt like cutting the line, but she held on. Just. 'I'm fine. How's Linda?'

'Linda? I'm sure she's fine too. We've just been tying up the loose ends. You know, on the apartment.'

'Right.' She went quiet.

Walter said, 'You all right, love?'

Love. Hah! 'Yeah. Sure.'

'Good.' Silence again. 'Something wrong?'

'No. I just . . .' She shrugged; it didn't travel well. 'I sold a dress.'

'You did?'

'Well, three actually, and one more with a deposit on it.'

'That's brilliant!'

'I suppose.'

'No suppose about it. It's fantastic – well done!'

'I really didn't do anything.'

'Bo**ocks! You did everything! Well done, you.'

She felt better then. He was genuinely enthusiastic. In fact, once she started telling him about it she could hardly stop. She only brought it to an end when she noticed a diminutive and elderly Chinese woman standing examining one of the remaining Primark dresses in the front window.

'Oh, I'm going to have to go, that must be May Li.'

'May Li?'

'She's making my designs up into dresses. Apparently she has access to all sorts of wonderful materials and half the price of anywhere else, though it beats me where she gets it because I used to scour the place looking for cheap stuff.'

'Well,' said Walter, 'it's Chinatown.'

'It's what?'

'It's Chinatown.'

'What are you talking about?'

'The movie, *Chinatown*. Jack Nicholson, anything that goes wrong or defies explanation, they say, "It's Chinatown".'

'I don't get it,' said Margaret. 'Are you saying this is all going to go wrong?'

'No, of course not! I was just joking.'

'Oh. All right.'

'It's just an expression that means nothing, and everything, at the same time. It's a brill movie. And *The Simpsons* do a great skit on it and maybe we could rent it out if you fancied.'

But Margaret wasn't listening. May Li was now peering even more closely at the dress. Then she turned her head slightly, and she spat on the ground. A great big hacked-up gob. Then she entered the shop.

'Oh Christ,' said Margaret.

'Margaret?'

'I have to go – I'll call you later.' She cut the line, her heart already thumping out of her chest. Had this little Chinawoman recognised the dress? What if she made Primark dresses as well and was about to expose it as a rip-off?

Oh please, oh please, oh please God no.

Margaret hurried back towards the shop. As she pulled the door open, Walter's words drifted back to her.

'It's Chinatown.'

On the other side of the city, Linda Wray was distraught. She knew she made attachments easily and could become dependent on people she hardly knew, but there was nothing she could do about it. She was what she was. But she had to do something, or as soon as the deal for the apartment was done he'd be gone and she'd go back to feeling wasted and used. She'd already half-frightened him off by babbling about her hysterectomy. It made her sound like some old middle-aged frump. She had to show him that she could do light and frothy and sexy, prove she wasn't a big ball of depression and insecurity. Walter was nice, and she had no idea if he was even better than that, but she needed at least the opportunity to find out, and that meant more than just a quick roll in the hay. But perhaps two rolls in the hay might help.

Linda liked candles. Not in a pervy 'melt that hot wax over my aching body' kind of a way, but designer candles in artistic shapes which wafted delicious perfumes. She also had a guilty attachment to the smell of old-fashioned straight white candles, the kind you kept about the house in case the power went off. And when you like something enough, you tend to presume that other people will like it as well, given half the chance. So, when she arrived at the penthouse apartment at Towerview half an hour before their appointment – no, *rendezvous* – Linda set about placing eighteen hand-picked candles of different hue around the lounge and master bedroom. She placed four bottles of Asti in the fridge. Then she slipped into the bathroom and took off her work suit. She pulled on stockings, attached suspenders, removed her bra and donned a baby-doll nightdress. She put a Frank Sinatra CD into the player. She applied make-up, perfume and practised sucking in her stomach. She drank two vodka miniatures straight down and hid the empty bottles back in her handbag.

Linda checked her watch. Three minutes until Walter was due. Perfect. She moved from candle to candle, lighting each one and then waiting a moment to see if the flame took. Just as she reached candle eighteen, the doorbell rang. Linda dimmed the lights. She felt tingly all over. She opened the door.

'Walter,' she said coyly. Then added, 'And Bertha. How lovely to see you.'

At that moment, the smoke alarm went off.

84

O Brother, Where Art Thou? (2)

Redmond, hung-over to hell, and with a surprisingly good recollection of his drunken behaviour in the public bar the night before, ordered a room-service breakfast and an *International Herald Tribune* rather than venture down. Besides, he didn't want to take the chance of his twin brother walking into the restaurant and accidentally exposing the fraud.

It was hardly an Ulster fry – oh, how he had dreamed of one of those in the preceding months – but it was greasy enough and fatty enough to quell the dry bokes. There was no mention of either Redmond or his brother in the paper, which was a relief. Interest was fading. Damian had clearly found it more difficult to organise safe passage for him than he had hoped and had been obliged to spend the night at the Archbishop of Bogotá's residence while all the details were ironed out. Redmond expected nothing less. His brother, although usually timid, was like a dog with a bone when he felt passionately about something. Damian was probably not only demanding safe passage, but first-class tickets as well. Redmond laughed at that.

Then the phone rang and a querulous voice said, 'Father Damian?' with a thick Spanish accent.

'Uhuh,' said Redmond.

'Oh, thank God you are safe!'

'I'm . . . yes, I am, quite safe indeed. God bless. Who would this be?'

'Damian – it is Ramón.'

'Ramón.'

'I was extremely worried. My driver was murdered last night.'

Redmond's eyes settled on a small book sitting on the bedside table beside the telephone. It was open to a double-page spread of photographs of ecclesiastical gentlemen. It wasn't exactly the *Penguin Book of Bishops* but it wasn't far off. There, on the right-hand page, was a circled picture with *Ramón des Quelia, Archbishop of Bogotá* printed beneath it.

'Murdered?'

'Shot dead and his car stolen. I cannot tell you how valuable that car was. Oh, this is such a relief. When the car did not return for many hours I was very concerned, and when they found the bodies at the city dump, it was natural to assume that you . . . well, thank God.'

Redmond's throat was dry enough already, but now it almost sealed over. 'Not just your driver?' he rasped.

'No. There was another man with him, but it was impossible to identify. His head . . .' The Archbishop sighed. 'It is not an unusual occurrence, Father, in this city of ours; there are many bodies found there. Do not let it concern you. Drivers are, as the Americans say, a dime a dozen. But a car like that is very difficult to replace. However, this is a relief, you are well. And I trust that you are happy with the details of your brother's journey?'

Redmond's mind was spinning. He managed a brief, 'Of course,' and the Archbishop chattered on, but Redmond was no longer listening. His brother was dead. Murdered for an expensive car. He slipped off the side of the bed onto his knees. Tears sprang. He rocked himself gently while the Archbishop of Bogotá debated shift versus automatic.

Then there was a knock. Redmond told the Archbishop he had to go and hung up. He wiped at his face and crossed, dazed, to the door. *Let it be Damian, let it be Damian, let it be Damian, let it be Damian . . .*

'Hiya Father – you all set?'

Redmond stared at her. Sinn Fein Siobhan, with her hair braided and a backpack over her shoulder.

'I . . . I . . .'

'Aw, come on, Father. I want to get there in time to do duty-free, you know? And I'm told the airport traffic's usually hectic, so will you come on?'

'My brother . . .'

Siobhan sighed. 'Father, I'm sorry. I know it's been traumatic. But the flights are non-transferable, so unless you want to dip into your own collection plate, you'll need to get your arse in gear. The Party's not going to shell out for new tickets.'

Redmond nodded vaguely. 'I'll just . . .'

'Be down in the lobby in ten minutes tops, all right?' Siobhan winked, then hurried off down the corridor.

Redmond closed the door and leaned against it. Damian was dead, there was no other explanation for his failure to return. Killed over a car, or mugged over a wallet. Dead in a dump. His head blown off, from the sounds of it.

Murdered trying to help me. Me. And whatever plans he carried or had agreed with the Archbishop to help me – lost with him.

Christ.

Death was a way of life for a terrorist like Redmond O'Boyle, but this was something else. Damian was a *priest*, for godsake. He wouldn't harm *anyone*. He was one of the few people Redmond knew who really did turn the other cheek. He was kind and meek and loyal, and the only reason he was in Bogotá at all was to bury his poor misguided brother. Whatever way he cared to look at it, Redmond knew that even though he hadn't actually pulled the trigger, he was the one responsible for Damian's death.

He was good.

I am evil.

Yin and Yang.

Redmond looked at himself in the mirror, dressed in his priest's habit. He gently flicked through his brother's passport. He touched the worn cover of his favourite Bible.

Thou shalt not kill.

My brother's keeper.

Redmond knew suddenly what he must do. A void had been created when his brother died, a void that had to be filled.

He would become his brother. He would carry on his good work. He would foresake evil, violence, and work for the common good. Damian had sacrificed his life for Redmond; now Redmond would *donate* his. They were twins, after all, almost identical. It would not be that difficult. As kids they were rarely mistaken for each other because their very different personalities were reflected both in their looks and demeanour. Redmond had always appeared cheeky and troublesome, while his brother looked like a choirboy. Their mother helped: dressing and cutting their hair to opposite extremes. It also helped their father, who was half-blind, half-drunk, to tell them apart. In addition, Redmond had a missing front tooth for a long time, where Damian had an endearing smile. Redmond had a permanently running nose, and if it wasn't one eye with a sty it was the other, or often both. Damian passed through puberty with barely a pimple, but Redmond's face looked like the collapse of Mount Doom. As they matured they grew more alike, but their interests and passions meant that they rarely spent time in each other's company. When he became a priest Damian served in outlying parishes, while Redmond was either on the run or on remand. They had not strolled down the street in each other's company for perhaps fifteen years. Nobody knew just how identical they had become. And now they never would.

I Predict A Riot

Redmond slipped his brother's passport into his jacket pocket, then quickly packed Damian's few possessions together into a small suitcase. He checked himself in the mirror again and found that he could hardly take his eyes off his own reflection.

'Damian,' he said, watching his own lips move.

'I forgive you, Brother,' said Damian.

'I won't let you down,' said Redmond.

85

In the Bathroom

'Linda – *please*.'

'No! Go away!'

'Linda! Come on, this is pointless.'

'That's easy for you to say!'

'Just unlock the door.'

'No!'

'Look, Bertha's a master of Tae kwon do. She'll smash the door down if you don't open it.'

Bertha said, 'Well, it's more of a defensive art, and my feet aren't what they were, and if you think I'm going to go damaging my own property, you've another think coming.'

From the other side of the locked bathroom door Linda said weakly, 'It's not your property, and now it never will be, not after this. I'm *mortified*.'

'If it's any consolation, I thought your get-up was very sexy,' said Walter. He wasn't lying. *Bizarre*, but sexy too. When she'd opened the door to Walter, determined on seduction, only to find his sugar-granny with him, she'd looked somewhere between Mrs Robinson in *The Graduate* and the mad old biddy in *Sunset Boulevard*.

God love her, Walter thought.

'Well, what do you want us to do?' Bertha asked.

'I want you to blow out the candles, turn the lights on, then leave. I'm sorry for embarrassing you. I'll understand if you don't want to buy the apartment. If you do, I'll send someone else to deal with it.'

'There's no need for that,' said Walter.

'There's *every* need.'

Walter sighed. 'Well, have it your way. I'm sorry, Linda. It was a nice thought. You've nothing to be ashamed of.'

They blew out the candles between them, Walter managing most because Bertha, though spry, didn't have the puff for it.

'All the best!' Walter shouted back, switching the main lights back on then ushering Bertha out onto the landing.

'Well, that was a bit of a shock to the system,' said Bertha. 'Had you been getting on well with her before?'

'No, no. Purely business. She's clearly, ahm, off her rocker.'

'Well,' Bertha said, 'maybe it's no bad thing.'

Walter's brow furrowed. 'How so?'

'We complain vociferously to her boss, and threaten to go to the papers unless he knocks a couple of grand off the price.'

Walter laughed. 'My God, Bertha, you're a wily old bird.'

'Less of the old,' said Bertha, turning towards the stairs.

Linda heard the front door close, and thanked God they were gone. She was sitting on the toilet, all Panda eyes and bunched-up toilet roll. Her baby-doll nightdress clung to her like a drenched nappy. She wanted to die. She had made a total and utter fool out of herself. She had lost Walter, lost the deal, and who knows, probably lost her job as well.

What the hell was I thinking of? And what do I do now?

She hauled herself up off the toilet seat, then cringed at her reflection in the mirror. *I'm like one of those idiots who go on* The X Factor *or* Pop Idol, *convinced they can sing, and then the whole world laughs at them.* The tears cascaded down her face again. She squeezed her eyes shut.

Stop it! *You were just trying a little seduction! If he hadn't brought that old bat with him everything would have been fine – you'd have been romping away! It's only a little hiccup!*

She didn't believe that for one moment. She firmly believed she had crossed the border from interestingly eccentric to certifiably mad. But thinking of hiccups reminded her of the bottles of Asti lining the fridge. *Exactly* what she needed right now. Linda splashed water onto her face, dried off, then unlocked the bathroom door and padded across the lounge and into the kitchen. She'd get drunk. There was the solution! Get pi**ed! She opened the fridge and removed a bottle. As she closed the door, a voice said, 'Pour one for me, why don't you?'

Linda screamed and dropped the bottle. Walter, stepping out of an alcove on the other side of the fridge, caught it.

'Good Jesus Christ!' Linda yelled. 'What the hell are you doing!?' She instinctively moved her arms to cover her breasts, which were clearly visible through her nightdress. She did not feel the sex siren now.

'Waiting for you to open the bathroom door,' said Walter. He smiled sympathetically at her. 'You look gorgeous,' he said.

Linda backed away. 'That's not fair,' she said. 'You said you were leaving.'

'I know,' said Walter, coming after her.

'Where's Bertha?'

'Away home.'

'Away laughing off into the night.'

'Not at all. She understood completely.'

'Yeah, bo**ocks.'

'No, seriously. She thought it was quite sweet.'

'Just wait there,' said Linda, finally reversing into the bathroom and closing the door. 'I need to get changed.'

'No, you don't,' said Walter, to the door.

'Yes, I do,' said Linda, turning the key. She had previously neatly folded her business suit onto the luxuriously tiled floor, and now she hurriedly began to pull it on.

'You must think I'm such an eejit,' she said, glaring at her reflection. Her hair was all over the place and her eyes were still badly smudged.

'Yes,' said Walter.

She laughed finally. 'I'm coming out now,' she said, 'but I have to warn you, I still look really scary.'

'I'll keep the lights low,' said Walter.

They sat facing each other in armchairs in the lounge, brimful cups of Asti in their hands and a second bottle waiting on the coffee table.

'What I don't understand is why you brought Bertha with you.'

'Well, as we didn't use protection last time, I thought I'd better do so this time.'

'That's not funny.'

'She wanted to make sure the papers were in order. She wanted another look at the property – I could hardly say no. And I didn't expect . . .'

'I thought it would be a nice surprise.'

'It was. Up to a point.'

'I get nervous, Walter. I'm sorry. On the phone today I talked such s**te, if you'll pardon the expression, and I was worried I'd scare you off, so I wanted to do something to keep you interested.' She shook her head. 'In retrospect . . .'

'It was a fantastic idea, Linda. I should have let you know. But I was just . . .' Walter sighed. 'I really like you, Linda.'

'If you're going to say let's just be friends you can f**k off now. I don't need that.'

'I was *going* to say I really like you, Linda, full stop.'

'Full stop?'

'Full stop.'

'Full stop what? I really like you, *but*?'
'But nothing. I really like you.'
'But let's just be friends?'
'No! For godsake.'
'Oh. Well.' She took a gulp of her drink. 'I really like you too.'
Thirty minutes later they were in bed. An hour after that she was lying in his arms thinking: *He likes me, he likes me, he likes me, he likes me.*
Walter was thinking: *I am such a b**tard.*

86
Arrest

Jimmy Marsh Mallow and Gary McBride arrived at New Allied Property Developments' glass-fronted offices at a little after 10 a.m. Gary had called ahead without specifying what they wanted to talk to George Green, the Managing Director, about. George Green knew that Jimmy Marsh Mallow wasn't coming to discuss parking tickets, but for such a smart man, hadn't yet put two and two together.

George was tall and thin, slightly stooped, and in his late forties. Many property developers start out building houses themselves, learning their trade from the bottom up, but George had never lifted a brick in his life. He came to property via Oxford University and the Classics. He was devoted to poetry and received some early acclaim for his own work, but was self-aware enough to know that ultimately it wasn't good enough for anything other than vanity publication, and he would not countenance that. So he dropped poetry with the same finality with which he later jettisoned his first and second wives. Family money and pressure got him his first, initially disinterested start in property, transforming a Victorian shell into three luxury apartments. But once he saw the real money that could be made, and understood that he could do it without getting his hands dirty, George developed an abiding passion which more than filled the void left by his rejection of poetry. He specialised in turning brownfield industrial wastelands into gleaming new shopping malls and upmarket housing estates, though he had no qualms about turning harmless greenfield sites into low-cost public housing either. He just liked making deals, wielding influence, building things, and creating wealth, his own. He was probably, with the exception of a pharmaceutical giant and an absentee landlord, the richest man in Northern Ireland. He was used to meeting powerful men, and dominating conversations, but he felt uneasy from the moment Jimmy Mallow and his sidekick were shown into his expansive, river-view office.

They shook hands. Marsh's grip was solid, and George matched it. Gary just nodded at him.

George slipped back in behind his desk. 'Well, gentlemen, what's all this—'

'That's some view,' said Jimmy Marsh, ignoring the chair George had indicated and positioning himself by the window.

'Yes, it is very relaxing,' said George.

'No shortage of apartments along here, is there? You build them all?'

'Not all of them. The Windsor, the Winston, the Towerview. We've another one going up a bit further along.'

'Business must be good.'

'It's up and down.'

'Can't have helped, that matter of the kid's body being found in the river right outside, what, the Towerview?' He turned to Gary for mock confirmation.

'Towerview,' said Gary, who had taken a seat.

'Unfortunate,' said George, 'but a three-day wonder. That's what you learn about the property business; you're in it for the long haul.'

Marsh remained motionless by the window. George looked at him for several moments, then switched his attention to Gary McBride. 'Do you want to tell me what this is about?'

'Well, he usually does most of the talking,' said Gary, nodding at Marsh. 'I tend to take notes and make smart comments.'

'Not that smart,' said Marsh, turning now.

'Well, that's a matter of opinion.'

Marsh smiled, then took a seat beside him and looked at George. George clasped his hands. Marsh clasped his.

'Gentlemen, I have a busy schedule. I find it better to come to the point sooner rather than—'

'Did you have a busy schedule on Thursday, June the sixteenth?'

'Why?'

'Usually I hate cops who say, "We'll ask the questions",' said Gary, 'but we'll ask the questions.'

Before George could respond indignantly, Marsh said: 'Are you married, George?'

'I'm divorced. Twice. No children.'

'What happened?'

'What do you mean, what happened? The marriages didn't work out.'

'You, ah, went over to the dark side, did you?' Marsh asked.

'I beg your pardon?'

'You decided to play for the other team.'

George's brow furrowed, and then abruptly he burst into laughter. 'Are you suggesting what I think you're suggesting?'

'I don't know,' said Marsh. 'What do you think I'm suggesting?'

George shook his head. 'This is ridiculous. I'm trying to help you, gentlemen. I wish you would get to the point.'

Marsh looked at him.

Gary looked at him.

George said, 'Do you want me to call my solicitor?'

Marsh said, 'Do you want to call your solicitor?'

'Oh for Christ sake. Inspector, I'm a—'

'Powerful man? Yes, we know. Mr Green, Thursday June the sixteenth, say around six p.m., where were you?'

George raised his hands helplessly. Then he pushed a button on his phone. 'Karen, check my diary, would you? Where was I on June the sixteenth?'

A young woman's voice, probably belonging to the pretty girl they'd stared at on the way in, said, 'June the sixteenth . . . Hold on.'

George said: 'Around six.'

'p.m.,' said Gary.

'Hi. June the sixteenth, you were in and out of the office all day, with half a dozen meetings – do you want me to read out the list? Closest to six was . . . the Europa at five.'

'Thank you, Karen. George pressed another button, then looked at Marsh. 'Does that help?'

'Us yes, you no.'

'Chief Inspector, please, you're starting to . . . Could you just be a little less cryptic? You know, half the secret of my success is that I'm always upfront about things.'

'You hired a rent boy in Castle Street. Maybe you took him back to the Europa – we'll find out – but you killed him. You chopped him up and you dumped him in the river.'

George's mouth dropped open.

'As we speak, Forensics are going through your car, George, and we already have your phone records showing you called a pimp called Benny Caproni shortly before the boy was picked up.'

'This isn't . . . I didn't . . .'

Marsh stood, Gary with him.

'We're taking you in, George.'

'But . . . but . . .'

'You can call your solicitor from the station,' said Gary, waving the tall, pale man out from behind his desk. George stood, then lifted an expensive fountain pen whose top had come off. He tried to fit the top back on, but his hands were shaking too much. 'I didn't do anything,' he said. 'Honestly, I can explain.'

'Looking forward to it,' said Marsh. He shook his head at George as Gary guided him past on rubbery legs. 'I'm telling you, George, you shouldn't mess with the wee lads. It always ends in tears. You of all people should know where to put your money. Bricks not pr**ks, George. Bricks not pr**ks.'

87

Chinese Whispers

Thinking in racial stereotypes can have nothing to do with being racist and everything to do with not getting out much, or watching too many old black and white TV movies because you've no real life of your own. At least this is what Margaret thought as she stood beside May Li as May Li pulled and poked at her dresses, and then rifled through her designs, pausing only to hit a spittoon from nine feet away. It wasn't actually a spittoon, of course. It was the bottom part of a ceramic plant pot which Louise had scrambled to put into place, based on past experience, and it served its purpose beautifully. The fact was that May Li spat. She spat on the footpath, she spat on the floor; if there was a spittoon, she spat in that, if there wasn't, she gobbed into the handiest receptacle. She hacked it up from the back of her throat. She did it without thinking. She had been doing it all her life.

The first time Margaret saw her do it, outside the shop, she thought, *Well, she's Chinese*. The second time, inside, she thought, *She's* really *Chinese*. But the third time, within a couple of minutes that is, she thought, *This isn't normal*. Because if every Chinese spat as often as May Li did, Peking would be drowning in phlegm. As the makeshift spittoon went *ping* again, Margaret concluded that it had nothing to do with the fact that May Li was Chinese, but a lot to do with the fact that May Li liked to spit. Margaret glanced at Emma Cochrane, who was looking queasy, and Louise, who was holding her stomach.

Margaret, who felt that she had her entire fantastical career riding on whether or not this little old Chinawoman guessed that she was a fraud and a charlatan, had decided as she re-entered the shop that she wasn't going to be intimidated, that she was going to stand up and fight. There were moments when she experienced stultifying wavers in confidence, but this was not one of them. She would brazenly insist that the dresses were hers, no matter what.

May Li *sniffed* one of the Primark dresses, then handed it to Louise.

She raised the small file of hand-drawn designs and waved them in Margaret's face. She opened her mouth, as if to speak, then let loose with another flying grot which landed in the dead centre of the ceramic bowl.

'You design these?' May Li asked in a smoky rasp, her eyes fixed on Margaret's.

Margaret eye-balled her back. 'You bet,' she said, then she too hacked one up and spat it straight across the shop floor towards the makeshift spittoon. It missed, landing on a summer dress, and dripped onto the floor. Neither of them had watched its flight, although Louise looked distraught.

May Li nodded slowly. She reached out and turned up the hem of the Primark dress. 'These, I don't like.'

'Fair enough,' said Margaret.

'These,' she waved the designs again, 'I like.' Then she smiled widely. 'Very clever, very bright, these will be very nice.'

Relief flooded through Margaret. Emma beamed. Louise held the dripping summer dress at arm's length and took it into the back room.

May Li was actually a *doll*, Margaret thought. A spitting doll, for sure, but still a doll. She was funny and quirky and smart. She knew *everything* there was to know about fabrics and materials and colour and zips and buttons and thread, and she did everything either by hand or on an ancient Singer. She spoke with a very strong Belfast accent. Margaret guessed she was about seventy years old.

'Have you been over here very long?' Margaret asked.

'Forty-one years.'

'And do you miss . . . home?'

'Liverpool? No.'

'You're from Liverpool?'

'Second generation. My family owned a restaurant right next door to The Cavern.'

'Really? Did John, Paul, George and Ringo pop in for a . . . Chinese?'

'No,' said May Li. Then she cackled. 'But one of Herman's Hermit's once came in.'

'So how come you ended up here?'

'I married a sailor. Merchant seaman from Sandy Row. He brought me home.'

'To Sandy Row?' May Li nodded. 'Gosh, that must have been hard.'

'It was . . . no problem. They did not mind that I was Chinese. As long as I wasn't a Catholic.'

Margaret smiled. 'And do you still live there?'

May Li shook her head wistfully. 'My parents went on what you

331

call the Long March with Mao Tse-tung in China in 1949. It was a march for change. I also went on a march for change, with the Civil Rights protestors in Derry in 1969. This did not go down well on Sandy Row. Our house was burned down.'

'My God.'

'There is an old Chinese saying. It says: *make sure you have good insurance*. We did. I have a nicer house now, in a quiet street.'

'And your husband?'

'He passed away.'

'Oh. I'm sorry.'

May Li nodded to herself, then said simply, 'Yes.' Then she hacked up again and . . . *ping*.

Margaret took a deep breath. It was time to take the bull by the horns. 'May Li, I think we're going to make a great team. But I need to ask you something, something personal. About the spitting.'

May Li looked at her, her brow already furrowed. 'What spitting?'

Margaret laughed involuntarily. 'The, you know, the . . .' And then she saw Emma and Louise gesticulating urgently at her from the door to the stockroom. Emma was making a cutting motion across her throat.

'Just . . . just the . . . you know.'

May Li looked genuinely confused.

'The uh . . . you know, all the spitting in Belfast. Everyone's at it, aren't they?'

May Li nodded in agreement. 'It's a disgusting habit,' she said.

Later, while she worked away in the stockroom, making notations and marginal comments on the designs, Margaret, Emma and Louise stood around the counter drinking coffee.

'But she can't *not* be aware of it,' said Margaret.

'My husband scratches his balls all the time,' said Louise, 'and he always says he isn't aware of it.'

'I think she gets so caught up in her work,' said Emma, 'that she does it without thinking.'

'He'll be on the bus or in a queue in a restaurant or waiting to see the bank manager,' Louise continued, 'and all you get is scratch, scratch, scratch.'

'But if she does it without thinking, how does she hit the spittoon every time?' Margaret asked.

'Or in the garden centre or during a christening and he once nearly got arrested in the swimming pool.'

'Perhaps it's just a God-given talent,' said Emma.

'And you never raised it with her?'

'I tried, but no – just a blank look. And I don't want to lose her, she's a godsend. So I just try to keep her out of the public eye and provide something for her to spit in.'

'It's really not a Chinese thing,' said Margaret.

'No,' agreed Emma, 'it's a May Li thing.'

'I just thank God,' said Louise, 'that he never asks *me* to scratch them.'

88
Blackmail

George Green, the property developer with a penchant for rent boys, was just being marched into an interview room downtown when Jimmy Marsh Mallow was called to a phone. He snapped the receiver up impatiently, so keen was he to observe Green being nailed to a table. 'What?' he barked.

'Mr Mallow?'

'Yes?'

'It's Julia.'

'Julia?'

Green was ushered in behind a desk. He was pale and sweating and demanding his solicitor.

'From the other night.'

'I'm not sure what you're talking about. Is there something I can help you with?'

'You pushed me down the stairs.'

She had his attention now. Jimmy Marsh stiffened. He indicated to two colleagues standing watching Green through the glass with him to leave the room, and they hurried out.

'Ah – right. Yes. Ahm – how are you?'

He didn't *care* how she was. His mind was going in five different directions at once, as if it was a one-armed bandit and someone had yanked the lever. How did she track him down? How did she get hold of this number? How did she know his name? It hit jackpot almost immediately: *the cheque*. He had somehow managed to blank the whole incident from his mind, dismissing it as a tragic aberration, but it had lurked in there, festering, and now here it was suddenly out in the open again, entirely focused around his own crushing stupidity.

I wrote her a cheque. It had my name on it. Thirty years of putting killers away on the most fiendishly complicated evidence, and I forget my name's printed on a cheque.

I Predict A Riot

'I'm not so good, Mr Marsh.' It was almost a little-girl voice, yet he knew she was as hard as nails.

'I'm sorry to hear that.' He could see Green with his head in his hands now.

'My lip is all infected, and my nose is broken, and in my profession, that's not good.'

'No, I imagine not.'

'So I was talking to a friend about this and she said I should report it to the police, and you know, get compensation.'

Didn't take her long to get to the point. Relax. You're an old hand. Slap her down, hard. Don't let her get her nails in.

'Well, Julie, I *am* the police, and I can tell you now, you haven't a cat's chance in hell of getting anything, apart from a shitload of trouble. Do you hear me? I don't know what you call yourself – an escort girl or a call girl or whatever – but we both know what you are. And what you're doing now is trying to squeeze me for some more money, and that's just not going to work because first of all, I did nothing wrong, and second of all, I'm big enough and powerful enough to make your life a complete f***ing misery, do you understand?'

There was a short silence, then Julie said: 'You threw me down the stairs.'

'I did *not* throw you down the stairs. I was only trying to get you out of the house.' *No, don't start arguing.*

'You hired me for sex and then you got cold feet, that's not my fault.'

Deep breath. 'Julie, don't f**k with me. I'm too big, I'm too strong, and I've been around too long. You made a mistake. You picked on the wrong man. Sort yourself out, move on, do you hear me? Because I'll tell you this now, if I ever hear from you again, you will regret it. Do you understand what I'm saying?'

'You're threatening me.'

'Yes, I am.'

'You're a cop. You're supposed to go to cops for help.'

'I *am* helping you, Julie. I'm sorry what happened happened, but I'm sure you've had worse. I wrote you a cheque – go ahead and cash it, we're even. All right?'

'All right,' Julie said weakly.

'Good.' Marsh hung up the phone. He sat in the darkened room, pulling at his bottom lip. His left leg jiggled up and down involuntarily. Through the glass he could see Gary McBride sitting on the edge of the table, passing photographs to George Green. Green was shaking his head a lot. Marsh flicked a switch so he could hear what they were saying. He usually liked this bit, when the enormity of their crimes,

335

which was usually lost in the frenzy of the act, finally began to register.

Green looked suitably revolted. His voice was anguished, half-strangled. 'Don't, please. I'm going to be sick.'

'So be sick. You can f***ing clean it up.'

'Just take it away.'

'They're only photos, George. Later, we'll bring the real thing in. The boy's head. Be in a plastic bag, like, but you can say hello.'

'Please, no.'

'It's no trouble.'

'My solicitor, is he here yet?'

'Let me just check. Oh, wait a minute, what am I, a f***ing pager service? When he's here he's here, George. But if you ask me, what's the point? I'm sure he'll cost you a f***ing fortune, but once he sees the evidence, he'll just laugh and ask for his cheque.'

'I haven't *done* anything.'

'Oh yes. That's right. You know, just before your brief comes in and rescues you, let's just review the evidence, George. Let's just review the prosecution case for the benefit of the jury. So you're feeling a bit horny, right? You phone your pimp mate Benny Caproni who knows exactly the right boy for you. "Ladies and gentlemen of the jury, take a look at the phone records – there's the call right there in black and white". You're so keen, you drive yourself round to Castle Street to pick him up. "Ladies and gentlemen, we're going to roll some CCTV footage for you which clearly shows defendant's car and the victim climbing in". Poor Michael Caldwell, he was never seen alive again. A few days later – "and if you'll look at the map now, members of the jury – Michael's body washes up here – and here – and here." Chopped up in a vain attempt to dispose of any incriminating evidence, except any damn fool with digital television and a fondness for CSI knows that it's almost impossible to get rid of *all* the evidence.'

'Please stop! I hear what you're saying, and I know how it looks, but it really wasn't me.'

'Oh, right. You promise?'

'I swear to God.'

Gary laughed out loud. 'Do your previous business friends know you're into the wee lads, George?'

'I'm not.'

'Do they know that you like to give it to the wee lads hard, eh, George? You like it really rough, do you?'

'I don't . . . it wasn't me.'

'What about your sister and her kids, George – what are they going to think?'

'It wasn't me!'

'But you phoned Benny Caproni, didn't you?'

'Yes!'

'And you hired the boy, didn't you?'

'Yes!'

'And you went and picked him up in your car, didn't you?'

'Yes! All right!'

'And you took him somewhere for sex, and it got out of hand, and you killed him and panicked and chopped him up and dumped him in the river?'

'No!'

'Looks that way. Eight out of twelve jurors would say it looks that way. Ten out of ten big scary men in prison will say it looks that way, just before they poke your eyes out.'

'Stop it, *please!*'

'Then tell us what happened!'

'Nothing happened!' George raised his hands and made a patting, downwards motion, as if he was trying to calm a rising tide. 'Look, I made the call; I picked him up. I took him to . . .' He shook his head in disbelief at his own actions. 'I got him for someone else. It was a . . . perk, a sweetener, a business deal. Christ, man, it happens all the time. Some people want money, some people want cars. He wanted a boy. But I had no idea he would . . .'

'What? A big boy did it and ran away?'

'Yes!'

'So, you'd have his name and everything.'

George looked down at the table. He shook his head.

'Might that be because he doesn't in fact exist?'

George swallowed. 'He exists.'

'Yeah – in your head. What are you, Gollum? Do you speak to your other half all the time?'

George's eyes stayed on the stained desk top. Tears ran down his cheeks. His voice cracked. 'He said he would kill my sister and her children if it ever got out.'

'Well, that's convenient,' said Gary.

'Why would I make something like that up!'

'In the vague hope that we might just say, "That's okay then, George, you can go on home, we believe you".'

Gary took one of the photographs of Michael Caldwell's severed head and set it back down on the table. 'Michael Caldwell,' he said simply.

'I know who it is.'

'Nice lad, was he?'

'Yes. I suppose.'

'This other guy, supposing for a moment that he really exists, must be someone pretty special if he can get one of the richest, most successful businessmen in Belfast to act as his pimp, not only procuring an underage boy, but also delivering him right into his lap.'

George's eyes flitted up from the photograph, then he nodded slowly, and there was something about the way he did it, the raw fear in his eyes, that made Gary glance up at the one-way glass for the first time, knowing that Marsh was watching and listening and thinking the same thoughts.

89

The Flying Priest

Somewhere over the Atlantic, Redmond nudged Siobhan out of a doze and said, 'Do you remember when Nelson Mandela got out of prison?'

Siobhan blinked groggily at him. 'What?'

'Nelson Mandela, when he got out of prison – what did you think?'

Siobhan yawned. It was a long, complicated flight home, heading out from Bogotá to Rio – this time without the option of topping up her tan on the beach – with just an hour's wait for the Heathrow flight they were on now, and she just wanted to sleep, not to have a mourning priest at her side bothering her. He hadn't talked half as much when he'd arrived in Bogotá. Now you could hardly shut him up. Grief, she supposed, affected different people in different ways. Thank God she had earphones and could turn up the volume when his talking or wailing became too annoying without him really being aware of it. Now, observing the earnest look in his eyes, she had the dread feeling that her interrupted sleep was going to remain just that for some considerable time.

'Nelson Mandela? I was too young. I think I knew about it happening, but I was probably out on my skateboard. Why?'

'Nothing. I mean, I was just thinking about him, being a terrorist . . .'

'A freedom fighter.'

'Yes, of course, and there was such a huge build-up to his release – you know for thirty years, really – and all the protests and embargoes and Elvis Costello doing that song, remember it?'

Siobhan, more alert now, began to sing, '*Free-ee-ee-ee-eee . . . Nelson Man-dela!* Loved that.'

'And it was all live on TV the morning he got out – wasn't it a Sunday morning? And you expected him to walk out and be like this *giant*, then he came through the gates and he was like this real little fella and I can remember being quite disappointed. My mum called him a *funny wonder*. And he was supposed to be this huge statesman, but all I ever really remember him doing was strange little African dances and meeting the Spice Girls.'

'What's your point, Father?'

'Well, that people forget, don't they? Nelson Mandela wasn't put away for his views, he was put away for blowing things up. But everyone seemed to conveniently ignore that.'

'Because what he started eventually led to the end of Apartheid and gave black people their freedom,' Siobhan said.

'So you could argue that Redmond was a bit like that – you know, fighting to give his people their freedom.'

'Well, yes. Although when Nelson got released he never went out and bombed some other country he'd nothing to do with, like Redmond did. Mandela believed in peace and democracy for South Africa.'

'But he still bombed his way to it.'

'Only in the early days. It became a peaceful campaign.'

'But what Redmond did in Ireland, it became a peaceful campaign as well. You could argue that without his sacrifice, there wouldn't be peace today. In some ways he was quite like Nelson Mandela.'

'Father, I know you're heartbroken by Redmond's death, and it was a tragedy, but he was no Nelson Mandela. I'm not trying to be disrespectful, but he was a bit of an anachronism, you know? Nelson knew when to lay down his gun; Redmond hadn't a clue.'

The flight attendant stopped beside them with her trolley. 'Can I get you anything, Father?'

'Perhaps a little whiskey – it'll help me sleep. If you could make it a double, I won't trouble you till we land.'

The attendant winked at him and gave him his drinks, and ice, and three bags of peanuts and one of crackers. Siobhan ordered water, but kept her tray-table up as she pushed and pulled through the bags of Minstrels and Starburst and copies of *Vogue* and *Cosmopolitan* she'd crammed into her seat pocket, then finally extracted the in-flight magazine. She removed a pen from her bag, brought down the table, then began to circle items she intended to buy from the duty-free trolley.

After a while Redmond said, 'Would you say he was more like Che Guevara, then?'

'Who?'

'Redmond. You know, he died taking the revolution to other countries. Just like Che.'

Siobhan shrugged. She was looking at a set of Ray Ban sunglasses and trying to remember what they cost at home.

'Do you think?' Redmond persisted.

Siobhan sighed. 'I don't really know.'

'It could get to be like a real cult thing, couldn't it? I mean, they rioted at home when I . . . when I heard that he'd died.'

'Father, you know what they're like, they riot because they like rioting.'

'I know, I know, but there's something romantic about dying in South America, fighting for a cause you believe in passionately.'

Siobhan flicked onto a page offering Toblerone and Jelly Beans. 'Father,' she said absently, 'I don't want to burst your bubble, but no one at home gives a toss about Colombia or FARC because frankly they haven't a clue what's going on there, and it wasn't as if Redmond sacrificed himself in the name of some universal cause we can all get behind. He just got caught with explosives, gave himself up without a fight and then succumbed to poisoned buttocks. It's not exactly Che Guevara, is it?'

'All right. Yeah. Okay.' Redmond mixed his drinks. 'But I'm sure Che wasn't all that fantastic either. I'm sure parts of his life were airbrushed to make them seem a little more heroic, don't you think? I mean, no one could be that fab. Maybe Sinn Fein could do a number on Redmond – you know, really promote him as a fallen comrade, a bit of an icon. God knows we need our heroes, don't we? What about a statue, eh? A statue, right in the middle of the Falls Road – what about that?'

'What, Redmond O'Boyle holding his sore arse?' Siobhan put a hand to her chest, momentarily shocked at her own sarcasm. 'I'm sorry, Father, I didn't mean—'

'It's all right, really.'

'It's just . . . Look, I understand how you feel, your loss, and yes, when Redmond died there was a kind of instinctive scrambling on our part to lay claim to him, but that soon died down. We realised that his death was more of a hindrance than a help. We've changed, you see: we've given up most of our guns and we've embraced democracy. So your Redmond, much as we appreciate the work he did for us in the past, it is *in* the past. What he did in Colombia was actually an embarrassment to us. I was only sent out on a damagelimitation exercise, and to be absolutely truthful, Father, as hurtful as this may sound, and I don't mean it as an attack on your brother at a personal level, in some ways it's better that he did die in such an ignoble fashion, achieving nothing, rotting away like that, because his entire reason for living was based on an outdated, outmoded concept which has already been rejected and quickly forgotten by every true Irishman. If Redmond O'Boyle is remembered at all, it'll be as a sordid little mercenary interested only in causing misery and mayhem.'

Redmond nodded slowly. He took a sip of his drink and ate a peanut. Siobhan returned her attention to the duty-free pages. She circled a Toblerone.

Redmond nudged her again. She glanced impatiently up.

'So, would he be more like Butch Cassidy then?'

90
Property Developments

Walter was just going up the steps to Bertha's front door when it opened suddenly and a white-bearded man in a grey suit, carrying a tan briefcase, stepped out, scowling. Walter did a quick mental calculation involving Bertha's age and fondness for Tae kwon do and surmised that she had mortally injured herself attempting a difficult kick and was therefore in no condition to sign the papers he had with him. The man on the porch had not yet uttered a word, but already Walter foresaw that his dreams of unbounded wealth and intimate relations with scores of attractive women were about to disappear. He was a real *the cup is half-empty* kind of a guy.

'Is everything okay?' Walter blurted out.

'You tell me,' the man replied bluntly.

'I'm sorry? Is Bertha all right?'

'That's a matter of opinion.'

'Well, well what's *your* opinion? Are you the doctor?'

'No, I'm the nephew.'

'Oh. Right.' Not quite sure what to do, and feeling suddenly uneasy at his own presence there, Walter hesitantly extended his hand. 'I'm Walter.'

'Oh, I know who *you* are.' The nephew's lip curled up into a sneer. He ignored the hand. 'It's "Walter said *this*, Walter said *that*".' He jabbed a thick finger at him. 'What *I'm* saying is, who the hell do you think you are? And what the hell do you think you're playing at?'

'Well, I'm . . . I'm . . .'

'That's my auntie in there. She's old and she's sick and she doesn't need some frigging chancer hanging around trying to take advantage. Do you hear me?'

Just as Walter took a step backwards under this unexpected

onslaught, Bertha appeared suddenly in the doorway. 'Eric, you didn't—' she began, but then she saw Walter, and smiled widely. 'Walter! I didn't know you were here. You've met Eric?'

'I've met Eric,' said Walter.

Bertha raised her eyes accusingly to her nephew. 'Eric, what have you been saying?'

'Nothing, Aunt Bertha.' Bertha gave him a *really* look. 'Nothing I haven't already said to you.' He nodded at Walter. 'You're a conman, sir, and if I see you round here again I'll have you arrested.'

'Eric!'

'It has to be said, Auntie. It's not *normal*.' He turned back to Walter again. 'First you knock her down in your car, then you insist on taking her home, then you sweet-talk her into financing some pie-in-the-sky property deal – what would *you* call it?'

'Eric!' Bertha's eyes blazed and she waved her own scolding finger. 'For your information, nephew of mine, *I* have done all the running in this *business* relationship. At no time has Walter asked me for money. Neither has he hung around waiting for me to die, like some close relatives I could mention. He has treated me with respect, with kindness, and occasionally he has taken the piss out of me. And if anyone is the conman in this relationship, *I* am that conman.'

'You are?' said Walter.

'I told you I was eighty-five. Actually I'm eighty-nine.'

Walter smiled. 'Well, you don't look a day over eighty-eight.'

'That's exactly what I'm talking about!' Eric exploded. 'All this sweet-talking, and then he steals our money!'

'*Our* money, Eric?!'

'You know what I mean!'

'Yes, I know *exactly* what you mean!'

They glared frostily at each other. Eric broke the connection first. He waved his finger at Walter again. 'I'm warning you!' Then he marched down the steps and along the footpath towards his car.

'Eric!' Bertha called suddenly after him.

The man stopped, took a deep, calming breath, then swivelled around to look at his aunt, expecting an apology and a hug.

'Missing you already,' said Bertha.

Walter made tea, then they sat at the kitchen table.

'He's not the worst of them,' Bertha was saying. 'In fact, he's probably the best, and he does care.'

'It's natural to be suspicious.'

'But he has no sense of humour, and no passion. He has a weak chin. I saw him punched at a school sports day forty years ago and he cried like a baby. He was sixteen.'

'It's funny the things you remember,' said Walter. Then: 'I took him for a doctor – I thought there was something wrong with you.'

'Eric? He could doctor your books. He's an accountant. *There's* a profession where having a weak chin doesn't inhibit you in any way.' Bertha nodded to herself. Then she examined her cup of tea. She stirred it. She turned the cup around in its saucer.

Walter said, 'What's the matter?'

'Nothing really.'

'Tell me,' said Walter.

'Eric – his heart's in the right place, and he is concerned. He didn't talk complete nonsense.'

'Oh.'

'I mean, I told him I was absolutely determined to proceed with this investment in property, and until that little outburst I thought he'd taken it on board, because he looked at the figures for me – a second or third or fourth opinion never hurts, does it? – and he even talked to some people he knows in the building trade. Walter, the thing is, he says that, putting aside the fact that he doesn't trust you, he really doesn't believe it's a good investment. He says Belfast's overrun with apartments right now, the prices have either stagnated or are going down, that it's overpriced for what it is and that the people who built them, they've a bit of a reputation for dodgy workmanship and it could easily turn out to be more trouble than it's worth.' Bertha took a sip of her tea. 'There, I said it.'

Walter was stunned. He thought he had researched the market thoroughly. Damn it, he *had* researched it thoroughly. 'But . . . it's a lovely apartment. The fridge is *fantastic.*'

Bertha moved her hand gently onto his. 'I know it is. But that's what Eric says – they tart these places up to appear spectacular, but really, if you look at them, they're just like Divis flats with a nice paint job. Like something out of the old Communist East Germany, he says.'

Walter tutted. 'Now that's not fair. They're *not.*' He put his other hand on top of hers, sandwiching it. 'Bertha. Isn't he laying it on a bit thick? Don't you think it's just that he doesn't want you to part with any money? Whatever it is, I want you to do what you feel is right. If you've reconsidered the whole idea, then just say so. He is right, up to a point. You don't know me from Adam.'

Bertha smiled indulgently. 'I know a good man when I meet one. I may be eighty-nine, Walter, but I've always been a good judge of character, and I haven't lost it yet.'

'Well . . .'

'Of *course* he's being negative. But that doesn't mean he's entirely wrong either. And yes, I have to admit I have had a few misgivings. There *are* thousands of apartments springing up, and the brutal fact is that they're really not selling well at all. If we buy now, we could cost ourselves thousands.'

'Right. Okay. So you're—'

'Eric says the real money's to be made in retail. Shops, Walter – city-centre shops. That's where we should invest.'

Walter blinked at her. 'Really?'

'Absolutely.'

'And forget about the penthouse apartment with the nice fridge?'

'Forget about it.'

Walter nodded slowly. 'You know something, Bertha? I think you could be right. There *are* thousands of apartments out there, and they're not moving. But the city-centre shops – they're bloody hiving, aren't they?' His brow furrowed suddenly. 'S**t. I swore blind to Linda that I was taking it; she's worked her arse off to get this through quickly.'

'Walter, she's an *estate agent*. People break their promises all the time. She's used to it. Water off a duck's back. Come on, give us a smile.'

Walter smiled, then looked quickly at his watch. He was due to meet Linda in the master bedroom of the Towerview penthouse apartment in twenty-five minutes. Even as he sipped his tea, she was probably lighting her candles.

91
Brought to Account

Eric McGympsey, of the beard and Walterish misgivings, was a senior partner in the leading Belfast accountancy firm of McGympsey, Styles & Cameron, which owned expensive offices on the Lisburn Road. Eric was pragmatic about every aspect of life and death. When it came to the design of the building, which was commissioned several years after the Ceasefire, and when the prevailing trend was towards glass-fronted edificies, Eric convinced his partners that it made much more sense to have virtually no glass at all, because the Ceasefire was bound to fail, they'd start with the bombs all over again, and then how much money was it going to cost if they had to replace blown-out windows twice a year? Like Walter, he was a glass half-empty kind of a guy, although the glass was actually a paper cup, to lessen the chances of it cracking or being knocked over accidentally and smashed.

As a result, the MGSC building was a dark and depressing place, but on the bright side, it made a lot of money.

Eric nearly always personally oversaw all the hiring and firing, but there were times when he was away on business trips when he simply wasn't available, so that the other partners had to take matters into their own hands. Therefore, there were always two or three members of staff who had not been personally recruited by him, and inevitably he found these unfortunate souls to be inefficient or boorish or lacking the balls he felt were required to be true accountants. In reality, you don't need balls at all, not even one, but senior partners in any profession tend to have an over-inflated opinion of the worth or relevance or difficulty of their chosen career. Eric saw himself as a Samurai warrior of the balance-sheet. If there was a chink in the armour, he dealt with it ruthlessly, particularly so soon after being faced down by his Auntie Bertha.

So Eric returned to work fuming. He cancelled a contract with the sandwich delivery company, telling them that their food wasn't up to scratch. He withdrew a display advertisement he'd reluctantly agreed to run in a programme being produced for a charity performance of *The Sound of Music* at the Opera House. Then he called Billy Gilmore into his office and fired him.

'It's no reflection on your work, Billy,' said Eric. 'It's the economic climate.'

'The economic climate? But we're rolling in it.'

'Yes, Billy, and that's precisely the time to divest ourselves of unwanted fat.'

'I'm unwanted fat?'

'It's only an expression. How long have you been with us now, Billy?'

'Eleven years. It's right there in front of you. There hasn't been one single complaint about my work, has there?'

'Not that I'm aware of.'

Anger grown of shock was soaking through Billy. His much-loved favourite tie felt strangulatory tight; sweat glistened down the back of his cropped hair.

'*Not that I'm aware of,*' he repeated. 'Why don't you just say *no*? Just by saying *not that I'm aware of* you're making it sound like there *have* been complaints – and you know that's not true, don't you?'

'As far as I know, yes.'

Billy had devoted himself totally to MGSC, working above and beyond the call of duty, and now they were stabbing him in the back. Eleven years. Another six months and he would confidently have expected to become a junior partner like they'd done with Alec upstairs. And that focused his thoughts.

'You don't want me to become a junior partner, that's it.'

'That's not it, Billy.'

'You don't want to pay the extra, you don't want me in on the profitshare, you don't want me using the executive toilet.'

'No, Billy.'

'There's nothing I can do or say to change your mind?'

Eric shook his head.

'Even if I agree to stay at this level, and not pursue a junior partnership?'

'No, Billy.'

'Well, what is it then!? You can't just cut me without a reason.'

'Yes, we can.'

Billy glared at him.

'There's quite an attractive redundancy package, Billy, and I'm sure you won't have a problem getting another position. Accountants and undertakers are always in demand.' Eric liked that line. He'd used it a dozen times before when sacking employees. Funnily enough, *they* rarely smiled either. 'Besides, you have a number of *extra-curricular* clients, don't you? They should keep you busy.'

So that was it.

'Is this about Pink Harrison?'

'No, Billy.' But there was a flicker of the eyelids.

'Yes, it is. Because I do his books.'

'What you do outside of work is your concern.'

'It was *you* put me on to him, Mr McGympsey. You took me to one side and said, "It's not good for our image to have Pink Harrison on our books, but we can hardly say no, so do us a favour and do him as a homer". You virtually ordered me to.'

'Well, I don't quite remember it like that, but he does seem to have been taking up an increasing amount of your time lately.'

'Only my own time. I meet him at lunchtimes. Or after work. At weekends. My work here doesn't suffer, you know that.'

'While we're on the subject, there's also the small matter of the police. They seem to be talking to you quite a lot. *That's* definitely not good.'

'I can't help that. It's what happens when you work with Pink. And you put me onto him in the first place!'

'I had hoped you would be rather more discreet.'

'I *am*! It's not me! When I started doing his books we were dealing in tens of thousands; now there's millions going through.'

Eric nodded. 'Yes, we're aware of that. In fact, we believe that Mr Harrison's reputation has evolved sufficiently for us to reconsider his being represented by this firm once again.'

'Well, then, I'm perfectly placed to—'

'Quite the opposite, actually, Billy. Your knowledge of his less salubrious business affairs would tend to preclude you from any further involvement. Much better to start with a clean balance-sheet, don't you think?'

'So you're firing me because you want to represent Pink Harrison again?'

'We're not firing you, Billy, we're making you redundant, and that would have happened irrespective of our desire to approach Councillor Harrison with a view to representing him.'

Billy sighed. 'I just don't believe this. Eleven years – and this is it?'

'Afraid so. But no hard feelings, eh? I've always thought we were just like a big, happy family, Billy. But now it's time to leave the nest, you know?'

'I'm being *thrown out* of the nest, Mr McGympsey.'

'Nonsense! You're ready to fly! And I want you to know, you'll always have friends at McGympsey, Styles and Cameron. That said, however, I'm afraid company security now becomes of paramount importance to us, so I would very much appreciate it if you would co-operate with Mr Dawson here,' and he nodded towards the door, 'who will escort you directly out of the building. You should not return to your office or attempt to communicate with any of your former colleagues. Your personal effects will be forwarded to you.'

Billy turned. Jeff Dawson, their security guard, a retired cop, was standing just outside the door, which he had silently half-opened. Billy shook his head in disbelief. 'You're treating me like I'm some kind of criminal.'

'It's just business, Billy.'

Eric stood and extended his hand. Billy shook it, despite himself. Eric walked him to the door. Billy's legs felt hollow. Eric pulled the door fully open and nodded at Mr Dawson.

'This way, sir,' said Dawson.

Dawson, with whom he'd laughed and joshed most days, walked him, eyes front, down the corridor. The doors to the other offices, most usually left open, were all closed, as if they all knew in advance, and didn't want to witness his humiliation. Or knew, and were turning their backs on him.

Eric shouted down the corridor after him, 'Give my regards to your wife.'

Billy waved back.

Billy left his pass on the front desk. The receptionist, who was always there, wasn't. Dawson held the front door open for him and Billy stepped out onto the footpath. The door swung back behind him and locked itself.

Billy buttoned his jacket. He fixed his tie. He walked purposefully away from the offices of McGympsey, Styles & Cameron. But as soon as he rounded the corner, he burst into tears.

92

The Name

West Bell, the Belfast boy-band which had reunited after its constituent members' solo careers failed to taxi, let alone take off, had played a sell-out concert at the Odyssey Arena the night before to 10,000 screaming kids and their mothers.

The car park was chocca till well into the early hours, but by 5 a.m. there were only half a dozen vehicles left. Usually the security staff ignored them, supposing that their owners had merely had a few too many drinks and would collect them in the morning. But they noticed the white Volkswagen with the peel-back lid because its lights were left on and there was a faint plume of exhaust smoke.

Two guys in orange Puffa jackets, with *Security* in bright yellow letters across their backs, approached the car, one of them saying what a groovy little motor it was, the other saying it was like a toy you'd get for Christmas. They peered in the driver's window at the guy sleeping behind the wheel. They tapped on the glass and told him he couldn't sleep there, he was on private property, but he didn't respond. So they tried the door and it opened. That's when the smell of petrol hit them. It was only by the grace of God that they weren't smoking, as they usually were, that late at night. The whole place could have gone up. They saw that the driver was dead. His name was Benny Caproni and someone had forced him to drink five litres of unleaded petrol.

Jimmy Marsh Mallow heard the news just before 6 a.m. He was already up and showered, so drove straight to the scene. Gary McBride was waiting for him. Marsh took a brief look at the bloated, blackened corpse, then let Forensics get on with it. As he turned back to Gary he said, 'What about cameras?'

Gary glanced up at the CCTV cameras which covered the car park and the various entrances to the Arena. 'On a quiet night we might

351

have been okay, but last night there were ten thousand kids here. It'll be like looking for a needle in a haystack.'

Marsh raised an eyebrow. 'But then that's our job,' and smiled. 'So the possibilities are: (a) a tragic accident (b) a very, very messy, not to mention well-nigh impossible, method of committing suicide(c) murder most foul. Or indeed(d), don't know.'

'I'd go for (c),' said Gary.

'And who would do a thing like that, and why?'

'Well, he was a dealer with a sideline in rent boys, so there could be hundreds of suspects.'

'Could be,' Marsh agreed.

Although true, they both knew that wasn't the case. Benny Caproni's death was a little *too* convenient, him being the link between the dead boy Michael Caldwell and the property developer George Green.

They went back to see George. It had only been a few hours, but he was looking twice as bad. They'd taken his shoelaces and tie; his eyes were swollen and his face hollow and shadowed with bristle. He was a man used to barking orders, being in control, but now appeared diminished and terrified. His solicitor was with him. Marsh knew all the top criminal solicitors, and Terence Black wasn't one of them. He was a company man, specialised in contracts, didn't know what he was doing in Castlereagh station. Hardly said a word.

'My sister, you've spoken to my sister?' George said when Jimmy Marsh Mallow and Gary entered the interview room.

'Yeah,' said Marsh, 'she's still alive. But I can tell you who's not.'

It seemed scarcely possible, but George's face blanched a little further. 'What? Who?'

'Benny Caproni,' said Gary.

'You remember Benny?' Marsh asked. 'Nice guy.'

'Oh Christ,' said George.

'Yes, indeed,' said Marsh, 'but no help to Benny.'

'Found him a couple of hours ago,' said Gary. 'He drank half the contents of a BP filling station.'

George looked from one to the other to see if they were joking.

'So what we were wondering, George,' said Marsh, 'was if this mystery man of yours might be responsible, or whether you've been blinking Morse Code messages to your nice solicitor here, and he got the word out to do a number on poor Benny.'

Marsh nodded at the solicitor, whose mouth was silently repeating the words but still failing to understand what Marsh was saying.

I Predict A Riot

'That's ridiculous! What're you talking about? He's really dead? And my sister?'

'Like I say, your sister's fine, although I suppose, if this mystery man of yours is responsible for Benny, then he might want to take out a little extra insurance by, say, kidnapping your sister or her kids – or, you know, maybe just one of her kids. Maybe he'll give her a choice, George – you know, like *Sophie's Choice* – you ever see that? Merryl Streep's fantastic. Did she win the Oscar for that, Gary?'

Gary shrugged. 'Was it not for *Kramer vs. Kramer*?'

'Might have been,' said Marsh. 'Or maybe it was *The Deer Hunter*. Anyway, point is, you know what Sophie's choice was, George?'

George shook his head wearily.

'Shame to spoil the film – or the book, for that matter – but Sophie's choice was, and it was like a Nazi guy doing this, "Which one of your kids do you want to save? Pick your favourite – the other goes in the ovens". You think you could do that, George, pick one of your nephews or nieces to save? Because it might come down to that. Right now, there's nothing to stop whoever the f**k it is walking right up her drive and taking one of them. *Do you hear me, George?*'

George swallowed. 'I hear you.'

'So what's it to be?' George glanced at his solicitor, but Terence Black was no help. 'Seems pretty simple to me, George. You see, this guy, if he exists, he can threaten you all he likes and there's not a damn thing we can do. You tell us, and we can lock him up. Sure, you might still need some extra security, but at the end of the day, you'll still be alive. So maybe your whole building thing goes pear-shaped. I'm sure you've good enough accountants. They'll have a nice big pile of cash squirrelled away somewhere, so you'll be all right. Ball's in your court now, George. What do you want to do?'

The solicitor started to say something, but George waved him away. He clasped his hands and leaned forward. 'I want my family taken to somewhere safe. I want my name kept out of it.'

'Not sure I can do that, George.'

'Take it or leave it.' George was used to business meetings where he always had the upper hand.

Mallow smiled. 'Okay, we'll leave it.'

'I . . . I don't mean . . . what I mean is, my family – you must look after them.'

'We can do that.'

'And the corruption charges?'

'Nothing to do with us, different department.'

'And what about the boy? Will it come out that I—'

'We might be able to sit on that.'

'Might?'

'Might.'

George's hands went from clasped to clenched. He gave a slight shake of his head. 'Why would he do a thing like that?'

'Why would *who* do a thing like that?'

'Pink Harrison,' said George.

93
The Truth, and Nothing Like the Truth

This time around, Linda decided to play it safe and went for just the three candles. Eighteen, in retrospect, had been a bit over the top. These candles were cubes of wax in red, white and blue. She lit them at three minutes to the hour, in the master bedroom of the penthouse apartment, then closed the door after her and sat on a bar stool in the kitchen, sipping a glass of Asti and thinking dirty thoughts. She was still wearing her business suit, but she had no underwear on underneath.

At thirty-five minutes past the hour she finished her third glass and blew the candles out. She sat on the bed. She took out her mobile phone and checked her messages. There were three, all relating to a house she was selling on the Antrim Road. She wondered if she'd got the time wrong, but knew that she hadn't. She stood out on the veranda and looked hopefully down at the car park, and then the roads beyond. Belfast was getting busier every year, but apart from during The Troubles, it had never yet experienced traffic jams that could delay anyone for more than twenty minutes. She didn't want to call Walter. She wanted to hear him ring the doorbell. She so desperately didn't want him to let her down.

She phoned him. 'Walter?'

'Margaret?'

'Linda.'

'Linda. How're you doing?'

'I'm doing fine.'

'Great. Good.'

'We had a date.'

'Yes, we did. Yes, we did.'

'So?'

'I've been delayed. I'm really sorry. I'm not going to be able to make it.'

'Oh. What's the problem?'

'It's Bertha. She's been taken ill.'

'Oh – right. I'm sorry to hear that.'

'Yes. Well, I'll tell her that.'

'What's the matter with her?'

'Nothing. I mean – you know, old age, basically.'

'Oh. Nothing too serious.'

'No. I mean, serious enough. In that – anything at her age . . . She's eighty-nine, you know.'

'Oh. Right. Walter?'

'Uhuh?'

'I'm sitting here with no underwear on. I've been waiting.'

'Yes, I know that. I mean, I didn't know you'd no . . . but yes, I know. I just – I just can't at the moment.'

'Well, can't you just, you know, tuck her in and *come on down*.' She tried to make it light and fluffy, but there was a horrible sinking feeling in her stomach.

'Well, I would, but I've – some other things to do as well.'

Silence. Nearly half a minute of it.

'You don't want to come, do you?'

'Yes, I do. Of course, I do.'

'You don't like me at all, do you, Walter?'

'Of course, I do.'

'I'm sitting here naked, and you don't find me attractive at all.'

'That's not true, Linda. I'm just tied up.'

'Then tie me up!' She blurted it out without thinking.

'*What?*'

'Tie me to the bed and beat me with a broomstick. Or don't. Walter, if you don't want to come and be with me, why don't you just say it?'

'I do want to.'

'No, you don't, otherwise you'd be here.'

'I just can't make it. And I don't want to buy the apartment.'

It was out, and not in the way he had intended, but he also had a tendency to blurt things out under pressure. He was sitting in his car outside Bertha's house and had been staring at his mobile for forty minutes, trying to summon the courage to phone Linda. He'd slept with her twice now, and while it might sound cruel to say that the novelty had worn off, it was true.

'You don't want to buy the apartment?'

'I don't want to buy the apartment.'

'Why on earth not? I mean, you've more or less already bought it.'

'I've not, I've not paid anything yet.'

'But you *signed* . . .'

'I know, but Bertha hasn't, and she's not going to. She says it's not worth it, and I'm inclined to agree.'

'But it's a fabulous apartment, Walter.'

'Yes, it is. It *is* fabulous. But Bertha says there's too many of them. That we won't make any money on it. She says it's better to buy retail. There's a glut of apartments, but there's a shortage of shops in prime positions. So we're going to go retail.'

'But I don't do retail.'

'I know that.'

'And I'm still sitting here without my pants on.'

'I know that also.'

'So I'm screwed on the property, but not screwed on the pants.'

'That would seem to cover it.'

'You're being cold and horrible to me, Walter.'

'I'm not trying to be.'

'A real man would have come here and told me to my face, not made up some feeble excuse.'

'She is unwell, and I do have things to do.'

'Like what?'

'Look at shops.'

'With your partner sick in bed?'

'I can look at shops by myself.'

'Walter, I don't think you can do anything by yourself. Apart from sex, you can do that by yourself, and that's exactly what you'll be doing. I thought we were good together, making love and eating chips afterwards – I enjoyed that.'

'So did I.'

'So what's changed?'

'Nothing. I just need to go retail.'

'I mean with me, Walter.'

'Nothing. Honestly. I'm just tied up.'

'So were you going to come later, or just leave me lying here without my underwear?'

Walter hesitated. The underwear talk, or lack of it, was getting to him. He had been determined to end it there and then with her, but what difference would a few hours make? Wouldn't it be nicer to leave them both with pleasant memories of their relationship? One more blissful night of lovemaking and chips, a tender, fond, passionate farewell? He could see her point of view completely now; he *was* being cold and callous. He wasn't being a real man at all. He should be completely upfront with her, after the sex. They were just two lonely people looking for everlasting love who were resigned to settling for just a few hours of it.

'Tell you what,' Walter said, not wishing to cave it entirely, 'if you give me half an hour to finish what I'm doing, I could be right with you.'

'No, Walter, you clearly don't want to.'

'No, really – it's not that, I really do have things to do. And I just felt really bad about not buying the apartment. But now that I hear your voice, you know, you're quite irresistible, you do know that?'

'I am *not*.'

'Yes, you are. In fact, those things I really do have to do, I'm not even going to do them. I'm going to drive round there right now and show you how irresistible you are.'

'You are *not*.'

'I am *so*. Listen to that, that's the sound of my car starting. I'm on my way. Are you going to be ready?'

'I am going to be ready.'

Linda made a kissing sound, then cut the line. She shivered with anticipation. She lit the candles again. She took off her business outfit and stretched out on the bed. She dribbled Asti onto her chest, deliberately.

Across town, Walter, flushed, drove like the wind. When he was within sight of the apartment block his mobile phone rang again and his sweaty hand darted out, feeling for it on the passenger seat and pressing the button while keeping both eyes on the traffic. 'I'm nearly there,' he said breathlessly.

'You're nearly where?' said Margaret.

'Margaret,' said Walter.

'Walter,' said Margaret. 'Where are you off to?'

'Going to see Bertha, she has a cold.'

'You sound pretty excited about it.'

'Not excited, concerned. She's eighty-nine.'

'Oh, well. That's okay. Just I had to run last time we spoke, so I was just wondering if you'd time for a cup of coffee.'

'Now?' asked Walter.

'Yeah, if it suits.'

'Okay,' said Walter.

94
Coffee, Tea or Me?

Margaret's quick cup of coffee with Walter lasted nearly two hours, sitting in a café in Fountain Street, talking excitedly about how her dresses were flying out of the shop and performing an impression of May Li's deadly accurate spitting, which nearly got them thrown out. They laughed and roared, then he said he had to run so she gave him a hug which turned into a peck which turned into a kiss which turned into tongue-on-tongue action. Shoppers stopped and stared. A passing photographer snapped them, imagining he was capturing lovers in Paris or a soldier and his girl marking VE Day. When they were finished, and she was walking off, she imagined Walter standing watching her go, but she didn't dare look back. It was a splendid fantasy, particularly as he'd ducked into a bakery for a gravy ring. Stuffing it into his face, he drove straight to the Towerview apartments.

Margaret was still smiling to herself as she approached her front door, but it faded fast when she saw Billy sitting on the top step, looking miserable. 'Billy,' she said. 'What do *you* want?'

'That's nice, that is. All those years together and that's what I get: *what do* you *want?*'

Margaret took a deep breath. She had her keys in her hand already, but she made no attempt to open the door. She didn't want him inside. She had been feeling fantastic, but the air of deflation that came with her ex-husband was already beginning to envelop her. Her ballon had been pricked, and Billy was the prick.

'Billy, what do you want?'

'I haven't done your accounts in weeks. You know what you're like.'

'Yes, Billy, I know what I'm like. And I'm quite capable of paying my own bills and writing my own cheques.'

Billy snorted. 'Yeah. Right.'

Margaret sighed, then folded her arms. 'Billy, get off the step, and move away from the door. I've had a hard day and I don't need this now.'

'You've had a hard day? What, wandering round the underpants?' She just looked at him. He stood up. 'I'm only trying to help.'

'Well, I don't need your help.'

Tears suddenly welled up again in Billy's eyes, and Margaret felt astonished. She'd never seen him cry before. Not at weddings or funerals or even at *Terms of Endearment*. 'Billy? What is it?' He came towards her and she couldn't help but put her arms around him and pat his back. 'What is it, love?'

Billy sniffed up. 'I got sacked.'

'Oh God.'

'Eleven years I gave them, never a single complaint.'

'But why would they sack you?'

'I don't know!'

She held him at arm's length. 'Well, they must have said something.'

'Redundancy, but I'm the only one. Because they don't want to make me a junior partner, because I'd be too expensive, or because I didn't go to f***ing Campbell College or Methody or because I don't play squash or cricket.'

'Maybe you got some sums wrong.'

'I don't do f***ing sums!'

'I know, Billy, I was only joking. Remember we used to joke about you doing sums?'

'Do I look like I need jokes now? Jesus Christ.'

'Right.'

Margaret slipped the key in and opened the door. Billy moved up behind her.

She turned, blocking his progress. 'No, Billy. I'm sorry you lost your job, but it's nothing to do with me any more.'

'I'm sorry, Margaret, I didn't mean to snap, I'm upset. I just came round because I needed to talk to someone and also because I need to sort your accounts out. It'll only take twenty minutes.'

'No, Billy.' She moved into the hall and began to close the door behind her.

'*Please*, Margaret.' The tears were rolling down his cheeks again.

Margaret sighed. 'Twenty minutes then,' she said.

Forty-five minutes later, on his third cup of tea and sixth custard cream, Billy was sitting on her favourite chair, paying scant attention to the bills and cheque stubs on his lap and ranting about his abrupt dismissal from MGSC. Margaret's initial concern had rapidly turned to frustration at being stuck with him, then migrated swiftly through annoyance to anger. She held it in check as best she could. There was a certain amount of residual sympathy, because they had been married, and, judged in the absence of such essential ingredients as love, passion, compassion, romance and friendship, that marriage could be looked upon as having had some successful elements, in that Billy had worked hard and been a good provider. Also, although they had argued interminably, he had never struck her, or she him.

It was just a few months since their split, and only a matter of days since her ill-judged attempt to pay off her hospital bill by sleeping with him, but if anything confirmed that their relationship, on whatever level, was now over for ever and ever, amen, it was the raw, savage anger that was growing inside her at the sight of him munching his way through her favourite biscuits. Offering one was being polite; taking two was being greedy; horsing down half a dozen was *brutal*.

Sitting behind him, pretending to look at her latest design, she tried to intellectualise it, telling herself it wasn't about the biscuits, it was about the anger she felt for the wasted years, the barren years, the years of turmoil and upset. Each biscuit represented a year of their marriage and in his rapid consumption of them he was actually swallowing their relationship, feeding on it, gaining strength at her expense. She firmly believed that if she allowed him to get to the end of the packet he would resume his position of dominance in her life, and she would return to her old, pliable, weak self. So she stood up and ripped the packet out of his hands and yelled, 'Leave me some, why don't you?'

She took them back into the kitchen, closed the door and placed them securely into the shortbread tin she used to stop them going stale. She pushed the tin against the back of the counter, then put three black bananas on top of it by way of camouflage.

When Margaret went back into the lounge Billy was holding up two cheques and carefully examining them. 'Who's Emma Cochrane, and why is she paying you so much money?'

'I design clothes, Billy, I've always designed clothes. And now it's starting to take off.'

'There's a couple of grand here.'

'Yes, I know.'

'And more to come?'

'Quite possibly.'

'I'm going to have to talk to you about your tax situation.'

'It's early days yet, Billy.'

Billy studied the cheques again. Margaret had her arms folded, and her mouth in gear ready to explode right back at him the moment he made one of his cheap cracks.

'Well – fair play to you.' He smiled, then made a note of the amounts on the small balance sheet he was working on. Half an hour later, he yawned and stretched, then began to put the books away. 'All sorted,' he said.

'Thanks, Billy.'

'Funny how things work out, isn't it? My life's falling apart, and yours is taking off. It's like *A Star is Born*, isn't it? Do you think one day you'll stand on some catwalk somewhere after you've had this incredible show and you'll say, "My name is Mrs Billy Gilmore"?'

'I wouldn't hold your breath, Billy.'

He smiled. 'Well. Perhaps not.'

She was standing in the kitchen doorway, leaning against the door-jamb. 'Anyway,' she said.

'I was just wondering . . .' he began, and gave her the look he always gave her when he felt horny.

'No, Billy.'

'I lost my job today, Margaret – it would really help.'

'No, Billy.'

'Just for ten minutes.'

'No, Billy.'

He gave a little shrug, then stood up. 'Just a hug, then.'

She gave in. He held her tight. She said, 'Everything will turn out all right, Billy, workwise.'

He nodded against her. His left hand caressed her bottom, his right cupped her breast.

Margaret shoved him hard in the chest. 'Just keep your bloody hands off me!'

Surprised, he staggered back several feet and for a moment his hands bunched up into fists. Then he smiled. 'Relax, would you? Just checking you out. You've put on a bit of weight. Those biscuits are addictive, aren't they?'

He winked and turned. Margaret didn't move until she heard the front door slam. Then she shivered. She went out into the hall to make sure he really was gone. She stood staring at the door, and tears sprang into her eyes. She hated him. She *really* hated him. She swore he would never come through that door again.

95

Slap Happy

There was a familiar moment of trepidation as Redmond approached passport control at Heathrow Airport; there always was, but this time was slightly different. In the past he had used Damian's passport quite regularly, comfortably slipping into the priest's outfit for just long enough to smile and bless his way through to baggage control, but he was no longer just a priest returning from holiday. His face, *both* faces, had been plastered all over the papers. If they recognised him they were quite likely to give him the third degree, and then the truth would out. They wouldn't be fooled by a slightly too large priest's outfit and a photo which showed that Damian enjoyed his food.

Fortunately, Siobhan was immediately in front of him in the line and she kicked up so much fuss about being asked the standard questions, claiming that she was being picked upon because she was a member of Sinn Fein, that the exasperated controller just waved Redmond through in her wake with only the most cursory of glances at his passport.

There was then a two hour wait for their connection to Belfast, with Siobhan alternating between the glass box of a smoking section and standing reading the magazines in WH Smith. Redmond, exhausted by the flight and somewhat overwhelmed by the sheer volume of people buzzing around the airport, sought sanctuary in the small inter-faith chapel set aside for passengers who wished to communicate with God before risking their lives in the air. It was empty. Redmond sat at the front. There was a tape of organ music playing subtly in the background. He rolled a cigarette for himself, and was just licking the paper closed when the door opened and a young woman appeared. Redmond nodded back at her and she hesitated before coming down a short aisle towards the front. She surprised him then by taking the seat right next to him. He imagined she was about twenty-five. She had short blonde hair and a slightly pointed nose. She said, 'I didn't realise there would be a priest.'

'I'm not,' said Redmond, then quickly added, 'I mean, I'm not on duty here. Just seeking a little peace and quiet, my child.'

'I need guidance, Father. I'm going on honeymoon, but the night before last I slept with the best man.'

'Oh,' said Father Redmond.

'I know. You look horrified. And I'm sorry to just come out with it like that, but my flight leaves in twenty minutes. I told him I was going for Maltesers. I go to church every week, Father; my relationship with God is very important to me, but I got drunk, and it happened, and I don't know what to do.'

Redmond lit his cigarette. He offered her a drag. It was what you did with a comrade, in the jungle. She looked surprised, but took it nevertheless.

'Do you love him?' Redmond asked.

'Yes, I do.'

'And will you sleep with the best man again?'

'No, of course not.'

'And will the best man get drunk at some stage in the future and tell your husband what happened?'

'No, Father. He lives in America now – we may not ever see him again.'

'And when you get drunk and have a row with your husband, as you will, will you shout it out in anger, that you slept with his best man?'

'No, I never will, Father.'

'Then let sleeping dogs lie, my child.'

The young woman nodded. She was twisting her wedding ring around her finger.

Redmond took another draw of the cigarette. He passed it back to her. She took another drag, but did not return it.

She said, 'It wasn't the first time, with the best man. We've been doing it on and off for months.'

'Oh,' said Father Redmond.

'The wedding, it was like a deadline, and we had to have as much sex as possible before the big day, because I wouldn't want to betray my husband once we were married.'

'I see.'

'And it really will be, 'cause once I make my mind up about something like that, there's no shifting me.'

Redmond moved his hand towards the cigarette, but she immediately took another puff, then switched it to her other hand so it was out of easy reach.

'What worries me is that usually we use protection, but the other night we got a bit carried away, so what happens if I'm pregnant?'

'I take it you're having relations with your husband?'

'Yes, of course. But up until now, on alternate days.'

'I see. So in fact, if you were pregnant, and it was the best man's, but you never saw the best man again, your husband might never know that his child wasn't really his child.'

'I guess.' She took a final puff on the cigarette, then stubbed it out on the rough, carpet-tiled floor. She put a hand on Redmond's sleeve. 'I know I've been bad, Father, I know there's no excuse, but I'm going to change my ways. I swear. And the great thing about God is, He forgives everything, doesn't He?'

Redmond, who had only ever been asked for advice on making bombs, was quite warming to this. He had promised to carry out God's work to make amends for causing Damian's death. This was his first test. God wasn't saying the actual words to him, but it *almost* felt like He was. God's intent was obvious, but He was entrusting the interpretation and delivery entirely to Redmond.

Father Redmond, flushed with adrenaline, took her hands in his. 'My dear, God has a word for fallen children like you. And that word is *slapper*.'

'It's *what*?'

'S-l-a-double p-e-r. Slapper.'

She tried to pull her hands away. 'I don't understand.'

'It's quite simple.' He held onto her hands. 'You're a slapper. See? It's not nice, is it?'

'Will you let go of my hands?'

'You're screwing around now. What're you going to be like when you get back from the honeymoon? Do the guy a favour: either tell him the truth or dump him.' Redmond finally let go.

'You're not supposed to speak to me like that,' said the girl, tears now dripping down her face.

'I know,' said Redmond. 'It's a change in policy. New Pope. Calling a spade a spade, and a slapper a slapper.'

She was crushed, but was beginning to see the truth in what the priest had to say. 'I *am* a slapper. I know that. But God will forgive me, won't He?'

'If you change your ways, and do the right thing by your husband, He'll probably have a think about it.'

She wiped at her face. 'You're right, you know. I've been awful. Why should I expect to be forgiven? I should expect to be punished. You know something? I came in here just looking for someone to tell me I'd be okay, not to worry. I was just panicked about getting caught out, more than anything. But you're right. *I* created this situation, *I* have to deal with it, or my life and my husband's life is just going to be one great bloody shambles. I always thought about priests – they've never been married or had girlfriends, what can they know about sex or attraction or jealousy or love? But you really do know, you really have an insight.' She took his hands. 'You've changed my life, Father. I came in here looking for a temporary fix, but now I know it would just have been a sticking-plaster over a huge gash. There's nothing I can do now but tell my husband the truth, and if I'm very lucky, *he'll* forgive me. Thank you so much, Father.'

She squeezed his hand, wiped at her face again, then hurried from the chapel.

Redmond sighed happily. He rolled himself another cigarette, and this time took his time over it. He wondered if Damian had seen him in action. Whether he was floating around here somewhere, like *Randall & Hopkirk Deceased.*

'What do you think, Damers?' he asked aloud. 'Pretty good going, no? You see, I may not know all the technical priest stuff like you do, but I can learn that. The rest – well, it's instinct, isn't it? Instinct and common sense and the truth. I'm going to be all right, Damian. I'm going to do good work. *Your* work. Do you hear me, Damian?'

There was no response, of course, just the piped organ music and beyond it the vague hum of thousands of anxious travellers.

96
Hail to the Chief

Jimmy Marsh Mallow was largely a law unto himself, but even he knew he couldn't just sweep Pink Harrison in for questioning without getting approval from on high. So he sat patiently outside the Chief Constable's office while the Chief Constable met a delegation of gypsies complaining about their lot. Inside, deep inside, Marsh was as excited as he had ever been about nailing someone. Pink Harrison had evaded him for so long. There was plenty he *could* have picked him up on over the past few years, but he wasn't interested in securing some minor conviction and putting him away for a few months. He wanted something major, so he could throw away the key. A crime where there could be no doubt, no allegation of collusion or corruption or an agenda, just an old-fashioned crime, like bloody, tragic murder, with the evidence there, on the table, indisputable. He had resigned himself to the fact that if he got Pink at all, it would be for his financial indiscretions, charges that depended on accountants and paper trails. But they were always a gamble. Half of those trials collapsed under their own weight, bogged down by tons of documents and confusing, often contradictory figures that served only to baffle juries and judges and often even left the obviously guilty with a bruised sense of injustice.

No, getting Pink for murder – that would be perfect.

As he'd sat in his office, waiting for the call to go up to see the Chief Constable, Marsh had turned the photographs of the dead boy over on his table, one after the other, as if he was playing a particularly morbid game of Patience. He kept saying, 'Got you now, got you now, got you now . . .'

Jimmy Marsh and the Chief Constable, Tony Martin, had a good professional relationship, but none at all outside of work. Martin was an English import, as they almost always were these days. It looked good on a CV, serving a couple of years in a trouble spot like Belfast.

When he was eventually shown in, Marsh shook hands formally, took a seat when invited to and quickly apprised the short, stocky Chief Constable of the current situation. Martin sat with his hands clasped into a church steeple, with the tip of the spire against his lips. He was a listener, not a talker. It helped to mask his basic ignorance of the city. When Marsh was finished, the Chief Constable said, 'So what do you want to do?'

'Well, with Benny Caproni being murdered, we've got to assume that Pink knows we're onto him. We have George Green and his family in a hotel at Aldergrove, and we'll shift them to Glasgow in the morning.'

'You think he'll try and get to them?'

'It won't be masked gunmen in the lift, but it'll be something. Pink will be panicking, that's for sure – not about the murder as such, but the fact that it's a boy. Everyone's suspected he's been fruity for years but he's gotten away with it because he delivers on his promises and spreads the wealth around, but if they think he's done this they'll hammer him. So he's going to do his level best to make sure there's no physical evidence left and no witnesses.'

'Are there other witnesses?'

'I doubt it. If he was messing with wee lads it'll be just him, somewhere private. He's not going to go parading him around the Rangers Supporters Club.'

'So where does that leave us?'

'He owns half a dozen properties – he could have taken the victim to any one of them. He'll have had the steam cleaners in, but he'll have missed something. A single hair. A fingerprint. Spittle. We'll get something. It's all we need. We go into all six at the same time, hit him hard and heavy. I have our people standing by. It's just a matter of the warrants.'

Marsh looked expectantly at the Chief Constable. Martin unclasped his hands and opened a file on his desk. He glanced at the top sheet. 'You've been after Pink Harrison for a long time.'

'Yes, we have.'

'Have you ever met him?'

'No, sir.'

'Nothing personal between you, no history?'

'No, sir. Nothing personal. He's been a UDA commander, a drug baron, a protection racketeer and now a politician willing to take a bribe. He has literally gotten away with murder for twenty years. And he hasn't served a day behind bars. He needs to *be* history. Especially if he's done this.'

Martin sucked on his lower lip for a several moments. 'The problem

I have with this, Jim,' he began, then paused to close the file back over, 'is the trouble it will cause.'

'Trouble?'

'A few nights ago we had half of West Belfast on fire because of that chap Redmond O'Boyle. I don't want the East to go that way as well. You know as well as I do that if we arrest Pink Harrison, he will call every manjack of them onto the streets; shops will be burned, buses will be hijacked, our people will be injured, ordinary punters will be hurt, millions of pounds' worth of damage will be caused, the economy will be unbalanced and the Tourist Board will have a stroke.'

Marsh gritted his teeth. 'And your point is?'

'Jim – my point is, we have to be sure.'

'We can't be sure until we search for forensic evidence.'

'I understand what you're saying, Jim, but if we go in there and find nothing, and half the city gets torn up, it's not going to look good for anyone.'

'We're talking about a murder, Chief Constable.'

Martin suddenly slapped his hand down hard on the table. 'I know what we're talking about, god damn-it! And I know all about Pink Harrison! And the truth of the matter is, Jim, that I may just be a blow-in from the Big Smoke, hardly know my way around, but I know you lot have had twenty f***ing years to put Pink Harrison away and you haven't managed it yet.'

'Well then, this is our opportunity.'

Martin closed his eyes and rubbed at his brow. Just for a few moments. When he opened them again Marsh was staring straight at him.

Jimmy Marsh spoke calmly and clearly. 'Pink Harrison took this kid off the streets, he drugged him up, he killed him, he cut him up and he put him in the river. We cannot take anything else into consideration.'

'With due respect, Jim, that's easy for you to say. Pink Harrison is in local government now, and that brings with it a whole different set of problems; maybe you don't have to worry about them, but I do. We go after Pink Harrison, we could have the whole Unionist Party on our backs.'

'Not if it's a boy.'

'You promise me that?'

Martin drummed his fingers on the desk. 'You're absolutely certain he's our man?'

'Yes, sir.'

'And you're prepared to let East Belfast go crazy?'

'Yes, sir.'

'A lot of people to get hurt, maybe killed?'

'It's unfortunate, but yes, sir.'

'There's no compromise in you at all, Jim, is there?'

'Not for this.'

'What do you do to relax?'

'*Sorry?*'

'What do you do when you're not working?'

This took him off-guard. Marsh gave a vague kind of shrug. 'This and that.'

'And you can go out and do this and that, without looking over your shoulder?'

'No, sir, most of *this and that*'s indoors.'

Martin nodded. 'I don't like this place. I'm never relaxed. I like fishing – can't do that here. But I do like my job, and I intend to keep it, and I intend to get results. I have to look at the bigger picture, Jim. What if keeping Pink Harrison on the streets helps maintain the Ceasefire and saves dozens of lives? Maybe we don't want to throw the baby out with the bathwater – do you know what I mean?'

Marsh's head nodded almost imperceptibly. 'Problem is, sir, this baby's already dead, drowned in the bath by Pink Harrison. I'm just not prepared to let Laughing Boy get away with it because you're worried about some windows getting smashed. The simple truth, Chief Constable, is that windows are always getting smashed around here. Then they get repaired. And double-glazed. We have more double-glazing than any country on earth. When buses get burned we get newer, better buses. It's like evolution, sir – you die or you come back better, stronger. Except for Michael Caldwell – he *can't* come back, his poor heartbroken mother can't just pop out for a new one. He's gone for good, and somebody should pay for that. That's why I'm going out of this door to arrest Pink Harrison. Are you going to stop me?'

97
Crossed Lines

Margaret wanted to make sure that there was absolutely no misunderstanding. *Last* time Billy had visited, Walter had appeared at the door and virtually caught them in bed, and that had almost destroyed their fledgling relationship. *This* time, although she'd only left Walter an hour before, on the other side of town, and he was off to do some urgent business, she wasn't prepared to take any chances. Walter was a romantic old Hector – what if he just decided to drop everything and come round and see her, and he saw Billy coming out of her house again? That really would be the final nail in the coffin. So as soon as she heard Billy drive off she snatched up the phone and called Walter's mobile, just to tell him that Billy had come round looking for sympathy sex but she'd chased him away. Besides, she wanted to hear his voice again.

Meanwhile, in the penthouse apartment at Towerview, Walter was snoring his head off. It had been another fraught few hours for Linda Wray. First he was coming, then he wasn't, then he was coming, then there was no sign of him. Then he really was coming. Linda lay beside him, her head propped up on one hand, watching his chest move up and down. She had never yet met a man who could sleep on his back and *not* snore, and Walter was no exception. If it had been the middle of the night, she might have dug him in the ribs to get him to turn over. If they had been an item for months, rather than days, she might have held his nose until he coughed and spluttered and turned. But they had only really known each other for a few hours, and it was still only late afternoon and there was plenty of time for her to sleep later, so she was quite happy to lie there and watch him, and could have continued to do so for the rest of the day, except for Walter's mobile phone ringing.

Walter, of course, slept on, even though the ringtone was loud and it was sitting right next to him on the bedside table. There wasn't even the slightest reaction. Linda's own phone went to Voicemail after six unanswered rings, but Walter's rang on, and on. Eventually she reached across him and picked it up. She should have just switched it off, but didn't. They were a couple now, weren't they? That meant no secrets.

'Hello?'

'Oh. Who's that?'

'Linda. Who's that?'

'Margaret. Linda – the estate agent?'

'Margaret – you fell in the river.'

'What're you doing with Walter's phone?'

'I thought you two were finished?'

'No, we're not, and why do you have Walter's phone?'

'What? Sorry, hold on a second, a bit noisy.' Linda glanced down at Walter's vibrating nostrils, then crawled out of bed and padded out into the hall, pulling the door closed behind her. 'Sorry,' she said.

'What was that?' Margaret asked.

'What was what?'

'Like a motor boat or tumble-dryer or a giant snoring.'

'Oh, vacuum cleaner. We have the cleaners in.'

'That's wild, you should get it serviced.'

'I just did,' said Linda. She pulled out a stool from the breakfast bar and sat down. The leather seat was cold against her bare bum. 'So,' she said, 'sorry about that. You were looking for Walter. He was here a wee while ago, and he left his phone.'

'Oh. *Right.* I didn't think he was buying the apartment.'

'No, he isn't. He just had to collect some paperwork. From the office.'

'Okay, right, fair enough. Is he long gone?'

'No, not really.'

'You two seem to get on like a house on fire.'

'Well, I wouldn't say that. He's a nice fella. You two are back together then?'

'Yes, we are. And he *is* a nice fella. Yes he is. They broke the mould when they made Walter.'

Then Margaret, despite feeling great pangs of jealousy, even over something so innocent as a good business relationship, found herself relating to Linda Wray the details of her first date with Walter, him turning up drunk, and her hair getting ruined and her heel broken, and him fixing it and being lovely and romantic, and then spoiling it all by using an assumed name.

'Gosh,' Linda said, 'that was a bit of an adventure. But you got back together.'

So Margaret told her about the carrot cake and the coma, and how Walter had mounted a vigil by her hospital bed.

'That is *so* romantic.'

'Yes, it was, and then I went and spoiled it all by sleeping with my ex-husband by accident, and Walter found out and dumped me.'

'By accident?'

'Well, it's a long story. Or a short story. You know the way sometimes with men, it's just easier to sleep with them? You know, to resolve something?'

'Tell me about it,' said Linda.

'Well, it happened with Billy, my husband, and Walter caught us out, and that was the end of that, for the second time.'

'But you got back together.'

'Yes – well, that was your fault.'

'My fault?'

'At the apartment. Your fault, but also fate, and serendipity, isn't that what they call it? Anyway, here we are. I feel like it's my lucky apartment! You know something? I'm just sitting here thinking, if Walter doesn't want it, and it's still available, it would be a real stretch, but I might want to think about putting an offer in.'

'It is a lovely apartment,' said Linda.

'I'd need another look, of course. My mind was kind of elsewhere when that door opened and there he was.'

'Of course it was. Why don't you come and I'll give you a tour?'

The bedroom door opened behind Linda, and Walter came wandering out, buck naked, his eyes half-open. He waved over vaguely, turned to the left, hesitated, then turned to the right and made his way slowly towards the bathroom.

'That would be great,' said Margaret. 'I don't suppose you're free right now, are you? Just once I get a bee in my bonnet, there's no stopping me.'

Linda glanced down the hall towards the bathroom. The door was open, and the angle was just right for her to see Walter standing peeing into the toilet. Linda sighed. 'I can't just at the moment,' she said, 'but I can certainly arrange a viewing tomorrow.'

Walter was just emerging from the bathroom when Linda snapped, 'Wash your hands, and put the toilet seat down. This is a showhouse, not a dosshouse.'

Walter blinked somewhat groggily at her, then turned wordlessly and performed the requested tasks. When he emerged, Linda had returned to the bedroom, and was sitting propped up against the pillows, her legs bent and the quilt pulled up above her chest. He climbed in beside her. Slightly more awake now, he put his hand on the quilt around about where her right knee was and caressed it. 'I'm glad to see you can squeeze in business calls in between bouts of furious lovemaking.'

'I don't think so,' said Linda, moving his hand.

'You don't think so, what?'

'I don't think so, full stop.'

'I'm not sure what you mean.'

'I'm not sure what *you* mean.'

'Linda – what's the matter?'

'*You're* the matter, Walter.'

'What have I done now?'

Linda shook her head. She was torn. She really liked Walter, and the fact of the matter was that he was with her, here and now, and not Margaret. They had made love. Or *had sex*. There was a difference, she knew, but it was open to interpretation. She had been making love. Perhaps Walter had been having sex. Did it matter? Did it matter that he had lied to her about Margaret? *Had* he lied to her? Or was he not telling her the same thing? He had dismissed Margaret as a looney who jumped into rivers. He hadn't actually said they were no longer an item. She wondered if she liked Walter enough to jump into a river for him. And if she didn't, why should she get upset that he was seeing someone else? Why not just enjoy it? Go with the flow. He clearly liked being in bed with her, otherwise why would he keep coming back? What was it that was supposed to make a perfect wife – being a whore in the bedroom and a chef in the kitchen? She was certainly halfway there.

'I'm sorry for leaving the toilet seat up,' said Walter.

'It's not about that.'

'And not washing my hands.'

'It's not about that either.'

'Well, what then?'

Linda shook her head. She sighed. 'Walter?'

'Uhuh?' He looked like a little puppy who'd just had his nose pressed into his own pee to teach him a lesson.

'I'm going to bake you a big cake.'

Walter blinked at her. 'I'm on a diet,' he said.

'Screw the diet,' said Linda.

98

Love To Love You, Baby

Mr Kawolski could hardly take his eyes off the new improved version of Maeve O'Boyle as she patrolled Primark looking for shoplifters. He followed her progress on the bank of monitors in his office, often manually directing the camera angles to improve his view. He had always fancied her, but since she'd turned up with her ebullient hair all shorn off and what was left dyed a delicious blonde, he had really, *really* fancied her. He was a short, rotund, mostly bald man, and was not naïve enough to believe that he could ever be more than her boss. He silently cursed his age and his genes. He had read in a woman's magazine once that women preferred men who could make them laugh, so he had done his best with Maeve but had rarely ever raised more than a sympathetic smile. He was doomed never to lie with her. Doomed never to suck popcorn out of her ears (which he did occasionally with his own wife, it having to do with their first sexual experience in the back of the Curzon cinema on the Ormeau Road). He wondered if any man was ever satisfied with his own wife.

In watching Maeve so closely, Mr Kawolski gradually became aware that she was being followed by a tall man, with a shock of black hair and a zipped-up leather jacket. As she moved down one aisle and passed out of shot, he entered. At first Mr Kawolski thought nothing of it – that he just happened to be moving in the same anti-clockwise direction around the store. But Mr Kawolski's staff were trained in directional stealth (fifteen minutes had been devoted to it during a day-long course in Lisburn) and knew not to give shoplifters the luxury of knowing where and when a security patrol would pass. So when Maeve abruptly changed direction and began a leisurely zig-zag between counters, and moments later the black-haired man followed the same course, Mr Kawolski knew for sure she was being followed.

It could be that he was merely doing what Mr Kawolski himself sometimes did with pretty female customers – on those rare occasions when he actually patrolled the store himself. That is, follow them slavishly, admiring the cut of their figure and the set of their hair and the turn of their nose, and occasionally, the glimpse of their ankles or flash of their brassière when they went into the changing rooms. Belfast, Mr Kawolski thought, was not over-endowed with good-looking women, so you had to take your opportunities when they came.

Or, if this man wasn't following Maeve because she was beautiful, perhaps he was following her because he was a reporter, and he'd recognised her or heard about her transformation from big-haired harpie to femme fatale. He wanted to slap her into a tabloid make-over exclusive or persecute her for observing an incredibly short period of mourning.

Or, indeed, he could be something altogether more frightening. Maeve was deemed by a large proportion of her neighbours to have sullied her martyred husband's legacy by having him cremated with undue haste. Her house had been burned out and she had been forced to flee. What if they had now tracked her down to Primark and this man had been sent to – *my God!* – shoot her. Assassinate her *here*, amongst the '3 T-shirts for a fiver'!

Three distinct possibilities, and each of them flushed adrenaline through Mr Kawolski's veins. Pervert, press or paramilitary – it didn't matter. If he saved her from her stalker – and, more importantly, she was aware of it – then he would be a hero in her eyes. He wouldn't have to woo her with crappy jokes then. She would be eternally grateful. Might be early days yet for the popcorn, but dinner wouldn't be an impossibility, and then once the wine was in, you just never knew what might happen.

Mr Kawolski opened his desk drawer and contemplated his weapons. There was a truncheon. There was a pointed Ninja star. There was a replica pistol. There was half a brick. There was a set of handcuffs. There was a Stanley knife. All of these had at one time or another been taken from kids brought up to his office for shoplifting or setting fire to things. He lifted the truncheon and slipped it into his left jacket pocket. He took the pistol and placed it in his right. He was tempted by the Ninja star, but knew himself well enough to know that if he threw it, an old lady would surely lose an eye.

Thus Mr Kawolski set out to save the woman he really, *really* fancied.

If he had spent just a few moments longer studying the security camera pictures, he would also have deduced that not only was Maeve O'Boyle being followed by a tall man with luxuriant black hair, but the tall man himself was being followed by a similarly tall man, but much thinner, and with a baseball cap pulled down low masking his face.

I Predict A Riot

Mr Kawolski stepped smartly out of his office. The small radio on his breast crackled, one of his staff guarding the front door wanting five minutes to use the toilet. Mr Kawolski told him to go ahead. He could have pulled his troops in around him, just to be safe. But he didn't need back-up. He wanted to do this alone. There was no glory in an army defeating a single enemy. There *was* glory in a small round Pole saving a damsel in distress.

When he emerged onto the sales floor Mr Kawolski urgently surveyed the terrain, starting at the exact point where he'd last observed Maeve and her stalker on camera, then, using his in-depth knowledge of her patrolling habits, he scanned along her probable line of progresss to the left of the T-shirts, across Men's Canvas Jeans and then through the columns of stacked, piss-poor trainers towards the changing rooms that divided the men's section on the left from the much larger range of women's clothing to the right. There she was, lifting a silky top, holding it up against herself; and there *he* was, on the other side of the counter, staring at her. Seemingly unaware, Maeve disappeared into the changing rooms. A moment later the man followed.

Mr Kawolski hurried towards the changing rooms, his heart pounding, his sweaty hand already easing the truncheon out of his pocket. He wouldn't use the replica gun, not yet. He wanted to inflict actual damage. This deviant, this media predator, this misguided patriot, would suffer for daring to attack this defenceless young-ish woman.

Primark looks after its own!

Mr Kawolski paused at the entrance. There was supposed to be a shop assistant on duty here to check the garments in and out and to make sure that people didn't emerge wearing four pullovers and three pairs of trousers, but typically, she was nowhere to be seen. There were four unisex cubicles on either side, each with calf-length doors. All of them appeared to be in use. One door, at the bottom left, was just closing, and he caught the merest glimpse of a tall, emaciated man dressed in black. Not that one, then. That left him with a simple process of elimination. Six would contain innocent shoppers or guilty shoplifters; one a silent killer and his victim.

Mr Kawolski ducked down and scurried along the floor like an arthritic Cossack, peering beneath the cubicle doors, looking for two pairs of feet where there should be only one. No . . . no . . . no . . . There! At the end on the right; one big pair of black Oxford brogues, and squashed between them, for all he knew lifeless already, a woman's daintier feet clad in the familiar pale blue stockings of the Primark security uniform.

Mr Kawolski pulled himself up to his full height. He raised the truncheon. He tapped lightly on the door. 'Only one person in a cubicle at a time,' he said. This was a late flash of inspiration. Just in case he had got it very, very wrong.

It was polite, but at the same time heavy with menace. It was the Primark equivalent of the police shouting a warning before shooting. He, like them, was obliged to do it. It would sound better in court. Failure to comply was a licence to unleash hell.

There was an immediate and apparently panicked response from within. The feet moved, straightened, separated. Maeve, clearly being forced to speak against her will, cried breathlessly: 'It's okay, I'm staff security.'

'You bet you are!'

Mr Kawolski exploded into action. He grabbed the handle and yanked it hard, busting the flimsy interior lock and flinging the door open. He surged forward, truncheon raised and swinging, determined to inflict major brain trauma on Maeve's assailant.

Except she was sitting on his lap, in her bra. She looked shocked, and horrified. As did the man with the lipstick stains smeared across his cheek.

'Mr Kawolski! Don't!'

The man ducked down, but almost too late. A second later, and he most certainly would have lost a lot of blood. As it was, Mr Kawolski's truncheon swung just above the man's head and cracked harmlessly into the cubicle wall.

Mr Kawolski glared down at her, breathing hard. 'Maeve? What on earth are you doing?!'

Her fingers went to her lips to stop them trembling. 'I'm so sorry!'

'You – your *bra*!'

'I'm really, *really* sorry. We wanted to join the Mile High Club, except . . . you know . . . like in work instead of you know . . . Mr Kawolski, it's not what you think. I mean, it *is* what you think, but it's not like we're complete strangers. This is Jack. Jack, this is Mr Kawolski, my boss.'

'Hello, Mr Kawolski.'

Mr Kawolski just stared at them.

'And we've moved in together . . .'

'In fact, we're getting married,' said Jack Finucane, the King of Carrot Cake.

Maeve's head shot to one side. 'We are?'

Jack nodded. 'Yeah.'

From somewhere close by there came a strangled kind of a sound, like a sob in a mangle. Mr Kawolski, recovering the powers of reasoned thinking, but damaged to his very soul, pocketed his truncheon and barked, 'My office, Maeve – now!' Then he turned on his heel and stormed out of the cubicle, slamming the door closed behind him. It rocked back on its hinges, then opened again.

Less than a minute later, Maeve was clip-clopping after Mr Kawolski while still battling to re-button her shirt. It was a losing battle. Jack's masterful hands had ripped it open with one swipe. She was mortified at being discovered, but as she pursued her boss across the shopfloor it also came to her that Jack Finucane had, in his lovably direct way, asked her to marry him. She'd only known him for a week, and been a widow for less than that. Marrying him, even considering it, was wild and reckless, and it filled her with tremendously warm and melty feelings. If it came to it, Mr Kawolski could stick his job up his hole.

As Mr Kawolski crashed through the doors leading to the security offices, Jack Finucane sauntered out of the changing rooms and made his way out of the store onto Royal Avenue. He had no more expected to ask Maeve to marry him than she had expected to hear it. But now that he had, and she had tacitly accepted, he felt on top of the world.

On top of the world was not what Redmond O'Boyle felt, trailing this *bastard* from shop to street. He might have been dressed as a priest, but he had the heart of a killer.

99
Necessary Evil

Mark, in his political thinking, had begun to use the phrase *necessary evil*. He couldn't remember precisely how he came by it, but he thought it was exactly right for the situation he now found himself in. He had been repelled initially by the physical excesses he had witnessed on the streets of East Belfast, but now that the monthly collections were over, and he was somewhat removed from the beatings Pink Harrison's men had threatened to inflict on tardy payers, he recognised that they might indeed have been a *necessary evil*. Most of these people failed to vote, it was a well-known fact. And yet they expected their politicians to jump through hoops for them. Most of these people didn't have jobs. Yet they expected the Government to provide for them. Most of these people yakked on about God and Protestantism, yet hardly believed in one and could hardly explain the other.

It wasn't an ideal world. Mark was beginning to appreciate that corrupt politicians, whether morally or financially or indeed both, were not the devils the media portrayed them to be, but courageous souls struggling to hold onto their ideals in a world which quite simply did not work according to ideals. Was it wrong if back-scratching resulted in improved housing conditions? Was it a catastrophe if a suitcase full of cash secured a thousand jobs? And if a broken leg inspired a hundred other people to come out and support the Party, wasn't it worth a bit of a limp you'd get compensation for anyway? The next time he watched *All the President's Men*, Mark rooted for Nixon. When he played *Trivial Pursuit* with his mother and the question came up about who said, *All it takes for evil to flourish is for good men to do nothing*, Mark went into a long diatribe about *necessary evil*, to which his mother responded, 'Just answer the question, Adolf.'

On Friday, having packed up his files and personal effects in preparation for his move on Monday to Office 12, Mark grabbed a quick sandwich from the Mace close to his home, then drove out to Pink

Harrison's house in Holywood for a strategy and policy meeting. He was feeling decidedly *up*. He was learning things about the realities of political life that you could never, ever learn from a book. That it was *okay* to have doubts; it was *okay* to feel insecure; it was *all right* to ride roughshod over the laws of the land as long as you were discreet and your objectives were noble. Even Churchill, *my God*, the greatest Briton, had murdered thousands at Gallipoli. But without that disaster there might have been no triumph in Normandy. You learned by experience and by sacrificing anyone but yourself. Leaders lead from the rear, otherwise they are dead leaders.

These, and other grand, self-deluded thoughts were flowing through Mark's excited mind as he drove through the gates of Pink Harrison's house – estate, really – but they were soon shunted sideways when a police officer stepped out from behind a tree and held up his hand. Mark stopped immediately. His eyes flitted to his mirror and he saw two others step out from hidden positions behind the massive gateposts, presumably to block any attempt to escape. As the police officer approached his window, Mark looked up to the house and was astonished to see half a dozen police vehicles parked there. As well as uniformed officers standing around the front door, there were several in white, hooded forensic boiler suits moving in and out of the house.

Mark rapidly wound his window down. 'My God,' he said. 'What's happened?'

'We're conducting a murder investigation, sir,' the cop said gravely.

'My God! Is Councillor Harrison—?'

'Councillor Harrison is not at home.'

'Oh. Is that like a euphemism for he's missing presumed dead?'

'No, sir, he's just not at home. Do you happen to know his whereabouts?'

'God, no, I was due to meet him here.'

'And you are?'

Mark told him who he was; this information was radioed up to someone at the house. Mark was then directed to park in front of the building and talk to an Inspector McBride; he was warned not to attempt to enter the house. Mark proceeded slowly up the driveway. His mind was racing. A *murder* investigation. But Pink was alive. His immediate thought was that Bull had gone one step too far and killed a tardy contributor. But that would hardly have happened *here*, on Pink's own doorstep.

As he parked the car, Mark noted several other vaguely familiar faces – councillors and Party workers who had also turned up for the policy meeting. Each of them was being interviewed by a uniformed officer. Mark climbed out of the car and was immediately directed to

Inspector McBride, a youngish-looking man in plain-clothes. He had the frustrated air of a man who'd planned a surprise party but the main guest hadn't shown up.

McBride took down his details – home address, work address and telephone numbers, his connection to Councillor Harrison, the last time he'd seen him, spoken to him, and if he knew where he was right now. Mark gave all this information politely and asked as many questions as he could, but McBride wasn't giving anything away. The other Party members, having finished their own interviews, were now gathered in a small group to the right of the front door, earnestly conversing. Mark started to cross to them, then remembered something and turned back to the Inspector.

'Just realised – I'm moving offices on Monday, in case you call up and I'm not there and you think I've done a runner and you issue an APB or something.'

Inspector McBride blinked at him.

'All Points Bulletin,' explained Mark.

'This isn't *The Streets of San Francisco*,' said McBride.

'I appreciate that,' said Mark. 'Sorry. If you ask for Office Twelve, I'm not sure of the direct number yet.'

McBride made a note of it. Mark quickly scurried across to join in the gossip. One of them was saying, 'I heard someone got found drowned in his pool.'

'Like Brian Jones,' said another.

'Who's Brian Jones?' asked one.

'From the Rolling Stones.'

'Pink knows The Rolling Stones?' asked yet another.

'Pink knows everyone,' said the first councillor.

'I knew he was trouble,' said the man who hadn't heard of Brian Jones. 'Leopards and spots, leopards and spots.'

'That's not fair,' stated the man who knew about The Rolling Stones. 'It may all be perfectly innocent.'

'There's been a murder,' said the man who hadn't heard of Brian Jones, 'and they're searching his house – and I say there's no smoke without fire.'

'Someone might just have sneaked in to use the pool, then drowned,' said Mark. 'He mightn't know anything about it.'

'It's bad for the Party,' said one.

'It doesn't help,' said another.

'We should cut our losses,' said one.

'Some would argue that The Stones were a better band without Brian Jones,' said the one who'd introduced Brian Jones into the equation in the first place.

'It's hardly the same,' said another councillor, who had thus far kept his knowledge of The Rolling Stones under his hat, 'because Brian Jones was a founder member of the band, but Pink wasn't a founder member of the Party. He's more like Ron Wood, a gun for hire. I don't mean gun, of course, I mean guitarist. Ron Wood looks like a Stone, he sounds like a Stone, but ultimately he's not really a Stone. He's quite dispensable.'

'We shouldn't jump to any conclusions,' said Mark.

'Hear, hear,' said the man who hadn't heard of Brian Jones. 'We have to give Pink the benefit of the doubt. We need more information before we expel him.'

There were nods all around the group. They agreed to retire to Party Headquarters and await developments. They drove out of Pink's driveway in a little convoy. As they emerged onto the main road, they were filmed by a BBC News crew. Mark phoned home to make sure his wife taped the late-night news in case there was a glimpse of him. He was filled with excitement. He had hardly been in the Party for more than a few days, and already there was a crisis, and it felt like he was at the very heart of it. And if Pink really was involved in a murder, or was felt to have compromised the Party by some connection to it, no matter how tenuous, who better to step into his shoes than Mark himself? Pink Harrison's sole contribution to the Unionist cause might yet turn out to have been to serve as the *necessary evil* which elevated Mark to a position of power and influence.

100
White Riot

The Chief Constable knew that beyond the bluff and bluster, Jimmy was right. It was difficult enough being a blow-in from the mainland. This was one of the few occasions when he could show the rank and file that he wouldn't pander to the politicians all of the time, that when it really, *really* mattered he would stand with his men. They had, after all, been after Pink Harrison for years.

So the warrants were duly presented for approval by the judiciary, and implemented. Co-ordinated raids took place on all of Pink Harrison's properties, but there was no Pink Harrison to be found. It was highly likely that he had been tipped off. The old RUC had been a predominantly Protestant organisation that struggled with a misjudged reputation for being lenient on Protestant paramilitaries; since it had changed to the PSNI, and more convincingly encouraged Catholic recruitment, it had successfully reversed that reputation while in truth the growing paranoia of its officers, faced with a quasi-Republican influx, meant that it actually did go a little bit easier on the Protestant paramilitaries. Often they condoned the sentiment that the paramilitaries espoused rather than the reality, i.e. they supported an organisation which professed to protect the Unionist state and culture, but couldn't work out how selling drugs and running protection rackets furthered that cause. That Pink Harrison knew they were coming for him was not therefore much of a surprise; but there were enough good cops like Jimmy Marsh Mallow to make the Chief Constable confident that he would soon be caught. He crossed his fingers that there would be enough evidence to charge him, because Belfast was already going mad.

The trouble started within an hour of the raids taking place. Word quickly circulated through the local East Belfast schools, and by lunchtime many classrooms were empty. Kids returned home, changed into their riot clothes, and began making preparations. Walls were torn down and pavements torn up for missiles. Huge numbers of bottles for making petrol bombs were a little bit harder to come by than during the heyday of The Troubles, as milk was now largely distributed in plastic containers and Coke in cans, but enough were eventually gathered. These were slightly healthier than the old-fashioned devices, as they used unleaded petrol. Bull, being a veteran of many kinds of trouble, supervised the rapid assembly of blast bombs, pipe bombs and drogue bombs.

Cars all along the Newtownards Road were hijacked and set on fire. Shop windows were smashed and contents looted. Stones rained down on passing buses, amongst them a red double-decker giving a dozen American tourists a 'We Love Belfast' guided tour; the driver and guide immediately abandoned it and ran for their lives, leaving the Yanks somewhat perplexed by this apparent re-enactment of a riot which appeared astonishingly realistic. The Bangor to Belfast train was hijacked at Sydenham halt and guided into Central Station before being set ablaze. City Bus announced the cancellation of all services and workers were released early from work (to allow them to make their own way home, or to join the rioting, depending on their preference). Unionist politicians (with the exception of Pink Harrison) called for calm but blamed the PSNI for causing the disturbances. The PSNI stated that it had a duty to uphold the law and reiterated that it wished to speak to Pink Harrison as part of ongoing murder enquiries. The police, backed up by the Army, remained stoical in the face of violent attack. A number were injured, burns and broken heads mostly, and although several gun attacks were reported, nobody was hit.

The Chief Constable, when asked for his reaction, said that, 'These rioters will only succeed in damaging their own environments. They're kids and they don't really know what they're doing, or why they're doing it; it's the shadowy figures who are manipulating these kids who have to answer for this.'

A *Sunday World* reporter demanded to know who these shadowy figures were.

The Chief Constable, in an ill-judged attempt at humour, responded with: 'I don't know, they're all shadowy,' which raised a laugh from the assembled press corps, but was then roundly condemned by the very same reporters when they went back to their offices and thought about it.

Walter, sent home early with the rest of the Civil Servants, was on the train that got hijacked at Sydenham. Although he had no clear view of the Newtownards Road from where it was stopped, he could tell from the plumes of smoke hanging over that part of the city, that the trouble was more serious and widespread than it had been in years. He did not think it was necessarily a bad thing. Commercial property prices in the areas affected would probably come down, making it a good time to buy.

In the city centre, Royal Avenue and the surrounding shopping areas took on the appearance of a ghost town. Margaret patrolled the eerily empty Primark aisles; Maeve, having accepted a one-week suspension from work without pay for being caught about to make love to Jack Finucane in the changing rooms, made her way to *Irma La Deuce* which, although located on the south side of the city, backed onto the rows of terraces around Windsor Park, the home of Linfield Football Club which, with its totally Protestant following, made it another potential flashpoint. Jack decided to close early. There were no customers anyway. He pulled down all the metal shutters with the exception of the one for the front door, and stood there, waiting anxiously for Maeve to arrive.

Across the road, Emma Cochrane and Louise brought the *Emma Cochrane* shutters halfway down, but wouldn't close them because May Li was due to arrive with the first of the dresses she had made up from Margaret's designs. First she was ten minutes late, then twenty, then nearly an hour. When they called her mobile phone, some yob answered with an evil laugh and told them to go and f**k themselves when they asked about May Li. Eventually she arrived an hour and a half late, with a back window shattered and deep indentations on the driver's door where rioters had kicked at it. Her handbag and one of her shoes had been stolen. But the clothes were safe. The shutters immediately came fully down.

Billy Gilmore, sitting at home feeling sorry for himself and watching the coverage live on Sky, got a phone call. He answered morosely.

'Cheer up, sunshine.'

'Mr Harrison, is that you?'

'No one else. And call me Pink, all my mates do. How're you doing, Billy?'

'I'm f-fine.'

'I called your work – they said you're no longer on staff.'

'I got made redundant.'

'You? I thought you were their top man.'

'So did I.'

'Gee. Life just sucks, doesn't it? Anyway, you watching the telly?'

'Yeah. God, Pink, it's mad out there.'

'Tell me about it.'

'They're looking for you.'

'They seek him here, they seek him there. Actually, if they opened their frigging eyes, they'd see me sitting here in my own car outside Police Headquarters. I'm just about to walk in, but wanted to clear a few things up with you first.

'Me?'

'Well, you know where the bodies are hid, don't you?'

'Bodies? Pink, I don't know anything about any bodies.'

'Ah, wind your neck in, Billy, it's only an expression. I'm talking about the accounts, the paperwork . . .'

'Oh – right, of course, Pink. Sorry, Pink. The accounts.'

'I just wanted to make sure everything was safe and secure.'

'Absolutely, Pink.'

'Move them around as you need until I come out the other side of this.'

'Understood.'

'Excellent. Thanks, Billy. I owe you.'

'No problem, Pink.'

'Just one more thing. Need a bit of a favour.'

Billy felt his stomach go. He didn't know what the favour was, but it probably wouldn't be like shifting a heavy television or helping him put up shelves.

'Yes, Pink?'

'I need you to take a run over to the Supporters Club. I've left some money in the safe and I'd rather Inspector Plod didn't get his hands on it.'

'The uh, Supporters Club? Which one?'

'*Which one*? Which one do you think! Just pop over, pick up the money and pay it into one of the accounts.'

Billy took a deep breath. 'But it's murder out there. I mean—'

'You'll be fine.'

'But surely one of your guys, Bull or someone, could just as easily do it.'

'Billy, I wouldn't trust them as far as I could throw them. But I can trust you. You're my accountant, my special accountant. All right?'

Billy swallowed. Pink gave him the combination and told him to be quick. Billy asked about the rioters. Pink said not to worry about them, he'd know half of them anway, and to say he was working for Pink if required because 'that'll put the fear of God into them'.

When Billy put the phone down, he immediately slumped back into his chair and sighed. *You'll know the half of them.* He somehow doubted that. He recalled now how he'd heard that Pink kept a retinue of accountants to handle his many and nefarious business interests, and how he'd wondered if most of the skinhead football supporters in the club were actually accountants, acting hard. He had a sudden and delightful image of rioting accountants on the streets of East Belfast. He made little jokes in his head about the police being called 'to account' and peace being in 'the balance', but it was a momentary respite. East Belfast was in flames, and that's exactly where he was going. Billy groaned, fingered his tie, then forced himself up and out of his chair.

101

In the Pink

Marsh was sitting in his office, watching the riot coverage on a small TV, when his phone rang and an embarrassed-sounding WPC said, 'Sir, Councillor Harrison is in reception.'

A grey police Land Rover was just bursting into flames on screen, so Marsh was only half-paying attention. His immediate thought was he didn't need any bloody councillor whining to him about how badly the police were handling all the trouble.

'Tell him I'm—' And then he stopped. 'Do you mean *Pink* Harrison is downstairs?'

'Yes, sir.'

Jimmy Mallow shook his head. Of *course* Pink Harrison was downstairs. On his own terms. There were never going to be any TV shots of Pink Harrison being hauled off in handcuffs.

'Is he with anyone – a solicitor?'

'No, sir, he's by himself.'

'All right – show him to an interview room.'

'Yes, sir. Should I have him searched?'

'Of course.'

'Should I put someone in with him?'

It was normal practice, and Pink was, after all, a murder suspect, but Marsh didn't want anyone in there with him. Pink's ability to charm, influence and corrupt, while doubtlessly wildly exaggerated, probably had some basis in truth, so the fewer people exposed to it the better. Police HQ was paranoid enough without allowing Rasputin in to weave his poison.

'No, leave him be. Get him a cup of tea, but don't talk to him more than you have to. There'll be someone down shortly.'

'Yes, sir.'

Jimmy Marsh Mallow switched off the TV and called Gary. 'How's it going?' he asked.

'It's early days yet, boss. I've spoken to all six forensic teams in the last half-hour. Nothing to report besides the fact that two of them have been bricked, but no one hurt.'

'No bloody handprints, no ghostly figure pointing us in the right direction?'

'No, boss.'

'Okay, Gary, why don't you come back here? Pink Harrison just walked in.'

'Under his own steam?'

'You bet.'

'And what does he have to say for himself?'

'Not spoken to him yet. I'll let him kick his heels for a couple of hours, but then I want you to have first crack at him.'

'Me, sir? I thought . . .'

'I just want to see him in action before I plough in.'

'Yes, sir.'

Marsh cut the line. He took one of the photos of Michael Caldwell out of his drawer and placed it face up on the desk. He switched the TV back on and watched more scenes of violence and destruction and wondered why a player like Pink Harrison was confident enough to walk into a police station without legal representation.

She set the mug of tea down on the table, and put a couple of sachets of *Canderel* beside it. Pink Harrison smiled and asked what her name was.

'WPC Winterson,' said Claudia Winterson.

'No, I mean your first name.'

Claudia flushed a little, and shook her head. There was a Constable watching from the doorway.

'You're very pretty, do you know that?'

'There's your tea, Councillor Harrison. Can I get you anything else?'

'A length of rope, maybe. I'm obviously in big trouble.'

She gave him a thin smile, and quickly stepped out of the interview room. Constable Miller closed the door behind her. He turned to Claudia and said, 'So that's Pink Harrison. What do you think?'

'Bit flash for me,' said Claudia.

'You see his watch? Rolex.'

'Probably a knock-off.'

'Looked real enough to me. And did you notice his shoes?'

'Can't say I did.'

'Armani.'

'I thought Armani was suits.'

'It's everything these days. But the shoes – did you see the soles?'

'Can't say I did. What about them?'

'You know when you buy new shoes and the soles are absolutely perfect? But the moment you walk out of the shop, or the first time you put them on and go for a bit of a dander, they're immediately all scoured and marked?' Claudia nodded. 'Well, his soles, when he crossed his legs when he sat down, his soles didn't have a single mark on them. Like he'd just put them on outside the front door.'

'You should be a detective, Colin,' Claudia laughed, turning to walk back to the reception desk, 'or get a job in a shoe shop.'

Constable Miller smiled after her, then took up a position guarding the door to the interview room. He remained there for forty-five minutes. He looked through the glass panel half a dozen times. On the first three occasions Harrison was sitting quite normally at the desk, staring into space. On the second three, he was actually sitting *on* the desk in what appeared to be either a yoga position or one of meditation. His legs were crossed and his arms were held out in front of him. When the Constable turned his head closer to the door and listened, he could just about hear a humming sound.

Constable Miller continued his vigil. There was no reason to inform anyone of Pink Harrison's somewhat unusual behaviour. There was nothing in the manual that specifically related to the practice of either yoga or meditation while in police custody. So long as he wasn't harming himself, or a danger to others, then he could do what he liked.

When Gary McBride eventually appeared, he too peered through the glass panel. He said, 'What the hell's he playing at?'

'Don't know, sir,' said Constable Miller.

Gary shook his head, then said, 'Right, let's go.' He indicated for the Constable to follow him in.

Pink Harrison, still sitting on the desk, had his eyes closed and did not react to the two police officers entering.

Gary said, 'Councillor Harrison, sir,' then introduced himself and the Constable, and told him he wished to interview him in connection with a serious crime; he said he was obliged to record the interview. Gary began to fiddle with the recording equipment.

Pink opened one eye, noted the Constable, then looked at Gary. 'No,' he said.

Gary, still setting the equipment, said, 'No, what?'

'Before we begin, I'd like to speak to your boss.'

'My boss?'

'Superintendent James Mallow.'

'Maybe later.'

'No.'

Gary half-laughed. 'Councillor Harrison, I'm afraid it's not up to you.' Pink had both eyes closed again. Gary pulled out a chair and sat down. Constable Miller took up a position against the back wall. 'Councillor Harrison, for the record will you please give your name, date of birth, occupation and present address.'

Silence.

'Councillor Harrison?'

Silence.

'Councillor Harrison, for the record will you please give your name, date of birth, occupation and present address.'

Pink remained silent.

'Councillor Harrison?'

One eye opened. 'A private word with the Superintendent. Just me and him, no one else.'

Gary glared at him, then pushed his chair back and signalled for Constable Miller to follow him out of the room. They closed the door behind them. Gary immediately hissed, *'W***er.'* Then he went to the desk and phoned Marsh.

Marsh said, 'What's your take on it?'

'He's so full of himself, only wants to talk to someone on his level.'

'First time I've been described as being on his level.'

'You know what I mean, boss. Look, I'll tell him to go jump.'

'No, don't. He'll just sit there for days saying nothing. And we haven't turned up any forensics yet. If we don't take a crack at him soon he'll be able to walk.'

'You're going to come down?'

'I'm going to shake the tree, see if anything falls out of the branches.'

'Isn't that just giving in to him?'

'Yes, of course it is. Helps him maintain the illusion of being in control. But we know better, don't we, Gary?'

'Yes, sir.'

Jimmy Mallow walked into the interview room alone, twenty minutes later. Pink was no longer sitting on the table, but was back in his seat. He stood as Marsh entered and extended his hand. Marsh shook it, their eyes met and held. Marsh introduced himself. 'Now then, Councillor,' he said. 'What's so important that you won't talk to my people? I'm a busy man.'

Pink, never taking his eyes off Marsh, reached into his jacket and took out his wallet. He removed a slip of paper and flattened it out on the table. 'I want you to phone this number and identify yourself to whoever answers.'

Marsh looked at the paper, and the numbers written on it. 'And why would I want to do that, Councillor?'

392

'Because I feel it would be in both our interests.'

'Really?' It was heavy with sarcasm. Pink didn't react at all. Just kept looking at Marsh, the man who'd been after him all these years, and Marsh kept looking at Pink, whom he'd been chasing for all that time. 'Well,' said Marsh, 'let's see, but if I do this, I want you to talk to my people, and get yourself a solicitor.'

'Be happy to oblige,' said Pink.

Marsh walked back out of the interview room, leaving the door open, and crossed to the reception desk. He reached down and lifted a phone up onto the counter, then dialled the number from memory. It was answered almost immediately. A tired-sounding voice said, 'Hello?'

'This is Superintendent James Mallow. I was asked to phone this number.'

'Ah, yes, Superintendent. I was expecting your call.'

'Who am I speaking to, first of all?'

'Oh right, it's Dan Starkey, *Belfast Confidential.*'

Marsh glanced back to the interview room. Pink was now sitting on the desk, apparently meditating. Marsh's brow furrowed, then he sighed. '*Belfast Confidential,* right. I've avoided talking to you lot since you crawled out of the sewer, so why should I change the habit of a lifetime now? I've nothing to say about this case, it's way too early. In case you hadn't noticed, Mr Starkey, Belfast is burning, I hardly think this is the right time for you lot to mount a campaign of support for Pink f***ing Harrison.'

'Ah, Superintendent. I'm sorry, we seem to have our wires crossed a bit. This has nothing to do with Pink Harrison. This is to do with *you.*'

'What the hell are you talking about?'

'Well, sir, a certain individual is trying to sell us financial records and tape recordings which show that you beat up a prostitute called Julie Mateer and then tried to buy her off. We really just wanted to get your side of the story.'

Jimmy Marsh Mallow felt the colour drain from his face. His eyes flitted back to the interview room. Pink Harrison remained in his meditative position, and his eyes were closed, but even from this distance, Marsh could see the smirk on his face.

102

This Old House

Redmond followed Jack Finucane all the way back to *Irma La Deuce*, almost impervious to the deteriorating situation all around him. He hardly noticed that the streets were emptying or that sirens filled the air or that plumes of black smoke were wafting over the city. Shutters were coming down and buses were hurrying past stops without stopping, such was their desire to return to the comparative safety of the depot. Redmond only had eyes for the man who was going to marry his wife. The man was was clearly already having sex with his wife. The man who, judging from the front window of his café, specialised in carrot cake. What sort of a man was it, Redmond wondered, who specialised in carrot cake? How could any sort of a *man* hold his head up in public and say that his life revolved around carrot cake? And what sort of a woman would choose a man who specialised in carrot cake over a man who waged war – a warrior, a patriot, a hero, even a martyr?

Redmond had kept his alter ego secret from Maeve all these years only because he wished to protect her. In that respect he was like Clark Kent or Peter Parker. But now that she knew who or what he was, and given her background in the Falls Road ghetto, how could she ever, ever, *ever* give herself to a man who made carrot cake? What an incredible come-down, after having a man who changed the fate of nations. It was like Mrs Churchill getting over her grief by falling for a cigar-maker. Or Mrs Mao seeking love from a ping-pong player. And to go from death to marriage in a matter of days, what did that suggest? Either that she had been driven mad by her grief, or she'd been carrying on with this maker of carrot cakes for more than just the brief period of her widowhood. That while he, Redmond, was out saving, or destroying the world, she was having sex with this carrot-caking conniver.

Redmond took up a position opposite *Irma La Deuce* as Jack

Finucane – although clearly, he did not yet know his name – entered the empty café. A few moments later the *Closed* sign appeared on the front door, his staff departed and Jack reappeared to pull down the main window shutters. He didn't yet shutter the front door. Redmond was tempted to walk across. Although he'd had ample opportunity to assault him on the walk up from Primark, he had been dissuaded not only by the presence of the general public, but also by a deeper moral confusion. He was dressed as a priest now, and had vowed to continue his late brother's good work. This clearly couldn't involve attacking, battering and generally killing a hated love rival. Yet the temptation threatened to overwhelm him, particularly as Jack Finucane was standing right *there*, in his shop doorway, without a care in the world, quite happy to break one man's heart and take advantage of a poor grieving widow. He not only needed to be assaulted, he *deserved* it.

As Redmond thought about all of this, a taxi drew up outside the café and Maeve climbed out. Redmond's heart jumped and his stomach did somersaults. She looked *fantastic*. When he had first arrived in Primark, intent on surprising her, he had searched the shop for her without success. There *was* a gorgeous blonde security guard just a few metres in front of him and he was about to ask her where Maeve was when a bright young shop assistant, seeing his apparent confusion, and alerted to the fact that he was standing in Ladies Underwear, said, 'Can I help you, Father?' And when she pointed Maeve out, and it was this gorgeous blonde, Redmond was absolutely staggered at the transformation. He found himself quite unable to approach her. He had always found Maeve attractive, but in an earthy, *she's no oil painting but I like her* kind of a way. Now, the way she looked, the way she moved, he thought she was just the sexiest creature he had ever seen. How soul-destroying then to follow her into the changing rooms and first of all hear her attempt to copulate with this stranger, but then also hear her accept his proposal of marriage.

As Maeve stepped onto the pavement, Redmond had a desperate urge to charge across the road and take her in his arms. He would proclaim his love for her, and she would surely reciprocate, once she got over the shock of discovering that he wasn't dead from a suppurated arse and cremated with undue haste in far-off Colombia. But before Redmond could galvanise himself, Jack Finucane had stepped down from his café doorway and Maeve had rushed into *his* arms. They snogged, and snogged, and snogged, while police vehicles and fire-brigade tenders raced past, their sirens wailing, possibly more loudly than Redmond's despairing sighs. As the sound of the emergency vehicles began to fade, Maeve broke away from Jack, took his hand, and led him into the café. Jack pulled the final shutter down behind them, and they were gone.

Redmond tramped forlornly along the Lisburn Road. From somewhere the expression came to him, *It is better to have loved and lost, than never to have loved at all*. But he thought that that was b***ocks. If he had never met Maeve he would not now be feeling this tremendous despair, and his mind would certainly not now be engaged in a tremendous battle between his brother's piety and his own longing. His brother would doubtless forgive her. Redmond's inclination was to search out his enemy and destroy him.

At the top of Windsor Avenue a skinhead teenager noticed his priest's collar and shouted, 'Look – it's the f***ing Pope!'

Another, in a Linfield scarf, shouted, 'You f***ing Fenian b***ard!'

Redmond heard them but walked on, his head bowed. They came after him, catching up quickly, and walking on either side of him.

'What're you doing round here, you Fenian c***?'

'Yeah, why don't you f**k off back where you belong, you Fenian f***er.'

The boy in the scarf stuck out his foot and tripped Redmond. He staggered forward, but didn't go down. He turned to the boys, who came up to him, all evil smiles.

'What're you looking at, Pope-head?' the first one demanded. 'Can't you f***ing walk?'

'You f***ing w***er,' said the other.

Redmond clasped his hands before him, beatifically. 'Boys, now, there's no need for language like that.'

'Is there f***ing not?'

The boy with the scarf took a swing at him. Redmond moved deftly to one side, then headbutted him, hard. The boy's nose crumpled. He let out a scream and collapsed down, blood pumping. The other boy had already swung back his foot, intending to plant it in Redmond's stomach, but as it came at him Redmond again sidestepped swiftly and grabbed his DM boot. He twisted it to one side, then walked the boy backwards towards *Pressed for Time*, a dry-cleaning shop. He stopped just short of the front window. Moving swiftly along the boy's leg, he grabbed his crotch with one hand, squeezing hard, and his shirt-front with the other. Then he physically lifted him off the ground and *threw* him at the shop window. The boy hurtled through it with an explosive crash, then landed in a heap on the tiled floor with shards of jagged glass raining down all around him. He let out a miserable groan and lay where he was in a crumpled heap. There were three customers in the shop. They stood and stared, first at the injured boy, but then, and for much longer, at the priest rubbing his hands together in a satisfied fashion.

As Redmond turned away from the shop, the boy with the broken nose staggered back, out of range. 'What the . . . what the hell *are* you?' he asked.

'New Pope, new policy,' Redmond said simply, and walked on.

Redmond didn't feel any better for his explosion of violence. It was a release, not a solution. And he felt even worse now, standing outside the burned-out remains of his house in West Belfast. He simply could not comprehend why they, whoever *they* were, had done this. Or how they could have been allowed to do it by the powers-that-be. Didn't the IRA or Sinn Fein maintain order any more?

Redmond stepped into the small front garden. The grass itself was blackened and strewn with rubbish. No, not rubbish – the charred remains of his, *their*, possessions. A curled and useless photograph of his uncle playing soccer. Wedding photos torn in two and boasting thug footprints. Redmond fought back tears. He had sworn to start anew as a way of making up for his brother's death, but always, always at the back of his mind there was the faint possibility, the vague hope, that one day he would be able to go back to his old life. But now his wife was gone and his house was burned. He literally had *nothing* of his old life left. The front door was missing and the dark, dank interior of the house beckoned, but it was too much for him. He strangled a sob and turned away. As he stepped back out onto the footpath he saw that an elderly woman, carrying two plastic Dunnes shopping bags in each hand, was standing there looking at him curiously. 'Are you all right, Father?' she asked.

Redmond nodded, 'Yes, thank you.'

'Terrible thing they done, wasn't it?' said the woman, nodding at the house.

'Yes, yes indeed.'

'That Redmond, he was some pup, eh?'

'I suppose, yes.'

'He showed them, didn't he? No stopping him. If you ask me, he's a hero, a real Irish hero. We should knock that house down and put up a statue, that's what I say.'

'Well,' said Redmond, genuinely surprised, 'that's very kind.'

She nodded, went to move on, then looked at him a little closer and said, 'If you don't mind me asking, Father, what's that on your head?'

'My what?'

'Your head – that red stuff.'

Redmond's hand went to his forehead; it felt a little tender thanks to his recent headbutt. He examined his fingers. 'Oh, sorry, just a little dried blood. I, ahm, struck my head accidentally.'

The woman smiled. 'Oh, right. Good job, Father. Thought for a minute there you were turning into a f***ing Hindu. Never f***ing know these days, do you?'

She cackled then, and walked on. Redmond nodded after her, rubbing the congealed blood between his thumb and forefinger. *She was right*, he thought. *You just never f***ing knew, these days.*

103
Fashion is a Passion

Experience and statistics show that rioting in Belfast rarely lasts for more than three days, no matter what the cause. Teenagers, the main culprits, get bored. They want to hang with their mates. Usually there's a mid-week football match on the telly to watch. Righteous anger isn't quite so righteous when Man United are playing. Indignation fades and hatred is put on the back boiler to simmer indefinitely, a stew for all seasons. That said, it was still day one, and with at least two days to go, spirits were not high in either the police ranks or in the hearts of the general public who had to endure the violence, fear, destruction and disruption.

Margaret was worried about getting caught up in it, of course, but she was equally determined that nothing was going to stop her getting to Emma Cochrane for the first, private showing of the *M & Emma* collection. Emma had corralled a group of thin women who frequented the shop, to act as models. Some of them were actually real models, but past their best years. Several worked exclusively with one part of their body – their feet for modelling shoes, their hands for showing off jewellery; one even specialised in showing off her varicose veins in campaigns for the Health Promotion Agency. Six out of the eight models Emma had booked actually made it. One who didn't said she was stuck in a three-mile tailback of cars caused by a petrol tanker being hijacked and parked across the Grosvenor Road, and she thought it safer to turn back home; the other phoned to say her car had Irish Republic number plates, and she was worried about it being seized or attacked, so was staying home.

Six was plenty. They squeezed into the stockroom and excitedly changed into the dresses. May Li clucked around them, pulling and prodding and fixing and even stitching on the hoof. Margaret, even though they were her babies, stayed out of the way, preferring to see the outfits for the first time as a customer might see them at a fashion show. She sat on the counter, shaking with nerves and counselling herself repeatedly not to burst into tears of joy when the models began to parade through that curtain.

Louise produced a bottle of champagne and poured Margaret and Emma a glass, one for herself, then opened another two bottles and took them back to the changing room. Laughter, together with the occasional *ping* of a makeshift spittoon, filtered through the curtain as Margaret sipped her champagne and wondered if she had ever been happier. Yes, Belfast was going to hell in a handcart, but her own, personal life was turning into one long victory parade. She was finally free of Billy, both physically and mentally, she had a new man in her life, she was about to purchase a luxury apartment, and now her first collection – *entirely* her own work this time – was about to pass by in front of her. Could life *get* any better?

Then the moment came. The curtain was pulled back.

'Wait a minute! Wait a minute!' Louise shouted excitedly, then dived to switch on some music. In a few moments, the sound of Eric Clapton's 'Layla' wafted across the store. 'All right! Okay!' Louise called. 'All systems are go!'

The first of the models appeared.

I'm just going to *die*, thought Margaret.

An hour later Margaret, giddy with excitement and champagne, wove her way across Belfast, skilfully choosing side streets and back roads in a largely successful bid to avoid the rioting and the rioters. The air was thick with the smell of tyres burning and echoed to the sounds of cheers and yells and shattering glass. At one junction a kid in a balaclava shouted, 'No surrender!' at her as she drove past, and Margaret shouted, 'No surrender!' right back. She didn't care if her dresses were never seen by another living soul; it was sufficient for her that she had seen them parade by in a magical swirl of colour and shimmer just once. It seemed to her that the models had almost *inhabited* her creations, as if they were a second, succulent skin. It seemed both to go on for ever, and to be over in an instant. It was like watching slow motion all speeded up. Emma kissed her and Louise kissed her and the models kissed her and even May Li kissed her. They all danced around and turned the music up and quaffed champagne. They could easily have drunk another half dozen bottles, but the off-licence just along the road had closed early because of all the trouble.

As she waited at one set of traffic-lights, virtually the only car on the road, she took out her mobile and phoned Linda Wray and confirmed that her appointment to take a second look at the Towerview apartment was still on and that Linda had made it there despite all the traffic disruption. Then she called Walter and babbled excitedly about her dresses and how stunning they'd looked and how the models had crowded around her kissing and hugging just like you'd see on the TV. When the torrent had eased and the apartment block was coming into view she finally managed to say, 'So how are you, where are you?'

'I'm trudging into the city centre. Our train got hijacked – they threw everyone off.'

'Oh God! Are you all right?!'

'Oh yeah, they're just kids having fun.'

'And did they like, *take* the train?'

'Yep. Steamed off into the distance. But it's not like hijacking a plane or anything. They can't say, "Take me to Cuba". They could only say, "Take me to Lisburn or Antrim", or something. They're kind of confined to where the line runs to.'

'But you're okay, that's the important thing.'

'Yes, it is. And what about you? What're you up to now? More mad fashion parties?'

'Nah, that's enough excitement for one day. I'm actually going to take another look at that apartment of yours.'

'That what?'

Margaret was by now pulling into the car park at the Towerview Apartments. 'You don't mind, do you? Just you said you weren't inter-ested in buying it, so my idea to rent it off you went out the window, but I couldn't get it out of my head, so I called you for a chat about it, because I value your advice, but you'd gone and left your phone *in* the apartment, and Linda, you know, the estate agent, answered your phone, so I thought that was pretty bloody spooky and possibly a sign from God. I got talking to her and she invited me to come over for another look. You don't mind, do you, Walter?'

'I . . . I . . . no, I . . . You spoke to Linda?'

'Yes, of course.'

'And she said she had my phone?'

'Walter, I was talking to her on it.'

'And, and she invited you over?'

'Walter, what's wrong? Your voice is all . . .'

'Nothing, nothing. I just, ah, you know, I'm still quite kind of taken with the apartment.'

'But you said you weren't interested!'

'I know, I know.'

'You said you were going into commercial property.'

'And I am, I just . . . well . . . Linda didn't say anything, you know, about me?'

'No, Walter, what could she say? You backed out. She seemed surprised that we were together again.'

'She did?'

'Well, last time she saw me I was falling into a river.'

'Right. Yeah.'

'Look, I'm here now – in fact, I'm a couple of minutes late, so why don't I phone you when I'm finished and maybe we can go out for a drink to celebrate?'

'Ahm, yes, that would be nice. Tell you what, speak to Linda, and then, yes, ahm, call me. I'm sure that would be – you know, fine.'

'Walter, are you sure you're all right? You sound a bit weird.'

'Weird, no. It's just, you know – Chinatown.'

She laughed. He laughed. She said goodbye. He said goodbye. She took the lift up to the apartment, still smiling happily. Walter thought seriously about throwing *himself* in the Lagan.

104
Safe

In a recent poll conducted on a well-known internet travel site, the two most popular tourist destinations in Northern Ireland were named as the swinging Falls Road, in the heart of Catholic West Belfast, and that corrupted artery which runs partially parallel to the Falls, the Shankill Road. Interesting, because the tourists chose to ignore the beautiful Glens of Antrim, the stunning Mourne Mountains, the emasculated shipyards where the *Titanic* was built, and the Giant's Causeway where the Isle of Man was heaved out of the ground by a steroid-enhanced Finn McCool. They were chosen because of their history of menace and because you can see nice mountains in any country – apart from Holland, obviously – but you can't always feel like you're being brave and daring, which you can by sauntering along the Falls or the Shankill with a camera strung around your neck.

The differences between the two are small, but important. Both boasted some of the worst housing and unemployment in Europe, which were a contributing factor to the Troubles. The housing has generally been sorted out, though unemployment remains high. Although the Troubles in the Province as a whole have receded, civil unrest continues. It is much greater in the Protestant Shankill, where the people feel that all of the benefits of peace have gone to their near neighbours on the Falls. A tourist with a camera will be welcomed with open arms on the Falls. They will be encouraged to spend their dollars drinking in the local bars and community centres with the locals, will feel Irish, and will toast earnest patriots. When drunk, their camera will be stolen, but it will almost feel like a friendly act and will be chalked up to experience and become a story to boast about at home. On the Shankill Road, however, a tourist with a camera will be nutted the moment they climb out of their cab, and that, frankly, is not much of a story.

Billy Gilmore felt like a tourist. He had chosen not to take his car to the Shankill to recover Pink Harrison's money because he didn't want it taken off him by the rioters, so he hired a taxi instead. For the very same reason, the taxi driver refused point blank to take him within spitting distance of the Shankill, dropping him just short of it at Millfield. To blend in, Billy had once again donned his Rangers top, but had neglected to do anything about his trousers, which were nicely pressed, and his brogues, which were polished to a reflective shine. He kept his head down as he walked past a line of parked police Land Rovers and two vehicles equipped with water cannon, all awaiting the order to go in. As he turned onto the Shankill itself he forced his head up. There were about a hundred teenagers, male and female, spread out loosely across the street; several cars were on fire, broken glass sparkled on the tarmac. Some of the kids wore bandanas across their faces, a couple had on balaclavas, but most couldn't have cared less about hiding their identities. Billy began to work his mouth, like he was chewing gum. He rolled his shoulders like a boxer approaching the ring. He made eye-contact. He gave a slight nod of his head each time, but moved through without speaking. He wasn't challenged. When he was finally beyond them he breathed a sigh of relief. But it was temporary.

The Supporters Club was dead ahead. There was a crowd of older men moving around the entrance. Cardboard boxes brimming with explosive devices of many different types were being passed out and loaded onto the back of a milk-float. Billy approached with the same studied nonchalance, but inside he was churning up. He scanned their faces, looking for someone he recognised, but they all seemed to blend together, middle-aged men for the most part, either pumped-up from exercise or too many pies, hair cropped short, arms bristling with tatooes. When there was a brief lull in the procession of explosives Billy darted through the entrance and into the bar, which was packed and drunk. Flutes were being played, a drum was being rattled, everyone was singing along to the Loyalist anthems. Billy squeezed through, then moved along the short corridor to Pink's office. He tried the door – but it was locked. Billy cursed. He turned back down the corridor and squeezed back through the punters to the bar itself. He had to shout to make himself heard to the barman.

'I need the key to Pink's office!'

'And who the f**k are you?!'

'Pink sent me – I work for Pink!'

'Houl' on.'

The barman went to the far end of the bar and spoke to a flat-headed guy there, who then walked off. The barman came back along and said, 'Do you want a drink?'

'No, no thanks. Yes, a pint.'

Billy sipped his pint of Harp and moved his mouth in time to the songs. He knew them, of course, every kid of his generation did, but he couldn't bring himself to actually sing them. After a couple of minutes he was tapped on the shoulder. Bull was standing beside him.

'Billy, right?'

'Aye. Pink sent me – he wants some papers from his office.'

'He never said anything to me.'

'He probably didn't have time, he was going into the cop shop.'

'Was he? So they have him.'

'Aye,' said Billy. 'Think so.'

Bull nodded. 'So what does he want?'

'Just some contracts, accounts; doesn't want the peelers getting them.'

Bull snorted. 'They'll have some luck, getting in here.'

'Aye, I know, but when things calm down . . .'

Bull nodded. 'Aye, I suppose. Hold on.' He reached behind the bar, felt around the underside of it, then there was a slight ripping sound. He held up a key with a length of Sellotape attached to it. 'There you go, mate.'

'Cheers,' said Billy, taking it quickly. He nodded at Bull, then hurried down the corridor, opened the door and slipped into the dark office. He flicked the lights on, closed the door behind him and locked it, then rested against it for a moment to catch his breath. It was cool in here, and apparently, for some doubtlessly nefarious reason, sound-proofed. The singing from the bar was almost totally muted. The walls were bare, unlike the bar, which was hung with football pennants, Ulster flags and UDA banners. The air smelled of Pine Fresh. Billy sucked it in. Although it was neither pine nor fresh it was better than the rancid mix of beer and burps and BO and testosterone and petrol that enveloped the rest of the building. He hadn't been in Pink's office before because Pink, believing it to be bugged, had insisted on their previous meetings taking place in a stockroom; so it took him a few moments to locate the safe, sitting on the ground behind Pink's stout desk with a trenchcoat loosely draped over it.

Billy brushed the coat off, then bent to a small digital panel on the front of the safe and typed in the combination from memory. The door swung open. Billy peered inside. Then he stood up and said, 'Holy f***ing shite!'

Billy had brought an A4-sized Manila envelope with him to carry whatever cash Pink had stored in the safe. But it was going to be woefully inadequate. The safe was literally *crammed* with money. It wasn't sitting in neat piles either. It had been crushed inside in crumpled fistfuls, squeezed into every corner. In fact, as soon as he opened the door, cash avalanched out. Billy stared at it. As an accountant, money was just figures to him; he rarely actually handled it. But this. . . there had to be *at least* a million quid here. What was he supposed to do with *that*?

Billy sighed. He had his orders. There was nothing for it but to find some way to transport the money. He checked around the office, opening drawers and cupboards. He looked behind filing cabinets. He found a briefcase, but it was locked and besides, how incongruous would that look, walking through a riot with a briefcase in his hands? He continued his search. At the back of the office there was a small bathroom, just a toilet and sink; but sitting on top of the cistern he found a sports bag with a Nike symbol. He took out a pair of trainers and a sweat-smelling T-shirt and football shorts. Then he knelt back in front of the safe and began filling the bag with money.

It fitted. Just about. He had to struggle with the zip. Then he heaved it up onto his shoulder. A million pounds isn't light. Billy puffed a bit, pushed the safe door closed with his foot, then left Pink's office. He locked the door and handed the key back in to the barman. He shoved his way back through the drinkers and stepped out of the club. The chain of explosives carriers had either retired back into the bar or proceeded down to the front line, but there were still half a dozen or so men in football tops milling around, all of them drinking cans of beer. Billy put his head down and started walking. Iniside his head he began to hum the tune from *Mission Impossible*.

When he was 100 yards away from the club, and approaching the lines of teenagers awaiting the police advance, he saw that they were being spoken to by Bull and two other men. He tried to move past as far away from him as he could, but Bull noticed.

'Get what you want, Billy?' he called across.

Billy kept moving. 'Aye, thanks. See you around.'

'See ya.'

But it was only once he was past them that Bull saw the sports bag over Billy's shoulder.

'Hey – Billy!' Billy looked back, but didn't pause. 'What're you doing with me football gear?'

'What?' asked Billy.

'You've got me f***ing sports bag there, mate.'

'I needed it to carry Pink's stuff. Sorry. I'll drop it back tomorrow.'

Bull was moving towards him now. 'You'll f***ing not, I've footie tonight.'

'I'll drop it back later, then.' He wanted to break into a run, but couldn't.

Bull came jogging up. 'This place'll be chaos later, Billy.'

'Well, can't you use a different bag?'

'No, Billy, that's my bag. Give it here, I'll get one of these dough-nuts to run up to the shop and get you some plastic bags.'

'No, look, really, there's too much for plastic. I'll get it back to you later, honest.'

Bull put his hand on the bag. 'Billy, I'm not asking you, I'm *telling* you.'

Billy moved a couple of steps back, taking the bag with him. 'I swear to God.'

Bull reached out for it again, this time taking a firm grip. 'Give me the f***ing bag.'

'I can't!' Billy suddenly yelled, and yanked it out of Bull's hand. 'Just let me go!' He started walking again, faster, but Bull was on him in an instant. He yanked at the bag, pulling it down off Billy's shoulder. One of the straps came loose and he grabbed that; Billy grabbed the other one. They each tugged at it.

'Let it f***ing go, would you?'

But Billy wouldn't. He was scared out of his wits. Bull now actually *looked* like a bull, all muscle and shoulders and snarling. The gang of kids with their rocks and petrol bombs were watching intently, moving closer as well.

'Billy, what the f**k is wrong with you?! Give me the f***ing bag!' 'No!'

They both went at it again with all their strength, a tug-of-war in which Billy was slowly being dragged forwards, until there was a sudden ripping sound and the base of the bag split from one end to the other. In being torn apart it caused both of them to stumble back-wards and land on their arses. For several moments they sat on the glistening tarmac looking at the tens of thousands of pounds that were spilling out of the rip and blowing away in the wind.

'Jesus Christ!' shouted Bull.

'Oh *God*,' Billy whispered.

Bull sprang to his feet. 'Get it! Get it!' he screamed as the money continued to blow. The kids didn't need a second invitation. As they scrambled after it Billy jumped to his feet and started to walk quickly away. Bull saw him and bawled after him: 'You were f**king ripping us off, you c**t!'

'No!' Billy shouted back, 'I swear to God. Honestly, Pink told me to—'

'F***ing get him!'

Billy broke into a run. He was not a fit man, and ordinarily he would have been caught within a few yards. But everyone was so preoccupied with all the money floating around that the only ones who came after him were two of Bull's comrades who'd been at the pies rather than the weights. As Billy charged down the Shankill Road the pie men, yelling abuse and threats, actually began to gain on him and might well have caught up if they hadn't stopped suddenly. Billy glanced back, surprised, but then when he faced the front again he realised why his pursuers had halted. The police Land Rovers, flanking the water cannon, were beginning to advance along the Shankill Road directly towards him.

105
Checkmate

Jimmy Marsh Mallow put the phone down, then waved Gary McBride over from where he was standing chatting to a colleague by the coffee-machine. Police HQ was abuzz with the news that Pink Harrison had walked in off the street of his own accord and was now in one of the interview rooms practising yoga, meditation or, depending on whom you spoke to, self-administered tantric sex.

'Boss?'

'Change of plans, Gary. Just keep him in there – don't let anyone near him. No coffee, no lunch, no phone calls, all right?'

'All right, boss. What're you thinking?'

'Just keep an eye on him.'

Gary shrugged as Jimmy strode off towards the lifts.

Marsh rubbed his knuckles into his brow as he rode up to the sixth. Tension headache. The doors opened and he marched along to the Chief Constable's outer office. His secretary glanced up with the beginning of a smile, but quickly dropped it when she saw who it was.

'Is he in?' Marsh asked curtly.

'Yes, sir, but he's—'

Jimmy stalked past her and opened the door into Tony Martin's office. The Chief Constable was on the phone, but when he saw Marsh, and registered both the serious look on his face and the fact that he'd by-passed reception, he quickly finished his conversation. Jimmy took a seat opposite him. To one side, on a plasma-screen TV, the rioting continued.

'Jim. I'm told Pink Harrison is downstairs and that he's reading a Gideon Bible at the top of his voice.'

'Yes, he is, and no, he's not.'

'What's he doing then?'

'He's sitting there looking pleased with himself.'

'Why so? Does he know we haven't a shred of evidence yet?'

'No.'

'Does he know George Green has disappeared?'

'Has he?'

'He walked out of his hotel this morning to buy a paper, and hasn't returned.'

'I don't know if Pink knows that.'

'So what *is* he looking so pleased with himself for? Is it because the city has ground to a halt? Because we're stretched to the limit dealing with riots here, there and everywhere?'

'That's possibly a contributing factor.'

'Well, what else then?'

Marsh took a deep breath. 'Because he knows I've been after him all these years, and just when I thought I had a chance of getting him, he's pulled the rug out from under me.'

'I don't understand.'

'Well, sir, it's like this . . .'

And so he began, and as soon as he started the Chief Constable knew it had to be deadly serious because Jimmy Mallow was never one to unburden himself, to give away the smallest personal detail. Yet Marsh was telling him about his wife dying and his daughter trying to help him out by signing him up for a dating agency. He told him about the date he didn't turn up for, the date he walked out on, and finally the date who turned out to be a prostitute. How he tried to rush her out of the house and how she fell down the stairs as a result. How he agreed to pay her and wrote her a cheque, and that now a journalist called Dan Starkey had that cheque and a big exclusive for his scandal rag.

'. . . so I don't think I've any alternative but to offer you my resignation.'

The Chief Constable had been listening with growing disbelief. The only part of it he didn't actually find quite incredible was Jimmy Mallow's offer to resign. 'Well, okay then,' he said.

It sat in the air for several moments.

Then Jimmy said, 'You're accepting it?'

'I don't see that I've got any choice, if what you're telling me is true. Obviously I regret the fact that you feel you have to resign, but given the situation you find yourself in, and in which you have now put the PSNI as a whole, I can really see no alternative.'

Marsh blinked at him. 'I was offering it as a common courtesy. You're under no obligation to accept it.'

'On the contrary, Superintenent, I *am* obliged. Jim, Jimmy, what *on earth* were you thinking of? Prostitutes – you must have known where it would end up.'

'I didn't do anything wrong.'

'That may be, but we live in an age of spin, and you know and I know that this will be spun to make us look bad. What do you expect? A big headline saying *Jimmy Mallow Comes to Aid of Lady of Night Who Falls Downstairs, Pays for Dental Work*? You know as well as I do that it's all about perception, Jimmy, and if our biggest, toughest cop, the one we hold up as a shining example of all that's good and incorruptible about our force steps out of line himself, then we have to come down on him like a ton of bricks.'

'I didn't do anything illegal.'

'That's neither here nor there.'

Jimmy stared at the ground. He had planned to go on for ever. 'There's nothing I can do?'

'I don't think so, Jim. If the press have it, you're pretty much dead in the water. No pun intended.'

'What happens if I stay?'

'You'll be sacked, Jim. You'll probably lose your pension.'

'And if I go?'

'We'll say we understand your decision and offer our full support. You'll keep your pension.'

'What about Pink Harrison?'

'Ultimately I'm responsible for authorising the raids, and seeing as how they've thus far achieved nothing, apart from millions of pounds' worth of riot damage, then I imagine we'll have to release him without charge. The powers-that-be will want someone to answer for it, and that someone will be me. So, I'll probably see you at the unemployment exchange.'

'We can't just let him go.'

'We may have no choice.'

'But I *know* that he did this.'

'Instincts don't stand up in court, Jimmy.'

'The evidence is there, Chief. Somewhere.'

The Chief Constable sighed. 'I'm not your Chief any more, Jimmy,' he said. 'If it's there we'll find it.'

'So that's it, then? Thirty-five years down the Swanee?'

The Chief Constable nodded slowly. Then he stood up and offered Jimmy Mallow his hand. Jimmy looked at it, then turned and strode out of the office.

Pink didn't even bother looking up as the interview-room door opened, so the punch came as quite a surprise. It connected with the left side of his jaw and knocked him flying back in his seat, which toppled over, throwing him to the ground. Pink looked groggily up and saw

Jimmy Mallow standing over him. The door remained open and other cops, alerted by the noise, were already crowding around the opening. None of them made a move to stop Mallow as he advanced again, towering over the prostrate paramilitary.

'It's not checkmate, Pink, do you hear me? It's not even *close*.'

Then Mallow turned on his heel. The cops at the door jumped out of his way, then watched as Jimmy Mallow walked out of the cop shop for the last time, his head high, his stare intense, and for all they knew, his whole being still formidable and unbroken.

106
The Balcony Scene

It was only when Linda showed Margaret the impressive fridge for the third time that Margaret thought to herself, *Do you know something, girl? She's drunk as a skunk.* Linda had conducted the tour of the penthouse apartment just a little too quickly, moving ahead of Margaret through the rooms without allowing her the luxury of a proper look, but her spiel was coherent enough, and she was certainly enthusiastic. But dwelling on the fridge – although it *was* a nice fridge – was a little bit weird, and it was only when Margaret felt obliged to poke her head into the ice-maker for a third time that she caught the whiff of alcohol on Linda's breath, and then it suddenly all made sense. There was no harm, of course, in having a glass of wine with your lunch, and it was a nice touch to offer a glass to your clientèle, but the fridge was stacked with half a dozen bottles, two of which were empty, and it was suddenly clear that Linda must have had a lot of viewers today and enjoyed a glass with each of them.

Only on this third trip to the fridge, did Linda offer Margaret herself a glass. She weaved a little as she crossed to the opposite counter and pulled two paper cups out of a plastic bag. She opened a fresh bottle from the fridge, twisting the wire and popping the cork, and began to pour.

'And what about some cake?' Linda asked.

'Cake?'

'Yes, cake.' This time she actually staggered as she moved back to the counter, as if her previous movements had been an elaborate act of defiance against the cumulative effects of the wine, but she'd now given up the fight. She reached up and carefully lifted a chocolate cake down from a high-up shelf. As she turned with it she staggered again and Margaret was forced to step sharply out of the way as Linda basically fell towards the counter. The plate the cake was sitting on cracked against the greystone top but didn't break; the sponge undulated slightly, but was otherwise unharmed.

'Looks lovely,' said Margaret.

'Should be. I was up all night baking it.'

'You were?'

'Absolutely. Put my heart and soul into it. I made it for someone special.' She giggled to herself. 'But then I couldn't wait, and took a big bite out of it.'

Now that she could see the full circumference of the cake, Margaret noted that some of it was indeed missing. There were no neat edges, as there would have been if someone had merely cut out a slice. But there *was* a definite hole, and as she looked closer she could just about make out slight indentations which she thought could only have been made by teeth.

'You really did take a bite,' Margaret observed.

'I know, I forgot to bring a knife.' Linda giggled. 'Take a bite, why don't *you*?'

'No, really, I'm fine. Are you, ahm, fine, Linda?'

'Oh yes, I'm fine.' She took a glug of her wine. 'I'm fine all right – why *wouldn't* I be fine?'

'Well, I don't know.'

'After all, I've got this wonderful job, and I'm going to sell you this apartment because I'm absolutely fine and *absolutely* at the top of my game. Come on, let's take a look at the view.'

Linda snatched up her paper cup, spilling some of it, and meandered towards the bedroom. She pulled the sliding door to the balcony with a little too much force and it smacked into the frame and rebounded back at her. Linda laughed and tried it again, a little more gently, before stepping out into what would have been fresh air if it hadn't been for the acrid smoke drifting across from East Belfast. Margaret took a deep breath, then followed her out.

Linda leaned on the edge. Margaret joined her.

'Look what they're doing,' said Linda, staring out at the plumes of smoke. 'The stupid bas***ds.'

'Yeah, I know,' said Margaret.

'Fighting over nothing.'

Margaret nodded.

'They should catch themselves on, the ar***oles.'

'Yes, they should.'

'Because this is a great wee city, given half the chance.'

'Yes, it is.'

'So what about Walter then?' Linda asked abruptly.

'Walter? What about him?'

'Isn't he just the bee's knees?'

'I suppose he is.'

'You two getting married?'

'It's early days for that.'

'Well, you should, although I don't think bees actually have knees,' Linda cackled, then suddenly lost her grip on her cup. They both watched it hurtle to the ground far below. 'Oh sh**e!'

Margaret said, 'I'll get you another.'

Linda clearly didn't need another, but as she would doubtless have got it anyway, Margaret volunteered, intending to water it down. But just as she extracted another paper cup from the bag, the doorbell rang. Linda, with the wind blowing about her, couldn't hear it on the balcony, so Margaret went to the door herself and opened it.

'Margaret,' said Walter. His eyes were wide and his face flushed.

'Walter?' said Margaret. 'What are you doing here?'

'I thought . . . is she here?'

'Yes, of course.'

'Has she said anything?'

'She's *pissed*. She's blathering on about this and that, and I just want out of here, but what are you doing here?'

'I just thought – second opinion, you know?'

'Aw, that's sweet.'

She leaned forward and kissed him. He kissed her back, but he broke it off quickly. 'If she's pissed, let's just sneak off, forget about the apartment.'

Margaret rolled her eyes. 'If only. Come on, come and say hello, then we'll get out of here soon as we can.' She took hold of his arm and pulled him into the apartment, then led him through the kitchen – his eyes settling briefly on the chocolate cake – and into the bedroom, where she announced, 'Look what the cat dragged in.'

Walter followed gingerly behind her. Linda saw him, and immediately let out a crazy kind of a bark. 'The chief bee-keeper himself!' she exclaimed. 'Walter! How're you doing?'

Walter held up a placatory hand. 'Fine, Linda, fine. How are you?'

'Oh, I'm fine too Walter. Isn't that great? We're all just *fine*.'

'That's er . . . good . . .'

'Do you want some cake, Walter?'

'No, thanks.'

'Ach, go on, I made it special. Then you could have your cake *and* eat it.' She laughed again, then turned away to stare out over the city again.

'What's she on about?' Margaret whispered.

'Maybe she's upset I didn't buy the apartment. Come on, let's just go.'

'We can't leave her like this,' Margaret hissed. She stepped up and touched Linda's arm. 'I'll just get Walter a wee drink, eh?' Linda didn't respond. Margaret shook her head at Walter, then whispered, 'Keep an eye on her,' as she made her way back inside.

As soon as Margaret was out of sight, Walter moved sharply up beside Linda and asked, 'What're you playing at?'

'Playing?' Linda snapped, her look withering, 'I'm not the one playing. You and her having it off.'

'We're just friends, Linda.'

'Yeah, *right*.'

'We are, honestly. Don't do this, please.'

'You love her, don't you?'

'I hardly know her.'

'But you don't love me.'

'I hardly know you either.'

'Well, you f***ing should, all the things we've been doing.'

'I know, I know. Look, I'll sort this out, honestly I will. Please, just let me handle it.'

Linda shook her head. 'Look at you. What the *hell* was I thinking? You're just a big barrel of lard.'

Walter nodded. 'That's right, that's right. Look – I'm just going to get my drink.' He hurried back through the bedroom and into the kitchen, where he took Margaret firmly by the arm and said, 'That's it, we're leaving. She's friggin' mental. Come on.'

'But—'

'Come *on*!'

Margaret grabbed her bag and allowed herself to be propelled towards the front door. Walter was just opening it when they were stopped in their tracks by a shrill scream of *'WALTER!!!!!!!!!'*

Margaret looked at Walter, then raced back to the balcony.

'Oh my good Jesus!' she shouted, and a moment later Walter saw the reason why.

Linda had climbed up onto the rail. She had her eyes closed and was holding onto the far wall for support, but one foot was hanging out over the edge already and she was leaning forward, preparing to let herself fall.

'Oh *Christ*,' said Walter.

107
Emergency Services

The phone rang and rang, for nearly a minute. Eventually it was answered with a terse, 'Yes, what is it now?' and Walter was taken momentarily by surprise.

'Is that 999?'

'Yes, it is.'

'Aren't you supposed to say *"Emergency, which service, please?"*?'

There was a sigh from the other end. 'Yes. Sorry. Which service, please?'

'All of them, I think. There's a woman here threatening to jump off a ledge. She's at the top of—'

'Your name?'

'What does it matter what my name is?'

'In case it's a hoax. Sir, Belfast is in a state of chaos.'

'Right. Right. Walter North.'

'And your phone number?'

Walter gave her his mobile number, then the address of the apartment block.

'Sir, that's going to be about forty minutes.'

'Forty minutes? Christ, I'm not ordering a pizza, there's a woman trying to kill herself out there.'

'Well, I'm afraid there won't be anyone free until then. Have you tried The Samaritans?'

'What, do they have ladders and safety nets?'

'There's no need for that attitude, sir.'

'Okay, right, sorry. Just be as quick as you can, all right?'

'Yes, sir.'

Walter cut the line and returned to the bedroom. He didn't dare step out onto the balcony again in case it set Linda to jumping. She remained standing on the rail, with one foot dangling over the edge, and holding onto the wall with one hand. The wall was exposed brick, so there were only the grooves between them to hold onto, which wasn't much, considering the strength of the wind so high up.

Margaret was still out there talking quietly and calmly to her. She said, 'Is there anyone you want me to call?'

'No!'

'Your parents?'

'Dead!'

'A boyfriend?'

'Hah!'

'Please, Linda, don't do this.'

'Why not?!'

'Because! Life is wonderful!'

'That's easy for you to say.'

'Linda – please. Look, I was stuck in a disastrous marriage and I walked out of it, but I ended up living in a real shithole with a dead end job and going nowhere. But I didn't give up, and now I've started selling my designs and I'm buying this apartment and my whole life is turning around. I'd even given up on meeting a nice man, and then Walter comes along.'

'Hah!'

'My point is, it *can* happen. I don't know what's worrying you, if it's your job or your lovelife, but my point is, it can change – but if you jump, well, it can't.'

'Don't you think I know that?' Linda snapped. 'I'm not brain dead.'

'Not *yet*. Look, I've met you before, and you weren't like this. You were lovely, really good at your job. You're so pretty, my God, you could model one of my dresses.'

'Yeah, *right*.' Linda bent out into the wind, and it caught her hair. She shivered. 'You just don't understand.'

'Well, tell me.'

'I just want it to end.'

'But why?'

'Why do you think? Because my life is rubbish and there's no point.'

'But it's not rubbish, Linda, and even if it is, it can get better. You've had too much to drink, that's all, and you're upset about something. It'll all look better in the morning.'

'No, it won't! That's the f***ing point! I'm a walking disaster area! Every time I meet someone, I give them everything and they just pee all over me.'

'Well, some of them pay good money for that.'

'*What?*'

'Look, it was just a joke.'

'You're making a joke? I'm about to jump off here and you're making a f***ing *joke*?!'

'I'm sorry, I'm just trying to lighten the mood.'

'Well, *don't*!' She shook her head violently. 'Where is he? Where's he hiding?'

'Walter? He's inside.'

'Why's he inside?'

'He says he has a habit of saying inappropriate things, so he thought it was better to let me do the talking.'

'Christ, you're like two peas in a pod. You deserve each other.'

'Well, doesn't that prove my point? There's someone for everyone, Linda, but there's no one if you jump.'

'And that's *my* point! I've had dozens of someones and I've loved dozens of someones, but I don't get it back, so what's the f***ing point? Tell me, what is the f***ing point?'

A mile away, Jimmy Marsh Mallow was parked halfway up the Newtownards Road. The only other cars visible for 100 yards in either direction were burning. A gang of kids carrying sticks and bricks was coming towards him. He wanted them to attack. He wanted a reason to get out and smack their stupid heads. He still had his gun. His head was throbbing and his heart was broken. He would shoot them. They drew closer and closer. He could hear their excited, bolshie talk. He rolled down his window so he could catch the slightest abuse. So he could look them in the eye and dare them to make the first move.

Then they passed on by.

Didn't even look.

Marsh rested his head on the steering-wheel and closed his eyes. His police radio crackled incessantly, but he couldn't bring himself to turn it off. There were appeals for support, reports of police cars burning and officers injured. It seemed as if there was scarcely a part of the city that wasn't in crisis. Even the Falls and the Ardoyne and Ballymurphy, all Republican strongholds, were getting in on the act, taking advantage of the fact that the security forces were stretched. Banks were being robbed, shops looted.

All because of Pink Harrison.

Marsh couldn't get that vision of him out of his head, sitting on the desk, pretending to meditate, that gloating smirk. Marsh had come out with big words, telling him it wasn't checkmate, but in reality it was. He was no longer a police officer. His offer to resign had unexpectedly been accepted. With all the trouble going on, and *Belfast Confidential* being a weekly magazine rather than a daily paper, he had perhaps a few days' grace before the whole Province knew what an idiot he'd

419

been, getting involved with a hooker; knew what an arrogant prick he was, beating her up. Humiliated. Hung out to dry. Career in ruins.

He thought of his daughter, thought of his wife. They would be ashamed. The hard times he had given them – such a hypocrite.

On the radio, the dispatcher said, 'Is there *anyone* free to cover the jumper?'

There were no volunteers.

Then one car responded: 'Maybe in twenty minutes. Give me the address.'

'Apartment Twenty-four, Towerview – that's the big new one on the river. Jumper's name is Linda Wray.'

Marsh turned the volume down and then, finally, off. He had to accept he was no longer a part of it; it had *nothing* to do with him any more. Whether it was rampaging rioters or Pink Harrison or even this Linda Wray jumping out of her apartment, it was none of his business. In just a couple of minutes he had gone from being one of the most feared but successful cops in the history of the city to being no one, a nobody, a has-been, a laughing stock.

But then he thought: Linda Wray . . . do I know that name?

It came to him. He was always good with names. Linda Wray, he thought. I left a Linda Wray sitting in that restaurant. *Could it possibly be the same one?*

Christ! He could see the headlines in *Belfast Confidential* already. *Jimmy Mallow beats up hooker! Next week – Jimmy Mallow drives woman to suicide!*

That's how scandal-sheets like that worked; never mind the truth, just pump it till it's dry.

Marsh started the car and pulled out. He was going to turn up for his date with Linda and apologise for being very, very late.

108

Suicide is Painful

Margaret, her nerves shattered, stood by the front door, keeping an eye out for the police or ambulance or Fire Brigade. She had had to physically push Walter out onto the balcony to keep Linda talking. She could understand that he didn't trust himself not to say something stupid, because she was a bit that way herself, but she needed a rest and there was no one else and she couldn't leave that poor woman all alone out there. She thought, *That could so easily be me. Just a few more knockbacks, a few more kicks in the teeth, it really could be me. Except I can't stand heights.*

She would have found some other way. Not slitting her wrists. And no putting her head in the oven, because she'd heard that the gas that was piped into houses these days wasn't lethal. It probably still exploded if you opened the valve and lit a match, but she couldn't imagine doing that. She didn't want anyone to have to pick bits of her off a wall. Nor drinking bleach or taking an overdose (she found it hard enough to get a couple of Paracetamol down). If she had to go she'd want to do it nicely. And pain-free. Perhaps sitting in bed watching *Casablanca* and stuffing herself with pink marshmallows. A sugar-rush suicide.

Then she had a terrible thought, and immediately cursed herself for having it: what would it do to the value of the property if Linda Wray did jump? If it became known that the estate agent had committed suicide, would it drive the price down, and make it easier to buy? Despite Margaret's great hopes for the future, purchasing it now would still be a bit of a stretch. She hadn't even really thought about a mortgage or what type to go for. Linda, who probably knew all about them, was a bit busy at the moment. Walter was into property, but he didn't seem able to make his mind up about anything. The one person she probably could depend on to give her good advice was the one person she had no intention of turning to – Billy. She didn't feel any sympathy for him at all now, losing his job like that. Perhaps his bosses weren't concerned about the extra expense involved in making him a junior partner – perhaps they just realised what a prick he was.

Margaret checked her watch. Fifteen minutes since they'd dialled 999.

Poor Linda. Maybe she just needed a good girlie chat. A night out on the town.

Looking back into the apartment, Margaret's eyes fell on the chocolate cake. She glanced at the lift doors, just down the hall a bit. No lights yet. She darted across the kitchen, prevaricated for just a moment over the lack of cutlery, then scooped up a handful of cake and bundled it into her mouth. She hurried back to the doorway. It was *lovely*.

Out on the balcony Walter said, 'Is this because of me?'

'No, Walter.'

'Well, what then?'

'Everything. You're just the . . .'

'Catalyst?'

. . . final straw. I've been thinking about you, Walter, taking a really long hard look at you. And what I think it is, is that you're surprised to find yourself with two women interested in you – and you don't know what the hell to do. I have to presume you like having sex with me?'

'I do, I do.'

'So I'm guessing you're maybe not having sex with her?'

'I'm not, I'm not.'

'But you really want to, except you don't want to throw the baby out with the bathwater.'

'It's not like that.'

'Well, what *is* it like?!'

'Okay! Yes, it *is* like that!' Walter gripped the handrail. 'Linda, you're right, it's exactly like that. I've never been in this position before, and I'm confused.'

'You're shallow.'

'Yes, I'm shallow.'

'And you're two-faced.'

'Oh God, yes, I'm two-faced.'

'And I'm standing here, and I'm going to jump in a minute, I swear to God, and I know exactly what you're thinking.'

'You do? I mean, I'm praying you won't.'

'Well, maybe you are and maybe you aren't.'

'What does that mean?'

'You're praying that if I do jump, I won't tell her in there about us before I do.'

'Well, I would appreciate it. I mean, I one hundred per cent don't want you to jump under any circumstances, and I don't give a damn what you say to Margaret. It's such a waste, you are lovely.'

'Don't! I've had enough of your crap! I really thought we had something.'

'We did! We do!'

'B***ocks!'

Walter sighed. 'Linda, don't do this. Please. I didn't mean to hurt you.'

Linda shook her head sadly. 'Don't flatter yourself, Walter. It could have been anyone. I just always dive in at the deep end and the truth is I just *can't* swim.'

'You should try armbands.'

'*What?*'

'I mean, no one can swim at first, but with the right support, with lessons . . .'

'Lessons in love, Walter? *Are* there armbands for that?'

Walter shrugged. 'Please, Linda, don't.'

'I've just had enough.' Her legs were tired now; she was cold. She wanted to get it over with.

Margaret watched the lift light move towards the penthouse floor. It had to be the Emergency Services – none of the other apartments were yet occupied. The doors opened, but there was just one man standing there, a middle-aged guy with a stern expression.

'Oh,' Margaret said, 'I was expecting—'

'Where is she?' the man said curtly.

'Down here.' She nodded towards the apartment's open door. The man set off towards it. Margaret hurried after him. 'Excuse me, but who are you? Where's everyone else?'

'Police,' said the man. 'The others are on their way.'

He turned into the apartment. Margaret followed in after him. 'And are you trained in this? She's very fragile.'

'I'm an experienced hostage negotiator.'

'She's not a hostage.'

'Isn't she? She's a hostage to fate.'

Margaret stared at him. That was a bit cryptic, she thought. But maybe that was what was needed. Something deep and philosophical to get Linda in off her ledge rather than the trite and facile arguments she'd been coming out with.

'This way?' the man asked.

'I'll show you.'

She led him across the kitchen, and through the bedroom. Walter

423

was standing just inside the doorway leading out to the balcony. He glanced at Jimmy Marsh Mallow, who looked vaguely familiar, then said: 'She told me to go in. After speaking to me, she said that if she hadn't been suicidal already, she certainly was now. I'm sorry, I did my best.'

Margaret took his hand. 'I know. It's okay. It's not your fault.'

'Yes, it is,' Walter said weakly, but she didn't pick up on it.

Jimmy Mallow said, 'I'm going out. I'm going to close the door behind me. When the rest of them get here, tell them not to disturb us.'

Margaret nodded. 'Good luck,' she said.

Marsh just looked at her, then stepped out onto the balcony and pulled the door closed behind him.

109

Last Rites

Redmond sat disconsolately in the main thoroughfare at Belfast Central Station, waiting for a train that wasn't coming. His plan was to go to his late brother's parish house and rest up, get his head together. His life of late hadn't been so much a roller-coaster as a ghost train, and he needed to climb off. Just pull the blankets up over him and lie undisturbed for a while. By assuming his brother's identity he hoped also to inherit the quiet, quaint, undemanding life of a parish priest. The only demands on his time would be the occasional baptism or funeral. He might listen to confessions, secure in the knowledge that he himself had committed acts one thousand times worse than anything the local farmers' daughters could imagine. He would tend the parish garden and grow his own vegetables. His old life was over.

There were several dozen passengers stranded by the cancellation of the entire network service milling around, unsure what to do with themselves. It had been dangerous enough just getting to the station and none of them were in the mood to venture out again. Most of them were anxious to get on the Dublin Express. They had been told that it was unlikely to run at all, as the smouldering remains of the Bangor–Belfast train were still being attended to by the Fire Brigade on the tracks below, but as *unlikely* wasn't an unequivocal *no*, they chose to wait in hope. The bar, at least, was open, but like most railway station drinking establishments it seemed more like a good place to get into a fight or be robbed than to enjoy a relaxing drink. Its atmosphere was heavy with neglect and violence, so most of the travellers were disinclined to stay after taking an initial look. They sat around the tiled plaza, chatting amongst themselves, strangers mostly, united by circumstance. Redmond kept himself to himself. He stared morosely at the ground and thought about his beautiful wife making love to a man who made carrot cake.

There was a bit of a commotion down towards the barriers leading to the platforms and for a moment Redmond's heart soared in hope that

425

the train schedule had been reinstated; certainly several of the stranded passengers were now hurrying forward. But as he looked closer he saw that they weren't approaching the ticket barrier, but rather were gathering to the right of it. Then some of what they were saying began to drift back across the echoing spaces towards him.

'I called – they said it would be half an hour at least.'

'Does anyone know how to do this?'

'You squeeze his nose and breathe into his mouth.'

'Christ, he smells like a brewery.'

'Don't say that, he could be your dad.'

'Right, here goes . . .'

There was silence for the next few minutes, and then someone said: 'It's no use. He's a gonner.'

'Does he have any ID? We should phone.'

'Here, look. A pension book, isn't it? He's Fintan Hennessey. I don't see any address or anything.'

'Christ.'

'We can't just leave him like this.'

Their voices dropped. Redmond looked up from studying the ground to find that several of them were looking at him. Then a girl, a teenager, in shorts and sandals, came hurrying up.

'Father, Father,' she said. 'There's an old man dead or dying over here. Could you say the Last Rites for him?'

Redmond blinked at her. 'Well, I'm not sure. He may not even be a Catholic, and I wouldn't want to send him off with the wrong details. It would be like putting the wrong destination on your luggage.'

The girl's eyes widened a little. 'Father, he's called Fintan Hennessey, and he had these in his pocket.' She held up a set of rosary beads. 'I think he's one of yours.'

Redmond reluctantly got to his feet and followed the girl back across to the small group of passengers. They parted before him, revealing the very obviously dead body of Fintan Hennessey. He was an old man in an ill-fitting farmer's suit; bald on top but with bushy hair on the sides. There was a rolled *Irish News* sticking out of one pocket.

Redmond knelt beside Fintan Hennessey and made the sign of the cross, then began to administer the Last Rites. In fact, he began to mumble. Redmond was aware of the concept, but had no real notion of the detail, of the actual words and phrases and acts that went to make up your official, approved Last Rites. It wasn't as if it made any difference: Fintan Hennessey was dead as a door knob.

'Father?' Redmond looked up. One of the passengers, a solid-looking man in a yellow wind-cheater said, 'Sorry, Father, but could you speak up a bit?'

Redmond shook his head. 'Son, it's between me and him and God.'

'I know that, Father, but still – I'm taking these young people on a retreat to Navan,' he nodded around the little group, and Redmond suddenly realised, with a dreadful sinking feeling, that they were indeed a *group*, 'and it would be tremendously inspiring for them to see this act of Absolution.'

Redmond nodded. He gave the sign of the cross again, then renewed his attempt on the Last Rites, but it was scarcely any louder or clearer.

'I'm sorry, Father, but we're, uh, just not getting it.'

'Getting what?!' Redmond exploded suddenly. 'It's not a fu— a floor-show!'

'We just want to be part of his journey.'

The little group all nodded and crossed themselves. Redmond sighed, and bent to the task again. His words grew louder, but conversely, less coherent. When he was finally done, Redmond stood and brushed dust off his knees. 'All righty,' he said.

'But . . . surely, you've not said the half of it?' the man in the yellow wind-cheater complained.

'How do you know, if you couldn't hear me?'

Redmond gave him a rather misplaced look of triumph, then bristled, ready for action as the man stepped forward. 'Could I have a wee word, Father?' Before he could move, the man had slipped an arm through his and pulled right up beside him. He whispered into his ear, 'Please, Father, it would be *very* instructive for us to hear what you're saying. This is the living Catholic Church in action. Some of these guys are considering entering the priesthood, but they need to see this done, and done well.'

'I've done it – *twice* now.'

'Just once more, Father, *please*.' He wasn't threatening, exactly; he was just very, very disappointed.

Redmond, despite his growing anger, felt disappointed himself. He was making such a hash of his pledge to Damian. He'd already pursued his wife's lover and only barely restrained himself from attacking him, then he *had* actually attacked two wee lads, even if they were asking for it. Now here he was, flummoxed by his first attempt to act like a real priest. He should just rip off the collar now, admit the deception and give himself up for arrest.

He looked at the little group, so young and hopeful and so clearly impressionable. His own soul might be damned, but how many others was it within his power to damage?

Redmond sank to his knees again. He stared at the poor, pallid features of the late Fintan Hennessey, then glanced up at the man in the yellow wind-cheater, forlornly hoping for some last-minute reprieve – and his own heart almost stopped. For the man's face was no longer stern and disapproving, it was no longer even *his own* face, it was *Damian's*, staring down at him, smiling, nodding encouragement. His ghostly lips weren't moving, yet Redmond could hear his voice, soft and familiar. 'You know this, Redmond, you really know this.'

Redmond felt tears in his eyes. He knew that it wasn't Damian, that he wasn't hearing his brother's sweet voice, that it was jet lag and lack of food and sleep, or some kind of weird cocaine flashback, but he couldn't shake the image or the voice, gently imploring him. He forced himself to look away, to look back at the body of Fintan Hennessey. He raised his hands again and made the sign of the cross, and when he spoke, the words were suddenly, unaccountably there. 'God the Father of mercies,' he began, his voice bold and true, 'through the death and resurrection of His Son has reconciled the world to Himself and sent the Holy Spirit among us for the forgiveness of sins . . .' Adrenaline surged through him. *I know it! I fu**ing know it!*

'Through the ministry of the Church may God give you pardon and peace, and I absolve you from all of your sins, in the name of the Father, and of the Son, and of the Holy Spirit. Amen.'

Redmond closed his eyes briefly to signal that the performance was over. When he looked up, there were tears in the eyes of the watching group, the man in the yellow wind-cheater was nodding appreciatively, and even Fintan Hennessey looked a little more at peace with himself.

Redmond felt *fantastic*. He almost wished there was a big bomb or something so he could do some more. He climbed back to his feet, nodded around the little group, solemnly clasped his hands, then passed through them, grinning beatifically.

110
Billy Whizz

Billy charged about his apartment, packing clothes into his Gucci suit-cases, fully expecting to hear at any moment the thunder of footsteps on stairs, for the door to burst open and for Bull or any one of Pink Harrison's other cronies to rush in, guns blazing.

I am a dead man.

I am a dead, dead, dead, dead man.

I did nothing wrong, yet I am a dead man.

There was no other possible way to look at it. He had been sent to Pink's Shankill Road headquarters to retrieve money, and he had lost it through no fault of his own. A million pounds. At least. What hadn't been gathered up by rioters was probably still floating around up in the stratosphere. Some farmer in Armagh would wake in the morning and find he had a new cash-crop.

His only saving grace was that, as far as he knew, Pink was still in the police station, and therefore *incommunicado*. He would be unable to issue orders for Billy's immediate execution. Then: *Oh, who am I kidding!* He'll have a solicitor who'll be feeding him news of how all the rioting is going on. And he isn't going to mention Billy Gilmore losing a million quid?

Oh, I am truly a dead man!

Billy crammed in socks and ties and pants and suits and shirts and photos of Margaret. These were the things he needed. But the things he *wanted* – they were all around, and he could take none of them. His sixty-inch plasma TV, his top-of-the-range computer, his microwave which blasted food so quickly it rendered the cooking instructions on the side of tins woefully inadequate. His fridge with the ice-making facility. How many kitchens in *Europe* even boasted such a fridge? He had virtually limitless ice *whenever* he wanted it, while the plebs out there were still struggling with little plastic trays which delivered *twelve* cubes at a time. These electrical marvels weren't just things, they were *his* things; they existed beyond a simple twelve-month warranty; they were the very symbols of his success. He had become one with his luxury goods; they identified and quantified and represented who and what he was.

And in the same moment, they were utterly worthless.

Because he could never return here.

He must leave this apartment, this city, this country, taking with him only what he could carry. Billy Gilmore, twenty years an accountant, married, defined by his spending power, came down to nothing more than a couple of designer suitcases and the trousers he stood up in.

Then he remembered what someone had said to him, he forgot who: that there would always be a demand for accountants and undertakers. He had certificates, diplomas; he needed to take those with him so that no matter what corner of the world he washed up in, he had evidence of his qualifications.

Billy hurried into his back bedroom where he kept three filing cabinets full of his personal papers, all scrupulously indexed. He found his qualifications quickly, but in extracting them his eyes fell on the folders devoted to Pink Harrison's business affairs. What to do with them? The way his luck was running, they would be seized upon by the police as evidence of his own criminal collusion with the paramilitary gang leader, with the result that he would not only be on the run from Pink, but also Special Branch, or for all he knew of his ultimate destination, Interpol.

Better to destroy them, surely?

When Billy flicked open the top folder, meaning to quickly analyse how incriminating the documents could be, his eyes immediately fell on the letter Pink had signed, granting him power of attorney over the companies and accounts he had set up to launder or hide the profits from his many shady business dealings.

This gave Billy pause for thought.

Billy had been on a reasonable wage at the office, but lately he'd been spending more than he earned, secure in the knowledge that he would soon be able to pay off whatever debts he had with the hike in wages he'd get when he made junior partner. With that gone, and the freelance work for Pink also gone for good, how was he to finance his life on the run? He couldn't just walk into a new job and a new house, and he'd be damned if he was going to slum it in some dodgy hostel while he found his feet in some unfamiliar city.

He had lost a million pounds of Pink Harrison's money already that day. What possible difference could a few hundred pounds more make? Or even a few thousand?

I Predict A Riot

Might as well be shot for a sheep as a lamb.

With any luck, Pink would be so mad over the missing million, he wouldn't even notice a few thousand being siphoned off from some obscure account he was barely even aware of anyway

I put my career on the line for him, Billy thought. I just need a few grand to get me started. Ten, tops.

Did he dare? He was soaked in sweat even thinking about it. But what choice did he have? Was he going to sit here and wait for Bull to arrive, and then try to reason with him? If Bull didn't shoot him in the head straight away, then the best he could possibly hope for would be a slight delay, just long enough for him to be dragged back to the Rangers Supporters Club and hideously tortured. *Then* he would be shot in the head.

It wasn't as if moving Pink's money around different accounts was new to him. He had all the passwords and access codes. So all he was doing was moving the money to a different account. He wouldn't even have to speak to anyone. He could do it all over the internet.

Billy powered up the computer. He quickly accessed the first of Pink's foreign accounts, based in the Hellenic Bank in Nicosia, Cyprus. He typed in the relevant codes, authorising a transfer of ten thousand pounds to his own personal account with the Northern Bank in Belfast. It was just a trial, to see if it worked. He hesitated over the *send* instruction. Outside, a car door slammed. Billy raced to the window, but saw that it was just a neighbour carrying in groceries. He calmed himself, then returned to the computer, took a deep breath, and pressed the button.

Done.

He checked his watch: it was after 3 p.m. He knew from past experience that electronic transfers, although claiming to be instantaneous, were still quite often authorised by hand, and that if instructions weren't communicated by say, lunchtime, it would quite often be the next day before the money actually appeared in the desired account. Or perhaps they were a little more efficient in Cyprus.

Still, ten grand – it was more than enough to get him started, cash in hand.

The thing was, now that he had started, he could hardly stop himself. He began to transfer money out of every single one of Pink's accounts, sometimes channelling it into different accounts within the same bank, sometimes into entirely new accounts in different banks in different countries. Before he knew it he had all but emptied every one of Pink's secret hideaways – at least those he operated for him – only leaving token amounts in them to keep them open. When Billy finally glanced at his watch he was amazed and somewhat distressed to discover that nearly two hours had passed. And yet he couldn't leave it; a kind of fever was upon him. He next found his way into Pink's own private accounts with the Northern and drained those as well.

Finally he stood, exhausted, but also exhilarated. He would no longer be shot as a lamb, but as a huge flock of sheep. Very, very rich sheep. Totting it all up, Billy reckoned he had siphoned over three million pounds out of Pink Harrison's many accounts. He giggled. It wasn't a maniacal giggle, but it wasn't far short. He switched off the computer. He pulled on his jacket and lifted his Gucci luggage. He took a final look around the apartment. Leaving the plasma TV, the ice-making fridge and the nuclear microwave now didn't feel quite so bad. Before, it had felt so dreadful because he sensed he would never again achieve such a level of luxury. But now with money in the bank, many banks, anything was possible. Even life.

111
The Balcony Scene

'I don't know what you think you're going to achieve,' Linda said as Jimmy Marsh Mallow pulled the balcony door closed, 'but you're on a hiding to nothing. I'm taking one more look at this stinking, messed-up city and then I'm jumping.'

Her legs were *really* aching now, but not half as much as her head from all the drinking, and her heart, from all the disappointment. She peered down at the ground far below. At least she would be spared the embarrassment of having a crowd witness her plummet to a bloody, pulpy death. The apartments were empty, the builders that remained on site had been sent home because of the trouble, and the emergency services, to judge by the sky, were detained elsewhere. Just her and her soul and this hefty-looking man in his out-of-date suit and polished shoes, leaning on the rail. She wasn't sure if he was a cop or a doctor or what. She wondered if he was man enough to say no when sex was offered at a price, because that's what she'd done, sold herself in order to flog a flat – she could see that now. Cheap.

He said, 'How are you doing, Linda?'

Linda snorted. 'You're not talking me down.'

'No intention of it,' said Marsh.

'Yeah. Right.'

'No, really. I just thought, before you jump, I should apologise.'

'For *what*?'

'Well, there's a bit of a story to it.'

'Can we cut to the chase then? Because I'm just about ready to go.'

'Oh right. Well. Sure, it'll keep.'

'What do you mean, it'll keep? I'm about to *jump*!'

'I mean, it's not that important. To me – maybe, but not to you.'

A gust of wind caught her suddenly and she wobbled. She had to dig her fingers into the tiniest grooves in the mortar between the bricks to maintain her position. Steadied, she saw that the man was staring intently at the ground below, and apparently hadn't noticed that she'd nearly fallen.

'Who are you?' Linda asked. 'Police?' Marsh gave a little shrug. 'Or like that *Cracker* Robbie Coltrane? You needn't think you're going to just bullshit me to safety.'

Marsh turned a little towards her. 'You don't recognise me?'

'Should I?'

'Well, you've seen me before, one way or another – I'm pretty sure of that.'

She studied his features, and decided quickly that he *was* sort of familiar, but she had no idea where from. Maybe he owned the building, or had once worked in her office. 'Like I care,' she said.

Marsh shook his head. 'Sure you do, and I'll tell you, if you let me, but it's kind of roundabout and like you say, you have an appointment.' Marsh did not doubt that Linda Wray was serious about jumping. But it was a calculated guess, not to mention a sweeping generalisation about women, that she would not want to die curious.

'*Okay* – tell me.'

'You're sure?'

'*Yes.*'

'Only I wouldn't want to keep you from anything.'

She snapped, 'Just f***ing tell me!' but even with it, there was a trace of a smile.

'Well,' said Marsh, 'I'm Jimmy Mallow. Head of the CID, possibly the second most powerful police officer in Belfast, and certainly the most experienced.'

'Am I supposed to be impressed?'

'Not at all, because it's not true. Not any more. Not as of about thirty minutes ago.'

'Thirty minutes?'

'Aye. I got the Royal order of the boot.'

'So you're not a policeman.'

'No.'

'So what are you doing here?'

'Like I say, I came to apologise.'

'For *what*?'

'Well, that's what I'm trying to tell you, if you would ever shut up and give me a chance.' He raised his eyebrows. She looked away, at the ground below. 'So do you want to hear me out or not?'

'Yes! If you must!'

'Well, y'see, the reason I got sacked, and you'll be reading it in the papers soon – I mean, *you* won't, obviously, but everyone else will – is that I beat up a prostitute and then tried to buy her silence.'

'You *what*?'

'Yeah, I thought that might get your attention. It's not strictly true, of course, but that's what you'll read, or not as the case may be. Anyway, as it happens, I was on a date with her. I didn't know she was a prostitute, and then when I did know, I tried to order her out of the house and she fell down the stairs and cracked her head. At least, that's my story.'

'*Why* are you telling me this?'

Marsh sighed. 'Because it all has to do with the apology, admittedly in a roundabout fashion. Y'see, I'm a cop, I need to get all the evidence out there, so you can make a fair judgement. Do you get me? So if you'll let me finish . . . Do you want me to finish?'

Linda stared at him. She *did* want to know, but not really because of the story, because of him. There was something comforting about him, something big and protective. He was like a childhood episode of *Jackanory*. She knew that he was probably being paid to get inside her head like some psychic gigolo, and make her feel better, but she couldn't do anything about it. He was just there and she could hardly resist. She gave a slight nod of her head for him to continue.

'Well, y'see, the reason I was on this date, is my wife died a few months ago. Cancer. Afterwards I was a bit miserable, so my daughter thought she'd help things along because . . . well, because she cares. The thing is, Linda, I loved my wife, but I never really showed her, until it was too late. I was married to the job, and I brought it home with me, and it can be a terrible job, so I was a terrible husband – and father. You know, regret is a dreadful thing, and doubly so when you can't do anything about it. It eats you up. Is that how it gets you?'

'Finally it comes round to me.'

'I was only asking, you don't have to answer. I haven't finished my story yet.'

'Oh Christ, if it's all going to be this depressing I should jump sooner rather than later.'

'Well, it's good you're considering later.' This time he gave the smallest smile. And she responded.

'I'm sorry about your wife,' said Linda, 'but it really hasn't anything to do with me. If you want to come up here and jump with me, that's fine.'

'Well, that's an option,' said Marsh. He stared at the ground again. But then he gave another shake of his head. 'The thing is, Linda, my whole life has just fallen apart. I think I was just about coping because I had my job, but then that got stolen from me today and just now . . . well, I was sitting on the Newtownards Road and I was on the verge of going postal, you know?'

'Postal?'

'Taking my gun out and shooting people just for the sake of it.'

'Oh,' said Linda. 'And did you?'

'No, because of you.'

'Me?'

'You were on the police radio.'

'Oh, right. You thought if you saved me, you could make yourself feel a bit better. Well, sorry to disappoint.'

'No, it wasn't like that. I heard your name, and I thought, "That's a bit of a coincidence. If it's you, I should come and apologise". You know, before you jump and I go postal.'

Linda rolled her eyes. 'Will you get to the f***ing point?!'

'Okay – you're right. I am being a bit longwinded. The point is – this prostitute, the date, I met her through a website called *Let's Be Mates*.'

'*Let's Be Mates*.' She was looking at him with greater interest now, although she only had his side profile to study.

'I had no intention of trying to meet someone again after my wife died. My daughter bushwhacked me with membership of this thing and suddenly there were these women on my computer dead keen to go out on a date. I went through their emails and membership files and photos, and the one I thought was the nicest by far, I arranged a date with her.'

Finally he looked at her straight on. 'We were supposed to meet for dinner – at *Lemon Tree*.'

'*Lemon Grass*,' said Linda.

Marsh nodded. 'Except when I got there, I couldn't get out of the car. I thought she was really lovely-looking, but I still couldn't get out of the car. I hadn't been out on a date for thirty years, and I missed my wife. I was just . . . scared. So I did something unforgivable. I watched her, watched her get more and more embarrassed just sitting there, and then I drove off. I went home.'

'You,' said Linda.

Marsh nodded. 'I'm sorry.'

'Is that it?'

'That's it. I just wanted to apologise. Now, if you wish, you can jump. And I can, you know, go off on the rampage.'

'Is that what you're going to do?'

'Well, I suppose. Don't really see much alternative. Unless you were in a particularly forgiving mood and you let me take you out for that meal. I've, uh, recently lost my wife and my job, and I'm about to be vilified in the press as a violent woman-beater, so I can promise you some interesting but miserable conversation. That said,

I Predict A Riot

I hear the food's lovely. And if you do come down off that rail you can think of it not so much as you chickening out of a suicide as you saving the lives of all those poor people on the Newtownards Road I am going to murder if you don't go out for dinner with me. So, what do you say?'

112

Credit Where Credit's Due

The rioting had already begun to wind down naturally when word went out that it should be completely called off. After three days of mayhem on the city's streets Pink Harrison was finally being released without charge, forensic teams not having been able to find a single microscopic dot of evidence linking him either to the murder of Michael Caldwell or the mysterious death of Benny Caproni. The city could get back to work, and play. Insurance companies could send out assessors; builders and double glazers could begin planning lavish Christmas parties. Chief Constable Tony Martin appeared at a press conference and denied that Pink's release came as a result of political pressure. 'Allegations were made against Councillor Harrison and we had a duty to investigate. No evidence was found and so he has been released.'

'Are you saying that you made a mistake?' one reporter asked.

'No, they were serious allegations and we treated them seriously.'

'And are you now satisfied that Pink has nothing whatsoever to do with these crimes?'

'There is no evidence to link him to these crimes.'

'Will you be apologising to Councillor Harrison?'

'No.'

'There's a rumour going around that Jimmy Mallow has been sacked – would you care to comment?'

'Jimmy Mallow is taking early retirement, for personal reasons. He has been a loyal and faithful servant to both the RUC and the Police Service of Northern Ireland.'

'Has he been sacked because of Pink Harrison?'

'He hasn't been sacked. The Pink Harrison arrest was part of a wider murder investigation and was handled with complete professionalism by all concerned.'

'Do you believe that Pink Harrison was behind the rioting?'

'I can't comment on that.'

'Do you believe it was orchestrated by his supporters?'

'I can't comment on that.'

'Is Pink Harrison no longer part of your murder investigation?'

'Councillor Harrison has been released. If new evidence emerges, he or anyone else can be detained for questioning.'

'Has Marsh Mallow been sacrificed because the politicians need someone's head to roll over all this rioting?'

'No.'

'Rumour has it *Belfast Confidential* has something on Jimmy Mallow – care to comment?'

'Well, you tell me. You're from *Belfast Confidential*, Mr Starkey.'

That got a laugh, and provided an opportunity for the Chief Constable to call the press conference to an end on a lighter note. A few minutes later, on a footpath just outside Police Headquarters, Pink Harrison held his own. It was slightly chaotic, being right beside a busy main road, and with Pink's supporters singing his name and chanting their support and drivers pumping their horns as they realised who it was.

Pink, having ordered that his expensive toiletries be brought from home (and which his equally expensive solicitor only found after some considerable trouble, Pink's house in Holywood having been left in a state of chaos by the forensic team), and having been allowed use of shower facilities by the PSNI, once it became clear that they didn't have any evidence against him, looked his usual suave and dashing self; his hair sat perfectly and the three-day stubble was gone; his skin shone and his eyes were luminous.

Pink immediately condemned the police for their actions and said his arrest was like something out of 'Stalinist Russia'. He grew visibly angry when a reporter accused him of calling his supporters out onto the streets to riot, and described it as a 'spontaneous show of support' which he very much appreciated. Although he 'obviously' regretted the amount of damage that had been caused, he said this had erupted because of provocation by the PSNI in their heavy-handed response to a peaceful protest. Despite this, Pink maintained his support for the rank and file of the PSNI, who he said were doing a difficult job, and instead blamed the Chief Constable for bowing to pressure from 'my political rivals'. He called for Tony Martin to resign, and welcomed the departure of the Head of the CID, James Mallow, who, he said, had chosen to fall on his own sword rather than face the humiliation of being sacked. He expressed sympathy for the families of Michael Caldwell and Benny Caproni, hoped that George Green, the missing property millionaire who was now the chief suspect, would soon be found, and prayed that he himself would now be allowed to get back to what he did best, representing his people and continuing the search for a permanent and peaceful settlement in Northern Ireland.

As soon as he got behind closed doors, Pink said to Bull: 'Have you found that f***er Billy Gilmore yet?'

'Not yet, boss.'

'Well, f***ing do it. I want him crucified, and I'll hammer in the nails myself.'

'Yes, boss.'

Pink had lost £800,000. There had been £1.3 million in the safe. Half a million had been recovered by Bull and his comrades at the scene. The rest had either blown away in the wind or been surreptitiously smuggled away. Pink's take on it was the equivalent of *plenty more fish in the sea*. Bull himself had stashed away a hundred grand. Pink was aware that his most trusted comrades had helped themselves, without being aware of the individual amounts. It was only to be expected. He didn't blame them at all. He blamed Billy for making such a mess of it. So he patted Bull on the back and told him to get on with it, and went back to the party.

They were in the Stormont Inn, not far from Police HQ, and overlooking Stormont itself, the vast white edifice (and occasional elephant) that was the traditional seat of power in the Province, and to which, hopefully, such power would soon be restored. It was every local politician's ultimate goal. Certainly Pink had designs on it. If this gathering, merrily drinking and helping itself to an elaborate buffet, was anything to go by, then that day, when he attained real power, Cabinet power, could not be that far off. The Unionist Party, from its grass-roots supporters to his colleagues on the City Council, was here in force. He assumed they had wavered when news of his arrest broke, but now they were back smiling, pumping his hand, telling him they'd never doubted him for a minute and what a grand chap he was. Pink lapped it all up. He was the man of the moment, the star of the show. He ordered champagne with abandon, he posed for photographs, he was witty and light, but also serious and incisive. He condemned the anarchy that had descended but also praised the people for making a stand. He snorted three lines of cocaine in the toilets.

Mark saw him emerging, and wondered why such a well-groomed man as Pink Harrison had dandruff on his shoulders. Before he could think more of it, Pink spotted him and enveloped him in a bear hug which made Mark feel warm and snuggly, and very much a part of the inner circle, although he wasn't sure which particular inner circle. He supposed it was like a pebble being thrown into a lake; there were lots of circles, and none of them were joined, yet they were still connected and all were all expanding in the same direction.

Pink released him, but then pumped his hand and said again and again how great a day it was, and Mark was inclined to agree. He had been a little disappointed to learn that Pink was being released without charge, as he had had his eyes on Pink's council seat, but was thankful now that he hadn't expressed that ambition to anyone at Party Headquarters. He had been in and out of there half a dozen times following Pink's arrest, getting his face known and beginning to forge alliances. He did not doubt that his time would come, but his initial jubilation at Pink's arrest had soon given way to a wider appreciation of the repercussions it would have on the Party if he was found guilty of murderous crimes. The Party was already teetering on the brink of extinction; having hastily adopted Pink as one of its own, his conviction for murder would surely have shown how out of touch and naïve it was and served as the final, fatal blow. But Pink being innocent – or at least, not being guilty – was a blessing, saving it both from acute embarrassment and serving as a wake-up call. Yes, they were celebrating Pink Harrison now, but in the quiet corners of Party HQ Mark had eavesdropped on earnest conferences and overheard whispered realignments as the comfy shag was pulled gently from beneath Pink Harrison's feet. This extravagant party was both his moment of triumph and a wake for his political career.

Mark sat at the bar, sipping an orange juice, and watched as Pink worked the room and encouraged favoured journalists to drink on his tab. Local celebrities – television weather women and showband crooners – sucked around him. Hoods in suits smoked cigars. Once in a while Pink disappeared to top up his dandruff.

Gradually the crowds thinned and the staff began to clear up. Pink stood by the door saying goodbye to everyone, glowing in their praise and promises of support. Finally he retreated to a corner table with a gang of his cronies and ordered shots. He waved Mark over, but Mark said he had to be going. Pink said, 'Nah, go on, stay, have a drink with the lads.' Mark didn't have an excuse, he just didn't want to. He was still trying to talk his way out of it when the bar manager came over with the bill for the party food and the champagne and the hire of the room, and Pink studied the docket, then clutched his chest like it was a shock and everyone laughed. He handed over his credit card then started to tell his mates some joke, with Mark still standing there not sure whether he needed permission to leave. When Mark laughed at the punchline Pink fixed him with a look and said, 'Pull up a pew.'

Mark was just pulling up a stool when the bar manager came back over, looking very red-faced. 'I'm sorry, Mr Harrison,' he said. 'There seems to be a problem with your credit card.'

113
What's For You . . .

Like any Civil Servant, Walter half-hoped that the rioting would continue into a fourth day and thus, robbed of public transport, he would be excused going to work. But it was not to be. By Monday morning the city was largely back to normal. It was just a little louder than usual; the air was filled with the sounds of hammers and drills as repairs were carried out and scaffolding erected, the scrape of metal as burned-out cars were dragged away for scrap; it was rich with the smell of fresh tarmac and planks.

It was a bright, cheerful morning as Walter sauntered towards the train station. If it had been a chaotic few days for the city, it had been a wonderful few days for Walter North. His formula for life: *hope + dreams = disappointment* had been radically re-imagined, particularly in the romance department. He had endured a Friday from hell, when it seemed likely that he would lose both his sex partner, Linda, and his life partner (to be) Margaret. He felt a *certain* amount of responsibility for Linda's suicide attempt, because he hadn't been straight with her. He also reasoned, however, that if every girl who got two-timed threw herself off a tall building then it wouldn't be safe for *anyone* to walk the streets for danger of getting clobbered from above. It was clear that Linda had pre-existing problems which couldn't be laid at his door. But thank God it had turned out all right. She might even have met a real, proper boyfriend in the process. The way that Jimmy Marsh Mallow had walked her off the balcony and into the bedroom, hugging her to him, and then hurried the rest of them – three paramedics, six firemen, two uniformed police officers – out of the apartment had been so impressive. He seemed to be full of compassion and concern and understanding. Linda barely even noticed the Emergency Services, despite all their regalia and equipment, and didn't even clock that the chocolate cake had been completely devoured. She only had eyes for her saviour. That surely suggested that there were romantic possibilities there.

It was a relief that she was safe, and over him, but even better that Margaret, despite numerous hints, had still not cottoned on to his fling with Linda. She had now been through three traumatic experiences with Walter – their initial disastrous date, her falling into the river and discovering the head, and now a suicide attempt. As they walked back to Margaret's car, waving goodbye to the firemen, she said, 'If we've survived this far, I don't think there *is* anything else can break us up.' He had glowed then, and he was still glowing now. They'd since been out on two further dates – one to a movie which they'd missed most of by giggling and snogging in the back row, and one to *Deane's on the Square*, a smart restaurant in the city centre. Walter had driven on both occasions, and not had so much as half a pint. He had been the perfect gentleman. He had taken her home on both occassions and they'd kissed passionately. At the end of each date he asked, 'Can I see you again?' which she thought was really sweet.

There was a fruit'n'veg shop on the road leading down to Botanic Station that Walter had got into the habit of calling into on a Monday morning because that was the day he always started his diets and he liked to stock up with healthy things. He would buy apples and pears and grapes, then spend five minutes squeezing the melons to see which ones are ripe. The melon squeezing had become a bit of a joke between Walter and the elderly shopkeeper, Geordie. Every time Walter bought a melon Geordie asked after the last one. Walter always said it was still sitting in the fridge at home waiting for company. And it was true. He loved melons, but they always seemed like too much trouble to prepare. So he kept buying a fresh one every Monday morning, then taking it home on Monday night to introduce it to the old one. It seemed he always had three melons in the fridge. One overripe and needing to be thrown out, one perfect but neglected, and one fresh and still ripening. *This* morning, however, the shop was closed and Geordie was up a ladder outside, hammering wooden boards across the open windows. Glass lay in brushed-up piles on the ground, awaiting clearance.

'Jesus,' Walter said. 'I didn't think the riots had gotten this far.'

Geordie shook his head. 'Ah, the bad wee ba***rds'll take any opportunity.'

'Did they steal anything?'

Georgie laughed sadly. 'What're they going to take? Bananas? Courgettes? Nah, they just did this for the hell of it.'

'Yeah, well,' said Walter, 'kids today. So, will you be open later? I've a melon at home pining for company.'

'Nah. Sorry, Walter, you'll have to go to Tesco's or somewhere. Tell you the truth, I've had enough. I'm boarding her up and I'm walking away. Selling up. I'm too old for all this crap.'

'Oh,' said Walter. 'Sorry to hear that. I always liked your fruit.' He nodded, and started to turn away, but then he hesitated. He looked back up at Geordie. 'You're really selling up?'

'Aye. First decent offer I'm taking the wife to Spain and I'm not coming back.'

Cogs were turning, circuits were firing.

'If you don't mind me asking, Geordie – how much d'you reckon you'd sell her for?'

Geordie's head tilted to one side, and his lips moved silently. Then he gave a little shrug and said, 'Had her valued last year, reckoned she's gone up a bit since then, but then all this rioting has probably knocked that on the head. Maybe two hundred thousand. Why, do you know someone?'

'I might. I'll give you a shout, all right?'

Geordie nodded and went back to securing his premises. Walter walked on, thinking about the possibilities. He'd agreed with Bertha that commercial property was the way to go, and here was one almost being presented to him, and maybe at a knockdown price. It needed a bit of fixing up, but whatever damage the rioters had caused looked reasonably superficial. The old fella was keen to move. *First decent offer,* he'd said. This was quite a smart, artsy part of South Belfast, not usually associated with riots; there was no reason to think that they would occur again any time in the near future. It wouldn't be like buying property in a danger zone. This damage was surely a one-off.

Still, patience is a virtue, thought Walter. If I've learned anything of late, it's best not to rush into anything. I'm older now, more mature. What was it his mother used to say?

What's for you won't go by you.

Walter smiled at the memory of it, and decided to phone Bertha from work to discuss the fruit'n'veg shop. A further 100 yards along, on a corner opposite the station, there was a bakery Walter usually stopped at on a Tuesday morning when his diet had collapsed again. It was a gloriously old-fashioned bakery, with little dusty old women who'd worked there for thirty years eager to talk about the weather while they sold you gravy rings and Paris buns and German biscuits. This property had also been targeted by the rioters, but to a much greater extent. The roof was missing and the upper floor was charred; downstairs all of the windows were smashed and the interior scorched. The owner, a moon-faced man called Paul, who was on first-name terms with Walter, as he was with all of his best customers, saw him standing surveying the damage.

'Jesus, Paul,' said Walter, 'what's the world coming to?'

Paul had a brush in his hand. It appeared to be smouldering. 'They just burned it,' he said weakly. 'No rhyme nor reason.'

Walter's stomach rumbled. He said, 'Don't let the ba***rds grind you down.'

Paul sighed. 'Easier said than done, mate. Had a structural engineer around first thing; he said the whole place has to come down.'

'God,' said Walter. 'But your gravy rings are the best in Belfast. You'll re-open.'

'I don't know, Walter. I mean, we'll have the insurance money, but it'll take a year to get her up and running, and once you lose that passing trade, they never come back.'

'Aw, don't say that. Couldn't you get somewhere else, nearby?'

'Round here – you joking? A shop this close to the station's rarer than hen's teeth.' Paul blew air out of his cheeks. 'Sorry, Walter, unless I find somewhere in the next few days, that's me. You'll have to look elsewhere for your gravy rings.'

Walter shook his head. 'That'll be a terrible pity.'

'Aye,' said Paul.

Walter began to turn, aware that he was already running late for his train. But then he had a thought. 'Paul? Say a property *was* to become available, roughly the same size, similar location, you'd be game?'

'Absolutely.'

'How much do you reckon?'

'Round here? Well, you'd be talking, let's say, about a quarter to three hundred thousand.'

'Seriously? Even with all the rioting?'

'Oh, aye. Hardly affects the prices at all. If anything, it drives them up – less available, you know what I mean? Why, do you know somewhere?'

'I might,' said Walter.

114

Last Chance Saloon

Billy could have chosen any city in the world. He had cash, and easy access to bulging bank accounts. He could have danced in Rio or gambled in Monte Carlo, but he chose to remain in Belfast, living it up in the Clinton Suite in the Europa Hotel. When I say living it up, it was living it up accountant-style. No mad parties for Billy, no wild women, no drugs. It was watching pay-per-view movies and not giving a *damn* at the expense of it; it was ordering three-course meals from room service and tipping above 15 per cent – sometimes 17 per cent, once 19 per cent. It was drinking from the minibar and not replacing their expensive cans of Coke with cheaper versions he'd brought with him, as he usually did on holiday. He even sent his favourite shirts out to the laundry.

Billy was living so extravagantly because he knew he was on borrowed time. He might have eked it out for longer if there hadn't been bit of a cock-up over his signing in. He'd decided to use a false name – Peter de Vere – which he thought sounded classy, and not at all like a 1970s sleazy playboy – but then the woman had asked for a swipe of his credit card. He said he was paying cash, but she still demanded his credit card in case 'he went mental' and trashed his room. He had no option but to hand it over, so it was clear to her that his real name wasn't Peter de Vere but Billy Gilmore. He was aware that it might only be a matter of time before it got out, but still, he couldn't bring himself to leave.

For one good reason.

Margaret.

She haunted his dreams. They were happy dreams too, with no arguments and lots of holding hands in the sun. He felt at peace with her. Removed from his plush apartment and luxury goods, and sleeping better than he had in years, despite the fact that Pink Harrison had gunmen scouring the city for him, Billy began to realise the error of his ways. He had concentrated on building his career rather than making his marriage work. He had not paid enough attention to Margaret in the bedroom. All she wanted was for him to love her, and show his love, and when that wasn't forthcoming, she had rolled up in a ball, to protect herself, like a hedgehog. She wasn't really cold and unfeeling, she was just hurt.

Well – things were different now. He no longer had a career, but he had lots and lots of lovely money. He would invest the majority of it wisely, but there would be some left over to lavish on Margaret. He could buy her jewellery – and negotiate a fantastic discount, which all rich people seemed able to do – and sort out her crap hair. They could sit on an exotic beach and order the darkies around, getting drinks and burgers.

Billy went over his speech a thousand times. Given the opportunity, he would have used flow-charts on his laptop to fully explain his plan for their life on the run together but, he suspected, such was her hurt that she wouldn't give him the time for that. He might only have a couple of minutes to make his pitch. It had to be short, sharp, to the point, and unencumbered by sophisticated electrical equipment.

The problem was actually getting to speak to her. When he phoned her house, her answer-machine was on permanently, and he wasn't stupid enough to leave a message telling her where he was. You never knew who was listening. The thought struck him that perhaps Pink Harrison had taken her hostage, and this freaked him out for a while. He felt sure a kidnapping would have made the local news, but then there was so much going on with the rioting and its repercussions that a kidnap mightn't be considered sufficiently interesting. Or perhaps the police already knew about it and were keeping quiet so they could mount an SAS-style recovery.

Or perhaps not.

Eventually Billy phoned Primark and asked for her, but was told that employees couldn't take personal calls while on duty. However, the receptionist at least confirmed that Margaret *was* on duty, and not bound and gagged in some dank cellar.

Billy had a choice to make – keep phoning her house, because she had to pick up the phone eventually, and retaining the relative security of the Europa – or actually venturing out to Primark and running the risk of being discovered by Pink's men. Time was the crucial factor in his decision to go straight down to see her at work. As soon as the decision was made, he felt good about it. Gone were the days when, if there was something deeply personal to be said, he would leave it on a Post-it on the fridge. This was the new Billy, with his heart on his sleeve and his cheque book in his pocket. This was the new Billy, not even wearing a tie as he ventured out of the Europa, baseball cap pulled firmly down, walking down Great Victoria Street and along Howard Street towards Donegall Place and Primark, all the while trying to avoid eye-contact, but at the same time not being able to help it, because if anything was going to happen he wanted to see it coming.

It didn't. He reached Primark in one piece, and located Margaret almost immediately, talking to an attractive blonde colleague, her face as happy and smiley as it had been in their early days; however, her expression froze as soon as she saw him coming towards her. There was an urgent muttering between the two security guards and then the blonde one moved away – but not, Billy noticed, very far.

'Billy,' said Margaret.

'Margaret, love, how're you doing?'

'Fine and dandy, thanks.'

'No, really.'

'Really.'

'Well – that's good. How's your fashion . . . thing?'

'It's great. Thanks.'

There wasn't even a hint of warmth, but he expected that. It was just a question of thawing her out. Rubbing her limbs.

'I'm going away,' he said next.

'Oh. Where to?' No hint of interest.

'Rio.'

'Where?'

'Or Cozumel, Mexico.'

'*Mexico*?'

'Or Palma – I hear that's nice.'

'You came down here to tell me you're going on holiday?'

'No – look, Margaret. I want you to come with me.'

'You want me to go on holiday with you?'

'*No*. I'm not going on holiday. I'm going permanently. To Rio. Or Cozumel, Mexico.'

Margaret folded her arms. 'You can't go to Mexico. You'd melt away to nothing. You don't even like the sun.'

'Yes, I— That's not the point. I want you to come with me. To live there. To start again.'

'With you?'

'*Yes*. I've rather unexpectedly come into some money. A *lot* of money. So I'd like us to start again.' Billy took a deep breath. This was where his prepared speech came in. 'Margaret, I'm aware that . . .' and then he stumbled forward as a big momma with half a dozen Primark bags banged into the back of him, then marched on without a word of apology. 'Sorry. I'm aware that I haven't exactly been easy to live with, that I haven't paid—'

Margaret's radio crackled. Mr Kawolski said: 'Everything all right?'

'Yes, fine, thank you. Just giving a customer directions.' Margaret looked at Billy. 'Well?'

He cleared his throat. 'I should have done better. I didn't treat you well. I was self-absorbed, selfish. I really don't blame you for falling out of love with me. But now I've come into some money and we have the opportunity to start again, and I swear to God, I will treat you well. You will want for nothing – diamonds, bangles, those wavy sort of scarves you always wanted to buy on holiday because they were made by local craftsmen but I never let you because I thought they were tat. You can have anything. Just, let's start again, let's put it back to the way it was.'

'But Billy,' said Margaret, 'you were always a pr**k.'

Billy laughed at the joke. 'You married me,' he said.

'Yes, I did. And I regretted it every single day since.'

Now Billy's brow furrowed. She wasn't laughing. 'But I'm giving you this second chance.'

'*You're* giving *me* a second chance?'

'I don't mean it like that. I mean, let's try again. Let me take you out of this place.' And he waved his arms around the store, then had to apologise for clipping the ear of a passing shopper. 'Margaret, I'm offering you everything you can possibly imagine. Please, let's try again.'

'Billy, I've met someone else.'

He blinked at her. It was lucky he was in a forgiving mood. 'That's allowed, darling, I won't hold it against you. But forget about him. Come back to me, live a life of luxury. Sun and sea and—'

'Billy, I've *really* met someone else.'

'Does he have any money?'

'No.'

'Well, then.'

Margaret's radio crackled again. 'You sure you're all right?' said Mr Kawolski.

'Yes, boss. He's just leaving.' She shook her head sadly. 'Billy, you should go.'

'I'm not going without you.'

'Yes, you are.'

'Margaret, I love you.'

'Well, I don't love you.'

'Then why the f**k did you marry me?' Billy exploded suddenly.

'I have no idea.'

Billy sighed extravagantly. He blew air out of his cheeks. He looked around him, anywhere but at Margaret.

She moved a little closer. 'Billy, I'm sorry, but I'm happy that you've come into some money. Maybe you'll meet someone nice in Coz . . . Comuzel?'

'Cozumel, Mexico. Margaret, I have *millions*. You have to understand, if you come with me, it's like winning the lottery.'

Margaret shook her head sadly. 'With last year's numbers, Billy. With last year's numbers.'

Billy looked baffled. 'What the f**k are you talking about? Why do you always have to be so bloody *cryptic*?'

'I'm not trying to be—'

'Shut up. That's just exactly it! You think you're being so smart – you like to think you're better than other people, but you're not, you're not even as good as other people. Just because you find someone mug enough to buy some of your funny wee designs, you come over all high and mighty, but you're not, do you hear me? You're a middle-aged woman working in Primark. And in five years you'll be an old woman working in Primark.'

'I think you should go now, Billy.'

His eyes were blazing. 'I'm not going anywhere,' he snapped.

'I can have you thrown out.'

'Yeah, right. You would do that, wouldn't you? Everything I did for you, you would do that? What was I thinking of? Taking you abroad would be a f***ing misery.' He looked about him. They were standing in the Young Adult fashion section. 'Okay. Where are the T-shirts? I need T-shirts.'

'Over there, on the right,' said Margaret.

'Thanks.' Billy moved away. Then he turned back. 'Last chance?'

'No, Billy.'

'Okay, all right. *Loser*. See you around.'

Billy stormed off.

115

Martini Girl

Gary McBride was sitting in an unmarked car outside Jimmy's house when Jimmy arrived home in his car. It had taken Gary a while to find the house, because although they'd worked together for the past decade, they had never socialised. In the end, he kind of stumbled on the house, recognising it not by a house number, which wasn't visible anywhere, but by the array of security cameras and the incongruous blocks of concrete (albeit decorated with flowers) which formed a protective barrier around it. Although there hadn't been a proper car bomb in years, the blocks were probably just too awkward to shift now. Marsh raised a hand as he drove towards the electronic gates. As they purred inward, Gary climbed out of his car clutching a bottle of whiskey.

Jimmy Mallow was looking surprisingly upbeat. Last time Gary had spoken to him, at Police HQ, he'd looked like thunder. He'd smacked Pink Harrison in the chops and then stormed out. But now he appeared quite calm, and even managed something of a smile as he extended his hand.

'Gary,' he said.

'Boss,' said Gary. It meant nothing, Marsh realised, but it was a nice mark of respect. 'Brought you this.'

Marsh examined the bottle. 'That'll do nicely,' he said, and led Gary into the house.

While Marsh fixed their drinks, Gary looked about the lounge, and was more than a little surprised at the extent of his host's music collection. There was no shortage of shelves, and every one of them seemed to be filled with LPs, CDs and singles. He'd never let any of this slip at work. Gary was quite into music himself. He was just examining a vinyl copy of The Rolling Stones' *Get Yer Ya Ya's Out* when Marsh appeared with the drinks.

'Look at this,' said Gary. 'This is the live one, right?'

Jimmy nodded. 'You into music?'

'Oh yeah – used to play the guitar in a punk band.'

'You?'

Gary smiled and nodded. He slipped the record back onto the shelf. Marsh looked down for a moment, debating with himself, then removed the record again and re-inserted it slightly further along. 'Alphabetical,' he said by way of explanation. Then added, 'And anal retentive.' He clinked glasses with Gary, then sat. 'So how's it going?'

'With Pink?'

'With anyone.'

'Well, I hear you're in line for a medal, talking someone down off a bridge.'

'A balcony. They won't be thinking about a medal when *Belfast Confidential* comes out on Thursday.'

'Yeah. I've my copy ordered.'

'Thirty years, and it ends like this. I just thank Christ the wife isn't around to see it.'

Gary took a sip of his drink, then looked at Marsh over the rim. 'You know, this journalist, Starkey – we can lean on him.'

'Yeah, I know. I appreciate the thought, but it's out there, it'll find its way into one paper or another; might as well get it over with. What're they saying, the rank and file?'

'They don't believe it.'

'Wait till they read *Belfast Confidential*, then they'll believe it.'

'No, they won't.'

Jimmy shrugged. 'So what's happening with Pink?'

'We've been told to stay clear of him.'

'And what about George Green – has he turned up yet?'

'Nope. No one has heard from him, his credit card hasn't been used.'

'He's gone for good, then.'

'It's looking that way. Boss, what are you going to do now? I mean, when you're not saving damsels in distress.'

'Well, there's going to be a shit storm when this comes out, so I'll probably just keep my head down.'

Gary nodded to himself. Then he set his glass down and stood up. 'I brought you your stuff from the office.'

'Oh right.'

'Come on, let's get it.'

Gary stood and crossed the lounge. Marsh frowned, but then went after him, down to his car. When Gary popped the boot, it was crammed with bin bags, full to the brim.

'What the hell's this?' Jimmy asked. 'I was expecting a couple of photos and some pencils.'

'This,' said Gary, 'is homework. Every single piece of evidence to do with the Michael Caldwell case, lovingly photocopied by yours truly and half a dozen of your most talented protégés. You may think you've been sacked, Superintendent, and you may think you're just going to sit on your arse listening to records, but we've decided otherwise. You've been after Pink Harrison for as long as I can remember, and there's no reason to stop now. And I, lacking an interesting hobby like stamp collecting or cultivating bonsai trees, need something to do with my spare time. So grab a bag, replenish our drinks, and let's go through the evidence, in the words of someone not a million miles from here, one last f***ing time.'

Gary lifted a bag out, heaved it up onto his shoulder, then turned for the house. Marsh laughed out loud, then reached for a bag himself.

Marsh sat up long after Gary left, drinking steadily, listening to Leonard Cohen, still leafing through the evidence, but mostly thinking about Linda Wray. He had sat in the apartment, watching her sleep off her drunkenness, until she woke, sick and embarrassed. He allowed her time to fix her face and check in with her work, then he took her to a café and bought her tea and toast. He got the impression that she was a natural talker, but there and then, she didn't say much. Like an injured bird. A pheasant, even, hiding her colours. He took her back to her house, made sure she had everything she needed, then left her his number in case she wanted to talk. It had now been three days, and she hadn't called yet. He checked her number in the book on the first day, and sat with it on the arm of the chair, but didn't call. But now, empowered by whiskey, he gave in to the temptation.

She answered, eventually, with a slightly groggy, 'Yes?'

'Hi. Hello. It's Jimmy. James Mallow.'

'Jimmy?'

'The apartment, the ledge – remember?'

'Oh God. Yes. Sorry. I meant to call, only I threw your number out. I mean, it must have got stuck to a newspaper and then I couldn't find it. What time is it anyway?'

'Oh – sorry. I didn't realise. It's gone one in the morning. Lost track of the time. I just wanted to phone and check you were okay, but I can call back if you—'

'No, really, Mr Mallow, it's fine.'

'James, please. Jimmy. Are you sure?'

'Yes, of course.'

Silence then.

And more.

Then Jimmy said, 'So are you all right?'

'Yes. Yes, I am.'

'You're sure?'

'Yes, quite sure.' It was heading towards another long silence, but then she suddenly blabbed out: 'Look, I'm sorry, I'm just absolutely . . . *mortified*. I've never done anything like that in my life. I was just upset and drunk and it's a bad combination. I'm sorry you or anyone had to see that. I've made a real eejit of myself and I just feel like crawling under a rock. I haven't been back in to work yet. I mean, they don't know what happened, but I just can't face . . . you know, *people*, not yet, anyway. And, so, how was your day?'

'My day was fine.'

'Well, that's good.'

'You're sure you're okay?'

'Yes. Absolutely.'

'So, then, now that I know you're absolutely okay, I was wondering if you remembered what we talked about – you know, the date that never was.'

'The date you never turned up for, you mean.'

Marsh chuckled. 'Yes, that one. I was wondering if you'd still like to go on it. Give me a second chance.'

'Mr Mallow, if you don't mind me saying, I have found that men who require a second chance, quite often require a third and a fourth.'

He hesitated, then asked, 'Is that a no?'

Linda sighed. 'James Mallow, you saved my life, you are my knight in shining armour, do you think that for one moment I'm *ever* going to say no? Of *course* I want to go out on a date. Any time, any place, anywhere.'

'Martini,' said Marsh.

'Whatever turns you on,' said Linda.

116
Father, Dear Father

Father Damian's parish was well out in the sticks, and straddled the invisible border between the counties of Down and Tyrone. While it was undeniably rough and ready, it had never quite been violent or dangerous enough to be considered part of 'Bandit Country'. If the IRA had been rating it for inclusion under that banner, they would have given it a 'must try harder'. With the weapons now put away, and love all around, it was a peaceful retreat of a place, a land for growing apples and tending cows. Redmond, standing in for his late, twin brother, absolutely loved it. At least, initially.

Damian had a housekeeper called Molly Malone – really – who took one look at Redmond's half-starved figure and immediately ordered him to the kitchen for stew. He feasted upon it three times a day. If she could have attached a stew drip to his arm, she probably would have. She was a kindly, florid woman who lived nearby in a little village with its little post office and little shop, which overlooked a little stream. There was a little pub and when Redmond ventured in for a pint and tried to listen in to their conversation it made little sense, the accents were that thick. The locals would clap him on the back with easy familiarity and set him up another one while they chatted excitedly about this and that, while Redmond nodded away and barely understood a word of it.

The pints, though, were few and far between. Although his strength was slowly returning, he found that he had little desire for alcohol. Instead he sat out in the sun in his front garden, and wondered how he would tackle the church service on Sunday, and the homily that went with it (there was no Saturday service in these parts due to lack of demand). Late on Saturday afternoon, with the sun still bright, Mrs Malone approached him in the garden. She said she'd left stew for him in the microwave and that she'd see him at church on Sunday. Before she went she said, 'Say hello to Father Benedict for me.'

Redmond nodded without really appreciating what she meant, at least until shortly after seven when he was just preparing to settle in for a night of Spanish football in front of the telly. He was standing at the sink in the kitchen, with the radio on loud, when he was suddenly blinded by two hands coming down over his eyes. A slightly high-pitched voice said, 'Guess who-oo . . . !'

Redmond, you understand, was trained to *kill*, so it was quite natural for him to swivel, duck down out of his assailant's grasp and ram one hand up hard under his chin, snapping his head back. He then pounded the other hand into his attacker's stomach. As he collapsed down, Redmond caught him by the ears, holding him upright, before turning him round and hurling him into the cutlery drawer opposite.

It was only when the man in the dog collar slithered down onto the floor, coughing and spluttering and groaning, that Redmond understood that this might not be a dangerous assassin, but Father Benedict.

Redmond immediately dashed across and put him into the recovery position. When his breath returned he gently eased him up and steered him across to a seat at the kitchen table. He poured him a glass of water from the tap and patted his back as he drank it down. 'I'm so sorry, I'm so very sorry,' he said.

'My God,' Father Benedict finally managed to say, still catching his breath between gulps and wincing as the water went down, 'you have returned *brutalised*. Did they do to you what they did to your poor brother?'

'No, no, not at all. You just took me by surprise. Please, let me get you something stronger.'

He made up a couple of whiskies for them. Father Benedict drank his down quickly, then studied Redmond intently across the table. 'My,' he said, 'have you lost some weight.'

'I hardly ate,' said Redmond.

'You hardly did. Look at you. Although – I quite like it. I didn't like to say, but you could have done with losing a few pounds. Anyway, you're home safe now. I'm very sorry about your brother, it was a terrible thing.' Redmond nodded sadly. 'But I have to say, Damian, a bad egg does not a good omelette make.'

Redmond nodded slightly less sadly.

'A black sheep who wanders from the flock will not come to market.'

Redmond took a sip of his whiskey.

'The bird that falls from—'

'How's your whiskey?' Redmond asked.

'I'll take another wee nip. Damian, I was being thoughtless. I was just so worried. It was a terrible tragedy – a miscarriage of justice.'

Redmond gave a little shrug. 'I was thinking about a statue.'

'I was thinking about something else.'

'I'm sorry?'

'Well – did you?'

'Did I what?'

'You know – did you bring me . . . ?' And he raised his eyebrows.

'Bring you what?'

'Oh, you're such a tease, Damian. Did you bring me something back or not?'

'Ah. Right. Ahm – no, sorry.'

'No wee prezzy for Benny?'

'No.'

'Seriously?'

'Seriously.'

'Oh.' Benedict drummed his fingers on the table. He was not pleased. 'I brought you one back from Rome.'

'Did you? I mean – you did, yes. And it was great. I just . . . couldn't. That is, I did get one, only it was too big. They wouldn't let me on the plane with it.'

'Honest?'

'Honest.'

'What was it?'

'A bird. A Colombian stuffed bird.'

'Aw. Well, that was sweet. Every house of God should have a Colombian stuffed bird.'

'That's what I was thinking,' said Redmond.

Saturday night, apparently, was DVD night. Father Benedict had brought with him the re-make of *The Dukes of Hazzard*. The priests sat in the front lounge, sipping whiskey. It was a truly dreadful movie, but it was a relief for Redmond to concentrate on something different, as he'd spent the previous hour recounting his – i.e. his brother's – experiences in Bogotá and he was worried about getting some obvious detail of the priesthood wrong. So Redmond kept his eyes glued to the screen, although he was only too aware that his companion wasn't watching it at all, but rather, was watching *him*.

Of course he suspects, Redmond concluded. Who wouldn't? I got away with it in Colombia and Belfast, but here, with another priest, he must notice the difference; he must be aware I'm floundering.

When the movie finally ended, Redmond made a great show of yawning and saying, 'Well, I don't know about you, but I'm bushed.'

'So am I,' said Benedict. 'Why don't you go on up, and I'll switch off down here.'

Redmond hesitated. 'Sure I'll wait and let you out.'

Benedict snorted. 'You're funny,' he said. He came right up to him, put his hands on Redmond's shoulders, then kissed him hard on the lips. He moved quickly to Redmond's cheek, then nuzzled his ear and whispered huskily, 'I've missed you, baby.'

117
Moving Day

Within fifteen minutes of arriving in work Walter had made a series of phone calls, first of all to Bertha, then to a surveyor, a bank and a mortgage provider. Finally he phoned Margaret and asked her if she thought it was a good idea.

'To buy a property in the morning, re-sell it in the afternoon, and make a huge profit? Why *wouldn't* I think it was a good idea?'

'Well, the fruit-shop man could put his price up, and the bakery guy could drop his offer.'

'Yes, of course they could, but as long as you're satisfied the fruit shop is a good investment anyway, then I don't see the problem. If the bakery guy doesn't offer enough, then don't sell it to him. There's nothing says you *have* to do it all in one day.'

'I know that, but I want to. There's something exciting about it; it's the way all those big entrepreneurs start out. They see an opportunity no one else sees, and really go for it.'

'Then go for it.'

They made kissy for a while, then Walter set about his next round of phone calls. Mark, making slow work of finally tidying his desk before his move down the corridor into Office 12, looked a little put out.

'Time was,' he said, 'you would have asked me for that kind of advice.'

'What's your advice then, Mark?'

'Don't risk it, you'll never pull it off, what's the point, life's too short.'

'I rest my case,' said Walter, and pushed some more numbers.

He had never ever felt this upbeat before. He just knew it was going to work. He was on course to make at least £50,000 profit in one day. It wouldn't *really* be one day, it might be six weeks before it all worked out, but still – to all intents and purposes it was one day. Property was a bit like his lovelife – you waited ages for the right one to come along, then two arrived at once.

I Predict A Riot

Towards lunchtime Bertha phoned to say she'd taken her glowering nephew to see the fruit shop, and he'd surprised her by agreeing that it was a good investment. He hadn't surprised her in the slightest by then saying that she should invest in it by herself, and cut Walter out of the deal. Walter's heart hammered at that, but Bertha quickly said she'd told him to *go f**k himself*.

By early afternoon the finances were in place, and Walter phoned Geordie with his offer for the shop. Geordie accepted on the spot, and Walter punched the air. Then he phoned Paul at the bakery and said he had a property for him, but didn't specify where. Paul tried to drag it out of him, but Walter stood firm, advising him just to get his finances in order so that he could sign straight away if he liked the look of it, because there were other buyers gagging for it. He found himself slipping into the patter so easily.

'I'm going to write it into the contract that you have to send me a box of gravy rings every week for a year,' said Walter.

'I thought you were on a diet,' said Paul.

'That's *two* boxes every week for a year. Anything else to say?' They both laughed. Walter loved it. He was getting cocky. But with reason. Paul hadn't seen the property, but if it was as well-placed as Walter promised, he said he could go as far as £310,000. 'Well, that's certainly an interesting opening offer,' said Walter.

Margaret, who seemed to be getting quite caught up in the excitement of it herself, phoned again to see how things were going and he excitedly informed her that everything was falling nicely into place, and that seeing as how he was going to be making such a profit, he'd like to buy her something.

'Me? Like what? A car or something?'

His voice dropped immediately. 'Well, if you really . . .'

'Walter! I was only joking! For godsake!'

'I know, I know.'

'You don't need to buy me anything. And don't count your chickens before they hatch.'

'I know, but I'd still like to. Is there a wee something I can get you?'

'Like what?'

'I don't know. A big box of chocolates. Or a nice dinner. Or both.'

'That would be nice. Or . . .'

'Go on.'

'No, seriously, it's okay. Chocolates would be lovely.'

'No, what were you going to say?'

'Well, my friend Maeve, she's had this fantastic kind of a makeover. It's taken years off her, she looks brilliant. And I thought, you know, with me going into the fashion business, I could do with looking

461

a bit more – with it. Instead of them just messing it around a bit, something radical. You know what I mean?'

'You look fine to me.'

'Fine is a word men use when they think you look distinctly average.'

'No, it's not.'

'It is, ask any woman. If you tell her she looks fine, it's like saying "you look like a pig in a wig".'

'Well, I think you look great.'

'Thank you, Walter, but I really do need a bit of an image change. She went to this place in Holywood, but it cost her a fortune.'

'What, like twenty, thirty quid?'

'Walter!'

'I know. I'm only joking. Fifty, then.'

'They wouldn't fluff it up for fifty.'

Walter took a deep breath. 'The point is, it doesn't matter. No matter what it costs, I want to treat you.'

'Are you *sure*?'

'Yes, of course I'm sure. And even if this deal doesn't work out, I still want to treat you.'

'Oh Walter, that's really *sweet*.'

When he came off the phone, Mark was sitting on the edge of his desk, looking forlornly across. 'Well,' he said, 'it all seems to be working out for you.'

'So far so good.'

Mark lifted his box of personal effects and paperwork. 'I'll be off then.' He nodded around their little office. 'We've had some good times here,' he said sadly.

'Have we?'

'Well, we've had some times.'

'Cheer up, Mark. It's not like you're moving to a different country. You're only going down the corridor.'

Mark looked down the corridor towards Office 12. Walter didn't really understand. Office 12 was *exactly* like another country. It operated according to its own standards and rules; it was a law unto itself. *This* office had been his home from home, his security blanket, his comfort zone, for so long. Office 12 represented a huge step up into the shadowy world of espionage, misinformation and intrigue. It was hugely exciting and completely terrifying at the same time. The thought of working closely with Steven rather unsettled him. Walter was a laugh. Steven was slightly creepy and very mysterious. He couldn't imagine laughing about girls and diets with Steven the way he had with Walter. But Walter was moving on as well. Probably in a few months he'd be gone too, the way his property thing was shaping up.

Come on, Mark, for godsake gee yourself up! Back straight, chest out, here's to a brave new world!

'See you around, mate,' he said, then winked at Walter and strode purposefully down the corridor towards Office 12.

'Mark!'

Mark stopped. Walter was standing in the doorway.

'What?'

'Missing you already.' Walter laughed, then turned back to his desk.

118
Bull by the Horns

It didn't matter whether you were a cop or a reporter, there was nothing to beat old-fashioned footwork. Marsh knew that as well as anyone, and the proof of it was there before him. The Bull, Pink Harrison's right-hand man, was just coming out of Billy Gilmore's house, the door behind him hanging off its hinges. It was a combination of luck and good timing that he was there to see it, with perhaps a smidgin of instinct thrown in. Marsh had spent twenty-four hours going through the paperwork on the Michael Caldwell case. Gary had promised to come round again, but then got called into work on a different case. Marsh wasn't put out. He didn't mind working by himself. He went to bed in the early hours, but only manged ninety minutes of sleep. He woke with a cricked neck and a sore head, and deciding to lay off the whiskey for a while. Gary phoned first thing with a story he'd heard about Pink's party in Stormont, that all his credit cards were refused. Word on the street was that his accountant had done a runner with Pink's money.

There had been no answer on Gilmore's home phone, and his mobile was dead, so Marsh went to see him. Now, with Bull pacing up and down in front of the house, talking into his own mobile, Marsh knew that Billy wasn't at home. The door off its hinges meant he was in big trouble, but Bull still hanging around at least meant that Marsh wasn't at a murder scene. Billy was still alive. And if he was alive he still knew all about Pink's bank accounts.

Marsh was about 100 yards away, sitting in his car with the sun visor down, far enough away not to be noticed, but close enough to see Bull smile suddenly and hurry towards his own car, then set off at speed, a hunter following a scent. Marsh followed, down into the city centre then behind the Europa Hotel and into an NCP car park. It was busy, so Bull had to go almost to the top level, and with the turnings being tight, Marsh was forced to stay well back. By the time he got parked himself, Bull had already made it to the lift and was gone.

Jimmy Marsh Mallow approached the hotel reception desk, flashed the warrant card he had somehow neglected to hand in, and asked for Billy Gilmore's room, but was told there was no one booked under that name. He thanked the girl and was just turning away when she called him back and told him about the Mr de Vere whose account was being paid for by a Billy Gilmore. She said she thought they were probably one and the same person, and that guys did that all the time when they were having an affair. She told him he was in the Clinton Suite, and did he want her to call the room? Marsh said no. He stepped towards the lift, wishing he'd brought his gun. Bull probably wasn't mug enough to use one in here, but he'd surely be carrying one. Marsh's gun was at home. He hadn't worn it in a while. A sign of the times.

Top floor – and there they were already. Bull was marching Billy down the corridor, one hand behind his back, either prodding him with a weapon or half-breaking his arm. Billy looked terrified. Neither of them recognised Marsh until he was right up close – Billy first. 'Please God!' he cried, and then the penny dropped with Bull. But he didn't panic. He just smiled, held onto Billy, and pushed the button for the lift.

Marsh said, 'How're you doing, Bull?'

'Fine,' said Bull. 'How're you doing? Hear you lost your job.'

'Yeah, and I hear your boss lost his money.'

'Yeah, so what?'

'So what are you doing with Billy-boy here?'

'We're just going for a walk, aren't we, Billy?'

Billy shook his head vehemently. 'No, please, you have to – Jesus!' Bull had twisted his arm up hard.

'Let him go, Bull,' said Marsh.

'Now why would I want to do that?'

'Because I'm asking you nicely.'

'And you'll do what, exactly, if I don't?'

'Nothing, Bull. I'm just appealing to your good nature. And better me than . . .' Marsh nodded at the lift.

Bull's brow furrowed. The lift pinged and the door opened. He looked at the empty space. 'Why, who's down there?'

'Well, who would be down there, Bull, if word was out that Pink was stony broke?'

'Pink's not broke.'

'So what do you want Billy for?'

'Because he was caught with his fingers in the pie.'

'No, I wasn't,' said Billy.

'So who's down there?' Bull asked again.

'About fifty cops who want to talk to Billy. They won't think twice about doing you for kidnapping. And for carrying a gun.'

'I'm not carrying a gun,' said Bull.

Marsh thumped him hard and sudden, right under the chin. Bull's jaw clamped shut on his tongue and he shot backwards, his head cracking into the wall. His legs immediately gave way and he slumped down, his eyes rolling back in his skull. Billy looked down at Bull in shock, then at Marsh. 'I've never seen anything like that in my life,' he said.

'You should get out more,' Marsh told him.

Marsh walked Billy across the lobby, the accountant struggling with his Gucci bags and looking all around him, wondering when all those cops were going to spring out and whisk him into protective custody. But Marsh kept him moving straight and steady out of the front doors, then guided him towards the NCP car park.

'It was a *bluff*,' Billy finally realised.

'That's right, Billy.'

'You saved my life,' said Billy.

'Probably did. So you owe me.'

'Yes, I do. Yes, I do. Do you want me to, like, write you a cheque?'

'Would that be with Pink Harrison's money?'

'It's my money now.'

'I don't want a cheque, Billy, I want to go through Pink's finances with you again.'

The NCP lift was ready and waiting. They stepped in and Marsh hit the button.

'But I've done that with you already.'

'Well, I want you to do it again.'

'I don't have the accounts – they're at my house.'

'Then that's where we'll go.'

'What if they're waiting there for me as well?'

'That's a chance we'll just have to take.'

Marsh negotiated the bends out of the car park in silence. Only when they had swept back out onto Great Victoria Street did Billy make him promise to give him a lift to the airport when they were finished.

Marsh stopped at a traffic-light, then looked across at his passenger. 'Exactly how much did you take from Pink?'

Billy told him.

Marsh laughed. 'Christ, Billy,' he said, 'you've some balls on you.'

'Not really.' Billy explained about being sent by Pink to collect the money, and Bull and him having a tug-of-war with the bag. 'It was an accident.'

'Draining his accounts wasn't an accident.'

'I have to live, don't I?'

'Sure, Billy, but did you have to pick on someone who's going to spend the rest of his life tracking you down?'

'Do you think he will?'

'I *know* he will.'

Billy sighed. 'You've no intention of taking me to the airport. You'll need me to stay and testify about all of Pink's accounts. That could take months, years. I'll never get out of here. He'll find some way to kill me. That's the truth of it, isn't it?'

Marsh shook his head. 'You know something, Billy? You recall Al Capone, the way he was done for tax evasion? I always felt sorry for the guys that chased him all those years. They wanted to catch him with a smoking gun in his hand. It must have been kind of an anti-climax, tax evasion.'

'Well, speaking as an accountant, I'd find it quite fascinating.'

'Yeah, well – fact is, the PSNI are washing their hands of Pink, and I haven't the resources to mount a full-scale investigation into his finances. Nor, to be frank, the interest. I want to get him for murder, Billy. I want to get him for raping and cutting up a little boy. I want to finish him off for good.'

Billy nodded. He studied the surrounding traffic for a few moments before looking back at the big ex-cop behind the wheel. 'You've got some balls on you as well,' he said.

119
Mack

Margaret was taken a little by surprise when she phoned Thomas Mack, Hair Design, in Holywood, and was invited to come the next day. It was so different from, say, her GP, where the receptionist would laugh in your face if you expected an appointment within a month. Clearly, money talked. When she explained roughly what she wanted done, she was told that Thomas Mack was prepared to work 'in that general area', but that he was usually a law unto himself. When she asked how much it would cost she was given 'an estimate'. Her mother had always taught her to go to three different plumbers for estimates before settling on one, but this was slightly different. Thomas Mack was in a league of his own.

When she told Walter how much the estimate was he looked a little pale and said he'd need to go to the cash machine. They were sitting in Pizza Express on the Dublin Road. Margaret agreed that it was a ridiculous amount to pay for a new hairstyle, but with an excited kind of a glow in her eyes. Walter said that amount of money would keep him, his children, and his children's children in haircuts for their entire lifetimes. 'He doesn't do children,' was Margaret's response. 'Or old women.'

'Is there like a sign on the door, *No Kids or Old Bats*?'

'I do believe there is.'

'He sounds a bit . . . eccentric.'

'He's won Hairdresser of the Year three times.'

'Well, Chelsea keep winning the League, but it doesn't mean they're anything special.'

'I would have thought it meant precisely that.'

'It just means they have a lot of expensive prima donnas, and nobody likes that.'

'Well, Thomas Mack is supposed to be a bit of a character. You've probably seen him on TV, he's always on those celebrity quizzes. Dresses all in black, he's about six foot seven, this big shiny head.'

'He's bald?'

'Completely.'

'Well, there you go. Never trust a bald barber.'

'He's not a barber.'

'You know what I mean. It's like fat aerobics teachers, and laser eye-surgery guys who wear glasses – there's something quite fishy about it.'

'There's nothing fishy about it at all. And I thought you were supposed to be getting *your* eyes done?'

Walter looked a bit sheepish. 'I missed my appointment.'

'You forgot?'

'No, I . . .'

'You chickened out.' Walter nodded. 'Aw, Walter, it's not supposed to be sore at all.'

'Well, they *would* say that.'

He promised to reconsider, especially when she said he looked really cute without his glasses. Later, outside, he went to the cash machine. When he handed over the thickish wad of notes she said, 'Are you sure about this?'

'No, but take it while the going's good.'

'This is very sweet of you, especially as none of your money's through yet.'

No, it wasn't through, but it would be soon enough. His first stab at a property deal was going like a dream. Geordie had been more than grateful to sell the fruit and vegetable shop to Walter, although for slightly more than he'd originally said – £225,000. But it was still a good price. Even before the paperwork was sorted out, Geordie had handed over the keys. He wanted rid of it that much. 'Thirty-five years of getting up at five every morning to buy apples. I'll be happy if I never see another Granny Smith again.'

Thus armed with the keys, Walter was able to show Paul the baker around later that same day. Paul offered less than he'd originally suggested, saying it was slightly further away from the train station than his original premises and that it needed some structural upgrading, but the offer was still well more than Walter was paying for it. He was going to make a very healthy profit indeed. Almost twice his annual salary at the Department of Education, in fact, which got him thinking.

The next afternoon, finishing work early, and making sure to change out of her Primark uniform, Margaret duly drove out to Holywood and parked outside a plush, chrome and mirrors edifice just off the High Street. What she was paying for this put even her one-off visit to Tony & Guy into the shade.

She entered *Thomas Mack* with some trepidation, but was immediately welcomed like a long-lost relative. She was offered a wide range of impressive coffees and then presented with a selection of carrot cakes. 'We have a special arrangement with *Irma La Deuce* – have you heard of them?' said Rhona, who had a badge with *Client Liaison Officer* on her chest, which was ample; she looked like Cameron Diaz, only with better skin. Margaret declined the carrot cake and was just about to try her choice of coffee when Thomas Mack swept in. He *was* impressive, but he was also only human. His impressively tall frame was, well, impressive, but it was also clearly causing him back problems, as he was wincing as he walked, which is like mincing, but more painful. His head *was* completely bald and shining, but it was also flecked with several black dots because 'those f***ing gypsies are tarmacing again'. As soon as he saw Margaret he looked her up and down, then said, 'Boy, have you come to the right place.'

Margaret had not previously thought that her hair was *that* bad, but Thomas Mack – 'call me Mack' – quickly put her straight. It was badly cut, badly maintained, thirty years out of date and the colour was atrocious. 'You've either been in a concentration camp, or you've been to Tony and Guy,' he said, then cackled. 'No, honestly,' he quickly added, 'I won't hear a word said against them. I was their top stylist for years, but then they just couldn't afford me.'

He sat her down and they had a thirty-minute discussion about what *she* wanted, he emphasised that time and again, although when it came to making an actual decision it seemed to be more a case of what *he* wanted. Still, she didn't mind that. That's what she was paying for – a new approach, a new look; out with the old, in with the new. Certainly she had his undivided attention – no conveyor belt here – even if the more she listened to him the more she realised how everything he said was about him and his career and his famous friends, and what his favourite restaurant was and who he met there and how wonderful the chef was, and where he took his holidays and how exclusive it all was. It was mildly annoying but also maddening, because she wanted to compete with him; she wanted to tell him all about *M & Emma* and how she was a bit of a player herself now, but there never seemed to be a suitable opportunity. She was sitting with silver foil in her hair under a heated lamp, sipping a cappuccino when Walter phoned to see how it was all going.

'I have no idea,' said Margaret.

'I can't wait to see it,' said Walter.

'Neither can I. When do you get out of work?'

'I am out of work. I'm sitting in my car outside. Look out the window – I'm waving.'

Margaret peered down the length of the salon, and right enough, there was Walter waving away from behind the wheel of his car.

'Jesus, Walter, I don't want you to see me like this.'

'I can't, Margaret, not really. I'm just waving in your general direction.'

'What are you even doing here?'

'I want to take the New Look You out to dinner.'

'Oh. Well, that's nice. But if we keep going out for dinner, at this rate we'll be as fat as fools.'

'I know,' said Walter, 'but the diet starts on Monday.'

It *was* sweet of him. He was being very good to her. It was such a refreshing change after Billy. She told Walter she would be ages yet and told him to go for a walk or something.

When she cut the line, Margaret noticed that there was a message waiting for her; it was from Emma. A little frisson of excitement raced through her. She loved the fashion world! As she waited for the message to play back, her only regret was that Mack wasn't standing beside her. She would have loved to have dropped Emma's name, then talked business with her. Maybe he'd even knock something off the bill, or give it to her for free – that's how it worked with celebrities.

When Margaret called her back, Emma sounded excited. 'Margaret, darling, you won't believe this. The ba****ds! We've had someone in from Trading Standards! Remember your dresses – the first ones we sold? Well, Primark are selling rip-off copies already! Trading Standards want to take them to court. We've definitely arrived now!'

120
Mack (2)

Thomas Mack was growing increasingly agitated with Margaret. 'Will you just *keep still*,' he said on more than one occasion. Margaret couldn't help herself. Her mind was racing, and when that happened her body tended to follow suit. She moved her head and crossed her legs and shifted her bum and rolled her shoulders. Mack tutted and said, 'What's got into you?'

'Nothing. I—' She stopped herself saying, *I'm about to be exposed as a clothes pirate!* Instead, she nodded at her reflection. 'Is it supposed to look like that?'

'Yes, dear.'

'That colour?'

'That's what we agreed.'

Margaret nodded. She had nonchalantly cut her conversation with Emma Cochrane short, mostly because of panic, but she was *dying* to know what was going on. A Trading Standards Officer was on the verge of exposing her fraud, and here she was sitting in an expensive leather swivel chair being talked down to by a bald man with scissors. She said, 'How long do you think this will take?'

'It will take as long as it takes.'

Margaret nodded. But then said, 'But how long is that?'

'How long is a piece of string, dear?'

'I know, but ball park.'

Thomas Mack pulled himself up to his full extraordinary height, even with the slight stoop. 'Thomas Mack does not do ball park,' he said.

'Okay. All right. Sorry.'

Thomas Mack hesitated, then returned to his cutting. His flow of stories about celebrities he had worked with dried up, and he worked on in silence until Margaret's mobile rang again, then he tutted when she went to answer it. 'I would really prefer,' he said, rather

472

testily, 'if you would switch that blessed thing off. I'm trying to concentrate.'

Margaret picked up the phone. 'I know. I'm sorry. Just this one.'

'Margaret – it's Emma.'

'Emma,' said Margaret, her throat dry.

'He wants to talk to you.'

'Me? I haven't done anything wrong!'

'Will you keep still?' Mack, behind her now, pulled her head forcefully back.

'*Aoow!* Sorry, Emma. I'm having my hair done.'

'Really?! Anything nice?'

'I don't know yet.'

'Where are you?'

'Thomas Mack.'

'Oh, he's such a doll! Tell him Emma says hello!'

Margaret glanced up. 'Emma says hello.'

Thomas Mack looked at her, then mouthed, *'Emma?'*

Margaret shrugged and said, 'Why does he want to talk to me?'

'He's just determined to nail whoever is ripping us off! He's a real crusader! He says that once he gets the bit between his teeth he never lets go! He wants the dates when you originally made the dresses, a statement, any corroborating evidence, then he's going to go after Primark. They won't know what's hit them!'

'Is he . . . is he still there?'

'No, he's away now, but he's left his card and wants you to call him straight away.'

'Could you *please* keep still?' asked Mack.

'All *right*,' snapped Margaret. '*This* is important.'

'And so is *this*,' Mack snapped back, and this time he jerked her head to the right.

Margaret felt a bone click in her neck. 'Aooooow,' she said, and glared at the hairdresser. 'Would you be careful?'

'Well, would you get off that bloody phone and let me finish this production?'

'I'll get off it when I'm finished,' said Margaret. 'Emma, look, I'm going to have to go. My hairdresser's not happy.'

'Mack?' Emma began. 'But he's such a—'

Margaret cut the line and closed her phone. 'Right,' she said. 'All done.'

'Good,' said Mack. Then he forced her head to the left.

Margaret took a deep breath. 'Do you think you could just take it a little easier?'

Mack glared down at her. 'Who's the expert?'

'I'm not doubting your abilities. I'm just saying, take it a little easier. My neck clicked there.'

'Necks are supposed to click, dear. It's when they don't click you have to worry.' He clipped away for another minute, then tried to move her head again. This time Margaret resisted.

'Go with me, now,' said Mack.

'Then take it a bit easier.'

Mack stepped back. 'Listen, dear, either you're working with me, or you're working against me.'

'I just have a sore neck.'

'Well, you should have advised us of that before we started.'

'I didn't have it before we started.'

'Are you implying that we've injured your neck?'

'No, I'm just saying, if you carry on like that you *will* injure my neck.'

'Well, if you would stay still, and didn't make phone calls, then perhaps I wouldn't have to keep moving your neck.'

'I wasn't making phone calls,' said Margaret.

'*Right*,' said Mack. 'Tell me this, if you were in hospital having liposuction, would you sit up in the middle of the operation to make a phone call?'

'What are you saying, that I *need* liposuction?'

'It was only an example. It could just as easily be a facelift.'

Margaret glared at him. 'Are you saying I *need* a facelift?'

'Dear, none of us is perfect.'

'You can say that again, you baldy f***er.'

Mack's mouth dropped open. All around the salon, where hairdressers and clients alike had been quietly enjoying the growing ill-feeling, mouths dropped open. 'You . . . you . . .' Mack was trying to say something coherent, but the words wouldn't come.

Margaret stood suddenly, pulling off her gown, and stood menacingly before Thomas Mack. 'You just listen to me, you f***ing big drink of water. You don't talk to people like that. Have you never heard of the customer always being right? I came in here for a hair*do*, nothing more, nothing less, not to have my neck half-broken because you object to me taking a phone call, all right? And *not* to be made to feel small and imperfect. And for your f***ing information, there's no comparison between being a f***ing surgeon and a f***ing hairdresser. You cut hair! And you charge more than a f***ing surgeon! And people respect surgeons! They save lives, not split ends!'

Margaret threw her gown down, grabbed her bag and stormed out of the salon, slamming the door closed behind her. Her hair was still soaking wet, and only cut on one side. She immediately burst into tears.

474

Within seconds, Walter was out of his car and holding her in his arms. 'What's wrong, love? What's wrong?'

'Look at my hair!'

Walter looked at her hair. 'What's wrong with it? It looks fine.'

'Fine?!'

'Fantastic! It looks fantastic!'

'Oh!' Margaret broke away from him; her head began to dart this way and that.

'What's wrong? What are you looking for?' Walter asked.

'A shop! I need a cigarette!'

'You don't smoke.'

'I'm starting!' She turned and glared back at the shop. 'That man! The nerve of him!'

'What's wrong? What did he do?'

'Nothing!'

'Did he try something on with you?'

'No!'

''Cause I'll go in and sort him out.'

'No – Christ, that's all I need! And a cigarette!'

The tears sprang again. He held her by the shoulders. 'Margaret, listen to me. Cigarettes won't solve anything. Can I interest you in a gravy ring?'

She laughed involuntarily. 'Oh Walter,' she said. 'What am I going to do?'

'About what, love?'

Margaret swallowed hard, then began to tell him the story of the Primark dresses.

121
The Seven Deadly Sins

Father Benedict woke with an aching head, a throbbing nose and a swollen lip. He was confused and groggy and handcuffed to the headboard. Boy, he thought, that must have been *fantastic*. Absence *does* make the heart grow fonder.

Yet . . . now he realised he was still fully dressed. And although he usually liked it quite rough, he felt like he had actually been beaten up. He tried to get his thoughts together, but it was hard, with his head so sore and his breathing difficult with his nose all stuffed up. At first he thought it was a cold, but then with his free hand, the one that wasn't attached to the headboard, he poked at it, wincing at the pain and then examining in the half-light the dried blood on his hand. My God, he thought, it's *broken*. My God, he thought again, what has become of Damian? He went out to that godforsaken country a meek and pliable country priest, and he's come back a raging beast. Benedict wasn't quite sure that he liked it.

He heard movement then, off to his right. The curtains were closed and the light above off, but he now realised that the half-light was coming from the bathroom across the hall; its door was slightly open and by twisting his head he could see the mirror, and reflected in it, the shower cubicle, with Damian inside.

Father Benedict didn't know what to do – whether to call out to Damian to release him or to try and get himself out. The problem was, he couldn't remember whether he'd volunteered for all of this. He remembered watching the DVD, then embracing Damian and kissing him, but everything else was a blank. Had they taken drugs? Had Damian brought something especially strong back from South America? But why the violence? And what if he'd done something equally bad to Damian? What if he was in the shower now, washing the blood off?

Oh my, this is getting out of hand.

476

The handcuff was on tight, and pulling at it only rattled the head-board. He tried to squeeze his hand out of it, but without success. The shower door opened and closed. Benedict closed his eyes immediately, but when at first Damian didn't appear, he opened them again and darted a glance towards the bathroom. He saw Damian standing naked in front of the mirror, drying his hair. He thought, *My God!* And suddenly things felt a little clearer.

Ten minutes later, Redmond entered the bedroom, back in his priest's outfit. He opened the curtains and light flooded in. Father Benedict blinked up at him, his face a mess of dried blood, his eyes already yellowing.

'Damian,' Benedict began.

'Shut your cake-hole.' Benedict fell silent. Redmond stood over the end of the bed. He looked furious. 'Haven't you ever heard of the Seven Deadly Sins?' he snapped out.

'Yes, of course. Brad Pitt—'

'Not the movie, you clampett! Our rules, our laws. Pride! Envy! Lust! Anger! Gluttony! Greed! Sloth!'

'Yes, yes, of course – but Damian . . .'

'Shut up!' He pointed an angry finger at him. 'People are supposed to look up to us! We're supposed to be an example!'

'We do our best,' Benedict said weakly.

'Our best? What about *lust*?!'

'Well, it takes two to tango.'

'Don't get smart with me!'

'Damian, please. I know what you're saying, and we've all struggled with our consciences, but we are but weak mortals, and we pretty much avoid the other deadly sins. Six out of seven isn't bad; in another field that sort of percentage would get you into a good grammar school.'

'I'm not talking about grammar schools, I'm talking about *this*. I'm talking about last night and you . . . you *disgust* me.'

Even this was a bit rich for Benedict. '*I* disgust *you*? Well, listen here, sweetie. They're your handcuffs – you were always more into this than I was.'

'My . . . ?'

'Unless of course you keep them in your bedside drawer in case a burglar comes by.'

Redmond shook his head. He didn't know what he'd thought when he'd found them while casting around for something to restrain the unconscious priest with. There had been no way of telling how long the headbutt would keep him out for, and he didn't want him charging off into the night screaming blue murder and probably giving the whole deception away. In fact, the thought had crossed his mind that they *were* for a burglar. But not, he ruefully thought, an a*se burglar.

'Damian,' Benedict said gently, 'I know what's going on.'

'You do?'

Benedict nodded. 'I knew the moment I saw you.'

Redmond swallowed. 'It was that obvious?'

'It was that obvious.'

'Oh, Christ. And are you going to tell anyone?'

Benedict smiled for the first time, even though it hurt to do so. 'Do you *want* me to tell anyone?'

'No, of course not.'

'Well then, I won't. Of course I won't. I'll just save it all for me.'

Redmond blinked at him. 'Save it?'

'Oh Damian. It's all clear now. I've read all about it, I've heard what they can do.'

'Who can?'

'Not who, what! It's the steroids. Or hormones. Or the medication.'

'What medication?'

'Damian, *please*. I saw you in the bathroom mirror. That *thing*. You went away a little finger, and you came back a thumb.'

'I what?'

'Damian, *please*. You went away a poodle and came back a Doberman.'

'What are you *talking* about?'

'Damian! You went away a sprickleback and came back Moby Dick!' This time he nodded at Redmond's groin, and the penny – finally, finally – dropped. 'I saw, Damian, and I'm impressed – and it explains everything. You attacked me last night, didn't you? That's why I feel like this. Ever since I arrived, you were moody and taciturn. It was as if you were a different person. I *know*, Damian. While you were away you met some glamorous South American surgeon and he did fantastic things to your little man, but you've paid a terrible price as well. You talk to me about the Seven Deadly Sins? Well, what about Vanity, Damian? What about that? You've interfered with God's will. And while the results are certainly pleasing to the eye, at what price, my darling, at what price?'

'I don't know,' said Redmond.

'Will you be on these drugs for ever?' Benedict asked.

'I don't know,' said Redmond.

'Will your personality be altered for ever?' Benedict asked.

'I don't know,' said Redmond.

'And will you ever love me again?' Benedict demanded.

'Probably not,' said Redmond.

*   *   *

Redmond released Benedict from the handcuffs and helped to get him cleaned up. Then he took him downstairs and made him a fry. Throughout Benedict watched him with sad swollen eyes, and not just from the beating he'd taken.

'It's like the ultimate confirmation of God's love for us,' said Benedict. 'He blesses the surgeon with the ability to do the operation, and you with the kind of personality who would want to undergo this appalling operation in order to please me – even though you'll recall that I hardly ever complained about your size in the past. And yet in doing this, He also visits a personality disorder upon you which renders what you've undergone completely irrelevant. It's like payback for vanity: "I'll give you this huge weapon, but you won't have any desire to use it at all".' Benedict cut into his Denny's pork sausage. 'Damian, what are we going to do?'

'Well, I've got a service to perform.'

'I mean about us.'

'Well, I'll obviously consult my doctor. But I do believe I was warned that I could be on these for a *very* long time.'

'It's a crying shame, and such a waste.'

'I'm sorry for attacking you, for handcuffing you.'

'It's all right, Damian. It's your condition, I understand that now.'

Redmond nodded at his fry. He had pulled it round, saved the day. He had been preparing to flee, so convinced was he that the game was up, but now he could relax. Benedict would leave soon, bruised and chaste, but at least still believing that Redmond really was Damian. It was, Redmond reflected, like a French film he'd seen once, *The Return of Martin Guerre*, except it was slightly less believable, and without the subtitles.

122
Paper Trail

When they got home, the first thing Marsh did was locate his gun and check that it was in good working order. Then he set it on the coffee table in the lounge. Billy eyed it warily.

'Is that for *me*?' he asked.

'No,' said Marsh. 'It's for *them*.'

There was also a half-drunk bottle of whiskey sitting beside it, but it wasn't on offer. Marsh made coffee instead. He set the cups down, then moved to the window and turned the Venetian blinds so that he could see *out* but anyone outside couldn't see *in*. He watched for a minute, then, satisfied, turned and nodded at the two stacks of documents he'd placed on the hearth earlier. One was made up of the photocopied files Gary had delivered to him, the other contained the paperwork concerning Pink Harrison that they'd managed to retrieve from Billy's apartment earlier. Bull had smashed his plasma screen, toppled over his fridge and ripped the door off his expensive microwave, but although the contents of his filing cabinets had been strewn about the room, they hadn't actually been destroyed or removed. All of the papers relating to Pink's investments were still there, and the laptop, which had further details, was untouched.

'Right,' said Marsh, 'let's get started.'

It was a slow, slow process. But they both worked (or had worked) in jobs where that was taken for granted. The devil was often in the detail. There was nothing to be gained from Billy reading interview notes and witness statements, just as there was no point in Marsh examining profit and loss accounts and bank transactions, but there was everything to be gained from Marsh shouting out a name from his pile and Billy trying to trace a match in his, or Billy saying such and such an amount had been paid by Pink to someone he had not previously encountered, and was he by any chance mentioned in one of Marsh's wire taps or surveillance logs? The only difference between this approach and routine police work was that Marsh usually had dozens of trained officers at his disposal, but now there was just him, and Billy, who kept drinking his coffee and asking for more Viscounts.

Marsh's daughter phoned in the late afternoon and asked breezily how his lovelife was and he said it was fine. She asked him how work was going and he realised suddenly that she had somehow managed to miss the news that he'd resigned from the PSNI. It probably wasn't such a big thing in England. So he said fine to that as well.

She said, 'You sound tense.'

'Busy, a case,' he said.

'At home?'

'Uhuh.'

Billy knocked over his cup, then raised his hands apologetically. Lauren – maybe it was the detective genes in her – quickly said, 'You've someone with you.'

'Yes, I have.'

'Is it one of your new lovers?'

'No, it isn't.'

'You don't want to talk, do you?'

'Can't,' said Marsh.

'In that case, I just wanted to say: I love you, Daddy.' She kissed the phone then, and cut the line.

When Marsh retook his seat Billy said, 'I wiped up as much as I could.'

'Don't worry about it.'

'Did someone die?'

'What?'

'You've tears in your eyes.'

'No, I haven't.'

Billy knew different, but he was too intimidated by James Mallow to pursue it any further. Instead he said, 'It's like looking for a needle in a haystack.'

Marsh nodded, and lifted his next stack of papers.

About an hour later Billy said, 'I've a receipt here signed by a Mark Beck. It's marked "political contributions" and it has the Unionist Party stamp on it.'

'Why would Pink have that?'

'Well, as far as I'm aware his people collect direct from local supporters and the money is counted down at Unionist Headquarters so at least it's seen to be going in the right direction, but there are two receipt books, so that half the money gets recorded for the Party, and the other half goes back to Pink.'

'Okay, nice work if you can get it. Anything else on Mark Beck?'

'No. Never heard of him.'

Marsh quickly leafed through his own pile and soon found what he was looking for – Mark's brief interview with Gary McBride at Pink Harrison's house in Holywood on the morning the search warrants were executed. 'Mark Beck, Party worker, Civil Servant, Department of Education . . . Office Twelve. That rings a bell.'

Billy nodded. 'I mentioned Office Twelve to you one time. Pink – well, Pink told me I should. He knew you were after him, obviously, so he thought mentioning Office Twelve would lead you on a wild-goose chase.'

'You were working for both sides, were you?'

Billy saw no point in denying it. 'I was just protecting myself.'

Marsh snorted. 'I'm glad it all turned out well in the end. So what *is* Office Twelve?'

'I don't know. He just told me to say it.'

Marsh drummed his fingers on the arm of the chair. Then he got up and checked his telephone directory for a number for the Department of Education. He called and asked to be put through to Office 12. The operator thanked him and put him through. To the canteen. The canteen said they couldn't transfer him, so he hung up and called back. He asked for Office 12 again, and a different operator transferred him through to Pensions Branch. Pensions Branch said they couldn't transfer him from there and put him back to the operator. The operator apologised and promised to put him through. Marsh waited and waited, then realised that the line was dead. He phoned back and explained that he'd been trying to get through to Office 12 for the last ten minutes, and what exactly was the problem? She apologised and put him through. The phone rang, and rang, and rang.

'Perhaps,' Billy ventured, 'if you tried asking for Mark Beck by name?'

Marsh glared at him. Then phoned back. 'Could you put me through to Mark Beck, please.'

'Which department?'

'I'm not sure.'

'Oh, right. Just hold on.'

The call was transferred. A moment later it was picked up. Marsh said, 'Mark Beck?'

'No, sorry – Walter North.' Marsh, who neither recognised the name nor the voice from Linda's attempted suicide, just sighed at being given the familiar runaround. But then Walter said, 'I can transfer you if you want?'

'You can?'

'Absolutely. Just hold on.' It went quiet for another minute, then Walter came back on the line. 'Sorry – I don't know what's up with these bloody phones, but I can't seem to get a connection. Look – he's only down the corridor. If you give me a minute, I'll nip down and get him.'

'I'd appreciate that, thanks.'

Walter put the receiver down, and hurried down the corridor. It was as good an excuse as any to see his old mate. He had exciting news to tell him about his property developments, and he had at the back of his mind to mention Margaret and her Primark problem, to see if the all-powerful Office 12 could lend a hand. Walter hadn't spoken to Mark since he'd shifted offices the day before. He hesitated for a moment, wondering whether he needed to knock before entering, then decided he should. Given the mysterious workings of Office 12, he didn't want to just barge in on something he wasn't supposed to see. He gave a little drum roll on the door, and Mark's slightly querulous voice came back, 'Who is it?'

Walter opened the door – then frowned. Mark was sitting to the left of Steven's desk, with his coat on and his belongings still in a cardboard box in front of him. There was no one else in the room.

'Where's Steven?' Walter asked.

'I don't know,' said Mark. 'He hasn't been in.'

'This morning?'

'At all.'

Walter nodded down at Mark's box, and the computer in front of him which wasn't switched on. 'So what have you been doing?'

'Waiting for him.'

'Didn't he call, or didn't you call someone?'

Mark shook his head. 'I thought maybe it was some kind of test.'

Walter sighed. 'Well, there's someone on the phone for you in our . . . *my* office.'

'Is it Steven?'

'No, Mark, it's not bloody Steven.'

123

The New Man in Office 12

'Mark Beck? You're a hard man to track down.'
  'Am I?'
'Anyone would think you're trying to avoid being contacted.'
'I'm sorry, but who is this?'
'This is James Mallow.'
'James Mallow? The . . . ?'
'Yes, that one.'
'You used to be . . . ?'
'Yes, I did.'
'It was only the other . . .'
'Yes, it was.'
'Oh my Lord. I mean, what can I do for you?'
'It's like this, Mark. I'm kind of working freelance now.'
'For the PSNI?'
'No, not for the PSNI. Shall we say, for other interested parties.'
Marsh let it sit in the air for a moment.
  'Oh. Right. I see.' Mark lowered his voice a little. 'You're Office
Twelve as well?'
  Marsh cleared his throat.
  'Right,' said Mark, 'I understand. Our tentacles reach far and wide.'
  'Okay. So, Mark. Tell me about yourself.'
  'Well, I've been sitting here waiting for two days and I'm not sure
whether it's a test or everyone's so busy they've forgotten that I was
meant to start yesterday. I haven't looked in any of the filing cabinets
or opened any of the drawers, if that's what you're worried about. I
was curious, but I thought maybe you had CCTV cameras hidden
somewhere – just, you know, to see how I coped with being left alone.
But I didn't touch anything, I swear to God.'
  Marsh had to think about that for a few moments, and that brief

silence was somehow interpreted by Mark as a confirmation that he had indeed been observed and possibly recorded.

'Okay, look, to tell you the truth, I was bored to distraction, I was just looking for something to do, so I thought I'd make some notes about what I'd like to do with Office Twelve, but I didn't have a pen, so I went to Steven's desk and opened the drawer and I saw the gun but I didn't do anything with it, and I didn't tell anyone. I just shut the drawer and went and sat down again.' Mark took a deep breath. 'Did I do the right thing?'

Marsh said, 'Yes, you did the right thing. Tell me, Mark, why do you think there's a gun in the Department of Education?'

'To protect ourselves?'

'Against whom?'

'Our enemies.'

'What sort of enemies, Mark?'

'I'm not sure. Insurgents.'

'In the Department of Education?'

'Likely here as anywhere.'

'But it was in Steven's drawer?'

'Yes, it was.'

'Steven – what surname is he, ahm, currently operating under?'

'Bradley. Steven Bradley.'

'Bradley. Right. Good. And is he in charge at the moment?'

'Well, he would be, if he was here. Is he on some sort of a . . . you know, special assignment? No – sorry, I shouldn't ask that.'

'All right, Mark, now just relax. But tell me, how would you describe Office Twelve to a complete stranger?'

Mark caught that straight away. 'I wouldn't describe it to a complete stranger.'

'Very good,' said Marsh. He paused again. He could hear Mark breathing heavily. 'Now, how would you describe it to, say, a young colleague, starting his first day in Office Twelve.'

'Well,' said Mark, 'I am that young colleague, and it is – was – my first day.'

'So how was it described to you, By . . .'

'Steve. Well, Steven described it as the Office of Misinformation.'

'Misinformation?'

'Black propaganda, a specialist unit – that's what he said.'

'What kind of black propaganda?'

'Just generally putting a spanner in the works.'

'In the Department of Education?'

'I think so.'

'To what purpose?'

'Well, we're fighting the Republicans, obviously, and then the DUP, I suppose. We support the establishment. The Unionists.'

'The Unionist Party, of which you're a member.'

'Of course.'

'You spoke to one of my colleagues the day we raided Councillor Harrison's house.'

'Yes, I did.'

'And you signed for the receipt of monies collected by Councillor Harrison for Party funds.'

'Yes, I did.'

'Funds which have subsequently gone missing.'

'Have they?'

'Yes, they have. Are they making their way to Office Twelve?'

'No, of course not. We're entirely funded by the Department of Education.'

'You're funded by the Department of Education, and your sole purpose is to disrupt the Department of Education.'

'I wouldn't say it was our sole purpose. I get the impression we'll disrupt anything.'

There was another silence. Mark eventually said, 'How am I doing?'

'You're doing fine, Mark.'

'Have you any idea when Steven will be back?'

'I can't tell you that.'

'Of course, I understand. I just want to do the job properly, that's all.'

'Very commendable. But Mark, I need you to do something else for me. You see the gun? If Steven's not there, we don't want to leave it lying around, do we?'

'I suppose not.'

'So I want you to take it out of the drawer, put it in an envelope, and when you're leaving work tonight, I want you to bring it with you, and I'll take it off you.'

'Really? Are you sure?'

'Yes, Mark. I think it's the right thing to do, don't you?'

'Yes, I suppose. But what if Steven comes back?'

'I'll return it to him in due course. Now listen carefully. When you're putting it in the envelope, try not to touch it directly. Let's not get your fingerprints on it, eh?'

'No, of course not, that's wise,' said Mark. 'I finish at five – I'll bring it with me. And I suppose I'll recognise you, as you're always on the telly.'

'Yes, you will,' said Marsh.

*   *   *

When Mark put the phone down, Walter turned from the window overlooking the dual carriageway to Newtownards. Even hearing just one side of it, he knew it had been a very disturbing conversation. Mark sat rather forlornly at his old desk, staring at the phone.

'Well?' said Walter.

'Well what?'

'Office Twelve business?'

'Yeah.'

'So all hush-hush.'

'I suppose.'

'You know, you don't have to work in there. You could come back here any time. I don't think they've even noticed you've gone.'

'Well, that's good,' said Mark. 'I don't think Steven even knows I've arrived.' He sighed. 'It's only my first couple of days – things will improve.'

Walter nodded. 'Yes, they will. You will soon be a man of power and influence. I sold a fruit shop and made some money, but you will decide the fate of nations.'

They both nodded solemnly.

Then Walter said, 'Polo?' Mark declined. Walter said, 'Anyway, now that you're a man of influence, I was just wondering . . .'

124
Trading Standards

Margaret did what she could with her hair before going into work the next morning, but there was no denying it looked like a dog's dinner. Maeve was straight to the point. 'You know when you're in the Chinky and they ask you whether you want rice or chips and you can't decide, and so you go for half and half. That's what you've got, half and half. Long on one side, short on the other.'

'It's a disaster,' Margaret said bluntly.

'Not necessarily. It's original. It could take off, you know, like the Rachel cut from *Friends* or the Purdy cut from *The New Avengers*. Remember her? Joanna Lumley.'

'This is not going to take off anywhere. I'm going to have to shave my head and start again. If he wasn't such an arrogant, up his own a**e sod I'd go in there and demand that he finish the job properly.'

'Well, why don't you?'

'Because I'm the one stormed out. I'm the one called him a baldy f***er.'

'*Seriously*?' Margaret nodded. 'God, you've some balls on you. What came over you?'

Margaret shrugged. She didn't want to get into the whole Trading Standards thing with Maeve. She had an appointment to see them in the early afternoon. It was more time off work. Mr Kawolski said she was bringing a new meaning to flexitime. It also meant changing out of her uniform. She was doing it so often these days she was starting to feel like Mr Benn.

'Anyway,' said Maeve, 'if Walter was paying for it, and no money actually exchanged hands, then he can still pay for you to go somewhere different, can't he?'

Margaret sighed. 'I gave the money back and I haven't the nerve to ask him for it again.'

'You've the nerve to call the most famous hairdresser in Ireland a

488

baldy f***er and you haven't the nerve to ask your boyfriend for money he's already promised you?'

Boyfriend? She hadn't even thought about Walter being her boyfriend. They were just . . . together.

'I know,' she said. 'I just feel funny about it.'

'Well, I think you should. And anyway, you're going to have to get it sorted soon, 'cause you never know what might pop through your door one of these mornings.' Maeve raised an eyebrow.

'Maeve? You're *not*.'

'I am. We are. We just thought, what's the point in waiting.'

'But you . . .'

'. . . hardly know each other. Yadda, yadda. Heard it all before. I know what I want, Margaret, and I want him.'

'As far as I can see, you've got him already. But it's still a big step.'

'I know. That's why we're taking it. We love each other. It's next Wednesday.'

'Next Wednesday!'

'Yeah, I know. I thought we'd have to wait months, but they had a cancellation. It's a bit like doing your driving test – you get your official date, which is months away, and then you ring up looking for a cancellation. Only it seems more people cancel their wedding than they do their driving tests, so they're not that hard to come by. I popped down after work yesterday and organised it all. Burst into tears like an eejit as well.'

'Well, it's an emotional thing, isn't it?'

'It wasn't that. To get the go-ahead I had to show them Redmond's death certificate and I only had this battered fax thing they sent from the British Embassy in Bogotá and they ummed and aahed over whether it was acceptable.'

'That would be upsetting.'

'No, it wasn't that either, since in the end it was no problem. But then they got onto this really trivial thing about what background music to play, you know, while everyone comes in, and I said, "What do you have?" So they played me some examples, and one of them was called "Pan Pipe Melodies", and it reminded me of Redmond in the jungle and I just couldn't help myself, I was blubbing away.'

'Oh, sweetheart,' said Margaret.

'I know. It was just a build-up, really. It was good to get it out of my system. I want you to be one of my witnesses.'

'Me? Seriously?'

'Absolutely. As long as you get your hair fixed. I don't want to be upstaged by the trendiest haircut in town. Or the worst.'

'Maeve, I'm really touched. But are you sure? Are there no closer relatives or friends?'

'Yes, of course there are. But they all want to have me tarred and feathered. It's going to be a *very* small wedding.'

'I like small weddings,' said Margaret.

'Good thing,' said Maeve.

Margaret was kept sitting in reception at Trading Standards for half an hour, flicking through a *Which?* survey of fridges and aware all the time of the bored girl behind the desk staring at her hair. Eventually an overweight man in a too-tight shirt and tie puffed over and introduced himself as Kenneth Buchanan. By way of chit-chat he said, 'You're not at all as I imagined.'

Margaret touched her hair defensively but didn't otherwise respond. He led her into a small, barely furnished office. Margaret thought it was like a police interview room, or at least what she imagined one to be like.

'So,' Buchanan said, settling in behind the desk, 'I imagine you're pretty peeved about this.'

'No, actually,' said Margaret. 'I'm quite flattered.'

'Really? You're potentially losing hundreds of thousands of pounds' worth of sales. It's not just the Belfast store, you know, that's selling these cheap copies. It's *all* of their stores.'

'I'm *extremely* flattered, then.'

'It's a blatant infringement of copyright, as far as I'm concerned.'

This is where it gets risky.

Margaret had considered getting legal representation, telling the truth to Emma, or following Walter's advice of hiring a hit man, but had decided in the end just to brazen it out.

'Have you considered the possibility that it might be the other way round?' she asked. 'That *I* might have ripped off the Primark dresses and passed them off as my own?'

'You mean copied *their* designs?'

'No, I mean just taken the dresses and stitched my labels into them.'

'Why would anyone want to do that?'

Margaret shrugged. 'To expose the fickle nature of the fashion business. That one man's burger is another man's steak. To show that none of these clothes are actually worth one figure or the other. That beauty and price are in the eye of the beholder.'

Buchanan cleared his throat. 'Well, this is all very interesting, but hypothetical, and I've a very busy schedule, so perhaps if we get back onto the beaten track? The fact is that a customer has lodged a complaint against Primark selling dresses at £18.99 which are *exact* copies of a dress she bought for nearly a thousand pounds in *Emma Cochrane*. As the designer of the dress, I take it you have your original sketches?'

'Yes, of course.'

'And is there anyway of dating those sketches?'

'No, but I can write the date on them.'

'That's not really what I . . . Would you have receipts for the purchase of the original material, evidence of where the dresses were made?'

'No, I'm sorry – there was a fire.'

'Oh, right.' He lifted a pen and chewed on it. 'That's unfortunate.'

'Have you spoken to Primark?' Margaret asked.

'No, not yet. I like to go in with all guns blazing when it comes to dealing with the big fellas. You see, Margaret, usually I'm dealing with paramilitaries and their bootleg operations. You wouldn't believe the counterfeit goods they control. So, from my point of view, it's good to have a case where there's no risk whatsoever of me getting beaten up or shot at. Do you understand?'

Margaret nodded. 'And this girl that complained. What does she want out of it?'

'Justice,' said Kenneth Buchanan.

125

Lemon Grass

Marsh was too old in the tooth to get excited about things, there were too many unsolved cases out there to prove the folly of that; however, he couldn't help but feel a certain *frisson* as Mark Beck came towards him with a bulky envelope. Perhaps it was because for the first time in thirty years he was out on his own. He had the moral support of at least some of his former colleagues, but actual physical aid had thus far been confined to the supply of documents and the few hours Gary McBride had been able to spare. Perhaps it was also because he knew this would be his last case. The job was gone now, and he was about to be exposed as the woman-beating corruption of everything he had stood for. And if it appeared as if he was clutching at straws, well, sometimes you had to. The gun might be nothing, or it might prove to be the only link between Michael Caldwell, George Green, Pink Harrison and Office 12.

It wasn't to be. The envelope, handed by Mark through the window of Marsh's car, was far too light to contain a real, proper gun. Marsh opened it up and slipped the weapon out. It was a replica, and not a very good one. You could hold a Post Office up with it, but you couldn't shoot anyone. Even hitting someone over the head with it wouldn't elicit much of a bruise. Marsh immediately slipped it back into the envelope and returned it.

'Put it back where you found it, Mark.'

'No use?'

'No use.'

'God, you know your guns.'

'That I do.'

Mark stood slightly bent into Marsh's car, the late-afternoon gloom darkening his features as he looked for guidance. 'So what should I do now? Just hang about for Steven to return?'

'Yeah,' said Marsh. 'And keep *this* under your hat. If I need anything else, I'll give you a call.'

Mark nodded. 'We should have signals or something. You know, codewords, or funny handshakes to show who's in Office Twelve.'

'I'll see what I can do,' said Marsh, then rolled up his window.

He drove back to Belfast. He had a date with Linda Wray later in the evening, and was already dressed for it. He didn't fancy going back home, though – he'd left Billy sleeping on a sofa. He wasn't sure what further use the accountant could be to him, but he was reluctant to let him go in case he disappeared abroad and refused to return. He'd left him a pile of papers to go through, and Billy seemed pleased to have a purpose.

Now, with time to kill, and still wary about being seen in public, because he had enemies everywhere, Marsh found a largely deserted car park and made some calls. He was intrigued by this Office 12. Northern Ireland was rife with all manner of secretive organisations, but they were generally paramilitary in nature or had been around for hundreds of years, like the Orange Order or the Masons or Hibernians. It was unusual to find one so deeply ensconced in a Government Department. He did not doubt that dirty tricks and black propaganda went on. In fact, it had been hard to escape being involved in it himself during the 1970s and 1980s, and he wasn't naïve enough to believe that it might have totally disappeared with the Peace Process – but discovering it was one thing, getting such easy access to it was something else. That concerned him. And also the fact that Pink Harrison had tipped him off to it. What if he was being sucked into a trap? Or perhaps Pink had his own reasons; maybe he'd had a run-in with Office 12 himself and wanted to get his revenge by alerting Marsh to its existence while at the same time taking the heat off himself.

Marsh was tuned into Radio 2, listening to Franz Ferdinand and thinking how much like a 1960s band they sounded, when Gary phoned him back. 'I've an address for Steven Bradley. You do realise who he is, don't you?'

'Do I?'

'Well, the name fits, and the address corresponds. So your Steven Bradley would be the son of Richard Bradley, the Head of the Civil Service.'

'Oh,' said Marsh.

'You didn't know?'

'No.'

'This is still Pink you're working on, right?'

'Yeah.'

'So what has the son of the Head of the Civil Service got to do with Pink Harrison?'

'I have no idea.' And Marsh meant it.

'But obviously, you will share it, as soon as you do.'

'Goes without saying.'

They both laughed. Marsh took a note of the address, then checked his watch. At this time of night, with the rush-hour traffic beginning to ease off, he could be out at Hillsborough in twenty minutes. But his date with Linda was less than an hour away. It didn't really leave enough time. And he couldn't risk letting her down again. Not with someone who'd so recently almost thrown herself off a tall building. But at the same time he didn't want to appear distracted during the meal. That's what his wife used to accuse him of – with reason – on the few occasions they did get out. Always thinking about work. 'Even Superman takes time off,' she used to say, which led to another crazy argument because he didn't think that Superman actually did take time off. He may not always have worn the uniform, but he was always alert to the world being put in danger, and it usually happened precisely when he *wasn't* actually wearing it, thus causing him always to be on the look-out for a handy telephone box or revolving door to get changed in, and to therefore appear distracted.

He could have phoned, of course, but he was sufficiently intrigued by this Steven Bradley to want to meet him face to face. So he killed some more time listening to the radio and thinking about his wife, until he was ready to go to *Lemon Grass*. He arrived five minutes early. Linda was already there, sitting at a table by the window. She smiled widely as he approached.

'They tried to give me the same table as last time,' she said, 'but I refused point blank. It was an unlucky table.'

'And this is a lucky one?'

'Well, you're here this time, so it's luck*ier*.' She reached across and gently rested her hand on top of his. 'Thank you for coming. It's very sweet of you.'

'I wanted to come.'

'I know, but . . .'

'But nothing. Linda, let's get this clear right from the start. I'm not here because you tried to kill yourself. I'm here because I picked you out of an internet dating site and then left you sitting here.'

She smiled wanly. 'Could you keep your voice down? The people at the table behind us now know that I tried to commit suicide and have had to resort to an internet dating site.'

Marsh cleared his throat. 'Well, that's because they're at the unlucky table. And sorry – I didn't mean to shout.'

'It wasn't shouting. It was just a little too loud.'

'I'm used to shouting. It's part of the job.'

'A job you don't have any more.'

Marsh nodded. 'That's true.'

'So you're not on duty now.'

'No, absolutely not.'

'So you can speak more quietly. When we show clients around, we speak in hushed tones. Due reverence for the magisterial qualities of our properties.'

'I'll keep it down.'

The waiter came and took their orders. While they were eating their steaks Linda asked, 'Why do you keep looking round? Are you looking for an escape route?'

'No. Sorry, I just noticed the table behind – they're smoking, and it's a non-smoking restaurant.'

'I hadn't noticed. Does it bother you?'

'No, not really. Just the waiters should say something.'

'They're just boys, they're probably scared to say,' said Linda. 'If it's not bothering you, let it be. That's half the trouble with this country: too many people stick their big noses in then they get all hurt when they get bitten off.'

'Okay,' said Marsh.

'I don't mean that you have a big nose, or you stick it in. I'm just talking generally.' She decided to change the subject, and quickly. 'Have you ever had a massage?'

'A massage? No. In my position, I can hardly go to a massage parlour, can I?'

'Your position. Would this be the one you were fired from?'

'I wasn't fired, I took early retirement. But yes.'

'So you've never had a massage.'

'No, I've never had a massage.'

'You strike me as a man in dire need of a massage. You've thirty years of tension in those shoulders.'

'I wouldn't know where to go. And I wouldn't feel comfortable.'

'With a stranger?'

Marsh nodded. 'And also I'd be worried about, you know, if it was a woman, getting . . .' and he raised an eyebrow.

'Aroused?'

Marsh blushed. Linda thought it was very endearing. She squeezed his hand again. 'I give massages, James. Everyone tells me I'm very good. I light candles.'

'Well,' said Marsh.

'Are you game?' asked Linda.

'I suppose,' said Marsh.

They decided to skip dessert, and coffee, paid up quickly and skipped along to Marsh's car, holding hands. She said her place was a mess and could they go to his. He said his place wasn't a mess, but he had an accountant sleeping on his sofa, and please don't ask for an explanation. They finally settled on the Towerview apartments. Sometimes Linda thought her fate was inextricably linked to those apartments, but at least they were convenient when she felt horny.

126

The Last Lesson

During the course of the morning Walter received three phone calls from different estate agents suggesting commercial properties or developments he might care to invest in. Word was clearly out about his fruit-shop deal. That he was, already, a *player*. And the thing was, they weren't wrong. He had money in the bank and a keen eye for his next venture. Everything was starting to smell of roses, or if not roses, at least fruit and vegetables. His lovelife had gone from roaming in the wilderness for more years than he cared to remember, to chaotic, to his current state of happiness. The Linda problem was resolved without his two-timing ways being exposed. He now even had friends in high places. Or at least, one friend in a high place. Mark was with Office 12 and had promised to help Walter out with his little problem. He would use his newfound influence and power to get Margaret out of her difficulty with the Trading Standards Gestapo. Walter had been a little surprised at her pulling such a stunt, but on reflection it fitted in exactly with where her life had been, prior to meeting him – drifting, anchorless on the stormy seas of life. She had lied in her *Let's Be Mates* web profile and at their first meeting. The scam with the dresses was surely just an extension of that. The good thing was that, since meeting him, her own, original dress designs had been acclaimed and she was firmly on the road to being as much of a fashion mogul as he was a property tycoon. They were truly a golden couple.

Walter, in between dealing with fawning estate agents, tried to call Bertha a couple of times during the afternoon, but without success. She was probably out at salsa classes, or kick-boxing. She was an example to every old bat in Belfast. She was full of vim and vigour. And she had her head screwed on. She was the sage of Omagh. She had helped to make him a small fortune, and now he was going to pay her back. After work he took the train home, got changed, bought a box of Milk Tray and a bunch of flowers from the garage, then drove out to see her.

Walter parked outside, climbed out of the car with the flowers and chocolates already in his hand, only mildly crushing them in the process, then approached the front door. He could see the glow of the television in the front window, and the top of Bertha's head, just visible above the back of her favourite chair – 'Frank's chair,' she called it – but she clearly wasn't hearing the bell. She had confessed to being a little deaf, so the volume on the TV was right up: Walter could hear the *EastEnders* theme through the double glazing. He tried thumping on the front window next, but he still couldn't attract her attention. Walter moved around to the back of the house, and found that the back door was unlocked. He made as much noise as he could coming in, and called her name out several times. He didn't want to just suddenly appear and give her a heart-attack or something.

He made his way through the kitchen and down the hall to the lounge. The door was half-open. He called her name again, and knocked on it before pushing it fully open and venturing in. 'Bertha,' he said, 'it's only me. I rang the—'

She didn't look up, even as he stepped in front of her. Her eyes remained fixed on the television screen, and her hand was hovering above the remote control on the arm of her chair.

'Bertha?'

She continued to stare through him as if he wasn't there.

'Bertha, love, are you all right?'

Still nothing. Walter touched her arm – it was cool, and vibrating slightly. Now that he was so close he could see the shallow movement of her chest and the small trail of drool from the corner of her mouth. She became aware of him for the first time; just a slight movement of her eyes, then she opened her mouth to speak, but instead of words of welcome and explanation, there came a groan, a long, sleekid groan like the yawn of an opening tomb. Walter stood back, shocked. The groan came again. She was trying to say something, but the ability had deserted her. She was left only with the most primeval of sounds. It was meaningless, yet at the same time said everything that needed to be said. Walter moved the remote control and turned the sound down. Then he eased her vibrating arm back down onto the arm of the chair and stroked it gently.

'I'll just call someone,' he said. He went back out into the hall, located the phone and called an ambulance. There was also a small black address book on the table. He checked it for her beardy nephew Eric's number and called him. It was his home number, but there was no response. There was also a work number. Even though it was late,

Walter called McGympsey, Styles & Cameron and Eric himself answered the phone. Walter quickly explained.

'I knew you were trouble,' said Eric. 'I'm on my way.'

The ambulance people, now that life was back to being just a matter of life and death, and not rioting, promised to be there in ten minutes. Walter sat with Bertha for a while, but she kept making those groaning sounds, so he took the remote control and turned the sound up again. Then he changed the channel. Then he checked the Ceefax for the latest business news. It wasn't particularly insensitive, there was just nothing else he could think of doing for her, apart from tucking a tartan blanket in around her to keep her warm. Then he remembered why he'd come, and took an envelope out of his jacket and held it up in front of her.

'BERTHA?' Walter shouted. 'BERTHA? THIS IS YOUR MONEY, THE MONEY YOU LENT ME AND A SHARE OF THE PROFITS, ALL RIGHT?' There wasn't even a flicker of understanding. 'I'LL JUST PUT IT ON THE MANTELPIECE, ALL RIGHT?'

Walter showed her the envelope again, then slowly moved it towards the mantelpiece, but as he moved out of her direct line of sight her eyes remained fixed on the TV.

He propped the envelope up against a photo of her Frank. He turned then and looked at her. Such a vibrant, lovely woman reduced to this.

'BERTHA?'

Nothing.

'I THINK YOU'VE HAD A STROKE. IF YOU CAN HEAR ME, BLINK YOUR EYES. ONCE FOR YES, TWICE FOR NO.' Then he thought about that and laughed. 'I MEAN ONCE FOR YES. CAN YOU HEAR ME, BERTHA?'

Nothing.

Eric and the paramedics arrived almost simultaneously. Walter rushed them all through to the lounge. He said, 'I think she's had a stroke.'

Eric said, 'Let them be the judge of that.'

A paramedic said, 'Looks like she's had a stroke.'

Eric thrust a pudgy finger at Walter and said, 'What happened? What did you do to her?'

'I did nothing. I just called round to see her, found her like this.'

'You had a row, you tried to rip her off, the stress of it set this off.'

'No, really. She was just sitting there when I arrived, moaning.'

'Moaning about what?'

'Just moaning. Or groaning. She was already away with the fairies.'

'She was what?'

'How she is now.'

'Away with the fairies? What sort of a way is that to talk about someone?'

'It's just an expression,' said Walter.

The paramedics were calling Bertha's name, trying to get a response, then talking her through what they were doing, checking her blood pressure, giving her a wee injection, then gently lifting her out of Frank's chair and strapping her onto a stretcher.

Eric said, 'Is she going to be all right?'

The paramedic said, 'I hope so,' but his eyes said the opposite.

Eric turned angrily to Walter. 'This is all your fault! She should have been taking it easy, not gallivanting about buying property.'

'Eric, she had more energy than you and me put together.'

'I know about your great deal – well, you needn't think you're going to rip her off now she's near dead. I'll come after you for every last penny you owe her.'

Walter pointed to the envelope on the mantelpiece. 'It's all there, Eric.'

Eric glanced at the envelope, but he wasn't about to demean himself by going across and actually inspecting it.

The paramedics were just lifting Bertha up when she began to try and say something. Probably it was the injection.

'What's that, love?' one of the paramedics said, bending close. Walter could see her lips moving ever so slightly. The paramedic listened, nodding, then smiled at her and patted her hand. He turned to look at Walter and Eric. 'She says, could someone cancel the Tae kwon do?'

Walter immediately burst out laughing.

127
Office 12

Marsh woke in agony the next morning. Every muscle in his body ached; every time he turned in bed he had to suppress a groan of discomfort. It was the massage, mostly. The massage and then the sex. He had never experienced anything quite like it – the massage *or* the sex. Linda was lying beside him in the penthouse apartment at Towerview, sleeping soundly. He felt terrible, but in a good way. The massage had been painful, and the candles might have worked their sensuous charms on a more supple person, but he'd been all but impervious to them; it had been difficult to appreciate them while his spine was being realigned. But the sex. *Wow!*

After the early years there had never been much sex in his marriage. They had both just drifted out of it. It was reserved for hard-drinking nights and as a make-up after arguments. But even then it had been quick and unadventurous. He had not been aware of quite *how* unadventurous until Linda had gone to work on him. She was *fantastic*. Or, perhaps, most women were fantastic, and he just happened to have been married to one who wasn't. Or most men were fantastic and *he* wasn't. Whatever. Last night had been an eye-opener. He had heard of 69 before, but 99? It was a variation of 69, but required the use of a Cadbury's Flake.

Marsh took a shower, dried himself on the showhouse towels, then dressed. There was no coffee or cereal, which was a relief, as he had neither the strength to fill a kettle or wield a spoon. It was a little after 8 a.m. and his plan was to get to Hillsborough as early as he could. When he pulled on his jacket, Linda opened her eyes and said, 'Is that it then?'

'Is *what* it?'

'Wham bam thank you ma'm.'

Marsh sat on the bed beside her, wincing slightly as he lowered himself. He took her hand. 'Of course it isn't.'

'I don't mind. It's sort of par for the course.'

'Linda, don't be daft. Last night was . . . painful. Painful, but also brilliant.'

'Yes, it was. But that doesn't mean . . .'

'It *does* mean. If I have my way, this one is going to run and run.'

'You think so?'

'I know so.'

'Well, why don't you climb back into bed then?'

Marsh smiled. 'First of all, I would die for sure. I need to rest. Honestly. I would love to. But also I have a job to do.'

'What sort of a job?'

'A case.'

'But you're retired.'

'I know, it's just something I have to see through.'

'But you're *retired*. They're not paying you any more.'

'I know that. It's just something I have to finish.'

'And this is the only one?' Marsh nodded. 'And when you finish it, is that you finished?'

'That's me,' said Marsh. He leaned forward and kissed her on the forehead.

She said, 'I'm not your sister, or your daughter. Kiss me properly.'

He kissed her properly.

In the old days there would have been a police guard on the Head of the Civil Service, but Marsh was able to negotiate the twisting driveway which led up to his impressive house unchallenged. Hillsborough Castle, where the Royals stayed when they deigned to visit, was just visible half a mile away as it emerged from the morning mist.

Richard Bradley, wearing a tartan dressing-gown and with his hair unkempt, answered the door himself. He was a slightly overweight man in his late fifties. He pushed his glasses further up his nose and said, 'Superintendent Mallow, isn't it?'

'Retired,' said Marsh.

'Of course. I forgot.' He put a relieved hand to his chest. 'Well, thank God. I saw you walking up to the door and I thought perhaps something had happened to Steven – you know the way, the higher up you rise, the more senior the police officer they send to tell you the bad news. But yes, you're retired. Unfortunate business, if I read between the lines correctly. Please – come in.'

Bradley led him down a short hall, and directed him into a lounge on the right. Ahead of him, Marsh saw a kitchen table and a woman's leg in an identical dressing-gown gently swinging to music from a radio. He didn't recognise the song. He smelled toast and bacon.

I Predict A Riot

'Can I get you a cup of tea?'

'Please, yes.'

Marsh stayed in the lounge. Every inch of wallspace was devoted to either family photos or official pictures of the Civil Servant posing with members of the Royal Family. In fact, there hardly seemed to be a single member he hadn't met, from the Queen down to her most distant cousins twice removed. Marsh ignored the Royals and concentrated on identifying Steven Bradley. His father returned before he could find him. He came in carrying two mugs, handing one over.

'So,' he said, 'you're not the bearer of bad tidings. That's always a relief.'

Marsh gave a little shrug. He sat with his mug and said, 'I'd like you to tell me what you can about Office Twelve.'

Bradley hesitated, then took a sip of his tea. He nodded to himself. 'James, you're not here in any official capacity, are you?'

'No, sir.'

'Well, is there any reason why I should wish to discuss Office Twelve with you then?'

'Your son works for Office Twelve and there is a possibility that that office might have some connection to a murder case I'm investigating.'

'Really? I understood you had retired.'

'Yes, sir. I'm doing this on my own time.'

Bradley pondered that for a moment. 'What makes you think there's a connection?'

'I'm not at liberty to discuss that.'

'James, I'm sorry, that's the kind of thing a police officer says. You're no longer a police officer.'

'Nevertheless.'

Bradley set his mug down on a coffee table. He sat back and clasped his hands. 'Tell me what you know, or think you know about Office Twelve.'

'As far as I can determine, it's a secret department set up within the Civil Service for black propaganda purposes, with the aim of destabilising the political situation here.'

A smile had appeared on Bradley's face as Marsh spoke. 'And your sources for this information are . . . ?'

'Again, I can't divulge that.'

'Have you spoken to my son?'

'No, sir, that's why I'm here.'

'Superint— sorry, James, have you any idea how easy it would be for me to cite national security concerns and slap an order on you?'

'I'm aware it can be done.'

'Yes, it can. And you're probably thinking that if my son's involved in Office Twelve, then I am as well, that its tentacles reach right into the top tier of Government. That I could lift this phone and call in a squad to pick you up and you might never be seen again. Are you thinking that?'

'It had crossed my mind.'

'And you wish to continue?'

'Yes.'

'Why, James? One last case before you ride off into the sunset? Something for us to remember you by, something epic, rather than going out with your tail between your legs?' Marsh just looked blankly at him. Bradley took a deep breath. 'I'm sorry, I shouldn't have said that. You have to understand – this isn't easy for me. James, we live in a world rife with conspiracy theories; there's one for every occasion. Except for this one. Do you want to know what's incredible about Office Twelve?'

'Yes, sir.'

'It doesn't exist.'

'I don't understand.'

'It's not difficult. It quite simply *doesn't exist*. There *is* no Office Twelve. At least, not as you imagine it. It is a figment of my son's imagination.'

'I'm sorry?'

Bradley sighed. 'You see, James, when my son followed me into the Civil Service, he was a bit of a high flyer, being groomed for the top and rising swiftly through the ranks of the Unionist Party. And then – well, he lost it. He became unwell. Steven, my beautiful son, was diagnosed as being borderline schizophrenic.'

'Oh,' said Marsh. 'I didn't know.'

'No reason why you should. I don't know all the hows and whys of it, but that's what he is. Good news is, it is quite treatable with the right medication. As I'm sure you're aware, James, it's very difficult to actually lose your job in the Civil Service – particularly when your dad is the Head. Steven was turning up for work every day but making a quite dreadful hash of things. It was a very difficult situation. So, with my full agreement, it was decided to move him into his own office, with only the simplest duties to perform, to give him the security and routine of employment with none of the responsibilities, in the hope that with time, and medication, he might return to his old self. The office he happened to move into was Office Twelve.'

128
Swap Shop

Margaret was driving through the Craigantlet Hills, looking down over Dundonald, trying to locate an address which she presumed belonged to a farm. It was her only option: to track down the purchaser of the Primark dress and make her an offer she couldn't refuse. The Trading Standards people wouldn't provide the information, citing client confidentiality, but Emma Cochrane was more than helpful: she remembered exactly which women had bought the Primark dresses, because they were all regular customers, and from there it was just a process of elimination. Margaret explained it away by saying that as the dresses were merely prototypes, she wanted to make sure that no problems had developed after purchase – that the stitches hadn't slipped or the colours faded. 'Wow!' said Emma. 'Talk about customer service!'

Now she was on the hunt for Kathleen Norton, peering up lanes and trying to decipher faded numbers. The radio was playing 'See My Baby Jive' as re-imagined by an electronic frog. It was weirdly hypnotic. Margaret drummed along on the steering-wheel. Just as it finished, she spotted a slurry-sprayed house number and a slightly bent marker pointing up a poorly maintained lane. She'd already gone just a little beyond it by the time she realised what it was, so had to reverse to the opening, then turn in. There was scarcely room for one vehicle; if a tractor came the other way it would have to reverse or plough up a bank and through a hedge to get round her. She was in that kind of a mood. Primed for action, and unwilling to back down.

Kathleen Norton's mother was as fat and uncouth as Kathleen was thin and proper. Clearly Kathleen was grooming herself for a physical, mental and stylistic escape from the farming life, and her mother was just as determined to hold onto her. She was, as Mrs Norton wasted no time in telling Margaret, as she sat in the parlour, their only child. 'She never eats nothing and there's more muscle on a twig,' she said, handing Margaret a brimful china cup of tea and a fig roll, no plate. 'She should be out there helping Jack with the cows, not sticking Carmen rollers in her hair.'

After ten minutes a somewhat flushed Kathleen came hurrying in dressed as if for a prom, but with a wilting look which suggested she still lacked an invite. She said, 'My gosh, you came all this way from *Emma Cochrane*?'

'Absolutely,' said Margaret, as if it was perfectly normal. 'When a tragic error like this occurs, we don't hang about.'

'An error?'

'Well, as soon as we heard we were absolutely mortified – *mortified*, I tell you.'

Kathleen sat on the edge of the armchair opposite Margaret and said, 'I'm sorry to cause such a fuss. I was just so shocked to see it on sale at such a price. It's not that I mind paying so much for it – it's just the thought of every other Millie in town wearing the same dress and thinking that I only paid £18.99 for it as well.'

'Well, that's perfectly understandable. The fact is, our suppliers made a mistake. A box of dresses meant for us was inadvertently sent to Primark, who obviously wouldn't know a thousand-pound dress if it walked up and slapped them. They just stuck their usual price tag on and put them out on display. Honestly, I think they *weigh* the dresses and then decide the price.'

'Does that mean there are *dozens* of Millies walking around in thousand-pound dresses?'

'I'm afraid so. It's a tragedy.'

'It makes my dress virtually worthless.'

'Yes, it does. And you had every good reason to take your complaint to Trading Standards. However, although they will sort this mess out, and wrists will be slapped, believe you me, it doesn't really help your situation very much, does it?' Kathleen shook her head. 'And also, the publicity would not be good for us, so Trading Standards, having been made aware of this unfortunate mix-up, have agreed not to pursue the matter if, and only if, you are happy with the compensation we offer you.'

'Compensation?' This wasn't from Kathleen, but from her mother, standing in the doorway. 'Spending a thousand quid on that crap when any fool could see it wasn't worth more than twenty; if you ask me, she's her own worst enemy.'

'F**k off, Mum.'

'No, you f**k off.' Mother Norton turned on her heel.

Kathleen rolled her eyes. 'Sorry. She doesn't approve of me. She thinks I should be out there with my fingers up some cow's a**e. No sons, you see. Soon as they kick it I'm going to sell up and open my own boutique.'

From somewhere beyond the door Mother Norton snorted. 'Boutique! You couldn't run a marathon!'

'Anyway,' said Margaret, 'about the compensation. I have been authorised by Emma Cochrane herself to offer you a full refund on the dress, and also, completely free of charge, to give you this.'

Margaret opened the plastic bag she'd carried in with her. (Not, thankfully, a Primark bag this time.) She withdrew one of the dresses May Li had made up for the upcoming fashion show, shook it out and held it up.

'What do you think?' Margaret asked.

'What is it?'

'What do you mean, what is it?'

'What label?'

'It's *M & Emma*.'

'I haven't heard of that.'

'It's the first *M & Emma* ever to be released to the public. When you wear this, you will be the only model – sorry, client – in the entire world to have worn an *M & Emma*. If any of the fashion magazines hear that one has been released early they will absolutely *kill* to get a picture of it.'

Kathleen was feeling the material. 'How much is it worth?'

'At the moment? It's *priceless*. By the time it hits the catwalk, you're talking thousands.'

'Thousands?'

'Absolutely. Why don't you try it on?'

Half an hour later Margaret emerged from the farmhouse, aware of Mother Norton's stern gaze following her, but barely able to stop herself from smiling. Kathleen was happy with her cheque, even happier with her dress, and had quite willingly sat and texted Kenneth Buchanan at Trading Standards that she was withdrawing her complaint. Now all Margaret had to do was phone him herself and repeat the lie that Emma Cochrane's suppliers had supplied Primark in error, and that Emma was keen to keep the mistake out of the public eye, as it could easily damage her business.

'And that is what we call a *fait accompli*,' Margaret said aloud as she started the engine and began to negotiate the potholes on the narrow lane. She emerged onto the open road, then found a lay-by just a few hundred yards further along. She parked, then sat for several more moments rehearsing what she was going to say. When she was ready, calm, she switched off the radio and dialled Kenneth Buchanan's direct line. As she waited for it to be picked up she stared out, down the sweep of the Craigantlet Hills and across the fields beyond. There were towns and villages out there, she knew, but the huge swathe of green seemed to stretch uncluttered to the Mourne Mountains in the far distance. She loved the country, although obviously she wouldn't want to live in it.

'Ken Buchanan's phone.'

'Ahm, is Mr Buchanan there?'

'No, I'm sorry, he's indisposed.'

'Indisposed? Is that a fancy way of saying he's popped out for a fag?' Margaret asked cheerily.

'No. May I help you with something?'

'Well, no, I need to speak to him. Will he be long?'

The man cleared his throat. 'Mr Buchanan may be indisposed for several months. I'm afraid he's in the hospital.'

'Hospital? But I was only talking to him yesterday.'

'Well, I'm afraid he's in the hospital. Broken legs, broken arms, fractured skull.'

'God Almighty, did he crash his car or something?'

The man hesitated, then said, 'Between you and me, he did actually pop out for a fag. But they were waiting for him. Paramilitaries. UDA, I think. Beat him really badly.'

'Christ. I'm sorry. When do you think he'll be back to work?'

'After something like that, who knows? Suddenly, tracking down counterfeit Calvin Klein boxers doesn't seem so important. So, is there anything I can help you with?'

'No. Ahm, give him my best, will you?'

'Sure I will. What's your—'

But she had already cut the line. It was funny, she thought, how someone else's bad news was almost always someone else's good news, and vice versa. It just depended which end of the equation you were on. It was, as Walter never tired of reminding her, *Chinatown*.

129

A Blast from the Past

By Wednesday, Redmond was still basking in the reaction to his homily during Sunday's service. He was a natural. An orator to rival Churchill. He had wowed the congregation with both a glowing appreciation and a damning indictment of his own lately departed self. He had championed war and condemned peace, then he had condemned war and championed peace; he had batted philosophies and morals back and forth, confusing, amusing, exasperating and finally convincing his eager listeners of the sincerity of his beliefs, their wisdom, his own humility, and their deep spirituality. They applauded when he was finished, where normally they were asleep. The collection plate spilled over, where usually there were a lot of Euro cents. He pumped hands at the doorway, where their priest usually quickly scurried away, ashamed of his own performance. Outside they turned to each other and marvelled at the change in their priest, and wondered if he'd been drinking or had developed a personality disorder. Whatever – the reaction was *good*.

Redmond felt more relaxed than he had in years. He was putting weight on again. Later on the Sunday and again on Monday he took long walks in the countryside and sat by passive streams, just enjoying them for what they were. For as long as he could remember he had felt weighed down by his own self-imposed responsibilities and felt obliged to fight whatever battle there was going. When he had exhausted the fight out of Ireland, he had transported it abroad. He had begun as a freedom fighter and patriot, and ended as a mercenary. It was like starting out in The Beatles and ending up in The Bootleg Beatles. You looked like a Beatle, you sounded like a Beatle, but you most definitely were not a Beatle. Not even Ringo.

On the Tuesday morning he did a little gardening. In the afternoon and at night he read theological textbooks from his brother's small library and practised the rituals of the priesthood. On Wednesday morning he visited two parishioners who were unwell; he sipped a whiskey with one, and played chess with another. After another hearty lunch he slept for a while, then made his way down to the church and sat in the front row, staring up at the icons and the stained glass. He felt a part of it now. He was finally at peace with himself.

And then he heard the doors open at the back, and heels. He turned to find a woman coming down the aisle towards him, her slim figure and short, blonde hair wonderfully illuminated by the sunlight flowing around her through the open doors. She stopped at the end of the aisle, crossed herself, then turned towards him, and in so doing stepped out of the brightness.

Redmond's heart threatened to beat out of his chest. 'Maeve,' he whispered.

'Damian,' she said, and sat beside him. She looked into his face and took his hand; a tear sprang from one eye. 'My God,' she said. 'I'd forgotten how much you looked like him.'

Redmond opened his arms to her and they hugged. He smelled her hair and breathed in her perfume. He fought valiantly to stop himself crushing her against him. She patted his back and smoothed the hair on his head. 'I know,' she said, 'I *know*.'

Redmond released her from the hug, but held on to her shoulders. 'What do you know, Maeve?'

'I know how much he meant to you.'

Redmond nodded sadly.

'I wasn't sure if you would speak to me. They've turned against me in Belfast.'

'I heard that,' said Redmond. 'They think you had him cremated with undue haste.'

'Do you think that?'

'I think it would have been nice to bring him home.'

'I just couldn't face it, Damian – the parades and guns and eulogies. He wasn't a hero.'

'Wasn't he?'

'A hero is someone who stays with his family and looks after them. He was never there, Damian.'

'I think he would do it all very differently now.'

Maeve nodded. 'We all would.'

'Did you love him?'

'Yes, of course. But . . .'

'You drifted apart.'

'Yes. And he lied to me, about what he was doing.'

'He was trying to protect you.'

'No, he was lying because he knew I'd throw him out if I found out.'

'He had strong beliefs, Maeve.'

'He just liked blowing things up.'

'That's unfair.'

'It's the truth. Everyone else gave up bombs years ago.'

'Sometimes everyone else is wrong.'

'You think he was right just to continue on with it?'

'Maeve – he thought what he was doing was right. You have to respect him for that.'

'Why? Do I have to respect whoever shot Kennedy or Gandhi?'

Redmond blinked at her. He hadn't even been aware that she knew who Kennedy was, although he had a vague memory of renting *Gandhi*.

'No, I mean . . .' Redmond sighed. 'Maeve, it's just good to see you.'

'It's good to see you too, Damian. We never saw enough of you.'

'Well, we had differences, Redmond and I.'

'He loved you, Damian.'

'Did he?'

'Oh, he used to talk about you all the time.'

'Did I? I mean, did he?'

'Oh yes. All the time.' She reached out again, this time taking his hands. 'Father, Damian, I came for a reason.'

Redmond nodded. 'You're getting married again, and you know you're doing it with indecent haste, so you want my blessing because you feel bad about it.'

'Christ,' said Maeve. 'News travels fast.'

'It's a small world.' Redmond wanted to squeeze her hands. He wanted to place them on his body. He wanted to kiss her fingers. 'Do you love this man?'

'With all my heart.'

'He runs a café.'

'God, you *are* well-connected. Yes, he does. But he has big plans.'

'Redmond's only been gone a few days, Maeve.'

'No, Father, he's been gone for years.'

'Was this going on before he died?'

'No, Father, of course not.'

'It's all a bit of a whirlwind then.'

'Yes, Father.'

'Maeve – you've heard of the expression, "marry in haste, repent at leisure".'

'Yes, of course. But it's not like that.'

'As every runaway bride has doubtless said.'

'He's the one for me, Father, I know it.'

'I like your hair. Why, in all the years you were with Redmond, did you never get your hair done like that?'

'It was Jack's idea. Redmond never noticed anything like that.'

'He was too busy fighting for his beliefs. Tell me this, Maeve, if Redmond was to walk back through those doors there, right now, what would you do then?'

'He's not going to walk through those doors, Father.'

'Aye, I know, but if he did, what would you do?'

'He's not going to, Damian, he's dead.'

'Yes, I know, but hypothetically speaking, if Redmond was here right now, sitting next to you, what would you say to him?'

'But he's not here, Father. I can't live with 'what ifs'.'

'Yes, I know he's not here now, and you may say you can't live with what ifs, but I'd really like to know, for my own peace of mind, what you would say?'

'I wouldn't say anything, because he's dead and—'

'Oh for Christ sake!' Redmond exploded. 'Will you just answer the question?!'

He jumped up then, and began to pace about. Maeve looked shocked, but recovered quickly. 'I'm sorry, Father,' she said. 'I know it's been very hard on you, and perhaps it was a mistake to come, but I had to. Please understand – I was married to your brother, I loved him once, but he's gone now. I don't want to be a bitter old war widow like the half of them up there. I want to start again, and this is my chance. The wedding is on Wednesday. It's in the City Hall, at eleven, and I would like you to come as my guest. I think Redmond would want me to be happy, and your being there will be like him giving me his blessing. Will you come, Father Damian, for Redmond, and for me?'

130

Caravan

It was a response from a different era, but just as appropriate. Marsh looked at Richard Bradley, almost crumpled in his chair now, and said, 'With all due respect, sir, but you would say that, wouldn't you?'

The Head of the Civil Service raised his hands helplessly.

'You actually expect me to believe that this Office Twelve is just something your son concocted?'

'Yes, I do, James.'

'Mr Bradley, there are other people working in Office Twelve with him.'

'That's impossible.'

'I've spoken to at least one of them.'

'Well then, I can only presume that they have been sucked into it in exactly the same way that you have. I'm sorry, but I'd no idea. I can only presume he's stopped taking his medication, that he's creating some kind of elaborate fantasy world around himself. If you met him, James, you'd appreciate how easy he would find that. He's a very plausible young man, even when he's ill. The point is, he absolutely believes what he's doing, there's no artifice to it. If he's set up Office Twelve, then it's up and functioning in his head. But I can't believe that it has gone beyond that. The phones in his office don't work, for goodness sake. His computer works but he uses it purely to surf the internet. There are parental controls on it to stop him accessing adult sites, and it freezes if he attempts financial transactions. Honestly, James, I'm kept well up to speed on this.'

'And this man I spoke to, who claims to be working for Office Twelve?'

'James, it's the Department of Education. It's full of idiots.'

Marsh set his cup down. 'Well. I don't quite know what to say.'

'It's simple. You've been misled. You must follow leads that lead nowhere all the time. Or, at least you used to.'

Marsh ignored that one. 'Is it possible to speak to him? Steven?'

'You don't believe me, still?'

'I'm not saying that.'

Bradley sat back and sighed. 'Well, he's not here.'

'Could you tell me where he is then, Mr Bradley?'

'I don't really see the purpose of it. But – yes, all right. In fact, I'll take you to see him. If he's off his medicine, maybe you're just the man to scare him back onto it.'

'I can do that,' said Marsh.

Bradley asked for half an hour to get ready, but spent a good half of that time bickering with his wife in the kitchen. Marsh tried not to listen in. It couldn't be easy, having an only son like that. Didn't matter how many Royals you knew or how much you earned. He was lucky with his own daughter, yet he had never spent time with his grandchildren. Married to the job. And a denial of mortality. He would have to do something about that. Perhaps he would go and see them in England. Take Linda with him. He wondered if his daughter would allow them to sleep in the same bed together and how she would cope with his screams of pain as Linda bent his spine.

Forty-five minutes later Richard Bradley climbed into Marsh's car, even as Marsh hurriedly removed crushed coffee cups and a sandwich box from the seat. 'Where for?' Marsh asked.

'Ballywalter.'

Marsh turned the car. Bradley stared ahead of him, saying nothing for a good ten minutes. Ballywalter was a small village on the Down coast, the kind that used to get a steady holiday trade from Belfast in the old days, but which now struggled. It could look picturesque in the sun, nice enough for day-trippers to think about buying property there, but interest quickly faded when the rain started and the grey drabness of the place reasserted itself. Marsh had spent holidays there as a kid himself. The memories were good. The beach was stony. If there was pollution in the sea then, they hadn't been aware of it. Just lots of skinny children with sunburn.

'We have a luxury caravan down there,' Bradley said suddenly. A *luxury* caravan. 'Had it for years, but never used it much. Steven likes it though, likes to get away by himself. Very peaceful. But like I say, he has a job, so it was sitting vacant a lot of the time, so he asked me if he'd be able to rent it out over the summer months, weeks here and there, weekends. It wasn't really the money – it gave him an interest.'

'Fair enough,' said Marsh. 'Who was he renting it out to?'

'Well, I'm not really sure. I imagine it was some of the ones he knew down at *Past Masters* – you know, the club?' Marsh nodded.

'And he used to socialise quite a lot with the younger elements in the Unionist Party. So I imagine there were a few stag weekends and such.'

'You're sure he'll be here?'

'When he's not home, and he hasn't been since Friday, it's as likely where he'll be. Unfortunately there's no phone, and he's never carried a mobile.'

'You don't worry about him, being off on his own?'

'He's not a danger to anyone, if that's what you mean. Steven wouldn't hurt a fly.'

But he'd f**k with your head, easy enough.

They didn't speak much for the rest of the journey. Marsh drove along the Outer Ring, then on to Newtownards, across to Donaghadee and then down the winding coast road to Ballywalter. They got caught behind a tractor and there wasn't an opportunity to pass before their approach to Baylands Caravan Park.

Summer rain was sweeping across its long, narrow band, carried on a stiff breeze which buffeted the caravans. Bradley directed Marsh to the far side of the park and a large, beige-coloured caravan situated in probably the best spot – at least on a good day, with easy access to the nearby beach, but what was probably a bit of a nightmare in the winter months. The Venetian blinds were drawn. There was a television aerial sticking out of the roof and gas cylinders lined up at the back.

Marsh went to open his door, but Bradley put a hand on his arm to stop him. 'If you don't mind,' he said, 'I'd better have a word first. He's a bit strange with people he doesn't know.'

Marsh sat back.

Bradley hurried up to the door, then knocked sharply on it. He waited just a few moments, then knocked again. 'Steven!' he called. He glanced quickly back at Marsh in the car, then added: 'It's Daddy!'

There was no response. Bradley nodded at Marsh, then tried the door handle. It opened. He took one step up, then stopped suddenly, began to cough, quickly stepped back onto the concrete slab at the caravan's base, then crouched down and threw up.

Marsh quickly got out of the car.

The smell hit him straight away.

Steven Bradley had been dead for approximately seventy-two hours, according to the pathologist. There were three empty bottles of prescription medicines found beside his body, which was sitting at a table in the small kitchen. He had left a note which said:

Daddy and Mummy – I didn't do whatever this is, but I'll be blamed for it.

I'm always blamed for it. I'm in pain all the time. I'm sorry. I love you. Steven. Xxx.

Gary McBride, standing with Marsh on the beach, gazing at the waves, said, 'What do you think?'

'What do *you* think? You're the one still getting paid.'

'On the face of it, paranoid schizophrenic commits suicide.'

'But . . .'

'It wasn't a long rambling note, like you might expect, so if he was as warped as you seem to think he was, he might have experienced some moment of clarity and didn't want to be the fall guy for something.'

'But what?'

'*I didn't do whatever this is.* Is it something to do with this Office Twelve you're talking about?'

Marsh turned from the water and looked back up to the caravan. 'I think, if you're planning suicide, and you're together enough to sort out your pills and write a fairly coherent note, then you're going to want to go out with a bit of dignity, not slumped across a table. If you were committing suicide, you'd want to lie down and wait for the pills to take effect. You'd go into the bedroom.'

'So why didn't he?'

'Maybe when he arrived down on Friday he found something that tipped him over the edge.'

'Like what?'

Marsh just looked at him.

'All right, boss,' said Gary, 'I'll go and find out.' He smiled, began to turn away, then stopped. He was used to having Marsh with him. 'What are you going to do?'

'Skim some stones,' said Marsh.

131
Casualty

Walter was pretty much surplus to requirements. Eric made that clear right from the off. Eric had arrived at the Ulster Hospital in Dundonald five minutes after Bertha, and twenty minutes before Walter, thanks to his shiny BMW. By the time Walter found a parking spot and made it into Casualty, Eric was waiting to stop him getting any further. Walter just wanted to see her again, and now that he'd seen the state of Casualty – overcrowded with drunks and punishment-beaten teenagers and footballers with sprained five-a-side ankles – to suggest having Bertha transferred to Psyclops Surgeries, but Eric was having none of it. He said, 'You're not a relative, you've nothing to do with her, you're not welcome here, so bugger off.'

'Will you tell her . . .'

'I'll tell her *nothing*.'

'Just say that I'm praying for her and I'll see her when she's feeling better.'

Eric laughed scornfully. 'You don't get *better* from this.'

'You really don't know her at all, do you? Of *course* she'll get better.'

Eric shook his head. 'You really do live in your own wee world, don't you?' Then he turned and went back through a set of swing doors.

Walter thought briefly about going after him, but decided against it. Eric was right, up to a point. Bertha wasn't a relative. She was hardly even a friend. And their business partnership was over. She'd lent him some money, he'd paid her back. That was it. He could just walk away.

He stood outside; it was spitting. He took out his mobile and phoned Margaret. She immediately launched into her meeting with Kathleen Norton and how well it had gone, and how happy she was with it, but that a little bit of the wind had been taken out of her sails when she heard that Kenneth Buchanan, the Trading Standards man, had been seriously injured after being assaulted.

'Really?'

'Oh yeah, he's in the Ulster, he's really seriously ill.'

'God,' said Walter. He stepped out from under the protection of the entrance to stare up at the dull grey face of the hospital. 'He's in here?'

'You're there?'

'Aye. Bertha's not well. I think it's a stroke.'

'Oh – I'm sorry. I never got to meet her.'

'I know.' Walter was looking along the windows, counting up the floors. 'So what happened to your man?'

'Loyalist thugs, they said. Just ambushed him outside his office. And you joking about hiring a hitman – what if someone overheard?'

'Then I'd be in deep s**t,' Walter laughed. 'So what are you up to now?'

'Well, I'm not home long. I'm going to have a bath. Open a bottle of wine. Then I'm going to invite my new boyfriend around. If he plays his cards right, we might end up in bed together.'

'That would be nice,' said Walter. And then after a moment, added: 'It is me you're talking about?'

'*Walter.*'

'Sorry. I just . . . well, that would be fantastic.'

'Okay, then.'

'Should I bring something?'

'Just yourself.'

'More wine. A Chinese?'

'Just yourself.'

'So it's just myself you'll be wanting?'

'That's it. How long will you be?'

'About nine minutes if the traffic-lights are with me.'

'I said I'm having a bath.'

'That's okay. I can watch. Or climb in.'

She giggled. Then she said: 'I really like this, Walter. Let's not spoil it.'

'I don't intend to.'

'But we are both people that things happen to. And they're usually not good.'

'No, actually I think you're wrong there. That's who we used to be. Now we've turned the corner, it's all downhill from here.'

'Downhill? Isn't that a bad thing?'

'Well, uphill sounds like a lot of hard work. Downhill is like free-wheeling. So that's good. At least until your brakes fail and there's like this articulated lorry coming right at you. Do they still call them articulated lorries? I don't even know what articulated means. Isn't that what solicitors get, articulated? Or accountants? Maybe your Billy would . . .'

'Walter?'

'Mmm-hmm?'

'Less talk, more action.'

She cut the line. Walter was beaming. But only for a few moments. Then he called Mark on his mobile and snapped into it: 'What the f***ing hell did you do?'

'What? Walter? What're you talking about?'

'What do you think I'm talking about? The Trading Standards guy!'

'What about him?'

'He's in the Ulster, fighting for his life!'

'He is?'

'Something like that, yes. I asked you to get Office Twelve to sort him out, but I was only talking about hacking into his computer and deleting his records, not nearly killing him.'

'Oh Christ. I should have known.'

'Should have known what?'

Mark tutted. 'Look Walter, I'm sorry, I was only trying to help. I've been sitting in Office Twelve for days, waiting for Steven, waiting for anyone to show up, but it's been just me on my lonesome, so I had to call in the favour somewhere else. There's a man I met through the Party, I don't even know his real name, but he's called Bull and, well, he was only too keen to help, but he doesn't really do hacking – unless it's with an axe. I'm sorry, I should have guessed. I just thought he'd lean on him a bit.'

'He did more than just f***ing lean on him!'

'I realise that now. Is he going to be all right?'

'Well, how do I know?! Do you think I can just waltz in there and enquire? "And by the way, I'm the one who organised for you to get beaten within an inch of your life"!'

'Walter, what more can I say? I did my best.'

Walter sighed. 'Yes. I know. Just, I've lived in this bloody city all my life without having The f***ing Troubles affect me one little bit. Then as soon as they're over I get mixed up in this pile of crap.'

The rain was a little heavier now, so he stepped back into the shelter of the hospital entrance.

'Walter, whoever told you The Troubles were over?'

'Mark – it was on the news.'

'And all that rioting, what would that be?'

'That's just them fellas messing about as usual. It's always been like that.'

'Yeah. Well. Fair point. Look – I do feel really bad about this. Do you fancy coming over for a drink or something? Make us both feel a bit better.'

'Sorry, mate, no can do. I'm going to have sex with my girlfriend for the first time.'

'Really?'

'Really.'

'Walter?'

'What?'

'That's too much information.'

'I thought that as soon as I said it. Nevertheless, I am. See you later, Alligator.' He cut the line. He was still smiling at the thought of sex with Margaret when he realised there was a skinhead standing behind him, sheltering from the rain as well, and smoking a fag. He was smiling too. As Walter turned his collar up, and prepared to dash for the car, the skinhead said, 'Hey – mate?'

'Yeah?'

'Give her one for Ulster.'

Walter blinked at him for a moment. Then he said: 'Okay,' and darted out into the rain.

132
Kilimanjaro

James 'Marsh' Mallow and Linda 'Jump Off a Tall Building' Wray were enjoying dinner in Pizza Express on the Dublin Road. From their table they could see BBC Northern Ireland, and the local celebrities going in and out. They played 'spot the newsreader'. They held hands across the table. She had taken his hand as a natural act – they were lovers, after all. Marsh found it awkward at first; he was unused to public displays of affection. He had not held his wife's hand in such a fashion in their entire marriage. It was not a wasted life, he thought, it was just a different one. There was *muzak* playing, a truly horrific version of 'Brown Sugar'. In the past it would have been enough to have spoiled his meal, but not any longer; in fact, the pizza itself was enough to spoil his meal, but even that didn't matter. He was happy.

Linda said, 'Look, there's Noel Thompson.'

Marsh saw the news presenter crossing the road outside. 'Delivering bad news since 1990.'

'That's not fair,' said Linda. 'I think he's quite attractive.'

Marsh nodded. 'All right. Delivering bad news since 1990, but still quite attractive.'

She smiled and said, 'What are you going to do now?'

'Well, now that my back's sorted and my muscles are in shape I was thinking about trekking up Kilimanjaro. Or another night in bed with my loved one. Both equally strenuous, both have a great view, but only one has a risk of malaria.'

'Am I your loved one?'

'Well, you're definitely in my top three.' But then he saw she was serious. 'Of course you are.'

'That's the first time you've said it.'

'Well, it just kind of slipped out.'

'It was nice.' Then: 'I would say the same back.'

'If you meant it.'

'I would mean it, but I've said it far too easily to too many people for far too long. So I'm going to hold back for now. Even if deep inside I'm dying to say it.'

'Well, you sort of have, then.'

'I suppose.' They played finger footsie for a minute, then she looked a little more serious. 'James, what are you going to do, now that you've retired? You're not the type just to garden, are you?'

'I don't know. Maybe write my memoirs. I'm covered by Official Secrets, but I'm sure there's a way round it, and I don't really feel like I owe them anything.'

'Not after the way they've treated you.'

'Although, that said, *Belfast Confidential* comes out tomorrow. I may actually *be* taking the Kilimanjaro option. It's not going to be very pleasant, Linda.'

'I know that.'

'You do believe me, don't you, about what happened?'

'James, I'm a *Let's Be Mates* veteran. Nothing surprises me. Although if you'd shown a bit of backbone in the first place, and not left me sitting in that restaurant, you wouldn't be in this mess.'

'It's all about the little decisions, isn't it? You can never guess what they're going to lead to.'

'Well, maybe you weren't in the right place to meet me then, so maybe we would have had a miserable meal and not hit it off the way we have now. Maybe we needed something dramatic . . .'

'Like jumping off a tall building . . .'

'Like me getting drunk and upset, to get our ball rolling.'

Marsh lifted his glass, Linda lifted hers. Just as they went to clink, Marsh's phone began to ring. They clinked, and kissed across the table. She said, 'Aren't you going to answer that?'

'It's my work phone. And I don't work any more.'

'Nevertheless.'

Marsh removed his phone. 'Yep?' he said into it.

'Boss, it's Gary.'

'You're going to have to get out of the habit of calling me "boss",' said Marsh. 'Me no worky no more.' He smiled playfully across the table.

'Right, boss,' said Gary. 'I thought you'd want to know about the caravan.'

'Okay, hold on a minute.' Marsh gave Linda an apologetic look. 'Will you excuse me for a moment?'

'Of course.'

Marsh dabbed his lips with his napkin, then pushed his chair back and crossed the floor of the pizzeria. He stepped out into the cool night air. 'Right, Gary, shoot.'

'Are you sitting down?'

'Yes.'

'Okay, first off, we took the caravan apart. The bedroom had been thoroughly cleaned in the past few days, but there was a small hole in the floor and blood had leaked through . . .'

'Blood?'

'Blood had leaked right through and dripped onto a concrete slab beneath the caravan. We have a DNA match, boss – in fact, two DNA matches. One for Michael Caldwell, and one for Pink Harrison. His blood, and a pubic hair.'

'Christ,' said Marsh.

'I know. We have him, boss. We f**king have him.'

'That's brilliant, Gary. Well done.'

'You led us there, boss.'

'Well. Anyway, tell me how you see it now.'

'Steven Bradley was in the habit of hiring his caravan out to his Unionist buddies and Pink was one of them. He had a thing for boys, but had to take them somewhere real secret, because if word got out, the hoods would have had him for breakfast. So he takes Michael down to Ballywalter, they fight over something, Pink kills him, maybe gets hurt himself in the process. He cleans up the murder scene, but misses the blood, takes the body back to town to throw everyone off-track, then dumps it in the Lagan.'

Marsh said: 'You should do this for a living – you're very good.'

'So should you,' said Gary. 'And maybe you could again. When this gets out . . .'

'No, Gary. It's done.'

They were quiet for a few moments, then Gary said, 'We've paper-work to sort out, but do you want to come along for the ride when we go to pick Pink up? It wouldn't be a problem.'

'No thanks, Gary. I've better things to do with my time.'

Marsh returned to the restaurant. When he sat down, Linda said, 'Something wrong?'

'No, not at all. Quite the opposite.'

'So why the long face?' Marsh shrugged. He turned his glass of wine between his fingers, then briefly told Linda what had happened. At the end she said, 'That's great news. Isn't it?'

'Yeah. Of course it is.'

'So?'

'I don't know. I suppose we're back to old Kilimanjaro again. I mean, I'm told it's absolutely miserable getting there, freezing cold and you're so high up above sea level you get a raging headache, so by the time you get to the top you're not the slightest bit interested in the view and you just want to lie down.'

Linda squeezed his hand. 'Well, maybe *we* should go and lie down. I don't know much about you, James Mallow, but I do know you've been fighting these people for thirty years, and now you've . . . hung up your gun, or whatever it is you do, but not before you got the last of them. It's been a hard slog and you're exhausted and you're in no position now to appreciate what you've done. But you've done something good, and in the morning maybe it won't be so cold, and your head won't be so sore and the clouds will have rolled back and you'll be able to appreciate the view, and think the effort was worthwhile.'

Marsh squeezed her hand back and said, 'I'll get the bill.'

133

Pink

The arrest of Pink Harrison could not happen for at least twenty-four hours, they had that much from their many moles within Police Headquarters. Even before the Chief Constable was informed of the breakthrough, word had already reached four of the five leaders of the UDA in Belfast. The fifth, obviously, was Pink Harrison, and he hadn't a clue.

Pink had been on the rampage for the past few days, arguing with and threatening banks, creditors and many varieties of financial institution where he could – but most of them were overseas, and you had to see Pink face to face to appreciate his terror. He wasn't getting far. With his cash still landing in gardens all over the Province, and his credit cards maxed out or rejecting him, he was forced to squeeze the protection rackets even harder. He demanded a 'special' contribution to Party funds, and those few businesses that he still had an interest in were ordered to hand over their reserves and sell off fixtures and fittings. yet something was different. Pink Harrison's desperation was apparent for all to see. It was the first time anyone had seen him rattled. Billy Gilmore was his Achilles heel. In fact, with the way Pink's luck was running, he had two Achilles heels, which was not only career threatening in football, but pretty damn risky in paramilitary circles. The second Achilles heel was, at least in the eyes of the UDA Brigadiers, much more serious. They had put up with his bullying ways, they had put up with his showboating and the press attention it brought. And murdering someone, well that obviously went with the territory. But being caught with your pants down with a rent boy – that was the final nail in the coffin. The good people of the UDA would stand for many things, not the least of which was having their country torn away from beneath them, but they wouldn't stand for a fruit in their midst.

He had to go.

There are no early retirements in the UDA. There are no pension plans, no golden handshakes. You are not asked to clear your desk immediately, or escorted from the building. The Brigadiers knew Pink well enough. They knew that if they stood him down, he would seek revenge in the traditional manner. They also knew that once the police had him in custody, pressure would be brought to bear on him to name names. Pink knew many names, and where they were buried. It wouldn't be allowed.

Shortly after the decision was made, Bull drove out to see him. Instead of pulling into the driveway, he parked in the next street along. He grabbed a plastic Primark bag from the front seat. It was full of cash he'd collected from the Supporters Club en route. He stopped just outside the gates, and stepped into the shadows as another car approached, then drove past. At that moment his mobile phone rang. He answered it in case there was a last-minute change in orders.

'Bull?'

'Yes.'

'It's Mark.'

'Mark?'

'Mark Beck. I called you about the Trading Standards guy.'

Bull tutted. 'Yes, what about it?'

'Well, I didn't mean you to go that far. He's in hospital and—'

'Mark? I'm busy right now.'

'Oh. Sorry. It's just that I'm pretty peeved . . .'

'*Peeved*?'

'I only meant you to warn him off.'

'Mark? We *did* only warn him off. If we'd been serious he would have been propping up the f**king fly-over by now. So take your *peeved* and stick it up your f**king a*se, all right?'

'All right,' said Mark.

Bull snapped the phone shut, then walked up the drive to Pink's front door. Every light in the house appeared to be on, and music was booming out. Bob Marley. It took several rings for Pink to answer. He was wearing white shorts and sandals. His upper half was naked, well-tanned and muscled. He had a dumbbell in his right hand and a glass of champagne in his left. He smiled at Bull and said, 'All right, mate? Come on in.'

There didn't appear to be anyone else in the house. Bull said, 'Am I late for the party, or too early?'

'Neither, mate, just chillin'. I'll get you a drink.' Pink led him towards the kitchen. 'You been in here before?' he asked, setting the dumbbell down on a granite counter and waving his hand around the ultra-modern design.

'Couple of times,' said Bull.

'Designed by Liam Miller. Cost me twenty grand, and I've never made more than baked beans in it. But see this fridge? Makes its own friggin' ice, twenty-four seven.' He pulled the door open. 'Beer or champagne?'

'Neither,' said Bull.

Pink glanced back, and saw the gun.

'Bull,' said Pink.

'Pink,' said Bull.

Marsh didn't hear about the murder of Pink Harrison until he switched on the radio news the next morning. It had been given blanket coverage by the local stations almost as soon as police arrived at the scene, but there was no TV in the penthouse apartment and besides, he had other things on his mind.

Now, driving home after another exhausting, fantastical night, he listened in to the local coverage, switching between stations. He didn't feel anything in particular: certainly not robbed, or angry, or even sad. In fact, he didn't even want to be driving home; he wanted to stay with Linda, but she had her job to do, and besides, he had to find out what Billy Gilmore was up to. Marsh hadn't been back to his house for two nights, and Billy wasn't answering the phone. There was always the outside possibility that one of Pink's last acts had been to track Billy down to Marsh's house and murder him, but he suspected he would have heard.

When he arrived home, the house was in neat and tidy order, but there was no sign of Billy. There was a note, however.

Dear Superintendent, Marsh read, *I see they got Pink, but I don't think I'm off the hook yet. So I'm off. I just wanted to thank you for saving my life, and also to say you're a bullying f**ker. You have a very interesting record collection. I know bugger all about music, but you've left me here alone for so long, scared out of my wits, that I've had time to price your collection on the internet. So I have selected your most valuable records and taken them with me. I will sell them on eBay. It's a small thing, but I think you'll agree, very annoying. All the best, Billy.*

A week, maybe even a few hours ago, Marsh would have flown into a frenzied rage. His music had been *everything* to him. But it no longer was. Or not quite. Make no mistake, he would absolutely thump Billy if he ever saw him again, but he wouldn't go out of his way. The music had been an escape – from everything. From his work, from his marriage. Now there was a brave new world opening up. Before, after his wife had died, he would have the music on constantly, and loud. Now the house was quiet, and he rather liked it. He made a cup of tea. He sat at the kitchen table and checked his mobile. Gary had called half a dozen times, but without leaving any messages. He called him.

Gary said, 'Where you been, boss?'

'Out,' said Marsh.

'You've heard about Pink?'

'Yeah. The usual suspects, right?'

'Just the one. We're just about to pick up the Bull.'

In paramilitary circles, it usually turned out to be the right-hand man. Marsh was just surprised that Bull had been fingered so quickly. 'You'd think by now he'd be well versed in getting rid of a gun and burning his clothes, and generally pretty good at giving Forensics a miserable time.'

'Oh aye, he did all that. But the stupid b***ard went and answered his phone right outside Pink's house about two minutes before he pulled the trigger. Those mobile phone people are all the same, aren't they? Doesn't matter whether it's your bill you're complaining about or some murder you've committed, they always get you in the end. Anyway, boss, we never did get Pink to court, but it's over anyway, isn't it?'

'Just about,' said Marsh.

134
Wedding

Redmond swore that he would not attend the wedding of his wife to Jack Finucane. He swore, and swore, and swore, and swore, until his housekeeper was forced to knock on his bedroom door and ask if everything was all right. He emerged pale and slightly drunk, and said he had to go to Belfast. In the end, he couldn't *not* go. He had no idea how he would react when he got there or what he would do or say when his wife walked down the aisle. Physical violence was second nature to him. Redmond could put a bomb together given five minutes and the contents of the average grocery trolley. He could construct lethal weapons out of twigs and nettles. But now he had other strings to his bow as well: he could give the Last Rites, as he had; he could baptise, as he had just the previous morning; he could listen to confessions, almost daily, and offer sage and appropriate advice; and he could bless and bless and bless and bask in the warmth, respect, and yes, love of his rural parish. He had eventually decided, after long, fraught hours of deliberation, that he must accept the fact that there would always be two of him. When he wore the black of the priest, then he would be that priest. But he couldn't wear it all the time. When he took the black off, he would become Redmond. It was a slightly schizophrenic approach, but he could see no other way of doing it. There just had to be some way to keep the two of him apart.

So he caught the train to Belfast. He wore his priest's outfit. He thought it might help to control his emotions, and anger.

Then he got to City Hall and saw Maeve, and his heart near broke in two. She was wearing a beautiful suit. 'Isn't it lovely?' she said. 'My mate Margaret designed it and had it made up as a special surprise. It's worth *thousands*.' She was getting a bit anxious because Jack hadn't arrived yet. Then she said she had a favour to ask Damian. 'Margaret's going to be my witness, but poor Jack – he doesn't have any relatives living here, and no really close friends to ask, so I was wondering if you'd be his witness.'

Redmond was stunned. He hadn't exactly expected the wedding to be packed with family and friends of Maeve's – as she'd been disowned by every right-thinking Republican in Belfast – but had presumed that her husband-to-be's family would make up the numbers. However, there appeared to be virtually no other guests. There was Margaret, and presumably the man with her was her husband, and then there was the short, bald, sad-faced man whom Maeve introduced as her boss from work. But that was it.

'What sort of a man has no friends to give him away?' Redmond asked.

'He has friends, Father – just they're all chefs. They work in different cities, different countries.'

'But I don't know him from Adam.'

'But you know me, you're family, Damian, and I think Redmond would approve.'

'He f***ing wouldn't, you know.'

He almost said it out loud, and would have if the Registrar of Marriages hadn't come hurrying up asking for the witnesses' names. When Maeve introduced Damian, the Registrar gave him a cool look and said, 'There can be no religious contributions to civil marriages. I'm sorry, but it's the law. If you want to act as a witness, you'll have to lose the collar.'

Redmond duly removed the collar and unbuttoned his shirt.

'Thank you, Damian,' said Maeve.

The Registrar said, 'Five minutes – we've a busy schedule. I'll start the pan pipes.'

As he turned away, Maeve gave a little gasp of excitement, then quickly pulled Redmond to one side. 'Here he comes now! Look at him! Oh Damian, I'm so happy! I have to get offside now, bad luck to see him before the ceremony, but sure I hardly saw him. Go on, you, and introduce yourself. I'll see you in a mo.' She reached up then and kissed him on the cheek, and he hoped against hope that such close proximity, flesh to flesh, might spark in her some belated recognition that this was truly her husband, returned from the grave, but there was nothing, nothing at all, and she was gone in a flash.

Redmond put out his hand. 'I'm Damian, Redmond's twin brother. Maeve asked me to be your witness.'

Jack grasped it tightly. 'It's very good of you.'

'No problem. It's strange though. I don't know you at all.'

Jack nodded. He looked nervously along the corridor and through the open doors of the Register Office. 'Is she here?'

'Aye, she's hiding round the corner.'

'Thank God. I wasn't sure. It's all been a bit of a whirlwind.'

'Yes, it has. And you're absolutely certain?'

Jack eyes drifted back to him. 'Sorry?'

'The whirlwind. You've only known her a few weeks, and she's only recently widowed.'

'I've never been more certain of anything, Damian.'

'But her poor dead husband . . .'

'Her poor dead husband treated her like sh*t for twenty years. She deserves a better life.'

The Registrar appeared in the doorway, and tapped his watch in Jack's direction. Jack took a deep breath. 'Okay,' he said. 'Let's go.'

Margaret said, 'She looks beautiful.'

'And her outfit's a cracker,' said Walter.

'Oh shush, you.'

They were holding hands.

'Do you think one day . . .' Walter whispered.

'Don't count your chickens before they're hatched,' Margaret whispered back.

'The chicken or the egg,' whispered Walter. 'Which came first?'

'You did,' said Margaret.

'It's lack of practice,' said Walter.

'We can remedy that,' said Margaret.

Maeve and Jack faced each other, standing on the blue and yellow carpet, with the Registrar between them.

Jack repeated, 'I do solemnly declare that I know not of any lawful impediment why I, Jack Patrick Finucane, may not be joined in matrimony to Maeve Delores O'Boyle.'

The Registrar nodded, then smiled at Maeve. 'Now Maeve, if you'll repeat after me . . .'

Maeve's voice wavered. 'I do solemnly declare that I know not of any . . .'

There was a sudden fit of coughing from behind, and they both glanced around. Mr Kawolski was looking purple in the face, and holding up an apologetic hand. The Registrar shot him an evil look, then prompted Maeve to continue. '. . . lawful impediment, why I . . .'

Redmond, no longer prohibited by his brother's collar, had almost, almost cried out. But he stopped himself. Because it came to him, standing there and observing how happy she was, that while he had indeed been a s**t to her for twenty years and this wedding would seem to signal the definite end of their relationship, what with him being dead and all, that in fact it wasn't over, and that time itself was relative. By taking the road less travelled, by imbibing the positive ambience of his new parish and the wonders of the natural world he had encountered in Colombia, he had grown to appreciate the value of life and the purpose of time. Also, that the words he was hearing now were only words and that in the coming days, weeks or months, Maeve might realise the folly of her rapid plunge into marriage. She hardly knew this Jack Finucane, so anything could happen. He might treat her every bit as badly as he himself had done, and if he did – *when* he did – he, Redmond O'Boyle, would be there, ready and willing to cast off his priestly garments, lure Jack Finucane down a dark alley and beat him to a pulp, before reclaiming his beloved Maeve.

Epilogue

There were two purposes to the trip. First off, James Mallow drove to Bangor West and the family home of Michael Caldwell. The mother was in by herself, and still looking red-eyed. She hesitated before letting him in, and he saw the reason why, sitting on the coffee table in the lounge: a copy of *Belfast Confidential*. He nodded down at it. 'I haven't read it yet, but I'm presuming you're thinking I'm a bit of a s**t.'

'It looks that way,' said Mrs Caldwell.

'Not much I can say.'

'You could say if it's true.'

'It's not.'

She shrugged. 'I heard that Pink Harrison was arrested, but you never called to tell me, so I thought maybe it wasn't certain. Then he was released and you took early retirement and you still didn't call, so I presumed it was over, and we'd never find out, and your promise to find him was just rubbish.'

'We did find him, Mrs Caldwell.'

'Then why did you let him go?'

'At the time there wasn't enough evidence to keep him. Then there was. He got killed before we had the chance to pick him up. I'm sorry.'

'I wanted the chance to look him in the eye, in a courtroom. I wanted to ask him why. Michael was only fifteen. I'm working part-time as an estate agent, you know, but I always make sure I'm home at this time, because this is the time Michael gets home from school.'

Marsh said nothing. She went to make tea. He sat in the lounge and looked at the family photos. When she came back in with a tray she said, 'Is this why you've taken early retirement?' She nodded down at the magazine.

'Mostly, yes. And, it was time.'

'And what will you do?'

'I don't know.'

'What about your wife? Is she pleased you're finished?'

'I don't know. She's in the car.'

Mrs Caldwell stood and peered out. 'Why didn't you say? Bring her in.'

He had parked away from the front window, so she couldn't see.

'No, I really can't stay. I just wanted to . . . I don't know, I was going to say put your mind at rest, but it sounds wrong. In case it never came out, I wanted you to know that we got him in the end.'

She nodded. 'It doesn't bring Michael back. But at least I won't be walking through Belfast thinking, Was it him? Was it him? Was it him? At least I have that.'

'It's something,' said Marsh.

He didn't feel any better afterwards, driving down to the beach at Ballyholme. Linda had predicted that he would wake in the morning and appreciate the view from Kilimanjaro, but he hadn't, not yet anyway. There was no great lifting of weight from his shoulders in meeting with Mrs Caldwell, in finally closing the file on his last case. In a better world they would have shared a moment of epiphany and healing. In a better world Dan Starkey would have phoned to say they'd chosen not to run the beating-a-hooker story because of Marsh's long record of good service. And in a better world the Chief Constable would have personally begged him to come back to lead the CID. But it wasn't a better world, it was just *the* world, and he would have to live with it.

Marsh parked by the green banks leading down to the beach, and lifted his wife out of the glove compartment.

He would scatter her here on the sand, with the wind blowing fresh off Belfast lough, taking care to stand upwind. They had walked here when they were courting. He was a cop even then, and cops had always come to Bangor because it was safe. Or safer.

As he began, there were couples walking their dogs. The women looked at him curiously, and then moist-eyed. The men were harder to read. There were tears in his own eyes, but it was mostly the wind, and the sand, blowing up.

Linda phoned as he was driving back to town.

She said cheerily, 'Whatcha doing?'

'Just finishing some stuff. Did you ever see that barn on the way out of Bangor?'

'The one with the big writing?'

'Yeah. I'm just passing it.'

It was on his right, a huge old barn with enormous letters on its side. They'd been there for as long as he could remember.

Linda said, 'What is it – *For God so loved the world that He gave His only begotten son?*'

'That's it.'

'I used to think it said *forgotten* instead of *begotten.*'

Marsh smiled. 'That would change the meaning a bit.'

'So, what about it? You're not joining the God Squad on me, are you?'

'Nah. Just thinking.'

'Well, if you're in a thinking mood, why don't you think about stopping somewhere along the line and picking up some candles.'

'It's going to be one of those nights, is it?'

'It's going to be one of those nights.'

The barn dropped away behind him. The clouds that had gathered earlier had shifted, the sun was out, bathing the city ahead of him in a warm summer glow. It was a city he knew perhaps too well. It was a cold, hard, unforgiving place. He had kept it at a distance for all these years, treating it with a surliness born of fear and contempt. But now, driving towards it, with the twin giant cranes of the shipyard and the soft curve of the Cave Hill dominating his view, he briefly allowed himself to imagine it as a gentler, more forgiving place. Yes, the sun would go down soon and the darkness would return, but the light would never fully be extinguished, even if it was just a solitary candle, burning either for a lost soul or redemptive love, depending on your point of view.

Thinking this, he had veered slightly out of his lane. The car beside him honked, and he glanced across. A kid gave him the fingers. James Marsh Mallow gave them right back.